About Author

Claire was born and raised in London. She graduated with a BSc (Hons) in Social Sciences from the OU, and a Creative Writing MA from Royal Holloway. She now lives in Surrey with her family where she is fulfilling her lifelong dream of writing, full-time. She makes her debut with her series, *Diary of an obstinate, headstrong female*.

Acknowledgments

Thanks to Jon, as ever, for putting up with my endless long days of being tied to my laptop so I could get this finished, whilst always keeping the cogs turning in my absence.
Thanks to all collaborators involved in making this publication possible:
Editor: Kemone Brown at THPeditingServc.
Cover artist: @vikncharlie.

Dedication

For all those who have been forced to fit into impossible moulds.

Appetence.

C. C. Burns

Copyright

First Edition. Paperback.
ISBN 978-1-7397984-4-4 **DISCLAIMER:** This novel's story and characters are fictitious, with the exception of those details already in the public domain. Certain long standing institutions, agencies, public offices and public figures are mentioned, but the characters involved are wholly imaginary.
Any resemblance to persons living or dead is purely coincidental and not intended by the author.

CONTENT WARNING: This book contains some explicit material, suitable only for adult readers, including depictions of violence and scenes of a sexual nature.

Independently published by the author, Claire Burns, 2022, England.

www. ccburns.co.uk

Introduction

Diary of an obstinate, headstrong female series.

Appetence is book 2 in this series, and continues on from the first book: Vanilla Kisses.

The series is intended to be read in order for the best reading experience, as links and references are made between them, that may not be otherwise, understood.

I hope you enjoy the next instalment!

Aftermath.

August 1821. - Eleanor.

When I awoke in the warmth and familiar comfort of my own bed, I felt instantly relieved. But it was short lived, as the respite of my escape last night gave way to the horror of my need to offer my parent's an explanation as to what I was doing here, and why I could not go back: never go back, to that vulgar man.

I was beginning to force my body into stirring against the aches and pains that were resisting my attempts to move, when Watts came into the room and it suddenly occurred to me, they may already know of my return.

'Good morning, ma'am. Your toilette is ready,' Watts droned as the heavy door fell shut behind her. She always sounded that way: years of loyal service manifested themselves in a multitude of creases around her heavy eyes and lingered in her sour tone. Today it was a comfort to hear her miserable monotone, and I could have almost believed the horrors of the past month quite an illusion. Like nothing at all had altered and I was still free. Still innocent. Untarnished. Unmarried.

'Just leave everything at the washstand,' I said, stifling a yawn and wiping the sleep from my eyes. 'Watts, who sent you here? Does my mama know I am home?'

'No, milady; twas the young maid sent me with an instruction to go first to you. Your mother has not risen yet.'

I felt grateful at this news. 'You must not tell her yet. Let her take her breakfast and toilette, then you will ask her to come to me. But do not tell my father, and if he is with her, you must not say a word, but report back to me. Oh, and I shall not require your assistance to dress:

I shall manage it myself.' I ignored her furrowed brow at the suggestion and buried my face back beneath the sheets until I heard the door close. I was not ready to surface. I felt sure I had merely blinked I was so exhausted and I needed time to think. I had placed myself in check-mate with all the cursed lies and scandals surrounding me; I hardly knew what miracle could be contrived in any amount of thinking time. Yet if I wanted their protection; I must consider what I could say that would earn it.

Once Watts had gone and I had stared into the pattern of the wallpaper a while— tracing the tail of a gilt painted feather—I threw the covers back and forced myself over to the mirror; the previous night's events dawning on me more vividly than the hazy, piecemeal details I had salvaged upon waking. I suspected my night's sleep had sobered me from that terrible draught Mariella forced me to take. But the sleep, however brief and inadequate it felt, must be responsible for sharpening my memory, as much as I wished it otherwise. But how much I wished *otherwise*. The power to undo so many things, unsay so many things...

I went over to the dressing table, carefully easing myself onto the stool and peered blankly into my reflection. My eyes were red and puffy with dark shadows beneath them and my complexion a sallow shade of grey. I pinched my cheeks but the colour did not rise in them, it simply left a blotchy yellow imprint in my flesh before disappearing altogether. Then I saw the bruises on my arms and pulled at my night dress to examine the trail that led all the way across to my chest; imprinted on my shoulders were the marks where she had buried her knees into them. *How had I been so gulled?* I had walked blindly into their entrapment never understanding their true character at all: neither of them. What a cat's paw she had proved. What a villain he had shown himself to be.

My head fell limply into my hands as I exhaled a deep sigh. If I could barely believe the revelation, how could I expect anyone else to accept such a twisted account? They would surely think me mad for the very suggestion of it: a fancy or figment of my imagination to justify my own sins in it all. I would have to find a middle ground somewhere between the absurdity of the truth and the palatability of another untruth, if I was to convince anyone to help me. Yet I felt contaminated, transparent, as though everyone would see the terrible secret that lurked within me and find out the whole. I could not bear it to be known: none of it. I wanted a hole to hide away in, like squirrels made in trees for the winter. A season of hibernation where I could sleep it all away, forget all, be beyond the reach of anyone's eyes, questions or demands. If only life was that easy. If only I was a squirrel.

No such lines of thinking were of any use at all.

I lifted myself carefully from my seat, bracing my weight and leant over to the washstand where the mess from last night had been cleared and a fresh jug stood, filled with warm water. I poured it into the porcelain basin and dipped my cloth. My reflection peered back at me as I sponged my face; I was so much paler than usual. The dead look didn't suit and yet it was the most honest look I'd worn in an age.

I swirled the washcloth around in the water and, for a moment, wondered what it would feel like to drown. I wrung it out and placed it over my eyes and held it there to try to improve the swelling. The last thing I needed today was my mother fretting over the look of me. I was not sure what I would tell her but I knew that I did not want anyone to see me in such a state, especially her.

With more than a little struggle, and a fair amount of agony, I managed to dress myself: Forcing my aching limbs into impossible poses in the process. Even though my lacing was loose and untidy, I found it hard to care, so long as my injuries were concealed beneath my long sleeves and high collar, it would do. But my hair and face proved more difficult to set right. My arms ached and trembled wretchedly and it took me the best part of half an hour just to arrange it into a simple bun and powder over the marks on my face. But my eyes would not improve, they were heavy, dark, and swollen from tears, and the bump on the side of my forehead was only partially obscured by the fringe I had styled to conceal it. I painted my eyes several times then washed it back off again in between, finding no improvement. My frustration was growing; my stomach was growling with hunger and my mouth dry and parched and my eyes looked, if anything, worse from all my efforts.

I was tempted to give in and call for the girl last night and remembered then, the image of her running off in tears, not to mention the matter of not even remembering her name to ask for her. Was it Annabelle, or something of that order? I could not be sure. I would have to manage for now. I peered back at my red ringed eyes and picked up my paint brush and mixed some more soot into oil to coat my lash line. When I smudged it again with my trembling hands and saw the hopeless sight I had painted myself into, I felt my frustration erupt into such a shocking rage I did not recognise myself. I screeched, and with more strength than I thought I had in me, flung my arm across the washstand. The half-filled basin crashed to the floor, followed by the jug and pile of neatly folded towels. I collapsed onto the floor beside them. Water sat upon the fibres of the rug, I watched it seep in slowly. Finely painted pieces of porcelain lay scattered around my feet: *I never liked that pattern anyway*, I thought, rubbing my temples in small circles and recovering my breath.

It was Watts, not my mama who came into me shortly after and I pulled myself up from the floor a fraction too late to prevent her suspicion or concern.

'Are you alright miss? You have had a fall,' she said rushing over to me.

I raised my hands in protest of her helping me and used the back of the chair to steady myself. 'A little accident but I am fine. Is my mama coming?'

'No, your father was in her company, taking their breakfast together, so I couldn't tell her and now there is a call and she attends it. So, I am sorry miss, I could not pass your message quietly.'

'No matter. Who is it Watts; that calls?'

'I didn't catch the name, ma'am. Shall I clean that mess up for you?'

My heart sunk, could it be them wretches come to look for me? So bold faced impudent, I could no longer suppose anything above their daring. But the fact was, my mama did not yet know I was here and could offer no intelligence on my whereabouts. 'No, never mind that,' I said to Watts, 'you will make a fuss and I will be discovered. Now, when she is done, you must send my message to her.' I dismissed her before the panic overcame me. I listened carefully at the door and when I was certain all was quiet, I went out and perched upon the top stair to listen in from a comfortable distance.

I could hear the din of voices from the drawing room, but I could not make them out, so I crept a few stairs lower and when I heard the door spring open, and a female voice order Grantley to fetch her parasol, I sighed my relief, recognising the voice of the dowager. I got up carefully and as I turned around to head back to my chamber, I heard the opening of a door along the upper hall and held my breath. I could not see anyone in the direction of my father's quarters and when I saw the flash of a maidservant's skirts behind a pile of linen she carried almost as high as her face, I calmed. As she passed me on the stairs, I recognised her as the girl from last night. I paid no further attention to her as she descended and was almost returned to my room when I stopped in my tracks hearing Mother's voice bellowing from below.

'Come here girl, at once...' I heard her say.

Footsteps padded along the lower hall, accordingly.

'Am I correct in thinking you are the maid covering Molly's duties at present?' Mother continued.

'Yes, ma'am,' she replied courtly.

'I thought as much. So, might you explain to me why my finest wool rug on the upper landing has mud stains all over it? It certainly wasn't there when I retired, and Mrs Crawford informs me you were responsible for the final duties.'

I felt my heart sink at the words and leaned over the banister and saw it was she my mother addressed. I knew I should have paid her a bribe. Just when I thought things could not get any worse. The last thing I needed was an interrogation from Mother on how I had arrived here: I had resolved to tell her I had come early by coach, but I had neither the strength nor good temper to face such an inquisition on how I might have managed it through the dead of night. What would I say? What could I possibly contrive within the next two minutes to explain it all? I held my head in my hands and peeped through the wooden rails; my stomach churning.

'I'm sorry, ma'am. I thought it cleaned...I had to help bring in the linens from the line as that terrible storm set in last night and I'm afraid I realised too late that my shoes were muddy from the yard. I must have had some on my shoes when I went to snuff the candles; I'm so sorry, ma'am. I did sweep the floors as soon as I realised, only I must have missed that bit in the darkness. I shall see to it right away.'

'Indeed.' There was a pause. 'On this occasion, as you are new to the upper bounds, and I have it from Crawford that *usually* you are a good worker, I am willing to overlook it. However...I might remind you that here at Cuddington, we do not entertain incompetence of our staff and I do not expect such carelessness in the future.'

'Yes, ma'am, thank you,' she squeaked, and Mother dismissed her with a wave of her hand before pulling on her gloves and marching out to the coach.

I felt both relieved and ashamed as I rose, hearing their footsteps taper off. Why had she covered for me? Taking the blame for me and offering such a tale. *She could have lost her job,* I thought uncomfortably, creeping my way back to my chamber. And after how horridly I had behaved to her last night when she had showed me nothing less than kindness.

I knew I was right to feel ashamed, but I had too much else to think of today to pay mind to other things of less consequence, so I pushed the thought away. I could not take on the strain of any further burden of guilt right now; it might just be enough to sink me entirely.

Later that morning when she was returned from wherever she had gone with the dowager, Mama appeared at my door, wide-eyed and confused to find me sat at the dressing table under a thick layer of powder.

'What the devil—'

'Sit down, Mama,' I said gravely and she studied me and came into the room and did as bid.

I turned about to face her, stifling the wince of pain as I twisted in my seat. 'I am come early this morning through the servants' entrance as I did not want to disturb you at such an hour.'

'But—'

'Please, Mama. I cannot go back there. I cannot go back to him.'

'Whatever can you mean; he is your husband. What the devil are you about?'

'He hurt me last night, Mama; so dreadfully, I cannot even begin to tell you the whole of it.'

'What did he do? Are you alright?'

'I will be I think, if you do not send me back there.'

'He raised his hand to you?'

'Yes.' I felt the sting of tears roll down my cheeks and suddenly realised I could not bear to tell her the vulgar details of precisely what had passed. So I showed her my head, the split across my lower lip where Mariella had slapped my face and then the bruises upon my arms and shoulders.

She jumped back in alarm and covered her open mouth with her hand. It had all the effect required without the additional sordid details.

'My poor girl,' she cried, bursting into sobs. 'Whatever did you marry such a man for, I knew he must be a horrid man the moment I set eyes on him. Oh, I did not want you to marry into that family, Eleanor, but what can be done of it now? If you set your face against him, he will surely grow more ill-tempered...'

'You must permit me to stay here. Do not send me back, I beg you.' I clung to her.

'No, no of course, I will not. But the trouble is my dear, how can we stop him removing you; you are his wife now.'

I sobbed too now, the relief of her allegiance gushing forth from me. I had not expected it. She was not an affectionate mother and she had shown me little more emotion than I had showed her in the past. But now I felt her presence. Her mind turning towards assisting me and I was moved by it.

'We must send you away to convalesce somewhere he cannot find you. I shall write to your sister and you can go to her whilst we think of some better resolution. In the meantime, we must tell him you are not here, so you must stay inside the house, alright? I will have to tell your father, he will know what is to be done.'

This was a welcome solution for now. An escape to Harriet's was the greatest remedy, for to be amongst my sister and her family would not only keep me out of his way, but restore me in her company. She knew more than anyone else in my family and I could trust the most to her. Not all. But more than anyone else I might be placed with.

On Mama's orders, I was to return to my bed if I would not permit her call the doctor. This point we argued upon but I would not submit to having any kind of examination now. The compromise was made that if the doctor was not to come, then I would at least accept bed rest, and to this I had no argument at all. Every fibre of me was exhausted.

My room felt as empty as before when Mama left it. I stared at the broken ceramics which were still littered about the floor like a tipped out jigsaw puzzle, reminding me of my earlier outburst. But I didn't care, I couldn't care even if I had wanted to; I hadn't the energy. I refused my meals and stayed to my bed. I was in so much pain I could only hope for the refuge of sleep to assuage it now I had refused the doctors coming, and in doing so, denied myself the relief of some pain soothing draught he would have bestowed upon me. But I could not have him look at me and see what my husband had done to me, nor could I hide from him the terrible pain that plagued me that was in an altogether different place than where my bruises could be found.

It was late when I awoke to find my mama sitting up with me.

'What time is it?' I asked, remembering not to try to move too much in her presence.

'Almost ten. It does not signify: you need the rest. How do you feel now?'

'Sore, but it is to be expected.'

'I have written to Harriet, and await her reply.'

'Has he come to look for me?'

'No, he hasn't and I have had a job preventing your father from looking for him. I did not know if I should send a coach for Miss Rosen and send her back to London? It seems a dreadful neglect to leave her in that house alone.'

'She has already gone, Mama. I think the whole affair frightened her off and who could blame her.'

'Well, that is a shame, for I hoped she would travel to Kent with you and tend you at your sister's house. We should find you a replacement when you are well again. But until then, you cannot dare walk out alone now. You will take the young footman too, for extra security if you go about in Kent. He is a strong looking fellow and it would ease my mind to have him about you.'

For a change, I welcomed this entourage if it would keep me safe from him.

On Mother's insistence, I took a little thin soup to appease her before she retired to bed, and whilst I felt weak to the core, I was not tired now, mentally at least. My mind had so many thoughts and images sliding in and out of it, competing for space, that forcing myself back to bed was fruitless. I tried to tire myself with a few lines in my diary, but I could not bring myself to write the words, so I tried the bed again, tried at ignoring the noise of my own head, to numb the feelings such thoughts provoked: but I could not, and the silence was tormenting.

In the end, I got up. Considered a dram of my father's Brandy might offer a little relief from the pain and insomnia.

Workload.

August 1821. - Annalise.

After dinner had been served to the upper servants in their parlour, Annalise went straight back to her room and dropped onto the bed to catch a moment's respite. It had been a long and miserable day and the bliss of their balmy evenings sat about the herb garden seemed a world away now. The only reminder: the scorching August heat that was turning even the smallest of tasks into an insufferable chore, the sweat dripping from their brows, the stifling vapour filled air from the boiling pots, the continuous swatting of flies buzzing around their heads as they toiled.

It had been manageable once a day for the servants' dinner, but now the family were back the number of courses took up most of the day to prepare for dinner time, and even Cook's attempts to offer summer apposite Salamagundi's and cold cuts for the menu's only went so far in alleviating the burden.

'You alright, luv?' Poppy said, coming into the room and finding her spread across the mattress still in her apron.

'Just tired and fed up.'

'Aye, well, we knew it wouldn't last forever eh. Anyway, you coming to the servants' hall? There's ice and lemon barley water set aside for us.'

'No, I've still got my evening chores to do and I would rather a rest.'

'Alright luv. I'll bring you a cup back with me,' Poppy said, hanging up her apron and slipping back out of the room.

After a half hour of watching the dust motes dancing in the light from the small window, staring into the cracks in the ceiling and counting the stockings on the airer, she pulled herself back to her feet, changed her apron for her housemaids one and headed off down the underpass over to the laundry rooms under the guise of taking over the days rice and potato water.

The laundry was deserted when she got there and the air was hot with the tang of soap and lye. She released the barrow she had been wheeling with the starch water urn upon it and peered into the copper to check on Eleanor's soaking dress; she hadn't had the heart to throw it away, despite her instructions, it was too fine for the rag and bone man. Giving it a stir with the dolly and waiting for the murky clouds to disperse, she was satisfied that most of the stains had lifted, and the rest would fade out in the sunlight with a good airing. She tipped the contents of the copper into the sink and filled it up with clean water to rinse it out, before carrying it over to the mangle. She was careful with it as she loaded it between the rollers, ensuring the delicate lace and ribbon trims were carefully wrapped in linen swatches before passing them through and turning the wheel cogs. She was no laundry maid, but had had enough years of washing her own laundry to know how it was done and since the state of the dress would have raised suspicion, she thought it best to manage it covertly herself than cause questions.

Perhaps the luxury of not having to tend to her own anymore lightened the task now as she heaved the heavy fabric and cranked the wheel, her own skirts damp with the drippings, despite trying to keep them out of the way of it. But despite the labour, there was something soothing in the task of it. She could imagine herself back in the kitchen at Gint's, pegging out her and her mama's clothes over the fire airer and meeting her in the housekeeper's parlour over a cup of chocolate and an evening read over Gint's discarded newspapers.

How she longed to open the wood warped door of that little parlour with its green floral tablecloth so worn it was faded almost to white, to find her mama sat in cap and fingerless mitts, one hand curled around a steaming cup and the other flicking through the pages.

Her joie de vivre had seemed to return to her these past few months and the melancholy spells certainly ran fewer and farther between than before, but it seemed that when they cast over her now, they were so stark and immersive; they were difficult to shake off. She was determined not to let them sink her and knew that when the mind could not be diverted, the body could be occupied until the shadows dispersed. She knew that's why she was really here, in the laundry after hours, washing a dress she was supposed to have discarded.

She shook out the wrung linen, folded it neatly upon the table before lifting it into a basket, tossing some clothes pegs into it as she passed the peg bag and headed up the steps and out to the laundry lines. The air was refreshing after the swelter of the basement humidity and she considered how nice it would be just to find a patch of grass to lie out upon and watch the sunset as they had so many nights before. She sought out the farthest line, which was closest to the kitchen yard, in order she might hang it close enough to nip out and inspect it tomorrow and take it down from the line before anyone noticed its tattered hems.

'I thought it was you,' came a voice the other side of the line as she stretched the heavy expanse of the dress out over it.

'Gosh, Will, you gave me a fright,' she said having taken the peg from between her lips and pinning a soggy sleeve up.

'Sorry, I didn't mean to scare yer. So, you're a maid of all work nowadays are yer?' he teased. 'I can't keep up, one minute your passing cloches through the hatch, the next snuffing the lights out upstairs, and now you're doing laundry at this time of night?'

'It's a one-off. What are you doing out now? Isn't the valet back to walking the dogs?'

'Aye, sadly. Miss it already I do. So, I thought I'd take a little stroll about for old time's sake. It's too stuffy in the servants' hall and it's not quite the same without you there.'

She ignored the latter part of his speech. 'It's a shame isn't it, to go back to how it was. But there's nothing for it I suppose,' she said, blindly shaking out a few creases and picking her basket back up.

'Here, let me take that for you.'

'Thank you,' she said not knowing how to refuse his help. She wasn't ungrateful; she just wasn't in the mood for trying to dodge his enthusiasm tonight. She had enough to contend with without their marked friendship falling to the notice of the upper servants. It was different before, when they were kept out of the sight of them, but she had to take care now they were back to the confines of the house. 'Actually, Will, would you spare me the task of taking it back to the laundry room? I'm supposed to start on my rounds now—'

'For you, anything.'

'Thanks, Will,' she said feeling relieved as he headed back down the way she had come. At least they would not be seen walking in together.

She passed through the kitchen unnoticed by the few scullery maids still at work and found her bark bucket, candle snuffer and replenished her stock of new candles in it. As she passed the servants' hall, she caught snippets of the gossip that was brewing over the daughter's impromptu return.

'To turn up like that it can't be the thing,' she heard Maud saying.

'Well, you know what it sniffs of?' said Fanny, revelling at the prospect of a scandal. 'Sounds like her sad marriage is on the rocks before it's even fired off. It was such a rushed thing after all.'

'Nah. I reckon she's in a delicate condition and can't get any rest at that Beddington house. Apparently, it's in a right state and the place is crammed with workman trying to fix it all up. My Charlie knows one of the builders over there,' Mary cut in and stole her thunder.

'Well, if she is, I wager she must 'ave been knocked-up before the wedding and that explains why it was so quick.'

Annalise rolled her eyes to the ceiling as she mounted the stairs. She'd heard little else all day and was getting fed up of the all the conjecture. She was perhaps the closest to understanding the circumstance, and whilst she didn't know precisely what had happened, she was certain all the stories she had heard the others put about, were all wrong. She had been trying to forget all about last night, to no avail with their constant conjuring up the topic and she was actually grateful for the peace above stairs when she left the din behind her.

The house was a striking contrast once she had reached the first floor jib, and her footsteps echoed in the silence as she scurried along the corridors with her equipment clattering in her hands. She paused to check her shoes and was relieved that they were clean, as was the landing rug, which she noted still held a damp patch where she had cleaned it earlier. She was still unused to the eeriness of walking about such a big house, alone at night. It was beautiful enough by day but in the evening, it took on a different tone and the loftiness of the ceilings cast into shadow and the localised amber pools of light about the candelabras gave a mysterious air that made her stiffen, often jumping at the unfamiliar creaks of the house, and walking quickly out of the rooms once all the lights were put out.

It had never bothered her at Hurley Street, but then you were never that far away from another soul. *Mr Gint's town house would have fit into this one at least six times over,* she considered as she snuffed out the candles in the long gallery which was so rarely used it seemed a waste of wax to even have it lit now. Although Mrs Crawford had been clear to her and Maggie that Lady Ashlyn liked all the rooms at least dimly lit on the front façade of the first floor should they receive an unexpected visitor who might arrive to find the house in darkness. It seemed a strange logic to her, as she tossed the burnt down candle ends into her bark bucket and replaced them with fresh glossy sticks of wax that would no doubt end up in there a few nights later.

She continued padding in and out of the rooms, snuffing and replacing, floorboards creaking, shadows falling behind her steps. She had learned to start in such a sequence that left the halls lit until she made her way towards her exit, having made the mistake of doing it haphazardly the first time. Now she had it down to an art and saved the best for last. Just one to go, then bed, she reminded herself, turning the handle of the library door.

The centre chandelier was roaring with sixteen flames above her, casting the Chinese rug pattern beneath into an orange glow and the heights of the surrounding bookshelves into shadow. This was quite easily her favourite room in the house, and she often imagined sinking into one of the cosy fireside chairs—cushions so plump they stretched the fabric—and piled high with a selection from the floor to ceiling bookshelves.

She had once guiltily considered the opportunity when the family were away and Mrs Crawford had shown her about the rooms she was to tend. But when she had returned to it alone, she had given up the audacious notion and settled instead for a cursory browsing of the titles whilst resting from climbing the ladder to snuff the chandelier lights out. She had found a copy of *The Passions* which had took her interest and induced her into sampling three of its pages before she remembered herself. Now, she read a page per visit and was up to page seventeen. It seemed a fair reward for her tiresome labours and she looked to it as she began up the stairs. What could be the harm in a page per day? This way, it appeased her want of reading it without it leaving the shelf beyond a few borrowed moments, and promised her a satiation she looked forward to on these lonesome nightly rounds.

She went straight over to its place now, no longer able to wait to tend the lights first; second bookcase on the left, four shelves up from the ground, five books along on the shelf. *There you are.* She ran a finger along its leather-bound spine as she recalled yesterday's page number to mind.

'Who is there?' a voice punctuated the silence and Annalise jumped, dropping her bark, and candle ends spilled out upon the polished floorboards.

'It is the maid, ma'am,' she replied, shrinking as she turned her head, recognising the voice that came from the far corner of the room.

'Oh.' Eleanor closed her open book and slid it back into its place on the bookshelf. She was stood at the opposite end of the room.

What kind of 'oh' was it exactly? 'Oh, it's *just* the maid,' or *'Oh,* it's the maid.' She could not decipher the meaning. How had she not noticed her there? She had scarcely looked about her, being so accustomed to finding it abandoned and her mind quite fixed on the task of getting to page eighteen tonight. She could not have seen her, could she? She had not taken it from its place yet. 'I'm sorry, miss, I hadn't realised the library was still in use. I'll come back later,' she said and scrambled down to gather up the sprawled-out pieces of candle wax.

'No, there's no need. I was just leaving,' Eleanor said, rushing over to help her recover them.

Annalise looked up surprised and as they rose simultaneously, their eyes met; an uncomfortable glance that seemed impossible to maintain and yet difficult to break from. She looked a little improved from last night, still pale and the cuts on her face more prominent, but her eyes were clearer and less puffy and there was something altogether more human about her now.

'Why did you cover for me?' Eleanor asked then, much to Annalise's surprise and she was glad for the moment, not to have to answer any questions on her going to the bookshelf. She thought back to this morning with a wince, taking the blame for the carpets and Lady Ashlyn mad as fire with her. 'In truth, ma'am, I am not really sure.' She wanted to take back the words as soon as she had spoken them. It had seemed favourable at first, to explaining that despite the vulgarity of her manners, she had felt nothing but pity for the despairing creature that crawled in last night in such a horrid state.

Eleanor nodded. 'Well, I respect your frankness.' She paused as though considering her words. 'I hope you will accept my apology... and my thanks.'

Annalise watched the words roll uncomfortably off her tongue, so surprised by this change of demeanour she almost forgot to make answer. 'Yes, of course, miss.'

A temporary silence hung awkwardly between them and Annalise tried to read what was beyond that carmelite gaze. She had deft skill at hiding the emotion behind her eyes, just as a hint of a clue appeared—a brief flash—it vanished as quickly.

'What is your name?'

'Tulley,' Annalise told her as she handed her a fistful of candle ends to add to the bark box which was once again restored to its full measure. 'Are you alright, ma'am?' she asked instinctively, noticing a flinch of pain in her gait as she moved.

'Quite,' she said quickly. 'Tulley, yes, I remember now. I will bid you goodnight.'

She remembered? She could not recall telling her her name, or being asked to. 'Goodnight, Miss.' She dipped a curtsey and was relieved to be alone again. Although page eighteen would have to wait now, she could not feel comfortable attempting it tonight.

The Library.

August 1821. - Eleanor.

I woke up feeling slightly better having got off to sleep after a couple of glasses of Brandy I procured from my father's study and a little distracted reading. It had eased the pain that had since returned to me this morning with the addition of a heavy dull ache in my lower back. I had a bath drawn for me after breakfast and asked Watts to procure me some soothing herbs and salves, and insisted upon taking it without any further assistance. I had managed to hide the worst of my injuries insofar and had no mind to jeopardise that feat now, even if it meant a little struggling.

It was worth the trouble. The relief was so restoring, I wished I had thought of it sooner, feeling the heat penetrate into sore muscles and achy places as I sank back into the tub and immersed myself as fully as I could. It was the first time I had been able to sit comfortably, having lately settled for a careful arrangement of cushions or lying down upon my side. I wondered if it might be sensible to proceed on to Bath after all; I had heard they had private baths for hire there in the healing waters which could restore all kinds of ills. I was not sure if this kind would be amongst them, but I would have given almost anything a try that might offer relief. But it could not be risked since he might expect me to go there. May even be there searching for me now. I was doubtful I would manage to sit in the carriage at all anyway, let alone make the fourteen-hour journey.

I was reminded then, that I must remember to write to Lady W. to update her. No doubt the staff would send word to her that we had not arrived and she might puzzle over it. I wished she was not so far away. I felt her counsel would prove invaluable right now and she might be the only one I could confess the full account to. It seemed strange to me that she should be, so recent our acquaintance. And yet there was a depth to our friendship and an authenticity to her character that made me feel she could be trusted with anything; however unsavoury the detail.

Perhaps London might prove safe to visit after a time. Perhaps when I was returned from Harriet's and knew how the land lie with Giles. Perhaps he would go onto Venice and I would be safe to visit her then. For now, at least, I must be content to keep my whereabouts out of his knowing until some resolution was found, whatever that may be.

I sunk my face below the surface of the water and felt the stinging of my lip and forehead, but comfort to my scalp that felt inflamed and bruised to the touch at the crown where he had pulled me by the hair. I diverted the memory as it attempted to replay again and rose back up, folding a wet face cloth and settling it across my eyes, steam carrying the scent of chamomile and feverfew flowers to my nostrils.

The afternoon I spent lying upon the chaise in my room, reading from several different books, but finding nothing that could hold my interest or keep me distracted from my own head stories. It did at least make my eyes grow weary and prompt me to fall into frequent naps, but by evening, this proved a curse as the idleness of the day caused my body to grow restless at precisely the point when the relief of my soothing bath and salves wore off entirely and I found myself rigid, sore and unable to settle to bed. What I needed was some exercise to exhaust me. A vigorous ride on the downs or a long walk on the park—neither of which was plausible in my current state and I knew weren't likely to be for some time yet. The very idea of mounting Samson ever again seemed impossible to me right now, but I hoped I might return to it sometime soon. I supposed I could try for a gentle walk tomorrow, but I was frightened of the prospect of being seen beyond the house having them for neighbours. And even though we were hardly overlooked and the woodland boundary was a good distance from the house, I would not have put it passed them to try at spying for a sign of my presence.

So, I followed the routine of the previous night: stopped in Papa's study for some Brandy en-route to the library.

I don't know why I felt inclined to go back to the library when I had already amassed such a pile of books from it that had been discarded to a pile beside the chaise. I had found myself both lacking in amusement and yet unable to settle to anything diverting. I had browsed a few, earmarked some pages of interest to return to in a better head, and puzzled over some of my selections, thinking them dull.

But I went there all the same, amassed another pile and curled up on the long sofa, a half-browsed copy of *La Belle Assemblee* abandoned to the floor. I supposed a change of scenery was my intention. I had spent so much time in my own chamber I had grown sick and tired of the pattern of my own wallpaper. Perhaps I should suggest a refurbishment of the room. That would at least give me a project to busy myself with, something to focus this mind on that would not switch off, nor be persuaded to any industrious use. But Mama would not be for it. It had only been refashioned two years ago, and in her mind, my staying here again was but a temporary arrangement, until things were "resolved". I wish it were so simple. But then I could never divulge to her just how bad it all was. It seemed preferable not to correct her than to relay to her such gross details that would no doubt send her into a fit of nervous apoplexy.

I must have been dozing off from my Brandy induced repose when I heard the click of the door and footsteps pad into the room. I could not see who was there from my position on the sofa, facing away from the door, so, feeling too sleepy to rise from it, I peered up into the mirror above the mantle and saw reflected back in it, the maid, Tulley, again. I stiffened a little at the notice of her. There was still something insufferable in acknowledging the state in which she had seen me. No one had ever seen me in such a monstrous rage; I had never been in such a head before. It felt like a self-betrayal to have permitted such a scene before an audience, and a shameful injury each time I saw her again, reminding me of what had passed and what intimate knowledge she had of me. Of all the scrapes, bumps and bruises she must have noticed, of all the tears I shed in her presence.

Still, I felt somewhat better for having attempted to make amends with her yesterday. The idea of her carrying a stifled contempt for me after my unreasonable treatment of her, causing her to bad mouth me or distribute my secrets below stairs, jarred me. I hoped that she would do neither now I had taken the opportunity to apologise. But my faith in servants grew ever frailer after the betrayal of Molly, then Miss Rosen, not to mention the spies installed at Half Moon Street.

I was just mustering up the composure to greet her now, as nonchalantly as I would to any housemaid, but with perhaps a slightly kinder smile for her. But as I began to push up from the sofa, I saw her put down her things upon the floor and slide a book from the bookshelf. I paused, intrigued; kept beneath the cover of the sofa back and waited. What was she about? She had gone directly to it. Was she? No...it could not be. Yes: She was reading from it. I held in a gasp. I had always held the assumption that, with the exception of some of the upper servants, they could not read, and yet here she was, a chit of a girl, reading from our library. It disconcerted me and I wasn't sure why. Perhaps because I had nurtured a false sense of security in writing my diaries or leaving my letters out upon my desk. She had rendered this presumption instantly false, in a moment of her sliding a book from its shelf.

So...was this why my bribe had failed to win her? I had offered her jewels when she preferred books. It seemed absurd and yet something in it could not fail to move me a fraction, see something admirable in such a preference, even if it was disconcerting.

She closed the book and slid it back into place. I quickly closed my eyes and feigned sleep as I heard her footsteps come in my direction, then heard her gasp of surprise, noticing me at last. I concentrated on not allowing my eyes to twitch and give me away. Then I heard her tinkering with her things and felt a little relief that she was no longer likely to be stood over me staring. I wondered then, why I had assumed the role of the guilty party, pretending I must not be seen when it was she that was at mischief. I supposed if she knew I was awake I would be forced to confront her on the matter and what would I say? Besides, it may prove useful yet to know this secret, to have some leverage with her: To know that we both had each other's secrets in safekeeping. I did not exactly know how it might prove useful yet, but I knew such insights were always worth collecting.

When she left, after a little more tinkering about, I got up from the sofa and went in search of the book she had taken from the shelf. I had not been able to see it properly through the glass' reflection and was none the wiser for perusing the shelf. But I went back a couple of nights later about the same hour, and this time hid beneath the desk so I could watch her. She was more cautious now, checking the sofas and glancing around to make sure she was quite alone. There was something quite thrilling about watching her through the crack in the desk in her oblivion. Once she was at ease, she repeated the pattern I had seen before, and this time, I noted the place from which she pulled the book.

This became a habit we both repeated, night after night: me crouched beneath the desk, she reading from the book a few pages before snubbing the candle flames and dusting the fireplace.

I could not understand or explain my fascination, and this odd ritual that had borne out of it. But every night, about a quarter past eleven, I would wait for her there in muted anticipation.

I had considered the possibility of my own madness. Had the taking on of the Craythorne name transmitted to me some of their insanity? I had also become increasingly partial to my father's Brandy decanter to help me get to sleep at night and had suspected that my increasing indulgence had perhaps got to my head a little, and blamed that for this peculiar routine.

The Passion by Rosa Matilda—I had discovered the book to be, eventually. I wondered how far she had read through it; she must have committed the page number to memory for the pages were unmarked and there was no place saver inside it. I had once read it, some time ago, when Harriet had first bought it, but the details had faded somewhat from my recollection. So, in particularly idle moments, I would go in the daytime to read a little and refresh my memory of it. Always making sure to put it back in precisely the same place.

Pain relief.

August 1821. - Eleanor.

It was half past eleven and I was sat at my escritoire over a candle. My eyes were stinging with the strain, reading back through Lady W.'s now finished letter. I had received her reply to my express this morning and was touched by her open-door invitation to me, should I wish to return to Grosvenor Square as her guest. I would have liked to, very much. I was falling into an isolated melancholy here in the country, confined to the house with no company or diversion. But I was in no fit state for travel or to receive company yet, and told her I would write to her again when I was in better health.

I was beginning to wonder just how long that would be. For even as I felt the small increments in my physical healing each day, bruises shrinking and fading to yellow, less cushions to mount upon the chair, it seemed to run contrary to my spirits which seemed to deteriorate further as time went by. Perhaps when I could get back to riding or walking again, I might lift these doldrums enough to take her up on her invitation. I knew it would do me some good to be about her. I sealed the letter and popped it into my writing chest.

Even the happy prospect of going to Harriet's was to be delayed on account of her being already set out on a journey to Malvern to visit her parents-in-law before Mama's letter had reached Kent. And so, I was to remain to the house for now, in the sweltering August heat, with the gardens in full bloom and tempting me to venture out into the sunshine. Mama had suggested I take on Fanny until she had arranged the Abigail interviews she was advertising for. That way I could at least go out to the walled gardens for air and exercise with her chaperone. But I was not keen on Fanny. Something in her countenance gave me the impression she was a slyboots, and having dealt with enough of those types of persons lately, I had no wish to have any more close about me. To deal with my toilette was manageable, so long as I took care to see to my own washing and change my shift before she dressed me, but beyond these necessities, I had no wish to be saddled with her. I would rather have taken my father's hounds out to guard me. Their company and loyalty could be relied upon entirely, although they would likely have half the kitchen garden overturned in an afternoon for the sport of it, and so I reserved that idea for when I was feeling more confident to venture out to the woods. Heaven knows I would have to do something soon if I was to tire myself enough to sleep at night. It had become such an ordeal just to go to bed with restless limbs and racing thoughts.

I tried the bed again now, and after another hour of tossing and turning, I found myself creeping down to Father's study for the Brandy doses that had become habitual and increasing with every restless night. I had tried to cap it at three this evening on my way to the library, thinking that would be adequate to convey me into slumber a couple of hours ago. Alas tonight would be four doses it seemed, and so I pushed my feet into my slippers and found my robe upon the back of the door. Noticing the lights had already been snuffed out in the hall, I went back for my candle and navigated carefully downstairs.

When I got to Father's study, I was surprised to find it was locked when I tried the handle, as was the wine cellar when I ventured down to the basement in rising desperation. I was later than usual and had never considered that the place was shut up like this at night, not on the inside at least.

It had seemed a wasted pursuit until I finally stumbled on an unopened bottle of Claret in the drawing room cabinet that had been forgotten. It would have to do, even if it would likely take the bottle to achieve what a few drams of spirits could. I would have to be better prepared tomorrow. Perhaps send one of the servants out to town to procure me some of my own. My father would surely begin to notice his dwindling supply if I continued helping myself. I headed back downstairs and padded carefully along the servants' corridors, the bottle beneath my arm and my robe cloaked carefully over it, in search of a corkscrew. I hadn't a clue where I might find one in the kitchens but I was sure there must be one somewhere in there.

I eased the door open carefully and was relieved to find it empty. The smell of the days cooking was dwindling and I recognised a whiff of the same musty dampness I noticed in the corridor. I put the bottle down on a nearside workbench and searched through the nearest set of drawers trying to make no sounds. I found all manner of strange looking ephemera and held them up to the light of my lamp, but I did not recognise any of them. I went through another and another, but still could not find anything that resembled a corkscrew. I turned around and held my light out to survey the room better, and as I turned from the doorway, I heard it open behind me. I tried not to gasp but it was too late and with the panic to hide it, I knocked the wine bottle to the ground.

'Miss?' came the voice, advancing on me and I knew when I saw Tulley's silhouette advance into the room, that a bribe would be no good to me.

'Is...is there something I can help you with?' she said, blinking with confusion, stopping the rolling wine bottle with her foot.

I was grateful that it did not smash.

She picked it up and handed it back to me and I quickly took it up beneath my robe. 'Yes, as a matter of fact, I am looking for a corkscrew,' I told her as confidently as I could contrive. I couldn't see her face properly in the dim light and was glad not to have to meet her eyes.

I watched her put down a pile of linen she had been carrying on the table and walk over to a draw on the opposite side of the room. I wondered how anyone might know the precise place of so many things in such a big room, so full of them. She rummaged around for a moment then shut it, walked over to me and held it out.

'Thank you.' My voice cracked over the words.

'You might have rang for it,' she said and I could see her face better now, I could see too that she was wise to the situation and it frustrated me. I was sure that anyone else, with the exception of Delores, would have not dared question me, would have had neither the care nor the cheek to look at me in such a way that told me she knew what I was up to and did not approve of it. I thought about offering her some coins but knew better of it. There was something unusual in her character, something of morals and wisdom beyond her class and it perturbed me greatly.

'Yes, yes. Well, my bell is not working and I was expecting someone to be here to ask. I didn't realise you had all retired.' My words were a clumsy effort and I felt the heat rising in my cheeks. I wondered what on earth I was doing, standing here, in answer to a maidservant? I was clearly on the brink of losing my mind, never mind my temper, but I quelled it, remembering the discretion she afforded me on the last matter. 'What are you doing up when everyone else is gone to bed?' I asked her when I could think of no other answer.

She pressed her lips together and I sensed her unease.

'I was about to do some mending,' she said, sideways glancing at the pile slumped on the table.

I followed her stare and walked over to it, held my light over it and recognised the ruby fabric of my dress. 'I told you to throw it away,' I scowled as I shook off a flashback from *that* night.

'I'm sorry miss, I know you did. But look...' she picked it up and shook it out, holding it to her shoulders. 'It is almost as good as new, just another night or two and it will be finished for you,' she said, looking pleased with herself.

I could not deny it was well restored from the unrecognisable mess it was in that evening, but neither could I explain that if I watched it burn on the fire I would be more satisfied. 'Tulley, you are a chamber maid are you not?'

'A tweeny at the moment, miss, but I am usually a kitchen maid.'

'Then why have you assumed the work of a lady's maid, and against my instruction?'

'I'm sorry miss, I have acted above my station, I know.'

I bit my lip at the temptation to scold her. I could see the fear in her eyes at the realisation and I had the leverage I needed now. 'Indeed. Well, you have done a very good job of it. But I will not miss it... You should keep it.'

'Oh, miss, I couldn't. I only mended it to please you.'

My patience was fraying. 'Yes, you could. I insist upon it,' I managed and turned to leave.

'But it is far too grand a dress for me and I would never have an occasion for it.'

'Then a relative or friend perhaps might make some use of it?'

She was silent a moment. Then she thanked me and I was relieved at last to have shut her up. I took the wine to my room and when I got there and realised I had forgotten to bring a glass, I drunk it straight from the bottle.

I woke late the next morning with a fuzzy headache and a dry mouth. The Claret was certainly not as forgiving as the Brandy and I knew I must make contingency plans today to prevent a re-occurrence. Mama had summoned me to her parlour to look over the applications she had received and I sat over them with her, trying to focus my eyes on the letters of recommendation as I sipped on strongly brewed coffee. They were separated into a shortlist and Mama said she would send out invitations to interview. But since I had insisted on taking on no local girls, she was in a quandary as to how we would manage them. I hardly cared. All I could think about was how to obtain a bottle of Brandy to set my evenings off a little smoother, but I could not decide on who to entrust the task to.

'Your father has discovered that Giles is not here any longer, but back in Half Moon Street,' Mama said whilst scooping the piles of letters from the table.

'He is?'

She nodded. 'So, perhaps you might go out for a little air on the park this afternoon, my dear. Take Fanny and the footman with you. You look so peaky, I'm certain it must do you some good.'

I nodded my agreement. If he really was away then I supposed I must be at ease about the park now at least. But I would take the hounds instead.

And so, I sent a message to my father's valet and asked him to meet me at the stable yard with Bess and Maximus at two. When I was greeted by excited wagging tails and bounding about my feet, I stroked them down a moment before taking the leashes he supplied me with and an instruction not to be out too long for Bess' condition was well established now and it might not do her good to over exercise in such heat.

'So, she is to have pups?' I asked excited and he nodded. 'When?'

'Likely within the next couple of weeks, the farmer says.'

'How exciting,' I said and bid him farewell and called the dogs to heel as I led them off towards the lawns. I thought, as I roamed the woodlands with them whilst they sniffed and urinated along the path, that I should like to keep one of the puppies for a pet when they were born. That was just what I needed; a loyal companion, something to cuddle and fuss over and take for walks like this. I would tell my father at dinner, beg Mama to let me keep it in the house once it was weaned. I should have to find someone to make up a sumptuous pillow bed for it so it may be comfortable in my chamber.

As we walked out towards the lake, I debated over whether I should like a boy or girl, trifled over possible names and considered whether they would be born in the shade of black of their father or yellow as their mother. I had no preference. Just a cheerful buoyant character and possibly the ability to launch an attack at the sound of the name Giles, I considered as I sat lakeside and watched them leap into the water and wade about in it. They were having so much fun I felt tempted to follow their example and cool off a while. But I had not come prepared for it, and even though I felt better for the news of Giles being in London, I did not feel fully at ease still and kept my wits about me.

When we got home, I felt far from invigorated for my troubles and found myself quite tremulous and lethargic. Perhaps it was the heat, or being so active after such a lull or perhaps the wine, I considered, deciding to take a glass with my luncheon. It seemed to do the trick, so I took another couple with my dinner and managed to get to the Brandy decanter ahead of the study being locked up tonight. But by the time I had sat in the library a half hour, I was already certain I needed more. It was as though the effect was lessening with every cup and when the library door burst open tonight and Tulley came into it, I was relieved at the sight of her.

'Good evening, ma'am,' she dipped a curtsey, hiding her surprise at finding me there.

I had not hid tonight, I wanted to see her, needed to. For all its discomfort, the fact was, she knew enough about my circumstances that I needed not pretend with her. And so outright, I asked her: 'Tulley, would you be so good as to have a bottle of Claret sent up to my room? I am going now, so I need not hold you up.'

'Of course, ma'am, I shall tell Grantley and—'

'No. I would prefer to keep the matter between us if you will.'

'But, ma'am, Grantley keeps all the wines locked up.'

'I'm sure you can figure it out. Be easy. I shall vouch for the request should you have any difficulty,' I said, rising from my chair a little unsteadily and departing for my chamber.

I rushed Fanny through my toilette when I returned, not wanting her presence to collide with my delivery. Half an hour later and I realised as I paced the floor that there had been no need to hurry her at all.

'I'm sorry, ma'am. I had some trouble managing it, but, here it is,' she said putting a tray upon the side table, with a glass and corkscrew beside the bottle.

'Thank you,' I said relieved and set about opening it.

'Will that be all, ma'am?'

'Yes. Thank you for your trouble. Is there something I might do in return, for you?' I had thought instantly of the book in the library, but had no wish to expose myself.

'No, ma'am. Good evening.'

And so, this formed the pattern of the evenings and my sleep came to me easily, my tremors kept at bay with regular dosing, and whilst I was far from in good spirits, I welcomed the numbing of my senses to a manageable level.

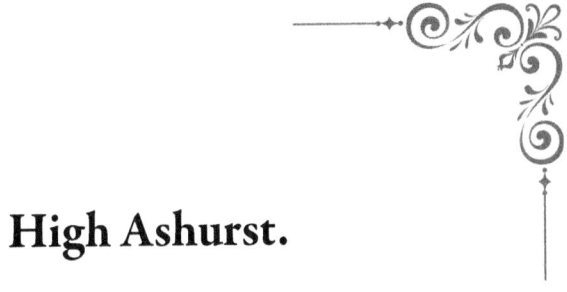

High Ashurst.

August 1821.-Eleanor.

I woke up in a pool of my own vomit. It had surprised me that I could not remember having even felt sick. I climbed out of the bed, covered the messy pillows with my sheet and rang for Tulley. 'I'm sorry, I know it is not your duty, and I do not ask you to deal with the unpleasant task, but pray, fetch me the things I will need to set it to rights without anyone knowing.'

'Very well,' she agreed, looking over the mess as I peeled back the sheet. There was something of dismay in her eyes and I thought it just my luck that the most dependable of servants was such a stickler.

When she returned, she tried to take up the task for me, but this was too much to expect and I accepted her guidance as I did my best to clean the debris from the bedding, strip the sheets and replace them with the new linens she had brought up. This I did need some assistance with as I was far too tremulous to manage the flapping and folding of sheets on my own in such a state and was binding myself up in a right fix.

I took a small cup of wine before going down for breakfast. Mama had specifically asked that I join her today after permitting me keep to my room for meals insofar, and so I took my seat bracing myself for conversation which I had no head for, feeling so fragile.

'My dear, do you think you are quite well enough for travel yet?' she asked as I buttered a crumpet with incredible concentration to disguise the shaking of the butter knife.

'Perhaps. Why? Is Harriet come home early?' I asked hopefully.

'No. She shall be yet another week at least.' She poured from the teapot into both of our cups, but I was in need of coffee today. 'It's Henry, it seems he wishes us to meet with a young lady he means to offer for.'

'Henry?' I almost spat out my crumpet.

'Yes. He has asked us to come up to London to meet her this week.'

'Why should we have to travel to him? Surely he should do the courtesy of bringing her home.'

'Not *we*, my dear, just your father and I,' she said carefully, stirring her tea and taking a long sip.

And then I understood. He was ashamed of me. Of all the scandal. Perhaps of putting this damsel off by his association as my brother. 'So, what shall I do? You know London is not safe for me with that beast there, even if I keep to the house and you are not in it.'

'Well. I had been troubling over the difficulty and, I was visiting Delores just yesterday to welcome her back after her wedding journey and, she has invited you to stay with her a few days in Dorking.'

'Is she well? Does married life suit her?' I asked, wondering how I could get out of this arrangement. I was not fit to stay under Delores careful gaze without her noticing my troubles; she was far too assiduous in her observations.

'Surprisingly well it seems. She asked after you and said it would be nice for you to stay a while.'

'It seems my only other choice is stay here alone.'

'We both know that is not a good idea. If he learns we are in London, who knows if he might chance coming home to find you here alone? I don't think my nerves could take the worry. We must sort out your lack of companion. Which reminds me, Mrs Bloxam made me the recommendation of a very good lady's maid at tea yesterday. A Swiss girl,' she said this with great expectation that made it difficult to explain to her that I would rather choose a knife boy over someone with Mrs Bloxam's recommendation.

'She was her cousin's daughter's maid for two years and Lady Rushton's before that. But the daughter is to move abroad at the end of the month and the maid has declined to go with her. Dreadfully inconvenient for her, but how fortunate for us. Mrs Bloxam will write to her cousin with our direction so she can apply directly to us.'

'But Mama, we don't have time for the wait if she's to go to Kent with me. I am sure she must serve out her notice until her Lady leaves the country?' It was the only point I could think to make in protest.

'Yes, there is that, but a good lady's maid is worth the wait, dear, and we both know those I'm to interview left us quite underwhelmed. Perhaps I should cancel them?'

'No, Mama, don't do that. Please take them as planned and if they prove a disappointment in person, then we might have heard back from Mrs Bloxam's cousin on our return.'

This seemed reasonable, even to her.

'Very well. But none of it solves our dilemma presently.'

'I will go to Dorking, Mama, so long as I can take my own maidservant with me.'

Her expression lightened. 'Of course. Fanny will surely be delighted to go with you and act as Abigail.'

'Not Fanny, Mama, I want the other maid. The kind one: Tulley.'

She blinked a little confused. 'I think she is a kitchen maid my dear, that would never do.'

'I don't care. She is sensible and calm and Fanny is excitable and skittish. I shall only go if I can take her and be comfortable in Dorking.'

She sighed. 'Ah well, if you insist, but I think you will create some discord for Mrs Crawford usurping Fanny when it would be her proper place, but—'

'It shall only be for a few days, and like you say, I shall have a proper Abigail soon.'

And so it was settled and I was packed off to Dorking the next day, with Tulley beside me and a couple of bottles of wine she had procured, packed in the bottom of my portmanteau.

Far from seeming content at this arrangement, she seemed uncomfortable and perturbed by having to wait on me, although she said nothing of it. I thought she might enjoy the respite from the heavier work she was used to and I asked little of her beyond assisting with my toilette and accompanying me on my exercise. She said little in these moments of proximity beyond courtesies and asking for directions on some such trivial task such as how she was to style my hair and what oils and lotions she was to use in my toilette. I grew into the habit of preparing what I could for her in advance and settled upon simple chignons, which seemed the only mode of hairstyle she knew how to craft. Since I was no better informed on the construction of more elaborate designs, it seemed best to keep things simple. Besides, I was hardly out to impress at some soiree. Now, just to be presentable was adequate and more effort than I could be bothered to commit to. If it was up to me, I would probably have given up on the trying and lived in undress and slippers day and night.

Delores was spritely and glowing with the contentment of her new circumstances. Married life did suit her very well indeed and I was surprised at not only how much altered she seemed by her new station, but how it altered the amiability betwixt us, now that she was no longer my chaperone and I no longer her troublesome charge. Things were quiet and slow in Dorking, but she was kind and sympathetic to me and my present difficulties, saying that "nobody could have known how ill it would turn out" and that she was "sorry to see me so downcast." I was grateful for her compassion, her willingness to overlook my circumstances when even my own brother could not do as much. Not that I cared a whit for it beyond the point of principle. He had done more to disgrace our family in his days as one of Prinny's set, than I ever could manage, but of course, he was a son and heir and so all such ills were explained as a natural course of his growing into his manhood, even if he was soon to be thirty.

The Squire too was kind and amiable and clearly very much enamoured by his new wife. I was truly happy for her, to see her come about with such bleak prospects, was such a victory for a female of Delores' years, and far too little of such stories were known of. The trajectory of her life had seemed resigned to service to my family before being pensioned off to a Cuddington cottage one day. Now, here she was, mistress of High Ashurst and with a glow of happiness in her cheek more akin to that of a young debutante than a woman of her late forties. It gave me hope. I was not sure how I could turn around the bleak looking future laid out in front of me yet, but it reminded me that it was possible for your fortune to turn, in even the most unlikely of circumstances.

We spent a pleasant few days in Dorking. She was not shy of taking me to pay some calls upon her new neighbours, and took me in the Landau to drive up to the top of box hill and walk some of the way down it. I took Tulley along too, and even though she said little, I could see a lightening in her countenance as we took in the fine air and felt the sunshine warm our backs.

She was a puzzle to me. Giving so little away whilst always seeming so much in earnest and propriety. Her toilette skills left a lot to be desired and it was clear to me she had never undertaken this kind of work. Yet I felt I could trust her. I felt safe with her. And that weighed heavier with me of late than friseur skills. Despite this, we didn't seem to see eye to eye, and I felt her disapproval of my wine sipping most fervently. I had noticed her habit of coming to check on me at night, rousing me and forcing me onto my side if I was not already, before snuffing the lights and going off to her quarters.

In the morning, she forced copious amounts of barley water down me before agreeing to let me take a small glass of wine to stave off the shaking. I knew I must try to reduce it, and eventually I meant to, once I was restored to a more normal and active lifestyle. When my mind was not shrouded in such misery. When the trauma of what had passed, and the fear of what may yet come to pass, did not haunt me every hour. But I was not there yet. There was much still to be resolved and recovered in my peace of mind. And even as my body physically healed with increasing resilience now, I knew my mind would not bounce back so fast. That the stain of that night would lay heavy in my memory for a time to come.

But these few days in Dorking had done much to restore me and I had managed to keep the wine to bedtimes, beyond a small morning glass, so that Delores did not discern anything unusual. If I could only keep the pattern when I got home this afternoon, then I might manage to hold things together a little better. I must try. If I was soon to go to Kent, I must try to get myself in better order first.

Under pressure.

August 1821. - Annalise.

'Eh? What is it? What's wrong, Anna?' Will asked, spotting her fleeing the servants' staircase at a run.

'Nothing, let me be, Will,' Annalise said between sobs, trying to push past him as he moved into her path.

'Slow down, will yer and don't tell me nothing when your face is sodden with tears.' He put an arm across the wall so she could not pass through and when she resisted, he gathered her up and held her. 'Hey, come, whatever it is, it'll be alright.'

'No, no it won't be, it never is. There is always something,' Annalise said through waves of sobs and stutters, giving in to his embrace now.

'That's just life, love, yer know that. But yer got this far, so I'd say you're weathering it pretty well.'

'Oh, don't make me laugh, Will; it's not funny.'

'Then why are you laughing?' He pulled back a fraction to study her better. 'Are you laughing, or crying?'

She let out another involuntary chuckle and wiped her eyes. 'I don't know!'

'Well, whatever it is, it's an improvement I s'pose.'

She batted him away playfully with the back of her hand and stepped aside a fraction.

'You obviously want to be furious at the moment, so, why don't you tell me what it is that's got yer into such a passion and we'll see if we can fire you up again and burn all the rage out?'

'Argh, Will, it's everything. One thing resolves, and another comes right up behind it to take its place, usually worse than the one preceding. When will it get better?'

'Aye, I thought you'd be 'appy now the new housemaids taken over all those over jobs you were doing. Thought you'd be getting more kip and soothing those bags beneath your eyes.'

The chance would be a fine thing, Annalise thought. He was right of course, she should be early to bed now, not staying up to check on a drunkard every night to make sure she wasn't choking in her sleep. She sighed and brushed a palm over her forehead. 'I do need more sleep,' she admitted.

'Then get yourself off to bed and get some!'

'I can't yet, I have something I must do first.'

'Then let me do it?'

'I can't.'

'Course you can, well, unless it's anything to do with chamber pots or ladies toilettes, that is.'

'Oh, Will, you are so daft. I wish it were so simple.'

'Well, tell me what it is and I'll tell you if I can 'elp with it.'

'I need to get access to the wine cellar.'

'What?'

'Not for me, Will!'

'But you who'll take the flack for it if Grantley finds you out.'

She nodded and bit her lip.

'How long do you need?'

'Long enough to grab a couple of bottles of, well, of anything really,' she said, thinking if Eleanor's habit was anything in the style of her mama's, she would not be fussy.

'Gimme twenty minutes, alright. He usually locks up the after-dinner drinks about ten. You be ready waiting down there out the way somewhere and I'll come and distract him for a moment so you can get in there.'

'No, Will, I shan't embroil you into my troubles.'

'Hey, a problem halved and all that.'

Annalise felt so wrong in accepting his help in such a scheme and yet so helpless without it. And whilst she was grateful to him, she was so bitter in having entangled him in such wicked mischief, twice as mad as she was for getting involved in it herself. As she packed the two bottles of wine up into Eleanor's travelling trunk, she felt such resentment coursing through her, it took all she could muster to keep a civil tongue with her. Had she any idea how others were suffering because of her selfish habit? How painful it was for Annalise to have to deal in her antics when they ran so close to the memory of her mama? Would she care if she or Will got caught and put out for it? Did she care for anything above her own selfishness?

It was in such a head of stifled fury that she was even unkind to Fanny that morning when she came marching up to her in the servants' hall with her hands on her hips.

'Why you going to Dorking wi' the mistress?' she demanded to know in accents far from friendly or enquiring. What perhaps she did not expect was to be answered in a tone of even greater irritation.

'Why's it pigeon pie on the menu today? Why do the candles need putting on in empty rooms, and why is the sky blue? God, Fanny, how should I know? I follow the orders, I don't give them.'

'Alright, keep your 'air on. I was only askin'.'

'No, you weren't. You were insinuating and I'm not in the mood for it today Fanny.'

'Well, I dunno why you're in such a fidget. It's not you who has to stay here working is it? No, swanning off to Dorking to change a petticoat once in a while.'

'Well, if you are that bothered about it, why don't you do us both a favour and go to the mistress and volunteer your going in my place?'

Old Mill Street.

August 1821. - Eleanor.

It only took a day of being back home to cull all the progress I had made at Dorking. I had not realised how much freer I felt there. How much more anonymity I had enjoyed at High Ashurst. How much I had benefited from the change of scenery and increase in walking and even social visits to strangers. It was like something of normality had grounded me again and now it was all set asunder: The return to four walls, bleak idolatry and wishing away the hours of my existence.

My parents had come home overjoyed, bearing the news of Henry's announcement to wed Lady Jane Yardley, a wealthy chit barely a couple of years older than me. I wonder if she knew what she was letting herself in for agreeing to Henry's offer. He was not violent at least, but generally useless and self-absorbed.

I was pleased to see the lift in my parents' spirits though. It had been their sincerest wish for him to settle down as long as I could remember, and I supposed none of us really thought it would ever happen. But I had little time for my eldest brother, and less interest in all the news and pomp as Mama set upon her grandest plans to date. I wondered whether she thought the brilliance of such lavish celebrations would shrink into shadow the infamy of my circumstances. That the Yardley-Ashlyn affiliation might usurp the Craythorne-Ashlyn one. They were an important family and it would surely do much to help recover us. If only I could contrive to take a holiday during all the arrangements and ceremony.

At least when Delores was here, she would have her ears to box with such details. But now it seemed I was to be the sounding board when I could think of nothing worse than the prospect of contemplating society affairs, grand balls and engagement parties, and had little beyond a sense of foreboding at all the talk. I tried, in good grace, to humour it for Mama's sake. I owed her that much I supposed, given the disappointment I had proved. But when a flurry of well-wishers arrived upon having heard the news of this impressive alliance, I grabbed my bonnet and darted through the open garden doors before Grantley had left the room to announce them.

I took a short cut through the kitchen garden, the aromatic scent of sweet marjoram and rosemary in the warm air. It was the quickest route to reach the woodland and I wanted to disappear as quickly as I could before Mama sent someone out to summon me back. She was of a mind that putting on a brave face was the best way to deal with prittle-prattles, and had counselled me to embrace them, directing me to endure insipid conversation with persons that were all to ready to play pretty to my face then throw me into the scandal broth cauldron. I was to put on smiles and airs of nonchalance to prove everything was quite alright as a rebuttal. But it was not alright. *I* was not alright, and I had tired now of telling others I was. Even if they could hear the words I forced out to the contrary, I was certain they could see the untruth of it in my face, my puffy ringed eyes, sallow complexion and general weariness that seeped its way out of me despite my attempts at concealment.

Unlike me, the world outside of the house and these troubles seemed to be well and vibrant. Summer colour springing up from every bloom, the woodland thick with leafy cover, sheltering its trunks and blossom from the harshness of the sun, the once muddy pathways now dry and walkable without the need for patens. It was beautiful. However ugly I felt inside, however lacklustre my life seemed, I was reminded that there was still good in the world. Still hope of brighter seasons—however distant from past or present they seemed now.

I walked on a good half hour or more before I was distracted by the notice of someone ahead. I was still on my father's land and had kept purposely away from the Beaulieu boundary, so I hadn't expected to find anyone else walking these woods and it made me nervous. I quickened my pace to investigate. The visibility through the woods was patchy but they were in my line of sight. As I drew furtively closer, I could make out a female figure, but still I did not recognise the peasant looking clothing and felt relieved that it was unlikely to be Mariella: unless she had assumed an elaborate clothing disguise to match the elaborate disguise of her persona falsum.

I was about to call out when the startled figure turned around to the sound of the twigs breaking beneath my half boots.

'Miss?'

'Tulley. I did not expect to see you here,' I said with more relief than she would have been able to fathom. 'You gave me quite a start,' I said, removing my hand from my throat.

'I am on my way to town,' she explained as if presumed guilty of some mischief.

'I see. Well, it is a nice day for it.'

'It is, miss.'

'Are you off shopping?' I gestured to the empty basket swinging from the crook in her elbow. I don't know why I said it. In answer to the awkward pauses perhaps. It seemed the more I said, the more discomforting the atmosphere seemed to grow. Why did everything I say seem always to have some suspicious sounding note to it?

'Just a few groceries, for my friends.'

Friends. I had forgotten what it was to be amongst them. I thought of Lady W. instantly and wished I might look to such easy company to be in. It seemed I had so very few left. Although the saying went, "quality over quantity," and at least that much was true.

'Miss?'

I blinked.

'Is there anything more you wished to say to me?'

'No. No, your private time is your own. I shan't keep you.'

'Thank you, miss, only I am already running behind.'

'There is no need to explain, as I said, your free time is none of my business.'

She bobbed a curtsy and set off again.

'Tulley,' I called and waited for her to turn back around. 'I would be grateful if you could likewise remember that what goes on in my private life is none of yours either.'

'I already know that, miss, and if you think I would betray your trust, you are quite mistaken.'

I searched her face, a few stray blonde hairs flayed in the breeze; her light brown eyes stared back at me, wide and uncertain.

'That's not what I meant.'

She frowned confused.

'I know what you think of me, Tulley. I know you disapprove.'

'I do not think ill of you Miss, if that is what you mean to imply. I am simply concerned for your health—'

Apparently, everyone always was until I really needed their concern. 'Well, you need not concern yourself with such matters. My request is that you bring the wine to my room, not pass judgement on whether or not I should consume it.'

'I was not passing judgement, miss. I was trying to help.'

'I do not need your help.'

'Of course.'

'What is that supposed to mean?' The cynicism in her tone irritated me far more than it ought to.

'Nothing.' She hastened her pace.

I chased on after her. 'I asked you a question!' I had raised my voice; I could hear it echo through the trees.

This stalled her and she turned around fully to me. 'Well, you needn't have. You certainly have no desire for an honest answer, so I cannot understand why you would pose the question.'

Her frankness shocked me and I was ill prepared for it. 'Says she who has no qualms in doing the dirty work of procuring it for me.'

'Yes, I did, and how I hate it. Because whatever you think, miss, I am not in the habit of stealing and deceiving others. I am a Christian and I know better than to take something that does not belong to me.'

'Oh, do remind me of the scripture that condones the voluntary telling of a lie, I will not be blamed for that.'

'It does not. I lied because of how terribly distressed you were that night that I thought my silence might afford you the time to recover and speak on the matter on your own terms, not because a simple maid, who knew no better than to mind her own business had betrayed you to your mother. Of course, if I knew then that your terms would be to drink yourself into a drunken stupor every night with my assistance, I would have told the truth to start with.'

'How very honourable.'

'No, not honourable miss; stupid I think. And I am sorry for it, and for lying when I should not have, because it is wrong and I am not too proud to confess it or learn by it.'

'What a shame you have not learnt in all your years, how to speak respectfully to those above you.'

'Well, as I said before, I did not think you wanted an honest answer.'

'There is a difference in being honest and speaking above your station.'

'No there is not, the truth is the truth whoever speaks it: the difference is in your willingness to hear it from one so below you.'

'How dare you!'

She did not answer me but hastened her pace and my body felt so weak I struggled to keep up with her. I stopped her with a tug at her elbow.

'This conversation is not finished.'

'It might as well be, it seems quite pointless if we cannot speak on equal terms, unless of course you are not seeking a conversation at all, but the satisfaction of having me agree with everything you say out of fear that you might punish me for it.'

'Fine, you want equal terms then let us speak plainly. I have had enough of your good Samaritan act. I do not for a minute believe you to be honest or without an ulterior motive, even if I have yet to fathom exactly what you want from this. But I do know that you have overstepped the mark and mistakenly think you can continue to do so just because you hold over me a secret that you think will prevent me from reminding you of your place. Well, you go and tell whoever you choose for all I care, because I will not be spoken to or treated like this by anyone, especially not you!' I hoped she could not tell I was bluffing.

'Very well, miss, if it is the truth you insist on then so be it. It is not my "good Samaritan act" that troubles you, nor my glances, comments or reactions that anger you. In fact, I have nothing to do with it at all really, I am simply a bystander. What you truly feel is not the judgement or opinion of a kitchen maid gnawing at you, but the weight of your own conscience trying to be heard. The voice of your own reason calling out to you to try and protect you from yourself. But you refuse to hear anything at all and instead send me on your unscrupulous errands to steal from your own father's cellar, and even though you know I want no part in it, even though I have never in my life stolen so much as a shirt button. And you try to stuff petty bribes into my palms like morality is a commodity that can be bought and paid for, then confuse yourself with the thinking that my refusal signifies an ulterior motive, and not because I do not want a reward for the acts I have sullied my hands with. It is one thing to surrender your morals under the duress of those who hold your fate in their very hands, but quite another to willingly profit from it! But despite whether or not I disapprove, I am made part of it, and am forced to take on part of the responsibility! I did not feel right to leave you unchecked all night after draining two bottles of wine, sleeping in your own vomit, your room dishevelled and the evidence sprawled about the floor. But perhaps I should have left you there for Watts or your mama to find you in the morning, unconscious or worse!'

I slapped her so swiftly across the face I shocked myself. I felt the sting of tears in my eyes, the pressure building in my temples, the tremor of my hands and I could not speak a word, even when she held her cheek against her palm and glared at me with such betrayal it shook me into brutal regret. I watched her eyes fill with tears before she turned away and walked the last of the woods before disappearing over to the small gatehouse and out onto the road. I took a seat on a tree stump to steady myself and let a few tears fall. Part of me felt better for it but the other felt nauseous from the candour of her words I feared may have more than a trifle of truth in them. Then I took a deep breath, wiped my cheeks, stood up and called out to her.

'Stop! Tulley, stop!' I called several times and when I realised she was not coming back, I mustered up the will to go after her.

She was further down the lane than I expected when I came through the gatehouse and I had to run most of the way to catch her.

'Tulley, that was wrong of me. Please—'

She paused and turned to look at me and I saw the injury in her eyes. I wanted to apologise, say sorry, but I was not accustomed to apologies and the words would not come forth naturally. 'Are you alright?' I said instead.

'Yes, I'll be fine,' she told me quickly before stepping up her pace again. A gentleman passed by in his curricle and the noise of the interruption afforded me a minute to contemplate my speech. 'Why don't we just forget about it all, pretend we had never spoken on the matter and there can be no harm done, hmmm?' It was only when she glanced sideways at me with incredulity that I realised how patronising I sounded.

'As you wish,' she said without looking at me.

'Well, I don't know how to please you!' I said despairing, once she had spent another five minutes or so marching her way ahead in silence. 'I have tried to make amends. I can't think of anyone else who would tolerate the tone you have used on me.'

'I thought it was behind us now?'

'Well, it would be if you would stop being so, so...' I couldn't find the words. I was on bad form today and felt desperate to take just a little wine to steady myself. 'Judgemental!' I eventually said.

'I do not judge you, miss. I only hoped to help you see things as they were, not to judge you by it.'

'Then why have I heard nothing but your opinion on what is right or wrong for me if you was not judging my behaviour to be unacceptable?'

'Opinion? I do not speak of my opinion, miss, I speak of my experience.'

'And what experience could you possibly have that qualifies you to dictate to me?'

'The experience of watching my own mother drink herself to her death, will that do for you?'

I wished instantly to take back the words. The silence was painful. 'I'm sorry for your loss,' I mumbled my inadequate attempt at compassion, but it only made us both more uncomfortable. I hadn't expected such an answer and wanted to sink into a hole and disappear. I racked my brains for some right sounding words but I just didn't know what to say to her. I wished I had the gentle wit to know how to handle sensitive matters like these, but I had rarely required such skills. I looked at her and knew she would have something appropriate to say to any situation and wished I was able to offer her something of the sort.

'How long ago?' I asked when the silence became too much.

'I don't want to talk about it,' she said calmly and we did not speak again until we got to town. It was only then I questioned what on earth I was even doing there, uninvited, dressed in my morning clothes. I presumed she had wondered the same but had thought better than to comment on it. I should have turned back long ago, and yet now I had ventured too far from safety to be walking about the place alone.

We were in the town centre, walking past all the usual shops I knew well. As was customary for mid-morning, ladies huddled in intimate groups of two and three, paraded the row of shops in their good dresses, chattering and pointing at displays of interest in the shop windows they passed. I was sure I spotted Anna outside the milliners. I put my bonnet on in the hope that I might not be recognised and kept my eyes to the ground. The last thing I wanted was to bump into anyone of consequence.

We made our way across the dusty carriage path towards Mrs Macoby's tearoom then crossed to the opposite side of the road. Passing the side street, vendors called out to us: 'Sixpence a pound for fresh potatoes.' 'Have your boots mended here,' they chanted. Women were stood along the stalls, poking at loaves of bread and examining apples. It was noisy and too warm suddenly. The road so dry it was kicking up dust into the air. The smell of fermenting vegetables and fruits sweating in the sun. It was all too much for my senses, my pounding head. My weary feeling limbs.

When Tulley took a turn through a gap in the lane, I was relieved to escape the crowded marketplace. We followed it through to the meat market lanes which were much quieter. The smell was always striking, especially in warmer weather, but thankfully we did not stop. We walked farther on and Tulley picked out some groceries from the stalls to fill her basket. Then she brought some worn out looking boots from a little shack of a cobbler's that was so grim and eerie I could not wait to leave.

Yet I didn't. And I could not fathom why I had seemed to have subconsciously invited myself on her journey and bound myself to it.

From there, we crossed the road and took yet another small lane leading away from the grocery stalls and north of the main streets. We walked for another five minutes or so, taking corners here and there into what seemed ever shrinking lanes and then almost alleyways before I found any reason to question my surroundings. These were certainly not streets I had seen in all my years of coming here.

'You might prefer not to go on now, miss,' Tulley stopped and said at last.

'I see,' her words filled me with both relief and embarrassment.

'I mean, you are welcome to, but I do not think this is the kind of place that will suit you and I have visits to make here that I cannot put off.'

'I understand,' but as I turned to leave, I considered more seriously that the risk of being caught out alone in town was one I really could not afford to take right now. 'Will you be long there?'

'No. A half hour at most.'

'Can I wait for you here?' I looked around me questioning the prospect of doing so. It did not seem like somewhere I would bump into anyone I might know. But nor did it seem like somewhere I would feel comfortable sitting out a half hour wait.

She looked me over, reading me as she often did. I wonder how much she could see. 'I am not supposed to be out, alone,' I said in answer to her stare.

'Very well, wait, or you can come with me. If you should not mind the place, I know my friends would be very happy to say they received a visit from a Lady.'

I could not vouch for not minding the place, but I had little choice now. 'Thank you,' I accepted the offer and, in my smile, I wondered if she knew she was forgiven it all. That somehow, she had chastened me with her outspoken audacity and far from feeling the rage I at first did, I felt impressed in some peculiar corner of my mind. As if that part of me realised I had received an overdue setting down. That part of me applauded her for delivering it. That part of me knew it was well deserved and was relieved to be put in line. It was the reactionary parts of me that were not so well accustomed.

As we journeyed on, it was the smell of the place that first caught me by surprise; it made the meat market seem tolerable. I covered my lower face with a gloved hand, and peered down at a stream of murky water, running along the edge of the dusty road. The stench was almost choking, and it was only when a woman stepped out from her house and emptied a chamber pot into the street, that I realised what was responsible for it and the swarms of flies buzzing about the place. And when I looked about at the grubby children sat upon their doorsteps drawing circles in the dirt with sticks, I had to stifle an involuntary retch. But nobody else seemed to notice or care. A shabby grey-haired dog, drinking from the puddles, beggars and drunks slouched against walls, whores hanging about the entrance of the small tavern; seemed perfectly overlooked by everyone else. The only thing that everyone did seem to notice; was me. I felt the gaze of everyone on me as I passed, following me with a raised eyebrow, a confused frown. I lowered my eyes to the murky ground to escape them and tried to ignore the fact that the bottoms of my skirts were trailing in all the filth.

We turned into a small square next, which apart from being slightly wider, resembled the formless streets we had just left: the buildings angular and featureless, the disrepair, disorganisation.

Tulley stopped then, and turned to one of the houses and knocked at the door.

'This is the Bartlett's,' she told me, and I tried to smile with interest. 'They are very inviting people,' she said, I think, to comfort me.

I looked up at the barely legible street sign that was attached to the wall of a house further along, *"Old Mill Street"*, it read. And when I turned back to the door, a pale faced, balding man stood in the doorway, beckoning us in.

'We 'ave two special visitors today,' he turned away and said to a lady who was nursing an infant by the fireplace.

'Oh, Miss Anna,' the woman said, looking up from the child. Her eyes seemed gladdened by her arrival. I had never heard a maidservant addressed as "miss" before. I did not even know her name was Anna. I supposed that everyone had their superiors.

Tulley made the introductions and I was welcomed into the small, musty smelling room.

'Your Ladyship,' said Mr Bartlett with half a bow.

'Ooh what an honour, Mr Bartlett; to have her ladyship visit us! You are very welcome!' Mrs Bartlett said, beckoning me to take a seat around the worn oak table that dominated the majority of the kitchen space, which seemed to account for the only real space in the place.

I smiled and forced back the urge to laugh at their ridiculous address when I caught Tulley's eyes upon me. She set her basket down and took off her bonnet before enquiring of their health and saying how long it had been since her last visit and apologising for it. She accepted the offer of some broth and begun to set out the contents of the basket on the table.

I was still looking about the small open plan room, trying to work it out when Tulley waved down my attention. Mr Bartlett was looking at me with the arm of a mug hanging from his grubby forefingers.

'Mr Bartlett asked if you would like some broth, Mrs Craythorne,' she repeated the question.

I looked about at the crumb laden table, the stained and chipped chinaware.

'No, thank you,' I said with half a smile. If it had been an offer of something with an alcohol content, I might have been tempted by it.

'How is work, Mr Bartlett?' Tulley asked him, sipping from her cup and blowing off the steam before mouthfuls.

'It's stable, for tha mom'nt,' he told her and she looked pleased.

'And the children?'

Mrs Bartlett shook her head. 'Nothing,' she said disappointed. 'Our Jack 'as been trying every day for the last month, but all the apprenticeships have been taken up and not even the farms are taking anyone for casual labour. Jane manages to find the odd day of laundry here and there, but nothing promising.'

'What a shame. I will keep my ear out for you, you know that,' Tulley told them and Mrs Bartlett thanked her.

'Fred sends us a lil' when he can; he's still doing well on the mines. If it weren't so far t'go I'd say we should find a place to settle up there an' we might all find some work. But with Rosie's condition.'

I looked over and realised for the first time that Mrs Bartlett's belly was full with child. I wondered how many they had and how they all managed in such a small place.

We had not stayed all that long when Tulley made her apologies for such a short visit and reassembled her bonnet and basket. I realised it was for my benefit and I was thankful for it. But just as she rose to finalise our departure, we all stopped sharp at the sudden sound of screaming from outside.

'Help, it's me ma; she won't stop sobbing,' came the voice followed by determined raps against the door that made it shake in its rickety frame.

Mr Bartlett leapt up from his chair and seized the handle.

A grubby looking boy of maybe eight or nine came bolting in quicker than the door could swing open.

'It's our Joe from down tha lane, Rosie,' he told her, recognising the sobbing little lad who had worked himself up so as not to manage to talk now he had finally arrived.

'Calm down, Joe. Catch some breath so you might tell us what's a matter now, lad,' Mr Bartlett tried to comfort him whilst Rosie put down her sleeping infant in the crib.

'Sit down, Joe. Don't speak just yet, steady your breathing,' she placed a gentle palm on his flushed cheek.

'Oh, miss, it's me ma,' he struggled and wheezed between words. 'Please miss, you have to go to her,' he said tugging at Mrs Bartlett's tatty apron.

'Alright Joe, you stay here with our Thomas and calm down, I'm sure your ma will be alright by the time I come back,' she told him, but I could see he was unconvinced. I wondered what on earth must be happening to account for such despair.

'Good grief, Rosie; shall I come with you?' Tulley asked her, replacing her basket back on the table.

'If you wouldn't mind, Miss Anna. I have a feeling this could be bad.'

Without further ado, she followed Mrs Bartlett out the door, and it took me a moment to grasp the situation and realise I had been left alone in here with these people I did not know. I charged out after them and followed them a few houses down the lane to a house where the door was already open. 'Moll?' Mrs Bartlett yelled as she made her way in, uninvited. There was no reply, but instead, the soft sound of a muffled lullaby coming from the back of the room where a curtain had been hung to divide the space up.

'Hush hush, little one...'

As we walked on to the source of the noise, I wondered what all the panic was in aid of, everything appeared calm enough. Before I could linger on the thought, Mrs Bartlett pulled back the curtain and sat in a chair was a small lady hunched over her half naked child, rocking her back and forth in time with the lullaby she was singing. I was surprised at this, the child was far too big to be rocked like an infant and I guessed that the child may be four or five.

Mrs Bartlett crouched down beside the singing lady who seemed oblivious to the fact that we had just walked into her home uninvited.

'Moll, Moll, put her down now, love,' Mrs Bartlett said softly. The blank faced lady ignored her but sung a little louder and faster than before.

'Moll, let me look at her then, eh?' she continued to probe her gently and this time persuaded her with open arms to release the child a little. The child's head fell loosely from the support of her mother's forearm and rested limply on her lap. Mrs Bartlett shook her head despondently.

Tulley's face dropped at Mrs Bartlett confirmation and I froze with utter disbelief at what I was seeing. Mrs Bartlett placed a stubby hand on the child's chest and then felt for the temperature. She shook her head. 'Let us take her to her bed eh, Moll?' she said softly and rubbed the lady's thin forearm. The woman stopped singing but did not release the child to Mrs Bartlett's outstretched arms. 'She's gone my love, let her rest,' she told her gently and this time, the lady let out a deep throated groan.

'No!' she cried—a guttural sound that made me instantly nauseous. 'Not my little Lucy. Lucy?' she let her go now, not in agreement but in despair, and Tulley scooped up the child in her own arms as Mrs Bartlett threw her arms around the mother to console her.

The groans and cries, so deep and affecting sent a shiver through me as I watched Tulley carry the limp child over to a small, tatty mattress held up by wooden crates.

'Dear god; Tulley, call for a doctor!' I said.

Tulley arranged the sheets around the little girl and stroked her curly tresses neatly about her face. She turned and looked up at me.

'It is too late, she has been dead at least an hour,' she said, feeling the coldness of the child's cheek against her palm.

I shook my head, 'I don't care, call one at once.'

Tulley frowned. 'They cannot afford one!' she said through gritted teeth.

'I shall see to the bill, just call a doctor for gods' sake!'

'Miss, it is of no use,' she said and placed an arm about me.

Something happened in that moment; a shift, the rest of the world slipping away. I stared at the breathless child. Her pretty chestnut locks about her pale face, her lips and cheeks still holding the barest hue of colour. A tear I had been willing not to fall, tumbled down my own. *Breathe,* I wanted to scream, willing her chest to rise and convince us all this was some terrible mistake.

Tulley covered the little girl with a sheet up to her shoulders and rolled her eyelids shut with a gentle brush of her hand. 'Come,' she said to me. 'We must leave.'

'But we can't...'

Tulley took me by the elbow, 'We must, there is nothing more we can do and we do not belong here. This is the place of her family and friends and we are neither,' she led me out onto the street and still as we walked on, the muffled cries followed our steps. We did not speak. I had no words, but I felt Tulley squeeze my arm, a reassuring pressure and when we reached the familiar front door, faded green and its paint all chipped and peeling, she turned to me and wiped my cheeks with her handkerchief before going back inside.

Mr Bartlett, who was still sat with a somewhat calmer Joe, stood up immediately, awaiting an explanation of the news. Tulley signalled him to join her out of earshot of the young boy and he handed him a mug of hot milk and walked over to join us.

'She has lost another,' Tulley told him in a whisper and his face fell staid with the news.

'Another?' I said without thinking.

Tulley shushed me with a finger to her lip and gestured towards Joe who seemed to be trying to work things out for himself. He may have only been nine or ten, but something told me, he was wise beyond his years.

'Dear lord, fate 'as been unkind to that poor family,' Mr Bartlett said after collecting himself again. 'Was it Millie or Lucy?' he asked.

'Lucy,' she told him.

'Aye, her oldest girl. Had three boys before finally having herself a young lass, and she was so pleased for it I tell ya,' he shook his head in disbelief.

Was it true they actually wished for girls here? Valued them.

Tulley nodded. She was fishing around in a worn-out leather purse. 'Here,' she said, 'take this for Moll, it is all I have with me now, but hopefully it will be of use.'

'You are too kind, Miss Anna, to all o' us,' he said, taking the coins. 'I know she will be grateful of it, she still has three to feed whatever else.' He turned the shiny coins in his hand '...although we shall have 'em here tonight. Where is Millie?' he asked, remembering the other sister.

'We did not see her, I'm sure.' Tulley frowned.

'She's up the lane with Fi-fe,' came a voice from beside them. Joe was stood next to them, his eyes glittering with tears and the remnants of those already cried staining his grubby cheeks.

'She's not gonna wake up, is she, sir?' he said to Mr Bartlett who squeezed his own eyes tight for a moment.

Tulley leant down to the boy and put her hand on his cheek. 'Hush now with such talk and go drink your milk Joe, your ma is waiting for the doctor,' he looked half calmed by the hope Tulley had given him and wandered back over to his steaming cup of milk.

I wondered if it were wrong to lie to him, but then I considered the harshness of taking such news from a stranger.

'Thank you,' Mr Bartlett said when Joe sat back down. 'I, I didn't know what to tell 'im.'

'Well, it'll keep for just a little while. I don't want to send him into one of those wheezing fits again. Might I do anything before I go? I own I wish I did not have to, but I must be back by two-o-clock.'

I wanted to tell her she need pay no mind to that. But she was no longer my stand in Abigail and she did not answer to me.

He smiled warmly at her. 'You 'ave done so much, Miss Anna, but no, I'll see to tea while Rosie's gone, and keep the boy with me—oh,' he said as though he had just remembered something. 'There is something...'

'Yes, of course,' Tulley replied, she was picking up her empty basket now.

'If you could just call our Jane in on your way out, she should be down the lane. I'll send her for little Millie and she can help me tend 'em.'

Tulley nodded. 'Of course. You are a good man, Mr Bartlett,' she gave him a gentle pat upon his forearm and this familiarity surprised me. 'Tell Rosie I will come again as soon as I am able, and Moll too, when she is fit for it of course.'

'Aye,' he said gratefully, and bid us both farewell.

Tulley called on the Bartlett's daughter as we left Old Mill Street. But as we walked the dusty lanes back into the town, I knew the memory of this visit would not be left behind us like our steps.

Everything seemed changed. I could not gather my thoughts or suspend the rushing of them. Shake the images from my head. Even the tears that I tried so hard to hold back kept getting the better of me.

'I shouldn't have taken you there,' Tulley said eventually.

I shook my head. 'You didn't,' I corrected her. 'I followed you there.'

'I should have known better—'

I stopped and turned to her. 'You have nothing to reproach yourself for. Quite the contrary.'

We walked on.

I spent the rest of the day in my room and took no meals. When Fanny came to dress me for dinner, I sent her away. I'd spent half the day crying until I could cry no more and only ache inside with an emptiness I knew not how to quell. I even prayed, and I didn't do that often at all. Not the real kind. The heartfelt ones that seemed to rip open every hurt and turn you inside out. I prayed for the young girl and her family, for all the children that perished so unjustly and for all their families that cried for them. I prayed for a better world full of more kind people like Tulley to fill it, and less of my own. This was the sticking point. The ugly truth. I did not know the first thing about being kind, and there were others who seemed not to know anything less.

I had just filled another page of my diary when the door tapped. 'Come in,' I sighed. I was not in the mood for Mama's attempts at coaxing me down to the dining room or asking my opinions on party decor. I closed the book and pushed it away.

When the door opened and Tulley came in with a tray of tea and fancies, I was surprised. She smiled and set it down on the table. 'I hope you don't mind, I thought you might need it since all your meals have been returned to the kitchen this afternoon.'

'Thank you. But you should not have taken the trouble, besides, I couldn't eat a morsel.' I had quite forgotten the fact that she had been set straight to work on our return. It seemed unfair that she should after such a day. How did she do it? Hold herself together with such composure.

'Then you must try to take some sweet tea—it is good for nerves.' She was already pouring the cup.

'What was her name?'

She put the cup down on the table beside me, a curl of steam rising. 'Lucy.'

'Lucy, yes I remember now, and how old was she?'

'I think she was five. You really should try to think of something else, you will do yourself no good dwelling on it so.'

'I can think of nothing else,' I paused to take a breath, feeling my throat begin to constrict again. 'What killed her?' I said when I could speak again.

'I think it must have been consumption. She had it since last winter. I remember Mrs Bartlett telling me.'

'And you said: "another one"?'

'Yes, her brother, George. They both came down with it at the same time, the chest cold that is, and the consumption remained after. They thought he had recovered it, but he fell ill again twice more before he died. They blamed it on all the soot and fumes making his chest weak.'

'Soot?'

'He swept chimneys, you see, and well, as you might imagine, the air is very bad inside them.'

I nodded vaguely. 'When will you go to them again? I would like to come, if you will let me?'

She nodded. 'In two weeks, when my next morning off is due. But I am not sure that is a good idea.'

'Please.'

'Perhaps, let us see how you feel nearer the time.'

'I want to help, Tulley. Although I don't know what could possibly be done. But if there was a way; I think you could help me to understand it.'

'That is very good of you, miss, and I'm sure they would be grateful.'

Good of me! I nearly laughed; it seemed that perhaps there was no good in me at all. The sorrow but also the guilt and shame consumed me fully. I was not a kind person like her, and the Bartlett's. I did not know what it was like to live in such wretched conditions and eat so little for the sake of poverty and work so hard to manage so many children. I did not even know how to prepare my own breakfast. The thought made me squirm with disgust.

'I had better get back to my chores,' Tulley said, as she finished stirring some sugar cubes into the tea.

'Yes, I have kept you.' I took the offered cup indifferently.

'Try to take a little.'

'I need something stronger, just a little,' I said to her and it was disappointment, not contempt in her eyes.

'I will come back later,' she agreed and I was relieved to be spared the confrontation. 'I had better get back to the kitchen.' She put the milk jug down beside my cup and instinctively I reached out to her.

'Thank you,' I said and yet it seemed not equal to what I wanted to say.

When she left, I pushed the tea tray aside. Nor did I open the wine that she later delivered to me as per our arrangement, despite the desperation half killing me. I took to my bed to try to allay the weakness, trembling and sweating, but I could not sleep, hanging in a torturous limbo between exhaustion and restlessness. But I could find no pity for myself: this was my own doing.

The offer.

August 1821. - Eleanor.

I don't quite know how I managed it. But I did not touch the wine at all that night. I felt for the first time: resistance. My own resistance. Real resistance. I *wanted* to drink it, ten times the amount to numb the monstrously grim thoughts and feelings of the day. But they had had an unexpected effect on me too. Something sobering. Something like the sting of a sharp slap or skin prickling gust of an arctic breeze. Unpleasant, but alerting. There was a truth emerging in that awareness that I had not before seen, or at least had not allowed myself to see before: there were others worse off than me who still lived meaningful lives. Still found their way to happiness. Still got up and faced the perils of their circumstances, however bleak they seemed.

A five-year-old child lost her life, and here I was frittering mine away, day after day. Things were difficult. Miserable. Uncertain. But. I had life in me yet. Perhaps a long one, unlike poor Lucy. One much less tumultuous and harsh than the residents of Old Mill Street. One I must turn into something better. And as much as I disliked owning it, the wine was not conducive to that. Not now at least. In the beginning, to numb the bodily pains that prevented my sleeping, it had helped. But I had felt nothing beyond fading aches and mild tenderness for days now. I was trying to numb *myself* now—all of me—in order to bear the bleakness of my life. But life was not simply to be borne, but to be lived.

If I continued on this course, I didn't know if I would end like Tulley's mama, drinking myself to an early grave, or simply wasting my life in a drunken tremulous stupor. But I did know, that neither appealed to me. I wanted my life to mean *something*. To find happiness. To find purpose.

So, as I scrambled in my sheets and stared at the bottle of Claret with its lopsided bottle label, I asked myself what I *really* wanted. My thoughts became a clash, like having the devil and angel at my ear. It quickly became tormenting. Head spinning. A few times, I reached for it, telling myself tomorrow would be the day of reckoning, that I would drink the whole, that I would drink just a glass or two, that I would pour it into the chamber pot to remove the temptation. But despite coming close to all of them, something told me that the time was now. That the strength to resist must come from somewhere inside myself. And so, I forced myself to keep to my bed without taking a sip and stared at the ceiling, tossed and turned for what felt like hours.

It was about a quarter past midnight when Tulley woke me. She was sat at my bedside moping the sweat from my brow. I supposed she had come to make her usual check on my inebriated state before retiring to her own bed. I felt a little pride in her seeing the unopened wine bottle, but it was a brief sense of accomplishment as I felt the quivering of my body and cold sweats breaking out all over me.

'Oh miss, you are ill indeed,' she said gravely.

I tried to sit up but the effort seemed too taxing and I gave up the trying. 'I think I have a fever.'

'I think you must take a little of that wine.'

'What?' *First you disapprove and now you encourage it.* 'Don't you see: I am trying to do the right thing.'

'Yes, I do. But this is not the way, it is too harsh on your health like this.'

I raised an eyebrow. 'Well, what do you suggest?' I snapped.

She was helping me up and plumping pillows behind my back, so I could not see her face.

'I suggest you take a small meal, then you take a small glass of wine afterwards; just enough to stop the trembling. Then tomorrow you do the same, but a little less still, and each day until eventually you take none at all. That way, your health will not suffer so harshly.'

What made her think she always knew best. I was on the verge of snapping at her again, then I remembered what she had told me about her mother and decided against it. Besides, I didn't mean it. I knew I ought to try to be grateful, but I felt like death and couldn't find the equanimity I would have hoped to muster. 'And you are certain this will work?'

'Yes, miss,' she nodded with certitude in her expression that reminded me that there was a great deal more to her than first impressions made plain.

I waited patiently for her to stop fussing with my pillows and bed clothes before I agreed. 'Very well then,' I said, and she went downstairs to fix something for me.

She had of course been right, and spent night after night encouraging me to take small meals and weaning me from the Claret until all I sipped was diluted orange wine. And whilst it proved a challenging and unpleasant time, it was less painful than the first night of my trying it alone. It had been incredibly hard on my nerves but I had turned a corner now and had begun to feel better and more like my former self again. I knew I could not have managed it without her help, and I had begun to find a strange comfort in her presence as she mopped my clammy brow and supervised my meals with a nanny-like air. It was a strange dynamic. We were not friends of course, but we had come to an understanding of sorts. The shared misery of Old Mill Street had bonded us in some peculiar way and erased much of the stiffness of our prior acquaintance. Smiles and occasionally even humour flowed more comfortably between us and I was grateful. Grateful to be on better terms, and grateful to feel the gradual return to myself.

It was the first time in days I had made it down to breakfast and I saw the relief on my parents' faces as I joined them.

'You look well my dear,' Mama said and Father smiled his relief to which was the most I might expect him to say on it.

'I feel it at last,' I told her and I was pleased that it was true.

'How happy it is to see you in better spirits. I trust it is on account of knowing Harriet will soon be home and you may take a holiday in Kent?'

'Yes. I do look forward to it,' I agreed, thinking it best to keep things simple. I *was* looking forward to it, to a change of scene, to Harriet's company, to not looking over my shoulder every time I ventured onto the park. But I could not say that my recovering bloom of health was owing to that, when it was owing to me slowly gathering the broken parts of myself back up and reassembling them in a somewhat softer and more earnest style. When it was because my body and mind had begun healing at last, not just from the trauma of that dreadful night, but the self-inflicted trauma of my cups. When it was because the support Tulley had offered me in meeting these challenges made me feel less alone.

Grantley came in and interrupted us with the post salver and I was grateful for the reprieve as she scanned through her letters. She opened one and pushed her spectacles further up the bridge of her nose. 'Oh, what happy timing,' she said distracted, scanning it quickly. 'Oh, perhaps not so good—you were right, she is to stay with her mistress until her departure,' she continued. 'I had hoped we might secure her ahead of your trip,' she said, taking her spectacles off and handing me Miss Pascal's application for the position of lady's maid. I had quite forgotten about it with so much else to distract me.

I read over the neat hand carefully, looking for any point I might make a matter of protest whilst Mother peered over my shoulder and read out loud the parts that were particularly impressive. And it could not be denied. She did have all the credentials to satisfy the position with ease, but those qualities were not important to me anymore; I knew that, above all else, I needed someone I could trust, someone who's loyalty and discretion was assured.

'I shall write to Miss Pascal today and tell her you accept and would like her to start as soon as possible,' Mama declared when I finished reading and put the letter down.

It was this that prompted me into realising, that I did not want Miss Pascal, or Fanny, or anyone else to be my Abigail. I wanted Tulley. I trusted Tulley. Even if I had to wear my hair in plain chignons and mix my own lotions for the rest of my days, I wanted above all else: someone

I could rely upon. Someone who had my interests at heart. Someone who knew loyalty. The qualities I had not yet managed to find elsewhere, were right here already. The problem was Tulley was a kitchen maid. And though I didn't mind it, whilst I remained at Cuddington, it would—as my mama had said on my taking her to High Ashurst—upset the order of things below stairs.

But as the day went on and I reflected more upon it, I knew that nothing else would do. That even if I was content to wait for Miss Pascal to arrive, even if she was as skilled and worthy of her recommendation as her letter implied, even if we went along amicably enough—we would never share the same bond or understanding that me and Tulley had. That with her, I could be myself, for she had seen me at my worst, my lowest and had helped me through such darkness. I did not know what lie ahead of me anymore. My future was more uncertain than it had ever been. But I knew that whatever was to be, I wanted someone like Tulley beside me.

'Mama,' I said the next morning. 'Have you written to Miss Pascal yet?'

'I own I forgot with Henry's engagement party arrangements to deal in. But I shall do it this afternoon, dear. A delay shan't matter in the least for you know she will not be able to leave her mistress until the end of the month anyway. We shall just have to manage until then as we have, and you may bring Fanny or that kitchen maid to Harriet's next week.'

'I shall do it, Mama. You have enough to contend with at present.'

'Will you?' she said, looking up from the pile of engagement party replies she was cross referencing with her list.

I nodded. 'I told you, I am feeling much more the thing now, and I have little else to do.'

'Very well my dear, it would be helpful. You see what I have to contend with today,' she said, gesturing to the pile of replies that had come in the morning post and sifting through it to find Miss Pascal's previous letter and handing it over to me.

Once I had taken a small bowl of oatmeal and been given the run down on who had accepted and declined insofar, and a progress report on all Henry's wedding arrangements, I went straight down to the kitchens.

'She is in the yard hanging laundry, miss,' said the young maid I found scrubbing the kitchen table when I came to look for Tulley. It was unusually quiet in there, I supposed on account that we were to dine at Delores' tonight. One of the few invitations I was willing to accept nowadays. It pleased me to think Tulley's load would be lightened a little in our absence and that she might get some rest. She always seemed to look so tired and I knew that my demands upon her this past couple of weeks had added to it.

I went outside to find her and waited for her to finish pegging the linen she had started on before interrupting her.

'You really are a maid of many talents,' I said and she turned to me surprised and smiled.

'Yes, miss, we are two down until the new girl arrives next week, and Mills is back in good health.'

'And yet you are one of the few at work? Where is everybody else?'

'Privileges of being the new girl,' she shrugged and I smiled at the proposition I was about to make her, *wanted* to make her.

'Well, there will be someone else to deprive you of such privileges at least in her coming.'

'Yes. There is that,' she said, but not with the relief you would expect for someone that seemed always to be busy with so many things.

'Will you walk with me?' I asked when I noted the basket was empty.

She nodded and put the surplus pegs in the pocket of her apron. It was an anxious nod and I could not be surprised by it. I had been nothing but trouble to her since our first meeting, so she had little reason to have faith in any better from me.

I waited until we had left the small yard before I began.

'What exactly did you do in your last position Tulley?'

'I worked in the house of Mr Gint of Hurley Street Miss,' she answered, searching for the relevance of my question.

'For how many years?'

'I hardly know. I lived there for as long as I can remember. But I was not put to work until I was perhaps ten.'

'I see.' This seemed a peculiar thing to me, but I did not wish to pry, I could already see the anxiety in her gaze at the direction of this conversation.

'My mother was his housekeeper, a real maid of all work you might say, for the house was small and apart from the butler, cook, a scullery maid and a live out maid that came in to help on wash days, she saw to most things.'

I saw the emotion of the memory glaze her eyes and did not know whether she was ready to talk on the subject of her mother on not. 'And you took up work there when you were old enough?'

'Yes, small errands at first. Mother would not permit it to begin with; I was always made to concentrate on my lessons. She wanted more for me you see, more than the life she had, and I realised when she had gone and I filled her position; why that was.'

'You were housekeeper then. But the work was hard on you?'

'Yes, but it was not that; it was my master,' she paused as if she had such too much. 'Anyway, he was a difficult man and I left as soon as I was able.'

I didn't press her. I feared I didn't need to for the graveness in her tone left me without doubt that his demands went beyond too much ringing of his bell. I felt instantly disturbed by the implication.

'And what lessons did you take?' I already knew she could read, sew, and converse well, so anything else would be an advantage in convincing my mother of the idea.

'Music, Literature and of course, Mother taught me the French that was native to her, and how to sew.'

It seemed an extraordinary list of accomplishments for a maidservant. French, I had not anticipated, but it gave me confidence in presenting my cause. I must have smiled too enthusiastically at her answer because she stopped and said to me:

'Is this what you meant to discuss with me miss?'

'No, well, yes. Shall we sit?' I offered as we passed a bench in the formal garden.

We sat overlooking the Parterre.

'I have a proposition for you, Tulley.'

She frowned.

'I am in need of a lady's maid.'

'I am not sure I am the person to ask for a recommendation Miss. Watts will be more help to you, I'm sure.'

'It is not a recommendation I need. I want to offer you the job.'

Her expression was so perplexed at the notion that I wondered how I would convince Mother of her suitability if she herself could not see the logic in it.

'Oh. Miss, you are very kind to think of me, but I have never tended a lady. I was only twelve when Mr Gint's daughter left home, and Mother always saw to her.'

'Tulley, you have been looking after me from the moment we met. Looking after me well.'

'But you know I don't know the first thing about a lady's toilette, or how to dress hair or make lotions. There is not much call for those things in a widower's house—'

'Those things can be easily learnt, the other things you are already more than practiced in.'

She fell silent a moment. It was not the reaction I was expecting and I hoped it was a mere lack of confidence that explained it. 'You can mend clothes and lay them out?'

She nodded.

'Make the bed? Tidy a chamber? Boil up water?'

She continued nodding.

'And we already know you can read and speak well enough. All the staff already know you, and you can start almost immediately. The mixing of a few cosmetics, the format of a lady's toilette and learning to pin hair is but a trifle to someone who can manage the work of a whole house almost single handed, don't you think?'

'Perhaps, but I am needed here, miss.'

'You said yourself, a new maid is on her way, and I'm sure Mrs Crawford can arrange for another on your going. The position is open immediately and my mother has found me someone that will take it up after her notice period.'

'Then why—'

'But I want someone I can trust, someone I know, someone who will come away with me as much as companion as maid. I do not intend to stay at Cuddington for much longer. I mean to travel about a little. Maybe just to visit relatives or to go to London or the spa towns. But however it is to be, I shall need someone to attend me. I hoped it would be you.'

She sat contemplatively a while before saying: 'I hope I do not speak out of turn, miss, but I don't expect you to make any allowances for me, just because I have done my duty to you. Anyone else would have done the same.'

I laughed. 'You have gone beyond your duty to me, Tulley, and we both know it. You might be surprised, but most would rather sell me out to my mother and who can blame them when I am such a terrible mistress!'

We both laughed then, and I wondered if the thought of having me to tend was not worth the promotion, however good the prospects. We had hardly got off to the best of starts. Although I was certain we had since moved past it. 'Listen, you needn't answer now, it is a lot to consider and I have sprung it upon you. But here are the details of the position.' I handed her the piece of paper Mother had drafted for my enquiry at the register office before Mrs Bloxam's interference had altered things. On it detailed the duties, character and requirements. The hours, the pay and the other details which mentioned a tea allowance and first refusal of my old clothes. I had read it over, and whilst I could not afford Tulley the credit of a reference that surpassed Miss Pascal's, my interview had established that she could meet with the requirements well enough that Mother could be placated by my choosing her.

'Miss I, I don't know what to say, you do me such an honour but—'

'Say nothing now. I am away to Dorking this afternoon. Tomorrow, I will return and you will give me your answer then, once you have had a chance to think upon it. That is the best I can do in delaying my answer to the other applicant, so think well on the matter.'

'Yes, miss, thank you, I shall.'

I could see the proposition turning in her mind but I could feel the reluctance as keenly and wondered as I watched her pad along back towards the house, if I should have perhaps upped the pay or benefits in some way. I assumed the wage Mama arranged to be fitting, and had been equal to that which Lady W. had suggested in drawing up Miss Rosen's offer. But I hardly knew if it was a good offer, or how much an improvement to her current wage. I would find out from Mrs Simpson. I had meant to see her anyway about affording Tulley some time off in recompense to all her service to me of late. If the difference was not adequate, I would increase it, double it or triple it for all I cared. I had little to show for my marriage. But the one thing I did have was money, lots of it.

I stood up and decided that since I was already out, I may as well take a little stroll now I was able to manage more exercise. I took a wonder through the gate, across the lawn and out into the woodland, absorbing the scent of summer with every step. Imagining as I trod, that I would soon have the company of one of Bess and Maxi's puppies chasing about my ankles. They had come early, I learned only yesterday. All nine of them, eight surviving now. I was desperate to go and see them for myself and find out who was to become my new companion, but Mr Morris felt it too early for any beyond those very familiar, to be about them. Apparently it was to be expected that Bess might become anxious for their safety and react poorly to such an intrusion this early on, and I had no wish to cause difficulties. So I accepted his offer to call back in a sennight or two and see how she went, maybe get to have a peak at least.

I was just considering names when I noticed, as I trod through a patch of narrow path and looked up through the trees ahead at a fleeting movement beyond. I jumped back startled when I saw the face of a man bearing a striking resemblance to Giles' manservant, Digby. His weasel like face and gangly gait was distinctive and I thought it an unlikely coincidence. But he was turned and gone from my sight so quickly at my notice of him, I could hardly be certain and did not hang about to check. I darted back through the trees the way I had come and spilled out onto the lawns moments later. I caught my breath as I walked calmly now towards the house, seeing some of the gardeners about the rose garden as I passed it, and feeling a little relief at the sight of them. It was then I began to wonder if I had been mistaken and whether it could have been some servant or groundsman going about his work. But if it had been, there would have been no need for him to cut a dash at the notice of me. It had been foolish of me to wonder off alone like that.

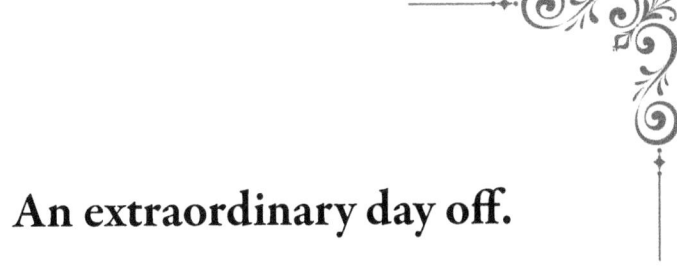

An extraordinary day off.

August 1821. - Annalise.

Annalise went back to the laundry in a muddle of competing thoughts. As she reloaded her baskets with more wet linens ready for hanging, she considered the implications of the offer she had just been made. It had stunned her. When she had finished all the pegging, she stole a moment to read over the details she had been given, thinking what it would be to earn such a wage. How fast she would clear the payments on her mama's headstone, how much easier it would be than wearing her hands out in such toiling in the kitchen and having every shortage of staff lumbered upon her on top of it. And then she thought too of what it would mean, to be in the ranks of the upper servants, to be separated from her friends, thought of like they were. Uppity. Disliked.

She folded the paper away into her apron pocket and headed over to the kitchen to make a start on her chores.

'What are you doing here?' Poppy said, selecting copper pots from the hanging rack.

Annalise frowned. 'What do you mean?'

'You are to 'ave the rest of the day as leave.'

'I am?' Annalise said confused.

Poppy shifted the pans about the overcrowded hob plate. 'So Cook says, she's not 'alf pleased about it though.'

'But why?'

Poppy shrugged. 'I thought you must 'ave had an arrangement with Crawford or something, for all the extra work you did.'

Annalise shook her head, not to her knowledge anyway.

'Well, I wouldn't argue it if I were you. Go and get that apron off and get out of here before Cook see's you and tries to reclaim it.'

It was too good an opportunity to pass up, however it had come about, Annalise thought as she changed into her own clothes and set out through the woodland. Besides, the family were to away today and so she could not be much missed. She supposed she had earned it in all the extra hours she had given Mrs Crawford, but she was surprised at such a generous token of gratitude. She would surely remember to thank her for it later. But for now, she was at leisure and for once, she had not planned every second of it away, since she never even knew it a possibility.

When she arrived at Old Mill Street, she braced herself for the solemnity of the mood here. It was still only a week since poor Lucy and she was only just moving past crying herself to sleep each night, so she braced herself for the relapse that would ensue after such a visit. There is something about grief—in losing someone dear to you—that seemed always to scratch open the wound in the face of other deaths. She had cried for Lucy of course, but she somehow knew that she was simultaneously still crying for her mother too. It was for that reason she had been at first reluctant to come. The contagion of so much melancholy seemed too much for her. Especially having such reminders of the perils of the cup foisted upon her in bringing Mrs Craythorne about to health again. It had resurrected so many painful memories that she was still not ready to revisit. But she would be needed at Old Mill Street. She knew that too. There were matters both practical and pastoral that she might be leaned upon to help in. This won out and she had taken some money from her savings to offer and filled her basket for both the households on her way through the market.

'Miss Anna,' Mrs Bartlett said, surprised at seeing her again so soon. 'Come in, luv.'

'Rosie,' Annalise put the heavy basket down and turned to hug her. 'How are you all?' she said.

'Bearing up, luv, it's been an 'ard spell to be sure. Sit down won't you.'

She pulled out a chair. 'How is Moll doing?'

'As you might expect. We 'ad the littleuns for the first couple of days. But she's getting back on her feet now. Says it better for her to 'ave 'em about and keep her busy.'

Annalise nodded. 'I bought her some things,' Annalise said nodding towards the basket. 'Will you take them to her? I'm sure it is too soon to pay her calls.'

'Oh, you are a kind girl, Anna! Of course, I will. But you can't keep spendin' your 'ard earned money on the likes 'o us. I say, we 'ave 'ad so much kindness it's been overwhelming. I don't think Moll's pantry as ever been so well stocked.'

Annalise smiled. 'I am glad everyone has rallied about.'

'Well, the truth is, we don't know where it came from.'

'What?'

'Well, the other night, I was just settling our Sidney to bed, and we get's a knock on the door, a delivery our Thomas says. A delivery, at this time of night? I say to him. Anyway,' she poured them both a cup of something, 'he opens up the packet and what do you think is in there?'

Annalise shrugged and begun unloading her basket. 'What?'

'Five guineas, or sovereigns as they call 'em now, but well—'

'Five guineas?' Annalise repeated, astonished.

Rosie nodded and slid a mug across the table. 'I know. It was such a quiz and I say's to him, it must be a mistake. It must 'ave been delivered to the wrong 'ouse. So, the next day we took it to the blacksmith—he reads for everyone around 'ere. It said;' she paused a minute to recollect the right words, 'For Mr and Mrs Bartlett, may this ease your...burden. Yes, that was it.'

'Oh my. How wonderful,' Annalise said.

'That's not the 'alf of it. Listen to this. I went round to Molls to drop the littleuns back to her. I wanted to make up a shopping list and see what she needed. So I'm 'aving a look about the larder and seeing what's what, and what do you think I see sat upon the side?'

'I don't know?'

'An envelope, just like the one we 'ad got.'

Annalise frowned.

'Moll, why 'aven't you opened your packet? I says to her. Poor love wasn't with it, she'd just chucked it on the side and went to bed that night. Anyways, open it I said.'

'Was it the same as yours, Rosie?' Annalise asked, beginning to grow suspicious now of who the donor may be.

She nodded. 'Except that she 'ad ten guineas inside it!'

'My goodness,' Annalise held her hand to her throat. 'So generous.' She had never considered her mistress as generous before, but...

'I know, we's never seen so much money in all our life. 'ide it away somewhere I says to her, and don't be breaking them coins down the market or we'll 'ave folk thinking we've turned to coining or the footpad line!'

'So, who is this mystery benefactor? What was the name upon the letter?'

'There wasn't one. So very odd. Like a miracle. Jane says it was from an Angel and she'd been praying for something kind to take everyone's tears away.'

Not an angel exactly, Annalise thought. But certainly of far more heart and generosity than she had perhaps given her credit for. She couldn't be sure of course, but it seemed far too much a coincidence that such an unlikely turn of fortune might be bestowed upon both these households within days of bringing her mistress here. She had not thought her the alms giving type and she had, at least initially thought her so far beyond the reach of decency, let alone empathy, that she almost dismissed the notion as ludicrous. But, she had, of late, felt a change in her, a softening perhaps.

She considered it at length when she left. She kept the call a short one, leaving herself the time she needed to walk the distance to Epsom and spend some time at her mother's graveside. It was harder to come as often now she was at Cuddington. She had been used to being close enough to pop out once or twice a week when she was at Gint's. But from Cuddington, it was over a leagues walk now, and if she spent every morning off there, there would be time for little else by the time she had completed each leg of the journey. It saddened her when she got there and found the shrivelled dead flowers crumbling into the soil and the weeds shooting up all over it. Had she really left it so long?

She dropped to her knees and let out the first rush of tears before starting out on clearing away the unkempt growth. *She will have a stone soon and it will not look so neglected then*, she reminded herself. She had been used to planting flowers to mark the spot whilst it settled but the weather had been so hot, they had long since been scorched to brown crepe and how sad they looked now amongst the vibrant foliage of so many weeds. She plucked the stubborn roots from the soil, nettle and bindweed twisted and tangling about each other. She could have done with a little more than her bare hands for the task and wished she had come better prepared.

Once it was cleared, she set out the carnations she had brought from the flower stall on her journey here and smiled through her tears to see it set to rights. It looked cared about once more, not abandoned and neglected as she had found it. She vowed she would not permit it to fall into such a condition again hereafter. She would come every month to clear it and once the stone was put upon it, she would begin planting so that it might always stay alive with blooms for every season. She wondered, as she sat upon the warm earth, her fingernails thick with mud and talking to her mother as she always did when she was alone here, that if she was to accept her mistress' proposal, and be off travelling all over the place, then she would not be able to keep such a promise and tend to her mother's grave. For even though the terms did state there would be a whole day of leave per month, it also said it was to fit around her lady's schedule, and who knew what that might be. Nor would she be able sit about in the servants' hall in the evenings or take her meals there, or be invited to Fanny's barn dances or to stay behind with the others when the family were away.

The Answer.

August 1821. - Eleanor.

The prospect of her answer gave me something to look forward to on my return home amidst so much I had to dread. This stay at High Ashurst had not been marked by the easy tranquillity of the last, and since this time I had agreed to bring Fanny along to placate any further upset below stairs, I felt lonelier without Tulley's measured company to rely on. Fanny's excited prattling was far from reassuring and coupled with all the animated talk of Henry's nuptials dominating our party's conversation, my head felt quite fit to burst.

I was of course, pleased to see the return of my parents' joie de vivre and was happy that this union had restored much of what I had put in jeopardy. But for me, the prospect of a house full of the ton this weekend for Henry's engagement party filled me with deep anxiety and an equal desire to find a way to escape it.

I had managed to keep such a low profile until now, avoid questions or explanations over my marriage situation and, steer clear of the two-faced slyboots that had once called themselves my friends. But now all of that was to be foisted upon me in unpredictable style. To top it off, Giles would unequivocally know where I had retreated to since deserting him, and although this would be soon countered by my disappearing off to Kent with Harriet, it did not allay my fear that this would prompt him to make some attempt to contact me.

The Craythornes, in their entirety, were kept off the guest lists for all events, as much for my sake as for my parents' wishes to keep as much separation between our family's mésalliance as possible, whilst Henry's union was cemented. But I had traitors amongst my own and I did not know how I would manage to do the pretty with Betsy, knowing that she had betrayed me to Mariella and could be relied upon to do the same again.

When we arrived back in Cuddington, I had no time at all to contemplate escape and avoidance strategies, for although the party was not until tomorrow evening, a few out-of-town guests were already arriving for the informal meeting of Lady Jane, and I had barely took off my bonnet and gloves when I was thrust around the parlour table to greet them with Mama.

'Ah, look, if it is not my little sister. Come and meet Lady Jane, Eleanor,' said my brother, Henry, with unusual marked affection. It rather startled me to be addressed so by him, but I smiled sweetly and shook Lady Jane's offered hand.

'Eleanor, so pleased to meet you. You are indeed quite as pretty as everyone said you were. I hope we shall be friends. I think we are close in years.'

'Likewise, Lady Jane. I am sure we shall. May I offer you my congratulations and best wishes,' I said.

'Thank you.'

'Ah, and here is my little brother, Ed,' Henry said and I moved along to find a seat.

When I spotted Aunt Orlagh amongst them, I went instantly to her side and settled into conversation with her before I was forced to acknowledge the pleasantries of the rest of the company. It was manageable for such a brief spell before I found excuse to leave them all to it, even if it had left me sipping tea with old acquaintances sooner than I preferred. It did at least assure me that my misdemeanours had been quite forgotten with all the focus on this wondrous engagement, and for taking the focus off of me, I was grateful for it. I seemed, for the most part, to be of little interest and I could not have wished it otherwise, for it might be my only consolation this weekend.

But as I sat up that night completing my diary, I fought the urge to resist the bell pull and summon Tulley to bring me a small cup of wine. Amongst other things, tomorrow would prove the first real test of my abstinence from it and the dread that grew inside me at the prospect of all the other trials I would face only further tested my will. I had hoped to see Tulley today. Had hoped for her answer. I had already penned a response to Miss Pascal, thanking her for her interest but directing her that the position had since been filled. It awaited only a date and seal, and I had hoped to send it off as soon as possible. But I resisted the urge to pester her. She would know now I was back and would surely come to me when she could. She was no doubt being kept busy with all the pomp and ceremony to prepare for.

But I found myself restless and impatient, unable to sleep and the lure of my father's Brandy decanter in the study called to me as I paced about my room, wringing my hands. At half past twelve, I gave in to the idea, the house seeming quiet once more, and I tiptoed down to the study as soundlessly as I could. I was to have only a small glass. When I turned the handle, I was relieved to find it still unlocked, but jumped back in astonishment to find it occupied.

'Edmund!' I said surprised.

'Ellie? What are you doing up so late?' he said, glancing up from some sprawled out papers.

'I—I saw the light on and thought Papa was still up.'

'No. He is to bed. He is letting me use his study as I have case papers to lay on Monday morning at the Old Bailey.'

'I see.'

'Is there something else?' he asked.

'Yes, actually, Edmund. May I sit?' I asked, still hovering in the doorway and he nodded and I closed the door behind me and took a seat the other side of the desk.

'Well?'

'What do you know about getting an annulment or divorce?'

'That it is nigh on impossible to gain either without very solid grounds, and even then, no small feat.'

'But it can be done.'

He glared at me incredulously before saying: 'Ellie, I am no expert in such matters. I am a criminal lawyer and these are matters for the ecclesiastical courts. But unless your husband is guilty of fraud or impotence then there shall be no annulment granted, for you are of age and I presume neither of you insane?'

I considered we might both be: he for his disturbing behaviour, me for marrying him. 'What do you mean by fraud?'

'I mean if you have found out he is not who he claims to be; a false identity? Or if he is unable to uphold his end of the contract?'

'I don't believe so. What about impotence?'

'Come, Ellie, you do not expect me to explain that to you, do you?'

I nodded. 'Well, I believe it means to be useless, and if that's the case, I would agree.'

'Not in the general, it refers to something very specific in this instance.'

There was a long pause before he said: 'Let's say; incapable of performing conjugal duties.'

'Oh,' I said surprised and shook my head. 'So, I have only insanity in my favour then.'

'Well, if you like the idea of Bedlam and even more social disgrace than you've landed yourself in already.'

'I did not mean me. Him. Would it be considered insanity for him to be having relations with his cousin who everyone believes to be his sister?'

He frowned. 'Is she his sister?'

'No.'

'Then unfortunately not.'

'What about divorce then?'

'You would need an act of parliament and a very large purse, more patience than a saint and compelling evidence. By gad, if the king of England hasn't even managed it, you might see what you are up against, and you a woman.'

'Can women not get a divorce?'

'Well, if a husband launches a crim con and has evidence his wife has been unfaithful, then technically, thereafter, if she is patient, rich and willing to become a social pariah, then there is a very slight possibility.'

'So, I must be unfaithful or mad?'

'Pretty much, and I do not think you are either. So, unless your husband drops dead, Ellie, I'm afraid your lot is dealt.'

'I wish he would.'

'That's may be, and I hear he is not all the crack, but come, Ellie, divorce? You cannot think that way. He is rich, is he not?'

I nodded.

'Then go and spend all his money and get him locked up in the fleet. It might not get you a divorce, but it will take him off your hands if you really want to be rid of him without declaring yourself insane or committing murder.' He laughed and I realised he was joking. To him this was all a joke, and an inconvenience.

'I'm glad someone finds my miserable circumstances so comical,' I said, getting out of my chair.

'Come, I was funning. I meant no offence.'

'Funning. Forgive me if I don't see the funny side. I have only just recovered from his brutality and am trying to figure out a way I might release myself from his clutches in case next time he actually kills me!'

His expression changed to something like regret but I did not stay around to hear any more. I ran from the room and straight to my bed, feeling the entirety of the hopelessness of my situation. At this rate, I might well be considered more suitable for Bedlam and wandered what might be the less of evils.

Morning came about too quickly and when I made my way downstairs, the house was alive and busied in preparations for this evening's events. Housemaids had been ordered to clean and polish every nook and cranny and set out the rooms in preparation for it and the dining room was full with breakfasting guests. It seemed there was nowhere to escape for a little peace; even my own room had been invaded by spring cleaning, although I knew this was not for the purpose of the party, but my mother's way of forcing me out from my attempted hibernation, which it seemed had not gone unnoticed after all, for she sent Watts to find me out and fetch me to join them. A temporary withdrawal from society had been necessary, even in her mind, to allow time for my name to cool on-dit, but she was determined that there would be no better time to face it out than under the distraction of this weekend's celebrations.

I waited until the dining room was half deserted before breakfasting, then took a walk in the morning sunshine, taking care now to stay out in the open and avoid the woods, spent some hours in the library and when my room was set to rights again, disappeared to resume my hibernation for the remainder of the afternoon. Still, Tulley had not come to me, and as tempted as I was to seek her out and berate her for avoiding coming, I chose again, to delay it. There was enough to contend with already today.

Dinner was, as I expected, an uncomfortable affair, for me at least; sitting around a dining table with Giles' absence glaringly obvious and questions on their lips I could not answer. But I was grateful for the arrival of my sisters to keep me occupied, and that the seating arrangements had kept me far enough away from my former set to keep me out of reach of any intimate conversation with them. It was quite disarranged now—Martha absent and still travelling about on her wedding journey; Clara keeping close to the side of her new husband; Anna and Beth seeming to have paired up; and Betsy hanging on to them like a poor relation.

I put on my brave face and kept as much out of conversation beyond the small civilities. It was not until we proceeded to the Long Gallery for the formal ball and the other guests arrived that things became difficult, and I thought myself weak enough to give into the wine on offer, just to get through it.

I met my brother in the hall on the way up to the gallery, and although I had already been subject to an hour of introduction to Lady Jane and her family upon their arrival yesterday, things had gone quite without incident and I gave the golden couple my felicitations in the proper style and had thought it all amicable enough. Even Henry was unusually charming, which was why I bothered to speak to him when the opportunity arose, thinking him perhaps changed and improved by Lady Jane, after all.

'Well congratulations, Henry. I own I did not see such news coming, but I am happy for you. Lady Jane is quite lovely and seems very happy,'

I said as we filled the ante-room, waiting for everyone to muster and be announced.

'Well, that makes one of us then,' he said flippantly.

I frowned. 'What?'

'You think I meant to be leg shackled so soon?'

So soon; he was hardly in the first bloom of youth, I was sure he was thirty now. 'Then why have you proposed?'

'Why do you think? With all the scandals you are firing off lately, it was thought I'd better act now before no one would have me.'

'Henry, that's absurd, you are a man of great consequence; heir to all of this. How can you think you would be cast aside over my trifles?' *Particularly*, I thought, *when you have a far longer list of misdemeanours than I.*

'Trifles? Is that what you think they are, Eleanor? Then perhaps Ed is right and you have lost your marbles. Take a look around you, half of society are not even come, the other half are doing their best to tolerate you for the rest of our sakes.'

'Many are holidaying at the moment.' I looked about the room, there was discomfort in the looks and contorted smiles I received. I could not pretend I did not understand their meaning, for I had made many such faces myself, more times than I cared to remember. The only true kindly eyes I noticed beyond my relations were Mrs Ponwiker's and Delores'. For the rest, I noted a hint of distaste, a gaze of pity, a squint of muted reprimand in their sideways glances. 'Henry, I'm sorry, I didn't mean to...'

'Tell it to Mama. Thanks to her quick thinking, I look likely to recover, but she is beyond that, I think. I hope it was worth it.'

'What do you mean?'

'Oh, you haven't heard the news? She has been asked to resign from her position of Almack's Patroness before next season.'

What? I held my hand to my throat. *Because of me.* I searched the room and saw my mama in conversation with Henry's new in-laws, an elegant smile across her mouth, a genteel sip from her glass. To other eyes, the grace with which she carried herself would have been disguise enough, but to me, me who knew how well schooled she was in behaving prettily, could tell from the slight tightness about her lips and heavier than usual powdering about her eyes, that even she was struggling to maintain it. I felt instantly appalled and wished myself to Jericho.

At precisely the moment I had decided to flee, Edmund came beside me and took me by the arm. 'Come little, sis, we are to be announced soon,' he said, pulling me into line.

'Did you tell Henry you thought I had lost my marbles?' I scowled at him.

'Hush. It was a passing comment. A jest. Don't give me cause to think it true.'

'What would either of you know of it anyway. You are never here. Mama speaks about the pair of you as if you were good sons but the truth is, she is lucky to see you but twice a year.'

'Ellie, this is not the time for family feuding,' he said tartly, casting a glance about us. 'Now, see if you might bear my company above a few minutes and take the scowl off your face and do the pretty, we are up next.'

'Do the pretty. That is all anyone in this family cares for, isn't it? No matter what miseries or true feeling lies beneath it, so long as we all smile along. Well, I've had it with such nonsense.'

He frowned and looked a little unsure of me. 'You really have gone queer in the attic,' he said, and I knew that had Grantley not announced us at that very moment, I would have shook free of his arm and likely shoved him out of my way and left. But even my training had cultivated an automated response of pressing my features into a smile when I saw all eyes turned towards us; and he was spared an elaboration on my point by Harriet coming directly up to us after our announcement.

'Is everything alright?' she asked, looking between us.

'Apparently not. According to Edmund, I have gone queer in the attic,' I said, casting him a sideways glance.

'Edmund, surely you would not say such an unkind thing,' she protested.

'My apologies. I should not have,' he acquiesced under Harriet's studying gaze.

'Apology accepted,' I said bitingly. I did not mean it, but it would be hard enough to bear the remaining hours of prattling and dancing amongst these people who would not overlook my reduced circumstances, without falling out with my family to deal in too. So, I took Harriet's arm and we went for a turn about the room as it slowly began to fill. We had not yet had a moment to speak privately with the house so overrun.

'Take no notice of him,' she said once we had moved out of earshot.

'It's not just him Harri. Henry boxed my ears just a moment ago, saying I am to blame for him having to wed and that Mama has been asked to resign by the patronesses.'

'Well, it is true that she has been asked to resign but Henry had no right to blame you for it. And as for him having to wed, I should think Mama grateful that something finally moved him to do so, for let's face it, he would have been no closer to it without a rush on,' she laughed and I joined her in it. 'Anyway, forget all of that. Tell me you are doing better now? Mama said you were in quite the state on your return, black and blue, I think she described it. I am so sorry, Ellie.'

'Thank you, Harri,' I said, pressing her hand lightly as it rested in the crook of my elbow. 'It was very bad. But I am doing better now. I just long to get today out of the way and come to Kent.'

'Yes, we will talk more then, away from all these prying eyes. Try to bear up, Ellie. It will be over with soon enough.'

I smiled and turned to see Betsy slip in beside us.

'Eleanor, Harriet,' she said serenely and I wanted to give her the cut sublime and turn in the opposite direction, but Harri, being none the wiser, smiled and stopped to converse with her.

'Elizabeth, how do you do?' she asked and I looked about me for someone else to turn my attention to, but there was no one else free. So, I listened absentmindedly as Betsy waffled on. It was only when Harri was distracted by her husband coming to claim her, that I looked up and found myself left quite alone with her.

'You're uncommonly quiet today. Is everything well?' she asked me and I could barely believe she had the nerve.

I cut her a sharp look but she ignored it. I was so distracted, that without thinking, I took a glass of wine from a tray and put it to my lips. It was the smell of it that reminded me just in time to put it down again. But it took all my will to manage it. I knew just a couple of glasses would be the difference between getting through this night with reasonable calm and not getting through it at all. My mind had been set on only two things tonight: avoiding confrontation and avoiding wine. Right now, I could not see how I would last the night.

'Am I?' I said nonchalantly.

She frowned at me through thick lashes that had been curled and powdered to excess and I wondered who she was trying her cap at now with the colonel off abroad. I knew she would be on the lookout for a better offer in his absence like she had been for the past three years. Now I understood why she had never found one. 'Is something wrong?' she asked me, looking more than mildly intrigued.

'With me? Nothing at all. Should there be?'

'No. Only, no one has seen you for the last couple of weeks and they've been asking after you.'

I bet they have.

'Well, you may tell them I am quite alive and well.'

'Indeed.' Her twisted smile was one I had come to know too well and yet only now saw it as plainly wicked as the rest of the world must always have seen it.

'How are you? Indeed, I do not believe I have seen you since Lady W.'s soiree,' I said pointedly.

'No indeed,' she replied and I noted the recognition of my point even though it remained unspoken. 'Not that we spoke a great deal at it, if I recall, you were, I believe: distracted.'

She was mocking me. It was just her way; usually I overlooked it with relative ease, but my patience was delicate and I knew it might snap at any time. I took a deep breath. 'Yes, I was quite distracted by other company.'

'Where is Giles?' she asked me then, and I knew now she meant to be incendiary.

'To Jericho, or the devil, I hope.'

'Trouble in paradise?' she asked.

I leant in close to whisper. 'Well, he wasn't too pleased to find I had been fucking Richards instead of him.'

Even she did not know how to respond to that.

'Oh, don't look so surprised, he was all over me from the moment we met. It was destined to happen eventually with him pursuing me so ardently. He even left me his card when he was engaged to teach you music. But well, I wasn't minded to refuse him when he made it plain to me that he hadn't the least speck of interest in you and the way was quite clear. I mean, he is very handsome, I can see why you threw yourself at him behind the colonel's back, and I cannot say I was disappointed in the least at caving.' If there was but a way to freeze the moment, her picture would have been an epic portrayal: her jaw dropped to the floor and eyes wide, betrayed. *Yes, have a taste of your own medicine.*

'You whore,' she spat.

'Not precisely, although I do remember thinking the very same of you when Richards described the way you pushed yourself on him and how he had to fend you off. Perhaps prefixed with desperate—yes, desperate whore seems more fitting to your circumstances. Still, if I ever had to turn to such a profession, I think I should have no trouble finding customers. Let's hope the colonel never finds out what you're about. Should you fall on hard times, you might starve to death if ever you must rely on such a trade.'

It happened too quickly to anticipate it, but as I saw her lip tremble, she raised her glass and threw the contents over me and screamed: 'You bitch!' before running out the room. It seemed to me it was about time there was a bigger bitch than her in Cuddington. I wiped my eyes with the heel of my hands and noted the silence in the room and shouted after her: 'I'm sorry, Bets. I won't tell anyone, I promise. Your secrets are safe with me.'

Harri was at my side steering me out of the room before I could utter another thing. 'What on earth was that?' she said furiously.

'Bets getting a dose of her own treatment at long last,' I said simply and looked up to see Henry bounding up the hall towards us.

'One damn weekend! Is that too much to ask for you to behave yourself?' he snarled.

'Oh, fuck off Henry. You wouldn't know the first thing about behaving yourself even at your age. I'll take my lectures from a better example than you.'

'You see, she is mad,' he said to Harriet as if I just evidenced the point for him. 'And vulgar and coarse, and a disgrace to us all! If my wedding goes to ruin because of you—'

'If your wedding goes to ruin, it will be because she doesn't love you, Henry. Because she realises what a great stupid oaf you are, or because she has learnt of your rakish dandy past, not because of your little sister. You really are pathetic to presume otherwise.'

'Stop! The pair of you!' Harri cried.

'Me? It's that little beast that needs her mouth washed out with soap,' Henry accused and I laughed.

'Oh, be careful Henry, who knows what I might be bought to doing next, dangerous little beast that I am. Don't feed it.'

'Ellie—'

'I'm sorry, Harri, but I'm sick to the teeth of all the hypocrisy in this family. You know what a disgrace and disappointment Henry has been and how he has broke our parents hearts a thousand times over, and yet here he is, thinking he can lecture me...'

'It's not the time, Ellie,' she said flatly.

'It never is, is it?' I said and speed walked my way up to my room.

My heart was still pounding in my chest when I got to it, and I drew in several breaths before the tears fell. I had given up on the idea of getting through this impossible night and wanted only the privacy and peace to find a pillow to cry into. I took the care to lock my door before flinging myself onto the bed. I had barely been there a minute when I heard it knock. I lay rigid and silent. I was not opening it, I did not care if it was Harri, or my own mother; I simply could not face any more of it without exploding. I wanted to implode instead and spare them the vitriol, but the goading was too much, my tolerance worn too thin now.

The door tapped again.

'Miss, are you in there? It's Tulley.'

I sighed with relief. 'Are you alone?' I asked, and when she confirmed it, I dragged myself off of the bed and wiped my face on the edge of my skirt. 'Are you sure there is no one else up here?'

'Yes, I am quite alone.'

I took a breath before turning the key and when I saw her stood in front of me, her gentle face, her eyes kind and unassuming, I felt such inexplicable comfort at the sight of her that I could not berate her for her lack of coming to me before, however much the slight of it had offended me.

I locked the door behind her and offered her to come over to the fire side chairs, the grate filled with nothing but a neatly swept pile of ash.

'I am so sorry, miss, for the delay in my coming. I saw you go by and thought I must catch you whilst I had the chance.' She looked tired, her eyes red and below them her pale skin had greyed. 'I have tried so many times to come, but with the big house clean and dinner tonight, I have not managed to break free of a chore for even the briefest moment. Cook is not in a mood to be trifled with and even Mrs Crawford didn't seem worth the trying.'

'It couldn't be helped then.' There was always such an honesty in her face that it seemed impossible to doubt her efforts. 'Will you sit?'

'Thank you, miss.'

'So, you have come to give me your answer?'

'Yes, miss.' She studied me carefully. 'Have you spilled something, miss? Shall I get you a towel?'

'Don't ask. No, I'll sort it out later. You go on.'

'Well, I thought long and hard about your offer, ma'am; I have thought on nothing else since. But...I'm afraid I cannot accept it.'

My throat seemed suddenly as dry as the ash in the fireplace and I couldn't speak.

'I am sorry. You have afforded me such a great honour and I hope you can forgive me for disappointing you, miss. But there are other reasons beyond my lack of experience that I felt could not be overcome.'

It is no great disappointment; I wanted to say. I would have said it to any other servant, but I could not to her. I opened my mouth to try. 'Can I enquire to what those reasons are?'

'I don't wish to leave this house miss, and I certainly don't wish to upset anyone down there when they have been so good to me... and if I took this position, they would think me above myself, bypassing others who have served your family longer than I, and outweigh my experience to boot.'

'So, you decline a promotion that could alter your life entirely for the sake of the judgement of the other servants?' I did not know whether to laugh or scream.

'They are my friends, miss, my family now, and Poppy is the nearest thing I have in the world to a sister, a mother...'

'But you will not have to suffer their disgruntlement forever, I told you, I am not to stay here.'

'Even if I could leave Poppy behind—'

I could see this seemed impossible to her, whoever this Poppy was.

'I only need look at Watts to see that wherever I was, I would be very much alone in the world and I don't think I could be alone again, miss.'

This was real no. I felt my lip tremble, my eyes gush with tears. I had banked too many hopes on her answer being yes. Had thought just moments ago, that with her chaperone we might set off to some resort early in the morning.

'Miss?'

I felt her come beside me.

'Here.' She dangled a handkerchief between my fingers but I did not take it. I could have dismissed her entirely for so many things, she knew I had the power to take all those things away from her, yet, somehow, she trusted that I would not. *I could not.* 'You may go now,' I told her.

'I cannot leave you like this; will you tell me what is wrong?'

'Everything is wrong, whatever I do.'

'I have disappointed you so much you think me ungrateful,' she said.

'Please go. Please leave me.'

But she refused, with that gentle obstinacy that she seemed entirely incapable of on looking at her face. But when I felt her arm around my shoulder, I could not continue my petition she leave. I felt instantly the comfort no one else could give to me, and I wanted her to stay.

I sobbed so much I think it shook us both. I had tried at holding strong for longer than I could have ever reasonably expected to manage. I could bear it no more, I was changed now. The walls that had once protected me from the injuries of life had begun to collapse all around me, crumbling away a little more each time I felt another blow, and like an open wound, my injuries of that wretched night had left me open to every kind of sadness: From Sheldon's betrayal to my own disgrace, the shame of Mariella, then Giles, my society blunders so narrowly recovered and the devastation of the poverty at Old Mill Street, to dead little Lucy.

My heart had grown so heavy that I did not know how I carried the burden of it all, or how I would carry it a moment longer. But her comfort alleviated the pain of it all for that moment as she held on to me despite my resistance, my stiffness, my reluctance to sink into her embrace. She seemed to know exactly what I needed, despite myself. The thought that I might not have her care in the coming weeks seemed unbearable. It was not the answer I had expected, but how could I fail to understand her reasons when my future depended on convention too, when being alone as I had felt so plainly, was a justified fear. I didn't want to be alone either anymore, yet when I was with her, I didn't feel alone.

When I calmed, she let me lean there for a while against her shoulder with no questions. I felt her stroking my hair. 'Miss, whatever my duties, my loyalty to you remains unchanged. I will do my best to support you in whatever ways I can. You may rely upon that.'

I sniffed back my tears and nodded. I knew it was true, for she had already proved it so from the moment we met; and yet it would be impossible now. I must get away from here. But I wanted to tell her everything, to have someone to confide in. We perched on the edge of the chaise-longue and I clung to her again as another wave of emotion stole my intended words.

'Let them fall,' she told me with a gentle squeeze that reassured me. Even through the noise of them, I could not fail to hear those strange and liberating words. I had never been given permission to cry, or scold or let my frustrations rise in me, or even feel; I realised then. Not truly feel or truly speak my thoughts. Everything I had known was an act, a game of pretend where my part was to deny my own feelings and agree with the demands of a society that expected nothing less and a family that knew no better. And here, whilst my heart was melting in my chest, I found more comfort and honesty in her embrace than I had ever felt before. She did not scold me for the tears that rolled down my cheeks because it was weak, improper, vulgar, or for the pain that wrenched at my gut, the hopelessness in my tone, for the feelings I was at last in touch with. Instead, she encouraged it and held me firm in her arms so I could not fall or drown in the flood that ensued.

Since she didn't press me for an explanation, when I cleared my throat and looked into her eyes for the first time, I wondered what compelled me to tell her the things I did—to speak with such frankness. The words seemed to want to spring forth from my lips, unrequested, uninvited. 'I have made such a hash of everything, Tulley.' I paused to steady my tone which was threatening to falter at each syllable. 'And I have let everyone down. I am not like you, Tulley: I am not good and kind and a feeling person.'

'That is not true, miss.' There was no flattery in her tone, yet I could not remember one kind thing I had done amongst all the terrible ones to afford her that assessment of me.

'If any of those things were true, then you would be quite unmoved and that clearly cannot be said. If it were true, then why did you send that money over to Old Mill Street?'

She knew?

'Little Jane decided that an Angel must have sent it, to stop everyone being so sad.'

I was stunned.

'They were very grateful, miss. Even though they don't know who their thanks are owed to.'

'It was only money.'

'Not to them. To them, it was the difference between full bellies and larders, less toil, to have the rent collector's coins ready for him when he come, for Lucy to have a proper coffin...' she added gently.

This made the tears come quicker, hot and stinging. Had I really been able to ease so many burdens with a few coins? 'I am glad it was help-ful,' I said when I was able to speak again. 'But it was one good thing out of so many bad things, Tulley. I have so many ugly secrets lurking within me that I fear the carrying of them have blackened my soul and everyone around me is touched by the curse—'

'You are not cursed. Whatever secrets you have, miss, and I think we all have some...'

I could not imagine her having any of any grave significance.

'I think you must make peace with them, one way or the other.'

'And how do I do that?'

'I'm not entirely sure. I suppose it is different for everyone. But for me, I try to accept that which cannot be altered and vow to learn by it, perhaps choose differently should the situation arise again, forgive myself for not knowing how to do better before so I can move on, but vowing to do so in the future.'

'It sounds simple when you say it, but I fear I do not have the sound-ness of your judgement in which to settle them so.'

'Of course you do.'

'No, in earnest, I do not. I realise now that my judgement cannot be trusted, or at least the values on which I have come to make them against.'

'Oh, miss, you are very severe with yourself.'

'You only say it because you don't know me.' And yet the irony seemed she knew more of the ugliness inside me than anyone else, for with her there had been little need to disguise or make excuse for the things she had witnessed. I looked up at her, and yet still she was at my side, without prejudice to me. Mother would have credited her with no more than due deference and knowing her place well, but I felt her kind-ness to be true, her words genuine. I had slipped enough bribes into ser-vants' palms in the past to know the difference. But she was not like that.

'Perhaps I do not know you well, but I do not need to, to see that you are suffering greatly by some means, and doing your best to overcome it.'

'Tulley, I don't think I can overcome it. I think it has overcome me, and yet I deserve it all, so how can I complain?'

'I do not know the circumstances that have led you here, miss, but I would find it very hard to accept that you might have provoked anything worthy of the pain I have seen in your countenance.'

'Why? You yourself have seen that I do not consider things beyond my own inconvenience. I have been unkind and harsh, even with you.' I paused and looked away.

'And it is quite forgiven and forgotten. I think you were not yourself.'

'I'm not sure I know what *myself* is, anymore, who it is.'

'I understand. When my mama died, I felt lost like that too.'

'And yet here you are, so together. How do you do that, Tulley?'

'I wouldn't say that. Perhaps slowly re-gathering myself might be more accurate. But I had to fall apart before I could steady myself again, sometimes I still do. But we go on. Life goes on and we must find a way. I think you need someone to talk to; to share your burden with.'

'I have no one—no one who would understand even if I had the nerve to confess it all. The only people that have ever given me comfort were my sisters and they are moved far away from here and I rarely see them. I am not like them. They made my parents proud; they married well and became the perfect ladies they were destined to be. I—I fear I am not made of the same stuff, I've made such a hash of it, like everything else.'

'I am sure even they have their troubles, miss.'

'Perhaps, but if they do, they have the sense to keep them out of the public knowing. Huh, look at me; here I am, trying to be something that I am not; a feeling person, but as usual, I am a fraud even at that.'

She put her palm to my face and wiped my cheek with her thumb. 'No, you are not. You do yourself the credit of an honest examination, which is more than most people do,' she told me gently.

I pulled away from her. 'But I am a fraud, Tulley. In twenty years, I have never known the devastation of my own town. I never knew that on my own doorstep children just like my niece and nephew were dead in their mothers' arms, because...' I got choked up again and paused. '...Not because of some ill that could not be remedied, but instead because they are too destitute to have good health and too poor still to have a doctor treat them. Then I sit in the home of people so poor they cannot afford the barest necessities, and they are kind to me and offer me their broth whilst my father sends his steward to rob them of their last few shillings for his rent.' My voice broke into tears again but I spoke through them. 'And my heart is bleeding, not only because of the shock I have felt at my own ignorance, but because I realise I have been lied to. The world is not the place I thought it. Society is not what I thought it. My friends and family are not who I believed them to be. And I am not even who I thought I was. It seems I am no better than they for all our differences.' The last words were swallowed in a sharp drawing of breath from the hysteria.

She pulled my chin up until our eyes met. 'You are better.'

'Why, because I finally found something potent enough to sting my conscience and gave a few alms.'

She nodded and held my face firm between her palms so I could not turn away.

'That is precisely why, miss. You were moved to do something. Do you understand the power of that? To recognise someone's suffering? That alone. Then to try to do something to alter things for the better, however great or small you may contribute.'

I looked up to meet her eyes. 'Yes, yes I think I do. You are the example.'

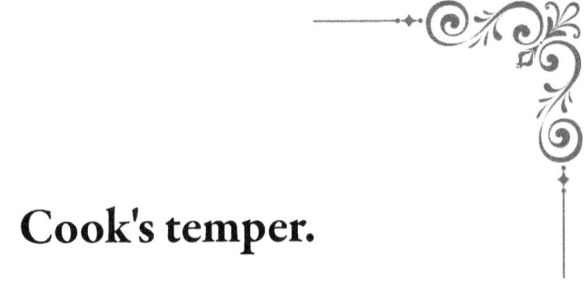

Cook's temper.

August 1821. - Annalise.

Annalise awoke to the sun's warm gaze upon her cheeks as it streamed through the unfamiliar tall windows. She squeezed her eyes shut and turned away from the harshness of it, then opened them again, startled to see Eleanor curled up fast asleep next to her. She studied the sight of her, still in her beautiful silk gown, flowers in her hair, her face so perfectly painted and now smudged by last night's tears. She rubbed her eyes and tried to pull herself to order. She had not meant to stay all night. She meant only to console her until she went to sleep. It seemed the only way to show her that she was able to confront her troubles without reaching for the liquor. And so she had lay beside her upon the bed as invited, and promised to stay until she fell asleep.

The washstand had not been replenished and she felt relieved that it was unlikely anyone had been in and seen her there. She rolled onto her back, covered her mouth to yawn and considered how strange it was to wake up in such a beautiful room. The handsome Chippendale four-poster bed, cloaked in the finest rose-coloured silk damask. The matching embroidered drapes and open white wood shutters, the tall windows flooding the room with brilliant light, unlike the tiny stream it cast across her basement bedroom through the narrow pane of glass.

A cosy window seat was fashioned beneath them, piled high with cushions, inviting you to want to sit there and admire the view from it. Every item of perfectly crafted furniture was polished and gleaming. Beneath the picture rail, many exquisite paintings hung ornamentally, framed in fine gilt wood. She could have stayed and stared into the stucco ceiling for hours on end with its complex, intricate design. She wondered what the scene depicted. Something biblical perhaps, she considered examining the cherubim's.

Her distracted thoughts evaporated as she turned her ear to the familiar stirring of the house coming to life for another day, and realised it was later than she had thought it.

She forced herself up from the soft still-made bed, and jumped down from it, the plush pile of the Oriental rug between her toes. She found her shoes on the floor, brushed the creases out of her uniform and quickly fixed her hair at the dressing table looking glass. *I've done it this time*, she told her reflection: Cook would be fuming if the kettles had not been set to boil before her rising. It would have been bad enough on any day, but leaving her understaffed after a huge party and with guests in the house, didn't even bear thinking.

She was not a woman well-disposed to accepting excuses of any kind—even half dead with the flu she would still find some small polishing of copper pots, or mending of sieves to occupy you throughout your recuperation, which was expected and encouraged to be swift. What on earth could she possibly say in answer to where she had been last night, all morning; that would appease as severe a woman as her? She could complain of having more duties above stairs? This might prove the one day she felt grateful of covering so many duties on top of her own. At least, she could stay out of Cook's way for long enough to think of a convincing excuse whilst she delivered the water to the chambers. Although she had yet to get around the small matter of having to go to the basement to fetch it first.

She crept out of the room cautiously, and was glad to see the household hadn't risen. Her heart raced as she took the service staircase, turning every corner, expecting to be confronted with someone she did not want to see. She consoled herself with the idea that cook might still be drawing up the day's orders, which would allow her to sneak off to her room unseen and change her apron. Then footsteps mounted the steps below and her heart sank at the sound of them.

'There you are!'

'Oh, thank god it's you, Poppy, I thought you were Cook,' she jumped back and gasped.

Poppy wasn't impressed. 'I've been worried half to death, where have you been all night?' She pulled her by the arm to lead her back up the stairs.

'I was with Mrs Craythorne, she was in crisis last night and—'

'Mrs who?'

'The Ashlyn daughter. She needed my help; it's a long story.'

'This will get you into trouble, Annalise. Have you lost all sense?' She shook her head and lowered her voice as they reached the hall.

'She gave me permission, only I didn't mean to fall asleep up there. Does cook know?'

'Asleep? Permission? It is Cook you report to, not guests, which is what your Mrs Craythorne is to this 'ouse now. And, of course, she knows; little passes her eye unnoticed. I tried to cover for you but I don't think she was convinced in the least.'

They were both silenced as Mrs Crawford came marching out of the dining hall, turning a beady eye over them as she passed.

Poppy shoved Annalise the grate equipment. 'I better get back to work. I put Fanny on the water, you're to go and do the grates in her place. We'll speak later.' And with that, Poppy disappeared back into the staircase.

She was grateful for being spared the fall out, but not so pleased for upsetting Poppy. But it had afforded her some time to think on what she might say, although, if Cook got to her before she and Poppy had a chance to agree the story, they would both be for it. The last thing she wanted was to get her into trouble as well. She wondered what had got into her lately, she never got in bother in all her months here and suddenly she seemed on a mission to make a habit of it.

'Stop dawdling, girl and get to work,' Mrs Crawford snorted in her passing.

'Yes, sorry, ma'am,' she said and rushed into the dining room to sweep the blown about ashes from the fireplace.

It was drawing near to breakfast time when Annalise completed her morning rounds. She had tried to drag them out as long as possible, hoping to think up a convincing explanation: but nothing. She trudged her way down nervously hoping that they'd all be in the servants' hall and she could wait in her room. Poppy was bound to check and then they might corroborate their story beforehand.

She sat on her bed, bored, rubbing bear grease into her hands and hoping Poppy would not be long. Her stomach seemed to disagree with her decision to skip breakfast as the salty smell of bacon filled the air. She walked over to the shard of mirror hanging upon the wall, dipped a rag into the jar of rosemary ashes and began cleaning her teeth. She was just re-pinning her hair when the door knocked. The dread rose inside her at the sound; Poppy wouldn't have knocked. She took a deep breath and went over to the door. Her heart pounded, Cook frowned at her and stepped into the room.

'You don't look ill to me.' She made her assessment with a brief look up and down her. Her platter faced cheeks flushed bright red and her nose crinkled up like it had been pushed against glass.

Annalise's lips began to twitch but she struggled to speak against the building anxiety. 'I am feeling much better now. I was just getting ready to come to the kitchen...'

She placed her hands on her hips which had the effect of rendering Annalise even more lost for words. 'I shall make up the time of course. I...I shall work twice as hard, you may be sure...'

Just as Cook seemed to be losing patience with her stuttering, the open door was tapped and Eleanor stepped into it.

'Mrs Simpson, I hoped I might find you here.'

Cook's expression froze before melting into a forged smile as she stepped aside and Eleanor came into view.

'Good morning, ma'am, would you like to speak privately?' she asked, although not really asking but assuming, stepping toward the corridor.

She put it down to her nerves, but Annalise had to concentrate hard to prevent herself from laughing aloud as she listened to Cook attempting to squeeze her gruff tone into something of a contrived genial accent.

'No, no. I wanted to thank Tulley as well,' Eleanor corrected her.

'Thank?' Cook squealed. It was clear that she was fuming at having her moment of tantrum usurped.

'Yes, thank you both of course,' Eleanor smiled. 'You see, when Tulley told me you might be displeased at her disappearing to my aid; I assured her that such a senior member of staff would certainly understand the urgency of attending a lady in crisis.'

'Yes indeed. But I thought Anna was unwell last night.' Cook looked suspicious, and hopeful of catching her out.

'Oh no, Mrs Simpson. It was I who was unwell last night. Although, between us, I think I had a little too much wine.' She lifted her brows fractionally. 'In any case, I just wanted to thank Tulley for her loyal service, and thank you for being so good as to spare her on such a busy night. And might I add whilst I remember, what a splendid effort you made with the dinner, the beef sirloin was a particular favourite.'

She'd done it, her smoothness had sufficed and Cook was sold. If you wanted to get on Cook's better side, allaying her fears that she was not about to be thrown over for a French chef was a good means of achieving it. Her pursed lips fell into a bashful smile. 'Well, I am pleased you enjoyed it, ma'am.'

'I was certainly not the only one, by the comments at the table.'

Cook's plump cheeks blushed a shade deeper than its usual mottled pink hue.

'Anyhow, I mustn't keep you any longer from your breakfast.'

'Oh, yes, if you might excuse me miss, there is much to be done. Good day to you.' She moved aside and dropped a curtsy on her way out. 'Oh Anna,' she called, looking back, 'Maggie left your breakfast on the stove plate when you're ready,' she added, as she pattered out of the room in far better spirits than she had entered with.

'Thank you, ma'am,' Annalise replied, smirking at Eleanor as they watched her disappear into the dimness of the corridor.

Eleanor smiled back.

'I can't thank you enough; I was about to be skinned alive.'

'I thought as much. It is the least I could do, you were a great comfort to me last night and I confess, I did not have the heart to wake you when I realised you were sleeping, so the fault is mine.'

She was glad to know she was not in any trouble on that count. She hadn't been sure who had fallen asleep first. 'Did you sleep alright, miss?'

'I did. Thank you.'

'And do you feel better today?'

'Yes. Yes, I think I do. Not as improved as I might if I could convince you to tell me not look for another lady's maid. Is there no hope of you changing your mind? I know I am not the meekest of mistresses, but I hope I might be found some improvement on Mrs Simpson?'

Annalise half smiled at the lightness in her voice. 'I wish I could. I think you might prove a very good mistress. But you see, that bed is Poppy's, we have worked together for as long as I can remember. She is the only one I have left in the world now, so you see...'

'It's alright. I know you have your reasons. We all have those. What is Poppy's role here?'

'She is undercook. One day I hope she will be Cook. She is very talented.'

'Well. She is very lucky to have such a friend. I better leave you to take your breakfast before it gets cold.'

Her stomach was pleased that she had not missed out on her breakfast when she took her empty plate to the scullery feeling content. Poppy followed her out to the yard where she was starting on plucking the game whilst Maggie scrubbed the tables down.

'What happened?' Poppy demanded, sitting down on Maggie's empty stool and examining Annalise for signs of a scolding.

'Nothing.' She smiled and Poppy looked confused.

'I don't understand. The old hen was smiling so sweetly when she came in to start the baking, I thought she had given you your marching orders!'

'She certainly seemed minded to when she found me, not that she could much afford to do without anyone of us right now.'

'Phew! Is that what changed her mind d'ya think?'

'No. It was Mrs Craythorne that changed her mind and sent her away smiling.'

'Who's Mrs Craythorne?'

'You know, the Ashlyn daughter—she's married now and that's her name.'

Poppy frowned again. 'Well, what does she have to do with the price of eggs?'

'She appeared at precisely the right moment to save my skin. It was actually mildly amusing.'

Poppy was not impressed. 'I'm glad you thought so! I, however, was worried sick about you last night, but I daren't alert anyone for fear of getting you sacked!'

Annalise's smile quickly faded, 'I'm sorry Poppy, I didn't mean to worry you. She needed my help. She was in a bad way last night. I didn't expect to stay so long, I didn't ...think at all.' She lowered her head.

'No, something you seem to be making a habit of lately.' She looked at Annalise's sunken gaze and softened her tone. 'Listen, I'm worried about you, Annalise. You are overworked as it is without being at her beck and call. Let her trouble Fanny with her errands. She's the one determined to win her way into her good books.'

'I do not think she is so keen on Fanny.'

'Well, not many are. But that's not your concern. She may have stepped in for you on this occasion, but how many times do you think either Cook or Mrs Crawford for that matter, will tolerate such meddling in their authority before they turn you out? Besides, you won't be fit for work if you keep missing your meals and now even your sleep.'

Annalise took up her bucket and flung a handful of feathers into it. 'I know. You are right. She tells me she will have a lady's maid soon so I'm sure I will not be needed much longer.'

'Good, because you are not in her employ and if you keep overlooking the chores you are assigned it will be noticed. The last thing I want is to see you get thrown out with a bad character and have to go back to Mr Gint's; I'm only thinking of you.'

'I know.'

A slip.

August 1821. - Eleanor.

I was on my way back from the basement when my aunt, Orlagh, called out to me as I passed the breakfast room. 'Love, you're alright, aren't you?' she said, looking concerned.

'Yes, thank you, Aunt. I am.'

'Your father told me about, well, about your husband. I'm sorry love. You know you can come to us whenever you like. London, Cork, whichever takes your fancy.'

'Thank you, Aunt. That is very good of you.'

'Tuh. Don't play polite wi' me. I mean it. You find yourself in a spot then you write to me and I shall send for you. I won't see you mishandled or forced back to that brute and I've told your pa as much. I know his type and I'd as leave go and pound the door down myself and have him answer for it. Your pa say's I'm not to interfere and I shan't with that. But, well, if you need some where to retreat to, or an ear, you only need to say.'

I felt my lip tremble. 'Thank you. I will.'

'Ah, come here, give your aunty a hug.'

She gathered me up and squeezed me, then said, 'What's say we go for a ride this morning? Your ma says you've been so worried about bumping into him, you've given up the habit. You can't do that dear. You can't let him win. I know you love your horses—it's the Ashlyn blood, you canny help it,' she laughed. 'What say you get changed into your habit and we trot over to the downs and get some exercise? That brute comes anywhere in sight, he'll have your uncles tiger to contend with.'

I laughed, if I remembered correctly, uncle's tiger was the inverse of a tiger, a brutish looking fellow of about six and a half foot high and as broad as two average men and quite the rough diamond. I was certain to be safe under his chaperone I considered, and wondered if I should look to hiring such a fellow myself. But it had not been only my safety that had prevented my riding, but my recovery. If I could just muster the confidence to trust my body to manage it now. I had suspected I had been healed at least a week and so it was as good a time as any to find out. 'I'll be down in twenty minutes,' I told my aunt and headed off to my chamber to ring for Fanny.

When the call was answered ten minutes later by a young maid I was unfamiliar with, I was puzzled. 'Where is Fanny?' I asked her.

She dipped a curtsey. 'She has had an accident, miss, so Mrs Crawford said I was to come. What may I do?'

'Goodness, I hope it was not serious. What happened?'

'I think, miss; she dropped the whale oil for the lamps down the stairs and slipped her way down to the bottom. She has a broken ankle and a very sore back.'

'Poor Fanny. How ghastly. You will give her my best wishes and tell her I will visit when she is up to it. Now, I will need your help to get changed into my habit as I am in a rush.'

It was a joint effort, the young girl not knowing where any of my things were kept or knowing the first thing about how to assemble my costume. I helped her find it and arranged it all upon the bed in step-by-step order. It was arduous for us both and I realised I must now write to Miss Pascal and offer her the position. I did not want to, on account I had wanted Tulley, and also due to my reluctance at having anyone upon a recommendation that was in any way connected to my circle. I wanted someone who had no loyalties to others over me, who might be prone to letting my confidences slip into the wrong ear. But I was desperate now. Tulley could not be moved and if I wanted to get away from Cuddington, then I needed a travelling companion and could not afford to delay it any longer. I would write to her when I returned.

After another ten minutes, I was finally dressed and the poor young maid looking as flustered as I. I sent her back to Mrs Crawford with a note, sending my apologies for Fanny's situation, but asking that she send Tulley in her place while Fanny was recuperating. Whilst Tulley was only marginally more familiar with my toilette, she was proficient and prompt once she had been shown a thing. Besides, someone would have to step in in the meantime, and I would like it to be her above anyone else.

Aunt Orlagh was already saddled at the stables when I arrived. 'I thought you'd changed your mind,' she said with a note of jest, already sat upon the back of her snowy white Irish draft.

'No; maid problems,' I said, patting down Samson and feeding him a few handfuls of apple halves before Thomas came beside me and helped me mount him. It felt strange to be back in the saddle. But I was relieved when we set off at a trot, that I found myself perfectly comfortable, and whilst I erred on the side of caution with my driving, by the time we had lapped the downs thrice and returned, I was certain all was well and I could at least return to this diversion again. Yes, I would no doubt ache a little tomorrow for having broken routine for such a time, but so long as it proved nothing out of the ordinary, I would have him drive to Kent so I could resume my riding there.

It was Mrs Crawford who came when I rang to be changed and I was quite astonished to have her assistance.

'Is Tulley too busy to come?' I asked her as she unlaced me.

'No, ma'am, Tulley is recuperating.'

'From what?' I said turning around to face her.

'She too was injured in the fall—'

'What? Is she alright?'

'She shall be,' she said prompting me to turn back around so she could continue unlacing. 'Doctor says she has broken four of her fingers and suspects a nasty sprain at the wrist, although he is to come back in a few days once the swelling goes down to make certain it is not broken.'

'Good grief, how did this happen? Both Fanny and Tulley in the same day.'

'It seems that when Fanny slipped down the stairs, Tulley was coming down the last steps of the flight ahead of her. When she heard the commotion, she turned about to help Fanny, but she was past helping and tumbling at a speed and came hurling into her. Tulley's arm got caught between the banister rungs as she tried to stop them both from crashing to the bottom. Thanks to her, the pair of them escaped cracked heads or worse, the doctor says.'

'That's just like her, thinking of others before herself,' I said without meaning to share my private thoughts. 'I must go and see her.'

'Well, she is on strict rest for the day.'

'For the day? And then what?'

'Well, a few days perhaps, before she can return to light duties.'

'Light duties?'

'Yes, restricted to things that can be done with one hand I suppose, so I doubt she will be much use in the kitchen.'

'Then she shall fill in for Fanny and tend to me. I shall make sure her duties are light and she gets enough rest.'

Mrs Crawford sighed, 'That's all very well, ma'am, but we are already short downstairs and she cannot be spared entirely.'

'Has the new maid come yet?'

'Yes, she arrived but yesterday,' she said cautiously and a little out of countenance that I should be abreast of such affairs.

'How quickly can another kitchen maid be employed?'

She blinked. 'Well, it depends, but we cannot be taking girls on for a few weeks then putting them out again when the others are back on their feet, ma'am.'

'No of course not. But here's the thing. I need someone to tend me and Tulley is not up to heavy work for a while. I also mean to change the staff at my London house, so, if I was to take on a kitchen maid, and even another housemaid to ease your burden, I could take them off to London with me once things were returned to usual order here.'

'Well, ma'am, that would have to be down to the mistress and—'

'No. Do not trouble my mama. She has enough to contend with with Henry's wedding, and so you see we cannot be short now when there are to be parties and breakfasts. If you will be so good as to find suitable persons, I shall pay the wages and contract them, only they shall start out here for now.'

'I don't know, ma'am. I shouldn't like your mama to think I went ahead without—'

'She shan't, she shall be glad you took the initiative to have spared her the worry of such trifles and that all shall run smoothly with two more pairs of hands. You are to spare no expense. In fact, I should prefer it if you would find skilled and experienced persons that might serve you well in this blip and serve me well thereafter.'

'Very well, ma'am. As you say.'

When she was gone and I was set to rights in a day dress fancy enough to account for our departing company's presence, but comfortable enough to sit about in, I headed to the dining room, for as soon as I had done my duty and waved them off, I was going straight down to the basement to see Tulley.

There was only family and the Yardleys around the table when I joined them for afternoon tea before they set off, and I was glad that Aunt Orlagh had saved me a seat with her. She had been so kind and warm, I was sorry that they would shortly be returning to Cork for the remainder of the year. Perhaps I might yet join them for a spell once I was properly attended. It was certainly nice to know I had the offer standing, especially still not knowing what Giles' intentions were. No one had heard a whisper from him these past weeks and whilst I was glad of it, hoped it served as a sign that he was too ashamed to enquire after me, I also felt uncertain over his intentions. Did he mean to simply let me slip away or just bide his time for now? Did he think I would return to him voluntarily or that my parents might force me in to doing so to quell the scandal? I hoped he understood now that they would not.

Although it was unclear to me what I would do now. How to plan my future. How I might settle. I had the right to spend his money, my papa had certainly contributed well enough in my marriage portion. I could find somewhere to rent, but I could not charge my bills to him whilst keeping my whereabouts unknown. At least I had no child to think of and have held to ransom. So, to travel from place to place for now, staying only a short while, ensuring my bills reached him only after moving on to the next, might be the best solution until I understood his intentions. I hoped that Mariella had dug her claws into him and was as resolute in keeping us apart as I was. Besides, he could not put off his trip to Venice forever. He might even be there now, for all I knew.

When I had finished saying my goodbyes, I went up to the library to find *The Passion* by Rosa Matilda and headed straight to the basement. When I tapped at the door, a servant I'd never seen before opened it.

'Oh, milady,' she dropped a curtsey.

'Good afternoon. Forgive me the intrusion, I was hoping to see Tulley. I am told she was injured.'

'She's a bit groggy, ma'am, and falling in and out of sleep,' she said opening the door up now so I could see the shape of her in the bed.

I stepped into the room. There was a rickety looking chair pulled up to the bedside where she was sleeping. 'May I sit with her?' I asked.

'Well, yes, miss. If you will,' she said a little taken aback. 'Doctor gave her some Laud'num for the pain this morning and she's been out since. If she wakes miss, will you send for me? I'd like to get her to eat something. She hasn't had a morsel all day.'

'Of course. Where shall I find you?'

'In the kitchen, ma'am,' she said and puffed the cushion on the chair before slipping out of the room and leaving me staring at Tulley, a pile of straw-coloured hair on the pillow so long and lustrous, I was surprised how well she concealed it all in the neatly pinned chignon she usually wore it in. Her lip was split at the bottom and bulged with the swelling, a clot of dried blood sealing it. Her cheekbone was bruised and her arm elevated upon a pillow where it was bound in bandages from fingers to elbow.

I sat down in the chair as quietly as I could for its creaking and was surprised at how choked I felt to see her in such a state. I did not know why I felt so moved. I supposed because she had done so much to care for me in my difficulties, I felt the same was due to her. Not that I quite knew what to do, for I had never taken care of anyone before. I had sat at my sister's side when she was confined and kept watch or company, but there had always been others to tend to her practical needs. There would be for Tulley too, I knew, and yet somehow, I did not want them to do it. I wanted to help, in whatever trifling ways I might. But I was to depart with Harri in a couple of hours for Kent, not knowing when I might be home again. In a fortnight for Henry's wedding I supposed. I dreaded to think of her being put to work again in but a few days without me here to ensure it otherwise, and yet she could hardly travel with me now. I looked about the room, its plain walls and cold flagstones. I should have liked to have her moved somewhere more comfortable, somewhere with at least an opening window, and less clatter and din coming through the walls, but it would not be borne. My very being here in the basement would be thought intrusion enough, without my meddling further.

I put a palm lightly to her forehead. She was warm but not feverish. A sheet had been tucked over her body and folded beneath her arms. It was at least cool in here, despite the August heat. I supposed owing to the position of the room and its small fixed pane of glass that peeped at ground level outside. I brushed a few strands of hair from her face, careful to avoid the bruising at her cheekbone. She breathed a little raspingly but soon settled back into rhythm. I wondered how much Laudanum the doctor had given her to keep her out so long. The rest at least would do her good. She worked too long and hard and needed it.

I flicked through the book I had brought down for her whilst she slept, refreshing my memory of the story which I only half remembered. I sat for at least an hour before she began to stir, trying to turn in the bed and struggle with the sheet that had been tightly tucked in to prevent her moving. 'No, no,' I said, reaching to stop her crushing her bad arm. 'You shall hurt yourself,' I said gently and she blinked her eyes open then focused on my face and frowned. 'It's alright, you are in bed resting. You had a fall.'

'How long have I been here?' she asked, lifting her head.

'All day I'm told. Would you like a drink?'

She nodded and I took a rye grass straw from the table and poured her a glass. 'Here, let me help you up,' I said, loosening the sheet and propping her up a little better so she could drink from the cup I held out to her, 'Mind your lip, it is sore.'

She stuck her tongue out to prod it and sipped from the other side.

'Thank you. You are very kind, miss, but I am sure you have better things to do than wait on me. Where is Poppy?'

'I *want* to wait on you and I do not know if Poppy was whom let me in here, but if it is, she is to be found in the kitchen, which reminds me, I am to let her know you have woken. Are you hungry?'

'I am nauseous.'

'That will be the Laudanum. Shall I send for something?'

She shook her head. 'No, miss, not yet.'

'I wish you would not call me, miss.'

'How would you like to me to address you, ma'am?'

'My name is Eleanor; you may call me by it in private. What is your name?'

'What, my given name?'

'Yes.'

'Annalise Tullier, but Cook thinks it better I am known here as Anna Tulley. Apparently, it is too fancy for a servant.'

She was too fancy for a servant, I thought fleetingly and we both laughed a moment, but hers was punctuated by a grimace of pain. I remembered the feeling of the same not so long ago.

'Do not strain yourself. Is there something I can do to make you more comfortable?'

'Would you mind mi—Eleanor? My ribs are sore. If I could just turn a little onto my side to take the pressure off.'

'Of course.' I supported her weight as she lifted onto her good arm and shuffled about until she lay back down upon her better side. 'Here, let me move the pillow so you may keep it elevated. Does it hurt very much?'

'My hand? I can't really feel it, I think it is numb. It is my ribs that smart.'

'I hear you were quite the hero, sparing you and Fanny more serious injuries.'

'So they tell me. I suppose I must be grateful they are not worse if this is anything to go by.'

'You shall need a lot of rest, and I do not want you to think about work at all right now. Just know you shall have all the rest you need and there is no hurry at all for your return.'

'I fear Mrs Simpson will disagree.'

'Well, I shall have my way on this head.'

She smiled and instinctively I reached for her hand to lightly squeeze it. She smiled and pressed it back and said: 'Thank you.'

'No need. You just rest, promise me you will, no matter what.'

'I do not think I have much choice in it.'

'I brought you a book from the library. I thought I might read to you, if you would like it. I know how dreadfully dull it is to be bedbound.'

'You are very generous mi—Eleanor; I promise I shall get used to it eventually. My head is still quite muzzy.'

'You may call me what you will for now under that excuse.'

We both looked towards the door as the handle clicked and the maid from before, stuck her head around it and smiled.

'Oh, luv, you are awake!' she said. 'Pardon me, ma'am,' she came into the room and dropped a curtsey.

'Poppy.' Annalise smiled and I noted such warmth in it that I felt momentarily...envious.

''ow are you doing, luv?' she said.

'Managing, I think.'

I stood up. 'Ladies, if you will excuse me. I shall pop in and see how Fanny does, and come back later, if I may?'

'Oh, ma'am, don't go on my account,' said Poppy.

I smiled. 'I have a couple of matters to see too. I shall come back soon.'

I had a hallboy give me Fanny's direction and spent a little while in with her. She was not the easiest character to go along with, but I felt sorry to see her like this—even more out of sorts than Annalise, with her broken leg balanced on a pile of pillows and the rest of her flesh covered in a patchwork of blue and purple bruises, her left eye black and not able to open for the swelling about it and a row of stitches at her temple. I left her with a promise to bring her some sugarplums on my return. Unlike Annalise, she was not minded to refuse a good offer and was quick to take me up on it. I made a request to Mary to bring them to my room, on my way back upstairs. I paused at the bottom a moment considering what a nasty place to fall with the jagged edges and uneven, narrow steps of stone. I would speak to my father and see if there were improvements that might be made to save it happening again.

'There you are!' my mama said when I passed the upstairs landing. 'I've had the footmen searching all over for you! Wherever have you been?'

'I was downstairs, visiting Fanny and Annal—'

'There is no time for that, my dear. Are you packed? Your sister is to leave in a half hour.'

'Mama, you might have a care, they are both badly injured.'

'Yes, yes, I know and I am very sorry for it, but you really must get a move on, my dear.'

'I am not going, Mama. I have changed my mind.'

'What do you mean? You have been waiting weeks to go.'

'I know. But I fear I am not good company and I don't want to be in a dudgeon around Harri and the boys. I can travel onto her in a few days when I am in better spirits. This weekend has taken its toll and I need to collect myself.'

'Is this about Henry? Harriet told me you had a falling out—'

'Henry, Betsy and society in general I think, Mama. I am not in good humour and quite out of patience with it. I think it best I have a little time alone to forget it all. Harri doesn't want to hear all my complaints, and I fear I have little else to say at present.'

'Very well, but I do think it would do you the world of good to go.'

'I shall, in a few days or so, once I am in a better head.'

A few days soon turned into a week and I had not much moved from the rickety chair at Annalise's bedside. I had looked in on Fanny and ordered more sugarplums and pillows than I could count, but Annalise wanted only for me to read to her and we had finished the first book I had brought and had now moved onto *The Libertine*.

She was doing much better now and was up on her feet at least, unlike Fanny who was expected to be laid up for another six weeks or more. Poppy had kept them both well fed on broths and vegetables to aid their healing and I had insisted that fruit be brought up from the farm to nourish them. Papa had promised to instruct his steward to assess the stairway for improvements on my unrelenting pressing of the matter, and Mama had thought me gone quite queer at spending so much time in the basement. How could I tell her that I was returning a favour, such an invaluable favour that had spared me from falling deeper into melancholy and danger at a time I had felt devoid of any hope? I could not confess to her the troubles I had privately battled over these past weeks, but even if I could, I did not think she would understand. Would no doubt say that any good servant should have performed such services. But it had been beyond that. I knew it. I felt it.

Annalise had accepted my arrangement with Crawford, to have her tend me until she had recovered the use of her arm and could return to her other duties, but the difficulty had been in trying to keep her from them. For although I needed a little help to dress, I wanted her to do little more than be companion to me whilst she was healing. This proved impossible as I confiscated dusters and cloths from her good hand and struggled to get her to sit still for more than a half hour at a time. 'I am not used to being so idle, miss,' she had said in complaint, 'I am sure I must do what I can now I am able.' My instruction she was to call me by my name now had failed almost as miserably as my instructions to keep her restful. I however, called her only by Annalise now, be it in private or otherwise. It bristled at me that she was to have even her name stripped from her by her superiors. And it was such a pretty name, so well suited to her that I refused to call her anything else, either directly or in reference to her.

I had eventually, quite by accident, discovered a way to keep her from working as she accompanied me on a walk in the park one afternoon. I realised, not only how much she liked being outside, but also how it rendered it impossible she could busy herself with any chores. So, with this realisation, our days turned quickly into sunny afternoons making daisy chains on the lawn and reading under the shade of a tree. Gentle walks in the shelter of the woodlands and some blackberry picking which we did more for the sport than the eating of them since there were too many to eat between us with the bushes so abundant. It seemed to prove good medicine for her spirit as well as her ailments and I was certainly gladdened to see her recovering, day by day, a little improvement, a little less pain, a lot more laughter. Her arm sling dispensed with, and just supporting bandages at her wrist and hand now. Her feeling coming back in her fingers and seeing her use them to lightly grasp a daisy stem as she threaded it with her good hand.

She was not the only one in recovery though; her presence was restoring me too: lifting me out of the shadows by small and steady graduations, helping me to remember how to feel light again. When I was with her, I felt different; alive in ways I had not known and she seemed to bring out the best in me, a best I did not know myself capable of. I wasn't sure how she had managed it, but there was something contagious in her sweet and easy nature that inspired me to do more, want more and be more than the wretched soul I had existed as for so long. I had realised in looking upon her easy smiles, that despite all that was lost, the most important things in the world to me remained constant.

My marriage, the season, the ton, my 'friends', my reputation; none of it mattered to me anymore, and I cared not for all the opinions and slights of those who set store by them. I had not even shame to offer them in return for their whispers and sideways glances. So unmoved I was by both their presence and absence now, I felt the alleviation of a burden I had not realised I had been carrying. The burden of expectation. Expectations that had been attached to me by others. Expectations I had never truly wanted to live up to. Expectations that were not my own.

Once we had plucked the blackberry bushes close to bare apart from the green and red new fruits that were not yet ready, we sent the excess blackberries to the kitchens for turning into pies and cordials, she told me as we dispatched our baskets at the kitchen door. She mentioned too that Cook had been frosty and gruff with her as though she had contrived to fall on purpose and deprive her of her help. Demanded to know when she was to stop "shilly shallying" about and get back to the kitchens now her arm was out of the sling. But I forbade it. The doctor had said that her fingers would still be mending for weeks, although her recovery had been swift and promising. I was not having her chopping and scrubbing a moment before he declared her completely healed. Besides, the new maidservants had arrived at last, redressing the balance, Mrs Crawford having sought the services of a registry for haste and me agreeing to pay the fees for an expedient solution.

My only wish, was that it might remain so, that these servants might stay here and she would change her mind and become my Abigail, yet I knew we had already become far more than that to each other, for their was friendship blossoming between us now and I did not know how I could do without it now I knew what it was to feel the authenticity of her easy company. She was such a comfort that I had quite forgotten all my troubles: they had vanished quite without me realising. I no longer looked over my shoulder when I was about on the park, did not stiffen at the sound of a carriage pulling up in the driveway, nor count the week down to Henry's wedding with such foreboding.

Instead, I awoke with a kindling sense of wonder every morning, looking forward to the day ahead instead of shrinking from it and wishing it away. I felt indomitable now, not just with Giles, but society, life, whatever obstacles it might throw at my feet. I knew now, I must rise in spite of them. I was not just determined not to fall back into melancholy or liquor dependence again, I was determined to live happier, better, to become something more than I had been schooled to. To follow my heart. To trust it. These were my new expectations and I vowed to skip to their tune now and no other. I would answer to no other master again.

This epiphany had come to me on a quote as we lay out upon the grass and I read the character Montmorency: "society corrupts the heart" was the line. I felt instantly resonant with the truth in this statement, even if it was but a fictional philosophy, I was the example of the truth in it. My heart had been corrupted for society's teachings and constraints. Now it was mending again, I would serve this, and only this master now, and society could go to the devil from whence it came.

Home alone.

September 1821. - Eleanor.

'Eleanor, you will need to get ready to go to Kent tomorrow,' Mama said over dinner.

I swallowed my mouthful. 'It is hardly worth the journeying back and forth when everyone will be here for the wedding on Friday.'

She lifted the top of a cloche to see what was beneath it. 'Yes, I see that. But the thing is, your father and I are to open up the house at Berkshire ready for Henry and Miss Yardley.'

'You are giving them Bourdon?' I asked surprised, for although I knew they would have to provide the couple somewhere to live, I did not expect them to gift them one of their finest houses, only a fraction less impressive than Cuddington.

'It is all to be Henry's one day my dear and I know he would not like to be too far away from London.'

No, I thought, *he should likely prefer to be in travelling distance of all his haunts and clubs whilst far enough away out of Miss Yardley's sight.* It seemed a travesty that all this grandeur and wealth would one day fall into the hands of the most profligate and least deserving of my siblings. I wondered how much of it would still be intact by the time his own children inherited. Harri, she was the most deserving of us all and most likely to preserve the estate. Even Ed, who I was on only marginally better terms with than Henry, would still have been safer hands to lay such privilege. He too might be a useless son and brother, but at least he had a sensible head on his shoulders.

'So will they be going with you?'

'Well, yes of course my dear. The Yardleys would like to see where their daughter is to live and Henry thinks it would be good for us to meet the wider family ahead of Friday. So, you see, we must set off in the morning and so must you. Harri will be expecting you and you may travel back with her in time for the wedding.'

I put down my knife and fork. 'So, I am not invited to Bourdon I take it... Well of course, Henry would not want the black sheep spoiling his pretence of being a gentleman.'

'Eleanor! Your brother *is* a gentleman!' Mama protested.

'By grace of title perhaps.'

'Eleanor, I think you may learn to hold your tongue,' Father cut in.

'Fine. I have no wish to go anyway. But I am not rattling down to Kent for such a brief spell. I will stay here and return to Kent with Harri after the wedding. I shall have Miss Pascal to attend me then.'

'Alone?'

'I shall hardly be alone when we have over forty servants about the house. I will be fine. I must learn to go forward in this style now and so where better to begin the learning.'

'I'm sure Delores—'

'Mama, Delores is a married woman now with her own family to think of. She can't be at our beck and call every time we have a need of her. I too am a married woman now, so what harm can there be in my staying home?'

'I only think of you. I thought you were fearful he might—'

'I can't live like that anymore. It is no life at all to be imprisoned so, and he might have rights to me, but he has none to trespass upon Father's land.'

'She is right, Helena,' said my father. 'It is only a few days. If we can't leave her under her own roof in safety, then where shall she be safe? The man's a coward, that's why he has not dared to step foot here and claim her. I will have a word with Grantley to ensure Craythorne is not admitted to the house under any circumstances without us being present.'

'Thank you, Papa,' I said surprised at this allegiance.

'You are a grown woman now, Eleanor, I hope you will act accordingly.'

'I shall.'

I felt a strange sense of liberation when their coach scuttled off along the driveway the next morning, like my invisible leading strings had been finally cut. I had had the briefest taste of the same in the gap between Giles setting off on his trip and returning to him at Beaulieu, but it had been all too brief. It was an odd feeling, the fizzing in my stomach as I looked about me and realised I was quite alone, quite free. I supposed this was why my brothers had spent so long avoiding the marriage mart. They had always known such liberty and were too attached to it to give it up willingly. Not that I believed for a minute that Henry would give it up at all. I could see visions of poor Lady Yardley being saddled with numerous children whilst Henry strutted about town as he always had. I hoped it otherwise, but feared it correct. Not that I thought Henry would be a cruel husband like Giles, but a neglectful and self-centred one, I suspected.

I had hoped and expected Giles to prove as such and was only too happy to accept such neglect in exchange for my freedom. I knew better now and was glad at least to find out sooner rather than later and be spared from becoming his broodmare, if nothing else.

I rang for Annalise once the coach had disappeared from my view and considered what we might do today.

'Sorry, ma'am,' she said coming into the room looking flustered. 'I was just helping Cal.'

'Cal?'

'I beg your pardon, Calverley. Cook said she was to be known as Cal.'

'Don't tell me: too fancy?'

She laughed and nodded.

'But is not Calverley the new kitchen maid?'

'Yes.'

'Then you have been working in the kitchen?'

'Not exactly, ma'am. I was asked to help with her training is all: Tell her the right way to do things, show her where everything is.'

'Annalise, you are in recovery and I have an arrangement with Mrs Crawford that means cook shall not expect you to return to the kitchen any day soon.'

She gave a sheepish wince. 'I know. Only, Cook doesn't quite see it that way and it really wasn't any bother. I only had to explain things to her.'

'Calverley has been a kitchen maid for the past five years I believe, longer than even you—so I think she will manage well enough. I shall have to have a word with Mrs Simpson and make this clear to her.'

'Oh, please don't, ma'am,' she said quickly with an imploring glance.

'Annalise, is Cook being difficult, for if she is—'

'No. It is just her way, ma'am. She has a particular order in which she likes things done and Cal does not know it well yet, that is all.'

'Alright, but anything more, you will tell me, won't you?'

She nodded but I was not convinced. I knew Annalise was not inclined towards lying, but I also knew that if she was keeping something from me, it must be for a good reason and suspected I might need to remind Cook of the order in which things were to go in this matter.

'Anyway,' I said, changing the subject. 'You are here now. What should you like to do today? We are quite at liberty.'

'What would you like to do?'

See you smiling again, I thought. 'Well, perhaps we could start with a walk for some exercise and whilst we are walking, you may think on what we can do next?'

We spent the morning on the park and the afternoon in the library when the sun peaked too hot. It was nice not to be expected anywhere by anyone and the house was quiet with most of the staff keeping below stairs except when summoned. But despite this, I could tell there was something quite amiss with Annalise. She was not her usual easy self and seemed preoccupied, easily distracted. I wondered if something had happened below stairs at dinner, for it was the only hour for which we had been separated since the morning.

It was evening now, the sky smelting into colourful hues of pink and amber beyond the garden wall. Me sat upon the bench and Annalise laid out upon a patch of grass, passing the bristles of a rosemary sprig between her half-bandaged fingers, the scent of the herb garden billowing sweet with the breeze. We were on chapter five of *The Libertine* now, but as I turned the pages and read from them, I could sense she was altogether somewhere else.

I stopped reading and put down the book. It took her a few moments to realise I had.

'Are you ready to go in now, miss?' she asked and dropped the rosemary sprig and begun to clamber her way up.

I stood up and reached out to help her to her feet. 'Is everything alright today, Annalise? You seem fractious, preoccupied I think?'

'Sorry?' she said looking up at me vaguely as she brushed her skirts down.

'Is everything alright with you?'

'Yes. Yes, thank you, miss.'

'Come, you know my secrets, will you not trust yours to me and lighten your mood? I see something weighs heavy there.' I saw a twitch upon her mouth and a desire in her eyes to accept my invitation, but then they clouded over with reluctance and I realised she must think it an inappropriate thing to confide in one's mistress. It probably was. No doubt my mama would be able to offer me a full half hour lecture on the perils of permitting such liberties. And yet improper or not, I wanted to know what troubled her. I wanted to know so I could fix it, lighten it, do whatever was required to alleviate her of it. For somehow, I could feel its weight too, like I was carrying it with her, although I couldn't fathom why. 'It is quite safe to tell me you know. I mean only to offer an ear.'

She lifted her eyes to mine and I saw the vulnerability in them, then tears welling, clouding them before one bled over her lash line and tumbled down her cheek. Instinctively, I drew close to her and staunched it with the tip of my thumb. I watched it seep into the fibres of my glove and then I watched her furrow her brow, puzzled as was I at this unexpected intimacy. What did it mean? I saw the question reflected back in them and could not answer either her or myself. So instead, I just withdrew—gently—found a handkerchief in my reticule and gestured her to sit down on the bench with me.

This she did, seeming slightly less uncomfortable now. That, or the burden of her sorrows had gained the greater advantage and as she began to sob, drawing her hands up to her face and sinking it into them, I found my arm about her shoulders, my other hand stroking her. Tenderly. So tenderly it puzzled me that I knew how to perform this art, this service. One that she had tried to render me so often: I did not understand it then, did not trust it. I understood now. I wanted to console her, sweep away all her tears: Her troubles too, if it was within my power to do so.

When she regained her composure, some ten minutes later, lifting her face—a streaked and blotchy mess now—her eyelids pink and slightly swollen, I asked her again what troubled her so.

'I am sorry, miss. I just have these turns sometimes. I am usually a little better at restricting them to private moments. I've had a bit of a strange morning and it's knocked me a little out of sorts.'

'I see. Will you tell me what has happened?'

'I do not wish to burden you with my troubles, miss. It wouldn't be right and, besides, it would seem such a silly thing.'

'I would not think it so.'

A fleeting flash of uncertainty came and went. She sighed. 'I got a letter earlier,' she wafted away a fly at her shoulder, 'and I have been troubling over what I should do about it, and I'm sorry if I have been distracted, I shan't let it impede my work again miss, you may be sure of that.'

'I do not care for the work, Annalise. May I ask who it was from?'

'From my old employer, asking me to pay him a visit as he wants to speak to me on a matter.'

I frowned. 'And do you want to go?'

'No. It's the last place I want to visit.'

'Then do not. Indeed, you are due your morning off soon, so by all means take it as you like, but if you do not want to go to him, why should you?'

'Miss, I did something I perhaps should not have done. I would not have done it of course if I had another way out, but you see, I did not. He says if I do not go, he will make it known.'

'What a nasty fellow,' I said feeling suddenly protective of her. 'What can I do to help?'

'Nothing. It is my matter and I shall deal in it. I'm just not sure how yet.'

'I will come with you if you want me to.'

'Thank you, you are very generous, but I should not like you to be introduced to such a man.'

'And I should not like to think you alone with such a man with him trying at blackmailing you.'

'He says he shall not tell it if I go.'

'What does he want?'

'That's the puzzle. I do not understand it.'

'Do you think he means to offer you your place again?'

'Maybe. But I shall not take it, even if he does threaten this one.'

'He threatens your place here? Ridiculous. Your place with us is quite safe, you know. He has no say in that matter, whatever he holds against you.'

'Well, that is not quite true. If cook or Crawford get wind of what I did, I might well be in trouble.'

'What did you do, Annalise? If I know anything of you, it cannot be a very bad thing.'

'I don't want you to think ill of me, miss.'

'Annalise, you can trust me. I have done my share of very bad things myself, so I doubt you will shock me.'

She bit her lip.

'You do not have to tell me. But I want you to know that it will not alter my view of you, you may be sure of it.'

She dropped her gaze to her lap. 'I wrote my own recommendation letter to Mrs Simpson. I did not overstate anything and wrote it quite as I had for all the other girls who'd worked there. But you see, there was no one else to do it for me, no one else more senior than I, or who could write, except Gint himself, and he would not have assisted my going. But I was desperate, ma'am, to go...'

'Is that it?'

She nodded. Her eyes searching and a pink flush about her cheeks.

'Then you speak of a trifle, Annalise. Really, it is nothing at all to concern yourself over.'

'I'm not sure about that. I think Mrs Simpson would be mad as fire if she found out and might send me packing.'

If she dared, I thought privately, *I would find a way to send her packing.* 'I would speak to my mama for you if it came to it, and I'm sure it never will.'

'Do you really think so? I'll hardly sleep a wink tonight worrying over it—I know it.'

"Then stay with me. We may set up the daybed in my chamber and we may be a comfort to each other; I will not be all alone up there and you will not be keeping Poppy awake all night tossing and turning with worries you need pay no mind to.'

'I couldn't miss. I am taking liberties enough—'

'You take no liberties. You could not. You do me the favour. Tomorrow you shall have your morning off and deal in this matter however you must so that it will set your mind at ease. If you choose to go, I am willing to come with you. Either way, this time tomorrow, it shall be settled and you may be comfortable again. But for now, until it is resolved, I think a distraction will suit. Shall we have a little music at the pianoforte? I do not forget that you told me you were schooled in it. What do you say?'

She held up her bandaged hand and I realised I had forgotten that detail.

'Ah, well then it seems you shall have to put up with my playing then.'

She smiled. 'Thank you, Eleanor, that would be merry indeed,' she said and it warmed me to hear her call me by my name unprompted.

We walked into the house through the tourist's entrance and I took care to slide the catch down on it once we were inside. The house would of course be properly locked up later by the staff, but I was taking a little extra care now I was home alone. I suspected my father was right though, Giles was a coward. If he was not, why did he not come here demanding my return in almost a month, unless of course, he did go off to Venice after all, in which case he was far enough away to be forgotten.

We went directly to the music room and I set about lighting candles and lamps, for even though a thin veil of muted evening light streamed through the many windows and the domed glass skylight above our heads, I suspected it would soon turn to dusk with the days beginning to shrink a fraction earlier now.

'It is such a beautiful room,' Annalise said looking from floor to ceiling with a note of wonder in her gaze.

It was indeed a beautiful room. My father had it commissioned as an addition to the house when I was in the cradle. Mama thought it a prudent investment given all the baby girls she was bearing and I supposed even then her mind was turned to our education, and showing us off in the best possible style. 'Have you not been in here before?' I asked her and she shook her head.

'It has been barely used since Harriet, my sister, left home,' I told her as I drew the cord for the drapes around the oversized bay where the pianoforte was positioned in its recess. I left the other drapes open, but did not want anyone to see me playing through the window, even if they might have to bear the hearing of it. For as much as I loved music, I preferred to sing and dance to it over playing it. I was not gifted like Harri or Caitlyn and my memories of my music lessons sat here in this very spot, were marred with angst at always trying to grow better and always disappointing my masters and my mama with my mediocre offerings. I suspected that was why it had not had the Holland covers lifted beyond an occasional visiting master's concert for the past few years. Mama had no wish to show me at a disadvantage.

I looked about at the plush pink seats set out in neat rows looking onto the bay. I supposed it was in such clean and ready order because this was where my mama had planned for Richards to play for Sheldon and I's grand wedding party that never happened. The irony was close to devastating now.

'What a shame, it is so very grand,' Annalise said running her fingertips along the white and gilt wood piano cover. It was a much grander piano than the little square ones we learnt on as children, which I remembered sat back-to-back against each other. The faded varnish and sun-bleached wood and raspy sounding strings we would learn on seemed prehistoric now. Caitlyn would often sit at one piano, Harri at the other as they duo'd on some fine and complex piece the maestro had selected for them. I suppose there was no need for two once Caitlyn left, for I would never have been capable of such displays, even with Harri to compensate for my blunders.

The old twin pair were replaced by this fine model that had been commissioned for Harri's coming out, designed to match the wood panelling upon the lower half of the walls and elegant Queen Anne legs to match the sideboards that sat beneath the windows. It had seen a lot of use that year, but very little since.

'So,' I said placing a lamp beside the music rack and lifting the top board and setting it on its prop. 'Let's see what we have. Any preference or requests?'

She pulled one of the chairs over to the piano side to sit by me as I flicked through the music sheets. 'Well, I do have a particular favourite: *Plaisir d'amour*. Do you know it?'

'I do; Martini. But I can only play from the sheet and I cannot see it amongst these. Why *Plaisir d'amour*?'

'It was actually my mama's favourite and she played it so beautifully, it reminds me of her.'

I smiled at the sparkle in her eyes and got up. 'Let me see if we have it over here,' I said, going over to one of the sideboards and sifting through the drawers. Once I had turned them out, I said, 'I'm sorry, we do not have it. But I shall order it since it is a particular favourite.'

'No need. But thank you. I have a copy downstairs. I can—'

'Yes, by all means. It will give me a chance to reacquaint myself whilst you are gone. I warn you though, I am not a good player and so you shall have to be easy on me.'

I watched as she scuttled across the polished wooden floor with all the excitement of a child. It was heartening to see. That was what it was about her that touched me so: she helped me to remember such states of being. Such easy joy as I had forgotten in myself. I selected Pleyels *Sonata in E-Flat Major, B. 579: II. Allegro* from the pile of sheet music and turned up the wick on the lamp a little. The flame flared and jumped and now the sky had fallen like a veil of gossamer, the glow of the lights all about the room reflected in all the surrounding panes of glass gave the illusion of double the number burning. I flexed my fingers and re-familiarised myself with the keys before beginning.

The start I made was rusty and a little cack-handed and took three times restarting it until my fingers began to fall into rhythm. By the time she returned to the room, I was halfway through Bach's *prelude no.1 in C major.* She put her sheet music down at my side and when I looked up briefly to turn my pages, I caught a glimpse of her as she swayed and turned to the music. It made me smile, but I drew my eyes back to the score so as not to lose my flow.

When I reached the end of the song, she carried on dancing without the music, moving softly and gracefully about the empty hall as though in her very own world where the music was still playing.

'Shall I play it from the beginning for you?' I asked her.

'No,' she said, opening her eyes as if waking from a dream. 'Thank you, that was wonderful,' she smiled shyly as if being caught doing something she shouldn't. I supposed she had not realised I was watching her dance and seemed suddenly conscious of herself. 'Forgive me, it has been an age since I have heard music... I think I may have got carried off by the moment.'

'Do not apologise; you move beautifully. Shall I play this next?' I asked, picking up the score she had put down on the seat beside me. It was well worn and creased, but I flattened it out and propped it up against the stand.

'Please,' she said and she stood at my side ready to turn the pages as I focussed hard on the fading print, wanting to play this for her as well as I could manage. I felt nervous knowing how much it meant to her. I concentrated and begun, a little shakily, but once I had moved beyond the first two pages, I improved. I looked up only briefly, but she was still this time, her eyes closed, totally absorbed in the listening. It took me a few pages to realise she was turning them, not from sight, but from memory.

We retired later than planned, having spent above a couple of hours at the pianoforte. I wondered what strange power she possessed to compel me into doing so. But we had sung and played merry, she even joining me one handed at my side. I was only grateful my mama was not here to see it, for she would think me very out of character indeed. But the truth was, I could have stayed up all night in that style: Seeing her smile and sway and sing with no marked air of self-consciousness about her.

We set up the day bed together and sat up a little while reading chapter six. This time, she took a turn at reading, the book propped on a pillow in her lap, and I sat back in the chair with my eyes closed, following the melodic tone of her voice as she narrated.

'Sorry, I don't think I shall manage another chapter tonight,' she said, pinching the flesh between her eyes, once she had finished chapter six. 'My sight is failing now.'

'It's late enough,' I said, lifting my eyes to the clock on the mantle where it read a quarter past midnight. 'Shall we go to bed?'

She nodded and closed the book in her lap and set about our toilette. I filled the basin with water and we washed our hands and faces, then she helped unlace me and then I realised as she stood, still clothed, that I would have to help her too tonight.

She offered me her back and I unbuttoned her dress, passed the sleeve carefully over her bandaged wrist and fingers so as not to snag at them; hung it on the back of the fireside chair and unlaced her stays. It felt strange to touch her. I wondered if this is how it felt to her when she tended my toilette. I was so accustomed to being dressed and undressed that it never occurred to me how odd it was to be the dresser. I supposed often attending upon a perfect stranger or little more than a distant miss, and unclothing her, seeing her so intimately; knowing the curves of her body, the smell of her hair, the profile of her face even better than she herself.

When she was down to her shimmy, I sat her at the dressing table and unpinned her hair and when the weight of it fell loose about her shoulders and trailed half the length of her back, I thought it so beautiful I nearly told her so. I wanted to, but the words got stuck in my throat. I picked up the brush and ran it through the lengths until it shined like gilt coated threads. 'You look so different with your hair out,' I managed eventually.

She smiled. 'I probably ought to cut it. It would certainly be easier to manage. But my mama forbade it. Thought it become me.'

'And she was quite right.'

She smiled and we climbed into our beds. Me snuffing the light out on my way. The sheets were refreshingly cool and though it had been a warm day, the evenings were beginning to calm nicely now.

'You must miss her awfully,' I said, reflecting on her words.

'I do; she was everything to me.'

I stared into the darkness and wondered what it must be like, to be so much alone in the world. I had felt like I had been in many ways, but I had others about me at least. Others to look out for me.

'I do not know if I am ready to go back there tomorrow, be confronted with all the memories that shall come rushing back at being in Hurley Street again.'

'I am sorry for it. I wish there was something I could do to—'

'You already have,' she said.

I woke first in the morning and had quite forgotten she was there until I stepped down from the bed and saw her upon the day bed, a length of her long hair trailing the floor. I opened the curtains and sat in the fireside chair looking at her as she slept. When she woke, we helped each other dress and I reiterated my offer to go with her to see this Mr Gint today. She would not hear of it and refused my offer to convey her there in the coach and wait outside for her. 'It would not seem right to have the other staff convey me—they would wonder at it,' she had said and so I relented. We took a small breakfast together and I waved her off anxiously at eleven-o-clock with her pledge to be back in a couple of hours.

Twenty minutes after she had left, I regretted letting her go alone and begun to worry. I did not know what he wanted of her and she had never told me anything directly, but her apprehension disturbed me and I suspected I knew why. I had Thomas bring the coach and drive me directly to Hurley Street.

I was not certain if she would have already reached the place by foot, for Ewell was not very far away at all if you walked the better part of the distance through the grounds and took the small gate out towards

Hogsmill. But I waited patiently in the coach a little way up the road and caught sight of her eventually, crossing it and going in through the gate of a house that stood but five windows wide. I instructed Thomas to creep forward just a little way and checked the time on the pocket watch I had put into my reticule on leaving. If she was not out in a reasonable time, I would have Thomas go and knock at the door to say he was here to collect her.

I sat there, watching the small hands tick on the face of the watch as the minutes passed wondering what a reasonable time was whilst simultaneously pondering all the different horrors that might have already occurred in those that had passed. I should not have let her go, I thought, as ten minutes went by. I should have insisted she take someone with her, arranged to have Poppy go perhaps. Anyone who might keep watch and make sure that lecherous man was not able to take advantage of her.

I was just about to give Thomas the instruction to head in when the front door opened and she came out of the gate, looking physically unruffled, but even from here, I could see she was distressed. Her steps hurried and her face red and sombre as she re-crossed the road and headed off in a different direction to the one she came in. I leapt down from the coach and asked Thomas to stay on my tail but keep back enough to remain out of sight and I followed the direction I had seen her go in.

I walked quickly, turned down the street she had vanished into then huddled quickly behind a tree, noticing her sat upon a bench in a garden square. She had her face partially covered with her good hand and it took me a moment to realise she was weeping. An impulse to go to her, comfort her, and find out what he had done nearly overpowered me. But I did not want her to know I had followed her after she had told me not to come. It was hard to tell whether it was because she did not want me there, or because she did not want to burden me with her troubles as she so often stated. I battled between staying and going to her until she eventually wiped her cheeks and stood up, took a breath and began walking towards my direction. I raced ahead before she levelled with me and waited until she set off towards the village.

I followed her on foot until she disappeared into a bookshop and I stepped back into the carriage to wait for her. She did not emerge for near to half hour later and nor did she come out with any books. I was quite baffled now and wondered what the connection was between this visit to Hurley Street and the bookshop. Had he sent her on some errand? She was certainly not headed in the direction of Cuddington as the carriage lagged behind her as she walked further on and then disappeared into the stonemason's shop. It had all become such a puzzle.

After the stonemason's, she finally took the route back to Cuddington and I felt such relief. I waited until she disappeared through the gate towards the Cuddington woodland path before I gave Thomas the signal to take us back at a gallop so I could get back home before her.

When she returned home that afternoon, I had already put my bonnet away and changed into soft slippers. I was sat at my writing desk with Lady W.'s half-finished letter in front of me when she tapped at the door and came into the room. All evidence of her sobbing quite vanished, and a complacent smile in her greeting. 'How did it go?' I asked her, gesturing for her to sit.

'Well, he will not inform on me, which is something I suppose.'

'But what did he want?'

She stiffened a little in the chair. 'To tell me he was dying and impart some parting words beforehand.'

'I see.' I did not think it right that I should probe after what they might be. I hoped instead she might just tell me. 'How have you taken the news?'

'I couldn't care less,' she said with uncharacteristic coldness in her tone and it surprised me to hear her speak so, especially after I had seen her rush from the place in floods of tears. There was clearly much more to her dealings with her old master than I realised or she had been willing to tell me. I had allowed myself to think that perhaps he had compelled her to perform improper services, but now I wondered if perhaps there had been a mutual regard of some kind that she did not wish to confess to me. I hoped I was mistaken, yet it did not make sense to me. 'Well,' I said, trying not to give away my understanding of her sadness. 'Will you go there again?'

She shook her head. 'Never.'

I frowned.

'You think me hard hearted, no doubt—'

'No.'

'You would not if you knew what he was like. What my mama had to endure in her time there.'

'Goodness,' I said. 'I'm sorry to hear it. Do you want to talk about it?'

'No,' she said flatly, vehemently almost before she lightened her tone and expression. 'Forgive me, ma'am, it has put me quite out of humour. I would very much like to forget about today entirely.'

'Of course.'

'Thank you. Would you like me to do anything, miss?'

I wanted to sigh that we were back at "miss" again when we had overcome that yesterday with such natural ease. 'Well, I am to go out for a ride now, so if you will help me with my habit, I shall not need you again until I return.'

Once I was saddled, I headed straight over to Ewell and dispatched Samson to the coaching house stable whilst I continued on to the bookshop on foot. I knew I shouldn't be out alone, especially under the circumstances, but I was determined to find out whatever I could about this Gint fellow and whatever he was about in blackmailing Annalise to the extent of bringing her to tears.

I knew I could not go directly to this house or I would blow my cover, but I could go into the shops and see if they held any clues.

The bookshop proved a waste of time. The old gentleman was very helpful with making suggestions of titles that I feigned interest in buying, but gave nothing away when I tried to ask some vague questions about the resident of Hurley Street.

I left with a copy of *Kenilworth* that I did not want, but thought best to make a purchase to throw him off the scent of my nosiness. *A nosy purchasing customer would surely be less suspect than a nosy non-purchasing customer,* I thought as I walked on up the High Street to the stonemasons she had visited earlier.

'Good morning, milady, how can I be of assistance,' said the gentleman behind the counter.

'Good morning, sir. Well, I wonder if you could help me with an enquiry. You see, there was a girl that came into your shop this morning, and I hoped you would be able to tell me on what business.' It seemed prudent to come straight to the point with him, since I did not plan on coming away having purchased something from here.

He furrowed his brow and seemed to consider me, sizing me up. 'Well, milady, the thing is, I was not serving customers this morning, I was out on deliveries you see, so I am sorry I can be of no help.'

'Then perhaps you could tell me who it was that served her?'

'John, my son, but he's gone off on his break.'

'Sir, please. I know it must seem quite an irregular query and forgive me for pressing you, but you see, it is very important. Admittedly, I cannot divulge why, for my mama; Lady Ashlyn, always taught me to keep confidences—'

'Lady Ashlyn is your mama?'

'Yes sir, are you acquainted with her?'

'Not very well, but I did, some many years ago now, make a pair of marble fireplaces for the drawing room at Cuddington.'

'You are the craftsman of that fine work?'

He swelled with pride and said, 'I daresay it was nigh on twenty years ago now. Anyway, this girl you speak of, do you know her name?'

'Yes, sir. It is Annalise Tullier.'

'Oh, Mr Glnt's old housekeeper, yes, I know.'

'You know him too, sir?'

'Indeed.'

'What can you tell me about him? I have heard he is not altogether a pleasant fellow.'

'Well, between you and me, and I don't like to speak ill of a gentleman, ma'am, but, well, every girl about this village knows to keep at arm's length with that fellow.'

'I see. He's *that* kind of character is he.'

He nodded and my heart sunk. It was as I suspected.

'Anyway, about miss Tullier—'

'Oh yes—I saw her come in here earlier and simply wanted to know what her business was here.'

'What time?' he asked, pulling out a leather-bound ledger and turning the pages.

'Umm about eleven-o-clock.'

'Ah yes, here she is. She was in to make a payment earlier. John has noted it down.'

'A payment?'

'Yes, an instalment.'

'She has a debt with you, sir?'

'She commissioned her mother's headstone and once it is half paid, she shall have it and pay the other half on credit.'

'I see, will that take very long?'

'Milady, I 'ave already spoken more than I should 'ave. If you will pardon me.'

'Yes, I realise I must seem very nosey. But you see, the thing is, I mean to settle the bill, in full today, if you are able to be so good as to tell me what is due?'

'Well, ma'am, 'tis not a mere trifle, but if you will bear with me, I shall go and find the agreement papers.'

'Thank you, sir.'

Unexpected news.

September 1821. - Annalise.

She had changed her mind several times about going to Hurley Street. Even as she walked in through the gate and knocked at the door, she considered turning back around. Her stomach was in knots and she could feel the tension in her gait as she forced herself to proceed, pulled the bell, stepped back and waited. 'Pike, good morning,' she said when the door opened.

'Oh, it's you,' she said in reply as if she had took the trouble of opening the door and wasting a smile on her for nothing.

'Yes. Mr Gint has asked me to come.'

She looked her up and down and said, 'I s'pose you better come in then.'

Annalise stepped into the hall, the familiar smell of turpentine and tallow lingering in the oak panelled room. It was airless and dim as it usually was and she followed Pike through to the anteroom, took a seat when Pike failed to invite her to do so, and waited whilst she went off to announce her arrival.

'You're gonna 'ave ta go up to 'im,' she said when she returned.

'I would rather see him down here.'

'Well, he's bed bound ain't he, and I ain't lugging him down 'ere for the likes o you,' she said flatly.

Just as charming as ever, Annalise thought, standing up and following her up the staircase. If he was going through one of his bad spells, then at least he could pose no risk to her. They walked along the upper landing, past the room that had once been her and her mama's, and the sight of it caught her in the chest and she held her hand to her ribs as she continued on. It felt like only yesterday whilst simultaneously feeling almost another lifetime away. She shook the thought and composed herself as Pike tapped at the door.

'Thank you for coming,' said Gint, when Pike left them alone. He was huddled beneath his blankets, a heap of bony limbs.

'Perhaps you will enlighten me, sir, on what was of such importance you summons me under threats of letters to my employer?'

'Come now. I was not minded to carry them out. I only needed some way to get you here.'

'And now you have, sir, and I am quite put out by it, I cannot deny the fact. So will you come swiftly to the matter at least.'

'Very well. Sit down. I have some news for you that I think you will find...difficult.' He lowered his spectacles. 'You must know I am not long for this world now.'

She sank slowly into the chair. If that was the "news", Annalise could only feel gratitude. One less man like he in the world could only be a good thing, she considered.

'And so, I must make plain to you something that has been long held a secret, and necessarily so.'

'If you might hurry this along, sir, I really have very little time to spare.'

'Well, you will have a great deal of time to spare hereon, if you wish it.'

If this was another of his threats, Annalise was minded to get up from her seat and leave the place at once. Of course, she did not want to risk losing her place at Cuddington, but to be held to ransom and forced to listen to this man, this curmudgeon she so much despised, was more testing than she had anticipated after seven months of reprieve.

'You see, Annalise, I have something for you. Something I think you will find, life changing.'

She was so entirely lost by this reference but took the offered paper he lifted from the side table. She stared at it, unsure of what it was, unfolding it and frowning into it a while trying to make sense of it. 'I do not understand?'

'It is yours.'

'What is it?'

'It's a banker's draft.'

She turned it in her hands once more, checking the wording, eyes tracing for the number again. A number so large she could not quite fathom it out. How much was six hundred pounds? She had rarely had cause to count beyond shillings, save for when settling some of Mr Gint's grocery accounts, but even they were nothing like this figure. It seemed a lot: A lot more than she could rationally understand. Perhaps he was losing his faculties now too? 'Forgive me, but there is no outstanding sum. I was paid up until my last day. I think you make some error, sir, some great error.'

He laughed at this. 'Oh well! I think you will find enough there to pay a housekeeper's earnings for life, so indeed it is not for that.'

Did he really mean to fun with her?

'Annalise, this money is for you. For your future. Your mother held me to a promise, that I would do right by you one day and see your future secured. It seems that day is come where I must acknowledge this duty.'

How dare he speak of her beloved mama as if he knew her better than she. As if they kept secrets from one another. As if he had any right to even think of her after what he put her through. How sad he made her. So sad she drunk herself to her grave. She shifted in her seat, feeling the heat of her rushing blood flaming through her veins. How dare he think she could be paid off for her mother's suffering. 'I do not know why you feel you should give it to me, but I do not want your money!' she said, flinging the draft back towards him and standing up. It landed, like a paper bird, on his upturned blanket.

'Hold your horses,' he said more sternly, jabbing a finger in the air. 'Your mother fought hard for this agreement; I shan't imagine her very happy to see it all come to nothing.'

'Oh, I know how hard she fought and I know you cared not a fig for her happiness. But if you think for a moment, there is any amount you may compensate me for the loss of my dear mama, you are even more bereft of feeling than I realised.'

'It is not compensation, girl! Well not for that. It is what is duly yours. It is what you were denied by your illegitimate birth.'

It was? Did he know her father? Had he been tasked with its safe keeping? Why he? Why had her mama not mentioned it? 'Why do you have it?'

'Because the debt is mine. Because I am your father, Annalise.'

Her ears must have deceived her. She could not speak. Had her heart skipped out a beat? She did not feel well all of a sudden. 'What did you say?' she managed through a choking lump of constriction in her throat.

'I said, I am your father.'

'It's impossible. You cannot be.'

'Yes, I daresay it will come as a surprise. But it is no less, the truth.'

'I think you are gone mad, sir! My mama did not even know you before I was born, so I am perfectly mystified as to how you come up with such a notion!'

'I daresay she thought it best to tell you so. But the truth is, Annalise, I took in you and your mama out of duty for my being responsible for her condition. You were born under this very roof and have always been here.'

Her mother would not have lied to her. Why would he tell such tales? Her breakfast seemed now to want to regurgitate. She swallowed down hard to quell the sensation. 'I think you are gone queer in the attic. I don't know what you mean by such an outrageous notion, but put it out of your mind at once, and utter not another word to its effect. This strange fantasy you have dreamt up is very disturbing. I take my leave of you now.'

She had stormed off in such a fit of fury and bewilderment she hadn't paid any notice to where she was actually headed. She found herself sobbing on the bench in Cadogan Square, but even spending tears could not release her from the insult of this ordeal. She got up, the need to walk, stomp in furious steps at a breathless pace to dispel the wound-up charge of energy attempting to erupt from her, required not logic, only action. So, when she found herself outside Mr Harrison's book shop, she went in, the familiar chime of the bell at the door, the comforting smell of musty pages and well settled dust, without having a notion of why she was come.

'Annalise. Are you alright?' he asked concerned, when she appeared at his counter, and she realised that how she felt and how she looked must have been in sympathy with one another.

'I am not, sir. In truth, I am quite bewildered and not myself at all,' she said, unfastening her bonnet strap and steadying herself on the counter.

'Sit down, my dear,' he said, dragging a chair around to where she stood. 'Are you unwell? What has happened to your hand?'

'Thank you, Mr Harrison. No, not unwell as such. I've just had the strangest encounter that has knocked me quite senseless,' she held up her hand, 'this is a healing injury—an accident at work, nothing to account. I should manage that ordeal all the better than the one I have just endured.'

'Will you tell me about it?'

'Yes. Yes, I think I must tell someone or else my head will implode.'

'Shall I put the pot to boil first? I think a cup of sweet tea might be in order.'

'Yes please,' she smiled through her tear glistened eyes, remembering what a welcome sensation it was to feel such warm regard and wondering what contorted expression she had been clenching her face into until now as her jaw ached at the joints. 'That would be very welcome. You are kind, sir.' She watched him shuffle back behind his cluttered walnut counter and out into the back rooms. It was nice to be waited on. To have someone else make the tea for a change. To be in the care of one of the kindest men she had ever known, having been forced to endure the company of his counterpart. She studied the pile of books upon the surface, diverting her thoughts, regulating her breath at last. Feeling a little more recovered by the time Mr Harrison pushed a steaming tea tray across the counter, she clearing a path of books away to make room for it.

'Now, why don't you start from the beginning?'

She nodded and stirred in a few sugar lumps until they dispersed into gravel and then dissolved. 'I hope you will not think badly of me, sir. But I must start with a confession. You see, when I took up the position at Cuddington, I had to write my own reference and sign it in Mrs Pike's name. It was not meant as an act of deceit, you understand, but one of desperation. I am not proud of it, but I had no choice, Gint would never have released me.'

'Annalise. Come. I know you well enough to require no assurances on account of your character. I know what that man is about, and I know you would not have done so if he was a man of proper sense and duty.'

'Thank you, Mr Harrison. I am grateful for your understanding. The truth is I haven't been comfortable with the means I had to take and it has disturbed me greatly since I started. Which is why I was so distressed at him summoning me to Hurley Street for an interview with him, under threat of him revealing my secret if I did not go.'

'He did what?'

'He insisted I go to him immediately, or he would write to Cuddington about the reference.'

'And you went?'

'Yes, against my better judgement and yet not feeling able to refuse. You see, I don't want to lose my position there, I like it very much, so I went...'

'And what happened?'

'The most extraordinary thing. He handed me a draft of money and said he was my father.'

Mr Harrison's face, far from seeming shocked by this absurd revelation, instead fell grave, the soft flesh of his cheeks falling downcast at his jaw line. 'He should not have told you that.'

Annalise frowned. 'What can you mean? You must see it is nonsense.'

He sat back in his chair and seemed to consider her a moment from over the top of his cup. 'Annalise, your mother did her best to protect you, you know. There was no price she would not pay to see you well.'

She felt a trembling in her lip and the hot sting of a tear roll down her cheek. 'I know.'

He searched his pocket for a handkerchief and handed it across to her. 'She never wanted you to find it out. She made him swear he would never reveal the fact to you. Just as she had kept to her word and never revealed it to his late wife.'

Annalise put down her cup. *It could not be.* 'Sir, are you saying you believe him to be my father?'

'I'm sorry, Annalise, but I know it to be true.'

'You cannot be serious? ...You are serious. But who told you?'

Mr Harrison nodded. 'Your mama told me. A long time ago, when she was just a little older than you are now.'

Annalise held her hand to her throat. The constriction had returned, the want of breath, the rushing blood...

'Annalise,' he said gently, soothing in his tone. 'Some things are beyond anyone's alteration. This being one beyond both your mother's and yours. Although I believe both of you would have preferred it otherwise.'

'But I—I don't understand. She hated Gint.'

'She did. But she loved you more and whether you like it or not, he was the only way ahead for her that would not see you starve or sent out to some baby farmer or orphanage.'

'But why did she—'

'She didn't. She had no choice. Women like your mama have little power over men of Mr Gint's standing.'

'She told you?'

'Yes, eventually. I was very well acquainted with the Tulliers, you know—your grandparents. They were good folk. Hard working. Honest. Good to do business with.' A mist of reminiscence captured him a moment. 'They didn't deserve the way things went for them.' He took up his pipe and began to stuff it with tobacco. 'Anyway, when the business went under and all the children were sent out to service or farm work, your mama landed herself a rather fortunate position as a lady's maid to Lady Dorothea Campbell. She was so well accomplished you see, that even at such a tender age, her mistress could tell she was wasted to the task of housemaid. She learned quickly and was getting on well considering what a diminishment in her circumstances it had been. Four years later and not a blemish on her character, not a word of reprimand from her mistress: and then *he* came to the house—a guest at a hunting party.'

'And that is how my mother came to know him?'

He nodded, tilted the candle to light his pipe and took a few chugs upon it, a curl of smoke rising, its earthy, woody scent swelling from it. 'He took a fancy to her. Even though his wife was under the same roof.'

Annalise could barely remember Mrs Gint. She scratched around for the vague recollection of a drawn cheeked willowy looking woman with glossy black ringlets, who she remembered always being sat in a rocking chair over her fancy work. She had died when Annalise was not above six or seven years old. 'She became his mistress?'

He exhaled a cloud of smoke and shook his head gravely. 'No. There was no affair. No affection—'

'You mean he set upon her?'

'I'm sorry my dear. It makes for hard hearing.'

Annalise felt the bulge of tears in her eyes once more. 'So, he was then, just as he is now; a predatory brute. That is from whence I came?' She shook her head in disbelief, for the first time, taking it in.

'None of us get to choose our parents, Annalise. But whatever your father may lack in goodness, you know your mother made up for it hundredfold.'

This heartened her a little. She nodded and dabbed away the tears with the corner of the handkerchief. 'I wish she had told me herself.'

'She never wanted you to know. Never wanted you to trouble your head with such details. Besides, the condition of him taking you in was in exchange for your mother's silence. So, she could not breathe a word of it anyway. I suppose by the time you were at an age to understand, where it could have been entrusted to you, it became too difficult to retract, especially since he had never taken an interest in you.'

'And yet it seems now he means to. Although I cannot imagine why.'

'Do you wish him to?'

'No. The very idea is abhorrent to me.'

'Well, you owe him nothing. Bank the draft and cut him off then. It is no more than he deserves. Although I am pleased he kept to his word on that head. Your mama will be smiling from the heavens at this news.'

'I did not take the money.'

'What?'

'I do not want his money. I want nothing from him. He disgusts me.'

He put down his pipe. 'I see that my dear and I understand your sentiment. But he owes you that much in the least.'

'What he owes me, he can never give back.' She felt another stream of hot tears roll down her face and caught them with the handkerchief this time.

'I know my dear, I know. But your mama wanted so much to see you have the happy life you deserved. The life she once knew. That is why she held him to this promise. Think of what comfort it would have been for her to know you are well established and enjoying a gentler way of life?'

Annalise nodded. This much she could not deny. She wanted not to displease her mama but she could not feel comfortable accepting anything from someone she hated with such vehemence. Someone who represented everything she abhorred.

'Why don't you write to him and ask him to send the draft onto Cuddington for you, eh? You shan't have to see him again then.'

She looked down and shook her head. 'I don't think I can bring myself to do it. When I left that house in February, I swore I would never set eyes on that man again. That I would start afresh, put the taint of so many bad memories behind me, and now I must have the taint of this knowing forever.'

'Well, if he is as sick as he says, then you may not get the chance to accept it again, Annalise.'

She nodded. 'But I don't know how to accept it—not the draft, the, the ugly truth of this matter, the knowing that I share—'

'No. Do not say it. You share nothing with that man, Annalise. You are your mother's daughter in every way, look at you; the very image of her, fair in face and heart. You have not a trace of him about you. You were born and christened a Tullier, you will always be a Tullier, well, unless you marry. And you might now dear girl. Think of that. You may have your own family and a home to call your own. None of this scrubbing down kitchen tables and waiting on others. You are too good for such a life of drudgery. So, please my dear: do what your mama wanted; bank the draft and go off into the world and find your way, make it a happy life.'

She wiped the rim of her eyes with the corner of her hanky and sniffed. 'I could pay you back for a start,' she said, coming slowly to terms with the idea.

He held up a hand. 'Come, Annalise, you offend me; that was not a loan but a gift I made, to a woman I–I held in great regard.' He blinked a few times and sighed. 'I want for you the same as she: for you to take the money and set yourself up prettily.'

She got up from her chair, walked around the counter and hugged him. 'You have always been such a good friend to us, Mr Harrison. We have been fortunate to have you.'

She had been grateful that Eleanor had gone straight out to ride when she got back. She needed a little time alone to compose herself and once she was gone, she spent a while cleaning up her quarters—the smaller items; the things set upon the dressing table, the small-framed pictures upon the mantle that she could dust with one hand, and plucked from the vase the limp flower stems that were past their best. There was not much to do. The housemaids had already been in to make up the bed, re-plenish the washstand and air the room.

But she was not ready to return to the basement right away, although she felt she should with so little to do. She needed time to think, without Cook on her case and Maggie in her ear and Cal asking questions and making sly comments about her dislike of Mrs Simpson. She had called her an ogre under her breath last night, and although she had privately thought it comical, she did not like to be put in such uncomfortable sit-uations.

So she looked about the room, wondering what she might do to be of use and buy herself just a little more peace to be with her thoughts be-fore she went back down and faced the noise. She should write to Gint, whilst she had the private opportunity to, but she had none of her things and she didn't mean to take liberties by helping herself to the ink and pa-per at Eleanor's desk.

Instead, she picked out a new day dress for her mistress, ready for when she returned. She spent a little while deciding over which to choose. She picked the sprigged coral one, thinking she looked pretty in any of them and so it hardly mattered which. She plucked some fresh stockings from the drawer and kept aside a small pile that she had identified for darning once she had the use of her hand back, though she then considered that she would likely not be serving her mistress then, for this Abigail was to come next weekend and she would go back to the kitchen for good.

She tossed the stockings back into the drawer with a sense of dismay. She was not sure she wanted the new Abigail to come now, but it was too late, she had already given her answer and besides, she did not know what she was to do yet. Everything was changed now. She neither wanted to return to the kitchen, nor leave Cuddington for this new life Mr Harrison spoke of. One day perhaps, but not this one. Besides, women could not just set up house alone and she had no sweetheart to sweep her off her feet and make an honest woman of her, and even if she did, she was sure she was not ready to settle to that kind of life just yet.

There were other things she might like to do before she was nursing infants. For a start, she would like to make the patchwork quilt she had saved her mama's clothes for and visit France and see the village of Colmar where her mama had grown up; admire the colourful houses and idyllic waterways she had described to her from her childhood memories of the place. And then there was dressmaking, she had always had a flair for it, although rarely the good cloth or money for it to really try out her skills. This would all be possible now, if she could bring herself to write to Gint.

It seemed so unfair to her that what would otherwise be possibilities that brought such joy must be tainted by the knowing it was on his account and knowing the why.

'Oh, you are up here.' Mrs Crawford came into the room without knocking and Annalise jumped and took the stockings she had selected for Eleanor over to the bed to lay out.

'Yes, ma'am. My mistress is out on a ride.'

Mrs Crawford crossed the room, opened the cupboard and restocked the linens from the pile she had dispatched to the chair. 'When shall she be back?'

'She did not say.'

'Then you might go down to appease Mrs Simpson awhile until she returns, she wants you to help the new girl understand the way we work,' she said, closing the cupboard and re-gathering the remaining linens on the chair. 'I daresay you prefer fiddling about up here, but you know she will only grow more uneasy at your avoidance.'

'Yes, of course, ma'am. I shall go to her directly,' she said, dropping a curtsey and following her out of the room.

Impromptu Visitor.

September 1821. - Eleanor.

I could see she was still out of sorts when I returned from Ewell. Her eyes gave away the sorrow in them, even though she smiled for me and talked pleasantries. I had come out of the stonemason's in a more buoyant mood having learnt of at least something I could help her with at last, but this melancholy undertone to her beautiful amber flecked gaze disconcerted me, and I wanted to ask her what had *really* happened with Mr Gint, for on this head I had made no real progress. But she was evasive, turning the conversation towards me at every opportunity as she helped me dress—this we had down to an impressive art between the pair of us—each using a hand to manage the tricky bits and knowing precisely how to work in accord in the task.

I dismissed her to her leisure for the rest of the afternoon, since I meant to finish my letter to Lady W. before things got too busy and I forgot to reply altogether. I told her of my plans to journey to Kent now I was soon to have a replacement for Miss Rosen at last, and that I would like very much to travel directly from there to London and pay her a visit before I decided where I would move onto before Autumn set in. I had considered Caitlyn next, but I had missed the festival now, and Scotland was not a place I meant to travel to for a short stint and unless I was willing to put up there for the duration of the winter and return after the snow laden roads were driveable again, I considered that may be a journey best left for the coming spring instead.

Once I had sealed it, I spent an hour at my diary, which I had neglected for the last couple of days, having been so much in Annalise's company. Which was preferable to this, but I had sensed she needed some time to digest her feelings on whatever was tormenting her and rest awhile. I hoped she would be improved for it when she returned after dinner.

I missed her company as I ate alone in the dining room with nothing but the empty chairs and candelabra to look at. Is this what my life was to become now? A lonely existence, a meal for one and a bored footman staring at the carpet, waiting for me to finish so he could retire from the room. I hoped not. I wondered how Lady W. had managed for so many years as a childless widow. Perhaps you grew used to it after a time. Although she was never short of company or occupation from what I could tell; always something to organise or attend to. That was what I must build for myself: things to occupy me, industrious things, interesting things that I could turn my mind to. New experiences, travel and friends...good ones this time.

I had made a winning start with Lady W. and now Annalise too. If my society was full of only such genuine persons, then I knew I should grow to like it very much and be happy with such companionship. As for realising the romantic companionship I had spent my girlhood dreaming up, that seemed an impossibility now. For if what Edmund said was true, then it was unlikely I would ever get the opportunity to divorce and remarry, even if I did ever find someone worthy, and I was growing ever more sceptical of the notion of true love's existence. I pushed the thought away, along with my plate and told the footman I was finished. But as I rose from the table, I stiffened and gripped the back of the chair, hearing the gallop of a horseman on the driveway.

'Peters,' I said to the footman anxiously, 'can you see from the window who is come?'

He put down the empty tray he was carrying to the table and looked out of the window. 'I cannot see properly, ma'am, but I think it is a lone rider.'

My heart began to race instantly, 'Is the house locked up?' I asked, almost tripping on the leg of my dining chair as I prepared to flee upstairs.

'I don't think so, ma'am, it is a little early.'

'Peters, I want you to abandon your duties here, go down to the basement and warn Mr Grantley we have an unknown lone rider approaching and I am not expecting anyone; he will know what to do. Then you are to convey the message that the house is to be locked up at once and checked thoroughly, and send Tulley directly to me please.'

He nodded and as the doorbell sounded, I fled through the jib, into the servants staircase and ran to my chamber and locked all the doors.

Once the bell had stopped ringing, I shortly after heard the gallop of the horse strike up again. I watched carefully from the window, but could see nothing but the black cloak that flailed in the wind as the horse galloped back down the driveway. I closed the curtains and sat down, recovering my breath. Moments later, Annalise knocked at the door and I unlocked it briefly to let her in. She came into the room looking puzzled, 'Is everything alright?' she asked.

'I don't know, do you know who was at the door?' I asked relocking this one.

'A courier I believe. Grantley asked me to bring you this,' she said, pulling a letter from her apron pocket and I sighed with relief and shook my head.

'I thought it was him,' I said in answer to her confused expression. 'My husband.'

'Oh.'

'I should not have let my thoughts run away with me so. Thank you,' I said, gesturing to the letter she handed me and I tore open the seal and instantly felt the return of all the terror I had just dispensed with.

Dear Wife,

I fear this sulk has gone on quite long enough.

I am willing to forgive and forget over Richards, and so I hope we may move on now.

Please return home. Your quarters at Beddington are finished now and you may be in comfort there. I know you have a wedding to attend shortly, but shall expect you home directly after this event.

We have been long enough estranged and I hope you will return and do your duty and I shall not have to file against Richards. If you are not home by Monday, I shall know how you wish to proceed and instruct my lawyers accordingly.

Giles.

'Are you alright miss? Eleanor?'

I looked up to see her at my side and folded the letter back up. I shook my head. 'Well, it seems we have both received unwelcome correspondence now.'

'What is it?'

'It is from my husband, asking me to return to him. I'd sooner throw myself from the roof of this house.'

'Eleanor, don't say such dreadful things,' she said with a tone of rebuke.

'Forgive me, it has thrown me quite out of countenance.'

'It's alright, I understand. Is there something I can do?'

I shook my head and found a smile for her. 'No, I thank you. I shall stay up a little while in the library before I retire. You will stay with me tonight, won't you?'

'Of course, I will,' she said with a reassuring pat at my arm.

'Thank you. I fear this has set me back a little, but I shall soon come about.'

She walked to the library with me and left me there, saying she was to go down and talk Cal through some more protocols as the kitchen was starting to make preparations for the wedding party and growing busy again. I asked her to collect me from the library at ten-o-clock in order we might both get an early night, for I was determined that this last couple of days of freedom would not be spent in worry over Giles' demands, but be made merry. It was to be the last time she was to serve as my Abigail and I felt this realisation with a growing sense of trepidation.

I scanned the shelves of the library carefully, looking to see if any of Edmund's old law books were lurking about in there. I thought it likely he had taken them with him but was pleasantly surprised to find a few well-worn books to thumb through. I took them over to the desk, used my candle to light the desk side lamp and sat down.

When Annalise came to fetch me, I was surprised I had whiled away a couple of hours in reading them. They had been no help at all, their subjects being matters of criminal law or trust law and nothing at all upon the ecclesiastical matters of separation or annulment. No less, they had kept me diverted and I took one of them back to my room for further reading.

'How is Calverley getting on?' I asked Annalise when we returned to my chamber.

'Very well. She is quick and thorough and tidy.'

'That's good,' I said sensing a vagueness about her tone. 'So, does that mean you shall not need to mentor her anymore?'

She shrugged. 'Well, they can use all the help they can get at present. The wedding party menus require a lot of intricate work.'

'But you cannot help them, Annalise.'

She did not reply but busied herself at the washstand and said, 'Shall we ready for bed now?'

'If you like.' I walked over to the stand and poured the water for her. 'What is it?' I asked her, noticing her wince as she rummaged the shelves for the facecloths.

'Nothing, I'm just a little tired tonight.'

I studied her carefully as she added the cloths to the basin. 'You wash first, I want to have a drink,' I said, sitting down and pouring some barley water from the carafe. And as I sipped from it, I watched her wash her face and hands, looking out for the wince I had just noted. When I saw it again, I got up and said, 'What is wrong, are you in pain?'

She looked up at me nervously, dabbing her face lightly with the damp cloth. 'It comes and goes, all part of the healing I suppose.'

I was unconvinced but set upon my own washing, supposing it better to get it out of the way if I intended on keeping to the early night I was minded to. I was not certain of what to do tomorrow, I had been minded to go out in the Landau with her and maybe find a picnicking spot, but that was before Giles' express had come and unnerved me. Now I felt reluctant to venture far.

I washed my face and hands and when I had dabbed my face dry, Annalise was already half undressed when I turned about. 'Here, let me help you, there is no sense in struggling,' I said, putting down the towel.

'It's alright, I am almost done, just my lacing if you will,' she said, trying to pass the sleeve over her bandages but the weight of the dress pulling against it.

'Nonsense.' I intervened and caught the other side of the dress and told her to hold it whilst I unruffled the twisted sleeve cuff and eased it gently over her bandages until her arm was free. It was then I noticed that her bandage, which was usually wrapped about a quarter way up her forearm, was now up to her elbow. I frowned as she stepped out of her dress. 'Why have you such a large bandage on today?'

Her eyes darted between me and her arm. 'Clumsy wrapping, there was no one to help me today.'

'You silly thing, why didn't you ask me? Sit down, I will adjust it for you so you may be more comfortable, I know how it itches you in this warm weather.'

'No, thank you miss. It's fine,' she said drawing her arm away. 'If you would just help me with my laces. I shall have it changed in the morning anyway.'

I unlaced her and set down her stays. 'Annalise, sit down,' I said, pointing to the chair. 'What are you not telling me? Let me see your arm. Did that Mr Gint hurt you this morning?'

'No,' she said reluctantly holding her arm across the table as I began to unwrap the bandaging. I was less than halfway done when I saw the angry blistering scald marks running the length of her inner forearm. 'Good good, what is this?'

'A little burn. It was my own fault.'

'From what?'

'I splashed it with hot kettle water, by accident.'

'You were supposed to only mentor. Have you been working in the kitchen, Annalise?'

'Just a little, helping out. Everyone is so busy, I could hardly—'

'Were you asked to help?'

'I didn't mind—'

'By who? Who Annalise? Cook?'

She nodded and looked down into her lap.

I felt a blood vessel might burst at my temple. 'How often has she asked you to help?'

'I don't know, just now and then.'

'I know you dislike lying Annalise, so why don't you tell me the truth? How many times? Once, twice, everyday?'

'I'm sorry. I just don't want to cause any bother. It was only a few jellies. It's just I forgot how heavy the kettle was if you try to lift it one handed and...' she began to cry. I rang the bell and comforted her until eventually a young maid answered it. I sent her to bring me a bowl of ice water, honey and fresh bandages and whilst we were waiting, I pressed Annalise for more details on what had happened in the kitchen.

When the young maid returned, I set down the honey jar and bandages and took the bowl from her at the door before dismissing her and carrying it into the room and towards the low side table I had positioned beside the chair Annalise sat in. 'Here,' I said setting down the bowl that I had managed to spill half the contents from on my short journey from the door. 'Let's cool these wounds.'

'You have taken too much trouble on my account, please miss, let me manage this,' she looked surprised at me but I ignored it. She had cleaned mud and vomit from me and put me to rights more times than I cared to remember, it seemed a small offering.

I knelt down on the floor beside her and supported the weight of her arm gently as she lowered it into the bowl.

'Miss, please, I can manage.'

'Does it sting?' I asked her.

'A little. But you really must let me...'

'Hush, it will not answer to complain when I am trying to concentrate,' I said, using a small jug from the washstand to trickle the water over the scold marks. 'My new Abigail arrives on Saturday,' I said re-dipping my jug.

She looked up and met my eyes. 'I see. Well, you must be relieved. You shall have a two-handed maid at last.'

'I shan't be. I was rather becoming fond of my one handed one,' I smiled, looking up briefly from my task and she met my gaze with a contrite expression.

'Will you go travelling now?' she asked me, flinching slightly as I trickled the water over an angry looking blister at her inner elbow.

I nodded.

'When will you go?'

'Monday. I shall go to my sister in Kent for a week or so, then up to London to see a dear friend and decide where to go on to after. Although I beg you keep the details to yourself.'

She nodded. 'Of course. Will your husband be looking for you?'

Her frankness surprised me. 'I fear he might.'

'Then you must keep moving on.'

'Yes, for now.'

'And thereafter?'

I sighed. 'I wish I knew. All I know for certain is that I shall not return to him.'

'Was it very hard, your marriage?'

I shrugged. 'You saw the state of me that night. It was the first occasion, but it was dreadful enough that I am determined to make sure it is the last.'

She brushed a gentle hand over mine and paused just long enough there for me to lift my eyes from my task. 'I am glad you shan't return to him. But sorry you shall be gone. When do you think you will return here?'

'I don't know. There is so much I do not know presently. That is half the trouble. Uncertainty. One minute I think I shall stay put in defiance and the next I think I would be better off vanishing across the channel and starting over.'

'To France?'

'Perhaps, I do not know what it is like there. But I speak the tongue, so if I should like it...'

'I mean to go one day. To Colmar, where my mama was born.'

'Perhaps we might go together and keep each other company,' I said without thinking. 'Is your father also from France?'

She stiffened a little. 'No. I believe he was English. I know very little about him.'

'Do you have any siblings?'

'No, it's just me.'

'It can be lonely, can't it? I mean, I have siblings, as you know, but they have not been much about me for years. I suppose that when you are an only child, it is like that all the time.' I put the jug down at the side of the bowl. 'Now, how does that feel?' I asked, lifting her arm from the water.

'Like it is about to drop off.'

We both laughed.

'Well, I suppose it has done its job then.' I wrapped her arm gently in a towel and moved the bowl of now-melted ice water to the floor. 'Now, if I remember correctly from my school room days, honey makes a very good balm for such an injury.' I poured a little into my palm and drizzled it over the skin, gently nudging it into place with a light fingertip.

'Eleanor...'

'Yes?'

'Thank you.'

'It's my pleasure,' I said, wiping my sticky fingers on the discarded towel and began unravelling the roll of fresh bandage. I knew she thought me insane and indeed it was against the grain of the way of things, but hadn't that become the story of my life? Perhaps, despite all my tuition to the contrary, that was who I had become. I certainly did not seem to know myself anymore. It seemed to me that if I was to be so thought and accused of such irregularity, I may at least use it for some good purpose, having insofar only used it to detrimental effect. And I owned there was some small satisfaction I felt in serving her in even small ways. But my next task, I knew must be a clandestine operation, for she would certainly not approve of it and I was not willing to let this go.

'Well then,' I said, neatly tucking the new bandage in place and getting up from the floor. 'I shall take these back downstairs and be back shortly. No, don't protest, you cannot carry them and that young maid has already lumbered it all up here. I shan't be long. Why don't you find our place in the book?'

I headed down to the basement thinking we would unlikely finish the story together now and it saddened me. I meant to make a gift of it to her so she could finish it. Although I wondered if she would find the time for such reading once I was gone. And the thought of her back down here in these gloomy confines, toiling away, made something catch in my throat.

Far from finding it frantic, I found the kitchen deserted, so I left the bowl and honey jar on the tabletop and went back into the corridor to find out the direction of the cook's parlour from the hallboy. When I found it empty, he showed me the way to the upper servants' parlour where he suspected I would find her, and I dismissed him with a few coins for his trouble.

I waited until I made out the sound of low voices stirring into chatter behind the door, the clink of glasses; the smell of tobacco rising. It seemed a stroke of luck when a footman rounded the corner with bottles in arm and tapped at the door looking disconcerted as he noticed me at the last.

I waited for it to open then seized the moment.

'Well, good evening,' I said in answer to their surprised faces as I came into the room behind the startled footman. There was about six of them huddled about the small table. The cards had been dealt, a small pile of coins sat at the middle of the tablecloth, an array of brandy and wine filled glasses, barely touched. 'My apologies, I have disturbed you, I think.'

'This is not what it looks like, miss,' said Grantley, rising to his feet; the rest of the staff following suit and rose accordingly.

'Please.' I waved them down and stepped in further, walking slowly around the room. 'Come, Mr Grantley, we must all take a little recreation from time to time; there is surely no harm in it.' I smiled and watched as they all took an inward sigh of relief. 'Bordeaux 1802, someone knows their wine,' I said, taking a bottle from the footman to examine, and I felt the discomfort growing in the room as they looked between each other nervously. I placed it on the table and turned to Mrs Crawford whose usually congenial smile had stiffened into almost a grimace. 'Mrs Crawford, am I correct in thinking that our arrangement with Tulley remains?'

'Why, yes, of course, ma'am. Is everything alright?'

'Not really. Tulley, who should have been *strictly* on Abigail duties until Miss Pascal arrives on Saturday, has managed to sustain yet another injury, a nasty scald. I am puzzled at how this could be when I have asked her to avoid any such tasks that might present such a risk. I am assuming Mrs Crawford then, that you have not—'

'No, ma'am,' she shook her head. 'She has not been tasked with anything.'

I caught cook colouring up in my peripheral vision and turned to her. 'Mrs Simpson, might I have a word—a private word?'

'Yes, ma'am,' she said uncomfortably and all the other staff in the room rose to take their leave.

Once they had vacated, I pulled up one of their empty chairs and sat opposite her. 'Mrs Simpson,' I said, eyes fixed on hers. 'I will come straight to the point. I know it was you that asked Tulley to undertake chores in the kitchen, despite your knowing my instructions to the contrary.'

'I—I forgot miss, the dates, it's so busy you see with your brother's wedding party, there's so much to see to and—'

'You forgot? Yes, you seem terribly busy just now. I shall be sure *not* to forget the fact.'

She shuffled in her seat, cheeks of flame red blush. 'I'm sorry, ma'am.'

'It is not me who deserves an apology, but Tulley who is nursing a scold to her forearm, having not even healed from the first round of injuries.'

'Yes, indeed and I shall make sure she—'

'You shall do nothing. Where Tulley is concerned, you shall do nothing and say nothing to her, without either my, or Mrs Crawford's leave to do so. Do you understand?'

She nodded.

'Good. Because the arrangement is that whilst you have Calverley, Tulley shall answer only to me and Mrs Crawford, is that clear?'

'Perfectly clear, ma'am.'

'Good, then perhaps your record will remain so too.' I got up from my seat. 'Good evening, Mrs Simpson,' I said and left the room.

Annalise was already up when I woke. I turned over to see her at the mirror, trying to brush out her long hair with a broken comb that even if intact was not much use to her with such long thick hair to tame. 'You should have woken me, Annalise.'

'I didn't like to. You seemed quite comfortable.'

'What is that dreadful thing you are scraping your hair about with? Put it away and pass me the brush from the dressing table.'

She did as requested, and I moved to the edge of the bed and patted the bed stairs. 'Sit here and I shall brush it out for you.'

'Thank you.'

'Have you ever tried plaiting it to make it easier to manage?'

'I don't know how.'

'Will you let me try?'

'If you like miss.'

I parted her hair and brushed it into two neat lengths before dividing it further and talking her through the process. It was one of the few hairstyles I did know how to manage, thanks to years of plaiting my doll's hair as a girl. There was something therapeutic in it, I remembered as I wove the lengths into neat ropes. When I was done, I made her hold the ends whilst I found ribbons to tie them with, and then I wrapped the plaits the circumference of her head, pinning them, before creating a chignon out of the remaining lengths. 'There, how pretty you look,' I said, and she blushed a little. 'You must know you are pretty?'

She stood up from the steps and patted her head. 'My mama used to tell me so. But she could hardly tell me otherwise.'

'Well, I have no cause to favour you, so you may take it as an impartial certainty that you are indeed, *very* pretty.'

She smiled and turned to the looking glass to examine her new hairstyle. 'Thank you, I like it.'

'Well, you shall dress in your own clothes today, no uniform. I am minded we shall go out and enjoy the weather, do a little shopping perhaps. And if you'd like to, we could visit your friends at Old Mill Street.'

'Really?'

'Yes, really. I want you doing as little as may be now you have another injury to nurse. How is your arm this morning?'

'It seems much better now, a little sore but the blisters have settled.'

'Good. Now, if you want to go down to the basement and fetch your own clothes, I shall wash and find my clothes, and perhaps we could take our breakfast in the garden? We have spent enough hours in this room and we shall soon be sorry when the good weather starts to fade and we no longer have the option.'

We were sat on the terrace breakfasting in the clement morning warmth when Mary came out through the open patio doors announcing Delores, who stepped out from behind her.

'Delores!' I said more surprised than I had meant to give away.

'Good morning, ladies. I hope you do not mind me dropping in on you, Eleanor, I was just visiting the dowager and thought I would see how you do.'

'That's very good of you, Delores. Mary, another place if you please.' As we waited for her to set it, I realised how foolish I had been to think my mama would not at least have her check up on me.

'So, how have you been?' she asked, settling into the chair Mary pulled up for her.

'Well enough. And you?'

'Very well. I do not believe we have been introduced?' she said studying Annalise curiously.

'My Abigail, stand in Abigail alas: Tulley,' I said, pouring the tea into all of our cups and I saw a flash of recollection in her gaze. I supposed she looked different from how she remembered her at High Ashurst in her dowdy uniform and plain chignon. Today, sat in her own saxon green day dress and pinned pleated hair, she looked radiant, beautiful.

'I see, well, good morning,' she said rather perturbed and I realised Annalise had turned pale and abandoned her plate.

'So, how is the Dowager?' I said to fill the uncomfortable silence.

'Yes, same as ever, I suppose. Gout, rheumatism and all the other complaints, but still merry for a round of backgammon, even at this hour.'

I smiled. 'Well, I suppose there are some benefits in the role of social pariah, for I have not been invited to call there for some time.'

'Oh, I'm sure she would very much like a call—'

'Come, Delores, she is a stickler and a brewer of scandal broth and we both know it.'

She shrugged and helped herself to a plum cake. 'Well, she is of a different generation. You young ones don't realise how much changed the world is in so many years.'

'Perhaps, but I should like it to alter a great deal more in my own.'

'And so it will, and you will one day be quoting to your own children how it was in your youth.'

'I shan't have any children, Delores. You know I shall not return to him and Edmund assures me I shall never get an annulment or a divorce, and so it seems I am to live out the life of a childless spinster after all.'

'But my dear, you are married, how will it be possible?'

'I don't care what people think of me anymore, Delores. Let them talk. Their scorn shall never be enough to induce me to return to him and suffer so.'

'Well, you have always known your own mind but, you are so young to be contemplating a life of solitude.'

'And so were you, and look at you now.'

'Well, yes, and so I know what I am talking about, Eleanor. It is not a life I would wish upon you.'

'No, but I'm sure you do not wish me to live a life of matrimonial misery and regular beatings either.'

'No, no, of course not. I suppose I had thought perhaps your father might have a word with him and, well, show his disapproval of this treatment so he may not repeat it again.'

'Men like him will always repeat it, Delores. Anyway, he deserves not even the mention. Tell me how things go at High Ashurst.'

She put down her teacup and grinned. 'Wonderfully. I am very fortunate, I know.'

'You deserve this happiness.'

'Thank you.'

We ate our breakfast and had the tea pot twice refilled as we chatted and I hoped when I got up from the table, Delores would make her excuses and permit us to go about our day as we intended. But when I dropped her the hint that I was to go into Epsom today for a little shopping, it quite backfired, for she invited herself along.

'Surely you have much to do, Delores. You need not play chaperone to me anymore. I have my maid with me, so I assure you I will be—'

'Yes, but for company. Besides, I have been meaning to stop in at the milliners and find some new bonnets.'

Of course, you have. I sighed inwardly and fronted a smile. 'Well then, I suppose I had better go and fetch my reticule.'

'Send the girl, my dear.' She nodded in Annalise's direction. 'I shall be with you in a moment, I just need to visit the water closet.'

'I'm so sorry, Annalise,' I said reaching for her as soon as Delores was gone. 'I had no idea she was going to come here, let alone attach herself to our plans.'

'It cannot be helped. But Eleanor, you must see how aghast she was to find me breakfasting with you.'

'Care not a whit for it.' I waved a dismissive hand. 'I am only sorry you shall have to be bored with our conversation all the afternoon when I hoped it would be a merry day, since it is our last.'

'I wish it were otherwise,' she said and this surprised me.

'Do you?'

'Of course, I do.'

'You know it is not too late to change your mind, about the Abigail position—Miss Pascal is not come yet—'

'But you have already given her the post and she will have no other to turn to at such a late—'

'I don't care. I mean, I will take care of that. I shall pay her until she finds such a place if—'

'No. It wouldn't be right and I am wishful thinking. I belong where I am for now and Miss Pascal at least can serve you well. I am useless as an Abigail, even more than usual,' she held up her hand. 'But I wish it were otherwise, know that.'

I smiled and nodded. 'So do I.' *More than you know.* 'I had better fetch my things and brace myself for an afternoon of hopping from every shop on Epsom High Street.' I sighed. 'How about I drop you off at Ewell? At least you can go and see your friends a while instead of having to be bored to tears.'

'I couldn't, I'm to be your Abigail yet another day and so I mean to.'

'Please. I do not want you worn out today. Go and see your friends so I might look to our last evening together without both of us being fagged to death.'

'Right, are we ready?' I turned about to see Delores and let go of Annalise's arm, which I had quite forgotten I had been holding onto.

It was precisely the kind of afternoon I had expected it to be, browsing every offering and walking until my feet were sore. I had at least dropped Annalise off in Ewell, telling Delores she was to run an errand there for me whilst we drove on to Epsom. The only thing that pleased me about the arrangement was that I had meant to be frivolous with Giles' money now I knew he meant to try to claim me back. And so, I returned to Cuddington that afternoon with every kind of article I could find a use for and a great many, I could not. As I surveyed the piles of bandboxes as they were unloaded from the carriage, I smiled to myself, thinking this could indeed become a rather satisfying hobby.

Decisions, decisions.

September 1821. - Annalise.

She spent the afternoon with the Bartletts at Old Mill Street and was pleased to see how much better they seemed. They had paid the rent up to the end of winter and had been able to keep the pantry well-stocked and even begin stockpiling coal ahead for the coming seasons. It heartened her to see them so at ease. And as much as she had resisted the writing to Gint for the money draft, she had begun to turn her mind to all the good she might be able to do, if she could bring herself to accepting it.

On her way home, she popped into Mr Harrison's, who had been happy to see her in better spirits than yesterday. They sat over a cup of tea all the same.

'So, have you had a chance to think about what I said; writing to Gint to ask him to send the draft?'

'I have and I am tempted to do it, but you see, my heart and my head are quite at odds on the matter. I want nothing from him and yet I do not want to waste my mama's sacrifice or forego an opportunity to do something useful. My mind changes by the hour.'

'Annalise, this could change your life.'

'Well, that's the thing you see, I have been thinking how many other lives it could change.'

'Oh?'

'Well, you see, he has not been a good man, but there seems to me something just in his money going to good causes. To help others, like my friends on Old Mill Street.'

'Well, that's a generous idea. But you are a good cause too you know. That money could spare you another day at the grindstone from here on.'

'I don't want to stop working, sir. For a start, what would I do with myself?'

He laughed at this. 'I'm sure you could grow accustomed to a gentler way of life. A little charity work perhaps, like Miss Lockheart.'

'Well, yes, I suppose there is that, but I don't want to be idle or wasteful. Especially when this money could do a lot for others; others who can't work or can't get enough work.'

'Annalise, you are all heart, and I admire your sentiment indeed. But have a care for yourself, for your future. No one can fix all the world's troubles, but we may share our bread, indeed.'

'But perhaps, sir, that is precisely how we might.—Mr Harrison, how much money is six hundred pounds? I mean, what can be done with it?'

'Enough to live on for the rest of your days. Plainly perhaps, but well; if you were to invest some of it, perhaps in the bank, or what say you to a business venture, or a house? You could end up very comfortable indeed with a wise head in how you use it.'

'Is it enough to rent a house with?'

He shook his head. 'Enough to buy a house.'

'Really?'

'Yes, and you could choose what to do with it. If you are happy to work presently, then you could put it up to let and generate rents from it. And when you have tired of working, or you come to retirement, well, what a comfortable one it would be.'

'I see.'

'Do you want to stay a kitchen maid, now you have a choice in the matter?'

'Not a kitchen maid, no, but in service, for now. It makes sense to keep my bed and board if I want to invest this money.'

'You could work for yourself you know. Set up a milliners or seamstress service—you always used to say you would like to be a dressmaker when you grew up. Well, now you have the means to set up such an establishment. I can see it now: *Tullier's Drapers*, the finest in the county.'

She laughed. 'Well, I do not say I would not like it. But you see, I don't only mean to help myself, sir, and if I throw all the money into such pursuits, I would miss the opportunity to help my friends.'

'Of course, you wouldn't, to the contrary. You would increase it, safeguard it for the future. Just think, you would consistently have more than enough to help them, not just as a one off, but for good. Besides, you could give them work, which most folk would prefer over charity.'

'That's true. But where would I even begin? I don't know the first thing about any of it. I have never even been inside a bank before.'

'Well, you're in no rush my love. You have youth on your side. You may take your time to decide upon things, once you have the money. Now, when you get back today, I want you to write that letter and when he sends the draft to you, you're to go straight to the bank to open an account. Then it's safe, while you make your mind up.'

She nodded her agreement. She had not realised what was possible. She still didn't fully understand the number or what such things might cost. But she did know that Mr Harrison understood such matters and would not have said so otherwise.

When she left Mr Harrison's, she bought some more flowers from the flower stall and decided last minute, to visit the cemetery whilst she had the chance. She had not meant to take liberties with the time even though Eleanor had assured her she would not be needed back until at least five-o-clock today. But she was to be back to her usual work soon and would not get the chance to go again for another two weeks. She had checked the time before leaving the bookshop—it was only a quarter past two when she had left it, so decided she had plenty of time yet to get back before five.

'Oh, Mama, what a secret to keep from me,' she said, arranging the flowers over the settling earth: the soil dry and dusty from the heat and the surrounding grass patchy and brown like hay. She settled on the ground beside it. She often spoke to her when there was no one else about to hear her and today, she had been lucky to find the church yard quiet. 'I forgive you of course. I understand why you kept it from me. I was better off never knowing such a father and so, you did your best to protect me. But oh, Mama, I wish you had not carried such burdens to the grave. How heavy your heart must have been,' she wiped a few tears from her cheeks. 'I know you did it for me. And I am grateful, Mama, for all that you did for me: the seen and unseen things. And I want to follow your example of selflessness, I want to find a way to help others. I know you would have wanted that too. I would like to make you proud one day, just as I felt proud to have you as my mama, to be of your blood. Oh, I wish you were here so you might tell me what to do for the best. So you might enjoy it with me. So you might have the gentler life you so deserved.

'But you are not. And so I know I must find a way to make good of all that you gave up, so this could be.'

After permitting herself a protracted release of tears and tidying the grave, she got up and brushed down her dress. It was her best dress and was so rarely worn it had lasted well with only the slightest of hem chaffing to give away its age. Otherwise, the beautiful green muslin embellished with cream floral stitching still looked as neat and vibrant as the day it was pinned to the dressmaking dummy. She had made it herself with the fine muslin her mama had given to her for her eighteenth birthday. She had made her mama a neat Spencer from the remnants too. The very same she was buried in along with her best ivory gown that Annalise had re-trimmed before she was laid to rest.

She was deeply thoughtful and reminiscent on her way home, but she felt lighter and more centred as she picked her way through the Cuddington tree's and meandered up the pathway to the house. But a sense of dread grew at having to enter through the kitchen doorway, dressed in her finest whilst the others sweated over the hotplates. When she was with Eleanor, she could avoid it, going through the house directly, but there was no excuse on her own. It was perhaps time to think of leaving this post. She could feel Cook's stifled resentment so tangibly now, in even the slightest look or word, that she doubted they could ever be on easy terms again, even once she returned properly to her duties in the kitchen and however hard she worked to compensate this spell. It was not about the work of course, for Cal had made up the number and was far more skilled than she in her eight months of learning the duties. It was about something else, something of authority and principle that had led to this hostility. But much to her surprise, as she came through the back door and edged her way through the room, avoiding pot handles and peeling buckets, Cook did not even look up at her as she passed. It was the others who seemed startled by her appearance and she felt guilty as Poppy looked up from the dough she was kneading and gave her a smile.

This was the sticking point: Poppy. If she was to find another place elsewhere or even if there was a way she might get a place under Mrs Crawford and remain, she would lose her proximity, not just in the kitchens, but in their little room together. She would be sent up to the attic if there was no need of her in the kitchen—and how little would she see her then? A passing half hour or so in the servants' hall of an evening. And though there might be a means to offer Poppy other options once she had decided what to do with this money, whatever else, Poppy was happy here, had plans to work her way up to the top, and she knew that whilst Cook was yet a little way from being pensioned off, she knew that one day, not too far distant, Poppy would have her place.

'Ah, I almost didn't recognise yer,' said Will as they near collided at the kitchen door.

'Will, forgive me. I was distracted,' she said, stepping out into the corridor now. 'How are you?'

'Better for seeing such an unexpected sight. You look charming. And like you should be off to somewhere much finer than the servants' hall.'

She felt a little flushed at the way he studied her. 'You are very kind, Will. But I am on my way back to my room. I had some matters to attend in town and now I am to wait for my mistress to return.'

'So, you're free for a bit?'

She considered her plan to write to Gint before Eleanor got home. 'Well, for a little while I suppose.'

'Well then, fancy the chances of that, for Grantley's just given us a half hour's leisure before we have the pleasure of moving about the furniture in the state rooms.'

'Then you had better enjoy the rest. It sounds tiresome and it seems for once I have the better bargain.'

'Aye, about time too, eh? Well, what do you say to sitting out wi'me on my break?'

'I don't know, Will, I am already getting daggers as it is for always lounging about with my mistress; at least that I can justify.'

''alf an hour tops? I 'aven't seen yer for an age. You're above stairs more than even I of late.'

She laughed a little. 'Very well, half an hour, but pray let us use the tourist door, I don't want to go through that way again.'

They sat in the shade of an old birch, out by the orchard where they were unlikely to be spotted. Will had picked them a couple of apples from the tree and they ate them as they chatted. He apprising her of all the hassle of converting the long saloon into a dining room capable of accommodating twice the number of the formal one: she explaining her dilemma with cook and how unpleasant she had been since her accident.

'Well sod 'er,' he said, having listened attentively to her account.

'Will, what language,' she protested.

'Aye well, I'll apologise for your sake, but as for that battleaxe—'

'Will, you must not speak so of our superiors.'

'Superiors? You are all of their superiors by far. If they had an ounce of your goodness and sense, well, maybe then I would respect them. But you don't see what I do, Anna. Take last night, they 'ad me and Peters waiting on them hand and foot whilst they enjoyed a gaming party.'

'Mrs Simpson?'

'Aye, 'er, Crawford, Grantley, and some of the tenant farmers, 'aving a right knees-up at the master's expense, fine food and liquor. Well, that was until your ladyship turned up outta the blue. Peter's described it as a right sight for sore eyes, 'er catching them at it.'

'Eleanor was there?'

'Oh, its Eleanor now, is it? First name terms and you've only been in her service—'

'Will,' she interrupted, sitting up. 'What was she doing there?'

He shrugged and tossed his apple core over the orchard fence and wiped down the blade of his flick knife he had been eating it from. 'Peter's said she wanted to see one of 'em. Said their jaws hit the flags when they see it was she, and with the evidence all over the place and no time to hide it. Master's wine on the table, cards dealt and bets cast,' he sniggered. 'I wish I'd answered that call, I tell yer.'

'Do you know what time this happened?'

He examined the blade of his knife, a glint of sunlight reflecting off its shiny surface and closed it and stuffed it back into his pocket. 'I dunno, about elevenish say. Anyway, what does it matter? The point is, respect is earned in my mind, and they don't deserve an ounce of it. You're worth ten 'o them you are, don't you ever forget it.'

She smiled. 'Well, so are you, Will.'

He cupped his hand to his ear, 'Was that a compliment?' he teased.

'Yes, I suppose it was.'

'Then I s'pose I'm the one that should be blushin',' he winked and rolled his shirt sleeves. He was still half liveried, having left his jacket in the basement and she thought him handsomely cut, as he stared into her eyes with such purpose. She had long understood the meaning of those looks, the fond regard in which he held her and yet she knew him a gent now, knew she was safe with him, even alone. He was not of Jack's mould, he meant to romance her gently, befriend her and one day, she supposed he might ask her to walk out with him in the proper style. Offer to make an honest woman of her perhaps. She revisited Mr Harrison's words: she might marry and have a family now. It was true. And perhaps one day she might like that, to keep house for her husband, a good man like Will and take care of her children, passing on the love and wisdom she had known in her mother's diligent care of her. But such things were a long way off in her mind. There were other matters to attend to first, like thinking of how to help the children she knew to be in need in Old Mill Street, coming to peace with the world now her mother was no longer in it, and doing something worthwhile with the energy of her youth before she settled to a life of domesticity. And so, remembering this, she broke the lingering gaze that had captured them both in its power, smiled meekly and said, 'Well, I think that is our half hour spent.'

'Aye, too short it was too,' he said with a hint of disappointment in his face as he jumped up to his feet and held his hand out to her. 'Come on me invalid, let's get you back to the 'ouse then,' he jested. But when their hands met and she drew level with him, there was no funning in his face or hers. They had both been stirred by some impassioned energy that seemed to slip into the moment uninvited. Possessed and incapacitated by its power for just an instant as they stood hand in hand a second beyond what was necessary. She went to pull her hand away and as she did, he lifted it to his lips and placed a kiss upon it.

'Will,' she said, a note of caution in her accent as she withdrew her hand gently from his grasp.

'I couldn't 'elp it,' he said apologetically, and they walked on towards the house in deafening silence.

She was spared the need to find a parting word for him, by the sight of Eleanor stood over a pile of bandboxes on the driveway as they came level with the front façade of the house. She noticed her instantly and waved her over, and she parted with Will sharing only a half-smile and glance before they split direction.

'Well, what perfect timing,' Eleanor said as they drew level. 'Who was that?'

'Just a footman,' she said nonchalantly.

'Well, you might have brought him with you, we shall need all the help we can get in taking it all upstairs.'

'What is all this?' Annalise asked, looking between the piles Jack and the groom were assembling upon the steps of the house.

'One way I can irritate my husband without even having to set eyes on him,' she said, looking pleased with herself and gesturing her up the steps. 'No, no, you shall not carry anything,' she insisted, stooping to pick up a couple of the lighter articles as they went. 'I have an altogether different task in mind for you. You shall tell me what I am to do with it.'

Annalise frowned, 'You mean you do not know?'

'Well, I have a few things I bought specifically, but that only accounts for about five of the boxes, the rest is... undecided, but, I knew that you would know best how to delegate them,' she smiled and hopped up the steps.

Annalise was perfectly puzzled as they sat in her chamber, pouring over the contents of the mountainous pile of boxes she opened up upon the carpet. She had separated the items into separate piles: toys for the children, comprising of toy theatre's, skipping ropes, hoops and tops, miniature china tea sets and baby houses, dolls and soldier figurines. And things for the ladies: fine Kashmir shawls, bonnets and caps, muffs, tippets and gloves, cloaks and mantlets, pewter brush and mirror sets.

'You look perturbed and I know, there is nothing much for the men. You see, I did not know what to buy for them, not without knowing what sizes would be suitable,' she said, flipping another lid and setting out the contents. 'There are handkerchiefs, which will suit the men I think, and cigars too... What, what is wrong?'

Annalise smiled kindly then bit her bottom lip.

'You do not like them?'

'Yes, they are very fine, exquisite things in fact,' she said, shuffling closer and placing a hand upon her forearm. 'Only, only they are perhaps, a little too fine. Folk at Old Mill Street do not wear such fancy things as this, and the children have little time for play beyond their infant years.'

'Oh, I see. I thought—I mean, I saw the children playing with sticks, drawing them in the mud and I thought how much nicer it would be if they had some real toys to play with...'

'Oh please, miss, don't be downcast. They will surely be very happy to have them. Only, well, my mind turns to the more practical things they are in need of: warm clothes and blankets for the winter season, extra coal for the fire...'

'Yes, yes indeed, you are right...how stupid of me. I knew I would somehow manage to get it wrong. I knew I could rely on you to set me right. That's why I wanted you to go with me, until Delores came and—oh well. I mean, I can take it back. Some of it at least—'

'No, no, we shall think of a good use to put them to, I promise. And the toys, well, I daresay the children would be sorry if they did not get to enjoy all these lovely things you have found for them.'

'I just wanted to help, do something good. I'm not altogether too good at that you see...'

Annalise saw the tears beginning to well in her eyes and gathered her up close with her unhindered arm, 'Yes you are, you are very good at it, look at all this effort you have been to. How thoughtful and generous. Little though it might count, I am proud of you and you should be proud of yourself.' And as the tears begun to fall from her eyes, quite forgetting herself, Annalise drew close to her face, kissed her eyelids softly and stroked her cheek with the thumb of her bandaged hand. She wondered as Eleanor fell silent and still, if she had overstepped the mark. Indeed, the lines had been much blurred betwixt them lately but perhaps she should not have let her emotions run so freely as to embrace her so, like a friend or near relation.

She was just about to draw back when she felt Eleanor wrap her arms around her back and pull close to her, so close she could feel her head resting at her bosom and could smell the fragrance of her hair pomade beneath her nose. She was soft and warm and gentle with her and it had seemed an age since she had been so held, remembering the last time she had crawled into the space beneath her mother's arm as she wept for her passing. It felt nice to be reminded of what it was to feel so comforted, to give such comfort and feel not so alone.

It was over dinner that evening, as she sat in the servants' hall chatting with Poppy, that she realised what was to be done with all the things Eleanor had bought. The toys of course could be distributed as intended. She would soon have enough money of her own to see to the winter clothes and more practical things they needed, so why shouldn't they have something nice for a change. But the ladies finery that she did not know the precise cost of, but was certain were of top drawer quality, she had an idea of how she might turn it to good effect when Poppy asked her if she was going to take her morning off to coincide with the harvest fair.

Miss Lockheart, the rector's daughter, always held a raffle at the harvest fair to raise money for various things that were needed in the community. She had noticed the poster up in Mr Harrison's window just yes-

terday. If the fine ladies articles were donated as prizes, she would surely raise a handsome sum, even greater than their cost perhaps, for it was
ladies of middling wealth who made up the largest number who fre-
quented the fair. Ladies who would no doubt find these luxury items
even a touch above their own pins. Then Miss Lockheart could be trusted to make sure the money raised went to the most urgent need. For
when she was not to be found in the church hall or at the back of Mr
Harrison's shop teaching letters, she was often seen throughout the district, visiting and bringing alms to the locals. It would be fairer that way.
One fine shawl might raise enough for many plain wool shawls and one
fine bonnet might be turned into many a warm fire this winter.

When she and Eleanor had finished their toilette this evening, she
made the suggestion of this scheme to her and she had accepted it with
good grace, saying it was indeed a more sensible way of doing things.
That tomorrow, even though they had only the morning before her parents would return home, they could take the things to Miss Lockheart
for the raffle, for she was not sure when else she would be able to. It was
to be her last weekend here after all.

It was that thought that weighed heavy on Annalise's mind, even as
Eleanor patted the space beside her on the bed and read chapter eleven
of *The Libertine* to her that night. The words seemed to wash over her
awareness and she was trapped in circular thoughts of Eleanor being
gone and her chance at being her Abigail gone with it, whilst thoughts
of leaving Poppy and her friends behind rebutted the temptation to go
with her. She had said it was still not too late, that she would still have
her, even now when Miss Pascal's arrival was but a couple of days away.
That she would have her, with her one armed cack-handedness, that was
only slightly more skilful even with both, over the spotless and impressive resume of this fancy Swiss maid.

It was peculiar. The shift in her life from only months ago. It seemed
as though the past eight months had flashed by in a heartbeat and she
had gone from utter hopelessness and melancholy to remembering happiness and companionship, to having opportunities thrown at her from
every direction. She did not feel worthy of such generous blessings as
had befallen her of late, but she was grateful of them. Grateful to have a

choice, grateful it seemed she was being steered into higher possibilities than she had ever conceived of. The challenge now, was to make sure she made the *right* choices, made the most of the opportunities presented. And this, she was not so skilled at determining, for she had never been faced with so much choice before in all her years.

'Are you tired? Shall we leave it there?' Eleanor paused and asked her and Annalise turned to face her. She had been staring up into the canopy of the bed. Now she was met with Eleanor's warm eyes peering across the top of the pages as she rested her head in her hand.

'Yes, I am a little, do you mind?' What she thought was that she was tired of running circular in her thoughts, tired of teetering on the edge of decisions, tired of countering every one of them and all the while, feeling a sense of impending trepidation, like a moment was about to slip from her grasp she might never recover, like the metaphorical stone after it was thrown. What she wasn't tired of, and knew she would soon long for, is the sound of Eleanor's dulcet tone in her ear as she read to her, the easy comfort they had accidentally fallen into, the conversations that they had on topics she couldn't have with anyone else, for they either had no time, interest or knowledge on them. Of those things, she knew she could never tire.

'Not in the least,' Eleanor said, closing the book and shuffling across the bed to slide it onto the side table. 'No,' she said moving back as Annalise lifted up on one arm, 'don't go. Stay in here with me tonight.'

Perhaps she was of like mind, thinking their time coming to a close. 'Are you sure?'

She nodded.

'Then I shall.'

With that, Eleanor got up, loosened the blankets from beneath her and blew out the candles before climbing back in and pulling the covers up over them. It was not cold, but it felt nice to be wrapped inside them. She felt the mattress sink as Eleanor rolled onto her back and the pair of them stared into the gloom, silent to begin with.

'Me and my mama used to share her bed. Sleep just like this. I thought I should never get used to sleeping alone. At least now my bed is small enough that I do not notice the empty space and I know Poppy is in the room with me.'

'Did you? I could not imagine having to share a bed with my mama, it was a rare enough thing that we managed to share a table without coming to grief with each other. I've never shared a bed with anyone before I was forced to endure my husband beside me.' She paused then asked: 'You did not have your own room there then?'

'No. I mean, I could have gone up in the attic I suppose, but Mama kept me close and her room was comfortable, big enough for the two of us.'

'Are you like your mama?'

'Everyone tells me so. But she was an esteemed beauty in her youth.'

'Then you are like her.'

'You flatter me. I found a miniature of her when I was packing up her things. I had never seen it before. She could not have been above sixteen.'

'How old are you?'

'One and twenty soon. It sounds quite strange to say it. I still feel like such a child.'

'So do I. Like an imposter. Like I am still playing at being a grown up.'

'Well at least I am not alone in that. How old are you?'

'Nineteen, twenty in February. When is your birthday?'

'September,' Annalise said, eager to think of some way to turn the subject, for it was to be her first without her mama and she had been trying to avoid thinking about it. Was hoping the day might come and go like any other, to spare her the need to feel the absence.

'Soon then. What day?'

'The seventeenth. When is yours?'

'February first. What do you like to do for your birthday?'

'Usually, my mama would apply to the master for us both to have the day off. It was the only time it was permitted. And we would do something together. Something special; a trip usually.'

'What kind of trip?'

'Well, we once went to the playhouse, and we would often go to the seaside for the day, if the weather was fair, and there was the time we went to the Menagerie at the Tower of London.'

'What was it like? I have always wanted to go but I was never permitted. Mama said it was too dangerous.'

'It was fascinating. Quite scary and altogether somewhere I should not like to visit again. The animals seemed so sad and contained and some of the visitors were unkind, taunting and poking them.'

'It is not how I imagined it then. Well, you shall have it off as you are used to, to spend however you like.'

'Eleanor, you are very kind. But you know there is no debt to settle between us. I do not expect—'

'Is that what you think? That I am still trying to settle the score.'

Annalise fell silent. It seemed that way.

'Well, I'm not. Not anymore anyway. I–I like your company. Is that so terrible of me? Besides, my pa has always given birthdays as a holiday, it is tradition here.'

'No. I'm sorry,' Annalise said and moved in closer to her, and pressed her cheek against her shoulder blade then felt her stiffen. Perhaps she should not have touched her. But it felt nice to be close to her. To feel the comfort of her beside her. She had slept alone for almost a year and this felt...familiar. 'In truth, I am inclined to want to forget the day altogether. I don't know how I am to bear it without her,' her words came out in a choke and her eyes began to well.

'Oh, Annalise,' Eleanor said turning her head on the pillow to try to make her out in the dimness, 'I'm sorry. I did not mean to sadden you.' She reached around for her hand and settled her own gently upon it.

Denial no more.

September 1821. - Eleanor.

I woke up at some point through the night to find her arm about my waist and the weight of her body pressed against my back. It was strange to feel her so close to me. I was not used to sharing a bed and the brief spell I had endured in my short marriage had been enough to put me off the notion entirely. But I had wanted her close tonight. As if it would somehow mollify the dread of our impending separation. I knew it could not. But it would give me something to hold on to, to remember when I was alone again. For I knew that without her, I would be.

I lifted the weight of her arm carefully to avoid aggravating her injury, and shuffled cautiously about to turn over. My shoulder was dead and I was sweating with the compressed heat of our bodies. She had me at the edge of the mattress and I tried to rouse her gently as I found myself nose to nose with her. 'Annalise,' I whispered a couple of times, but when she stirred a fraction, it was not to roll away as I had meant to encourage her, but instead she rolled further into me and put her arm back around me, and I felt her breath against my collarbone. I stiffened and tried again to wake her, to no avail.

After several minutes of staring into the darkness, thinking of how to get her to move over, I gave up and shuffled just a fraction to encourage her into my arms and stroked her hair gently as she made the occasional murmur. *God how I shall miss you.*

In the morning, our position had barely altered and when I opened my eyes, I was met with hers smiling up at me. 'Good morning,' she said, lifting her head.

'Good morning,' I smiled before a yawn interrupted it. 'Excuse me,' I said having cupped my hand over my mouth just in time and it was only then it struck me that I had pulled my hand out from around her and it suddenly seemed to have nowhere to go. 'Sorry, I—'

'For what, don't you like cuddling?' she said, frowning. I was not sure I had ever really cuddled anyone since my nursery days where I would often climb into nanny's lap. 'Um, I don't really know,' I said, too tired to consider a better answer.

'I can move if you want me to?'

'No. No, don't do that,' I said and she paused, then snuggled into me, resting her head upon my chest again.

'This is nice,' she said and I wanted to agree, but I was distracted by other thoughts that I did not wish to entertain, especially now, with her so close pressed against me. I had not felt such stirrings in what seemed like an age, and even then, it had not been like this. This strange and new affection I felt myself both drawn to and yet resisting. It puzzled me and reminded me of chewing on an unfamiliar food and trying to work out whether or not I liked it. I liked her, whatever else. Even if this tactile arrangement was a touch out of my comfort zone.

'You talk in your sleep you know,' she said to me a moment later and I could feel her cheeks shift into a grin.

'Do I? And what do I say?'

She laughed. 'Nothing I could fathom out, but plenty of mumbling.'

I felt relieved at that, although I wasn't sure why. What did I think I would have said? Something I would not want her to hear or know... 'Well, I do not think you talk in yours, but you have quite mastered the art of taking up the lion share of the bed space, even if you are the smallest.'

'I am not that small,' she protested. 'And anyway, I wanted to be next to you. I fear I am missing you before you have even gone away. Is that even possible?'

This warmed me. 'Yes, yes I think it is.'

She hugged me tighter. 'You will come back at some point, won't you?'

'Of course, I will,' I said, wondering how I would manage to stay away at all now. I had gone from being desperate to escape this place and now I felt an altogether different desperation emerging from a space I did not want to pay mind to. It seemed the more I tried to close my heart and repress it, the more it rebelled against me and opened a little farther.

'Well, I hope it shan't be too long, I think we have become quite attached. Is this what it is like to have a sister? I mean I have always thought of Poppy as a sister, but, well—'

'No,' I answered. *More like a sweetheart,* I considered, but those were not thoughts I was willing to share with her at all. Besides, she was innocent of such notions and I was not going to be responsible for altering them. 'So, what time will your Miss Lockheart be about to receive us? We should probably go as early as we might, for once my parents are back, the opportunity will be lost.'

'About ten-o-clock I believe. But if she is not, Mr Harrison shall know when to expect her.'

'Mr Harrison?' I said trying to place the name.

'Yes. He owns the bookshop in Ewell. It is where Miss Lockheart will be this morning if she still takes her classes in the same pattern.'

So that was why she went in there—to find Miss Lockheart perhaps. Why she came out without a book. 'So does Miss Lockheart work at the bookshop?'

'No. But Mr Harrison lets her use the back room to teach women their letters if they want to learn them. Her father does not permit her to use the church hall for that, only for boys, for he thinks it a bad idea to teach women such things.'

'Does he indeed.'

'Yes, she tries to counter his thinking by forcing Fordyce's sermons upon his notice, to no avail. But she has never let the obstacle stop her, even if she has to go about it a little more carefully.'

'Well, good for her. I think I shall rather like Miss Lockheart by the sound of her.'

'You shall, I am sure of it.

She was correct. I was quite taken with this serious looking woman of about thirty who dressed demurely and had a gravity about her countenance, and a frankness about her speech that was quite striking. Her warm eyes were all that gave away her kind nature, for her manner was pragmatic and business-like. But it was the greeting we received on entering the shop that had intrigued me. The elderly man I had spoken with only the other day, addressed Annalise with such warm familiarity, I was quite astonished as he emerged from his book cluttered counter, took his pipe from his mouth and greeted her casually, offering her tea, and realising that I was come with her, extending the offer to me.

'Thank you, Mr Harrison, but we are actually here to see Miss Lockheart if she is about today?'

'Just got in. Go straight through,' he said.

'Miss Tullier. It is you indeed. Well, what an age since I saw you last,' said Miss Lockheart brightly, who was distributing books to empty seats about the tables in preparation, it seemed.

'It has been a while. I hope I find you well, ma'am?'

She smiled. 'You do indeed. But how are you bearing up?'

Annalise nodded. 'I'm managing better, I think.'

'Marvellous news. Now, who is this you bring along?'

'My new mistress, Mrs Craythorne.'

She strode right up to me, smiled and held her hand out. 'Pleased to meet you, Mrs Craythorne. How do you do?'

'Well, I thank you,' I said, receiving her short, sharp handshake.

'Now, what can I do for you ladies? You will forgive me I hope, but I have ten minutes until my pupils begin arriving, so we shall have to be brief.'

'Actually, it is what we can do, I hope,' said Annalise.

'Oh? Have you finally reconsidered joining us?'

'No, sadly not, ma'am. But my mistress here has quite a significant contribution to make to the raffle prizes this year, for the harvest festival.'

'Well, that is very generous of you, Mrs Craythorne. I confess I have not yet put out the call for donations, but it is never too early.'

'It is not an insignificant number of things. I don't know if you would rather us convey them to the church hall for you?'

'Oh? Well, that is very good of you to offer. But father is out ministering this morning and my mother is laid up with a head cold, so you will find the hall quite shut-up. Hmm, are you sure you might not leave them with me and I shall convey them back later?'

'Well, we can if you would like, but you shall need a carriage to deliver them.'

She frowned and came outside with us to the coach where she took one look at the contents and declared that indeed, she would be grateful if we could convey them directly to the Rectory for safekeeping, and sent us along with a note to the housekeeper to make the necessary arrangements to store them in the interim.

From there, we went on to Old Mill Street to distribute the toys and were received with the warmth and kindness of old friends. We sat at the table with the Bartletts in a room too hot for the weather, even with the little windows opened. Annalise composing a list of the families with children and Mrs Bartlett and Jane apprising her of their number age and sex so that the toys could be appropriately allotted. It had taken Jane and her siblings an age to decide upon their own choices, their eyes wide with delight and their minds changing with each new inspection of their options. In the end, Jane settled on a toy theatre, and the boys a soldier figurine and a spinning top.

'Georgie will like this one,' Jane said, examining one of the options her brother had discarded. 'And Sarah will want the baby house, for she is always taking care of 'em.'

I looked up at the young girl and considered her to be about eight or nine years old. 'Well,' I said to her smiling, 'how about you help me arrange them accordingly?'

She nodded enthusiastically and I took the seat beside her on the upturned crates she was sitting on and began to compile them according to her instructions.

Once the list was complete and we realised we had enough to go around, Mr Bartlett fetched a barrow from the yard and the children filled it with the gifts and set about delivering them. It heartened me when we drove off down the lane to see them spinning tops in the street and jumping skipping ropes.

'You have brought more joy to this street in a day than these children have known all their years,' Annalise said as she waved out of the window.

'Thank you.' She took my hand in hers and held it there lightly. I looked up and smiled and thought her beautiful with the glow of joy in her eyes. The animation of her features, bright and effervescent. *And you have brought more joy to my soul, than I ever thought possible.*

When we returned from our errands, it was a quarter past eleven and I was glad that we had managed it all so promptly, so that we might have our last couple of hours' peace together whilst I was still at liberty. We were just gathering up the things we needed to take a picnic out to the lake when the crash of hooves descended upon us. I had thought to make quick out of the basement door thinking my parents home early, but just as we headed in its direction, a young lady emerged through it and announced herself as Miss Pascal, lady's maid, here to report to Mrs Craythorne.

'Miss Pascal,' I said surprised. 'We were not expecting you until Saturday.' I did not mean to sound so unwelcoming, I was usually more tactful, but all I could think about as she strode through the kitchen, in her impressive travelling dress and bonnet, was what her impromptu arrival meant to mine and Annalise's arrangements.

'Mrs Craythorne?' she said, looking me over and presumably distinguishing me from one of the staff.

'Indeed. Welcome, Miss Pascal. I hope your journey was—'

'Quite sufficient, thank you, Mrs Craythorne,' she said, bobbing a curtsy and I glanced at Annalise who was looking between us apprehensively. Had she too sensed that this marked the premature severing of our time together? I tried to think quickly. 'Miss Pascal, you must be tired after your journey, why don't you let Mrs Crawford—our housekeeper here—show you to your room and get you settled and we might meet this evening to discuss things further once you are rested and refreshed.'

'Oh no, Mrs Craythorne. I am not in need of rest, but ready to begin my duties at once. You have already been good enough to wait zee best part of a month for my arrival. You find me quite at your disposal.'

'No. I insist. You are to take some refreshment and rest beforehand. Mrs Crawford—'

'Very good, madame,' she nodded deferentially and Mrs Crawford swept her away towards the corridor and sent the footman out to fetch up her things.

I headed straight out of the back door behind him, quite forgetting the picnic-ware in my panic to quit my audience before the swelling tears began to fall.

'Eleanor?' Annalise called, running up beside me. 'Eleanor, slow down,' she said tugging at my elbow and I paused and brushed the tears from my face.

'I'm sorry, I had to get out of there quickly.'

'You are crying.'

I nodded, fearing that if I was to speak another word, I would not be able to stop myself from begging her to reconsider her place with me.

'Come, let us sit down.'

'Not here,' I managed, and we went off towards the periphery of the woodland where the house begun to fade from view. We sat beneath a shady birch and when the tears came thickly again, she huddled me up until my head was in her lap and she stroking my cheek as if soothing a disgruntled infant. It was calming to be so caressed. To feel her there so firmly in this moment, knowing I would soon wish to reach into it and pull her into existence from my memory. I could not cope well with that line of thought and so I focussed instead on tracing the pattern on her skirt with my fingertips as I snuggled against the softness of her thighs.

'Well, she seemed pleasant and keen,' Annalise said once I had recovered myself. 'I'm sure she will know all the fancy hairstyles and modes.'

'I care not,' was all I could say to this. *She's not you.*

She sighed and brushed my hair from my face. 'It saddens me too you know. Who would ever have thought we might become such friends?'

I did not want to be only her mistress or friend, that was the trouble. I had been trying to avoid acknowledging this fact for so long now that it was grievously sobering to disrupt the fallacy. But it was the truth I had hidden under so many layers of self-deception and avoidance and now I was to face the harshness of it, and I wasn't sure how I would manage.

When I returned to my chamber after dinner, I slumped into the chair and stared at the day bed which had been stripped of Annalise's bed linens and pushed back into its usual place beside the window.

I had endured a full recount of my parents' trip to Bourdon and all the particulars of the arrangements this weekend before leaving the table. It reminded me of all the reasons I needed to get away from here, reinforced my determination to set off on Monday and for the briefest reprieve, gave me the reassurance that it was for the best. And yet, within a glance of the derelict daybed, it was all undone. I neither wanted to stay or go. But there was no in-between.

If I stayed, Giles would pursue me and I would remain under my parents' authority and be forced to endure the kind of society I was relieved to have broken from at last. If I went, I would lose the only thing that really mattered to me anymore. The only thing that brought me joy.

I scratched about for a solution, but the only one was for her to agree to take Miss Pascal's place and come with me, and I realised now I understood her circumstances better, that in doing so, she would be placed in the same impossible quandary as I and would have to sacrifice what was essential to her peace. It was funny, but I realised that whilst she had no family, she had something like it, better perhaps. People who cared for her, truly. People who accepted her, fully. People who she could be easy with, always. It was no wonder she did not want to give that up when I knew what it was to be surrounded by people who never really saw me, less still, really cared. There were the exceptions of course, and it was in reflecting on them and what they meant to me, that I realised I could not press her and ask her to give them up.

It was in the midst of this melancholy that the door knocked and Miss Pascal came into the room bobbing a curtsey.

'Madame,' she said in that strong French accent I had paid no mind to earlier in the surprise of her arrival, 'I did not know what time you like to 'ave your toilette?'

'Miss Pascal,' I said wiping my face and sitting upright in my chair. 'Yes, I suppose now will do well enough,' I answered, getting up from the chair and supposing that an early night was best, given the early start of tomorrow's "big day". Although I knew as she stripped me out of my gown, that I wished only for the reprieve of sleep to relieve me of my thoughts.

Once I was set in my robe and soft slippers, my hair brushed down to mid-back and my cheeks slick with the shine of night lotions, I instructed Miss Pascal on my wardrobe for tomorrow and showed her about so she knew where to find everything. The atmosphere between us was stiff and unfamiliar, and though I could make no complaint to her diligence and proficiency, I felt disappointed by this return to such formality and wondered how we would go along together comfortably on our travels. For she was not just to tend my wardrobe; she was to be my nearest companion now and the prospect filled me with crippling lassitude.

So, to counter it and as a preventative measure to guard myself against changing my mind at the last, I had her start on packing up my trunks for the journey and having my winter wardrobe integrated into it, in order to make sure I was set for a long enough duration. This at least was in abundance, since I had never had it transported to Beddington after the wedding. In fact, so little was taken with me owing to the poor condition of the rooms and the house renovations, that I had not missed much and was grateful of the fact now. What little of my things remained there could stay there, and rot with the crumbling walls.

'Will you require your hooded cloaks, madame?' Miss Pascal asked, holding one up to me.

'Yes, thank you,' I said, wondering where I would be when the weather turned chill enough to require it next. Over the worst of the trials of this year, I hoped by then, whatever the geography.

When the trunks were packed and my bed turned down, I dismissed Miss Pascal, slipped beneath the blankets and felt the space beside me. I knew I would sleep ill tonight and fill my head with imaginings of feeling the weight of her arm at my waist and the mist of her breath against my skin.

Au Revoir.

September 1821. - Annalise.

It seemed odd to be sat back around the table in the servants' hall that evening, having grown used to retiring to Eleanor's side after dinner. The conversation poured over her as she gazed into her beer mug and watched the amber liquid fizzing to the surface. Will had insisted she join them in a mug and raised a private toast to her being returned to them at last. She wished she could share his merriment, but she felt altogether disjointed and preoccupied.

'Well, what do you think of the new girl?' he asked, referring to Miss Pascal.

'She's very fancy,' said Maggie thoughtfully.

'Seems a right stiff-rumped miss from what I've seen of 'er,' said Poppy, brushing crumbs off of the tabletop. 'She did put Jack in 'is place though when he tried at sniffing about her, so she's 'er 'ead screwed on, I'll give 'er that.'

'Well, I found her quite impressive,' Cal put in, which caused Annalise to look up and consider her point. She had been impressive, it was true. Neat as a pin with a manner and accent to match it. Pretty too she supposed, and confident, exuding the sense that she knew her job and her worth.

'Annalise?' Will pressed her.

'Um, she seems fitting, for the post I suppose,' she said vaguely.

'Not a scratch on you, though. I say your mistress has downgraded losing you. Eh, don't look so down in the mouth—the loss is hers. She should 'ave had the sense to 'ave given you the job after all the running around you've done after her these past weeks. But, I'm not complaining, we have you back at least.' He winked and drained his cup. 'Anyone for a top up?'

She shook her head. 'No, I think I'm for bed actually.'

'Bed? What kind o' welcome party will we 'ave without our guest of honour?' he teased.

'A party for one I imagine,' Poppy said, 'we're back to the kitchen now.'

'Now?' Annalise said puzzled.

'Aye, last of the wedding breakfast preparations,' she said, collecting up the empty mugs.

'Then I will come and help,' Annalise offered, rising from her seat.

'No. Cook says you're not to be back in the kitchen for now. Strict orders until the doctor declares you fit.'

'I am perfectly capable of scrubbing down—'

Poppy shook her head. 'Not yet a while, lass. You're under Crawford's direction till you're better. Now, go and get yourself off to bed for it will be all go up there tomorrow and there'll be plenty for you to do.'

She sat at the small table in her room, penning her letter to Gint absent-mindedly in the half light. Today at Old Mill Street had been the decider, seeing the happiness spread in just a morning. She planned to go back there at the next opportunity and take her measuring tape to measure up for winter clothes for them. Hopefully her fingers would have mended by then and she could sew again. Although it would have to be quick if she was to manage it in time for the turn of the weather.

When her letter was complete, she paid the hallboy thrupence to see it delivered first thing in the morning and then went off to find Mrs Crawford, to see if there was anything she wanted her to do; half hoping she would task her with putting out the lights upstairs so she might pop in to Eleanor and say goodnight. But she wanted nothing. Everything was in hand and she was to report to her in the morning for directions.

She should have been grateful for such an early reprieve, but she sunk into her bed feeling empty and off kilter.

In the morning, she was tasked with helping Mildred with the chamber linens, and whilst she was proving to be more hindrance than help, she was grateful to find an excuse to pop in to Eleanor.

'Good morning, miss,' she said when she came into the room and set down a fresh pile of cloths and towels for the washstand.

'Annalise,' Eleanor said, turning around from the dressing table and standing up.

'Well, look at you, how pretty you are,' Annalise said thinking that Miss Pascal certainly did know her stuff, whatever else. Eleanor was dressed in the utmost finery: Laylock satin with white lace trimming and an elaborate arrangement of her hair with a bead of pearls framing her face. She looked radiant. Impressive, she supposed, and glanced briefly over to Miss Pascal who had begun gathering up pins.

'Miss Pascal, if you could fetch my tea tray now, I thank you,' Eleanor said, dismissing her, and when she was gone from the room, she beckoned Annalise over and took her by the hand. 'Thank you,' she smiled. 'I'm to look the part and play the part today,' she said, rolling her eyes. 'Come, sit down with me a moment, will you.'

'I can't be very long. I am helping Mildred—'

'Do not let them overwork you, Annalise, you promise me? You need only say.'

'They are not, I assure you. I am of very little use to any of them at present, but I am trying. How goes it with Miss Pascal?'

Eleanor sat thoughtfully a moment before answering. 'As well as can be expected, I suppose.'

'Well, she seems to have done you justice this morning. No more plain chignon's,' she jested but the truth was it was taking everything to contain her sadness.

'Well, I rather liked my plainer looks; there was more time for other things then. All this sitting about in the mirror to impress people I care not a fig about, whilst—well...it will be over with soon enough.'

'You are anxious, don't be.'

'I am trying. It turns out that being the black sheep of the family can be a little taxing and well, now I cannot even look to a little champagne to help me through it. Oh, don't look like that, I shan't you know.'

'Well, you say black sheep, I can't help thinking you are more of a rare gem. You shall certainly outshine the bride today.'

Eleanor let out the beginning of a laugh then lifted her eyes and steadied her features. 'Well, I shall try to be worthy of your high praise and behave myself today, if I can.'

A frown crept over her brow. 'You are packed already?' she asked, distracted by the notice of the trunks piled up at the side of the wardrobe.

'Yes, well I doubt there will be much time to attend to it later on with the house full.' She sighed. 'That reminds me, I wanted to give you this,' she got up and took the copy of *The Libertine* from the side stand.

'I cannot take your book.'

'In truth, it is not mine to give away, I think it was Harri's, not that she would likely care for it now. But you may borrow it. Return it to the library when it is finished.'

'Thank you.'

She paused and held her gaze for a moment and Annalise wondered what was in her thoughts when she looked at her so ardently, as if the words were written behind her eyes but she refused to read them.

'Well, I had better not keep you any longer, and I am to be down to the coach by nine—' she said eventually.

'I'm sure it will go quickly and not be half as bad as you fear.' Annalise stood up and Eleanor rose simultaneously.

'I hope you are right.' She wrung her hands and then put them out. 'May I, may I hug you?'

Annalise smiled and stepped into her waiting embrace and sighed inwardly as she felt the warm skin of her shoulder against her cheek. She smelt sweet, of her fragrance waters she supposed and she inhaled the scent as if committing it to memory.

'If I don't get the chance to tell you so before I go, I just want you to know, I am thankful for everything you have done for me Annalise. Truly.'

Annalise squeezed her a fraction tighter before stepping back, kissing her lightly on the cheek and jumping back startled as Miss Pascal entered the room with the tea tray. She peered up at Eleanor who had also taken a step back a moment after raising her eyes to her in bewilderment. Perhaps she had heard her coming up the hall before she did. 'Well miss, I shall be off now, if there is nothing I might—'

'Thank you, Annalise. Don't forget the book,' she said with a look that said something altogether different. '*Don't forget me,' perhaps,* Annalise wondered as she exited the room, ignoring the suspicious glance Miss Pascal cast over her on the way out.

Once she and Mildred had finished upstairs, their next task was to arrange fresh flowers for all the vases to be placed in all the main rooms, both formal and guest accommodation. The farm hand wheeled barrows of pre-plucked flower bunches into the yard for them to transfer into baskets and they filled them to the brim and trotted from room to room filling the vases with fragrance and colour. It was a pleasant and manageable task this time and even though she worked at half the pace of Mildred, she was content to be busy and have somewhere to focus her mind, for it was constantly seeking to drift into some private matter or another. It had become heavy carrying so many secrets. She had never kept secrets from Poppy before, perhaps that was why she felt so out of sorts in containing it all. But she could not speak to her on these things. She did not want to confess to Poppy that Gint was her father, for the shame of it was too much, and she couldn't tell her of her other troubles for she could barely articulate them herself.

By lunchtime, the house was in pristine order and the set dining table looked palatial, she thought, as she stole a glance at it on her way back from lighting the pastel burners.

'You done now?' Will asked, meeting her in the staircase. He had been polishing the silverware until he saw her.

'Yes, I think so.'

'Looks pretty grand up there, don't it?'

'It does. Very beautiful.'

'Eh, you gonna tell me what's wrong, I know you're not yourself.'

'I'm fine, Will.'

'No, you're not. And it's no use trying t' gull me 'cause I can see it in your face. Is it something I've done?'

'No.' She paused on the stairs and gripped the banister to steady herself. The last person she wanted to fall apart in front of was he. But it was too late, his probing had been enough to tip her over the edge.

'Come Anna, come 'ere,' he said, putting an arm about her shoulders and guiding her to sit down on the step beside him. 'What's a matter, love?' he said, furnishing her with his handkerchief and squeezing her lightly. 'It's a clean one, I promise.'

She laughed at this and dried her face with it.

'That's better, I've missed that bonny smile.'

'I'm sorry, Will. It's just been an odd week. Lots to take in.'

'How so?'

'Can I trust you, Will?'

'Cross my heart and hope to die,' he gestured, drawing the shape of a cross upon his chest.

'I mean it. I haven't told anyone else this.'

'I'm in earnest. You can trust me with anything, Anna. Don't you know that?'

She nodded. 'I can't tell you the whole, but I found out the other day who my father is.'

He frowned and cast his mind back. 'I thought you said your pa was killed in the war whilst you were a bairn.'

'Yes, which is what I believed, what my mama told me. But it turns out he is alive.'

'Well, that's smashing news Anna—'

'No. No, it's not.' She shook her head and a hair pin slipped from it and landed on her lap. She picked it up and ran it through her fingertips. 'Do not think me cruel, but the man who it seems *is* my father, is not a good man, Will. In fact, I have spent my whole life hating him, without realising who he was.'

'You know 'im then?'

She nodded. 'I went to see him the other day. He asked to see me.'

'And how did it go?'

'I felt sick to my core. I cannot bear the sight of him. I am disappoint-ed and ashamed, Will. I thought my father was a hero, a good man, a man of honour and duty who was gone too soon. But this man is none of them things and yet his blood runs through my veins.' She traced the bluish line of a vein at her wrist with the tip of the hair pin.

'Listen, I don't know who this man is or what he's done, but I do know, that if there's one thing he got right in his life, it was you. And if he's not worthy of your love, then he must be worthy of your scorn for you are one of the kindest people I've ever known. And there ain't noth-ing wrong with you, girl. Do you hear me?'

She nodded and sniffed back another wave of tears.

'I mean it. I don't care who your father is. You're as perfect as they come and anyone who knows you will tell you the same. Come 'ere,' he said, squeezing her about the shoulders. 'Now, dry those pretty eyes and I'm gonna take you downstairs and fetch you a cuppa.'

She should have felt lighter after unburdening that ugly secret, she thought as she sat over the steaming coffee cup with Will trying at cheer-ing her up. But that was not the only one, and for the rest, she would not entrust to anyone. It was to be borne alone, for no one would understand it if even she could not. But his kindness and silliness did lift her mood a fraction and she set about her afternoon chores feeling a little less fragile. The rest of the day had proved too busy to dwell in any case. The wed-ding party arrived by one-o-clock and the basement sprang into chaos. First, all the footmen were saddled with trunk carrying, whilst she joined the housemaids in relieving guests of their bonnets, top hats and gloves and organising them in the cloakroom. Then she was tasked with show-ing the guest servants to their quarters and explaining house protocols to them. Then she assisted in the servery busying herself with a cloth, clean-ing up spills as the food trays coming up from the kitchen were deposited into the serving room before the footman carried them through to the long saloon.

When the final courses were on the table, she helped set the tea trays about the drawing room for the ladies to retire to and it was then, she caught the briefest sight of Eleanor as she came into the room chatting to someone on her arm and laughing at whatever they were conversing on.

She had not even noticed her as she slipped out of the room, but what difference would it have made if she had? She could hardly wave or greet her and ask her how it was going. They were of different worlds, and in this one, she was invisible to her.

The thing was, she had never felt invisible to her when they were together. Quite the contrary in fact. Like she had been a dear friend held in warm regard and not a mere servant to be overlooked and side-lined.

She saw nothing more of her at all as the day wore on. She was busy cleaning up the trails left in the wake of the wedding party and helping Mrs Crawford account for the fine china once it was collected back in that evening. She had been tasked with putting out the lights tonight, though. However, when the house finally settled enough to begin, she felt reluctant to find an excuse to go into Eleanor's chamber again. What would she say? There was no fire to quell and Eleanor was quite capable of stubbing out her own candles when she was ready to retire. Besides, she was probably in with Miss Pascal attending to her toilette and she had no wish to be reminded of the fact.

So she went off to the library instead and as she was collecting up the discarded day's newspapers, she had a thought that she might take them back to her room with her and sift through them before sending them down to the cloakroom for the bootboys. They'd certainly have plenty of need of them with the number of boots to polish in the morning.

She sat over the creased pages with a tallow candle and a pencil and scrap of paper, pulled the classified pages of them all out and disregarded the rest to a pile on the floor. Then she scanned them for places to let and places to buy; since Mr Harrison had said there would be enough to do so, it seemed worthy of consideration. She was determined to find the most sensible way to make use of this money and since she knew next to nothing about what would be most prudent, she knew she must make an effort in the learning if she wanted to use it wisely. A start was to know what the cost of things were, so she could begin on the sums. She scanned the pages, circling appropriate advertisements and set out a corresponding list of the various prices until she got a fair idea of the going rate.

When Poppy came in a little while later, arching her back and complaining of the ache in it, Annalise turned around to her and asked: 'Poppy, have you ever thought about any other kind of work? I mean outside of service.'

'I think only an 'ot brick is in order, not a new job, luv. Although, if it were like this every day, I might see your point. 'ow was your day?'

'Not too bad. Anyway, I didn't mean that. I meant, if you could do anything, or say, you won the lottery or something, what should you like to do?'

'Well, for a start, I don't play the lottery so that would be a surprise indeed. But no, you may be sure I'd certainly not waste my years in service. Cooking though, I like. Maybe I'd open a pie shop or sumin' simple where you're not at someone's beck 'n call all the hours. Where you can get to bed at a decent hour. Why, you been staking on the Hirsh's lottery?'

'No. I was just thinking about it, that's all.'

'Waste o' money if you ask me. Too many frauds and forgers, and the ticket prices are a pinch. Save your coin, luv. You'll only waste 'em and you don't wanna be getting into them kinda habits.'

Annalise nodded, folded the papers into a neater pile and stood up.

'Where you going?' Poppy asked, discarding her damp and stained apron to the basket.

'To get you a hot brick.'

As she sat over breakfast in the servants' hall, the table cluttered with the tacked-on place settings of the travelling servants, she felt an ache in her chest with every breath. She would leave today; be gone for weeks, months perhaps. She stirred her oatmeal around the bowl, breaking up the congealed lumps that had formed as it cooled against the china. There was nothing to be done now. She had made her choice. All that was left to do was bid her farewell. Something she knew she would put off if she did not get it over with and so she gathered up her bowl, stood up from the table and as she made for the scullery to discard it, Alfred caught up with her and held out a letter in his hand.

'This just came for you, Anna. Grantley said I was to bring it to you.'

She put down her bowl on the nearest surface and took it. 'Thank you,' she said and slipped it into her apron pocket and headed straight for the backdoor, through the yard and over to the stable courtyard where she perched on the low perimeter wall. She broke the seal and found inside it the draft for six hundred pounds bearing Gint's signature. She caught her breath and turned it in her hands and felt a sense of disbelief as she stared across the empty plains in a veiled mist of early morning light. *This is not any old morning though,* she thought as she looked up and caught sight of a migrating flock of pigeons overhead making patterns in the dewy veil of sky. *It is the morning my life is to change. The lives of many will change,* she thought with a spike of goose bumps rising at the nape of her neck. And since she could not bring herself to offer thanks to Gint, she directed the overwhelming gratitude rising in her, to her mama. Casting her eyes to the heavens she mouthed, 'Thank you, Mama. Thank you.'

There was much to attend to now and she realised she would have to ask one last favour of Eleanor before she departed today and see if she would grant her a day off so she might go to the bank and deposit it. She did not want the burden of its safekeeping for two weeks and besides, she could not be certain her usual half day would even be granted her given all the time she had been at leisure of late. Her fingers had started to regain some movement and she felt it likely they would be functioning again soon enough. Her wrist, although weak, was rotating with relative ease now and no swelling remained. She might even be back in the kitchen in a fortnight and if cook had her way, she would task her from dawn to dusk to make her point.

The cock crowed and surprised her. She folded the paper back up and stuffed it into her bandage. The basement had risen an hour earlier today to deal with the party of guests and she knew Mrs Crawford would be expecting her promptly.

She was set to her tasks alone this morning given all the other housemaids were tasked with supplying all the guests with warm water in their chambers, emptying the pots and answering the bell calls. She was to do her best with stripping the guest beds of their linens as the early departee's prepared to take advantage of the quiet roads. She was glad when she learned that Eleanor was not amongst them, and once she had finished with what was vacant on the top floor, she went to Eleanor's chamber, hoping to catch her before she went down for breakfast. As she knocked, she interrupted laughter and went into the room apprehensively.

'Annalise, come in,' Eleanor said, a peel of laughter still in the air as Miss Pascal sat upon a footstool rolling a stocking up the length of Eleanor's thigh.

'I can come back later, ma'am.'

'No, no. I shan't be long. Forgive me,' she said with a chuckle. 'The funniest thing,' she continued, recovering. 'Come see out of the window,' she beckoned her and pointed through the glass.

Annalise came up behind her and craned her neck to see the spectacle.

A gentleman was chasing what appeared to be an escaped goat from the farm who had made off with the gentleman's top hat in his mouth.

'Oh my,' Annalise said, realising what had happened. 'How did it get out and cross the ha-ha?'

'I have no idea. It's my brother Henry,' she laughed out again as he ran in circles cursing as the goat evaded him. 'You know, moments like these give me the impression our creator has quite the sense of humour.' She trailed into another fit of laughter before steadying herself. 'I daresay you would understand the comical sight of it better if you knew him. This is to be Cuddington's master one day,' she roared again.

Annalise wasn't sure whether to join her in the laughter or not with Miss Pascal's cold gaze upon her.

Eleanor wiped her eyes and steadied her breath, 'Sorry. It has cheered me up a little more than perhaps it should. Sit down, we are nearly done.'

Annalise lowered herself gingerly into the vacant chair and waited as Miss Pascal fastened shoe roses to her slippers and set them on each foot.

Then Eleanor said in French: 'Thank you, Camille, that will be all for now. If you would check with my sister what time we are to depart and make the necessary arrangements.'

Miss Pascal rose from bended knee, bobbed a curtsey and cast a studious glance over Annalise before leaving them.

'You speak in French now?'

'Oh, yes. Well, call me over cautious, but I had the idea that if we got into the habit of conversing in French, it might help to keep my plans more private—if we are overheard, I mean. I expect Giles shall be looking for me after today and I don't mean to leave any hints.'

'I see, but aren't all of your society taught the tongue?'

'Yes, it is not so much that, but...' she looked suddenly mindful of her words.

'It is the staff you wish to keep it from,' Annalise finished her sentence for her, feeling more disappointed than she knew she ought.

'Not only that,' Eleanor said quickly. 'I mean, even those taught in it rarely use it, not regularly in any case and so it will evade them better. One of the reasons I thought we might get to practicing it now, for I myself am very rusty—I am talking myself into a corner, aren't I? Forgive me, Annalise, I did not mean you of course. I know you are proficient in the tongue. I did not mean to offend—'

'I know. I am not offended. You must do what you think best to keep him off your tail. It's important. Anyway, how was the wedding?'

'Pretty enough I suppose, and altogether not as bad as I feared, but I am glad it's over with to be sure. The last twenty-four hours have reminded me of all the reasons I am to go...' she answered and then rested her gaze a little uncomfortably on Annalise's a moment. 'Have you been alright?'

Annalise nodded. It seemed favourable to an outright lie. 'Miss I—I hope you do not mind or think me taking a liberty, but I wondered, if I might ask a favour of you before you go?'

'Why of course, what is it?'

'I need a day off miss...I have some matters to attend to that I thought could wait until my next was due but—'

'Of course, when should you like it? I shall send a note to Mrs Crawford directly.'

'Thank you. Not today, we are too busy. But perhaps tomorrow or the next.'

'Very well.'

'Is it possible you could, send me on an errand of some sort, to justify my taking it early?'

'Well, I don't have any, but I am happy to say so if it will make you feel better about it?'

'No. I don't wish to embroil us in lies, I just thought there might be something—'

'Leave it with me, I am sure I can find something. Come to me after breakfast once I have had a chance to think on it.'

It turned out that it was Eleanor who came to find her out after breakfast, with the not so welcome news that she was leaving directly, for her brother-in-law had a wish to get back to Kent before the children grew over-tired and miserable in the carriage.

Annalise put down the stiff brush she had been using to brush down the footman's liveried jackets and led her into her own room where they could escape the distracted glares of Mildred and Mary, who had paused to listen in.

'I did not realise you would be going so soon,' Annalise said once they were inside the poky room that still held the dying scent of the tallow in the air from the previous night.

'I know, I had hoped I might have a little more time here,' she bit her lip.

'Well, it is probably for the best since you will likely be safely out of the way before your husband even realises you shall not be returning.'

'Yes, that is very true. Anyway, I have just spoken to Mrs Crawford and you are to have tomorrow off to go into town and run my errands which I did not have time to see to before my departure. You are to begin with posting this parcel for me.' She set a small box down upon the desk which still had the scraps of newspaper cuttings upon it, but she did not seem to pay mind to them. 'Then you are to go to Harrison's bookshop for me and procure me a copy of *Lovers and Friends: Ann of Swansea*, for when I return home next—for I know you shall waste no time in finishing *The Libertine* by then.' She smiled but it ran contrary to the glaze of sadness in her eyes. 'And finally, you are to take this draft to Miss Oliver's drapery and settle the balance upon my account with her. I have written the address upon the envelope so you may find it.'

Annalise felt her voice falter just a crack as she thanked her. She had been so thoughtful in taking the trouble and it overwhelmed her and for a moment she felt an erratic stream of thoughts overcome her. That she might just say, instead of thank you and goodbye; I have changed my mind, let me go with you. That she knew she was not as useful or impressive as Miss Pascal, but her French was immaculate—native almost—and that she would work so very hard at learning all the fancy styles of hair dressing and toilettes and— She interrupted the thought chain, glancing at the newspaper cuttings upon the desk. She had much to do here. She was needed here. The children of Old Mill Street would not have their winter clothes if she swanned off with her mistress till who knows when. Then her eyes fell upon the brick beneath Poppy's bed and she wondered who would go and heat it for her when she was next bent up in aches and pains after toiling in the kitchen all day. And when would she find the time for learning all the things she must about the prices of things and how to go about renting or buying or investing if she did not have Mr Harrison's counsel to rely on.

'Annalise?'

'Yes?' she said, looking up and finding Eleanor's perplexed gaze upon her.

'Is there something on your mind? Something you wanted to say to me before—?'

'No. I mean yes. I—I wondered if you might think of writing to me now and then, if you were minded to. To let me know how you are getting on and that you are well and safe from—'

Eleanor half smiled and brushed a strand of hair from Annalise's cheek. 'You may rely upon it. And I expect the same in return. Only you shall have to have a care to burn the letter's after and commit the return address to memory, and only memory for—'

Annalise nodded. 'I know. I would do nothing to compromise your whereabouts, your safety. You may depend upon it. You forget it was I that found you down here that night...' She trailed off, realising they had never actually spoken of that night beyond a passing reference.

'No. I shall never forget it,' Eleanor said, stepping in closer and gathering her up, this time, without asking. She pressed a kiss upon her forehead, pulled back and smiled at her with the glisten of tears showing in the corner of her eyes. 'Now, I must go. Au revoir my dear friend. I shall look to our reunion,' she said and then fled from the room so fast Annalise wondered as she sank onto her bed in a flood of tears, if she had really been there at all.

Restlessness.

September 1821. - Eleanor.

The carriage journey was close to unbearable. I had barely recovered my tears when I dashed up to vestibule to embark on the waiting coaches. Harri and Lord Osborne already sat inside, with a child each perched upon their laps. Nanny beside Lord Osborne and Miss Pascal, squeezing in beside me and Harri. 'Sorry, I forgot something,' I told them, trying to hide the raggedness in my voice.

Harri frowned and looked me over and I knew from her expression that she could tell I had been crying but did not want to press me in the company. Instead, she just smiled and placed a reassuring hand upon my lap. But I did not feel reassured. I felt—contrary to all my logic and reason—that I was making a grave mistake in leaving Cuddington. That I was somehow working against the grain of the instinct of my soul, whilst unable to reason it out. I needed to escape. To be out of the way of Giles and to be diverting the accompanying trouble that may arise from that direction, away from my parents; who I feared were quite at the end of their tether with me, and deserved to finally bask in the glory of their heir's handsome match and forget about the curse of my own.

Yet as the coach ventured further into the depths of the countryside; plains of farmland forming the view out of every window, I felt something tugging at me, growing tauter as I grew farther away and I felt an overwhelming desire to tap the roof, stop the carriage and find my way back. If it were not for my niece and nephew distracting me with their innocent smiles and easy uttering's, perhaps I might have given into it. But I had taken my share in entertaining them through the boredom of the journey, singing rhymes and answering impossible questions as best

I could. Such as, how do birds fly and why is the sky blue? Why don't I have a tail like the horseys? And my favourite of which was: why does Papa not get told off by nanny when he doesn't eat all his dinner up?

But when we finally arrived at Chauston, and I was sent off to freshen up from the journey, I collapsed onto the bed and left Miss Pascal to the unpacking, whilst I tried to hide from her the sobs that were heaving in my chest. Her attempts to console me, rather than improve me, made me worse, for she was not my Annalise and I wanted to say to her: it is she that should be here with me, not you. And then when I saw the confusion in her face, I felt guilty and tried harder at composing myself so that I might spare us both the discomfort. Then I had her set up the escritoire with ink and paper and set upon writing to Annalise to soothe the disconnection I suddenly felt in the unfamiliar room beneath the roof she was not under.

Dear Annalise,

I just wanted to let you know I have arrived safe and well.

I shan't return address this letter for obvious reasons, but if you look in the top drawer of my Tulipwood dresser, you will find inside it a note containing this address and the one I plan to move onto next. Please burn them after you come to know them and keep them safe and out of sight until then.

I shall write to you now under the pseudonym of Gabrielle Montmorency—yes, I thought that would make you laugh—and remind you to find some time for reading. You are still to remain in recuperation, you know (just because I am not there in person, it doesn't mean you can return to toiling for sixteen hours a day!). If you could direct your letters to the same then I hope they shall attract no undue attention—and yes—I am no doubt being over cautious again, but for now I fear I must.

Anyway, I shall write again soon. I just wanted to say adieu for now and tell you I am missing you already. I look forward to receiving word from you once your hand is recovered enough to take up the pen.

Yours affectionately, GM x

Even as I fell into pace with the quiet rhythm of the Kent countryside and the warming company of my sister and the children, the emptiness failed to shift. Miss Pascal had been efficient and attentive in her duties, but it had been a distant and perfunctory bond that had developed betwixt us and I knew it was I at fault. That I could only let her in so far to the space that was overflowing with the want of my Annalise. And even in the happier moments where Harri and I grew towards our old familiar habits and confidences, I felt a parallel distraction running alongside it, where the aching grew deeper and more tormenting with the passing days. I was certain that at some point the tides must turn and I would start inching towards improvement. But even when Sheldon had secured my affections and I had longed for him, it had not hurt like this, or proved so enduring.

This was different somehow, like the ache was not only in my heart, but etched onto my soul and I could not divert it. Like the pining I had witnessed in the puppies in the barn when Bess was away from them a while and only her return could placate it, no matter how many playmates and admirers they received in the interim with the farmer's children scooping them up in their arms caressing them. I wondered if perhaps I should write to the farm and ask Mr Morris to set aside one of the pups for me. I had changed my mind on seeing them, thinking it too difficult to set upon the training and nurturing of a new life when my own was up in the air and I was to be rattling around from one place to another, no fixed abode. It seemed unfair to subject a new puppy to such disturbance and unsettlement in its formative months and yet I could have perhaps managed it with a little more forethought. Perhaps I needed such a companion to pour my love into: One that could not disappoint me or fail to cheer me in such moments of utter melancholy as I felt every morning upon waking. And remembering. She was not here.

And it was not only longing I felt, but worry, anxiety over how Annalise was getting along. If she had remained to the bargain and not overworked herself. If her injuries were healing well. Her lack of written reply suggested she was still incapable of directing the pen and so I hoped that meant she remained out of the kitchen at least. If she had received her birthday presents and news of the celebrations I hoped had been merry in my absence. I remembered placing the very parcel of the vanity set in her hands for posting and wanting so much to give it to her then. To tell her it was for her. To tell her the birthday she was in dread of would not be so dreadful. But I could not. For if I had dared to start out in such a fashion, then I knew not how to prevent myself from saying other things that would rise to the surface and sit at the back of my throat as I tried to swallow them back down.

But ten days in Kent proved long enough to wrestle out this battle of heart and head beneath my sister's studious eye. It was time to move on to Lady W.'s society and try to find some equilibrium. It was a week earlier than I had planned it, but I was certain that she would not mind a bit if I turned up early. She had said as much in her correspondence, an open door.

And so, I kissed my sister and the children goodbye and set off for London with Miss Pascal, thinking for this, I was grateful to have her. To be able to go about freely now, unhindered by fears of lone travel and impropriety. And so, we conversed on our shared knowledge of the capital in reasonable spirits until I begun to feel the tug again, the sense of distance growing...aching, and before I paid the doubts forming too much consideration, I tapped the roof and gave the direction to the coachman: 'Turn around, sir, take us to Cuddington.'

Happy Birthday.

September 1821. - Annalise.

The remainder of the guests did not depart until Monday morning and it was upon this proviso of helping to see to the morning needs of the house, that Annalise was given leave to go off into town afterwards and set out upon Eleanor's errands. She made no mistake of the brief glance of contempt she caught from Mrs Simpson as she exited through the kitchen with her basket in hand, containing the parcel she was to convey to the post office.

However, her first priority when she arrived in Ewell was to deposit the banker's draft she had carefully concealed beneath her fresh bandaging this morning. And as she walked along the familiar parade of shops, she looked up at the signage for *Barclay & Bevan*, took a breath and opened the heavy door. She had walked past the place more times than she could count, but had never been inside it. Why would she? She had always lived on coin and never had a need for it. She was instantly met by the sight of a prestigious shop floor, carved walnut counters and pillars and oversized vases of floral arrangements, not dissimilar to the type she and Mildred had set about the house just the other day. She approached the counter and was met by a searching look from the clerk behind it. 'Can I help you...madam,' he said.

'Yes, sir, I thank you. I would like to open up an account today. I have a draft to deposit,' she told him, unfurling the fragile paper and placing it on the polished counter in front of him.

A glance at this seemed to sway him and he said, slightly more politely, 'Well, madam, if you would like to have a seat, I shall be just a moment,' he gestured to the chesterfield sofa with a bony, long fingered hand.

'Thank you,' she said and turned to retrieve her draft when he said:

'Oh, if you wouldn't mind, I shall be just a moment with this,' he said, picking it up and disappearing beyond a cubicle wall as high as his armpit and bent over what she presumed was a desk. A moment later, a pair of eyes rose above the cubicle wall, looked her over and disappeared again.

She felt inexplicably anxious and was relieved when the willowy looking clerk emerged from behind the cubby and led her over to a desk where the man who had peeped to glare at her was sat.

'Miss?'

'Tullier,' she added for him.

'Miss Tullier,' he said with an air of scepticism in his tone, 'I am Horace Knavelsby. Will you have a seat.'

She pulled out the heavily padded chair and sat down, putting her basket down at her feet.

'So, Miss Tullier, my colleague tells me you would like to open an account here today and bank this draft for six hundred pounds, is that correct?'

'Yes, it is, sir. I have been advised that it would be prudent to invest it here, that I would receive an interest on it.'

'Indeed, five percent. Yielding thirty pounds per annum interest.'

She was delighted at this news, and considered that she would have about two and a half times her usual wage without doing anything for it, nor upsetting the sum deposited whilst she figured out how she was to dispose of it. 'Well, that is very good, sir. I would indeed like to invest the draft, well, most of it that is,' she added, remembering that she meant to buy fabrics for the winter clothes at Old Mill Street and settle her debt with the stonemason first.

'Very well. We shall need to take down some particulars beforehand,' he said, fetching a ledger of some sort from his desk drawer. 'Now, we shall need your name, address, date of birth, marital status, occupation *if* applicable, and I shall need to see a notarised letter or affidavit from either your parish clergyman who holds the record of your birth in the parish register, or a person of known standing who may vouch for your identity.'

'I see. Well, I can furnish you with the details, but I own I did not know I required any paperwork sir. I did not bring any letters with me.'

'I see,' he sat back in his chair and interlinked his fingers, 'well, unless you have some way of proving you are Miss Tullier, I am afraid we will not be able to open the account. What is your address, madam?'

'I am kitchen maid at the Cuddington estate, sir—that is my present address.'

'And how does a kitchen maid come across a draft for such a sum?'

She didn't like the ingenuous inflection of his tone. 'That sir is private,' she said standing up. 'My draft, if you will,' she held out her hand.

'Miss Tullier, you do know that fraud and forgery is a very serious offence.'

'How dare you. I bid you hand me back my draft this instant for when I do bank it, it shall not be in this establishment!' She cast him a determined glare of outrage and he seemed unsure.

'Calm down, Miss Tullier. If you would just wait here a moment—'

'I will not wait here another moment. Now, hand me my property, sir, for I'm sure you too are aware that theft is a very serious offence.'

He held out the draft which she snatched out of his hand and fled through the heavy doors, opening it as if it was paperweight light and marched on to Mr Harrison's.

She was in floods of tears when she found him at his counter, mending books.

'I'm sorry, Mr Harrison, it is becoming quite the habit; me rushing in on you like this. I didn't know where else to g—'

'And you came to the right place,' he said, pulling out the stool and listening attentively as she gave him the whole.

'It is not your fault, my dear. You were not to know. You do not always need letters of verification if your name is known to them, but alas yours would not be. But that gave them no right to treat you like a criminal. That's bankers for you, the biggest criminals around, parading behind expensive tailoring and fancy neck cloths, thinking honest folk are as deceitful as they.'

'But sir, what am I to do with this now?' she held out the draft. 'It is useless to me if I cannot bank it.'

'Well, that may be easily resolved. You can either visit the parish register keeper and have a verified letter drawn up and sworn at a solicitor's offices, but it shall demand a fee, or we can go to Gint and obtain his vouching for you for free, if he will accompany you to the bank. They shall know of him there for this is one of their own drafts,' he said, examining the emblem upon the paper.

'No, no, not Gint. I shall pay the fee, sir. The only trouble is, I don't have time to manage all that today, even if I knew how to go about such business.'

'Well, you do know books. So how about you man the shop for me whilst I pay a visit to my legal man, have him draw up the documents for you and see about when we might manage to effect them?'

'Really? Would you, sir?'

'Of course, I shall. Now, I don't know how long it shall take me. He is a very busy man but his offices are just off the Cheam Road, so it shan't take long for me to find him out and see what can be done.'

'But won't he need the letter confirming the parish register?'

'Well, I should be able to vouch for you; I've known you most of your life and he has known me since I inherited this place. I hope he shall bear the same in mind when deciding upon your fee.'

'Thank you, sir, I am so grateful to you, but how am I to know how to manage the shop whilst you are gone?'

He pulled out three heavy ledgers. 'For a girl of your aptitude, it shall be a trifle. Accounts and balances payable here. Subscriptions in here, and cash purchases here, any orders made for which we do not have the stock, make a note of and advise them to call back in a fortnight to collect it,' he said, picking his hat up off the coat stand and putting it on his head.

And so it was, as Mr Harrison set off, she took his place behind the counter somewhat anxiously awaiting the next customer and trying to memorise the various ledgers so she would not stumble when her first came into the shop. Then she remembered that she was in fact her first customer, well Eleanor more precisely, and she found the envelope containing the coins and title of the novel she had asked her to procure. She scanned the shelves under both M and S, wondering what *Maria of Swansea* would be shelved under. But instead, she found it in the shop display window and when she removed it from its podium, tried to decide what to replace it with. Once she had found a copy of *The Village of Mariendorpt* in the stock room to put in its place, she entered the sale into the cash purchases ledger and dropped the coins into the money tin.

Is this what it would be like, she considered, this comfortable to become a trader. She had visions then of her own bookshop, then Poppy's Pie shop, then a Seamstress parlour and flitted between them as she envisaged giving jobs to her friends in Old Mill Street and training them up in the various skills. Poppy could teach them cooking, she sewing, and she could send them off to Miss Lockheart to take lessons in their letters and numbers. Then, she thought she would go into *Barclay & Bevan* and tell them where they may stick their stuffy account and interest, for when she did obtain the right papers, she was not depositing it with them. Even if it meant she had to travel farther.

When Mr Harrison returned an hour and a half later, she was in the middle of serving a customer; a lady in want of recommendations, and he doffed his hat to them both and left her to it as she continued in conversation with her. When she had made her purchases, she entered the sale into the accounts ledger and sent her on her way with three books more than the one she had come in for.

'Well, I think we might make a habit of this,' Mr Harrison tittered. 'Four books in one sale. I'm impressed.'

'Well, it is just as well, sir, for she has been the first customer I have had. Well, except a purchase I made on behalf of my mistress.'

'Yes, well, Monday mornings can sometimes be slow. We should pick up shortly when the ladies begin to promenade in an hour or so. Anyway, the good news is that I have spoken to my man and there is to be no fee to pay. The bad news, is that he cannot draw up the documents for signing until next week.'

'I see. I am very grateful to you, sir, for arranging it. The only thing is—I shan't have another day off for a fortnight at least and what am I to do with this in the meantime?'

'Keep it safe for now and you shall be able to bank it the very same day if we go to him early enough.'

'That's the thing, I feel in constant anxiety that I might lose the thing, such a flimsy thing it is that holds so much value at stake. I own I prefer coin. Is it possible, would you mind sir, keeping it for me?'

'Well, I can if you wish it, keep it in my own safe. But Annalise, I would rather not be responsible for it. Even I do not keep such sums in my own safe.'

'Surely it will be secure enough in there until then. Only I have nowhere lockable to keep it at Cuddington.'

He agreed and they sat over a pot of tea and chatted for a little while before Annalise realised the time and headed over to the posting office to relieve herself of the parcel, and then she headed for Mrs Oliver's and waited patiently at the unmanned counter to be served. *This too is a very fine establishment,* she thought, examining some luxurious brocade half stretched from its roll to display it. This was indeed the kind of establishment she could see herself in one day.

'Good morning,' came a voice from the back parlour eventually and a small middle-aged lady in a neat apron emerged from it and apologised for the delay, for she was in the middle of a fitting. Annalise handed her the envelope and told her she had come to settle Mrs Craythorne's account on her behalf and went to turn away when she called her back and said, 'Miss, hold on just a moment, won't you.' She went out to the back before returning and saying to her, 'Yes, it is as I thought it, there is no balance to be settled. Mrs Craythorne, you say.'

Annalise nodded and begun to worry if she had misheard her directions or made some mistake. She had been so distracted that morning she had come to say goodbye.

Mrs Oliver tore the seal and read from the pages, 'I see what it is,' she said and Annalise felt a wave of relief. 'It is for an order and it seems you are to place it.'

Annalise was perfectly mystified. Why had she not said so. She had no idea what it was she was to order when she was certain she had made no mention of it. 'I'm sorry, ma'am, I do not know what the order is to be.'

'Well, according to this, anything of your choosing up the value of the fifty guineas enclosed.'

'What? May I see it?'

She handed her the letter which did state: "items as my maid sees fit, to the value enclosed, for the winter clothes at Mill Street." It was then she realised what she had done and it brought her so close to tears she could barely speak. It had been one of her greatest anxieties in not managing to bank the draft today: That it would delay her procuring the fabrics she would need to begin on the winter clothing, although she hadn't a clue how she would sew them presently.

'Well, my dear, I don't mean to rush you, but I am in the middle of—'

'Yes, forgive me, ma'am. Um, well I should like to see some samples of your warm linens please.'

'Very good,' she said, and handed her some fabric swatches bound with a piece of thinly woven rope.

'The prices correspond with this list,' she said, sliding it across the countertop. 'Perhaps you would be so good as to decide on your selections whilst I unpin my lady and you may ring the bell when you are ready?'

'Yes, of course, ma'am, thank you.'

'Do make yourself comfortable and find a seat at the table.'

Annalise did as bid and felt her way through the patches of cloth as she looked up the corresponding prices. They were certainly not of the kind she was used to paying from the rag and bone man stalls at the pauper's market. But nor did she ever have fifty pounds at her disposal for the making up of them. So, she decided to make the most of the generosity that would afford them some more comfortable things. These linens were not scratchy and worn like the usual market offerings, and so she worked from feel more than sight, deciding that she would pick them the heaviest and hardiest choices for the thermal wear, the softest for shirts and underclothes and perhaps resort to the market for the trousers for the boys which would no doubt end with holes at the knees within in a week.

Once the order was placed and she was apprised that it would be delivered to her at Cuddington the very next day, she decided, checking the time as she departed, that she could still squeeze in a visit to Old Mill Street if she was quick. She might not be yet able to sew, but if she had the fabric and measurements, there was nothing to stop her cutting out the patterns with her good hand, in preparation for when she could.

It turned out, much to her surprise, she was to have her next day off sooner than she had expected, being given the news, when she reported to Mrs Crawford, that she was to have the day off for her birthday as was custom and the Master's tradition in affording thanks to his staff. She was not aware they even knew her birthday, then considered that Poppy must have told them. She was initially delighted at this unexpected reprieve, but had felt sorry that she and Poppy could not go off together and celebrate it, just as she and her mama once did. This had been the sour point of the realisation. She had reasoned that if this birthday was to pass in a day of working from dusk till dawn, at least it would not remind her so painfully of the cleft in it. Now she wondered what she would do with the empty day stretched before her. It was not like she could even put it to some pragmatic use and prevail upon Mr Harrison's legal man to get the business dealt in at such short notice, which would have been something.

But she tried to be grateful and merry as her friends sang the birthday song to her in the servants' hall at breakfast and Maggie let slip that Poppy had baked her a cake for after supper tonight. Even Will had surprised her with a posy of flowers and tied them with a pretty length of jonquil ribbon that he said was for her hair once she had made use of the flowers. It was nice they had taken the trouble, and yet she felt more alone than ever.

She decided to go back to her room once the basement had dissipated into the day's toil. She had meant to go back to redress out of her work uniform, but once she was there, she sunk upon the bed and found herself staring into the ceiling thinking first of bitter-sweet memories of birthday's past and then of Eleanor, wondering if she had quite forgotten her by now. If her and Miss Pascal had become friends yet. If she was feeling her absence as painfully as she felt it, even now almost a week had been and gone. What it was like at Grosvenor Square where she would be headed to next, according to the list of addresses she had left for her in the dresser drawer, which had already been committed to memory and burned in the kitchen grate.

Then, after an hour of subdued and thoughtful melancholy, she sat up, wiped her eyes and pulled from beneath her bed, her pattern box and the parcels of linen that had arrived from Mrs Oliver.

She had settled on cutting a new pattern every night on retiring, which had proved much earlier than she had been used to when acting as tweeny before, and maid for Eleanor. But she considered that today she could get much done, and beyond indulging in a walk about the park this afternoon, she could not think of any better plan. And so, she laid her patterns out upon the flags and her fabrics upon the bed and began pinning them in accordance with her measurement list. She was cutting coats out for the boys and hooded capes out for the girls when Poppy come into the room.

'What's the meaning of this on your birthday?' she said surprised. 'It's bad enough you sitting up every night at it, without spoiling your birthday.'

'It is already spoiled, Poppy. I'm not sure I'll ever look to it again in the same way.'

Poppy came over to where Annalise was knelt upon the floor, crouched down and hugged her. 'Come now, luv. I know what this day always was to you and I know 'ow much you miss 'er, but that doesn't mean the rest of your life is to be condemned to misery.'

'Then why does it feel as though it is?' she cried.

'Because you're sitting in this cell of a gloomy room whilst the sun is burning bright in the sky just waiting for you to make the most of it. What did your mama always say, eh—you are not always responsible for an un'appy circumstance, but you are always responsible for what you do with it.'

Annalise hugged her tighter and smiled as she envisaged her mama sat about the parlour table speaking the words.

'There we are. Now, what's say you go and catch some of that fresh air and see if it don't make you feel better?'

Annalise nodded and got up from the floor.

'That's the spirit. Now, are you gonna get changed or sit about in your scratchy work dress all day?'

Annalise accepted her offer to help her change and she picked out her best green day dress on account that it was her birthday and that she should walk into Epsom and spend a moment with her ma whilst she could. And then, once Poppy slipped out of the room, she came back in, saying she had almost forgot why she had came in the first place, which was to give her this letter from the post that came today.

She opened it and found a letter from "Gabrielle Montmorency" which instantly brightened her.

Dear Annalise,

Happy birthday!

I do hope you are well and that I shall hear from you soon, telling me as much. I have thought of you oftentimes as I sit about the lawns with my niece and nephew. And when I sit up at night reading, with no one beside me, I remember the sound of your voice. It seems so long since I last heard it. It is worse still because I don't know how you do.

So I had a thought—I have self-addressed a letter (enclosed) and thought you might send me a pressed flower from the garden's or some-such token by return, so that I might know you received my letters and you are well.

But my purpose for writing to you today is to tell you that you are expected at the church hall on your birthday, by the hour of three. I am sorry to ask it of you on such a day but since I was aware you would be at leisure, it was the only one I could be certain of. It is on some important matter over the harvest donations, so please make sure you go. Miss Lockheart will be in expectation of your coming and explain all.

And again, Happy Birthday, dearest. I hope your day is filled with joy.

Yours, as ever, affectionately, GM x

When she unbuckled the rectory gate and approached the church hall, she was surprised to find it so quiet. She had had much time to contemplate the purpose of the visit as she walked the quiet lanes and stopped a while at the cemetery. She had considered that perhaps Miss Lockheart needed some help in organising the donations, there were so many of them after all. Then she wondered if perhaps she wasn't selling enough tickets for them and needed her help shifting some more. Or whether she was holding an event to show off the prize collection to encourage purchases. What she couldn't understand was the urgency of it when the harvest festival was still some weeks off.

She knocked at the door but no reply came and when she tried the handle, it was open and she pulled it slightly ajar and called out: 'Miss Lockheart, Miss Lockheart.'

Then suddenly, she heard a raucous cheer of 'Happy Birthday! Surprise!' She jumped back out of the doorway a stride and held her hand to her throat in complete astonishment. But when she looked up again, Miss Lockheart was beside her, taking up her arm, leading her into the room where she saw the crowd of people about it and a table full of food platters. It took her a moment to recover her senses and work out that she was at a birthday party—her own birthday party—and as she looked about the well-wishers, she noticed they comprised of her friends from Old Mill Street, some of the villagers she knew on polite terms, a number of the ladies from Miss Lockheart's secret school room and, yes, even Mr Harrison was there. Her eyes filled with tears and she smiled through them as Miss Lockheart took to the pianoforte and they all sung the birthday song to her. She had never had a birthday party before. Never even been to one. She had seen them, at Hurley Street when Gint's daughter was still at home—she had never given a thought to the fact that this missish girl was actually a sister of sorts. She shook the thought and tried to compose herself as they all sung "for she's a jolly good fellow..." Then they clapped for her and the crowd broke up and Mrs Bartlett came over to her and hugged her. 'Well, don't you look pretty in your fine dress, I say! Happy birthday, Miss Anna. This is for you,' she said, holding out a small package.

'Thank you, Rosie, and thank you for coming, it is quite the surprise.'

'We've been looking forward to it all week. The kids have been driving us up the wall with the excitement. Well, aren't you going to open your present?'

She smiled. 'Yes, thank you,' she said and opened it up to find inside a silk wrapper a bar of olive soap. 'Oh, Rosie, you should not have bought me such an expensive gift. It is too much, I cannot—'

'Didn't I tell you she'd say that Thomas,' she turned to her husband who had slipped in beside them.

'Aye, you did and yes, Miss Anna, you must accept it, as it's a small token o' what we would 'ave liked to 'ave given you. You are such a dear girl and do so much for us. Let us 'ave our way and get to spoil you for a change, eh?'

She felt fit to burst with tears but restrained herself. To be given such a present from her friends that spent more time worrying about how to keep the fire burning and the children's bellies full, felt altogether wrong and humbling. She hadn't a clue what such a fancy soap would cost but she knew it above and beyond their means. 'Thank you, both of you. I am overwhelmed by so much kindness.'

'Come 'ere, let me give you a kiss,' said Mrs Bartlett. She squeezed her into a hug and kissed her on the cheek before saying, 'Well, we better not keep you to ourselves when you 'ave all these people come to wish you well. You go on now and enjoy your party.'

She turned about to find Mr Harrison waiting to embrace her and wish her merry and this was the style that continued for nigh on half an hour as she worked her way about the room, an ever-growing collection of gifts and embraces and it was all so very hard to take in. To receive.

When, eventually, Miss Lockheart gave up her place at the pianoforte, Annalise went straight over to her.

'Miss Lockheart, I cannot believe you went to all this trouble for me. I am sure I don't know what to say.'

'Well, I would happily take the trouble for you, but I own I cannot take the credit. It was your mistress that asked me to assist her in the planning of it, and who has paid for it all.

Eleanor? She was baffled. 'She did?'

'Yes, she asked me to pay a visit to her and, oh and to be sure I don't forget, tasked me with giving you this.' She turned about and lifted a large gift-wrapped box from on top of the piano forte and presented it to her, 'She was very sorry she would miss your birthday and wanted to make sure it was a special day for you all the same.'

An involuntary tear rolled down her cheek.

'Oh, come, dear. This is a merry day,' Miss Lockheart said, squeezing her gently by the elbows.

'I know. I am just, everyone has been so kind and so very generous, I—'

'Well, it is fitting, for that is what you have been to every one of us, and we do not forget the fact, even if we scarcely have the opportunity to celebrate in such a style. You deserve it my dear. So, enjoy it.'

She turned her mind to doing so, even though she was struggling to contain the overwhelm. It was true, whenever did her kind of folk have an opportunity to be so merry, she considered as she watched the children of Old Mill Street prancing about the hall to the music of the folk band that had just started up. Some of them were sat at the table enjoying sugar plums and cakes. They had likely never even seen such delights before, she was sure. So, when Mr Harrison invited her to dance, she took up his offer and gave herself permission to feel the joy that she saw in everyone else's smiling, happy faces. It was contagious, and as she spun and reeled about the floor with her friends, the more the feeling allayed all those that came before it, and she found herself as light as air.

When she stopped to catch her breath, she was tapped upon the shoulder, 'May I have this dance,' said Will in formal style and she was astonished to see him there, and notice Poppy and Maggie, waving from beyond his shoulder. How was it possible, she wondered, to permit her the day off was one thing on her birthday, but another three of the staff when the family were in residence. She flung her arms about them all and said: 'You knew about this too?'

'Aye, we did.' Will winked.

'But how?'

He tapped his nose. 'You gonna keep a fellow waiting with your an-swer?' he said, gesturing to the dancing and she took up his offered hand and re-joined the merriment.

They returned to Cuddington that night by hired hack, for there was so much to bring back, it could not be carried such a distance on foot. Besides, their legs would likely have been unable to carry them the walk having danced so many hours and drunk so much ale and wine. For Eleanor had thought of everything, and there were all sorts of choices on offer, and whilst Annalise was not much inclined for anything beyond a mug of ale, she had entertained the offer of a couple of glasses of wine and had danced an extra hour on account of it. They had even had fire-works lit into the sky just after sunset and it seemed that everyone there became child-like with awe at the spectacle of it.

When they returned through the basement, they were all three of them met with disapproving glances from the rest of the staff who saw them in passing. It was to be expected she supposed, the resentment of those who had had to work extra to cover the duties of they who had been dancing the day away.

'What's up? Eh, don't pay no mind to those sour-pusses,' Poppy said audibly enough to be overheard.

Annalise cast her gaze to the ground. 'Poppy,' she said quietly. 'Shh, the wine has loosened your tongue.' And she pulled her on towards their room as quickly as she could.

'Well, she's right enough,' Will said as they came into the room, him carrying the lion share of Annalise's gifts for her.

'They don't mean it Will, they are just tired from the extra workload and—' Annalise said and sat Poppy down on her bed.

'Are behaving like jealous misers. It's yer birthday for god's sake,' he said, and set down the boxes on the table. She had quite forgotten the newspaper cuttings and realised when she looked up that he was inspect-ing them. 'You looking to rent something?' he said, holding one of the clippings up.

'What?' said Poppy sitting up from unlacing her boots.

'No, no. I was just trying to work out the cost of things,' she said, crossing the floor and taking it from him and sweeping up the rest of the pile. She was obviously not the only one who could read down here and it had been clumsy of her to leave them about like this.

'I told you to leave off that lottery gaming,' Poppy interjected. 'It's filled your 'ead with wishful notions. Like's o' us can't be thinking of renting on our pay.'

'You're right. I got carried away. Thank you, Will, for carrying them for me,' she said, offering a hint that it was time he said goodnight, and accordingly, he did so. And whilst Poppy got undressed, she began distributing her gifts from the tabletop. She had been truly overwhelmed. She put her bar of soap upon the washstand, deciding she would cut it into halves tomorrow so she and Poppy could have their own piece. She put the wax candles from Miss Lockheart into a box beneath the bed—they would come in handy for the sewing when she was ready to undertake it. She put her new book from Mr Harrison upon the bed-side shelf, and with it, Eleanor's new acquisition which she planned to deposit into her dresser drawer tomorrow when running an errand up there. Poppy's gift: a fine pair of Worsted stockings, she folded away neatly. And Eleanor's which she knew was in the large box Miss Lockheart had given to her earlier, she felt self-conscious of opening in front of Poppy. She waited up reading a while until she heard Poppy snoring. She only snored when she was in her cups, which was not very often at all thankfully.

She put down her book soundlessly, lifted the box and carried it over to her bed and carefully untied the bow about it and lifted off the lid. Beneath it laid a layer of paper and beneath that a bulging layer of white fabric with pink buttons. She lifted it carefully out and spread it the length of her bed, for it was heavy and voluptuously layered. Then as she unfolded the sleeves, she made out the shape of a beautiful pelisse with a high collar at the back, beautiful thick pink frogging and sleeves a la mamelouk. *It is beautiful and fine...and not made for the likes of me,* she considered as she flattened out the fold lines and edges. She was used to her heavy wool cloak in colder weather, which was not elegant at all, but did the trick and at least it suited the rest of her wardrobe. In this, she would be laughed at, she felt sure. She peered back into the box and found another small, wrapped parcel and out of it came a fine horsehair brush and mirror set in ivory with a painted gold filigree pattern on the back. They were beautiful and well-made and she unpinned her hair with one hand, and run the bristles through a length of it. It reminded her of when Eleanor had brushed out her hair and she felt instantly choked.

She had gone to so much trouble and expense for her, so much planning and organising covertly and yet she would have traded it all in exchange to be sat back in the easy chairs by the fireplace, conversing, reading together. She swallowed back her tears, set everything back in its box as carefully as she could, and put it back on the table. She would need Poppy's help tomorrow to lift it to the cupboard top for there was no room for such a large box beneath her bed with all of her mama's things and the sewing parcels pushed tight beneath it. And when she carried her light over to the bedside, she saw a note upon the blanket that must have fallen out of the box.

'Dear Annalise, I hope you have had a very special day with your friends. I thought that since you were turning your mind to winter clothes for your friends, I would follow suit with my friend. I hope you like it. Any necessary adjustments, Mrs Oliver has agreed to undertake for you since I did not have you present for the measuring. E x

She lay down on top of the blankets and held the little note card to her chest and sighing deeply before leaning to turn out the lamp, catching sight of Will's flowers sat in a chipped mug of water with the pretty ribbon tied about the circumference; a vibrancy of colour in the otherwise colourless room.

A mystery benefactor.

September 1821. - Annalise.

A week later.

After waiting anxiously for the opportunity as she spent days dusting, scrubbing and polishing upstairs with Mildred, Annalise finally set off for Mr Harrison's this morning in her fancy new pelisse. It had been an intentional decision to wear it, arising from the unpleasant memory of her treatment at *Barclay & Bevan,* and since today she was to go to a rival bank with Mr Harrison once they had signed the papers at the legal man's office in the Cheam Road, it seemed a fitting choice. Even if she did have to smuggle it out in her basket and put it on in the woodlands to escape being noticed by the other servants. Poppy had declared it a work of art when she tried it on for size, and said she would have no hesitation wearing such a lovely thing. But she feared the rest would either find it ridiculous or think her haughty, and she wished for neither response.

But it had all gone smoothly enough today and she did not know if it was owing to her fancy dress, Mr Harrison's presence or whether *Smith & Hobbs Provencal Bank* was formed of better mannered clerks; but her treatment was congenial and the process smooth and timely. And the clerk soon announced she was now an account holder, furnished her with a little book and some papers, and asked her if she would like to bank her draft and invest the sum. She agreed to invest five hundred and ninety pounds of its value and asked to withdraw the excess to which the clerk began counting out paper notes to the value of ten pounds. She peered at the wafer-thin paper upon the desktop and said to him: 'Sir, if you please, I should like coin, not paper.'

He looked up and she could see the look of incredulity in his face, although he seemed minded to keep his tongue and say only gently, 'Well, of course, ma'am, if it is your wish, but you know the paper is just as good and much easier to carry about.'

Yes, and much easier to lose or misplace, she thought. Besides, how could they be commensurate, paper was paper and coin was real gold, silver and copper. And what was more, the tradesman she bought things from were of much the same mind. She had never in all her years seen Mr Tubbett of the meat mongers stall presented with paper in place of coin, nor the shoe mender or rag and bone seller. She could imagine having as much trouble trying to shift these paper promises at the market as she did in getting the bank account at *Barclay & Bevan.* With the exception of the stonemason perhaps, who was to have the lion share of the money, she considered. But even he might suspect her of some counterfeiting were she to present these paper notes, having already agreed instalment terms with him. But good solid coin that could be felt and counted in the palm could not be so suspicious. So, she insisted that she would indeed like the ten pounds in coin and watched him twist his thinned lipped mouth into a contrived smile as he disappeared from the desk a while and came back, counting coins into piles.

She was happier with this arrangement and even though her purse was over-stuffed to the point of the seams tautening ready to split, she felt a sense of reassurance that she would not get into any further bother now. She stuffed the weighty bulge into the pocket of her new pelisse and kept her fingers curled around it as they walked the journey back to Harrison's.

She had wanted to do something nice for her old friend now she was finally able to. His help, as ever, had been indispensable and generously given, and for a change she was in a position to reciprocate. But he had already closed the shop to accompany her this morning and she was only on a half day leave. *Next time,* she thought. *Next time I shall see about taking him to the old inn and having a dinner in one of the supper rooms at my expense.* They could pose as father and daughter and nothing could be suspected if she wore her fancy coat and ribbon in her hair. Besides, he had been the nearest she had ever come to knowing a father, so it was not such a long stretch of the truth. So, she fixed the date with him and parted after a quick cup of ale and set off to the stonemason's with her sagging pocketful of coins, which she was relieved would soon be lightened for her going.

'Good day to you, sir,' she said when she came in through the door. I am here to make payment upon my account. Well, to settle it in fact.'

'Morning, miss. Fine day, isn't it? You look very fine too, miss; if you don't mind me saying so.'

Annalise smiled, 'Yes, Mr Gadsby, it is very sunny out there,' but unlike that of her admirer, her smile was limited to one of civility. She knew the stonemason's son had taken a liking to her that was beyond common courtesy. She knew it had been on that account that the option of instalments had been accepted in her case, when this facility was usually reserved for persons of greater means than she. She was grateful for the kindness, but she could not return it, not in that way alas. She was in no mind for entertaining such ideas and certainly not to one so above her touch. Whatever *he* wanted, his father would surely have designs upon a woman of class, or at least birth... Strangely; it occurred to her, rather resentfully now, that she *was* of his class, above it perhaps in terms of her 'gentleman' father. Although she was illegitimate so it answered for nothing.

Her illegitimacy had always felt to her a point of shame. Now she was grateful for it. She could deny any familial connection to Gint forevermore because of that fact. When it come to bearing shame, her relation to him was the greater of the pair. She knew she must one day confess the matter to Poppy and that there would naturally be questions over her sudden change in fortune, but had no need to widely state whom her father was, only that he had settled on her.

'It is Miss Tullier, isn't it?' said Mr Gadsby eventually. He had been thumbing through ledgers and frowning for a while now.

'Yes,' Annalise nodded. He knew full well what her name was, he had at length discussed the French origin of her name with her on her last visit, holding her up nigh on ten minutes, telling her how unusual it was and how well he liked the ring to it. If this was meant as some ploy to keep her here longer or illicit some further conversation, she did not appreciate it. She had much left to do with this precious morning off and half of it had already elapsed, so she was minded to deal in this matter swiftly and get on with it. 'Sir,' she said, watching him flicking back and forth, frowning and biting his bottom lip. 'Is there something wrong?'

He looked up from the page he had been tracing with a finger. 'Sorry, Miss Tullier, I am having a little trouble working out your account. Tell me, when did you last come in to make a payment?'

She searched her memory. 'Well, exactly two weeks ago.'

'Yes, that's what I thought.'

'Is the payment not recorded, sir?'

'It is recorded. I did it myself.'

'Then forgive me Mr Gadsby, but what is the issue?'

He scratched his head. 'You don't seem to have an outstanding balance; your account seems to have been settled, in full.'

'What?'

'Yes, it seems a payment for six pounds was forthcoming on the very day of your last visit?'

'But sir, I do not understand? Forgive me, but perhaps you made a mistake in your recording it in the book—' *You certainly were distracted enough,* she thought privately.

'I trust you are not aware of it?'

'I would not be here if I was, would I?' she said a little more sharply than was usual of her manner. She felt a pang of regret for it, realising the injury in his eyes as he glanced up a moment before returning them to the page.

'No, no, of course not. Will you mind waiting here for just a moment? I will see if I can find out what has happened.'

'Yes, of course,' she said more kindly, remembering herself. It was likely a simple oversight she supposed. There was obviously some error to answer and he perhaps wasn't even to blame for it, else... She shrugged away a thought that was fast forming in her mind but far too outrageous to pay any consideration to. Although he had been very particular in his attentions to her, she could not imagine for a moment that he would do such a thing; stage this mishap in order to write off her debt? It was a ludicrous notion, ripping off his own father to make up to her. No one would do so contemptible a thing, surely? Certainly, any such behaviour would have precisely the opposite effect of what might be intended and disgust her quite marvellously.

She shuffled about impatiently, waiting, staring at the polished stone and marble headstone examples about the place. Then she remembered suddenly, admiring the copperplate lettering upon her mother's headstone just last week and realising that although it had been her original choice, she had changed it to the plainer style upon understanding the extra twenty shillings difference it would make to the sum. And yet she had received the copperplate lettering all the same...

Now she scratched her head, wondering how she could have failed to realise it before. She had been distracted the day of her birthday, so much in a head full of thoughts and memories, that finer detail had not been a feature of them. Perhaps, had she not been so overwhelmed at seeing, for the first time, the headstone in place, she might have thought about it. But she had not expected to see it for another few weeks yet and there it was in place, as she picked her way through the other moss covered and sinking stones. Standing out amongst them, just as she had so fervently imagined seeing it, stood brilliantly gleaming in the morning sunshine marking the spot. Its polished façade with her mother's name emblazoned on it. She should have realised it before; this discrepancy. Paid it some mind before now. Queried it and attempted to see what could be done. Perhaps she could pay the extra now, or the mason might consider dropping some of the interest for his part in the mistake? But she had not considered it at all. She was so caught up between raptures of tears of both pride and then sorrow at the sight of it. At knowing that her mama was laid to rest in a style that befitted her, even if she was denied living out her years in such a way. That she would never be forgotten to the world, even once she herself was gone from it. That of all things that played out in her thoughts that poignant day as she gathered flowers to lay, she had paid no heed to the detail of the lettering beyond thinking it all so beautifully crafted.

'Well, Miss Tullier,' he said, coming back into the room now. 'It seems the account was settled by a person wishing to remain anonymous.'

'Excuse me, sir, but I cannot see the likelihood. There must be some mistake.'

'I know. Quite extraordinary, but I've had it from my father's own lips, he banked the notes himself. It seems you have friends in high places Miss Tullier.'

She rolled her eyes without meaning to be so explicit. She had thought better of him than to stoop to such attempts to win her. It was an absurd length to go to whether he could afford to take such liberties or not. 'Really? Well then, I would like to speak with your father directly and know for myself who this person was?'

'A Lady, he tells me. Didn't want her name given; expressly wished it to remain anonymous.'

She frowned at this. If he meant to throw her off the scent, this line was even more unlikely, she considered. Even if she was open to the possibility of this mystery benefactor, then there were only two people she could think of her acquaintance with the means to discharge such a debt and neither were ladies. It would not be Mr Harrison for he would not have resorted to secrecy. Either—she shivered at the thought—it was Gint, or this lad was scheming. She did not like either prospect well. Then she considered Eleanor's generosity but remembered she knew nothing about her mama's resting place or her debt with the stonemasons and so she dismissed it and reverted to the former possibilities.

She left the stonemason's in a miasma of muted fury. No closer to resolving the mystery and uncomfortable with either choice of benefactor. Gint's direct involvement would have felt the ultimate of insults and Mr Gadsby Junior, she supposed she would not have to see anymore at least.

She was annoyed too that she still carried around a heavy purse full of Guineas that was meant to be two thirds empty now. It sagged in her skirt pocket and hit against her thighbone with each stride. She felt vulnerable carrying such a sum into the slums with her as she journeyed over to Old Mill Street to see the Bartletts. If she did not think it would attract unwanted attention or expectation, she would have emptied it along the journey, Guinea by Guinea to begging bowls and street urchins as she passed. But she was too frequent a visitor to these parts not to put herself at risk if she was thought to be of means. She had already taken a care to remove her Pelisse and put it back in the jute sack in her basket to disguise it. Which was a relief on account of the weather too, for there was no need for a coat at all on such a day as this and she had been sweating beneath its weight all morning. So now she was left with two things of great value to protect through a walk that was always thick with footpads and swindlers, but where she had always been safe to walk about in perfect anonymity.

Besides, as tempting as it was to drop the coins into a beggar's palms, she considered that she must also be prepared for the possibility that this mystery may yet be resolved, and when it was, she would be ready to settle the sum to discharge her debt. Of course, if this proved to be Gint, it left her in a quandary for she wanted to offer him no consideration whatsoever, nor permit him the satisfaction of knowing that he had paid for half of the handsome stone memorial. Her mama would surely turn in her grave to know it. To expect him to secure his daughter's future was one thing, but to insult her from beyond the grave with his coin would be quite another.

Anyway, she could come back with smaller coins next time that wouldn't cause any suspicion or particular interest to the beggars or market sellers. And she was sorry that she hadn't thought to ask the bank clerk for just one of the guineas made up in shillings, so she might stop and get her friends the usual supplies. But she had taxed him enough with even this request, without provoking more disapproval. Although she regretted that she would come empty handed today and had decided to see if she might slip a few of the coins upon the fire mantle without Rosie noticing until after she'd left.

It had been a short and sweet visit, but she was glad to see how well they were doing and equally as glad to have arrived back at Cuddington ten minutes before she was due, leaving just enough time to put away her Pelisse and coin and slip into an apron before she would be expected to join Mildred in the remaining brass polishing upstairs. But as she was checking the time on the stable clock tower as she passed it, she paused and frowned a moment, certain it was Miss Pascal she recognised directing the groom and footman in unloading the coach. Did that mean, could it be?

She turned about and saw that yes, it was Eleanor who was approaching the tourist entrance just ahead of her, bonnet swinging from her wrist and her curls dazzling like shiny conker skins in the sunlight. Without thinking, she called out, 'Eleanor?' and she turned around instantly, broke into the widest smile and came running back in her direction and threw her arms about her.

'Annalise!' she shrieked, squeezing her into an embrace and burrowing her face beside her ear and saying, 'Oh, how I have missed you, my dear, dear, friend.'

Annalise smiled through her tears, pulled back to look at her and then kissed her on the cheek and held her by the hands, lightly. 'I have missed you too! But what are you doing here? Are you breaking the journey to London? How long shall you be here for?'

Eleanor fell into gentle laughter and said, 'One question at a time if you will.'

'Forgive me,' Annalise said beaming bright with excitement, 'I am just so surprised to see you. I thought it would be weeks, months perhaps...'

'So did I, until I realised how insufferable it would be to be so long without the company of my favourite friend.'

Annalise laughed off her astonishment at this answer for it seemed both too implausible to be true, but also in such affinity with her own feelings that it seemed absurd to doubt it. 'So you mean to stay?'

'For now.'

'But what about your husband—'

'Well, I have decided that I shan't run from him, if it means that I must run from other things I have no wish to at least.'

Annalise smiled and gathered her gloved hands up in her own and pressed a kiss against them.

'Your hand is better? You can use it now?'

'Yes, it is only my fingers that are limited, but even they are improving,' she said, demonstrating it with a wiggle of them. 'It is my grip and coordination that is poor, although I can just about scrawl my name now, in the style of a child's hand, anyway.'

Eleanor laughed and lifted her less heavily bandaged hand and pressed a kiss upon her bare fingertips, which shocked Annalise and she

withdrew and looked about herself to make sure no one else had witnessed her mistress behaving so. She could barely imagine what the upper
servants would make of it, less still the Ashlyn's had they been passing the
window that very moment. She caught sight of Miss Pascal in the corner
of her eye but since she was back facing her, felt sure she could not have
seen it.

'What, what is it?' Eleanor said, searchingly.

'Nothing, I'm just being silly. I have had a strange morning and it has
left me in a puzzle, that's all.'

'Oh, well, how about we go inside and you tell me all about it.'

'I can't, I'm sorry. I am to be back to my duties now. Mildred will be
waiting for me and I—'

'Very well. What hour can you be free?'

'About ten or eleven perhaps, depending on what Mrs Crawford—'

'Come to me when you can then, whatever the hour. There is much I
wish to talk to you about. But for now, I am sure I must face a hundred
and one questions from my parents, so if you will excuse me.'

'Yes, yes, I will come as soon as I may.'

'Until this evening then,' Eleanor smiled and went on into the house.

The Abigail's Apprentice.

September 1821. - Eleanor.

It felt good to be back beneath the same roof as her, even if I did have to wait until a quarter past eleven until she finally came to my room. It was worth the wait to see her at last. I pulled her into my embrace once more, as if to convince myself I was not imagining it, like I had all the other nights in Kent. Then, I invited her over to the fireside chairs and we slumped into them with the familiarity we'd grown used to.

'So,' I said, still beaming, 'tell me how you have been in my absence?'

'I have been alright. It has all been rather busy for one reason or another. I want you to know how very touched I was by all the pains you took to make my birthday so, special.'

'You are special to me, Annalise, and I wanted you to have a reason to remember it fondly. Even if it wasn't quite like the ones you have grown used to. I only wish I could have been there.'

'I shall remember it very fondly. It was my first birthday party and so it shall be hard to forget. And it was not just me you brought happiness to—my friends, the children...they had never seen the like or been so merry. So many smiles, such laughter and gaiety in their faces. I thank you for that. But the gifts Eleanor, you gave me too much—'

'Did you like them?'

'Of course, they are beautiful—'

'You are beautiful, Annalise, inside and out and I have ached to see your smiling face every moment of our separation. It is the only thing in this world that brings me joy. That is why I am here. Why I could not stay abroad.'

'I have been tormented by the same misery. I did not realise it was possible to become such firm friends in so little time. I am glad you are come home. Truly.'

It heartened me to hear the words, to see the truth of them in her eyes as she spoke them. But I knew she did not understand the extent of my regard and perhaps never would. Her love was innocent and sisterly in devotion, mine was growing into something else out of all proportion to anything I had ever known. 'Well,' I said more seriously, 'I am going to be honest with you, Annalise. I have not come home for the sake of it. I have returned to make one last try at convincing you to spare us both the need of separation, and offer you the post of lady's maid once more.'

'But Miss Pascal?'

'Is very good at her job. Excellent perhaps, which is why I want to keep her in my employ to teach you, properly, so you may learn it until you feel confident about it.'

'You would do that for me?'

I would do anything for you. 'Yes, but only if you want it. I don't want you to say so because you feel in anyway obliged—I want to offer you the chance to flourish, Annalise, and if I thought you would accept that alone, I would have it my way and take you on as just my companion, which I shall you know, if you would prefer it.'

'You know me too well. I should not prefer it at all. You know I like to be useful. Anyway, I do not feel obliged. But I do feel compelled to want to try. I own I felt it all the day of your leaving. But Miss Pascal seemed so professional and proficient that I did not dare to ask you to reconsider your offer, and of course you are not leaving now, which means I need not leave my friends behind anyway. So, if you still want me, then: yes and thank you.'

I swallowed down the lump in my throat. 'Then it is settled.'

'Yes, although what about once I have learned the tasks and grown competent in them? I would hate to be responsible for pushing Miss Pascal out of her job.'

'Well, I shall give her the choice to stay and share the duty with you, or to go with a handsome reference and bonus for teaching you the skill. I think that is as fair as I can be. Besides, she shall have no difficulty in finding places, she is indeed very good you know. But, she is not you, and above all else, I want a friend beside me, Annalise. Do you understand?'

She nodded and broke into a warm smile. 'I do.'

'So, I have not had a chance to consider how this might best work, for I own, I feared you might decline again. Do you have any thoughts?'

'Well. If it would meet your approval, I should not like to just vanish from below stairs. I mean, if this is to be a shared role, then I would surely take the place of an apprentice of sorts, and so I should expect to be paid accordingly and not in the range that Miss Pascal receives. It would not be fair and it might please her to know that I am more of an under-maid, if there is such a thing.'

'Very well, it shall preserve her pride better I expect.'

'And please, miss, if there was any way I might keep my place in the room with Poppy—'

'But Annalise, you would have a nicer room, in the attic, your own private space, better equipped and more comfortable.' I had Nanny's old room in mind for her. It would need some freshening up, but it was by far the biggest and the nicest, second only to Mrs Crawford's own apartments.

'Thank you, but I do not care for that. I want to be in reach of Poppy, it was my reason for trying for a place here. I mean, I was trying for a place anywhere to get out of that house, but to be with my friend I was happy to reduce my position to kitchen maid. And although I don't always like the work or rub along perfectly with Cook, I shall need to continue on as kitchen maid for now, if I want to keep my room with Poppy, whilst I am learning from Miss Pascal at least. We are only afforded it because of its proximity to the kitchen, and if I was to give up my position, well then it would be offered to Cal, or Maggie perhaps. And you see, if I am to spend much of my time above stairs, well then I should never really see Poppy anymore if I was moved into the attic.'

'Well then, it shall be as you wish it. If I negotiate mornings in the kitchen with cook and afternoons with me, would that warrant your staying put?'

'Yes, I think it would.'

'Well, are there any other terms you would like to negotiate?'

She shook her head. 'No, I know I already ask too much when you have made me such a generous offer.'

'Then I shall ask you to meet my terms now: You are to start by being properly fitted out in the style of a lady's maid. Secondly, you are to begin in the main, by watching and observing and taking Miss Pascal's instruction only—at least until your hand is fully recovered. I would like you to take particular interest in wardrobe care and preparation and in hair grooming and cosmetics. Whilst I shall not leave to go abroad as planned, I will expect you to accompany me on some trips as they arise and, most important of all, when we are alone, I am not to be addressed as miss, ma'am, or any such salutation, but as Eleanor, your friend.'

She laughed. 'I think I can manage that.'

'Perfect, you shall start tomorrow afternoon. That will give me the time to speak to the upper servants and Miss Pascal in the morning. So, for now, we can move on from this talk, and speak as friends who have been parted for too long.'

As we talked on other subjects: the account of her birthday party, the fabric patterns she had been cutting for the children in the slums, my trip to Kent, the hilarious and impossible utterings of my nephew who had a question for every answer, I felt a wholeness return to me. An easiness in my being that was effortless and reassuring. But in her, although I sensed an affinity, I also sensed she was holding back somehow, like there was something she wasn't telling me.

'Would you like me to read to you?' she offered when the mantle clock chimed the hour of twelve and I rose to remove my robe and ready to go to bed.

'It is late and you have to be up early,' I said, pecking her on the cheek and climbing into the bed.

'And we have been parted for so long. What difference can another half hour make?'

'You are not tired?'

'No. So, shall I fetch your new book from the drawer? I forgot to say I put it there.'

'No. I would like you to talk to me,' I said. 'Tell me what is troubling you—and do not say there is nothing, for I can feel it.'

'Very well. May I?' she gestured to the bedside chair and I patted the mattress beside me and waited for her to climb up and sit against the pillows with me.

'Well, a strange thing happened earlier. I went to settle a bill, a rather substantial bill with the stonemason this morning. I commissioned a headstone, to mark my mother's grave. I have been making payments towards it for almost a year now and I went today to settle the balance, only to find it had already been settled by some mystery benefactor. Or so I am told.'

I shifted in my sit. 'Well, that is a surprise.'

'Most peculiar since I do not believe it to be either of the two acquaintances I know with the means to do so.'

'Well, it is mystery. But surely a happy one, I mean if the debt has been discharged and you are free of its burden?' I said brightly.

'Perhaps. But I have my suspicions as to who is behind it and I am not at all comfortable with the notion, nor do I know what to do to solve it. If he will not confess it, then I am left in a precarious position of being unable to pay him back.'

'Oh, why is that?'

'Promise you will not think me vain or silly. For I am not so inclined and I assure you I do not accept followers. Only this fellow is always trying to coax me into protracted conversation and make favours to me even when they are not asked for. And so you see it was impossible for me not to understand his intentions.'

'I see. Well then, you think he has settled this in the hope of winning you?'

She nodded and tears began to fall. 'And it will not have that effect and I want only to know for sure that it was he before so accusing him and forcing him to take back the money and freeing myself of any obligation. I have no wish to be indebted and no need either, for I have the money to pay it.'

I hadn't foreseen this complication. I patted her lap reassuringly. 'What if it was not him? Perhaps it might be someone else who holds you in kind regard and knew it must be done in such a way for you to be accepting of it?'

She sniffed back her tears and sat thoughtfully a moment before replying. 'Precisely the difficulty I find myself in.'

'Does it really matter who settled it? I should certainly be happy to be deserving of such surprises.' Why didn't she seem happy? Six pounds was a lot of money, even to my mind, surely, she should be singing her relief, not contorting her pretty swollen, tear-streaked face in anguish. 'Annalise, perhaps you must try to move beyond the question of who discharged the debt. Is it not to be celebrated that someone thinks kindly enough of you to wish to do such a thing? That they have done a little good by their purse in the hope of seeing you relieved of it?'

'In truth, I do not feel that. Or at least I cannot without knowing from whence it came. I have a dear old friend that paid for my mama to have a private burial. To this date, he will not disclose the sum but I know it was vast. He has already done so much for me, that I cannot believe he, being of moderate means himself, would be in a position to do this too, and if he was, I feel certain he would not hide it from me. But I should like to pay him back if it is so.'

I wondered if this fellow was a sweetheart or another of her admirers, or at least desirous of so being. It seemed unsurprising to me that she would gather such a following. 'But whyever would you wish to pay it back? It was obviously not intended as a loan but as a gift, without expectation of repayment.'

'It would not be right for him to pay it. He has already done so much for me. I had been with him all morning before I went to the stonemason's. I should have gone back and asked him there and then. I shall write to him and go on my next day off.'

'Write to him?' I said anxiously.

'Yes, ask him if it was he, so that I can take the coin to him in two weeks. I don't want to carry that wretched purse about with me again if it was not him.'

'Annalise, I cannot see you brooding for two weeks. You need not pay a visit to your friend on that account. I can solve your mystery, although I had no wish to do so, but I see I must. I thought it would never need to be revealed.'

'You know?'

I nodded.

'You settled it?' she said, eyes wide with realisation and something accusatory about her tone.

'I meant it as a kindness Annalise, not a puzzle or a slight, and certainly not to cause you distress.'

She paused, taking it in a moment and I could not read her, was it relief or indignation?

'Why?'

'Because I had the means to and I did not like to think you indebted for such a time. The term was so long you would be working it off for years I'd imagine, with the interest.' It was true and yet the opportunity to do such things for other servants had always existed and yet never compelled me to such action. Why indeed? Why did she have this effect on me? Was this a natural softening that happened with age or with trauma, like bruised fruit, forever altered soft after the injury? Or was this an effect produced by her and her alone? I did not know. I wasn't sure if I liked this new vulnerability I saw in myself either. It was heavy to feel the suffering of others so vividly. But it was there and it could not be denied or silenced.

'I see. Then I am grateful, miss, truly. But I have the money and can pay every penny back to you at once.'

Where on earth would she have got six pounds from? I was certain Miss Crawford had said her annual pay was only twice the sum. 'Like I said, it was a gift: nothing more, nothing less. There is nothing for you to repay.'

'Eleanor, that is very generous but I—How did you come to know of the debt?'

I swallowed. In the moment of spontaneity that had compelled me to make this confession, I had not considered that in revealing this part of my involvement I would now have to expose the rest. 'I saw you go into the place.'

She frowned at me puzzled and I felt a pang of shame rising in me. 'You followed me?'

'No!' *Not followed exactly.* 'Yes, yes, I followed you that morning after you received that letter. I was worried about you; you would not let me go with you and yet I could see you were frightened and I feared something might happen to you. Then I saw you come out of that house all upset and I feared he had hurt you. But you would not tell me and so...I made enquiries as to what your business was there.'

Now she looked perfectly baffled.

'I'm sorry. I should have told you. But I didn't want to upset you with such questions, so I thought it would spare you...'

'I see. Well. The mystery is solved. And I shall pay you back.'

'Please, don't take offence.' I placed a hand over hers. 'You have done so much for me, let me do something in return. And it is not a bribe or any such sordid thing, but a kindness meant for one who has shown me kindness in my darkest moments.' I felt the sting of a tear in my own eyes now.

She stiffened. 'You can't keep doing this. The gifts, the donations, the birthday party and now following me about finding out my debts and settling them without even telling me? Don't you understand, my silence, my loyalty is not for sale. Is that what you think is necessary to be sure of it, still, after all the time...' she broke off into another trail of sobs and I felt devastated that she thought so little of me to think this a bribe.

'No. That's not why I did it, any of it. That person I once was, when I did try to bribe you: I am ashamed of her. I do not recognise her. And I am not her, anymore. You changed all that.'

'I thought we were friends...'

'Then why won't you trust me, Annalise? Why did you pretend on returning that all had been well at your visit to Hurley Street when I saw you; distraught, sobbing in the square, wanting so much to come to you and comfort you—'

'Because I am ashamed, alright. That is why.'

'What did he do to you, Annalise?'

She made no answer and would not meet my eyes.

'You have no reason to be ashamed with me. I understand; I have felt shame, blamed myself for all of what passed that night you found me. I know you understand what happened to me that night, don't you?'

She nodded.

I brushed a stream of tears from my face. 'It is because of you, I have moved beyond those feelings—perhaps not entirely, but enough, enough to stop destroying myself. It is because of you I have come to know my own heart. It is because of you I know what it is to give, for the sake of doing some good, bringing some ease, joy, giving something when all I have ever done is take.'

There was a glow of sympathy in her eyes now that seemed to neutralise the hue of indignation in them somewhat. 'Are you telling me, that if I was to go and visit my husband, all alone, and would not let you go with me, you would not do the same?'

She sighed. 'Yes, of course I would, I would not want you to come to harm...'

The resounding sobs were entirely my own now.

'But I do not want your money, Eleanor.'

'I know. But it is the one thing I have a lot of and so why shouldn't it do some good for a change?'

'It should, you are right. But I am not your charity case. I do not want to be that.'

'You are not. You are so much more to me than—'

'Is that why you have offered me this post—'

'No. I offered it to you because I—I have come to care for you so deeply that I had to find a way not to be without you. And if I thought you would just agree to come away with me, be my friend and my...companion, well then, I would have just asked you. But I know that will not do for you: you mean to work and be useful, stand on your own two feet and I admire that Annalise, I do, for I want to be useful too.'

She looked up at me, and this time I could read something of a softening behind her bewilderment. A clearing, an understanding perhaps.

'Then I thank you. If that is truly your wish, then I will find another good use to put the money towards instead.'

I did not care what use she put the money towards, only that she would not be labouring the next eighteen month or more to pay it off. 'So, you will forgive me?'

She nodded. 'If you promise, no more secrets and no more buying me gifts or settling my debts.'

'I promise.'

'There are other ways to show care you know, that cost not a penny. They mean more too.'

This was humbling for I had little idea what they were precisely. 'Will you show me, how?' I said sheepishly.

'Yes,' she smiled. 'Come here,' and she pulled me into her embrace, rested my head into her lap and stroked my cheek. 'My mama used to stroke my cheek like this, when I was upset or would not sleep, and you know that is what I miss now, things that money can never buy or re-place...'

A part of me did understand. But is that what she wanted from me? To be tactile and comforting with her? It was dangerous territory, even if I was willing to soften to her wants, her needs. But how could I yield to such intimacy with her, when doing so would lead me to wanting an al-together different kind of intimacy? I did not know how to manage the line between the two. To quell it was the safest thing and yet the thing I wanted least. 'Annalise, have you ever thought...about marrying. You said before that you do not accept followers, yet I am sure you must find your-self catching their attention all the same?'

She stopped stroking my cheek and looked at me thoughtfully. 'Why do you ask it?'

'I don't mean to pry, I just—well it is natural is it not, to think of such things?'

'Well perhaps. But in service it is not often liked. Mrs Crawford is very strict on the matter and forbids it.'

'But that does not mean you cannot think it. Cannot feel it.'

She shrugged. 'I do sometimes, wonder. But I don't know. There are things I want to do first, before I turn to such matters. My mother was the best of mothers, but I have no wish to be so saddled. And look what happened to poor Molly. That blaggard Jack gets her in the family way and she is to bear all the misery of it.'

'He did not get away completely scot-free you know. I have the steward dock his wages every week and send off payments to her.'

'You did?'

'I could not save Molly, it was beyond my power. But, it was within it to make sure Jack shared at least some of the responsibility and that neither her or the child should be penniless.'

'That was good of you. I hope she shall be alright. It will no doubt be difficult to manage work with a baby to care for when it comes. Which must be soon I think.'

'Yes, you are surely right. Perhaps we could send some things on, for the baby?'

'Yes,' she smiled brightly, I have already cut the patterns out for several baby dresses and caps.'

'Then I shall help you sew them, so we might send them soon. What, why are you smiling like that?'

'Because I knew you did not need me to teach you how,' she said with a sense of pride and I felt a different kind of tenderness in the way she resumed stroking my face.

'Eleanor, can I ask you something, something personal?'

I nodded and braced myself.

'I don't want to remind you of things you would rather forget, but, your husband, before well, you know, you came home; did you love him?'

'No. Not in the least. I didn't even know him. Now I am certain I feel only the deepest disgust of him.'

'What if, what if you had had to bear a child to him? Feeling as you do. How would you—'

'I am only grateful I was spared that fate. I could not begin to imagine passing on his blood. For some poor child to have him for a father... What, what is it?' I said sitting up, noticing how her face had turned into one of deep sadness. 'Have I said something out of turn?'

She shook her head. 'No. It's nothing you've said. Would you still be able to love the child, do you think, I mean truly as if it were made in love and not disgust.'

'Well, I have never had one, but I do not see how you could refuse to love a child, it seems it would run contrary to everything. I mean, I do not particularly like my brother-in-law, but my niece and nephew, well, they are the bonniest things and I have so much love for them. When I see them, I see my sister's children and they are beautiful, just like her.'

'Thank you.'

'For what?'

'For putting my mind at ease, I suppose. What I did not tell you that day, when you followed me—'

I felt the heat rise in my cheeks at the mention.

'I found out some unhappy news about who my father was. You see, I was illegitimate—I always knew that. But the man who I believed my father to be, whom I own I never met, for I was told he died in his youth, in the war but—well, it was not him. He was a fiction my mama contrived to conceal from me, who my real father was.'

'But why would she do that?'

'Because she knew I would be better off never knowing it.'

'So how did you find out?'

'I found out when I visited my old employer.'

'He knew? He told you?'

She nodded. 'That's as much as I can face the telling of right now. But I want you to know that I do trust you. And when I am ready to tell the rest of that story, you shall know it first.'

I wrapped her up in my arms instinctively and this increasing responsiveness of my body to her needs was ever surprising to me. It was still so odd, I felt it almost in third person. And yet when I held her there, it seemed like the most natural thing in the world.

'Can I stay with you tonight?' she said, looking up into my eyes, hers still heavy with tears.

'Of course, you can,' I told her, wondering as I spoke the words, how easily I had relented on my promise. It was the promise I had made to myself privately, the last time we shared a bed: That I must not permit it again for how out of sorts I felt all morning on waking up with her beside me. Like she had undone me somehow. Like she had stirred in me things I did not want to think or feel. Things that made me not trust myself. That made me fear she could not trust me. But there was an internal war going on inside of me in these moments and the losing side stood no chance at all when in her presence.

Even as I got up and helped her undress for bed, I found my thoughts and feelings all asunder. Like she had disarranged me from the inside out. All of my good intentions unpicked at the seams and all of my deepest concerns running ragged about my mind as I lay back down and she shuffled in closer than we had ever been: Her head upon my breast, her arm about my waist as I stared into the shadow of the bed canopy and became startlingly aware of my every breath. Of the rise and fall of my chest beneath her cheek. The lightness of her fingertips as they snagged against the muslin of my shift on an inhale. The echo of her words through my flesh as she spoke now and then. Telling me how nice it was. How she had missed me. What a comfort I was to her. How unlikely it had all seemed. How it was our little secret that others thought our relationship to be formal and when we were alone it was the most beautiful friendship. And who would have thought that there could be any common ground between us. Our lives so different. And yet sharing something so alike, so indescribable. An invisible bond. One I must have a care not to break, I thought, as she lifted her head and kissed me on my chin. I supposed she had meant to aim for my cheek but had missed in the darkness. My body had not missed it though. My instincts were oversensitive. It took every power within me not to dip my chin and meet her with my own kiss. Not to sigh out at the accidental brush of her face against my nipple when she adjusted her position or lifted her head to speak. And then she would settle again, and I would settle again, eventually, until the next time.

Is this what I had put Sheldon through? What he accused me of not understanding. Of what drove him to...

I could never even look at another whilst my heart was so bound to her. No matter how this was fraying me. Perhaps this was my comeuppance. There were those who believed in such natural forms of justice, of reaping what one sowed. I did not fancy the penalty in this. I did not know how I would endure it. And yet I knew I had no choice. She was an innocent. Just as I had once been. Naïve. Not understanding her own power.

In the morning when I woke, we were quite entwined, her limbs and mine. The delirium of sleep having no regard for where we placed them. For how I had twisted my shift so tight about me I could hardly move; bound mummy-like beneath the weight of her. For how the ribbons of hers had slackened and fallen loose about her neck so I could see the slightest ridge of her ribcage at the centre of her chest. She was sound asleep, her breath willowy as she exhaled it. I lay there, just watching her a while. Thinking her beautiful. Thinking how neatly formed her mouth was. How the cleft above the bow in her lips held the faintest sheen of sweat. A wayward strand of hair caught upon it. I carefully swept it aside and then giving into the temptation, run my thumb across her temple. She opened her eyes and immediately beamed at me at the very moment I heard the latch on the door and twisted about to see Miss Pascal come in. 'Camille!' I said more guiltily than necessary. For nothing untoward had occurred, not beyond my mind anyway.

'Good morning, madame,' she said going straight over to draw back the curtains and when she turned about, I saw the change in her expression as she noticed Annalise beside me in the bed. It was certainly not the best of starts given what discussions I was yet to have with her today. I shared an awkward glance with Annalise as we both sat up in the bed and created some distance.

'Did you sleep well, madame?' Camille said next and even though she asked the same every morning, I could not help noticing a note of brackishness in her tone today.

'Yes, thank you. Camille, I shall take my breakfast before dressing to-day—if you would be so good?'

She curtsied and left the room.

This had not done much to improve the awkwardness of the conversation I had to put to her later that morning once she had gone about her morning tasks and I beckoned her to sit down with me for tea. I had already expected it to be difficult to balance my choice of words in such a way as to cause the least offence. And even though I tried wherever possible to emphasise that it was on account of her superior skill and manner that I wished her to play mentor to Annalise, I could tell she had taken it ill. It was only when I explained to her that once she had done her part in showing Annalise the way of things, that she was to enjoy every afternoon and evening off at her leisure, that she seemed to come about again.

Nonetheless, all the business was dealt with by noon, both with Miss Pascal and below stairs, and when Annalise reported to me at two-o-clock, which was to be the time of the shift change, I had my sewing workbox set out ready and sent for all her cloth and patterns to be brought up. If she could not sew yet, I would be her hands until she could. If she wanted me to express my care in some non-monetary fashion, this was to be my first attempt. For I hated the craft and usually could not be persuaded to take up even a little fancy work—despite Mama and Delores' efforts and attempts to shove a hoop into my hand at any idle moment. But this was different, this meant something to her and so it meant something to me. And just as Miss Pascal instructed her in her duties through the passing days, she instructed me in sewing practically, not just fancy.

For whereas I was taught the delicate art of fancywork, she had been taught the practical and labour-intensive work of garment making up and mending. It required an altogether different kind of stamina and speed that I knew would take time to master as I massaged the aches from my stiff knuckles each evening. But it had started to pay off, and as she sat trimming and pinning patterns, I sewed their parts together until they began to take form and I recognised them as heavy coats and hooded capes, plain shifts and long johns, baby dresses and caps. And we got creative with our work-times, taking it out upon a picnic rug upon the lawn if there was no rain, moving about the house to afford a change of backdrop, one evening the library, the next the music room, we had even resorted to one of the basement stores one evening when my parents had dinner guests to stay and I did not wish to be prevailed upon and made to join them.

It kept me busy, first making up the basket we were to send on to Molly, then trying to complete a few things for the harvest festival for Miss Lockheart to distribute with the food parcel donations. I found that even when she was not with me, I was working at it most of the time.

My mother had thought me unwell I dedicated so much time to it. But was not displeased by my settling to something she felt more suitable for a lady's occupation. It had even helped to distract me from the increasing frequency of Giles' communications that had resumed, all saying the same thing: 'Come home, do your duty or else there would be legal action.' Did he not see that that was music to my ears: that I wished he would do something that could sever or limit this contract? So, I made no replies, and grew used to throwing them into the grate without even opening them once I had ascertained the hand.

Jealous.

September 1821. - Annalise.

Annalise could hardly believe her luck when she came down to the basement that morning with a bounce in her step and a smile upon her mouth, even though there had been no one about to smile at. She could not believe how much things had turned for the better, in just half a year.

The decision to leave Gint's, however necessary, had been the most frightening she had ever faced. Leaving the security of the only home she'd ever known. Leaving the place where her mother's memory was etched into every room. Going out into the world with every kind of uncertainty haunting her half-hearted hopes of finding something beyond the gloom. And it had proved to be the best thing she had ever done.

Her life was unrecognisable from the one she had left behind. *She* was unrecognisable too: A lightness of heart she had not known since her mother's passing. A new-found confidence she did not know existed in her. And potential, so many possibilities she could never have foreseen, not even in her wildest imaginings.

And she wanted to share it: the joy, the possibilities, with everyone she could. Let her blessings ricochet and be felt by others. Her first thought was to give the four extra pounds in her purse to Poppy so she could treat herself to some new winter things. She usually knitted her some warm mitts and stockings at this time of year, but she was not going to be able to this time. And when her fingers were finally capable of sewing, she had much to get on with, for she had cut so many patterns and still had yards upon yards of fabric still untouched.

The six pounds Eleanor had refused to take back, she was to donate towards the harvest food parcels, and then when she got her first interest payment from the bank, she meant to take Mr Harrison out, for she knew he would never permit the insult of her paying him back for her mother's burial.

She got back to her room unnoticed and assumed everyone still at their breakfast. She would join them once she had brushed her teeth and washed her face. For there had been little time to get ready properly in trying to vanish from Eleanor's room before Miss Pascal's return with the breakfast tray.

She was just rinsing the ashes from her mouth when Poppy came into the room. She spat and dabbed her chin dry. 'Poppy,' she said, smiling and excited to give her the coins.

'There you are.'

'Yes, sorry, I—'

'I know where you were and so does half the basement now Miss Pascal's had her say.'

'What?'

'Yes, thought she would make mention that she found you upstairs sleeping in the mistress' bed. What are you thinking, girl? Do you want to be sent away without a character, Annalise?'

'Of course, I don't. Who did she tell?'

'Well, thankfully none of the upper lot were about to 'ear it but you may be certain the rest 'eard 'er alright.'

'It was late, we got caught up talking and, she needs me you know Poppy. We have become friends.'

'She always needs you! And does she not care that you are needed here and when you are not you need your bed? Friends. Friends, Annalise? She is your mistress, your superior, not your friend.'

'She does care, Poppy—in her way. And yes, I own it's strange, unlikely, but it is true.'

'Her way, whatever other way is there in her world?'

'She is not like the others, Poppy. She has a heart, I have seen it, she has done so—'

'And will she have a heart when you are dismissed without a character for keep pushing Cook to the edge of her tolerance? 'ow do you think this news of your taking to sleeping above stairs will go when she gets wind o' it. You know she's already gunning for your job, don't yer? Is only this 'and of yours and you being under Miss Crawford's authority that's saving yer. For now. But when you return to the kitchen, she'll make your life a bloody misery until you give up the place yer know, and even I can't stop it.'

'I think so. She offered me a position. So, you see, you need not worry. I'm sorry if I've made you anxious for me. I didn't mean to. Nor to anger Cook—'

She relaxed the reprimand in her expression now, her interest piqued. 'A position?'

'Yes. She is to have me trained up as a Lady's Maid by Miss Pascal.' She considered how good a start this was likely to be if she was a blabber mouth.

Poppy sighed her relief and put a hand to her throat. 'That is why you've been pushing your luck! Well, you might 'ave told me before and saved me the worry.'

'I'm sorry. I didn't know she would renew her offer and on such happy terms, so you see, I only knew last night, that it was to be official.'

'What do you mean, renew 'er offer? This is not the first?'

Annalise shook her head, feeling a little conscious of just how much she had withheld from Poppy of late. 'No. She offered me a few weeks ago, more perhaps, I don't quite remember. But I declined it, so there was really nothing to tell.'

Poppy's mouth dropped. 'What?'

'I couldn't take it then.'

'Whyever not? You got pigeons flyin' about that 'ead o' yours or somein?'

'It wouldn't have been right to take it then; I had no experience in the duties of it. You know I am positively useless in matters of dressing hair and mixing cosmetics and the like. My years of service to Mr Gint were hardly conducive to teaching me the ropes of a lady's care. The wardrobe care and dressing was fine, or at least, it would have been until this...' she held up her hand.

Poppy smiled her agreement at that fact before she fell serious. 'But if she 'as offered you the job, she must realise this, because I can't imagine you had the sense to keep that to yourself.'

'No. She knows it.'

'Then why don't you tell me why you really refused?'

Annalise sat down on the bed. 'Lots of reasons. You know, Poppy: everyone will hate me for it. I'll be like Watts, everyone dropping to whispers in her presence and so much alone and friendless down here. And then she was to set off travelling and I did not want to be away from you all—'

'Well, everything in this life comes with its price, luv. And the others might turn on you, but you know I never could, and you would never be without a friend here.'

'Oh, Poppy, you know I have no stomach for such ruffling of everyone's feathers and I own, for a while I let that stop me.'

'I do, and anyone worth the knowing will also know it, and those who don't wont dare to say a word to yer, any more than they would to Watts or Mrs Crawford.'

'But they will think it, and I will feel it all the same.'

'And that's what you 'ave to consider in the price of the bargain. But you know, Annalise, an offer like that is not likely to come again for you.'

'I know and I know you shall say that my mama would have wanted me to take it. And now I have. Anyway, I hope it may not go down in such a style now, since I am to be an apprentice to it and I shall be working half the day in the kitchen too.'

'Well, let's 'ope not eh, luv. I'm 'appy for you. You deserve this chance and if anyone wants to say otherwise in my presence, then I shall set 'em down on the spot.'

'Thank you, Poppy, I knew you would be pleased. It's thanks to you I even have the chance.'

'Nah, was bound to 'appen whatever. You're made for better things, luv. That's what your mama brought you up for, and someone was bound to notice the fact sooner or later. Now, come 'ere and let me give you an 'ug. Congratulations. We shall raise a cup later.'

Annalise squeezed her back. 'And so are you, Poppy—made for better things.'

She waved away the comment.

'I love you, Poppy. Thank you for everything. And I know you don't like all that talk, but I want you to know that even though I might not be about as much as usual now, I shan't forget myself, or my dearest friend.' She placed a kiss on her cheek.

'I know it, luv. Now, get away wi' yer before you 'ave me in tears and Cook won't want them going in the soups.'

Annalise laughed. 'There's just one more thing before you go,' she said, rummaging in the boxes beneath her bed until she found her purse. 'I want to give something to you and I don't want any protests or fuss. Only know that I have been fortunate, come into some extra money, and I want you to have this,' she placed four sovereigns in Poppy's palm and closed her fingers around it.

'You're full o' surprise's today aren't you,' she said, then lifted the coins to her face. 'I can't take this, Annalise. You been betting on that lottery again?' she said, trying to hand them back to her.

'No, but I have it spare and I want you to take it; get some winter things on your next morning off. You know I can't knit you any till these splints come off me fingers—'

'Winter things—I should 'ave enough here to replace me whole wardrobe, boots an all. Luv, it's too much.'

'It's not,' Annalise said, pushing the offered coins away. 'If you don't take them, I shall only have to go out myself and buy it all for you. Wouldn't you rather have the choice? You know we don't have same taste in colours.'

'You really 'ave it spare?'

'I promise you. And there shall be more too, but we will talk about that another time, once I've figured it all out. Just trust me, alright, things are going to get better for us, soon. I just need a little time to make all the arrangements. Just trust me until then.'

Poppy nodded then folded her into another bear hug before they both went out to the kitchen and Annalise took her breakfast into the servants' hall and ate it quickly, so she could report to Mrs Crawford on time.

As she made her way to the upper servants' parlour to find her, she was presented with her first problem. As Miss Pascal opened the door to her, she looked her up and down in disapproving accents and ignored her when she said good morning. Mrs Crawford, however, was her usual self at least and she had detected no hostility in that quarter and hoped that meant Miss Pascal had the sense not to tittle-tattle in their company.

She was relieved when she broke her chores for the midday break, that the rest of the servants in the hall appeared to be at ease with her.

'Ah, here she is,' said Will, who was sat at their usual end of the table with Maggie and Cal and a couple of the dairy maids.

'Where's Poppy?' she asked, taking a seat and pouring a cup.

'Her and Cook are waiting on the roasting spits. She should be in in a minute,' Maggie said, then she leaned in and lowered her voice. 'Is it true, Anna?'

Annalise almost spat out her mouthful of lukewarm broth. 'Is what true, Maggie?'

'Of course, it's not true, Maggie,' Will cut in. 'Gawd, you'd believe anyfing, you would.'

'Not that. O' course I don't think she was sleeping in the lady's bed. I'm not stupid you know,' Maggie said a little resentfully and it seemed suddenly unwise and impossible for Annalise to correct her. For it became clear to her in that instant, that the reason everyone was fine with her, was because they didn't believe what Miss Pascal had said. She was an outsider after all and it would certainly seem like a fantastical tale she supposed.

'I meant the other fing,' Maggie continued. 'What Poppy said about you becoming a lady's maid, a proper one.'

Annalise saw the surprise in the faces of the others, then the contorted frowns before all eyes turned on hers. 'Well, what exactly did Poppy say, Maggie?'

'Well, she didn't exactly—not to me. It was what she said to Jack when 'e was saying unkind things about you to Cal.'

Cal stiffened in her seat and Will puffed out his chest. 'Oh, did he now? Perhaps he wants to try saying them to me.'

'Oh, no need to worry. Poppy didn't 'alf give 'im what for. I doubt 'e'll breathe another word o' it,' Maggie added with a hint of relish in her speech. 'Anyway, she told 'im, he wants to be careful who he talks about, for Anna was to be a lady's maid soon and she 'as her lady's ear. This seemed to scare 'im right off and he said sorry about five times before Poppy told 'im to get lost for she had these spits to jack up and if he weren't careful, he might find 'is 'ead on one.'

Annalise covered her mouth with her hand to conceal the laughter that sprang to her lips at hearing this. She could just imagine Poppy flying into one of her rages, and as lovely as Poppy was, as patient as they come, if you stepped on the wrong side of her, you would surely meet her polar opposite. And it was no surprise that such a threat would scare Jack to his wits having learned that Eleanor was already having his wages docked.

'Well, Anna?' Will said, looking confused now. 'Is it true?'

She leant in too now. 'I didn't want anyone knowing just yet, so keep it quiet, won't you. I'm not even sure if the upper servants have been informed, so you promise?' She looked about the table to see nodding heads. 'Well, I am to be, eventually. But today, I begin my training, half day's down here and half day's in the learning.'

Maggie's face broke into a wide smile. 'Really?'

'Yes, really, Maggie.'

'So, it's proper. You'll get a proper position after that and get the wage that goes with it? I don't want you being strung along to wait on 'er for free again,' Will put in, a cynical twist about his mouth.

'Yes. I shall be under Miss Pascal's instruction for now. But once I've learned everything and can do a good job, then yes, it shall be official. And until then, no one else needs to know. So, keep it to yourselves, won't you?'

'Aye, we will. Well, I'm made up for you, Anna. You deserve a chance like this,' Will said, relaxing into a smile and the others about the table offering their congratulations. Maggie the most fervent, nodding and smiling like a Cheshire cat.

'I's remember when Molly said it never 'appens to the likes 'o us,' Maggie said, 'But it does. Anna, you're proof of it.'

Annalise smiled. 'Yes, Maggie, it seems there are more things possible than we realise.'

Cal got up then and excused herself from the table.

'Where's she going, we got another ten minutes left yet?' Maggie frowned, checking the clock.

'Probably to go smooching with that rotten one,' said one of the dairy maids.

'Well, more fool her,' said the other.

Annalise frowned. 'Do you mean Jack?'

They nodded.

'Oh, no. Has anybody warned her off him?'

'We tried. She'll 'ear none of it. Thinks she's some kinda princess and we're all just jealous. Stupid girl, she'll find out.'

Annalise did not want her to find out that way. There was a baby to be born any minute because of that way of finding things out and she had no wish to see it repeat itself. She would try speaking to Cal privately, later. 'Anyway, that's enough of my news, how are you?'

'Same as always,' Maggie said and the dairy maids agreed.

Will winked, 'Always grand in this fine company,' he said.

Annalise smiled and pretended not to notice that his expression was angled at her, even if his words were addressed to everyone. 'So, will anyone be going to the Harvest Festival in Ewell Village?'

'Aye, the whole lot of us.'

'Everyone?' Annalise said, wondering who was to do work. 'Are the family away then?'

Will put down his mug. 'No. They always give it us. Only a few hours after church mind, but it's good enough.'

'Then who looks after the house?'

'A few of the old bores who don't wanna go. Grantley never does, nor the steward or the farm lot. You'll be going won't yer?'

'I hope so. I have to see what my mistress says. I'm promised to her from two-o-clock onwards so it's whether I could be back in time—'

Will looked a little disheartened at this. 'Well, ask 'er, won't yer?'

'Of course.'

'Well, I better make me way back, Grantley's in a stinking mood, so I'd rather be early than not.' Will stood up.

Then from out of nowhere it seemed, came a creaking and ranting noise from somewhere up the corridors.

'What's that racket?' Will said, frowning in the direction of the doorway with an upturned ear.

They didn't puzzle over it for long, seconds later, Fanny came into the servants' hall in a wheeled chair, squawking at the hallboy pushing it, to go faster whilst the young lad protested "it's 'eavy."

'Fanny,' Annalise said brightly, 'you're up.'

'Got you a carriage of your own an all,' Will said in jest. But Fanny did not have a note of good manner or humour in her face at all.

'You!' she said jabbing a finger in Annalise's direction. 'You cheating, backstabbing bitch!'

'Me?' Annalise said, astonished.

'Eh,' Will said, stepping in between them as Fanny's chair slowly creaked towards Annalise. 'Wash your foul mouth out, talkin' like that.'

'I ain't talkin' to you, am I?' Fanny scowled and the hall fell silent. Even servants, who hadn't been in it, began to pile up in the doorway to see the commotion.

'No,' said Will, raising his tone. 'You're talkin' to the girl that saved your bloody 'ead from cracking on them stairs, so why don't you change your tone.'

'Will, it's alright, you don't need to protect me. I'll deal in this. Fanny, what is wrong? If I have done something to upset you, then pray tell me so I can understand you.'

'Pray tell me—look at yer, always thought you were better than all o' us with your fancy words and your writing letters,' she spat.

'Fanny, I have never thought that, you are wrong.'

'Is that why you skived behind my back to take my position whilst I was trussed up in my room with a broken leg? That job should 'ave been mine and you know it.'

How did she know about it? 'Fanny, I have never skived behind your back at all. And if you think I take any pleasure in your injuries you are much mistaken. I wouldn't have tried to help you and ended up with a useless hand for my trouble if I wished you ill. And I don't. You said to me only yesterday that I was the only one who bothered looking in on you now.'

'Yes, well that was before that French maid tells me you're to pinch 'er job from 'er and 'ave been making up to the mistress to get it.'

Annalise felt her cheeks flush hot with blood; rage and embarrassment boiling up in her. 'I am not pinching anyone's job, Fanny, not Miss Pascal's or yours. For Miss Pascal may share it with me once I am trained, and you never had the offer in the first place.'

'Yes, what, because I don't make up to the misses and pretend to be 'er friend and talk all fancy with 'er and read to 'er. Oh, you think I didn't notice how you sweetened 'er up to make me look bad.'

'The only one who is making you look bad right now Fanny is you! Shame on you; you ungrateful girl. I have never wished you any harm or ill will. What a spiteful mouth you have,' *And I'm not pretending, I am her friend,* she wanted to add, but looking at the audience that had gathered, she decided against it.

'Well, I 'ope she shits on your efforts like she did on mine, and Molly's before that. So go on Miss Uppity, go and take what's not yours to take because I've been to lame to watch over you whilst you stab me in the back. You selfish bitch—'

'Oi,' Poppy came thundering into the room, pushing her way through the crowded doorway. 'Shut your blimmin' trap you 'orrible little cow. I've 'eard just about as much as I can bear o' your poisonous nonsense. Jealous, that's what you are. Cause she's worth ten o' you and the mistress had the sense to see that and give the position to someone worthy. Who won't go about rummaging through 'er wardrobe when 'er backs turned and jumping off the beds and spilling 'er secrets too, I wouldn't doubt. Ah, you think we don't know what you're about.'

A flush of colour came up on Fanny's cheeks now and the other housemaids in the room looked to the floor. 'Get lost, Poppy, you don't 'ave any authority over me. Course you'd come running to defend 'er—she's your friend.'

'And who will defend you, Fanny? Who's your friends down 'ere when you say that the only one who's bothered to look in on yer these past weeks is who you're cussing at now? Anyone wanna stand up and defend their friend Fanny? Tell us that she don't play dress up in the ladyship's chambers when the family are out? Tell us she's a nice kind girl and not a selfish, immature brat? Anyone?' she said, casting a glance about the room and met with only dropped gazes or fascinated faces.

'Sod you, Poppy. You don't know anything about me. You can't tell me what I can't say—'

'Well, she might not, but I certainly can!' Mrs Crawford seemed to apparate from thin air. 'Fanny Larkin, to my parlour. Now! And the rest of you: back to work!' She clapped her hands and everyone vanished from the room as quick as they could funnel out of it.

Annalise ran straight to her room once she broke free into the corridor and Poppy came in behind her, 'Don't you listen to a word 'o it, luv. She always was a spiteful nasty miss,' she said cloaking her in a heavy arm and rustling about for a hanky with the other.

'That's what they think of me,' Annalise sobbed. 'That I swindled my way to the job. I told you this would happen,' Annalise sobbed.

'Don't be daft, no one ever listens to Fanny, she's always full of theatre that one, you know that. She's just jealous, luv, surely you see that.'

'Aye, she is,' came Will's voice and she looked up to see that he, Maggie and the dairymaids had come into the room quite uninvited.

'Are you alright, Anna?' came Maggie's sheepish voice.

'I will be,' Annalise said, trying to recover herself.

'She should be ashamed o' 'erself,'

'Always was a poisonous little cow, you got that spot on, Poppy.'

'Thank you, all of you,' Annalise said, trying to steady her breath. 'But I—'

'Leaves 'er wi; me luvs. I knows you mean well, but let 'er 'ave a cry eh – then you can see 'er later once she's pulled 'erself together again,' Poppy said gently and ushered them out of the room.

She had her cry and straightened herself up after one of Poppy's pep talks that usually perked her up. But as she went about the fire blacking with Mildred and sensed her mood, she felt as miserable as before. She had not said anything out of turn to her, or been directly rude, but there was an air about her, of distance and muted contempt that flowed thick between them as they went from room to room. She was obviously camp Fanny, for she realised that that's how it was to be now. You were either camp Anna or camp Fanny in the whole, and the few impartials that claimed not to be involved or to take a side, kept their distance from the pair of them.

The only thing that had cheered her up after that, was finding Eleanor at the sewing box when she arrived for her afternoon shift. It had brought her almost to tears having felt so unsure of whether she should go ahead with the scheme of her training now. And in that moment, when she looked up at her with her needle and thread poised and said: "Well, what will you have me do? I am ready to be your hands for the afternoon," all her doubts fell away again and she realised that she would not let them destroy this, for it was not a matter of sweetening or making up, she had a friend in her and she was not going to let their jealousy destroy it.

This she reminded herself of when Miss Pascal came into the room to dress Eleanor for dinner and she showed her how to style her mistress' hair 'al la Grecque' and mix various toilette waters and pomades. She remained aloof but behaved better in Eleanor's presence and so Annalise went along with it, thinking she did not want to become a tattler and bring Miss Pascal into disfavour with Eleanor on her account. So, she made no mention of any of what had happened in the basement that morning and went on with Miss Pascal with due deference and diligence.

What she did speak to Eleanor about later, however, was Cal. Not to tell tales on her, but because she was worried for her and weighing up the less of evils, decided that Cal ending up stranded by Jack, pregnant and out on her ear was definitely the worser fate than Cal taking offence if she found out it was she that told.

'Silly girl,' Eleanor said. 'You did right to warn me, and now I shall put a stop to it before it runs in the same way.'

'You won't mention me telling it, will you?'

'No, I don't want you in any bother over it. Anyway, I don't mean to speak to her about it. I shall speak with Jack.'

'Jack?'

'Yes. It will do no good warning Calverley off him and threatening her with sanctions. I doubt the same would have worked with Molly either, if I had known in time. He obviously knows how to charm them and an innocent will fall for it, believe me, I know. Anyway, he is the problem, not Molly or Calverley, and if he's not careful, he'll soon have his wages docked for so many babes that he shan't have a penny to his own. I shall simply remind him of the fact. Advise him to gently give Cal the brush off if he ever wants a character from this house.'

This brought Annalise a sense of relief. With all that had gone on to-day, she had had quite enough of her own ears burning and was glad not to have to be down there much right now. And as the days passed and she noticed Jack giving Cal the cold shoulder, she realised that her own name was on no one's lips in the matter and the snippets she caught were ones simply telling Cal, "That's what he's like, we tried to warn you."

But things were still stiff downstairs, even though there had been no renewed arguments and Fanny had kept to her room since. But the animosity between the two camps was felt in every quarter, like the fight was now between others who had been little more than bystanders. Will with his hackles up and Poppy giving scowls to anyone who looked at them the wrong way. It was upsetting, for they had always seemed like such a merry bunch in the main. Yes, there were your odd Jack and Fanny 'types', but they had always proved the exception. But now the divide could be felt painfully around the table, no one wanting to sit the end closest to their enemies if they arrived at it late. It distressed her more to think that whilst she got to escape from the worst of it half a day at a time, it endured around the clock, even in her absence.

But even her absences were becoming more tenuous with Miss Pascal's ever increasing poorly stifled resentment bubbling closer to the surface. She seemed a naturally aloof person anyway, which only added to the ambiguity of her behaviour, snatching up pins from Annalise's hand when directing her in a new style, cutting glances and eye rolls when Eleanor could not see. And on the rare occasions they brushed shoulders in a corridor or stairway, she would lift her chin and nose in the air and turn away from the sight of Annalise's smile and ignore her greetings. She had learned now not to bother granting them and tried, wherever possible, to avoid her when she could.

But despite these tensions, Annalise was getting along well and Eleanor was pleased with her progress. And in the gaps between all these hostile lines, she would sit out with Eleanor, cutting patterns and directing her in how to sew them together. When their sight and fingers were fatigued by the effort, they would take walks about the grounds arm in arm, talk in increasingly intimate matters and fall into such easiness of mind and being that it sometimes seemed they were friends of old, not new. That they could guess each other's mind and words before they were expressed and would often fall into laughter with just a look or twitch of the others mouth.

It was perhaps this that helped her bear the other side of life more easily than she might have. It was the perfect antidote to a morning of awkward pairing of tasks with a resentful Mildred, or an intolerant biting lesson from Miss Pascal. And sometimes when it had felt a little too much to bear, she would look to the evening where Eleanor would often lay upon the bed and open an arm out to the space next to her and allow her to crawl into it and feel the comfort of her embrace. This seemed a cure capable of alleviating all ills and she wished she could agree to stay there with her through the night and not be forced to leave the comfort of her behind. But with all that had passed the last time, she could not afford to add any further fuel to that fire, and she was sure Miss Pascal would be on the lookout for any evidence of a reoccurrence to fuel the basement gossips with.

And so, she made a habit of pulling herself up from the warmth of her and padding downstairs by bedtime. Reluctant as she was to do so, it afforded her a little time to sit over the day's discarded newspapers and study the advertisements for places for sale. They rarely offered the prices without an application and so she scribbled question marks against those that sounded of particular interest and considered whether she might take them to Mr Harrison's on her next day off, for his opinion. She knew she could afford the lettings advertised for they had been readily given in prices and her bank interest alone seemed capable of covering the cost at a trifle. But it seemed pointless to be so wasteful when she had no intention of leaving her employ or the bed and board already provided here. So, she was minded to take up Mr Harrison's idea of purchasing somewhere and letting it out until she needed it one day.

But she would have to keep the matter perfectly quiet; if this was the response she got from gaining a promotion, what might she be faced with if it was found out she had come into money, property. How would she answer the questions that would arise about where it had come from?

What she did know now, was that in spite of all those who wished it otherwise, she meant to become the best of lady's maids to her mistress; and whilst she was not of Miss Pascal's skill set yet, she was making every effort to ensure that one day she would be, and the sooner these fingers of hers mended, the sooner she would be able to prove herself worthy of the opportunity. For there was one skill she certainly did have that outshone Miss Pascal's and that was a dressmaker's eye and hand, and once she was able, she meant to demonstrate it.

These were her thoughts as she stood in Mrs Oliver's shop that morning, being fitted out for her new wardrobe to attend her mistress in. A dozen smart fine muslin day dresses, a few simpler ones for undress and chores with full length aprons to protect them, a couple of fancy ones for outings and as many crisp new shifts, stays and pairs of stockings to accompany them. She dreaded to think of the expense of it all and did try to bargain with Eleanor into ordering just one or two from Mrs Oliver to get by on until she could make her own at a trifle of the cost, but it was easily rebuffed on account that once she was able to join her at the sewing basket again, she would be too busy helping her in the clothes for

Old Mill Street to have time to make her own, and on this point, it could not be argued. For although Eleanor's commitment to the undertaking had been unrelenting, only the baby clothes and a few cloaks were complete, and whilst the weather remained warm and bright in the day, the nip of an evening chill was starting to be felt below stairs at night and she knew it would not be long before they were needed.

So, she stood patiently as she was pinned and measured and gave her preferences for patterns and colours and trims when asked to. And she endured the same at the shoemaker's as she was fitted out for beautifully shiny new leather half-boots and soft slippers and then on to the milliner's to pick out bonnets to accompany her new wardrobe. She felt almost ashamed as the orders began to arrive and fill up her and Poppy's little hanging rail. She wondered if perhaps she should have taken up the room in the attic where she might not hog the space so. But she could not be parted from Poppy. The precious couple of hours or so they would spend together chatting of an evening when Poppy downed her apron and Annalise swept away her newspaper clippings, was too precious to abandon. Besides, when Poppy came back from her own morning off that week, the expansion of her wardrobe made Annalise feel a little better about it and the bowing rod of dowel all these new garments hung from.

Harvest.

September 1821. - Eleanor.

'Camille, you are to have the day to yourself after church tomorrow. It is usual for the servants to go onto the Harvest Festival afterwards, so you may join them if you wish it.'

'But madame, who will take care of you all morning?' Camille replied as she laced up my half stays.

'Annalise will take care of everything.'

'Is Annalise not to go too, madame? I mean, if it is zee usual thing?'

'No. We have other plans and she does not mind missing it.'

'But madame,' she said, coming around to face me and with the most peculiar caress of my shoulder, said, 'you know I do not mind missing it either.'

I pulled away. 'Well, that is very generous of you, Miss Pascal, but as I said, it is all arranged. Perhaps if you do not wish to go to the festival, you may find something else at your leisure that is more to your taste.'

'But madame, I only wish to serve you. Have I done something to displease you, madame?'

'No, no, not at all. Quite the contrary in fact. You are doing a very good job of teaching Annalise and I am very grateful for your efforts. It is only that... Well, Annalise and I have something to do that only she can help me with. You do understand, don't you?'

She cast a sultry gaze up through her dark lashes and it made me a little uncomfortable as she ran a finger the length of my corset boning. 'I understand perfectly, madame. But you know, I can help you with anything you wish me to, you know. My skills are not limited to those I am used to performing for you. You need only say.'

I swallowed and stepped over to the dressing table and sat down. 'I'm sure, Miss Pascal, but really, there is nothing else. I thank you,' I said, feeling increasingly concerned over her meaning. I neither wished to suspect or insinuate more than was intended by her speech and yet I felt certain she was not referring to a new hairstyle or cosmetic trick. 'Miss Pascal, everything is alright, isn't it?'

'Well of course, madame. Ah—I cannot deceive you. Well, only I overheard Annalise telling her friends 'ow sorry she was zat she could not go to the festival, and I thought, since I did not care for it, zat I might take her place and spare her zee upset.'

'Upset?'

'Well, perhaps it was her friend who seemed more upset zan her but—'

'Poppy?'

'No, no. Zee manservant. Zee one she is very fond of.'

I felt a sudden shift in my concern, she had never mentioned being fond of anyone. 'Which manservant?'

'Will, they call him.'

'The footman?'

She nodded and I used the table edge to steady myself. He was handsome, I supposed. But surely, she would have told me if—

'Are you alright, madame?' Miss Pascal came rushing over to me and took up my hand then pressed a palm to my forehead. 'You are warm, shall I open the window for you?'

'I am?' I said pressing my palms to my cheeks. 'Yes please.'

When Annalise came to me at two-o-clock, I wanted desperately to ask her about Will, but did not know how to hide the raging jealousy inside me at the fear of her answer. And if she suspected me of insinuating anything, I knew she would take offence, for she had been very clear with me about her staunch resolution to not take up followers, nor think of marrying for many years to come. I had readily believed it because I wanted to. Because I wanted to believe she was implying that she had no romantic interest in men. *Is it possible she could have meant to deceive me?* I wondered as she set out the afternoon tea tray at the table and congratulated me on the first boy's jacket I had managed to finish this morning. 'Annalise,' I said carefully, 'do you mind not going to the Harvest Festival tomorrow?'

'Not in the least, I already told you. It is more important that we distribute the clothes that are ready before the weather turns.'

'But we could do it another time, if you wanted to go. I could ask Mrs Crawford to give you the morning off and we could deliver them before the festival, that way you could do both and need not miss out.'

'There's no need. I am not missing out. I am doing something of greater importance and besides, I can go to the festival next year and all the years beyond it. And I should rather not upset Mrs Crawford's chores.'

'But your friends—surely they shall miss you and want you to go—'

'Well, yes, I daresay but they understand perfectly—'

'Annalise, you would tell me wouldn't you, if you felt...unhappy, I mean with the arrangements. You know I wouldn't be displeased with you for saying otherwise.'

'Of course, I would. But I am not unhappy. What is on your mind?'

'Nothing. I just thought it could be otherwise arranged if you were.'

'Well, I thank you. But there really is no need. Besides, look:' she held up her bandaged hand and wiggled her fingers a fraction. 'I think I may be able to begin helping with the sewing tomorrow. I think I am almost mended!'

I broke into a wide smile and quite without thinking, pressed a kiss to her cheek. 'That is wonderful news,' I said and she beamed back at me.

'So, if we do have some extra time tomorrow, I can be more useful here than at a festival.'

I called for the doctor that afternoon to check up on her hand and make sure it was safe to remove the splints and for her to begin using it again. When he confirmed that they could remain off, seemed to be healing well and that movement in fact would be beneficial to recovering her strength in them, I was willing to let her join me in the effort to get one more jacket ready in time for tomorrow. I also let her practice some of the hairstyles Miss Pascal had been teaching her and was pleased to see how proud she was when she had managed it without any help. And this mood of merriness and progress helped me to forget my concerns of earlier and feel reassured that there was nothing she could be hiding from me. She was too much in earnest. Too free and open with me to be hiding such a secret as some clandestine romance with a footman. After all, it was she that warned me of the danger Cal had put herself in and she seemed perfectly aware of the foolishness of such a scheme.

Moreover, I was growing increasingly convinced that my feelings, however much they remained unuttered and unexpressed to her, were reciprocated. She was so tactile and caressing when we were together. Innocently perhaps, but in her eyes, I could see something deeper behind them. Something warmer than her words gave away. Something more than a generous compliment when she admired the look of me after helping me dress, or receiving Miss Pascal's instruction in my toilette.

In my doubtful moments, I told myself I was wishful thinking; that I was reading too much into nothing. That it was all a fantasy and figment of my imaginings. But in others, it felt undeniable. Every night when she kissed me on the cheek goodnight, I felt the tug of her not wanting to go at all. I felt the desperate want of her to take up my invitations to stay, even though she said she could not. When she arrived promptly at two-o-clock each day to take over from Miss Pascal, I sensed an enthusiasm in her to be there, with me. A brightness in her countenance. Whatever her feelings, I knew they were growing in ever increasing degrees of fondness. It was like watching a seed sprout and blossom under the warmth of the sun and it was inevitable something must flourish.

So, I paid no more mind to my doubts, for we were happy and content in our endeavours and I felt certain she would soon be ready to fully take up her position as my Abigail. Whilst I knew I must offer Miss Pascal the option of remaining on, I sincerely hoped she would not wish to. That I could appease her handsomely with a generous settlement and glowing character, for although she was proficient and skilled, there was no rapport betwixt us, no friendship or trust beyond the superficial and perfunctory that permitted us to go along amicably. But I was sensing that Annalise's growing presence and proficiency was starting to put her nose out of joint and had no wish for angst or ill temper to fester.

So, despite Miss Pascal's evermore determined attempts to impress and please me, I did my utmost to keep a cool and measured distance between us, and as Annalise progressed in her training, between the two of them as much as possible. I no longer required Camille to tutor her in my evening dress or hairstyling, and only on occasion did their paths come together, such as when I had them rotate my summer and winter wardrobe and clean and store the jewellery I had accumulated for the season, which seemed redundant now I had only dinner with my parents to dress for. I kept aside a few plain strings of pearls and a diamond set that could compliment any outfit. But a want of simplicity in all things was growing in me and calling me to question so many of my previous fussier habits. Yes, there were times and occasions that would warrant something more, but in the whole, I wished only to invest my time and efforts into things that brought true value to me, and increasingly, to others. If there was something to be said of being abandoned by your friends and society, it was the pressure such isolation caused you to grow comfortable with your own company. To delve deeper into understanding a self you had never really took the time to acquaint yourself with. To find a sense of peace and companionship in your own occupation. To realise that the company of a good friend outweighed the company of many a poor excuse for one.

She made up for them all in droves. Our easy companionship was unlike any I had ever known. There was no need for pretence and cautiousness about her presence. No fear of being disapproved of or failing to meet some societal standard or pressure held in higher regard than one's own happiness. No need for even talking at times, just companionable silence would suffice as we sewed or sat beneath the sunny skies. And rather than come away from her company feeling drained or irked as I had been used to amongst the company of my set, with her I felt somehow replenished, motivated and nourished from our time together: It was like she had some power to illicit the better parts of me that had lay dormant for so many years that they were a surprise to me as I came to meet those aspects of myself. I had even begun to feel less and less concern or hostility for Giles and Mariella. Even when his letters persisted with demands and threats. Their significance had diminished and I found myself throwing his letters into the grate now, not with anger and contempt as before, but with something of a letting go...a gentle release of what was and what I was certain never would be again.

The only struggle I faced now all the rest had fallen away, was how to contain my own feelings in a style that would not put our friendship in jeopardy. For I knew that I risked doing so if I was to act upon them, and as much as I felt the temptation and overflowing want to set them free, I was resolute in maintaining our equilibrium above all else. Annalise was a gentle creature, sincere and trusting, and I did not want to breach her trust or expectations of me, which I knew were still gaining ground.

Carshalton.

October 1821. - Annalise.

Annalise arrived at Mr Harrison's promptly for nine-o-clock as per the arrangements he had made with a vendor who he had been in correspondence with on Annalise's behalf on account of a dwelling-house that had come up for sale in Carshalton. It was a little further afield than she had in mind, but Mr Harrison was convinced it would be worth the three-and-a-half-mile journey given the reasonable price and potential of the place. It was an old timber building of two storeys at number sixteen on the High Street, close to the pond. She had a vague memory of passing through the village on one of her birthday outings one year and knew of its popularity for drinking from Anne Boleyn's well, but it was otherwise little known to her. But she trusted Mr Harrison's good judgment, and if he thought it too good and rare an opportunity to pass up the looking over, then she was happy to spend her morning off in the consideration of it. Besides, it boasted one of the finest inns in the area and she had long wished to treat him to a fine supper at her expense.

She had expressed to him a desire for something which might hold the potential for the opening of a pie shop or dressmakers in the future when she and Poppy were ready to move away from the world of service, and Mr Harrison said that it was on this basis the property was worth the seeing. For he told her that Carshalton was the perfect place to open such an establishment, given the many sporting men and tourists frequenting the town with plump pockets.

When the hack pulled up outside it, she saw the house had already had the downstairs front window converted into a shop façade although the old signage had been removed. The aspect was pleasant enough with views to the pond and its oak and chestnut sprigged banks beyond it. And it was prominently placed betwixt other establishments: a bakery, a barbers, a bank, The Kings Arms public house and opposite stood the post office. Surrounding the merchant buildings, public houses and inns, lay beautiful parkland, manor houses and fields of all kinds of medicinal herbs, the scent of lavender and peppermint billowing fragrant in the breeze and the rush of the river Wandle coursing through the pretty village. It reminded her of sitting about the kitchen garden in the height of summer when she caught the note of fragrance in the air as they disembarked the hack and waited for the house agent to arrive.

She was not certain of the premises yet, but the village she liked a great deal upon a first glance and when Mr Morgan met them at the door, she kept an open mind.

'Mr Harrison, miss?' he said, reaching out a hand to Mr Harrison and offering her a bow and doff of his top hat.

'Miss Tullier, sir, pleased to meet you,' she responded as he held the door open for them to pass through. It was a double fronted aspect with the doors set in the middle of the windows either side in the traditional style of timber framed glass. A scent of ink and musty air hit her instantly as she stepped over the pile of unopened mail that had accumulated upon the floor. Mr Morgan stooped to collect them up as she and Mr Harrison walked into the centre of the small shop floor. Empty bookshelves of mahogany lined the walls and a counter of the same ran the width of the room with a lift up panel to reach behind it.

'Well,' said Mr Morgan as he stuffed the pile of neglected mail onto an empty shelf, 'As you can see, we have a fine blank canvas of a shop front here, suitable for any type of trade. Extremely well situated—'

'What was it previously used for, sir?' Annalise asked him.

'A stationer's shop, paper and ink in the main. Supplier to Mr Reynolds at the manor house. A profitable trade long enough established so it could indeed be resurrected to the same if you were so minded sir,' he said to Mr Harrison.

'Oh, it is not I you shall be doing business with, but my niece here, Mr Morgan. She has come into an...inheritance and is looking for a sound investment.'

They had previously agreed to assume the position of niece and uncle for their visit and Annalise liked the sound of it, the sound of a good relation when she no longer laid claim to any of her own.

'Well,' he said a little surprised and looking over Annalise a little more studiously, 'then you need look no further Miss T...'

'Tullier,' she smiled.

'Well, have you in mind what you should like to do with the place?'

'Not precisely, sir.'

'Well, there's no end of opportunities. As I said, the closing down of this establishment has left a gap in supplies, the nearest stationer is in Sutton and with the convenience of having the paper mill just along the Wandle for supplies, it could not be easier to re-establish it. The post office just across the way,' he pointed through the window in its direction, 'makes a convenient companion to the trade.'

'I don't think that would be of interest to me, sir.'

'Well, the advantage of a fine premises like this, is that it can cater to any purpose. I mean, all this is but a fraction of the floor space.' He stepped through the lift top counter pane and wrapped his knuckles against the timber panelled wall. 'This is a simple partition, can be easily pushed back to extend the space should you require it. Come through, see for yourself,' he ushered them and they followed through the countertop gap and out the jib-style door that lead into a pleasant—if dated—parlour room with a comfortable looking armchair and footstool set before the fire place.

'So, you have a parlour room here as you see. All in good order as you find it but lending perfectly to alteration. You see, you could double the shop floor space and still keep this room half intact. Keep the fireside area, and a table could be made to fit here, if need be,' he gestured to a space before the rear window. 'Then through here is a kitchen, small but perfectly adequate, everything you need. A little modernisation might be desirable, but a mere trifle. There's a well esteemed builder just off West Street who can be called upon for renovations at very reasonable rates.'

'And a garden?' Mr Harrison said, pointing to the back door.

'More of a yard, but a useful space no less, enough to stable a horse if required.' He fiddled about his set of keys to find the one that opened it, then nudged the swollen wood from the door frame and stumbled onto the doorstep when it gave way.

They followed him out to the yard space which had little to recommend it; plain, straw strewn gravel and mud with a number of small pots and old barrows filled with mossy soil and dead stems curling over the tops. A privy shed with cobwebs billowing in the breeze. But it was a long, if narrow strip of land that could be made pleasant again, Annalise thought, with some grass seed laid, a new fence enclosure and some colourful floral plantings. There was space for line hanging and a bench to sit upon on sunny days and perhaps some storage if required. It seemed to her it had been used as a place to stable a horse and trap once upon a time. A discarded rusty old trough and only the posts remaining of what could have been a shelter with the roof long rotted away.

Next, he took them back inside and up a narrow wooden staircase that led into three rooms that he insisted would be better converted to two to make more comfortable sleeping quarters if Annalise was planning on owner occupying, but left to three if she was considering renting the rooms out.

'Well,' Mr Morgan said as they returned to the shop floor where they had started, 'I hope you find it all to your liking?'

'And why did the last owner cease to trade?' Mr Harrison asked. He was examining cracks in the plaster work and casting searching glances up at the ceiling.

'Passed away last winter, sadly. So, you see, the sale is in consequence of his death. The trustees of his estate are keen to achieve a swift conclusion, hence the very reasonable price.'

'If I may, sir, what did the gentleman die of?' Annalise asked and he frowned at the oddity of the question.

'Old age, I believe. He was a centennial I am told, outlived his heirs. Hardly surprising living in such a place as this: The finest air and clearest of springs, it is renowned for being conducive to good health living here, as I'm sure you must know.'

She did not know, but could see that it would be; a pleasant balance of nature and amenity in happy harmony with each other.

'Indeed,' said Mr Harrison, checking the aspect from the windows now. 'And the price – is it negotiable?'

'Hardly, sir, you must see that four hundred and eighty pounds is practically a giveaway for such premises. The rents alone would yield an easy nine or ten pounds per annum. Freehold and exonerated from land tax too, you know.'

'Yes, I see that,' said Mr Harrison smoothing the ends of his white moustache. 'The trouble is sir, the dry rot that is eating away the timbers in the roof. And then of course the entire place is need of a little refurbishment, the garden space too will take some bringing about.'

His face dropped a little as if he had been caught out. 'Well, these old buildings can be prone to a little wear, which is to be expected. I think a modest reduction to reflect the fact would not be beyond negotiation.'

'Four twenty,' Mr Harrison proposed.

'Sir, be reasonable, I beg you.'

'Cost of a new roof, scaffolds and builder's rates, inconvenience and time wasted whilst the work is done...'

'Four seventy,' Mr Morgan counter offered.

'Cost of the new timbers and renovations required after all the disturbance of the works... Four forty.'

'Sir, we are both businessmen, are we not?'

'We are. And my own shop is twice the size with abundant full gardens and five good rooms above stairs and still I would not value it above four fifty.'

'This is Carshalton, sir. Stagecoach to London running twice a day from just outside the Greyhound, tourism, sporting and trade merchants with money to spend passing through every day, and but a ten mile to the capital.'

'Four fifty...cash.'

'Cash you say?'

'In full, ready and waiting. Your clients require a fast sale if I recall?'

'I shall put it to them, sir.'

'Well, what did you think of the place?' Mr Harrison asked as they parted with Mr Morgan and walked the High Street up towards the park-
lands where Mr Harrison assured her that the gentleman owner permitted the public to roam his lands freely.

'Well, I see it has potential, but the sound of all that work and expense—'

'About that; likely a couple of new beams and a patch of new roofing
tiles at most, it is barely set in but will need to be attended to swiftly.'

'But you said—'

He patted her hand which was looped through the crook of his arm,
'I said what was necessary to bring him down to a fair price, but the
building seems sound, and if they are willing to accept an offer of that
number, then you would indeed come away with quite the happy bargain. It is small, but so very well situated that he was correct; you might
turn your hand to anything in such a place. And renting it out should
match your interest from the bank until then. I do not say that the bank
is an unsafe place, but bricks and mortar might be safer still.'

'I do like the village,' she said as they reached the splendid gates of the
park. 'And I like the aspect, the banks upon the waters are so very pretty to look at, and the yard, I think could be made into a pleasant garden
with some work. I can see the planting of a few fruit trees and shrubs and
herbs...But I am not altogether certain of the space being adequate to accommodate both a pie house and a dressmaking room. It seems to lend
well to one or the other but...'

'Well, you may prefer to keep looking a while. I mean, you are in no
rush. You seem happy with your new promotion and it suits you very
well.'

'Thank you, sir. I am indeed very happy. And as you say, I doubt very
much that I shall think of leaving service anytime soon and I daresay I
could live very happily on the bank interest and my wages anyway. But I
want to invest this money in something more. Something that invests in
the people I care for. Poppy for a start and then there are the children she
could train up and give work to, a trade for life. It is like that saying: you
can give a man his bread for the day or give him the tools to mill his own

wheat. It is not about the money for me, but about the opportunities it can bring.'

'You always like to think of others, you are just like your dear mama,' he said poignantly, then turned away as his eyes began to glisten and bulge a little. 'If she could see you now: dressed in such finery, maid to a Lady and maybe even soon to be an establishment owner...well, she would be so very proud of you...'

Annalise squeezed his hand back now with the newly returning strength in her own. 'I know you miss her very much,' she said, wondering, as she often did, if there had been something more between the pair than simple friendship. She had always known them fond friends but it was only since the decline in him after her mother's passing had she begun to question if there had been something of a deeper kind of love between them, perhaps unspoken. He must be near twenty years senior to her mama, and yet he had never seemed his age to her, still sporting a fine head of hair and full set of teeth and the kindest of eyes. Her mama had spent a lot of time at Harrison's when she could, and he had always assumed a fatherly air towards Annalise, as far back as she could remember. If only one could choose their family, she considered then, casting a glance over him as he looked up into the trees and surveyed the parkland which was still thick with leaves, despite the dawn of the autumn.

Once they had spent a merry hour exploring the village offerings, after a little persuasion, Mr Harrison agreed to procure them a table in the supper rooms with the innkeeper at the Greyhound and they were shown to a comfortable dining parlour with a low fire in the grate and handsomely dressed tables. They were brought wine and offered choices of soups, roasted meats, fresh trout caught from neighbouring streams and a selection of game pies. Annalise thought instantly of Poppy and chose a course of potato soup and bread, followed by the game pie with seasonal vegetables and Mr Harrison settled on a brace of pigeons and joined her in the potato soup.

'Well, this is nice,' Annalise said looking at the sparsely filled tables around them, a couple of gentlemen sitting over their plates and discussing their catches after a morning of fishing, a couple, finely dressed discussing the times of their stagecoach journey into the city and a fellow sat alone by the window chugging on a cigar over a decanter. The tap room had been much busier, she realised as they'd passed it, with gentlemen hunched over tables shoulder to shoulder and the inn staff floating about depositing and collecting tankards and glasses.

'It is indeed,' Mr Harrison said, pouring wine for them both. 'Perhaps we might make more of a habit of it, now you are to be a lady of business.'

She chuckled. 'Well, I don't know about that, I am still just a servant for now. But yes, I suppose one day I will be more at leisure to decide, and certainly we shall do this again. Perhaps we could take the stagecoach into London one day if it really is not above an hour and a half?'

'I'd like that. But you are no more just a servant than I am just a bookseller.'

'Very true. You are, in my mind, the type of man I should choose to have as a father if ever such choices were our own to make.'

He smiled warmly. 'And you are the daughter I wished I had had.'

'Thank you, for everything. It has been a very hard year, but I know not what I would have done without you and Poppy. You will always be family in my mind.'

'Then a toast,' he held up his glass, 'to friends that become family in heart if not by blood.'

She clinked her glass and they settled to their plates.

They passed another happy hour supping and talking and discussing the merits and pitfalls of the shop at number sixteen. There would be refurbishments to pay for and tradesmen to procure for the work. But Mr Harrison did not think the sum would be too obscene and if the offer was accepted, it would be readily worthwhile. He would wait to hear back from Mr Morgan and she could enjoy a little time to think things through. She would still be left with one hundred and forty pounds in the bank and though she would likely need to draw upon some of it for repairs and tradesman, it was likely with the new pay rise she would receive upon completion of her training, that it could be easily replenished again over time.

It was then she considered whether she would have been tempted to withdraw from service right away if she had not been promoted to Eleanor's employ. She was certainly dreading the prospect of returning to the kitchen tomorrow and facing out Cook's hostility. If that had been her lot, it might have been easy to come to a decisive conclusion on the shop. She had a fleeting image of seeing a sign up for "Poppy's Pies and Puddings" set above the quaint façade. Then she thought of the rooms above stairs which would be good enough for dress making and fitting—at least if they had no need for lodging in the very same. And even if they were willing to economise and double up in just one room, where was she to store all the fabrics?

Mr Harrison advised her that there was space enough for a small extension to the rear of the building if she was willing to lose half the garden land to the cause and a fair bit more money in the works. He would make some enquiries with the builders when he asked for quotes for the replacement tiles and timbers.

On this head, he spoke to the innkeeper for recommendations and was given the direction of a couple of local men who were well reputed for their work, who had undertaken the very same for him but a few years ago when they discovered the dry rot in the cellars. This progressed on to their business in the village and interest in the shop and moved beyond that to the details of other places he knew were up for auction or private sale in the locality. There was the quirky cottage by Anne Boleyn's Well, which was an oddity of a structure but with eight rooms and fine gardens, a merchant yard along the river by the paper mill, and a fine house for a gentleman's family up at Strawberry Lodge. All of which were out of her price range or otherwise unsuitable. Mr Harrison left his card with him so that he might let him know if he heard of anything else in the area that his details might be forwarded, but more and more, Annalise was growing passively persuaded that the shop at number sixteen would suffice.

Where she had not fallen in love with the building, she was certainly losing her head with village itself and could see herself here, with Poppy, carving out a new way of life in some distant future. Having time to walk the park and river trails, sup in such places as this and take day trips into the city when they were at leisure. Then of course there was the garden, or whatever might be left of it if it required alterations.

She had never dreamed of having her own garden before and even if it was to be dainty and modest in size, she would make sure it was colourful and fragrant and perfect for sitting in the afternoon sunshine now and then.

They were just settling the bill with the innkeeper which Annalise had insisted on giving Mr Harrison the coin for, when the cigar chugging gentleman who had been sat alone at the table came over to him and said:

'I'm off now old, fellow. Will you be so good as to add the bill to my account?'

'Right, you are Mr Craythorne. Good day to you, sir,' replied the innkeeper and he turned back to the coin he had been counting and began again.

The familiarity of the name had instantly piqued Annalise's interest and she watched as the gentleman was fetched his coat, hat and crop by the innkeeper's wife and he exited her view.

'Was that Mr Craythorne of Beddington, sir?' Annalise asked, quite without thinking.

'Aye, up at the manor house,' the innkeeper said, looking irritated at having to perform his third recount. She had given adequate for the leaving of a tip and once he had realised the fact, thanked them congenially and summoned his wife to fetch their things. They had declined the offer of having the hack called for them as Annalise felt an inclination to at least go and take a glance at the quirky cottage by the well that he had mentioned earlier, before they left.

When she returned to her room at a quarter to two, she had little need to alter her dress beyond removing her Pelisse and adopting her full-length apron to take above stairs, so she reported to Eleanor with perfect punctuality. She was surprised to find Miss Pascal still in attendance of her mistress and in the middle of changing her out of her riding habit.

'Annalise, how well you look!' Eleanor said when she came into her view. 'Who did your hair for you? It looks very nice like that.'

'Thank you, miss. I did it myself, thought I should practice now my fingers need the exercise.'

'Well, it suits you. Didn't she do well, Camille? See how well your teaching is proving?'

Camille gave the faintest of nods without looking up and continued undressing her.

'What has happened to you this morning?' Annalise asked, peering over the mud laden skirts discarded beside her.

'I slipped getting off of Samson. I wasn't hurt, just very soiled as you see.' She held up her arms where she could now see the crusting mud about her wrists where her riding gloves had protected her hands, but not above them.

'My goodness, I didn't realise it was muddy. It had all seemed very dry and parched to me on walking it. You are sure there is no injury?'

'Quite sure. And it isn't in the main, but it seems a spring has come up in meadows and saturated the surroundings. Took me quite by surprise. Samson approved of it though and helped himself to a drink. Anyway, I am having an impromptu bath drawn, so you can relax a little while.'

'Don't you need me to help? I can take over from Miss Pascal?'

'Zat won't be necessary,' Miss Pascal said in a defiant tone. 'I shall set madame to rights and you might take over from me zen.'

'Very well,' Annalise said.

'Actually Camille, perhaps Annalise can help, and you can show her how the washes are mixed and done?'

Eleanor was not of a view to catch the rolling of Miss Pascal's eyes. 'Yes, of course, madame.'

'I suppose we haven't gotten around to that yet. Have you seen the bathing room before, Annalise?' Eleanor asked.

She shook her head.

'Perfect, then you shall have the learning today and then some good would have come of me getting into such a scrape.'

It was an unusual water closet Annalise thought as they stepped through a jib in Eleanor's chamber that Annalise had never noticed before, and took a winding enclosed staircase to two floors below. It was a novel idea she supposed, situated on the basement floor for ease of the pumped water, but the direct course of the stairs rendering it a much quicker journey down than the one she was used to taking. She wondered where it could be accessed from noting the door on the far side of the wall which she presumed opened out into one of the basement corridors. She would see about using it for a short cut if it was permitted, especially when carrying things up or down. It would surely take less than half the time. But she would save that question for when Miss Pascal was not about to hear the asking, for she sensed an even deeper hostility in her now than she had been used to receiving. Before, she seemed irked by having to explain things to her. Now, she seemed irked by merely her presence.

'How unusual it is,' Annalise said as she studied the charming lounge room with a floor of Italian granite tiles and a beautiful chaise and armchair set out by a fireplace. Then beyond it, a wood panelled arch way with sliding doors which offered a view to the room where even prettier tiles were laid over the walls as well as the floors and a zinc tub painted in cream and embellished with blue design sat upon ornate feet in the centre of the room. Around it were various closets, that she soon realised held a number of lotions and canisters and kettles for setting over the fireplace in that quarter where a couple hung over it, bubbling away.

'It is a little unusual I suppose,' Eleanor said in reply. 'My father took his inspiration from the Duchess' bathroom at Ham and thought to improve on it further. There is another just the same that serves my parents' chambers.'

'Sit down, mademoiselle. I shall see if zee water is ready,' Miss Pascal said as she laid out the fresh shift she had taken from one of the drawers over a rack before the fireplace. Then she looked up at Annalise and said, 'Madame shall not want to be draped in cold linens, so you must always warm zem first. You may 'elp me with zee water.'

'No, Camille, her hand is still weak and I shall not have her recovery jeopardised in the carrying of heavy things. Why don't you show her where to find the lotions and toilet waters instead?' Eleanor intervened and Annalise pretended not to notice the note of stifled defiance in Miss Pascal's face before she nodded in Eleanor's direction and went over to the room through the archway.

'Follow me,' she said to Annalise and she led her over to one of the whitewashed cupboards where all manner of potion bottles and jars were revealed to her once she drew back the cupboard doors.

'My goodness, there are so many,' Annalise said instinctively, thinking she had only just grown familiar with the various concoctions used in ordinary washing and toilette.

Miss Pascal rolled her eyes again and said as she selected the ones she required, 'Scented soaps for washing zee skin and in an emergency like zis, the 'air. If you are planning on washing zee 'air in advance, see Mrs Crawford, who will 'ave zee still room maids prepare a fresh wash for zee 'air zat is kinder to it. A day's notice is usually sufficient.'

Annalise nodded.

'Oils of every kind to go into zee bath water: in zee winter, Eucalyptus, mint, lavender, ginger if suffering from chills or aches to warm zee blood. In zee summer months, lavender and rose and perhaps a little rosemary if madame likes zee scent.'

'I am very fond of rosemary scent,' Eleanor put in.

'Oils for zee skin for using after zee bath to prevent zee skin drying out and looking chalky: almond oil or olive oil. You can add a little rosehip or some of zee bath oils to zis for fragrance if madame would like zee skin to smell sweet. Just a drop or two though, no more, zay are very strong.'

Annalise lifted one of the bottles and asked, 'Olive or almond today?'

'Almond will be fine. If she 'as dry skin or patches, zee olive oil is better, but not for zee face, on zee face, it shall cause pimples.'

'And what is this for?' Annalise asked as she watched her pluck another pot from the shelf.

'Pomade for zee 'air, not to be kept in but rinsed away after zee soaping has been done. Even better, 'ave zee stillroom prepare a cream of avocado and egg whites, and a little vinegar for zee rinsing. Zis shall have to do today. Take zees over to the trolley,' she pointed to a wheeled table that was empty and sat tucked in a recess beside the cupboard. 'Fill it with zees,' she pointed to the assortment of jars she had picked out. 'And go to zee other cupboard and get bathing sheets and wash cloths, zen take it over to the tub. I shall get zee water,' she added with a glint in her eyes.

Annalise did as bid and creaked the wheeled table across to the bathtub whilst Miss Pascal carried heavy kettles of water from the fireplace and mixed them with buckets of cold water collected directly from the sink on the opposite side of the wall. This reminded her of a much fancier and smaller version of the scullery apparatus. Although, this seemed to be made of polished stone, not lined with lead, and you could just about wash a cup in the space of it.

'Never put zee kettles in first, you will 'eat zee metal tub and cause madame a scold. Cold water goes in first, zen zee kettle. Zen you blend the two until the temperature is nice and warm. Now you can add zee bath oils and make sure madame tests zee temperature after you have, before getting in. Madame?'

Eleanor rose from her chair in the other room, crossed it, and with the support of Miss Pascal's hand, stepped into the bathtub, approving of the temperature and thanking her as she sat down in it. Annalise wanted to ask why she did so in her shift which was now soaked through and bubbling up trying to rise to the water's surface, but since neither Miss Pascal nor Eleanor appeared to be concerned by this clothed bathing, she closed her open mouth without utterance.

She could not remember the last time she had taken a bath. When she had been a smaller child, her mother would often fill up one of the small coppers to dunk her in, but it had always been in nothing but her skin. That was what it was for though after all, to soak the grime from it? She had taken them occasionally since to soothe her monthly cramps when they had been particularly cruel, but when her mama got ill, she could never find the time to manage even the occasional hip bath. It had never even occurred to her to ask since she had been here, since no one had ever made mention of it for either they or the family, although she recalled some of the boys taking a dip in the lake when the family were away, although she had no desire to resort to such drastic measures for a soaking. Her flannel and water basin would suffice if that was the option open to the servants. Perhaps, she thought, revisiting the wonders of her day in Carshalton, she and Poppy may have a tub at number sixteen, and her thoughts carried her off over the details of where it may be placed, thinking the kitchen too small and the parlour too open and likely draughty in cold weather.

'Are you listening, Annalise?' Miss Pascal said impatiently and it caught her notice and she turned to her to see she was passing jugs of water over Eleanor's hair as she arched her head back. 'Zee soap!' Miss Pascal said and Annalise peered across to the trolley and passed it to her. She lathered it up in her hands before rubbing it into Eleanor's hair which she noticed now seemed long with her curls stretched flat carrying the weight of the water. 'Zee first wash is to remove zee dirt from zee hair. Massage gently to zee ends and rinse.' She followed her own instructions then gestured for the soap dish again and re-lathered her hands. 'Zee second wash is for zee scalp, and you want to make a firm pressure with zee fingertips, massaging zee 'ead thoroughly.' She proceeded to demonstrate and through the duration of these rituals, Annalise had a care to follow them precisely and not drift away in her musings again.

It had all passed rather uneventfully, even if seeming overly laborious and particular. Her childhood memories had consisted of about five minutes of a scrub and buckets of water rushing over the whole before being wrapped and dried and put into a fresh shift. The clock on the mantle showed that half an hour with two top ups to the bath water had already passed when Miss Pascal declared the protocol complete and Eleanor stood up with the drenched shift hanging off of her like a soiled sack, sagging and wearing thin in places so that they were as good as transparent anyway.

However, when she was relieved of this at last and wrapped in bath sheets, it seemed another ritual was about to begin as Miss Pascal led her over to the chaise and begun lessons on massaging oils into the skin and pomades into the hair before brushing it out to dry in front of the flames. *No wonder it is not often partaken in if this is how timely the investment,* Annalise considered as Miss Pascal instructed Eleanor to lie back against the pillows she had arranged whilst she demonstrated the technique for massaging oils into the face. Sweeping pressure of both hands in symmetry, followed by circular motions and tapping about the jaw line.

'Zis keeps zee muscles supple and youthful to prevent zee jowls,' Miss Pascal appraised her when she frowned her confusion over this bizarre display.

For the most part, Annalise feigned interest and found her eyes wondering over the trompe de d'loeil ceiling, which she had found quite fascinating and the fine mirrors that hung about this room in full length proportions so you could catch every angle of yourself in it through the reflection of another. They had misted now and the steam filled room where the tub was set had carried out into the lounge room and condensated about it. There was a small set window in the bathing room just like the one in her own and she supposed that it could not be opened either. The dry heat of the fire would burn the damp air out eventually she supposed.

'You see, always upwards, it's good for zee blood,' Miss Pascal intervened in her musings again and Annalise nodded and held her gaze until it dropped again. Her tolerance for Miss Pascal's patronising style of tutelage was wearing as thin as her tolerance for Annalise's presence seemed to be. She was certain she was correct and proficient and even seemed to rather relish in her task as she brushed her palms all over Eleanor's skin in various styles and manoeuvres, but Annalise sensed it was all done with a passive jeer at her own ineptitude.

Even on the occasions Annalise did something well and Eleanor commented on it, she would either grow silent and nod or find some improvement that could be made upon it. She had no doubt she would forget half of what Miss Pascal had demonstrated today, but had the basics well enough to not need a running commentary on every motion of her hands, which seemed peculiarly elaborate, and if she dared to say so: intrusive, she considered as she palmed as far down as her décolleté and missed only the most private places out of her attentions to the lower half. There was a smile in her eyes as she did this and asked Eleanor every now and then: "How is zis feeling, madame?" to which Eleanor would reply sometimes with "Very good, Camille," and others with a sigh of relief and occasionally with: "I think that shall do."

No less, once Eleanor was back in her chamber cloaked in a robe and soft slippers, Miss Pascal was thanked and dismissed, seemingly to her chagrin, and Annalise felt she could at last be at ease and talk freely to Eleanor again.

'Well, that was quite a lesson,' Annalise said with the hint of a smile in her eyes.

Eleanor joined her in the smirk, 'Indeed she is very...thorough and severe with you I notice. I am sorry for it, Annalise, it is difficult to reprimand her when she takes such pains in your learning and she is very knowledgeable. You are learning from the best. But do not think I don't notice her menacing tone. I find it most disagreeable and had wondered at saying something but did not want to make things ill betwixt you.'

'Please don't,' Annalise said. They are already ill enough, she wanted to say. 'I think she feels threatened by my learning. She does know she is to remain on after I am proficient?'

'Yes, I have told her that, although...' She took a thoughtful pause before continuing, 'Well, I'm not sure how desirable that shall be if she continues in this style.'

'Well, our paths need not cross once I am trained, so I suppose it shall be of no significance by then.'

'So, are you all set for returning to the kitchen tomorrow?'

'Yes,' she thought with a sense of dread, realising she was but a matter of hours away from returning to Cook's authority and she knew that in comparison, Miss Pascal would seem a trifling irritation against Cook's gruff reprimands that had the power to make you want to quake and disappear.

'Are you sure it is not too soon?'

'No, the sooner I get back into the swing of things, the better I will adapt to them again,' she said, wondering how long that might take after such a time and she had visions of the cracked and peeling knuckles of her early days return to her. She looked down at her hands now which were soft and neat once more, no sign of the ragged and chaffing skin, red raw and itching that she had tolerated before now. She would be ashamed to press such rough hands—as they were likely to become again—against the softness of her mistress' skin in the styles Miss Pascal had just demonstrated. Besides the unpleasant look of them, they would scratch and chafe at her they grew so coarse from all the starches and scrubbing.

'So, how was your morning off?' Eleanor asked her, as she ran her fingers through her half dry tresses that were beginning to lighten and shrink up into curls now.

'Very nice, it is a pleasant place,' she said careful not to elaborate too fully. She had told Eleanor of her plans to take a dinner with Mr Harrison but nothing about the meeting with Mr Morgan or the plans to find a dwelling house. She hadn't told anyone beyond him and meant to keep it that way for now at least, until things were settled and decided. Even then she was not sure how well such news would bode with Eleanor. Would she think her wasting all this time in her training for nothing? Would she believe her when she explained that she had no plans to abandon her or her post in the foreseeable future? She knew she could not, even if she wanted to. She would miss her too dearly now.

'And where did you dine?'

'The Greyhound Inn. Mr Harrison had to give the line that I was his niece so they admitted us without suspicion.'

'So that's why you are dressed so fine and pretty today.'

'Well, I thought I had better look the part if I was not to embarrass him or be turned away.'

'As if you could.'

'Eleanor, there was a gentleman there. I noticed him only briefly before, sitting alone at one of the tables, I think he had finished his plates before we got there. Anyway, when he spoke to the innkeeper on leaving, he referred to him as Mr Craythorne.'

'He did? And what did he look like?'

'Tall, dark hair that curled about the ears. Handsome I suppose, perhaps about five and thirty?'

'It was him then. The senior Mr Craythorne is mostly balding. Was there anyone with him? A lady, smartly dressed with red hair?'

'No one as far as I could tell. Like I said, it's possible he could have been in company before our arrival, but he was quite alone upon my first notice of him.'

'Well, he is not abroad as I had hoped or expected by now. He was supposed to go to Venice for a time to tend to some business there. It seems he has altered his plans.'

'Have you had any more letters from him?'

'Lots; about one every three days. I daresay he is sticking around to keep a watch over me, perhaps to see if he can scrape together any evidence on R—well, it doesn't matter. He shall find nothing.'

'He did not look as I expected him to. I mean—I expected a brute.'

'Don't be fooled by the outward charm Annalise, you saw first-hand what he is capable of.'

'Yes indeed. I suppose looks can be deceiving.'

'Anyway, I don't want to talk about him. Why don't I get dressed and we can take the carriage into town and pay Miss Lockheart a visit and see how the raffle went. She might be able to give us some hints on what we need to make up next?'

The next morning, she was up sharp to report to Cook on time, dressed in her dowdy grey skirts, hair pinned back in plain neat style. It was Miss Pascal that alerted her to the stark difference in her looks as she passed her in the corridor saying: 'Oh, yes, zis is much more your style.'

She ignored it and gave no rise. They must bear each other a little longer yet and things were fractious enough, but it seemed to set the tone for the morning and whilst she worked hard, fast and attentively, Cook seemed determined to put her through her paces this morning, just as Poppy had warned her.

'Just go along with it, keep up and make no complaints,' Poppy had warned her. 'She'll get bored of it after a time if you show no weakness. I wish there was somein' I could do but I know what she is.'

'It's alright, Poppy. I shall manage, it is only half a day after all, how bad can it be?'

Bad enough, she knew now, but she endured, ignored the sting of her rapidly declining skin and the tingles in her fingers as she adjusted them to the grip of the knife and endless peeling and chopping. Perhaps it had

been a little too soon. It mattered not now and Maggie had stepped in
for the carrying of particularly heavy pots or kettles which had spared her
the worst of it.

It was merry to be back in the company of her friends again, though.
Maggie always had a way of brightening the most mundane of tasks and
she knew that if she was to succeed in agreeing a contract for the sale of
number sixteen, there would be a place for Maggie there once they set
things up. The more she washed and scraped and peeled and softened her
smiles and face against Cook's relentless provocation and demands, the
more certain she grew that she was to take up the purchase. She hoped
it would not take long for Mr Morgan to send word of a reply so she
knew whether or not her forming plans and imagined renovations were
to come to fruition.

She had imagined the extended shop floor housing tables and chairs
laid for the eating of pies and soups and warm drinks. The dark mahogany white-washed with bright and cheerful watercolours of the village upon the walls above the panelling. The countertops brimming with
Poppy's offerings laid upon crisp white cotton doilies and pretty chinaware. The smell of freshly baked pastry in the air as she came in
through the doors. Their back parlour furnished with another fireside
chair to match the one already there and their own dining table looking
out through the rear window into a colourful neat garden. The kitchen
stoves and sink replaced with piped water like those in the scullery here.
And perhaps a bathtub too, she thought as she felt the stirring of her men-
strual cramps threatening. She would have to fetch her rags in the sustenance break.

But it was these musings and imaginings that kept her spirits buoyant against the tide of hostility, and she could not wait for it all to be settled so she could put the prospect to Poppy, see what she wanted to do
about it. She might choose to stay on in the learning a while here or jump
at the chance to set upon her own venture and start as soon as the works
were completed. There was no reason she should not begin ahead of her
if she wished it. Get the pie shop up and running before Annalise joined
her later when she was ready to set upon her dressmaking. Perhaps once
she was trained, Eleanor would consent to her living out in Carshalton

and travelling in to her to take up her shift at two o clock. It would be a lot of miles to walk though and she could not ride or justify the expense of such regular hiring of hacks. But she was sure there would be a way to manage things when the time came. She did not need it all figured out just yet, so long as the sale was settled and the place made ready.

She changed into her fancy dress and fetched her rags before heading up to Eleanor today with a sense of such relief as she left the din of the kitchen behind and climbed the service staircase. She had forgotten to ask about the bathing room short cut last night and would be sure to re-member it when she got there. Her turn around times were tighter now she was back in the kitchen and even a few minutes spared would be worth the taking if she could. Besides, she would not have to bump into the housemaids on her journey who routinely snubbed her and fell into low chatter as she passed. Or, as she considered, meeting her on the land-ing, Miss Pascal either, who was making her way down.

'Well,' she said, stopping to speak to her and casting an up and down glance over the look of her. 'An improvement on zis morning but now you carry zee air of an imposter again. You really cannot win,' she said tartly with a laugh in her eyes.

'Well, so long as my mistress is happy with me, then I am happy,' An-nalise replied after having bid herself remain silent.

'Yes, well we know why zat is, don't we?'

'Oh?'

'Don't play zee innocent with me. I know how you keep your mistress 'appy and it is not your work.'

'What is that supposed to mean? If my mistress has an issue with the standard of my work, she would tell me.'

'Would she? Or would she suffer it to retain zee *extra* comforts you bring to her?'

Annalise frowned and got the distinct feeling they were having two parallel conversations with entirely different threads. 'I don't know what you mean, Miss Pascal, but I will say that I mean to progress in my training and your attempts to undermine the effort shall not interfere with it.'

She made a sniggering sound and said: 'You think you are zee only one who knows how to put your 'ands up zee madam's skirts and relieve her?'

'What?'

'You know exactly what I mean. Sharing zee bed with her, I have seen it.'

'Yes, you have seen us share the bed once, and what of it?'

'You shan't have zee monopoly on her always you know, she grows very fond of me too. Soon you will see.' And with that, she flicked her head up in the air and continued down the stairs.

She felt a strange sense of wanting to laugh and wanting to recoil in disgust at the insinuations she was sure Miss Pascal was making. Did she really believe that she performed some inappropriate service to her mistress? Could she be that crack-brained to believe her mistress would make such a peculiar and unnatural request as to expect them fondle each other? It seemed most ridiculous and disturbing simultaneously. And what did she mean she was growing fond of her too? Did she mean to suggest she was willing to participate in such behaviours? *It is women like her who give the French a bad name,* she thought as she climbed the remaining flight of stairs.

Rising tensions.

October 1821. - Eleanor.

I had taken care to send Camille away ten minutes before Annalise was due to attend me today. After yesterday, it seemed a prudent effort to keep them as much apart as I could manage. I could sense the growing animosity and realised now that once Annalise had completed her training, I must see to encouraging Camille elsewhere. It would have been easy before, with so many persons to make recommendations to in my circle, but now I could not think who might take her on. But she was excellent in many ways and I felt certain that she would surely find a situation without difficulty if I could only prompt her into doing so.

I did not think it would take much longer for Annalise to come about now her hand was mending. She needed practice more than instruction now and so I was minded to ensure that she got plenty and make at least two changes of dress each afternoon, even though no more than one for dinner was much needed given the flatness of my social calendar. But I meant to pay a visit to Lady W. soon in London, even if a short one of just a few days to compensate for the longer one I had abandoned. Our correspondence remained lively but it had been a while now since we had last been in company and her society was so merry that I knew it would be worth the journeying, however brief the stay.

So, when Annalise came to me, I discussed with her the possibility of her accompanying me to London for a few days.

'Oh, Eleanor, I would love to go,' she said to me with a hint of regret about her tone. 'But I have only returned to the kitchen this morning and to be quite honest, I just don't think Cook would tolerate my going just yet. And I know you could smooth it all out with her, but you see, in the long term, that only makes her more resentful. Perhaps this time it might be best if Miss Pascal attends you.'

'I see,' I said, trying not to let my disappointment show. For I was disappointed. Not only because I had planned to take her out to see some sights too, but because the idea of her being so willing and able to deal with days of our separation felt painful to me, knowing I struggled to count down the hours to her coming each day.

'I'm sorry,' she said placing a hand upon my knee. 'I wish I could go. I should much rather be at your disposal than Cook's, I assure you. But for now, I must placate her. You do understand, don't you?'

I nodded. 'Of course. If you are sure, then I shall ask Camille instead.'

'Next time, hopefully.'

I smiled against the rising sadness in me. At times like this I wondered if I truly mattered to her the way she did to me. But there was nothing to be done and so I contrived my best effort at turning the conversation to something else. I did not know why I felt so sensitive today. There was the matter of another letter from Giles this morning that I had actually bothered to open today since Annalise's sighting of him yesterday had brought home to me his proximity. And I supposed there was the growing want in me to break away to an independent way of life, where I could have my own home and my own staff and arrangements to suit me. It was becoming increasingly impossible to see how I would ever achieve this whilst remaining out of his reach. I wished he would just disappear across the sea somewhere on one of his merchant ships not to return again.

But I did not mean to sit about in melancholy counting my troubles. The sun was out and the weather still warm, but for how much longer I did not know. So, I encouraged Annalise out on to the park with a promise to teach her the game of Battledore as I had meant to before she had injured herself.

'Now,' I said to her showing her how to hold the bat and adjust her grip more flexibly, 'the shuttlecock is light as is the bat, but have a care with your hand and if it feels fatigued, we shall stop, alright?'

She nodded.

'So, I am going to serve first; like so,' I dropped the shuttlecock onto my racket and bounced it up into the air and prompted her to do the same. 'It's easier if you drop it from a little height. Have a practice at hitting it up and once you grow familiar, we shall serve to each other.' I watched her as she dropped it clumsily several times before growing more proficient. The concentration in her face was focused on the movements of the shuttlecock as it flew up into the air and she broke into a smile as it landed and she caught it, sending it high above our heads.

'I did it,' she said as her distraction cost her this landing.

'You did,' I smiled and as my eyes settled on hers, I found it difficult to draw them away. The lifting of her features and the dimples that formed in her cheeks only upon smiling, had the effect of sending me into a temporary paralysis where I wanted only to look at her, admire her and cast the image to my memory for later perusal. She was so pretty, effortlessly so and whilst I tried not to get carried off in such thoughts, there were moments like this when I felt totally suspended in the sight of such affecting beauty.

'What, what is it? Am I making a terrible hash of it?' she asked me with a light frown across her brow.

I drew away and collected my own shuttlecock from the ground to shake myself out of this infatuated gaze. 'Of course not, you are doing very well and I think we are ready to try out a game.'

We got off to a rather haphazard start with more time spent re-gathering the dropped shuttlecocks than actually hitting them between us. But we grew steadily improved and enjoyed longer bouts of passing it back and forth between gathering it. We had both got into the rhythm of things and were leaping and bounding across the grass to catch it and it felt merry and invigorating to spend such energy. I was glad I had managed so much of the sewing lately, but the hours of sitting about in the task did little for my health and although I made a habit of a morning walk and ride on Samson, it was not always enough to dispel the fidgets that accumulated as I sat for hours at my sewing box. I liked the feeling of my blood rushing through my limbs and my breaths growing raspy with the effort. It felt good. I felt alive. And as I paused to catch my breath a moment whilst she gathered up another missed serve, I considered what other sports I might introduce her to before the weather changed. We might go boating in the lake. Swimming even, although I doubted it was quite hot enough for that now. Perhaps in the peak of the day. We could try at skittles and even some archery if I could have the groundsmen set the targets up in one of the meadows.

'Ready?' Annalise called, poised to serve and the sunlight caught across her eyes making them sparkle and showing up all the lighter coloured flecks in them.

I adore you.

We had been at it for quite a time when we finally gave into the exhaustion and laid upon our backs on the grass, recovering. Looking up into the blueness of the sky and frowning against the sun when it burned too bright in our direction.

'Well, that was merry. I liked it more than I expected, even if I am not very good.'

'You are good, it was your first attempt too. I am glad you enjoyed it. What say you to shooting arrows?'

She turned her cheek to the grass to look at me head on, 'It depends what at?'

'At targets, that's all.'

'Well, why not then. So long as it's not some poor unsuspecting creature, then I would give it a try.'

'I rather thought I might make sketches of my husband for the purpose, that would no doubt improve my aim,' I said half funning and half serious.

She laughed a little, no doubt thinking me in only jest. 'What will happen if you continue to refuse to return to him?' she said more seriously now.

'Well, not a lot since I am already a social pariah these days. I suppose he could file for separation and it is my earnest hope that he will be brought to so doing once he sees I shan't be persuaded back.'

'Would that render you free again?'

'Well, to an extent, free of any marital obligations to him, but not free to re-marry if that's what you mean.'

'No. You would need a divorce and no one ever gets them, or at least I am told. In Old Mill Street years ago, one of the sailors that lodged in one of the tenements sold his wife to the blacksmith's son—said since he couldn't divorce her, he would be happy with a guinea.'

'Madness, isn't it? I should like to be able to sell Giles though, if I could. I rather like the notion in reverse—husband selling.' We both laughed a little harder at this.

'But what will you do if ever you do fall in love again?'

'Again? I was never in love to begin with. But I suppose we would have to become secret lovers. That or disappear to some place where we aren't known and attempt to start afresh, change our names, something like that.' But even as I spoke of it, I knew it to be fruitless talk. I would never want to remarry. I would likely never fall in love with someone I *could* marry anyway. Not unless I changed more than my name and assumed a male persona.

'What about children, do you not want a family one day?'

'Yes, I did once upon a time and I suppose there is a part of me that still would, one day. But I could never bear his children. The idea is abhorrent to me. And so, I must grow content with being an aunt I suppose. I should like to see more of my sister's children. They are merry company and I miss so much of their growing up.'

'Perhaps you should go to stay more often?'

I would, I considered, if it did not mean leaving you behind. 'Well, I would need my maid with me to travel on my own.'

'Give me a little time to pacify Cook and I shall attend you, I promise.'

'She sounds like a right old scratch-cat.'

Annalise grinned before straightening her expression. 'I must not say so, even if I cannot disagree.'

'You can say whatever you like in my hearing without concern you know.'

'I know.'

'Do you want to have a family one day?'

'Yes, I do. Just not anytime soon. I have...other things to settle in my life before I consider those kinds of things. I am just getting used to standing on my own feet without my mama's protection, I certainly am not ready to become one yet.'

'Who would you marry, if you could?'

'No one I could name. But a kind man, I think. And one that wants more than a free maidservant and child bearer.'

We laughed. 'Well, I think you might be on quite a quest.'

'Yes, well, all the more reason to be in no great rush.'

'But don't you get lonely sometimes. Have a want for passion and...comfort?'

'No. I suppose you do not miss what you do not know. Do you miss that?'

'Sometimes, but not with him.'

She reached out and held my hand and gave it a little squeeze. 'Well, I suppose we must be grateful for friends.'

'I am grateful for you.'

She smiled. 'And I for you.'

A spell of silence fell between us then and I wondered what she was thinking of. I was thinking of ways to prevent myself speaking out of turn and confessing to her that I would be quite content for it to be just the two of us, alone and under a roof where we were both free of surveillance and restriction.

I wondered, if I could set up my own home—if I could figure out a way—if she would come and join me. She would miss her friends below stairs but I could offer them places, promotions, pay rises, whatever it took to make her happy, to make her come. But I could not see a way through to such an end without him discovering me and forcing me to flee. Here, I was safe. But how could I argue a trespass against a home that was of his paying and obtained on account of his name? It was impossible. Unless—I considered sensing something of a brainwave—I found an alternative way of paying for things.

Drawing on banker's drafts and accounts of credit would always leave a trail behind me. But what if I used them to buy goods I could sell or pawn for cash? Coin would leave no trace at all. I could buy expensive things, begin collecting them. Things that were easily resalable: Jewellery, silverware, even horses and carriages. I was entitled to all of these things under my dowry alone. I could not believe I had not thought of it before. The idea of wasting his money and driving up bills for him to settle on: yes, but only to irritate him and encourage him to dispense with an expensive wife which he enjoyed none of the pleasures of. But to use this tactic to create an untraceable bank of savings, I had never advanced the idea, until now.

It would not be a quick solution. God knows how many things I would have to buy and what I might lose in the selling of them before I accumulated anything capable of long-term sustenance. But I must start. The sooner, the better. I must familiarise myself with the dealers of such wares who would pay readily in coin and ask no questions, and discover the best things to buy to get a quick return. Rarities and collectables might be a place to start. The auction houses would give a clue to the type of thing worth looking out for. I need not even make a profit or crack even on them, so long as it added to the sum.

I sat up then. 'I think I am going to go up to my room and take care of some correspondence,' I said to Annalise, planning to write off to Christie's and some other auction houses to request their catalogues. I would scan the papers too—that would surely be one way to sell things—placing advertisements and letting the buyers come to me.

'Alright. Shall I bring you a tray up, something to eat or drink?' Annalise said, lifting up to her elbows.

'No, no, I will be fine. Why don't you take an hour's leisure and we can perhaps take a little refreshment together afterwards if you would like it?' I said, getting up and brushing grass from my skirt.

'Oh, Eleanor!' she said and I turned about puzzled at the alarm in her voice.

'What's wrong?'

'You have a stain upon your skirts,' she said getting up to her feet too now.

'Is that all?' I said trying to reach around to see.

'I fear it is your monthly blood,' she said then and I felt instantly embarrassed. I'd forgotten entirely to keep abreast of my dates lately—there no longer seemed any need—and I had had no hint of discomfort to remind me. 'Is it very noticeable?'

She nodded and lifted the fabric so I could see it.

'Goodness.'

'It's alright, I shall walk behind you when we go into the house and no one shall see.'

There was little choice but to attempt it since I had nothing to cover myself with. There had been no need for a shawl or Pelisse on such a warm afternoon and we hadn't bothered bringing a rug or blanket to sit on since we had all of the battledore things to carry. We gathered them up and set off for the house with Annalise hovering behind in case of any onlookers.

'Shall we go through the basement? You can use the staircase from the bathroom?'

'Good thinking. Although I expect it will be locked and my key is in my escritoire.'

'Well, I imagine Mrs Crawford will have one, I can fetch it from her?'

'Yes, if you will. I shall just have to stand against a wall in the wait for you.' Which is what I did, for at least ten minutes until she came bounding up the corridor.

'Sorry, she was in her parlour around the other side of the house.'

'Thank you,' I said as she unlocked the door and eased it open. 'Make sure you lock it back up won't you,' I said once we were inside. I didn't like the thought that it might be left open and go forgotten. Although I kept the access door in my room locked, there was something spooky about the idea that someone could be stood right behind it without my knowing. It was a fear I had had as a child but since it was first Caitlyn's, then Harri's room, I never had to trouble over the thought of waking in the night to find it open or someone standing over the bed. A brief image of waking up to seeing Giles stood over me with the jib ajar sent a shiver over my shoulders and I shook the thought.

'Shall we get you sorted out down here since we have everything to hand? Shall you want a wash or the bathtub filled?' Annalise asked as we passed through it.

'No, you go and have your break and I shall call Miss Pascal to help me.' I could not bear the embarrassment of her finding me in such an in-delicate mess and having to deal with my soiled rags and water. I didn't know what I would do if she ever did replace Miss Pascal completely. I supposed I would have to learn to see to it myself for I could never bring myself to permitting her to wait on me in such matters. It was the very same reason I was happy for her to take the later shift and not have to deal in my chamber pot each morning. By the time she arrived, it was all replaced clean and afresh and I would send her on an errand if I was ever desperate to use it in her company.

'Don't be silly, I can go after you are made comfortable.'

'No, really, I insist. Come and open up my door for me and I shall ring for Miss Pascal.'

She conceded with a puzzled look upon her face and I wished I could explain. But what could I say? I was shy of her seeing me in such inelegance because I did not want her to hold such images of me in her mind? That I didn't care if Camille did for I had no reason or care to impress her?

Perhaps had Annalise been an Abigail before and grown used to such unpleasant tasks it might not have seemed so daunting to have her undertake them. But she had not been, and I did not want to be the source of such a memory.

Camille was not phased at all by it and dealt in all my soiled garments whilst I sat over a bowl of water and cleaned up. She did not protest at being called upon during Annalise's shift and I told her simply that Annalise was on another errand and so I had to call for her. She accepted it without question and I thanked her for her trouble and declined her rather peculiar offering of performing some kind of massage to my abdomen to ease the cramps. She assured me that her previous mistress had declared it a marvel and never hesitated to summon her to rub away the pains each month. I knew her to be thorough and attentive in her work but this was a little too thorough for my liking and I sent her away with thanks and said I would call for a hot brick if I grew uncomfortable.

I considered, once she had gone, that had Annalise made such a suggestion, I might have been open minded to trying, but not for want of pain relief. More for want of feeling her touch, being that close to her. It was the thing that had become most crippling now, the desire, the longing to hold her and caress her when my heart felt fit to burst. Whilst we were tactile in our way, even this I had had to be careful of now for fear of reading it wrong or making some slip up and taking it too far. When she had used to stay the night with me it had been more acceptable to let her lay close against me for such a time, but it was inappropriate outside of that circumstance and I longed for her to agree to stay again, so we might curl up like that and feel the warmth and sweet proximity of each other.

But I had ceased in the asking after so many apologetic refusals. I did not mean to pester or beg and so I did not repeat the asking as she kissed my cheek goodnight, even though I wanted so desperately to throw caution to the wind and make another try. I had hoped by now that she would have felt the urges I was feeling. That she would have shown some sign or gave a clue by now. And whilst there were moments when I felt she came close or gave away some hint, they were too infrequent and ambiguous to be certain.

'Zis is 'ow you blend zee liquid roses,' Camille said to Annalise, picking up the jar of Pears and smoothing a dab into the apple of my cheek. I had a rare invitation to dine out this evening at Delores' and it seemed opportune to give Annalise a painting lesson since we had not covered the use of cosmetics yet. Not that I frequently used them, but a little enhancement, if done with a delicate hand was always worth the knowing.

'Can I try?' Annalise asked Camille and she handed her the pot.

'No, no, just a little, a dab,' she corrected Annalise and directed her to wipe the excess onto a cloth before proceeding. She did as bid and leant in close to my face—I presumed examining the symmetry of where to place it and I tried with all my will not to look too carefully at her. Not to show my delight in feeling the soft mist of her breath against my face or the pressure of her fingertips as she applied the lotion to my cheeks.

'More blending, more blending,' Camille said with increasing impatience. It was this that had almost convinced me to forego the lesson, but with so little left for Annalise to learn, it seemed silly to delay it.

Annalise stepped back holding a red fingertip in the air as she considered her efforts.

'No, no she cannot go out like zis, look, come behind and look in zee mirror—see? It must not be detectable. It looks like you have stamped her upon zee cheek. Zis will not do.'

'Camille,' I cut in, not liking her tone. 'It is her first attempt, have a little patience, will you?'

'Of course, madame, but she does not follow my instructions. I told her light touch, a dab.'

'I'm sorry,' Annalise said to me, 'I am not very good at these things.'

'It is only practice that makes perfect. Do not be disheartened,' I said and she smiled at my reassurance. 'Now, how about we remove this and start again from scratch?' I ignored Camille's sigh as she reached for the cloth. She was never like this when we were alone. Quite the contrary; she was helpful, overly sometimes, enthusiastic as if nothing could be too much trouble. Yet in Annalise's company, she was waspish and impatient and it had begun to nip at me now.

'Right zen, zis, is how we take off zee cosmetics,' Camille said, pouring more hot water from the kettle into the basin and immersing the cloth. 'You use zee prong to pick it up or it will scold you,' she said, lifting the steaming cloth from the water and letting the excess drip off. 'After a few seconds, you may squeeze it out while it is still warm, and apply it to madame's face like so.'

I felt my face enveloped in steaming warmth.

'Do not cover zee mouth and nose, she must breathe. When it begins to lose its warmth, you may remove zee residues with a little pressure, like so. If it does not all come off in zee first try, you may repeat—here.'

Annalise repeated the process and once again I was engulfed in steam and the pressure of her hands was welcome. We went through the process again from the start now and this time got as far as the lash and brow darkening before Camille started up again in irritable style.

'Goodness me! I said a little, and to 'old zee paper below to catch the excess! Now look at it, she 'as black ash all over 'er cheek and we shall 'ave to start again!'

'I'm sorry, my coordination in this hand is still a little shaky.'

'Camille, enough of this. She is learning for goodness' sake. It doesn't matter if we must try over.'

'She will never learn,' she said to me in French this time and I supposed she mistakenly thought Annalise would not be able to understand her. I was about to appraise her of the contrary when she set off in a rant rendering me unable to get a word in.

'You waste your time and generosity with her, madame,' she continued again in French. 'She is better off in the kitchens where you found her. She has no talent in this work. She is clumsy and heavy handed and does not pay attention to what I show her.'

'How dare you, Camille? It is not your place to comment or decide, but mine.'

'Eleanor, please, she is right. I am a liability,' Annalise cut in and Camille frowned.

'I'm sorry, madame, but it is the truth,' she continued on, still in French. 'If you want me to train someone, you must give me someone who can be trained. She is a waste of effort. I have shown her everything and look what she does...' she gestured at my powder spattered cheekbone. 'It is impossible.'

'Camille, I beg you hold your tongue. You are coming dangerously close to being dismissed.'

'Eleanor, no—' Annalise cut in and placed a gentle hand over mine which was gripping the arm of the chair as I got ready to rise from it.

'Me dismissed, madame? Me? When I serve you so well and tend to you properly. You shall dismiss me for telling you the truth?'

'Yes, Camille, you do, and then you go and ruin it all by forgetting yourself and being unkind.'

'I would never be unkind to you, madame.'

'Well, in being unkind and impatient with Annalise, I deem it just as bad. Leave me now, Camille, before I say something you will regret.'

'Then who shall get you ready for the dinner party? She cannot manage. You will end up looking like Marie Antoinette.'

'Enough! Get out of my sight.'

'Fine. I know she is your favourite. I have seen the way you look at her, the way you want her. But not me. For me, you have no care. It is her you lust after and she doesn't have a clue.'

'I can understand everything you are saying, Miss Pascal,' Annalise said as my cheeks flamed with embarrassment and I could not find any words.

'Parlez-vous Francais?'

'Oui, je le fais même si je ne suis qu'une femme de ménage! Je pense que vous devriez faire comme madame et partir maintenant.'*Translation: Yes, I do! Even though I am only a kitchen maid! I think you should do as madame bid and leave now. *

With that, Camille put down the dish of ashes she had been holding, lifted her chin in the air like a spoilt child, crossed the room and left.

I let out a long-drawn sigh. 'I'm sorry, Annalise, she had no right to speak so ill of you. I know you are trying and you are coming about, you really are.'

'Perhaps, but I have a long way to go and I don't blame her for growing frustrated with me. I am not a natural like her.'

'No one is a natural, Annalise, it is merely practice and experience. Everyone makes mistakes in the learning. Molly once gave me talc to clean my teeth with instead of tooth powder and burnt a strand of curls from my head with the irons.'

'Well, I suggest you keep those irons away from me, if I really am as useless as Miss Pascal thinks I am.'

'It doesn't matter what she thinks, Annalise. I think you are wonderful and nothing will alter that.' I realised quickly I had said too much as a mist of uncertainty crossed her expression and in the light of what Miss Pascal had just disclosed to her, it was a stupid thing to say at such a time.

'Well, I shall try to be worthy of your confidence. Shall we have another go?' she said in an even tone, but I could see her mind ticking over in other lines of thought.

'Yes, I suppose so.'

We had a couple of little mishaps in the retry, but thankfully the sort that could be corrected along the way rather than require our starting from scratch. I helped her this time. I could manage this part myself, if necessary. Even if not as well as Camille could, it was perfectly adequate. And with my hair, she did a good a job, for this she had had more practice in and once she had adorned me of my jewellery ornaments, I was in perfectly good style for the evening. 'See,' I said to her as she stood back and examined me. 'I told you you could do it.'

She half smiled. 'Well, that is partly owing to your help and in the other part how pretty you are anyway,' she said, and it made my heart skip with joy to have such a compliment from her.

'You think me pretty?' I asked her again for want of confirmation.

'Of course, you are.. Uncommonly so. Even without all these concoctions. Now, shall I get you a pelisse or a cape? It might be a little nippy now the sun has set.'

'My green cape will do, thank you,' I said, struggling to repress the wide mouthed smile that wanted to erupt from me at her words. The joy of this hearing had seemed to wash away all the bitterness that was simmering after Camille's outburst, even to the degree that when she implored me not to be hasty and dismiss Camille, but give her a chance to make apology, I agreed. I did not really want to after her embarrassing me in such a style and knowing that she understood my feelings for Annalise was a further risk I could have done without. But, it was true that she did not know Annalise could understand her speech and I knew Annalise would think ill of me if I did not give her a chance to be forgiven. And so, I promised to sleep on it and see how things were in the morning.

Sham Abram.

October 1821. -Annalise.

It was an early break for Annalise tonight once she waved Eleanor off looking beautiful and elegant for her evening out. She had spent not above an hour tidying up her quarters and setting out her bed things ready for her return tonight. But she had found the whole ordeal of these cosmetics quite arduous and could not entirely disagree with Miss Pascal's assessment of her talents, or lack thereof. Give her a chicken to pluck or a fish to gut any day over that fussy rigmarole.

She went into the servants' hall to keep herself awake. There was a danger of her falling asleep and failing to answer the bell call when Eleanor returned if she dared to keep to her room. She hoped it would not be too late, but was not sure what Eleanor had meant by "country hours" and so was left guessing. Her return to the kitchen was tiring her more than she had expected and even though it was only half the day to bear, it seemed to take more toil than before.

The servants' hall was quiet and she realised that it would be a little while until the others retired and joined her. So, she gathered her sewing box and fabric and laid it out upon the table in the hall and set to work on it. She would clear it away when the others filtered in, but for now, whilst it was deserted, she meant to take advantage of the better working space and light.

She was pinning a paper pattern to a ream of thickly weaved calico when she heard footsteps into the room and looked up from her work. Of all the persons she did not expect to see in here it was Miss Pascal. She had her own parlour to retire to with the upper servants and had not made a habit of frequenting this one. But she did not look dressed for relaxation with her Redingote buttoned up to her chin and her bonnet in hand.

'Oh, it's you,' she said. 'Who do I see about getting a carriage?'

'The groom, I suppose. But where are you going?'

'I am leaving. I will not stay where I am not wanted and I will not be fired, so I 'ave quit.'

'No, she is not going to dismiss you. You are overreacting.'

'You heard her say so, didn't you?'

'Yes, when she was angry, in the heat of the moment. But once she had calmed down, she saw reason and is not minded to dismiss you. At least, she shan't if you have the sense to make her an apology.'

'And she said zis?'

'Yes.'

'Well, it makes no difference; she has made her feelings clear. It is you she wants, not me.'

'Don't be ridiculous. We have an equal share of the role. She needs us both. As you said, I am not up to standard...yet.'

'It does not matter. She will be pleased with anything you do and I will remain invisible to her no matter how well I serve her.'

'Of course, you don't. She often sings your praises, telling me I am learning from the best.'

'Perhaps, but you have her heart and I can't compete with zat.'

'Compete? There is nothing to compete for. And I own we have grown as fond friends, but in time you shall too.'

She laughed wryly. 'No, she does not think of me the way she thinks of you. If you ask me, she is in love with you.'

'Don't be so absurd. I don't know what you mean by all these unnatural accusations, but you are quite mistaken if you think—'

'I am not mistaken. It is you zat cannot see it. She did not deny it either, did she? Hmm, you did not think about zat, did you? She could not, for she knew it was true and she could not deny it. Oh, you think it unnatural or impossible zat a woman may fall in love with her own sex? Enjoy the comforts of her own sex? Zen you are very green my child.'

Annalise did not know what to say to this. Was she green? Was this possible? She could not imagine it so being. 'Look, it is late. Why don't you go to bed and think about it? In the morning, with a fresher head, you can decide whether to go to her and make apology, or if you remain of this mind, have the coach convey you to wherever it is you mean to go. But I hope you will see sense by then.'

'Sense, I am seeing sense. There is no room for me here.'

'Oh, and where else will you get paid so handsomely for having half a day at your leisure? And a kind mistress like this?'

She seemed to consider these points. 'Why do you try to convince me to stay?'

'Because there is no need for you to go. No need for us to be enemies either. We may all start over tomorrow and put this behind us. What is it?'

'Perhaps I have ill-judged you. It is perhaps zee only thing I have been wrong about, but—'

'Well, I prefer not to hold grudges. I mean it: we may start again tomorrow,' and with this saying, Annalise held out her hand as a peace offering.

'I cannot take it. I do not deserve your forgiveness.'

'Well, you have it.'

'No, you will change your mind when you realise what I 'ave done.'

'What have you done?' she asked, dropping her outstretched hand.

'I told Fanny. I'm sorry. I was angry. I should not 'ave.'

'Told her what?'

'Zat madame has a tendre for you.'

Annalise's heart sunk.

'See, I told you I did not deserve it. I will go now. I am sorry though. You did not deserve my unkindness.' She turned on her heels and got almost to the door before Annalise called out:

'Miss Pascal.'

'Oui?'

'Go and tell Fanny you were mistaken and go to bed.'

She gave her an incredulous look. 'Zat is it? You are not angry with me.'

'I am upset. But I am not angry.'

'I did not mean to upset you. I meant to upset madame. And even if you are good enough to forgive me—she will not.'

'She need not know.'

'You will not tell her?'

Annalise shook her head and sat back down at the table.

'I will speak to Fanny now...thank you, Annalise.'

When she picked her sewing work back up, she realised she had no head for it now and began to gather it up instead. She did not know what line of thought to follow. There was so much swimming about in her head now: The peculiarity of Miss Pascal's accusations. The oddity of Eleanor's lack of denial. The dread of what would be doing the rumour mill by morning now Fanny had this notion in her head. Miss Pascal might well try to retract it, but Fanny would not care for that. She would run with it anyway and she must prepare herself for the onslaught tomorrow.

If it was not for the promise of her plans to buy the dwelling shop in Carshalton, she might have sunk into a despairing misery over all this business. But she knew now that her future did not rest solely on her remaining here anymore, and so if it really did get too bad, she had alternative options. Well, she would, if she had had confirmation from Mr Morgan, but still, she had not.

She spent an hour about the table with her friends when they came in, trying to forget all the bad business for a while and made no mention of what had passed. How could she even begin to broach such a fancy as the accusation that had been levelled at her mistress? In love with her own sex, her own maid? It seemed such an odd kind of fancy to contrive and yet she was resolute that it was borne of a fiction and had not an ounce of truth to it. They were friends. Close friends perhaps. But love. Romance. What an idea.

It was an idea that plagued her no less, and when she was called at close to midnight to tend to Eleanor on her return, she could not help but feel a tad more cautious around her even if she did do her best to hide it.

'How was your dinner, miss?' she asked her as evenly as she could.

'It was nice to go out for a change, I suppose. But I would have rather been in your company.'

Annalise contrived a thin-lipped smile and untied the ribbon on her cape.

'How was your evening? I hope you have not taken Camille's unkindness to heart. You look a little forlorn, I must say.'

'No, I know she was just frustrated. I'm sure she did not mean it.'

'You are too good, Annalise. You only like to see the good in people. Oh, don't look like that, it is not a fault. It is part of your beautiful character. I just worry that you will permit yourself be so abused by such persons and you do not deserve it.'

'Do you think me green, miss?'

'What an odd question and what's with the miss? We are quite alone now.'

'Sorry, I forgot. But do you? Honestly?'

'Well, perhaps in some matters, but then in others where I am green you are knowing. So, I suppose we just have different experiences.'

'Do you believe that it is possible for two females to be in love?'

'Annalise, what is all this about?'

'Just answer the question.'

'Very well. I suppose many things are possible that might seem, foreign to us.'

'Have you ever been in love with your own sex?'

'No. Have you?'

'Of course not. I'm sorry, I'm just tired, I did not mean to speak out of turn.'

'Well, let's concentrate on getting me changed and you might retire.'

She nodded and focused on her task, feeling an unusual awareness as she stripped her to her shift. An awareness of her scent, her flesh, the tang of something sweet on her breath when she leant in to remove the cosmetics they had spent such pains applying. It was as though her senses had swelled and made every sight, sound and sense swell with it. The creak of the floorboards as she stepped about her, the swish and crease of fabric as her clothes were discarded, the sound of an exhale after a suspension of breath.

When she had tidied away her things, drawn the drapes and turned down the bed for her, she instinctively went towards her to kiss her cheek goodnight as was the normal routine, but tonight she felt a hesitancy and simply said: 'Goodnight, sleep well,' and made for the door.

Annalise laid awake half the night in thoughtful anguish. Where her body longed for sleep, her mind was overactive and would not be subdued or turned to other matters. She felt ungrounded and lost in a maze of impossibility. She wanted to call out to Poppy, just to hear her voice; an anchor to help her remember herself, to feel herself again. But Poppy was snoring lightly into her pillow and even if she had been desperate enough to wake her at times, what would she say? Am I green, Poppy? Do you think my mistress has a romantic tendre for me?

Morning came about cruelly in a mist of thin grey light as Poppy fidgeted about the room getting dressed and stirring her. 'Come on, madam, we got 'alf hour before we're to work, wake your sleepy 'ead up and come and get some breakfast.'

'I can't,' Annalise said, covering her reluctant eyes with a hand. 'I think I'm ill.'

'What's wrong, luv?' Poppy pressed a palm to her forehead.

She tried to construct a story through the inertia of half sleep, 'I've got stomach cramps and a headache. I've hardly slept a wink all night,' she lied.

'Oh, luv. Do you want the pot?'

Annalise shook her head. 'No, I just need to sleep.'

'Alright, luv, I'll tell Cook for yer. Must be somein you've eaten.'

'My tummy hasn't been quite right since I dined at the inn,' she lied again.

'Daresay that's what it is. Hopefully it's almost through your system. Get some sleep and I'll come and check on you in a bit.'

When she was gone, Annalise felt engulfed in such guilt for lying to Poppy like that. She had never feigned a sick day in her life or told Poppy an outright lie. Yes, she had of late kept much from her knowing, but to gull her like this was a new low. She cried herself back to sleep wondering what she had come to, to be unable to talk openly with her best friend.

When Poppy returned later with a mug of peppermint tea and a letter for her, she came better to her senses and told Poppy she was feeling much improved and would return to the kitchen once she was up. That if she could prevail upon her to send a message to Miss Pascal, she would ask her to cover her shift with Eleanor so she might make the lost time up to cook. She agreed to the undertaking, made a little fuss about her looking peaky and suggesting she get a little more rest before throwing herself back into the kitchen so soon, then left her to her letter and mug of steaming tea.

If everything else was going ill, it seemed that one thing was to come about. The letter was from Mr Harrison saying Mr Morgan had consulted with the trustees and would accept an offer of four hundred and fifty-five, what should he tell him. She scribbled a hurried reply saying: "Yes, four-fifty-five is fine. Let's proceed as quick as possible."

Cook was pacified by her willingness to work the whole of the day in compensation for her late start in the kitchen and whilst she remained harsh and aloof with her, she knew that prioritising her duties to the kitchen over her mistress' had seemed to go some way with her. She did not like her authority usurped and it was this, she knew, above all else that had caused her to grow so wicked with her. So, she worked tirelessly and had very little to say to anyone, even Maggie, as she ploughed through one task to another, and it was on her sustenance break that Miss Pascal came into the servants' hall to find her. Immediately, she stepped out into the yard with her.

'Thank you for taking over today. I appreciate it,' Annalise said when they were out of hearing.

'It is zee least I could do. But I thought you were sick?'

'I am feeling better, but I am needed in the kitchen to keep Cook happy and make up for the time.'

'I see.'

'Did you manage to smooth things out with madame?'

'Yes, she gave me a setting down all zee same, but we are alright now. She wants me to apologise to you—'

'You already did, and like I said, you are quite forgiven. How did you get on with Fanny?'

'Well, zee good news is zat she agreed to keep quiet from now on. Zee bad news, is she already told a couple of zee 'ousemaids last night before I came to 'er.'

Annalise felt a genuine cramping in her gut now.

'But she assures me, she has sworn them to keep it quiet and insists that zay will take 'eed of her.'

'Thank you.'

'I am sorry, Annalise. I did not think. And I want you to know zat I really do feel terrible about it.'

Annalise smiled thinly. 'I know.'

'Anyway, madame is concerned for you. She asked me to check and see 'ow you do. What shall I tell her?'

'Umm... Well, tell her I am unlikely to be able to return to her for a couple of days, that the kitchen is busy and Cook is displeased.'

She cast an incredulous glance over her but said only: 'Very well. I will take care of madame until you are back.'

It became clear to her that evening which of the housemaids Fanny had told as they sniggered and dropped to low voices in her presence. The hostility from them she had grown used to since Fanny's outburst, but there was a new flash of relish and ridicule in their sideways glances now. She had readily ignored them before but this time it got to her. It was the concern over what they were thinking and saying: Who else they might tell.

So, she huddled close to her friends that evening in the servants' hall and for a change did not mind entertaining Will's attentions a little more openly. She knew she hoped that a counter impression might help to dispel the other narrative a little quicker and so she let down her guard a little, even sat up with him a while with her sewing box when all the others had retired to bed. It mattered not now if they thought something betwixt them. Her letter would be with Mr Harrison now and she would soon have Carshalton to fall back on should things continue growing so impossible here.

The question of setting up there now seemed ever less of a question and in her exchanges with Mr Harrison that followed she gave him the go ahead to undertake a visit with the builders ahead of the preparation and signing of the sale contracts. He was to have the builder look the place over for any more rot or issues and to give a quote for the improvements. He was to have his own legal man look over the contracts too and was minded to have this done before anything was signed, although she was anxious to hurry things along without further delay. She could break the news to Poppy then at last, once it was all signed and certain. All of it—from the beginning—her visit to Gint's and all that had come after. If Poppy wanted to leave her post, she would have it set up as a pie shop. Help her in the task whilst they found their feet and got things off to a start. Later, she could concern herself with her dressmaking. If Poppy wished to remain for now, she would reverse the order and focus on the dressmaking room so she could get started. For she felt increasingly convinced that to go sooner rather than later, might prove the better choice after all.

Disappointment.

October 1821. - Eleanor.

I felt instantly miserable upon waking, remembering that she had left me without a goodnight kiss upon my cheek last night. My eyes were still sore from the tears I had spent in revisiting that moment before I finally got off to sleep. Was she frightened of me now? Did she understand what Camille had said? Her questions last night certainly seemed to indicate it. Camille's apology and beseeching for forgiveness only added insult to injury now I had realised the damage she had done. But I could not give Annalise any further cause to distrust me and I had given her my word, so I made certain to keep it, despite the fury bubbling beneath my measured speech.

But it was when she returned to me after breakfast explaining that Annalise was unwell, that I really begun to understand the extent of the damage. Then later when she advised me she was doing better but did not expect to be able to come to me for a couple of days that I fell into deeper despair and I feared for the first time in all seriousness, the prospect of losing her.

On the first day of her absence, I set my mind to diversion from these worries and went into Epsom to begin on the stockpiling of valuables I meant to begin trading in. I found little of great spending there, but returned with some pretty ornaments of gold and precious stone. London would be the place for such shopping and yet now things were so ill, I knew I must postpone the going until I had tried to settle things between us again.

By the end of day two I had begun to reconsider my idea of giving her space to calm down and began turning my mind towards trying to bring her around to remembering our fond friendship. Perhaps a day out somewhere or a nice picnic by the lake, or having the groundsmen set up the archery targets like we had spoken of. But when Camille came again to put me to bed that night bearing another apology that Annalise would not be returning tomorrow either, the panic really set in. I knew I must go to her directly and speak to her. Nip this avoidance in the bud and try to convince her to return to me. Give me a chance to show her there was nothing altered between us, nothing to be fearful of.

So, I wasted no time in having Camille dress me in my night robe and slippers and take me down to the basement via the bathroom staircase where I waited for her to summon Annalise to meet me in the bathroom. I sat nervously on the chaise picking at a snag in the upholstery whilst I waited for her to come. But it was not her who came through the door, but Camille...alone.

'I'm sorry, madame, I cannot find her.'

'What do you mean?'

'I went to her room like you said. Poppy said she is not yet come to bed and was still in zee servants' hall. But when I went zer, it was empty and all the lights are put out down zer now.'

I was perfectly mystified but had a nasty gut feeling at this news. 'Not to worry, Camille, it shall have to keep till morning. You go on up to your room, I am going to use the sink down here to clean my teeth since I am here now.'

'I will wait with you, madame.'

'No. Go up to bed. It is late and you started early. You may go back up through my room. Goodnight.'

Once the sound of her steps had tapered off into the distance, I picked up the candlestick and stepped into the basement as soundlessly as possible. I did not know my way well, but I knew the kitchen and servants' hall was at the other extent of this corridor, and I would start there to try to navigate myself to her room from the kitchen once I had my bearings.

I thought it likely she was in bed and had asked Poppy to send Camille away to avoid having to answer. It saddened me so much I felt I could hardly breathe against the constriction of my own chest as I walked the flags, cold beneath my thin slippers.

The servants' hall was indeed deserted, I cast a light fleetingly about it just to be sure and done the same as I passed at the kitchen door. But it was there I felt an inexplicable instinct to go in further, even though it was in darkness and silence. But then I noticed as I held still a moment, the vaguest rumble of voices and I set down my candle in the corridor and went quietly into the room. I had stepped halfway in when I noticed the back door ajar and that sitting upon the doorstep were two people, one of them Annalise, I recognised from her voice and a man sat beside her. I put my hand over my mouth to prevent it from betraying me and crying out in despair. For that is what I felt now, beyond all reason and proportion as Camille's words of the other day came fresh to my mind now: "the manservant she was fond of."

I knew, even with his back turned to me, that it was he who sat talking to her on the doorstep. It was like a knowing without knowing and all my worst fears began to sink me as I listened to their talk, which seemed innocent enough in subject—something on the topic of Carshalton Park, I gathered. But the tone and familiarity in which they spoke is what disturbed me: Him playing at charming her with a little funning, she laughing gaily along with it. Why did I never feel so aware of my heart as when it was close to breaking. I was sure that it could not bear another crack, another shattering, and yet I knew, instinctively, that I was heading for a fall. That I had betrayed myself somehow into thinking it could be otherwise. That the moment of reckoning was upon me.

I recognised the very same from that day Lady Caroline emerged from Sheldon's room. A fracturing of everything in a moment and I wanted to run before the moment caught up with me, yet I could only stand rooted to the spot, waiting, flinching, bracing for the crash of it all to be confirmed.

Then I saw her stand up and say; 'It's late. I need my bed,' and realising they were about to depart in my direction I rushed back out into the corridor, blew the flame out on the candle and took refuge in a shadowy corner, seeing only the shape of them through the glass pane beside the door. It was not a clear view, but adequate enough to see him rise beside her, close the kitchen door and press a kiss to her cheek. And there it was: the moment of fracture I sensed was coming. I held in my tears so I might watch them longer. I had not intended to spy on them but here I had led myself, to the facing of this unbearable scene. Holding my breath as they passed me unseen, departing in opposite directions as I mustered all the restraint I could summons to keep myself from leaping out in some fit of emotional rage.

Painstakingly, I waited to hear the click of the doors behind them, echoing along the corridor and only then did I let the hot tears spring from me as I moved away from the wall and found my way back to the bathroom in the thickening darkness. I trudged my way back up what seemed an abyss of total blindness as I felt my way up the winding stairs with my palms stretched out to the walls beside me to guide me along its bends and turns. Then I reached an end to the climbing and palmed my way to the door, a slither of light emanating from about the frame and I fumbled in my pocket for the key.

It was then, as my dazzled eyes were flooded with the glow of light from my room and I locked the door up behind me, I expected to collapse into torrents of tears. But nothing more came. Only a stunned silence; a sobering sense of familiarity at the sight of the room before me, seeming to be in perfect order. Like I was still in perfect order. That any moment, Annalise might walk into it and turn down the bed and put a kiss upon my cheek. Could all I have dreamt of lately really have been snatched from me again?

I walked straight past my bed and to my escritoire and found my diary and ink, took it over to the window seat and begun writing in automaton fashion, just like Maillardet's strange doll I had seen exhibited at Petworth.

I awoke with my head against the windowpane, my diary in my lap and a blob of now-dry ink bleeding through the pages where I had abandoned my pen. I frowned against the breaking first beams of sunlight across the horizon of trees and realised as I wiped the dew from my temple, that a headache was forming from the cold condensation that misted around the panes of window glass. I got up, stiff and a chill in my limbs as I staggered over to the bed and wrapped myself in the warmth of a blanket. The mantle clock read a quarter to seven and I knew it too early yet to prevail upon her. She might be up, breakfasting I supposed, but I meant to catch her alone, not in company. I had planned it all out last night. I was not to be so easily defeated. I knew she was worth the fighting for and I would never forgive myself for conceding without at least trying.

I would order a fine picnic to be set out by the lake this afternoon. There was talk of a mini heatwave and the sky had indeed been red last night. It was too early to tell yet, but so long as the rain kept off, it would be pleasant enough. But Camille would not be in for another hour and so I dozed upon the bed in an awareness of half misery, half hope, until I could set upon my plans.

I had considered sending my instructions for Grantley down with Camille, but she was too quick minded not to suspect my plans, and I wanted no hindrance or interruptions today. We were to be alone, without anyone else to influence our time and that meant nobody else could know, including Camille. So when I had poked about at the breakfast I had no appetite for, I had Camille dress me much more finely than she normally would for this hour. I gave her the story that I meant to set upon another shopping trip today and would not be back until dinner time.

But when I sent her away, I went down to find Grantley and give him directions to set up the picnic in my favourite aspect upon the lake for two-o-clock. I wanted to go earlier, but I knew that stealing her away from her morning shift would distress her and so I bid myself to keep to the hour of her coming. I only wished she demonstrated as much regard for displeasing me as she seemed to for Cook, who she was forever stepping around furtively as though trying to avoid waking a sleeping dragon. But it seemed of late she was of no mind to consider me at all, and it hurt like nothing else to consider how little I must mean to her. How little store she set by my disappointment.

But I was not for dwelling, I promised myself as I went down to her room and let myself into it, having a hallboy call her to join me. I assumed she would prefer it over me going into the kitchen and disturbing her and I was not to be shunned today. We were to deal in this once and for all.

Her face was a picture of astonishment at finding me there; horror, I thought more fitting and I stifled my despair a little tighter.

'Eleanor?' she said, frowning and trying to compose herself. She looked tired and scruffy with what looked like chicken feathers clinging to the fabric of her apron.

'Forgive the intrusion, but I thought you would prefer to talk privately.'

'Eleanor, I—'

'I see you are feeling better, yet you tell Camille you shall not come to me today?'

She bit her lip. 'I shan't lie to you. I have been distressed over all this bad business with Camille. She is right you know: I am better suited to the kitchen than playing at being your maid.'

'Don't say that, you know it is not true.'

'I'm not sure I know what is and isn't true anymore.'

I stepped in closer and lifted her hands in mine. 'Truly? You doubt the friends we have become?'

She looked up and met my eyes at last. 'No. Things just seem so, difficult now.'

'They don't have to be. Will you come out upon the park with me today? Give us a chance to talk more freely when you have time, away from the house?'

'I don't know—'

'Please. I ask you as your friend, not your mistress.'

She nodded.

'Two-o-clock, shall I meet you by the rose garden?'

'I will be there.'

Picnic on the Lake.

October 1821. - Eleanor.

She was there as promised, promptly upon the hour. It was only my coming early in all my anxiety and excitement that made it seem like she was late. It was hot today. Uncommon for this time of year and I was certain somewhere above twenty-five degrees. But I'd come prepared and brought parasols for us both. I popped one up and passed it to her as we set out. Little beyond stiff greetings passed between us and I felt poignantly aware of the distance that had grown in just a few days.

We walked far in the heat, to the furthest extent of the grounds where the towering walls of Cuddington quickly disappeared from our view beyond the screen of woodland. I had taken care to avoid any attempt to elaborate on our conversation in her room earlier. 'Let us wait until we are entirely out of earshot, we can talk properly then,' I insisted, keeping the conversation directed to lighter topics, such as how prettily the Salvia blossomed for this season, and how scorched the grass had turned in places as we trod it. Even the unfortunate topic of how the heat had caused the manure heap to sweat out a most offensive odour as we passed it, hands cupped over our noses until it faded.

As we came through a small clearing in the trees, the lake came into view, water twinkling in the gaze of the sun, a breeze sending ripples across its surface. I was pleased to find the rowboat stationed in place as had been requested, tied to its post beside the jetty, bobbing gently at the water's edge.

'Eleanor, who is going to drive this boat, there is no one here?' Annalise said, eyeing it suspiciously as we peered over from the edge of the riverbank.

'We will,' I told her.

Annalise glanced between me and the boat. 'You cannot mean it? But I know not how.'

'Nor I precisely, but how difficult can it be? I have seen it done many a time.'

Her gaze searched for a clue of me funning and when she realised I was not, it transferred to one of wide eyed alarm. 'But what if we drift astray or the boat tips over?'

I laughed at this. 'It will be fine. The water is calm and fairly shallow. When we were children, we used to swim in it on hot days like this. Besides, we cannot drift any further than the other side of the lake, so we are quite without the risk of ending up abroad,' I told her, taking in its view. It was narrow at this point, cutting a cleft through the woodland before snaking around beneath an ornate stone footbridge and opening up to its full expanse. It had been landscaped by Capability Brown many years before it was home to us, and it was every part equal to the compliments always received by visitors.

I bent down to unfurl the rope from its mooring, taking care to leave one loop in place to steady us whilst we alighted. 'Will you prefer me to go first?' I asked, already knowing the answer before she nodded it. So, I lifted my skirts to my knees and lowered one leg into it, allowing a pause to test the rhythm of its sway before bringing the other down to join it. 'There,' I said, crouching low, holding on to the sides as it adjusted to my weight. 'See, there is nothing to it. Come, step in,' I beckoned her, daring now to stand upright and outstretching an arm to her.

'I don't know, Eleanor, it seems unstable,' she said, unconvinced.

'Perhaps a little, but it's quite safe, look,' I said rocking from foot to foot to show her that it did not turn me out of it with the motion.

'Stop, Eleanor. Have you lost your senses? You will tumble out.'

'Probably,' I said, laughing, ceasing the rocking now. 'I shan't fall... come, where is your sense of adventure?'

She edged forward a fraction closely examining the boat, lifting a tentative foot.

'Now take my hand,' I felt how she trembled as I caught it. 'It's quite alright, do not be alarmed. On the count of three...'

Taking a steadying breath and a final conspicuous look about her, she lunged forwards on the note of three and I pulled her into it. The boat made an erratic sway with her leaping so frightfully, and I caught her in my arms, enjoying how she clung to me until it regained its balance.

'I cannot believe I am doing this. I warn you, I cannot swim a breadth.'

Oh. This news made me a tad nervous but I did not want to show it and cause her unnecessary concern. 'You need not swim,' I said, encouraging her to loosen her grip upon my arms, her fingertips so tight pressed into my flesh I could imagine the bruises starting to form beneath the muslin. *You are too close.* 'Just, sit, gently mind. I shall take care of the boat.' *I shall take care of you.*

I watched her lower herself gingerly into her seat and when I felt certain she was stable, leant across to unravel the last loop of rope from the mooring. As I coiled it around my forearm and sunk to my own seat, the boat drifted away from the riverbank towards the middle of the lake, a briny breeze rippling around us. I peered across to her, thinking her so pretty in that fawn muslin dress she had been fitted for at Mrs Oliver's. She was sat stiff with a look of mistrust about her. If it was only for the sake of the safety of the boat, I might have felt less anxious, but I knew that was not all she mistrusted.

With the shrinking of the riverbank, I noticed how her fingers gripped the sides, her gaze fixed longingly on it, as if willing it back within reach.

'Annalise, will you pass me that oar,' I asked in the hope of distracting her, and I passed the other through its rust ringed loop. Had I realised she was nervous of water, I would have chosen the archery or a trip in the Landau.

'Here,' she said, lifting it towards me one handed, the other still firmly grasping. 'Are you sure you know what you are doing?'

'Yes.' I slipped the other one through and adjusted them until they felt balanced in my hands. They were heavier than I had expected them to be. My brothers had always given the impression they were next to weightless. 'It may take me a moment to warm up to it, but I am quick to learn. Be at ease.' I lifted them in a circular motion in the air at first, deciding which way to direct them and when I was decided, plunged them into the water and felt the tiniest shift in the boat as we lurched backwards. 'Oh dear,' I said, realising my mistake.

'What is it?' she asked with unnecessary alarm and I wished I had not spoken aloud.

'Nothing to be concerned of, only, I realise I am facing the wrong way. We shall travel backwards if I row this way and I mean to take us forwards. No matter. Let me try at rowing them the other way,' I said, and lifting the oars in the opposite direction, bought them crashing down so unsteady in this fashion that a cascade of water flew up into the air and drenched us as it landed.

We both gasped with the shock of it and wiping the wetness from my eyes; I noticed the surprise in Annalise's a moment before we both broke into a trill of laughter. 'Oh Annalise!' I said in breathy pauses.

She had a hand clasped to her mouth.

'I am sorry!' I said, examining our flattened hair and saturated attire that we had taken such care to avoid contaminating thus far.

'Well, since I remain inside the boat, I will forgive you it!' she teased me. 'But Eleanor, I cannot find confidence in your driving!'

'A little practice is all,' I said, reclaiming the oars and making a more gentle and controlled attempt now, edging us back and forth before finally working out that using one oar, I could turn us about in a circle and correct our direction. It was perhaps not the greatest start, but I was glad of something breaking the frigid atmosphere between us and for a moment, as a smile danced in her eyes, I knew she was back with me.

'Look at the state of us. What would your mother say?'

'I dread to think, so I shan't.' I resumed my grip on both the paddles now.

She sat thoughtfully a while before saying, 'Oh, Eleanor, I wonder what it would feel like to be so free? Not to be confined to the scolds and expectations of others.'

'Chaos, my mama always tells me, and so there must be order. But I cannot help but think it would be a beautiful kind of chaos.'

'If it is of our own making you mean?'

'Yes.' I smiled. *Like the beautiful chaos you unleash in me.*

'What would you choose?'

'To be happy, of course. Isn't that what we all want?'

She nodded and cast a gaze about the boat returning to her reverie.

As we finally began making headway, she remained rigid in her seat, as if expecting the boat to capsize with each stroke of the paddle. That's how trust was lost wasn't it: just a little hiccup was enough to undermine the whole and it could take ten times the effort to earn it back. 'It's quite alright.' I smiled. 'I seem to have mastered it.'

'Yes,' she agreed, peering across my shoulder as I worked in rhythm and the boat cut its way through the water, the accelerated breeze dispersing the sun's intensity a fraction. Brilliant shades of willowherb and buttercup now shrinking into sprays of mottled colour, lining the forest edge. It was beautiful. *You are beautiful.*

Annalise peered at me a moment. 'You seem deep in thought?'

'Oh, no, I was just thinking,' I blinked away the sight of her and renewed my focus on the task of steering the boat, '...how nice it is to be out here, with you.'

She beamed at me, a furtive twinkle flashing to her eyes for such a brief and fleeting moment, I might have missed it if I had sunk the oars a moment sooner.

'I have missed your company, Annalise. I have sorely felt the pain of its deprivation these past days, having spent so much time in it recently.'

I watched her shift in her seat and thought her growing uncomfortable at this line, but gave no signal that I understood why. That I knew that she had grown frightful of my presence, that I knew she had been with that footman last night. 'I almost came down to seek you out last night, see if you were alright, but then I considered it so late you must be to bed.'

'Oh,' she muttered, lowered her gaze and began fiddling with the embroidery of her dress. 'It was a dreadful busy day yesterday. So much preserving to do since so much has been harvested from the farm. We have to work quickly before it all starts to spoil. '

'Annalise, what is troubling you?' I asked, fixing her in a more direct gaze and releasing the paddles, allowing the breeze to carry the boat along a little way whilst I enjoyed a brief reprieve. Rowing had proved harder work than I expected. I wiped a stream of sweat from the nape of my neck.

'Nothing,' she answered without meeting my eyes. She feigned interest in a bevy of swans gliding a trail aside the riverbank. 'Aren't they beautiful?' she said, pointing.

'Yes,' I agreed. *Not beautiful enough to hold my attention when you are in my view, though.*

'Oh, Eleanor, actually that is not at all true. Might we clear the air? I really do hate this discomfort between us.'

I nodded. 'Well, we are at very little risk of being overheard here, so whatever you are minded to say...'

'I feel quite ashamed of myself for behaving as I have—'

'How have you been behaving? I own I cannot say I know, so little I have seen of you.'

'Yes, and you must know by now, I have been avoiding you. What you don't perhaps know is how I hate it.' A flush of colour rose up from her neckline to her cheeks.

Her frankness, however well intended, was painful to hear. 'But why, Annalise? Have I done something—'

'No,' she shook her head despairing. 'It is nothing you have done, it is just... Well, I should have been more honest with you.'

'You should?' A knot was forming in my belly. Was she about to confess some plan to run off and marry this footman she had stayed up late with whilst feigning illness to avoid sitting up with me?

'I don't know if you are wasting your time on me.'

'You have let Camille's bitterness infect your thinking.'

'No. I realise she is competitive. But there was truth in some of what she said, and perhaps it would be best if I relinquished it to her and kept to the kitchen.'

'Is that what you want?'

'No. It is what I think will answer.'

'To what?'

'To everything, in the long run.'

'I see,' I managed, though the thought of losing her fills me with so much dread I can hardly breathe.

'I have offended you. I am sorry. I knew it was a mistake to come.'

'You have not,' I said quickly. 'Look, I understand that I have made your working life difficult and that the ill mood between you and Miss Pascal has taken its toll on you and I am sorry, for that was never my intention, Annalise. I want only to make things better for you, not harder.' I reached across and placed a hand lightly over hers. I wondered, as I looked at it cupping her knuckles, who I meant to comfort with this gesture.

Annalise cleared her throat. 'I know you must think me terrible ungrateful. I'm not, you know.'

'I do not think you ungrateful, Annalise,' I sighed. 'I just wish you had the confidence in yourself, I have in you. I know you shall make a splendid ladies maid, you have already proved yourself equal to the task. I just don't understand why you can't see it.'

She frowned against the sunlight. 'I wish I could explain myself better. But, well, people of my class, we might work decades to progress in service. I have been here less than a year. You must imagine how many persons I have upset and how odd it seems.'

I flinched inside and drew back slowly. *To the devil with the lot of them.* 'Yes, in my experience, people will always try to make ill of those they are jealous of. But tell me Annalise, where are we to draw the line between appeasing such persons and finding our own way in the world? Choosing our own happiness, finding that beautiful chaos?'

She sat thoughtfully a moment.

I did not expect an answer. I poised the question as much in my own direction as hers.

'Honestly, Eleanor, I do not know.'

'Nor I.' I felt the regret of my next question in advance. 'Annalise. Is there a particular person you are afraid of disappointing?' I thought of this footman as I waited for her answer.

She tilted her head a fraction, trying to read me. 'No.'

'No one whom you have grown particularly close to?'

Her expression hardened and I noticed a glint of resentment in her eyes but before she contrived an answer, I yelled, 'Dash it.' My distraction had caused me to become complacent. I realised, a moment too late what was about to happen as the paddle slipped through its ring and splashed into the water. I made a flustered attempt at grasping for it, my arm stretched out shaking with the strain, but it was too late. I peered into the water and watched it swallow it entirely. 'Damn.'

'Oh my,' Annalise gasped. 'What will we do?'

'I think I must go in and get it.'

I felt her tug at my arm. 'Are you gone mad? Absolutely not!'

'Well, I cannot paddle us the rest of the journey with just one oar. It will take all morning.' I looked ahead; we were soon to pass beneath the bridge. Beyond that, the lake opened up to its full expanse and I did not think it sensible to attempt to navigate that part of the lake with just one paddle. We had always been forbidden to swim beyond the bridge, and I assumed that the more shallow waters we enjoyed here made way to greater depths beyond it. 'Let me see how deep we are.' I pulled the remaining oar from its support, tightening my grip about it before leaning as far over the edge of the boat as I could.

I plunged it into the water, holding it with both hands and probing to see if there was any clue to the depth of the riverbed. It bobbed and swayed without obstruction and I lunged a little further.

'Eleanor!' I heard Annalise scream, and before I could turn to see the cause of her distress, I felt the boat sway beneath my weight and managed to inhale a quick breath of air before I hit the water.

It was cold. Freezing. And as I felt myself sink into its arctic depths, plunging me into darkness, I splayed my fingers out wide to pat about for the oars. We were not that deep yet, perhaps six or seven feet, I estimated from the time it took to reach the bottom. *Where are they?* I was frantic in my search now, feeling the buoyancy threatening at any moment to pull me back up. Pebbles and gravel against my palms, until, yes, the smooth round wood. I clenched my fingers around its circumference and when I had a certain grip upon it, hit out against the floor to propel myself up.

I broke the surface with a pronounced gasp for air and was met, as I blinked through bleary eyes, by the panic-struck glare of Annalise leaning out of the boat.

'Good grief! Take my arm,' she called, reaching out to find my hand.

I handed her the oar instead. 'Carefully, put it in the boat,' I instructed her, catching my breath now.

She flung it into the boat so carelessly, reaching back out for me with a strain in her neck so pronounced I thought a tendon might snap in it and spring out from the side.

'Annalise.' I paddled to keep afloat. 'I am fine. Sit back in the boat before you tumble out as I did.' This, could not happen. I at least could swim.

'Eleanor, get out of the water. Let me help you up.'

'No,' I said, water fizzing and lapping about my ears, drowning out syllables in her sentence. 'I'm going to go back down for the other.'

Her eyes bulged. 'You cannot, get out of there for goodness' sake!'

'I am perfectly well, don't you see.' I was. In fact, I was no longer even cold. I felt invigorated now, the coolness of the water, the warmth of the sun against my face. I took a greedy breath and used the side of the boat to thrust myself below its surface once more, sinking to its depths, but this time, not landing at its bed. I had not propelled myself with adequate force to make the distance, it must be deeper than I realised. I broke the surface again and made a more determined attempt this time. Pulling myself up on the boat edge before plunging my weight down, still to no avail.

'You are unbelievable!' Annalise scolded me, unimpressed as I came up again, a shaft of sunlight blinding me, and this time I paused, regulating my breath. 'Will you give up on this madness and get back into the boat!' Her tone now, reminded me of Delores in an exasperated fervour. 'What is so amusing?' she demanded.

'You are. I'm sure I've never heard you use such accents.' I pressed a hand against the side to steady me. 'The look upon your face.'

'Well, I'm glad you find yourself amused.'

'Alright,' I relented. 'Don't get into such a fidget. You had better help me back up then,' I said more gently, holding my arm out.

She reached for me. 'I can't get a hold of you properly. You are too slippery.'

'Let me go. I am going to try something else.' I held on to the boat, bobbed myself up and down a few times to build momentum before lifting my weight out of the water with a leap. I held my weight steady at its side and attempted to hoist my leg up, but my dress was heavy and weighing me down and I had no arms spare for untangling it. 'It's no use, I shall have to swim to shore and pull you in.'

'No. You cannot leave me alone in this thing.' She reached out more determined to pull my weight up and this time I managed to hook one foot over the edge. But before I could bring the rest of my body to clamber into it, the boat tipped to its side again, throwing me back into the lake and very nearly Annalise spilling from it too. I clung to it only long enough to stay in reach of her, then pushed against it to keep her inside it. 'The other way, Annalise, lean the other side,' I called out to her and caught my breath as the boat sprung back into balance.

She had been spared going into the water, but had not been spared the water going over her. Its brief dip had been enough to fill the bottom of the boat with a shallow pool of water lapping about her feet and saturating the bottom of her skirts. It was without any further debate, that I took the mooring rope, tied it about my waist and swam to the nearest stretch of riverbank, stopping periodically, to tug the boat along whilst Annalise attempted to assist me with the one remaining paddle. It had hardly gone to plan and if I had understood her to be nervous of the water and unable to swim, then it would have seemed a very mad brained idea to bring her out here. It had been the novelty and romance of the boat ride that had bought it to mind, the journey around the lake was perfectly walkable and it seemed we were destined to walk the remainder anyhow.

When I finally found the lake shallow enough to stand up in, I pulled the rope with haste and the boat landed in as near as I could bid it. There was no mooring to rely upon, and Annalise had little choice but to disembark it where it stood.

'It is shallow now, look,' I told her as I helped her down into the water and it rose to a little higher than her waist level, lapping beneath her bosom, the fabric of her beautiful fawn dress darkened drab by its saturation.

'Huh... It is freezing!' she said, clinging to me still, like her life depended upon it and I dealt myself a silent reprimand for enjoying this proximity.

'Yes, but very refreshing once you become accustomed to it,' I teased her as she found her footing and the water resettled around us. Still, she continued her hold on me, adjusting it only slightly now. Where she had both arms wrapped about my neck, she now slipped one into the crook of my elbow as we waded our way over to the bank. To feel her so close to me was sweet torment and I was certain I nearly gave a clue to the fact, a momentary lapse in my composure as I swept a few drenched strands of golden hair from her face and allowed my gaze to linger a fraction too long over the task. It had not gone unnoticed, although she said nothing in response. But the uncertainty in her eyes was plain and she turned away and urged us on.

I realised then, how long it had been since I had swam, how I had long neglected that playful part of me. She had awoken it again, that sense of mischief and want of adventure I had long since consigned to the follies of youth.

I hurled the rope up onto the grassy bank and clambered my way up, caking my dress in mud as I tangled my feet up beneath it in the effort. When I reached down to pull Annalise up, she had a smile in her eyes and was biting down on her bottom lip.

'Look at the state of you,' she said, her face effervescent with laughter.

I peered down to see the sagging linen of my white muslin dress, now a more reliable shade of brown. 'It's just as well it wasn't a favourite,' I said and she laughed harder now, her cheeks dimpling and a crease quivering at the corner of her eye. I paused to take in the image of her, realising as I did, that I could not be without her.

I took her hands and pulled her up onto the bank and when she stood examining the state of her clothes now, I laughed at the sight of her.

'Oh, Eleanor, what are we to do? We can hardly go back to the house and traipse in like drowned rats!'

'Oh well, we should dry quickly, the sun is hot,' I said, winding in the boat closer to the bank to gain some more slack on the rope.

'I think, if we rinse the worst of it out now, it might come out clean in the wash.'

'You are never happy unless you are thinking of some work you must find,' I complained. 'Anyway, we are not going back to the house yet. I told you, I have a surprise. Come.'

She came over to help me and I stretched the length of rope to the nearest tree trunk to station it. Then leaving it secure, we walked the meandering path around the river, Annalise's boots squelching and me almost barefoot, having lost my slippers to the riverbed and torn through my stockings.

We passed over the moss speckled bridge and walked below a canopy of vines trailed over a wire archway, brilliant purple heads of wisteria draping above us. Then eventually, we came to a clearing laid to lawn, which was softer on the soles of my feet if I took care to dodge the discarded clumps of grass that had been cut and left to die upon it.

'Now if we walk up just a little further, we should arrive in the right spot.'

'The right spot for what, what is this mystery you keep from me?'

'You will have to wait and see,' I said, leading her through a willowy copse, the other side of which was my favourite aspect, a natural windbreak, scooped round in a cove like recess.

'Oh, Eleanor, how lovely,' she marvelled at the lavish picnic set before us as it came into view.

'It is delightful, isn't it?' Our position afforded a complete view of the lake and the rolling hills beyond it in the distance. When I needed somewhere to escape to, this was my haven. Inconspicuous enough to be forgotten, but set high enough above the wider landscape to survey everything about it.

'But you cannot mean all this, for my sake?' she said, her brow knitted as we gained on it.

Grantley had done a splendid job. A large, quilted picnic rug was out-sprawled upon the grass and a mass of small pillows were scattered on either side. In the centre stood a picnic basket and two place settings, perfectly laid as though they ought to be upon a dinner table, complete with a small, tubular glass vase holding a clutch of wildflowers in it. 'Of course, I mean it for you, silly.'

'But all this trouble...'

'Well, it is Grantley's handy work, so I cannot claim the credit for that.'

'I, I don't know what to say...I know I don't deserve it.'

'Of course, you do. You have looked after me. Now, let me have my way and spoil you a moment. Now, come and sit down and let's recuperate from all this excitement.

'Very well, but I must get out of these wet clothes first. I don't want to ruin all the lovely silk. Besides, it weighs a ton upon my shoulders.' She peeled the wet linen from her skin, sleeves first. 'Now, tell me, is it likely we should expect any passers-by here?'

'No, I would not imagine as far out as this. But Annalise...' I broke my sentence, watching in awe, as she wiggled her waist out of the soggy dress and allowed it to slip to the ground. I studied how her chemise clung to every impression of her shape as she bent down to knock the water out of her boots.

'Yes?' she said, looking up brightly, a shaft of sunlight casting a gleam around her.

'Never mind.'

'Ah, that is such a relief.' She stepped out of the heap of linen slumped around her feet.

'I think though, you must leave your stays on, just in case,' I warned, as she bought her hands to her back ready to untie them.

'But it's so heavy with all this water.'

'Yes, but they are short stays, they shan't take long to dry out in this.'

'True,' she acquiesced and I swallowed hard against the constriction of my throat and willed my eyes away from the sight of her.

'Here, let me help you with yours,' she offered, coming beside me where I was pulling at ragged threads of silk from my torn stockings to try to pull them off without snagging my toes. I had meant only to take these off, nothing more, and yet I found myself complacent to her instruction, turning my back to her to be unfastened and feeling the weight of my saturated skirts release me.

'Here, pass me your dress. I will have a try at rinsing out the worst. Though I have to say, I don't hold out much hope of turning your muslin white again.'

'No,' I agreed in vague consideration. I didn't care much for mine, but I would be sorry to see hers ruined, so prettily it became her. 'I can help.'

'It's no trouble,' she said waving me off and gathering it up in her arms with her own. 'I'll take care of this, you sort those stockings out before you find yourself in a bind.'

I sat down on the grass to tend them but found myself distracted, watching her as she wandered over to the riverside, her shimmy billowing in the breeze, clinging almost see through in the damper patches. I wished I could feel as easy as she seemed to manage. A subtle bounce in her step and a hum about her as she padded her way through the grass. I felt suddenly made of wood, stiff and inflexible.

She knelt down at a shallow pool of water that shelved its way up the bank and began plunging the dresses into it one by one.

'Ouch,' I gasped, looking down at my toe where it had grown pink and engorged as I pulled on a thread around it. It seemed I had quite forgotten it in my distraction and had been slowly strangling it from its blood supply. I slipped a finger beneath the razor like yarn and loosened it off more carefully, watching the colour disperse. I cast the sagging stocking to the ground and proceeded to untangle the next, considering the paleness of my ankles for a moment, unused to seeing them bare. Then stealing one last open glance at Annalise, her hair trailing down her back, glittering golden in the sunlight, I recomposed myself, pulled myself up off the ground and went over to her.

'Here, let me help.'

She looked up at me, and handed me a weighty pile as she lifted it from the water. It was her beautiful fawn dress, looking more a shade of cameleopard now. 'It will take some wringing,' she said, plunging the other back into the water.

After much grappling and squeezing, until our hands were raw and chaffing with the strain, we shook them out together and found a lofty tree branch to drape them over.

'There,' she said, looking pleased with herself. 'They should dry in no time in this heat.'

'Yes,' I smiled, peering at the sagging branch, turning myself to the sun to enjoy its warmth as a breeze prickled my damp skin. However much good we might have done in lessening the stains from our spoiled dresses, we had regressed in the drying of our shimmy's, now so heavy with water they stuck like a second skin. I dared not look at Annalise, I looked anywhere but her direction.

We settled on the picnic rug, opened the lid of the basket and pulled out a carafe of lemonade and filled our glasses. It was much needed but disappointingly warm, despite the wilting ice blocks Grantley had taken care to set about it. If I had had a notion of the fix we would get into on the journey here, I would have asked him to pack us up some towels and a change of clothes too, I considered, shivering a little now as we settled in the shade of the Wych Elm.

Annalise drained her glass and reclined down onto her side, propping her head up with her elbow. 'It's such a lovely spot. So peaceful.'

I stared into its horizon with her. 'Yes, it's a marvel,' I agreed, taking another lukewarm sip and sinking back onto the pillows. 'I went to see the puppies yesterday.'

'Oh, how is our little one?'

'He seemed well, well enough to nip me in any case,' I held up my finger to display the teeth marks. 'But he's hanging on, growing a little fatter. Mr Morris said he might wean the others soon and leave him an extra week or two to catch up.'

'Ah, yes, that would do him much good, I'm sure. Eleanor...' she began, stuttering over my name.

'Yes?' I said, lifting my head up to look at her a moment, wishing I had not, forgetting the damp shift.

'I cannot pretend as you do, that I have not behaved terribly.'

I closed my eyes to the sight of her and reclined back upon my pillow, the skin inside my eyelids turned orange against the bright sky as a stream of dappled sunlight broke through the shade of the tree overhead. 'Then we are even at last,' I said quickly, dismissing it. I was not minded to revisit staler topics now we were at last at ease again. 'Are you hungry?'

'A little.'

I sat up, opened the hamper and began to set out its contents, offering her the selection: A colourful platter of salmagundi, a small pie of pigeon, pickles, Queen cakes, a handsome heap of strawberries, and a lemon syllabub that was fast turning to a watery mush in the heat. A quart of Elderwine, I left inside to keep cool.

'Well, it is a splendid offering, but how many did the kitchen think they were packing it for? It must have been Maggie's work,' she said stunned with the setting out of plate after plate.

'It does seem a little excessive for the two of us, and strawberries in October?'

'Well, we shan't go hungry whilst waiting for our dresses to dry. Yes, they were done in the glass house; some experiment of Wilson's. These are the last we shall taste until next year I expect.' She picked up a strawberry, pushed it between her neat teeth and snapped it from its stem.

As the day moved towards its peak and the linen of our shifts grew dry and stiff, the conversation drifted easily at last and the past days of anxiety seemed almost forgotten. We picked at our luncheon, bathed our foreheads with the limp ice blocks, and I read to Annalise as she made daisy chains and decorated us in the products of her labour.

I did not remember drifting into sleep, so when I opened my bleary eyes to an irritating buzzing about my head, I was surprised to see Annalise sound asleep beside me, her head lolling to the side, her mouth hung open as her breath rasped in and out.

I blinked myself awake and rolled onto my side, swatting away the irritant fly that had seemed a moment ago to be part of a dream that was fast slipping from my consciousness. 'Annalise,' I whispered, wondering what time it was and how long we had slept. She was beautiful, even in this unflattering style. I blinked again, thinking myself mistaken by some remaining trick of sleep at noticing the crimson flush of her skin. I sat up and leaned forward to examine her better, lifting a silvery lock of hair from her cheek. 'Goodness, Annalise, you must wake up,' I nudged her gently.

She did not stir.

I looked about me, seeing how the tree now cast its shade on a different patch of ground leaving us sadly exposed. We had slept too long. I pawed through cushions until I found the parasols we had not needed earlier, amongst them. I snapped one up and held it over her. It seemed even more severe a shade in the shadow. I called out to her again and brushed the rest of her hair from her face, held her cheek softly against my palm and felt the burning heat radiate into it.

A small groan escaped her and she flung an arm out to one side before sinking into a hum of restfulness again. I took a pillow and lay back down beside her, taking care to keep her under the protection of the parasol. I traced a finger along the length of her arm, a line of pink scored it in half and I regretted not having a care to prevent it. I pressed a gentle kiss inside her elbow without thinking, her skin smelled sweet and felt clammy against my cheek. *I'm sorry.* I rolled onto my back and stared at the sky, wondering how I would ever resolve this discrepancy between my heart and my head, or if in fact I ever would.

I was staring into the leafy arms of the tree above when I heard her sigh. I turned my head and found her eyes upon me, looking momentarily confused before realising where she was. She was seized by a lengthy yawn before smiling up at me. 'How long have I slept?' she asked, leaning upon her elbow and pulling a crushed chain of daisies from her neck.

'Long enough to be scorched by the sun,' I told her sheepishly and was met with a puzzled frown.

'Ow,' she started with surprise. 'I feel it! My face is tight and stingy.'

I recognised the description, for my own skin felt this way and I realised I had not given a thought to my own exposure. I peered at my arms and chest; I was not very red but most definitely darkened. 'I have an idea,' I said, noticing the remaining strawberries that lay sweating in the sun, turning to shrivelled burgundy mush. I picked up the plate, found a fork still wrapped in a cone of starched napkin and began mashing them beneath it, fishing out the wilting stems. 'Watts' trick,' I said in answer to her puzzling glance and with this memory of being caked in a mask of strawberry in childhood, being scolded for licking it from around my mouth, came also the memory of my mother's outrage at finding me blackened by the sun. "You look like a brood of the tenant farmers children!" she would accuse me and my siblings, before turning her reprimand to nanny.

"I's sorry, milady. They was just playing in the park and they was havin' so much fun we didn't notice it. I won't let it happen again," she would say guiltily, before soothing us into compliance as Watts spread strawberry paste over our faces and we grew bored with being made to lay still whilst it worked upon us. I was surged by a sudden rush of affection, remembering nanny now, telling us stories to keep us occupied and promising us a sherbet dish of ice cream, or a sugar plum to reward our patience. I hadn't thought of her in such an age it near bought a tear to my eye, thinking of her now, so kind and so much loved by us all. I wondered if we ever recovered from the heartache of her leaving.

'Eleanor?'

'Yes?'

'What on earth are you doing?'

I followed the direction of her stare and peered into the pulp of strawberry flesh I was still squishing in a habitual rhythm. 'For your face, to help the sunburn.'

'Oh,' she accepted. 'Will it work?'

I could not remember in truth. It had never been a concern of mine at such an age to consider its efficacy, only to placate Mama and spare nanny any further scolding. 'I think so,' I said, checking the consistency, satisfied now that it was how I remembered it. 'Move your hair aside, and lay back down.'

She weaved her hair blindly into a chunky plait and shuffled upon the scattered pillows that still held our impressions in them. I scooped a handful of the paste up and began spreading it over her cheeks, patting it across the bridge of her nose and beneath her eyes where the skin was shinny and raw. A patch of skin between the strap of her stays and the expanse of her décolleté also shone pink, but I dared not apply it there.

'Is it working?'

'Don't be so impatient, I've barely set it down.'

'Will you do yours now?' she asked, a glob of pink paste falling from her chin as she spoke.

'Have a care not speak or you will undo it,' I warned her, re-patching the mask.

'Sorry,' she said through her teeth, straining not to move her lips this time.

'I shan't do mine now,' I said, staring at the empty plate that had only a few tracks of remaining slush upon it where the fork had left them behind.

'Well, you are very dark, although I think I like it. It suits you.'

I caught another wobbling fragment of the paste upon a waiting fingertip and pressed it back into place. I had been about to silence her again, but... 'You do?' I said instead, feeling the sting of my own frown contorting my face.

'Yes, it becomes you I think; your eyes seem brighter somehow. I mean, you always look pretty, but there is a certain something about the look of the brown stain upon you.'

Always pretty? I felt a flutter from somewhere deep inside my belly.

'Your nose is a little pink though,' she added. 'Is it sore too? Mine does pinch.'

'A little,' I replied and let my hand rest against her shoulder. 'It will soothe it, give it a chance,' I said reassuring, for this much I remembered to be the case. I was minded to add that I would happily endure my mother's scorn and keep the tan upon my own face if she preferred me with it. I would sit every afternoon in the scorch of midday heat and discard my parasol to the briar bush, if it induced her to think me pretty, to admire the shine of my eyes as I did hers. Gazing into them now, with so much longing I had to turn my face away from her entirely to break it. *Only she,* I thought, turning about, stacking the plates and cutlery back into the hamper, *can induce me to wanting so much to lean forward and kiss her with a plateful of crushed strawberries smothered over her face.* She looked ridiculous, an unfortunate victim of some dreadful malady or accident, and yet all I could think of as I stared into those warm whiskey eyes, a worm of paste clinging to a length of her lashes, was how much I longed to press my lips against her.

I folded the scrunched and spattered napkins into halves and stuffed them into the top of the basket before closing the lid. It seemed a wonder how it had all came out of it, so laboriously I had to force things into nooks and crevices to allow the lid to close flat and the leather straps to be tied. I had kept one of the cleaner napkins aside, reserved for the task of wiping the mask from Annalise's face and for now, there was little left to do but wait for it to work its remedy.

I plucked a few discarded daisy chains from the picnic rug and brushed away crumbs and ants that had been drawn to them, before settling back down beside her, propping myself against a pillow and allowing my eyes to settle over the view of her. A breeze carried with it the sickly-sweet scent of over ripened strawberries and rippled at the parasol, inching it away a fraction, flooding us with a brief flash of sunlight. She blinked her eyes against it and bought her hand to cover them, forgetting, for the briefest second as she pressed her hand against the mush.

'Oh no!'

I laughed. 'I think you are determined to prevent this course of action,' I said, putting the parasol back in position and reaching for the napkin.

'You know I am not such an ungrateful creature!' she protested, and as I settled back again, surprised by such an irregular turn of mischief from her, I shrunk away too late as she threw me a menacing grin before wiping her hand across my forehead and breaking into a trill of hearty giggles. 'I'm sorry. I could not resist it,' she warbled through them and I was left to feign offence as her laughter, combined with the spectacle of her mottled face was too contagious not to join her.

'You terrible mischief maker!' I accused, using the napkin to scrape the mess from my own face.

'Forgive me,' she sang in the final waves of excitement. 'Here, let me,' she offered, sitting up now, taking the napkin from my hand and wiping from my face what I had missed. 'There,' she said satisfied and I took the cloth from her and began cleaning up what had not already fallen from her own. I took care to be gentle in my strokes, not wanting to provoke the delicate looking skin any further. Shaking out the napkin before making another tentative sweep of her cheeks, even brushing the fallen remnants from her décolleté before realising how dangerously complacent I had allowed myself to become.

'Is it better?' she asked expectant, and I hadn't the heart to tell her I could notice very little difference in it. 'It feels a little better,' she said, and I put down the cloth and used my fingertips to tease from her hairline, a few tangled silvery strands it clung to.

'That is good, although I'm not certain it was on long enough. But it doesn't matter, we have many remedies at home for this very thing and we will try them when we go back.'

'It seems a shame we must go back, doesn't it? It's so lovely. I would love to stay and wait to watch the sunset,' she said, making a brief study of the view and turning back to me, a smile in her eyes.

'Would you like to Annalise? We can do it if you want to?'

'Perhaps another time,' she said, her face clouding over for a moment. 'But thank you for today,' she said then, embracing me with such enthusiasm it threw me quite out of countenance. I took a steadying breath as I felt her arms scoop me up and press me into the crook of her neck.

Oh Annalise, how will I ever learn to bear this?

I was not sure how long she held me there against her, her fiery skin setting flame against my own as the heat poured out of her. It was as though time had, for that moment, stopped counting itself, the way the antique clock in the drawing room would often stick its needles at a number on the clock-face, twitching, until someone remembered to wind it up again.

When she pulled back, brushed my hair from my cheek and kissed me lightly upon it, I knew my face had betrayed me the instant I read the question in hers.

'What is it?' she said pensively, releasing me entirely now and sitting back upon her heels.

'Nothing,' I replied, a conscious effort at reorganising my expression and hoping I had shaped it into something less conspicuous now. 'I am only a little concerned that you are quite badly burnt, you are flaming with heat,' I offered, hoping that this line would not only serve to divert us away from this insufferable atmosphere, but also act to prepare her for just how bad the circumstance of her burn was, before she was to discover the fact for herself.

'No, not that,' she said, waving it away with a dismissal and glaring at me so inquisitively I knew myself discovered, and not how to undo it. 'Why did you look at me that way? What was that?'

'I don't know what you mean,' I said, tripping over my own words and feeling queasy.

'That look, you have looked at me that way before and I do not know for what purpose it is intended, but it makes me feel...strange.'

'I'm sorry,' I said, pinching the flesh between my eyes. I hated lying to her. 'I did not realise I was looking at you in any particular way.'

'It's alright, it doesn't matter.' Her tone seemed a curious one and I could not make it out. 'I think we must get dressed and go before we burn anymore,' she added.

'Yes, yes, I will see if our clothes are dry,' I told her, getting up with haste, grateful for the excuse to hide the shame displayed across my face.

The clothes were crisp and warm when I pulled them from the branch and tossed them upon my shoulder as I had seen Annalise do in the past. When I returned, she was tying the laces of her boots, an aloof look upon her face as she noticed me beside her.

'All dry!' I said in an accent of such unnecessary enthusiasm, I shrunk at my own absurdity, handing down her share of the laundry.

'Thank you,' she said without looking up, but reaching blindly for them.

'Annalise, I did not mean to alarm you.'

'Let us just forget it.'

We dressed in silence and without each other's help, and once we had managed the task, took pains to tidy up the picnic arrangement to spare the staff the need, beyond carrying it back to the house. 'One of the footmen will bring the tow cart for it,' Annalise said, and I wondered if she thought of Will when she said this. That she thought of him at all was enough to sink my heart to such depths of melancholy I could not allow it to linger in my mind.

The journey back was ill at ease and sobering. We spoke nothing more than a few insignificant sentences to each other, such as me reminding her to keep her parasol poised and her occasionally pointing out some rough or ragged patch of path for me to avoid in my shoeless amble. *Had I lost her?* I could not entertain it.

It was fast approaching late afternoon when we arrived back at the house. We returned via a small underground tunnel I never knew existed. The staff used it to move between the dairy outbuilding and the kitchens, Annalise told me. She had expected it to be quieter than any other route at this time, and since she was anxious to avoid anyone's notice of her, I agreed. But as we scurried along the narrow corridor, with our heads buried beneath our sunshades, we passed a maid girl who startled at the fright of seeing us and I shut down my parasol and apologised for it as Annalise lowered hers to completely hide her face beneath it.

It was not until we were back in the house that this fractious mood lifted a little. I wondered why she held such store by what the other servants thought of her. Unless it was Will she meant always to be thought well of. *Oh god,* I hoped it was not that.

As we passed the long mirror in the corridor, Annalise stopped and turned back to it.

'My goodness, Eleanor, what am I to do? I am as pink as salmon!' she exclaimed, checking her reflection in the looking glass. 'I will be a laughingstock down here, not to mention the irritation I will cause at displaying the fact that whilst everyone else has been hard at work, I have been outdoors at leisure.'

I hadn't thought of this complication. 'Don't panic,' I said, joining in this study of her reflection and realising how severe it seemed in the dimness of the basement light. 'Where is the still room?'

'It is along the eastern corridor, beside the laundry. But it is always locked; Mrs Crawford keeps a key for it on her chatelaine. Have you a proper cure for this then? Pray, tell me that you do, for I don't think the strawberries worked.'

'Not precisely a cure,' I pulled her on from the looking glass, for it seemed this study of the damage only encouraged her into a passion. 'But if I can find the right lotions, we might tone it down somewhat, and certainly soothe it before it has a chance to dry and crack our skin.'

She gasped at this and I instantly wished to swallow the words. 'It will crack our skin?'

I supposed she could not know this, having never suffered a sun burn before. 'Not if we take care,' I told her reassuringly and was glad she was at least speaking with me in ordinary tones again. 'Now, you keep out of the way, go to the bathroom and we shall draw a bath, I will find the supplies.'

Mrs Crawford needed little explanation for my request for the still room key. I found her in the laundry, carrying an over-piled stack of pressed linen beneath her chin. She put it down a moment.

'Pommade de Seville?' she said wisely with raised eyebrows. 'Your mother will have something to say.' She looked me over as if I was a small child who had just come in dirty from playing in the mud. I was tempted to remind her I was now a married woman, not a child in leading strings, but I resisted. 'Yes, it was warmer than I realised, it is certainly not a typical autumn day.'

'Well, you are in luck; Watts made fresh batches for your mama a couple of weeks ago. Shall I send for Tulley to come and see to you?'

'Thank you, no. She already attends me.'

'Of course, she does,' she said, handing me the key she had just detached from the heavy bundle at her hip. 'Second shelf down on the far wall,' she told me and recovered her linen from the bureau.

I scanned the shelves and filled a cloth with everything I could think of: rice water, *Pommade de Seville, Crème L'Enclos, Milk of Roses* and *Olympian Dew*. I tied the cloth into a bundle and made my way back with the bounty. Considering now, as I walked, how exactly Watts had used these concoctions on me on past occasions.

When I came into the water closet, the fire was aglow and she had already begun filling the tub with water. It seemed so oppressive to have to resort to having a fire alight in such stuffy weather, and yet what choice was there when we needed water to bathe in. I set out the lotions, towels and cloths and waited for more water to boil up. It was a laborious task to undertake without assistance, but I knew Annalise would sooner heave every boiling pot herself, than have me send for help and be discovered, so patiently we shared the task between us.

We stripped back down to our shifts; they were a colourful shade of filth, carrying stains of mud, grass and strawberries over the white linen.

'I think I'll soak these later before they are sent to the laundry. I shall not want to explain to Benson how they came to be in such disorder,' Annalise said stretching out the fabric in her hands.

I looked over at her and smiled at the memory of her pasted speckled face earlier and was pleased she gave way to a reminiscent laugh.

'I am covered in stickiness,' she complained, pulling apart tacky fingertips. 'But I think it had better be a very shallow tub or it will take us hours before we are set to rights, and we are seen now.'

'Yes.' I swirled a hand around in the shallow water. 'It is warm enough now, get in,' I told her.

'No, you must go first.'

'I am not needed anywhere and I have come off less severely from the sun,' I protested and was astonished into silence when she lifted her chemise over her head and stood there in only her skin.

'Thank you.'

'Of course,' I managed, but I could not meet her eyes. I was shocked at the sight of her and instantly aware of my discomfort. I had not expected her to go in bare skinned.

'Are you certain you don't mind my going first?' she asked, stepping out of her stockings.

I swallowed hard, turned away and made busy with the kettle. 'No, please, you go,' I said as nonchalantly as I could muster and wondered for a fleeting moment, if I should explain; tell her she was supposed to keep her chemise on. But I hadn't the heart to embarrass her and I was already so much flustered I did not want to bring particular notice to the point. So, I waited for her to settle into the water, and fetched her the lotion. 'Here.' I poured a blob of Crème de L'Enclos onto a cloth and gave it to her, keeping my eyes determinedly on my task and not beyond it. 'It's a wash lotion; it will help to remove the tan.'

She took it instantly to her shoulder and screwed her face up in pain, flinching beneath the cloth as she pressed it against her crimson flesh. 'It's so sore, how violent it stings.'

'Yes,' I said guiltily. 'I'm afraid it will get worse before it gets better. Here, let me try,' I offered and dabbed tentatively at her face and around her shoulders before pouring rice water into her hands for her to rinse it with. Seeing her now without her clothes to hide away her usual paleness, the contrast was quite alarming. Bright red patches at the back of her neck and tops of her shoulders already having a scaly texture about them, save the small pale strips where the straps of her stays had spared her the injury. She would sleep ill tonight in such discomfort, I thought uneasily. My own skin, taught as it felt, was but only a fraction in the way of a burn, even if it was very brown and certainly enough to send Mama into a fit of lectures.

'How many washes you give me, did the others not succeed?' she asked me as I poured another pomade into her cupped hands.

'Not yet. But do not fret, we have not yet completed the regime,' I said more reassuringly than I should have, for I feared, now realising the extent of it, that it was more likely to take many days to fade such a burn, however many regimes she endured.

I patted off her face and the other sore areas before massaging in a generous offering of Milk of Roses into her skin. I was careful in my application, fearing to cause her pain as I dabbed at the scorch marks beneath her eyes that seemed particularly red and crêpey.

'Oh my, even my feet are affected,' she said with surprise, lifting her foot above the waterline and prodding it with a tentative finger to test the severity. 'Look what a terrible mark there is upon my leg,' she said, pointing at a line of demarcation a few inches above her ankle.

I glanced up only for a moment, glad she could not see the view upon the back of her neck as I could, for it was by far the worst. Besides, I dared not look beyond what I must; it was taking all my concentration to divert myself from the sight of her and even this gentle touching was a dangerous undertaking that I would not have entertained had the situation not necessitated it. I poured a few jugs of water over her back to rinse off the excess and realising the risk I had exposed myself to in such proximity to her, and feeling that I could do little more to improve her condition, I stood up and held out a bath sheet.

'Thank you, Eleanor,' she said, stepping into it. 'I am so grateful to you.'

I stared into the mosaic pattern of the tile. 'Can you feel any improvement in it?'

'Yes, I think it has brought some relief,' she told me, tucking the towel beneath her arm.

'Good,' I said and turned away, busying myself with adding more warm water to the tub and setting out new cloths as she took to drying herself. 'Do not dry off the sore areas, will you? I think it better left upon the skin to absorb, and do not forget to rub some into those ankles either,' I told her, handing her the bottle.

I hesitated at removing my own shift before I climbed in, but I didn't want to draw attention to the matter of her faux pas, so I decided I must. It was an odd feeling settling into the shallow water, feeling the cold metal sides of the tub against my bareness. I was sure the benefit of not being restricted by soggy linen would have felt refreshing if it was not for my company and my curious state of mind.

I had never been uncomfortable with my own nudity before; a lifetime of being washed and dressed by others ensured it. But every time I caught a glimpse of Annalise, it sent something surging through me that I wasn't ready to face. She was standing with her back to me patting herself dry. I told myself not to look, not to think; not even to imagine the sights my eyes were determined to draw me to, but my will was easily broken by the temptation. With her back turned to me, it afforded me the privacy to permit a shy glance, then another, until I could barely remove my eyes from her at all. She was so beautifully formed. I had never felt so affected. Any previous idea I had conjured in my mind about such a moment, fell miserably short of the reality of beholding her.

When she turned around and caught the direction of my stare, I looked away instantly. The embarrassment of it all was overwhelming. I remembered then, the book of Genesis where Adam and Eve had first become ashamed of their nakedness after they sinned. I felt the shame only when I looked at Annalise, but knew, like Eve must have, before she reached out for the apple, that she was destined to sin despite herself.

'Give me a moment and I will come and help you,' Annalise said as she combed fingers down the lengths of her blond hair which hung straggled beneath her shoulders.

'Thank you, no. There is no need,' I said quickly. 'I am practically finished.' I swished my cloth about my shoulders and cupped a few handfuls of water over myself before scrambling up to find my towel, which it appeared I had overlooked the preparation of.

'Are you quite well?' Annalise frowned.

'Yes, it was just a little cold to draw it out. Will you pass me a towel?' I lied; a ridiculous lie too for between the fire roaring and the steam rising it was certainly not cold. But my senses could not bear having her wash me into the bargain.

'Yes, sorry,' she said and I watched her come towards me, wrapping her own towel firmly about her now and gathering up one for me on her journey.

'Here we are,' she gestured, unfurling it and holding it out for me. I tried to ignore the bounce of her bare breasts as her own towel slipped. I peered at the floor, tried to keep my gaze away, but it was hard not to follow the perfect lines and curves of her body so presently set before me. I let her wrap me up and I tucked it beneath my underarm and picked up the lotion.

'Well let me at least see to that for you,' she insisted, taking the bottle from my hands. 'I don't pretend to have Camille's expertise, but I can apply it for you.'

'No, please do not trouble yourself,' I said, snatching it back, pouring a larger measure of it than I had meant to and splattered it clumsily about my shoulders. 'I am done now, it's not very sore at all,' I said, attempting to re-cork the glass bottle in my slippery hands.

Annalise laughed at this. 'Well, it is dripping everywhere, at least let me rub it in for you.'

'No, I can do it; you go and dress.'

'Nonsense, give it here,' she insisted and took the bottle from me, put it down on the side and stood so close to me I could feel her breath as she began rubbing at my neck and my shoulders. I ceased in my protest and tried to recompose myself. *Think of sobering things, Eleanor.* I tried to conjure a point that would usually bore or distract me, but I could not find one. I felt her warm palms spread across my neck, shoulders, the length of my arms, a silent purr vibrating beneath my flesh.

'You are tired I think.'

I hadn't even realised I had closed my eyes until her question. 'A little, the heat is to blame.'

'Yes. But it was such a lovely day.'

How she could think or talk of such ordinary things as the weather now was beyond me.

When she stopped and I felt her move away, I thought I might die. I opened my eyes, not expecting to see her standing right in front of them, her bare breasts sprung but an inch from me as she stood patting out another blob of lotion from the bottle.

'Hold your hair back, bring your chin up,' she directed me. 'I want to put some on your face. It is very dark.'

Not as dark as my thoughts had become. I noted the curve of her breast in my peripheral vision and closed my eyes against the sight of her. Her hands felt imbued with a soothing kind of sorcery as she offered them again, even the gentle, tiny strokes her fingertips swirled the lotion in about my cheeks. The sensation was barely perceptible, certainly not something I would have found otherwise compelling, but my senses were grown fragile, oversensitive and difficult to allay.

'Does that feel better?' she asked brightly, wiping the excess lotion into her own hands.

'Yes,' I smiled back, knowing what I was about to do, powerless to prevent it. I inched in closer and felt my heartbeat pulsing in my throat, took up her hands in mine and pulled her closer still. I was overcome; my stomach fluttered with anticipation and before I had a chance to answer to her perplexed gaze, I leaned in and kissed her gently on the lips. *She did not draw away from me.* I probed her compliant mouth with my tongue; slowly, tenderly coaxing her to follow suit. *Oh Annalise, how much I have wanted this; wanted you.* I lifted my trembling hands and pulled her face so close against mine our bodies touched, pressed briefly against each other and at this, she stiffened, stepped back and withdrew.

I opened my eyes. She was staring at me. A bleary gaze to begin with but as it cleared, I saw the bewilderment in them turn a staler shade of despair.

'Eleanor?'

Don't be alarmed my sweet. I stroked her arm gently to reassure her, but she held her palms to her cheeks and shook her head.

What I saw now in her eyes was not simply questions, but fear.

'What are we doing?' she said with such horror in her face, it made my blood run instantly cold.

I reached for her hand. 'Annalise, do not be alarmed.'

She edged back. 'No, Eleanor.'

My heart sank. *Please don't break it.*

She shook her head again. 'This is wrong... All so wrong!' She moved a hand across her lips now, as if to reprimand them for what they had permitted.

'Is it? Truly?' My voice cracked over the words and I felt the threatening sting of tears.

'You know it is!' The accusation in her tone sent a shiver coursing through me.

I suddenly felt unable to breathe. Her words resonated so harshly. I thought I might vomit, such knots my stomach seemed suddenly to twist in. 'It does not feel wrong, in my heart it does not.'

'I have to go,' she mumbled, pulling up her bath sheet tight around her.

For the first time, she seemed aware of her nudity and I recognised the discomfort in her clumsy movements as she searched for her things.

'Of course. Take your time. I will dress upstairs,' was all I could say to stop my welling tears from falling and have her witness it. I re-gathered my towel about me and unlocked the jib door, taking one last glance behind me.

She hadn't replied or seemed to notice at all. She was pulling on her clothes as fast as she could manage. I turned and made my way up the staircase feeling like a part of me had just expired and I tripped upon the steps and fell against the wall. I was not injured but I stayed there, leaning against the steps, huddled to the wall. I let the tears come now, quick and warm, stinging my sunburned cheeks as they fell. *I was mistaken to try.* The sobriety of my rejection struck me with such violence now I was free to permit it. I wished I could take back the whole, erase it from both our memories. At least then, I would not have the knowledge of how beautiful it was to kiss her. I would not have her still, but at least she would not glare at me so hatefully. Was it really true? Had I imagined her regard? Were my hopes of succeeding nothing more than the folly of my own creation? Suddenly, I felt such a fool for reading her so poorly. For allowing myself the notion that these shameful feelings could exist in her too. I covered my mouth with a handful of my towel to stifle the volume of my sobs. *I cannot lose you; you are everything that helps me remember how to smile.*

Unrequited.

October 1821. - Eleanor.

I had no appetite for dinner. I sat picking at my plate, scoring out translucent bones from the turbot which had grown cold on the table, the sauce upon it congealing, the greens wilted and limp. No one else seemed to notice the fact and so I said nothing to it. Pushed the plate aside and tried at the cheeses instead. Surely, I could not find fault with this plate.

'Eleanor?' my mother demanded, seeking a response to a part of the conversation that I had not heard. I swallowed my wine and looked up from my plate; she was staring down her spectacled nose with a beady looking gaze upon me.

'Sorry, Mama, what did you say?' I was preparing for an inquisition on abandoning my plate and made ready my defence.

'The state of your face.'

I had forgotten this point entirely. 'I fell asleep in the shade but awoke in the sun. I have applied lotions. It will fade,' I said disinterested.

Her lips set up in a pucker and I prepared myself, but before she could set her question to me, I was distracted again, this time by the brief capture of Annalise dashing across the hall towards the servants' stairway. The sight of her was jarring. 'I'm sorry, Mother,' I stood up immediately, 'you'll have to excuse me,' I said, slamming down my glass and fleeing clumsily from the table.

'Eleanor, Eleanor!' my father bellowed from his chair as my mother watched on in amazement.

'I don't know what has got into that girl,' I heard her despair as I disappeared into the dim light of the hall.

'Annalise? Annalise, wait!' I called out, chasing her along the narrow corridor that tapered off from the grand hall. But she ignored my calls, not even looking back once and continuing through the jib door to the servants' staircase. *Still, she could not face me.* I had not considered how I would face her. It was all very well chasing her through the house, but when I caught her, I must manage to look her directly in the eyes. I was not sure if I could do it, yet still I followed on, hurrying my steps as she did. The stairs creaking as we bounded, the shuffle against the boards giving away the urgency in which they were trod.

She had already rounded one flight when I caught up with her. She had run on faster in my gaining on her, but in her efforts, dropped the pile of linen she was carrying in a heap at her feet. It seemed ridiculous to me that she would attempt to run from me. What did she think would happen? That I could not catch up with her, or that there was some place to run to in which I could not follow? I would have followed through a path of hot coals.

'Annalise, please, just a moment of your time,' I said when we were too close for her to continue to feign ignorance.

She turned to me, but would not meet my eyes. 'I think we have said all that we needed to say.' Her face was still a brilliant shade of pink and I wondered why none of the preparations seemed to work on her. She bent down to reassemble the pile of fallen linen.

'But that is just it, we have not, or at least there is something I did not explain.'

'There is nothing to explain. Now, I must get these to the laundry,' she continued to dismiss me, and looked ready to make an escape now she had re-gathered what she had dropped.

We cannot hide from this Annalise. 'Wait.' I felt a recklessness surge from somewhere inside me and I grabbed her arm and pulled her blindly through a door and into the near side storeroom. The linen fell to the floor once more and this time I warned her to leave it.

'What has possessed you?' she exclaimed and I knew it was not only the sunburn that caused her colour to intensify. She was angry with me, I could feel it, see it in the narrowness of her gaze, hear it in the way her voice seemed to nip at me like a petulant lap dog.

'I have to tell you.' I slammed the door shut behind me and stood against it, securing her full attention at last. 'When you asked me today, why I kissed you, why I looked at you that way, I was dishonest with my reply—'

'It does not matter! Eleanor, please hold your tongue that you might spare us both the complication,' she pleaded, meeting my eyes in greater earnest.

'I cannot. If you are to despise and forsake me, do so only in the full knowledge of my intentions.'

'I do not despise you.'

Oh, but you do mean to forsake me! 'I looked at you in such a manner earlier and so many times prior, not unintentionally, but because sometimes... Sometimes I look upon your handsome face and cannot tear my eyes from you. Because the feelings and desires that churn inside me are longing to be spoken in a thousand different tongues. I kissed you because I could not help myself, and it was beautiful and enchanting and everything I imagined it would be.' Her gaze slipped away from me again and I took efforts to reengage it. 'Can you tell me, in earnest, that you did not feel it move you with such conviction?'

She cleared her throat. 'I felt nothing resembling what you describe.' She looked past me now, to the door. 'Now, may I be excused, ma'am?'

My heart sunk like lead. 'Your tongue deceives you. I see it in your face and hear it in your voice. Annalise, why won't you speak openly? I know you are afraid. I was afraid too...'

She squeezed her eyes shut and raised a protesting hand up between us. 'You know not what you ask of me!' she erupted and I watched a single tear roll down her cheek as she pulled her arm free of my grasp, pushed past me and fled the room.

I turned to go after her. *No. No I must not pursue her.* I slammed at the door with angry palms. 'Damn it,' I said through gritted teeth and dropped my head into my hands. *You have to let her go.*

I waited for the scurry of her footsteps to dissipate before going out. When I stepped out into the staircase, she was nowhere to be seen, and all that was left, was a heap of white linen, slumped upon the floor.

The next two days passed slowly. Agonisingly. Annalise had done all in her power to keep clear of me, abandoning me entirely to Camille's care. I had taken this as her resignation. I had wanted so much to inquire after her, demand her to come to her mistress (her mistress, I reminded myself, was all that I was now) but I had made a pledge to myself to leave her alone a while, give her time to forgive me the ill regard I had shown her and let the dust settle on it. I knew it was the right thing, but the knowing did little to make easier the doing, and the only way I could manage it at all, was to get completely out of the house. So, I set upon exaggerated rides on the downs, having Mrs Oliver fit me out for new gowns just to run up Giles' bill a little further, spent some time with the puppies and made the very few visits my sorry want for society now afforded me.

The day before, I had visited Miss Lockheart, taking a lengthy tea with her and a walk about the pretty gardens at the Rectory. Today, I went to the Bartletts', and it felt so irregular that she was not with me. But they had grown used to our coming on a Wednesday afternoon and it seemed they must not be neglected by us both, with neither word nor explanation. So, I packed them a basket and set upon the journey to Old Mill Street, alone. Reminiscing as I walked the muddy streets, spattering my muslin, on memories of her going with me.

By the time I arrived there, these memories had stopped comforting me, but now only marked my notice of the lack of her. The lack in me, without her. There was something about being in the cosy room with all the family animated in conversation and repartee, the smell of Rosie's cooking and the easiness between them all, that I longed to be part of, even if only for a while. I would have been willing, if it were the only way open to us, to live as humbly as they did to have her beside me. I knew now that my riches were a poor substitute for that which really held dear to me. And so, if I was pushed to choose in which to give up, I would be ready to submit to such a life. I was sure I could rake together enough to make such a circumstance possible. It was other circumstances that could not be so easily resolved.

It lifted my mood to be amongst them. I had few friends here now I had been cut or grown distant with them all. Even those I could still regard with some degree of kindness, like Martha or Beth, I had avoided to keep myself apart from those they associated with.

Lady W. and her bookish set were the only ones to stand by me through the whole of it without a sniff or a care. But they were in London and I could not risk my going back there unless I knew for certain Giles was out of the city. His recent presence in Carshalton made me nervous of the possibility since I had now received a letter postmarked from Westminster.

The need for the comfort of a good and honest friend grew ever desperate when I was without company and I felt the misery set so thick in my veins I feared I might sink into a paralysis of mind I could not climb out of again.

I sipped at the cloudy mug of broth Rosie had prepared for me, and for a moment, as I looked above the steam rising from my cup, I imagined Annalise sitting opposite me at the busy table. She would always choose that chair if it was vacant. I wondered if I would ever sit around this table with her again.

Later, as I walked back home through the secluded meadows, I attributed my sudden despair to being with them. Watching the simple satisfaction in their eyes; I realised how I longed for that kind of happiness and sense of completion I had watched in Mr and Mrs Bartlett's kindness to each other. I didn't want to be alone, nor married to a man I despised. I wanted the impossible, the forbidden and yet I feared, the only thing in the world that could make me happy.

My despair turned a duller shade of desperation by the time I reached the foot of the staircase with the promise of more loneliness afore me. I was either to remove to my room alone or make company with my mother's relentless questions. "What is wrong?" "Has something happened?" "Is it Giles?" "Why do you have such dreadful grey bags beneath your eyes."

I couldn't let this go on, I told myself firmly and turned on the stair. I was about to do something I would never do, something I would otherwise think below decency. But I was desperate, and still her mistress. Whether she liked it or not, Annalise would have to answer to me.

I hated myself for it even before it was done, for allowing myself to sink so low; but love made people foolish and I had fallen as much a victim to myself as Annalise was about to. I took the narrow staircase down to the basement, battling with my conscience which had decided to flee after a few valiant attempts at turning me back. *I must see her. This avoiding game cannot continue.* I navigated towards the sounds along the corridor. Nervously, I twisted the handle without knocking and quickly found myself confronted with a disturbed table of speechless faces. Mrs Simpson and the rest of the staff rose simultaneously.

'Is there something wrong, madam?' Mrs Simpson asked, half concerned, half vexed at my appearance in the servants' hall.

'No, nothing is wrong,' I said more evenly than I felt and turned to Annalise and settled my gaze upon her, noticing that she was the only one at the table not staring agog at me but looking down towards the floor. 'Forgive my disturbance to your meal; it is Annalise I want.'

This caught her attention and she shot up to meet my eyes, making a poor disguise of her disgust.

'Annalise, I would like a word, if you will be so good as to come to me when you are finished.'

'I will come now,' she said quickly, ignoring the suspicious glances that followed her steps from the table.

I realised instantly how I must have embarrassed her and a prickle of self-loathing scratched at me. But it was not enough. I *had* to see her.

'You can come to me after your meal,' I said again as she walked the corridor with me.

'I have lost my appetite,' she said with a tone of ice and I pushed the guilt from my thoughts and led her to the bathroom lounge.

We did not speak until I had closed and locked the door behind us.

'Well, I never expected you to treat me so much like your maid,' Annalise said to me at last, no longer avoiding my eyes, but instead conveying her anger through hers.

I took a breath which failed to steady me. 'Well, you refuse to be anything other than a maid, so what must you expect?' I realised that it was the old Eleanor speaking such twisted words. The Eleanor I had removed from these past months with hardly any effort at all, only to find that she was not as deeply buried as I had thought.

I saw the pain in her face at my cruel disregard and it sickened me to see the injury. But she had ignited this frustrated fury within me now and there was nothing to be done but let it burn itself out.

'Well done, even I am surprised at how quickly you can lower yourself.'

I had never heard Annalise speak so unfeelingly, in fact, I had never heard her speak an ill word of anyone; but something in her tone warned me she was not afraid to speak her mind on this occasion and it made me nervous.

'You are right.' I stepped in to narrow the gap between us. 'It was a low move, I should know better; in fact, I do, but...' I paused and sighed into my palms. 'Can't you see how this has driven me wild and so reckless? By god, Annalise, I am nothing without you to tame me.'

Annalise stepped back. 'Your sanity, miss, does not depend on me. You managed for many years before your knowing me and I am sure you will manage perfectly well again!'

Her words were guillotine sharp and I felt the last of my dignity slip from my grasp. I edged her up against the wall without even realising it until we could go no further. 'Please, stop pretending. You're killing me.'

'Pretending?' She turned from the weight of my stare.

'I know you care for me, Annalise. I have felt it and yet you act like you despise me when I know it cannot be true.'

'I do care. But not in the way you ask it of me and I cannot be persuaded to so I wish you would not go on trying.'

'Is this what you want? Do you want me to beg you?'

'Of course I don't. I wanted none of this! I want never again to think of the unnatural suggestions you have made to me, but you will not allow me even that.'

'Unnatural? I have never felt anything so natural in my whole existence; I have been living dead until you stirred my senses. And yes, they have been stirred before, Annalise. I have known what it is to have others lay their affections and kisses upon me. Persons that I should feel some regard or at least flattery by. Persons others have found to be a catch. Persons I know, upon a simple observation, must be thought of highly. And yet none of them, not one, has compelled me to return them with any earnest that compares to what I feel for you. It is only now, that I understand it, what it is to be so moved, that I realise it was with them I felt it an unnatural attachment. But this; this is beautiful, it cannot be called otherwise. And if it is unnatural, then let me be damned. Let me!'

'You will not damn me with you!' she spat and managed to pull away from my grasp.

'Then be a liar unto me and to yourself! Pretend as you do that you do not recognise the pain I speak of, that you do not feel this urgency; that you have not thought and wished for the love I want to make to you!'

The volume of my voice had risen to such heights we were both a moment silenced.

'It is wrong, can't you see that? It cannot matter what you want, not this time.'

A silence lingered again. I broke it lowering my voice to a whisper. 'But it will not be silenced or corrected; it will not alter the feelings imprisoned inside of you or me. God knows I have tried to quell it!'

'Not hard enough!'

I let out a dry laugh and pulled back. 'I never thought you dishonest, Annalise; little miss holier than thou! What is the price of your honesty, I wonder? Do you want to see me beg, because I'll beg, look, on, my knees.' I slid down her skirts until I was knelt at her feet. 'God damn it, Annalise, I'll do anything you want, name it.'

'For goodness' sake; get up,' she finally said and I did. 'All I want is for you to leave me alone.'

This was too much to bear, her eyes told me one thing and her words another. 'You do not mean what you just said.'

She looked away. 'Yes, I do! Look at us, what good can come of this?'

'So much good, if you will stop pretending there is nothing between us.'

'I do not pretend.'

I grabbed her face but firmer than I had intended. 'Then why do you keep looking away. Look me in the eye; I dare you to let yourself.'

She shied away from the invitation, despite my fingers about her chin, holding her firm, sinking dimples into her flesh. *You do not want to hurt her.* I relaxed my grip and without warning, pressed an uninvited kiss against her mouth.

But she did not move or respond this time; she froze against the wetness of my tongue. Could it be true? Did she really mean to cut me?

Then came her tears, fast and warm as they gushed and I broke my attempt, pulled back.

'Don't you see how this is killing us?' she said through her sobs. 'This is not what you want.'

'Yes, it is, more than anything. Please, Annalise, you're the only one that can remove this suffering from us. Please.'

'You want me like this, do you—against my will? Just as your husband dealt to you? Go on then, take what you need if that is who you have become. Go on...after all, I am merely your maid. Who am I to refuse you? Is this how I'm to serve my mistress?' She stepped in closer to me and I felt her stiff against my body. 'Take me,' she demanded in a tone that sent a chill to creep the length of me.

I stepped back. 'I've never treated you like my maid!'

'No, not until tonight.' The contempt in her stare was unbearable and I suddenly wished myself gone.

'Well, why do you delay? Kiss me then. That is what you want from me, isn't it? My friendship was not enough for you, was it?' There was such violence in her voice, reflected in her eyes; I could barely recognise her.

What had I done? Who had I become? I fell to my knees in tears. 'I'm so sorry, Annalise, I never...'

She let out a sigh. 'Why did you have to ruin everything?' She shook her head in despair. 'We were so happy.'

'I...I couldn't stop myself,' I cried and watched her slump against the wall and rub her forehead against her fingertips.

'I never wanted to hurt you, Annalise. I only want to love you, but not like this.'

'Stop this, get up now.' She offered out her hand to help me rise but I did not take it.

Instead, I fumbled in my pocket for the key and placed it into her hand. 'Go,' I said through quivering lips. 'Go before I make you stay.'

She hesitated and I saw the pity welling in her eyes.

'GO!' I screamed at her, before collapsing fully onto the floor, my cheek pressed against the cool granite tiles as I sobbed so violently, I trembled and convulsed until it eventually gaggled and choked me into whimpers. I do not know how long this fit endured but when I opened my eyes again, Annalise was gone.

The Search.

October 1821. - Eleanor.

After exhausting myself so exceedingly with such sobbing and then penning a pleading letter to Caitlin to ask to stay with her in Edinburgh, I made my way across the south east lawns and followed the cobbled pathway over to the small chapel that sat perched on a low hill. I had not been there for so long it seemed foreign to me, as did the words of my own prayers when I knelt at the altar with my trembling palms pressed together.

'Dear Father,' I began and could not find the words. 'Dear Father, I am a wretched creature who kneels before you now; too ashamed to ask your forgiveness and yet too tainted with sin to deny the necessity.' I lowered my voice, it was echoing all about me.

'I cannot hide from you, Father, although I have tried to these past months. I understand now. It is indeed an unjust world in which a wretch like me should have so much, whilst those truly deserving are the ones who seem to have nothing at all. All my life, everything I have wanted I could demand to have, and yet I cared not for it. I held that privilege in such little regard. Took it for granted. Considered it little more than my birth right. I was as much a disgrace then, as I am now, although of a different making.' I searched my pocket for a handkerchief and wiped my cheeks. 'She taught me, Father. I do not know if she was sent to do so, but I am changed now. She opened my eyes and my heart with her kindness; her example, and for the first time: I *feel*. I feel gratitude and compassion, humility and love inside me where before there was none, and I am angry, Father, that now I know how to feel such emotion, I am to be mocked by it. For I crave the affection of the only person who cannot return it to me. And now I see the justice in this lesson, and worst of all, I cannot pretend it is undeserved for I have been a selfish person all my life. Which is why I cannot be anymore. So here I am. I come to you, Father, to seek my forgiveness, and to ask you for the strength to do, what I myself cannot: and let her go.'

I was making my journey back across the courtyard when I heard footsteps beside me. I pulled my hair about my face instinctively to hide it better as I recognised Poppy headed for me.

'Miss, I beg your forgiveness for my coming to you like this, but I didn't know what else to do.'

'Good heavens, Poppy? What on earth has happened?'

'It's Annalise, miss... She has gone.'

'Gone?'

'I hope you will beg my pardon, miss, but I couldn't go to anyone else or she would be for it anyway.'

I composed myself. I had been crying so fitfully, I was sure she would notice the state of my face, the still recovering rhythm of my whimpering breaths. 'You were right to come to me, Poppy. Are you certain she is gone? Has she taken all her things? Did she leave you a note?'

She shook her head. 'She left her new dresses but her other clothes are gone. And she would not leave me a note, miss, because I would not be able to read it without her help. But, she left me this.' She pulled an embroidered handkerchief from her aprons. 'It is my birthday present miss, I caught her working on it before. But you see, it is not my birthday for another week, and I am worried sick, because apart from me, she has no one else in the world to go to.'

'Does she truly have no one at all, not a relative somewhere she might prevail upon?"

Poppy shook her head. 'Not like that. I am the nearest thing she has.'

I thought of the Bartletts, Miss Lockheart; *Would she go to them?* 'How long has she been gone?'

'I do not know, miss. I have been in the kitchen all evening, but I would guess an hour. Perhaps two at the most.'

'Does anyone else know she is gone?'

'No, not yet. They think her with you.'

'Right, well it must stay that way. Make any excuse you have to, but do not let on to anyone that she is gone. Go to the stables, have them saddle up my horse. I will find her and bring her home,' I told her with a conviction I could not convince myself of. Even if I could find her after such a time, I was perhaps the person with the least power to change her mind now.

'Oh, thank god, miss,' she said with such relief in her tone, pressing her palms to her chest, that I realised she had far greater confidence in me, than I did.

'And when I do, she will need your support.'

It was a quarter past nine when I climbed up on Samson's back. 'Come now, quickly please, Thomas. I must hurry,' I said to the groom as I grew more and more fearful that someone would come and discover me setting off alone so late, and try to prevent it. I would go anyhow, I was decided, but I could not afford the delay.

The evening had turned the sky a soft haze of indigo as I set across the downs at full speed. There was something liberating about tearing off across the empty meadows, the wind against my face, the night chasing my tail. I felt strong. Invigorated. And it numbed the dread and panic that was pulsing through me. I must keep my focus, keep my head. I was a fraction away from falling apart entirely if I lost sight of my task and gave into the prospect of not returning with her.

It wasn't until I had rode a good twenty minutes out and took a slow trot around the town, that the exhilaration of such a gallop, turned quickly to despair, having caught no sight of her. How far could she have got to at this hour? She had had no time to plan a journey on the stage-coach and she would not get far on foot before nightfall. I scanned the cobbled streets and checked for lights in the bowed windows. Everything in town was closed up and silent, with only the lights behind the windows of the ale house on the corner, a clue to any life behind them. The emptiness disappointed me; there was no one about to even ask after their having seen her. I brought Samson to a halt and surveyed every angle and corner about me, hoping, half expecting to see Annalise's slight frame padding along the street somewhere ahead. But nothing. I trotted on towards the ale house, dismounted Samson at its door, hooked his reins around a lamppost and took a breath before going inside.

The minute I stepped in, the merry hubbub fell into silence and everyone turned to examine me. It was full to capacity with every seat and table occupied, persons stood about the bar and huddled in little clusters about mismatched tables. I certainly stood out in my neat riding habit, and even though there were other women present amongst the hoards of men, they were certainly no ladies.

I ignored the stagnant smell of stale ale and cigar smoke and cleared my throat. 'Excuse me,' I said, taking advantage of their attention. 'I am looking for a young lady, about this high, blonde hair, pretty face. Has anyone seen her?'

'Aren't we all?' one of the men shouted out from a crowded table and sent the others into a fit of laughter.

'She may be dressed in maids clothing. There is a reward available.'

'I 'aven't seen anyone like that, milady,' said the landlord, who was pushing over-spilling tankards across the crowded bar.

'Thank you, sir. If you, or anyone else happens to know of anything, I can be reached at Cuddington, and you will be rewarded for your assistance.' I searched the crowds with a few hopeful glances, some shook their heads and shrugged their shoulders, most had returned to their tankards and chatter.

As I climbed back up onto Samson, I fought back the despair and doubt that was setting in thicker now. There was only one place left I could think of now, and the prospect of going so deep into the slums at this hour was an uncomfortable one, but the hope of finding her outweighed it, and I rode on towards the Bartletts' with the darkness falling behind me.

I took a moderate canter along the main street, keeping my speed up enough not to make myself vulnerable, and slow enough not to burst into a gallop and draw any more attention to myself than necessary. Not that there seemed to be anyone about to notice me, beyond a few stray cats scratching at the remnants of the day's market wares. I wasn't sure if I found this near desertion reassuring or eerie. The lanes were poorly lit, many not at all, and as I scanned my surroundings, my eyes played tricks on me and made shapes out of the shadows. When I reached Old Mill Street, the horizon of cluttered tenements in the backdrop, the familiarity comforted me and at once, I slowed down, until I was outside the Bartlett's green paint chipped front door.

'No, milady. We haven't seen Miss Anna since she came with you last,' said Rosie, as she stood in the doorway of the small cottage, tempting me to go in. I could see the fire flickering through the small window and the family sat around the table. No sign of Annalise and no reason to suspect they would lie to me.

'Thank you, Rosie, but I have nowhere to tie him up,' I said, referring to Samson. 'I am so sorry to have disturbed you like this at such an hour. I didn't know where else to try.'

'Oh, I do hope she is well, miss. Such a lovely girl. I'm sure she can't have gotten far.' She put down the toddler who had been perched on her hip and opened the door up wide and gestured me in again. 'We're just about to have supper, you're very welcome.'

'Thank you. No. I must carry on before nightfall. Mrs Bartlett, you must go back to your family, I will be on my way.'

'Then will you let me send Thomas and the boys out to look with you?'

'No. You are very good, but there is no need for so much trouble this late.'

'Well, if you are sure, miss, but you'll let us know, won't you? When you find her, let us know she is safe and well?'

'Yes, yes, of course. And please send word to me if she should arrive.'
Mrs Bartlett nodded.

'Goodnight.' I smiled and remounted Samson, fighting back the well of tears and hopelessness that were building so heavily in my eyes and at the back of my throat.

When I had got far enough down the street, I let a few of them fall. *Where are you, Annalise?* I was out of ideas now and for the first time seriously contemplated the possibility that I might not find her at all. It was too much to bear. What if she was gone for good? What if something terrible had happened to her—some accident or attack and that was why I could not find her? *Please, no!* I sobbed.

I was so preoccupied I had forgotten my precarious surroundings quite entirely, not realising that I had driven into a narrow lane where a rowdy crowd of young men were hanging about. 'Whoa!' I commanded Samson as I searched the vicinity; there was not enough room to turn him back.

'Ooh, what 'ave we got 'ere then boys?' one of them said. His slurred speech gave away his inebriation. *This I could do without.* I stiffened and felt them close in around me as Samson jibbed.

'Well, well, well, this is no time o' night to be trotting about in your finest m', luv,' said another greasy looking man who had crept up beside me and stood patting Samson's thigh. I wished Samson would kick him.

I kept my composure. 'Yes, I am very late, and would be grateful if you might let me pass so I can get on my way.'

'Well, she's a fair one alright.' I heard from somewhere ahead, but could not make out the face in the shadows.

'I'd say so,' said the greasy haired man again, and I felt his hand upon my leg and him patting it like he had patted the horse.

I stared into his sallow face. 'Sir, please take you hand off of me. I am leaving, now make way.' I held my nerve and tried to tap Samson gently onward, but he was aware of the lack of space to turn around in and the block they had formed ahead of us, and wouldn't budge.

'A gutsy one.' They laughed and made sneering, mocking noises.

'Look, I don't know what you mean by stalling me like this, I wish only to mind my own business and get on my way.'

'And what kind of business does your sort 'ave 'round 'ere exactly?'

'I was calling on friends.'

They burst into a greater fit of laughter. 'I can't imagine you have many friends here, my love, you sure you're not lost?'

I could smell the liquor and tobacco on his breath. 'No, I am not lost. I know my way perfectly well, if you stupid oafs would just get out of my way and let me pass!'

I hadn't realised I had raised my voice so severely until they fell silent at last.

'Listen 'ere lady, you need to quieten down, people are sleeping round 'ere.'

'What do you want from me? If it is money, I have none with me, so you are wasting your time.'

'Well, I say I don't believe you, and that we should see for ourselves lads,' said the one at my side and he began frisking my leg more aggressively now.

'Get off me at once!' I warned him again, and someone else told him to "Leave it, Bill," but he took no heed and before I knew it, I had kicked him hard across to the wall and he crashed right into it.

'You little bitch! You'll pay for that,' another ran at me. I slapped him swiftly across the face with my riding crop before he reached me. Then before I had time to contemplate it, I was thrusting and swinging the crop around violently in the air beating them out of my way, screaming words I could barely decipher in my rage. They bounced between the moss-covered walls in thumping echoes.

'You will all pay for this tomorrow when my father sends the constable and has the magistrate string you up for this,' I screamed until my throat felt scratched and when I paused a moment, crop mid-air, I realised I had beat them far enough away to give Samson space to manoeuvre. I set in my heels and he pelted off with such speed that the men were left to clamber to the walls either side to avoid him mowing them down.

I rode at full gallop for a good ten minutes, trembling with the shock, crying with both anger and relief. It wasn't until I reached the downs again that I began to slow to a canter and calm down a little. It was almost pitch black now, and the visibility was poor, the merest slither of a new moon above me. It was per chance, that I managed to spot the small figure of someone walking the middle of the meadows in a crack of the moons light. 'Annalise?' I called out. 'Annalise!' I steered Samson to the right and rode on towards her.

When I grew close enough to make her out properly my heart gushed at the sight of her. *She is alright.*

'Please go home, Eleanor,' she said flatly when I caught up with her. She seemed neither particularly surprised nor interested at my sudden appearance.

'Oh, thank the Lord it is you.' I reined Samson in and slid off his back. 'What on earth are you about? I have been everywhere looking for you!'

'Well, I never asked you to!' She scowled. 'In fact, I do not know what gives you the idea you have a right to come following me about. I am no longer in your employ or your family's. I am leaving.'

'I have been worried sick! And so has Poppy.' This at least seemed to produce some effect as at last she looked up at me. 'She came to me despairing of what to do and I told her I would bring you back safely.'

'Well then you have lied to her, because I cannot return with you, Eleanor, and you know that, so why must you make this any more troublesome for either of us?'

'You have nowhere to go, Annalise. This is ridiculous.'

'No, what is ridiculous is that I cannot seem to escape you, wherever I go!'

'Please.' I tugged at her arm to stop her walking on. 'Please, Annalise.' I stood in front of her to block her path. 'Just hear me out. Five minutes is all I ask.'

'You have said enough, Eleanor: too much, don't you see?'

'I promise you, if you give me just five minutes, I will let you go on undisturbed if you still wish it.'

'And if I refuse?'

'Then I will petition you all night through if I have to and we shall journey together to wherever it is you are headed.'

Reluctantly, she sighed her agreement and we made our way over to a nearby tree stump where she slumped down upon it. I walked Samson over by his reigns and tied him to a low hanging branch before sitting next to her, careful to keep a distance. I watched as he began to crop a patch of grass at the foot of the tree whilst I mustered my words.

'Annalise, I am so sorry to have hurt you to this degree. I have never wished to hurt you at all, but I see such injury in your eyes that I am ashamed to be the cause of it. For that, I apologise sincerely.'

'Very well. I am grateful for it,' she said, her eyes fixed on the dark horizon ahead, her hands tangling a reed she had pulled up from the ground.

'What I cannot apologise for, and will not take back, is what I have confessed to you of my feelings.'

She threw down the reed and went to stand up.

I tugged gently at her sleeve. 'I cannot apologise for it, because it is truly how I feel and I am powerless to forbid myself from feeling it. But what I can, and must do, is find the strength to quell it, until it passes. I will do that much, if it kills me, I will do it for you.'

Slowly she lowered herself back into her seat. 'Well, it will be an easier task for my absence, so you must see why I have to leave.'

'You have nowhere to go.'

'I will find somewhere; I will go to the registry tomorrow and seek another position.'

'But you love the one you have, the people you are amongst, the comfort of a good friend like Poppy; you cannot throw all of that away so lightly.'

I saw the glisten of tears in her eyes. 'Believe me; I do not do so lightly! It breaks my heart! But it is all sullied now.'

'Oh, Annalise, let me break mine instead that you may stay at Cuddington without me ever saying another word to you, as if we never met. I promise you that what happened today; it will never happen again.'

'I cannot, it would never work now; too much has passed.'

'It will if you let it. I will do whatever you want me to, to fix this.'

'You can't just fix this, Eleanor. Not everything can be fixed! Do you think that because you can put a few coins in the palms of the poor and make clothes for their children that everything in life can be so easily amended? Well, you are wrong!'

'Very well. If I cannot reason with you, then you force me to act against my conscience, Annalise. If you do not return with me right now, then you will not be the only one to leave the house tonight.'

'What are you talking about; what do you mean by that?'

'I do not care to know the details of what went on between you and that footman. But I have enough on him to see him turned out without a reference this very hour! My parents may be good employers, Annalise, but you well know what they expect, and you know what happened to Molly. If I tell them what it was I saw that night when you sat on the doorstep together, it will not go well.'

I could see the shock in her face; divided by contemplation of my issued threat and admission of witnessing the kiss her and Will had briefly shared.

The disgust in her face was painful to look at. 'Even you are not so malicious.'

'Why not? You seem to think me capable of everything else?'

'Why? Why must someone else suffer in this mess?'

'I know you have a low opinion of me, and I realise I have earned it. But despite what you think, or whether you believe it; I am doing this for you. I am trying to make amends.'

'By causing an innocent man to lose the position of his making?'

'You will not allow that to happen to him, no more than I will watch you journey on to nowhere in the dark, and give up a place that you love.'

She bit her lip and seemed to consider the situation.

'Now, I am planning to away this week. That will give us both a chance to put the memory of this wretched business behind us and move on. When I return, Camille will officially take up the full-time position of my Abigail and it will be as it was before we met, you have my word.' I held my hand out. 'Now, shall I take you home?'

She said nothing, but took my offered hand. I untied Samson, remounted him and pulled her up to saddle in front of me. I took a blanket from the saddle bag and arranged it around her shoulders despite her flinching at my every touch. 'It is chill and you will feel it more up here.'

Still she said nothing, but took the corners of it and pulled it tighter around her shoulders.

I looked ahead and was grateful now for the darkness, so I could not be easily seen straddling. I hoisted up my skirts and pulled the reins taught and felt the weight of Annalise between my forearms as we started up a trot. I refused to entertain my imagination at the idea of feeling my arms wrapped fully around her, however much my body yearned for such proximity. I tapped my heels and we sped off into a gallop across the hazy moor. I was in no mind to draw this out and add encountering highway men to this evening's adventures, so I rode hard and fast. The sooner she was out of reach, the better. For despite my implorations and assurances, it was taking everything I had not to throw myself helplessly at her mercy and beg her for another chance to put things right between us. All the restraint I could summon to divert the instinct to pull her closer as I felt her cling to me with fright as Samson picked up speed and bumped us about. She was not used to horses, I remembered. I wanted to tell her it was alright, that there was nothing to fear, that I would let no harm come to her. How could I when I cared more for her welfare than even my own? But I dared not say another thing in case some other words entirely, came to pass.

We didn't speak at all for the rest of the journey. It felt strange, to be so close, and yet the distance between us wider than that of strangers.

It was a bittersweet relief when we dismounted Samson and went on our separate ways with only the merest uttering of a 'goodbye' between us.

Giles or no, I would away to London at first light and put up in Berkeley Square until I heard back from Caitlin. This was a promise I could not break.

Consolation.

October 1821. - Eleanor.

My parents were reluctant to let me go off to Berkeley Square without them the next morning, but a well-placed hint that their refusal would only result in my petitioning Lady W. for an invitation instead, had the intended effect and it was agreed I could go for a week if I took Miss Pascal with me.

So, I took her, despite wanting to be alone and away from her fussing over my sad decline. But when we got there, I had her shown to her quarters and avoided calling on her for anything above the absolute necessary.

It was a strange feeling: the house all shut up and no company about it except the occasional appearance of a servant here and there. I was pleased the drawing room windows had been opened ahead of my arrival. There was a beautiful breeze that washed over me as I slumped onto the chaise and stretched my legs out in front of me. It was another exceptionally hot day for October and an unpleasant one to journey in. But I was here now, and quite relieved to be far removed from Annalise as well as to have so much privacy at my disposal to let my tears out. No prying or questions to answer about the puffiness around, or the pink streaked whites of my eyes. No trifling excuses to conjure to explain away the cause.

How could I tell anyone I was heartbroken when no one even suspected me in love?

I pinched the flesh between my eyes and pushed my fingertips into the sockets to massage them. A persistent dull ache behind them had refused to abate, like a splinter of glass had lodged itself somewhere behind them in my skull.

'Cook would like to know what hour you wish to dine this evening, ma'am?'

I turned to see the butler at my side, placing upon the table a glass of lavender lemonade. It was just the thing. 'Thank you, Bentham. I shan't dine tonight. I have no appetite.'

'Very good, ma'am.'

'Bentham, I think it unlikely at this season, but should any visitors call, or cards be left, please be so good as to turn them away and deny my being here.'

'As you wish, ma'am.'

I took a sip from my glass and when I heard the door close behind him, got up and ventured over to a window, taking care to keep behind the veil of tulle curtains as they flayed about in the breeze. Berkeley Square was all but deserted save a nanny, sat back-facing me, upon a bench in the gardens watching two young children play on the lawn whilst she rocked a perambulator to and fro. I looked across to number thirty-eight—the Jerseys had likely removed to Osterley. Which seemed a shame for of all the ton who had deserted me, I felt Lady Jersey might be one who might be relied upon to accept a call, despite it all. Even Lansdowne seemed shut up and deserted. With a bit of luck, not a soul would have seen my carriage dispatch me, and if I took care at the windows, no one should suspect me here at all.

I was still not sure of Giles' whereabouts; his most recent letter which came only this morning was postmarked from Portsmouth. I hoped such a distance indicated him setting off abroad on some business or other. Otherwise, the half-mile between here and Half Moon Street may not prove enough distance to prevent my presence coming to his notice, even if I was lying low. So, as I journeyed the short walk over to Grosvenor Square to leave a card for Lady W., I took care to keep my hair tucked tightly beneath my bonnet, my gaze low and my wits about me.

'I am sorry, Mrs Craythorne; she is away to Bath. Due back next week,' explained her butler when I arrived.

I was more disappointed than I expected at this news. I had barely been in town three hours and I already felt the Lombard fever setting in.

I took Crampton's offered cup of chocolate and sat in her parlour drinking it just to kill some time. *Now what?* I wondered, turning the cup to swill the last of the settled cocoa back into the mix. Then it came to me; there was another friend I *could* call on, although it had been a while...

I knew, as I thanked Crampton for the refreshment break and made the journey over to Old Chapel Street, I really should not go.

I walked through St James' Park in an attempt to avoid passing traffic. It was quiet at this hour, I noted as I scanned the landscape, neat beds of flowers lining the path, an autumnal turn of colour around the periphery of the leaves. If Giles was not away on business, it was in this quarter I was at most risk of crossing paths with him. But he never walked the parks; I was safe if I took care with my route.

There was something soothing in the park's desertion and as I scanned my surroundings and drew deeply on the milder evening air, I felt a sense of sanctuary within its tree lined enclosure.

I took a seat on a nearby bench and thumbed my copy of Cary's Pocket book to check my direction. The view before me drew me in as I closed the book: dappled crimson sky reflected off the lake. I took in its view and let the stillness suffuse. I could have stayed there at length, but it would not be safe, alone after sunset.

A pelican padded along the path ahead of me, stretched out a wing like a giant fan and jabbed its large yellow beak beneath it several times before retracting it and bobbing back towards the water's edge. *I should go,* I considered, as notions of streetwalkers and bandits came to mind in my mother's voice. I pulled my slipper from my foot and shook it about until a single shard of gravel that had been irritating me for nigh on twenty minutes was dislodged from it, before pulling it back on and resuming my journey. It seemed a shame to depart it when I exited the gates onto Queen Street. The peace I had felt there had been a brief reprieve. *I really should turn back. No damage has been done. Yet.*

When I arrived at Old Chapel Street with a mind for distraction, I was relieved to make eye contact with no one of significance and seemed to pique no interest at all in the few passers-by. I almost did turn back though, as I found myself outside number eight, hand poised to tug at the bell. But then I thought of going back to Berkeley Square all barren and friendless and pulled at it until it sounded. *It was done.*

'Good evening.'

'Good evening, sir, I am here to see Mr Richards.'

The landlord, a rather prim, weasel faced fellow, showed me up to his lodgings with a look about him that told me he was suspicious of my visit, but not stupid enough to question me.

We trod an exceeding high staircase that left me slightly fagged as we reached the landing and I noticed his eyes follow my hand in search of a wedding ring, I presumed, as I pulled off my gloves and rested a second. I noted a flicker of reassurance in his face as he found the gold band on my finger. Perhaps he had me for a sister or a cousin? I didn't much care, so long as it satisfied him enough to deliver me to Richards. It was just as well he obliged too, for I had no clue as to where his rooms were, having only ever written to him and never been inside before.

'Mrs Craythorne? Is everything alright?' Mr Richards said, puzzled at the sight of me as he opened the door a crack.

'Yes, thank you. Will you let me come in?'

He stepped aside. 'Of course. You will forgive me; I was not expecting visitors. I am hardly suitably attired,' he said, rushing to clear a pile of musical scores from an armchair where I presumed he had been working before my interruption. 'I am not accustomed to receiving them, in fact. You will have to excuse the disorder.'

'I'm sorry. I shouldn't have come unannounced like this.' He was wearing his night shirt and I realised he was minded to make an early night.

'Not at all, please; sit down.'

I took the offered seat obligingly and he settled in the opposite. The room was humble, a hint of faded glory and shabbiness in the furnishings and a chaos of things cluttered about the tables and fire mantle. But it was not unpleasant, there was a cosiness about it, and the proportions of the room were fair.

'You must tell me what I can do for you. I own I am a little surprised since you returned none of my calls.'

'Forgive me, sir, I am sorry for it. I hope I did not cause you any offence. You see, my marriage was—at that time—a priority for me, and I was given counsel to give you up before we were found out. There were rumours that reached my family's ears.'

'I see. Well, I expected it to be something of that order.'

'You did?'

'Yes. I am the man everyone's wife and daughter wishes to make love to, so long as it can never be found out.'

I was a little shocked by his candour but I supposed I should not be, given that we had been so much more intimate before. 'You say it most unaffected, sir.'

'You get used to the way of things do you not, after a time?'

'Yes, some things I suppose.'

'Not you though, I confess. You, I was sorry to part company with.'

I found a smile for him. 'And I you, sir, for it's plain that you are not in short supply of admirers and yet you have always been so attentive to me.'

'Oh, Eleanor, I think you mean to gammon me! You must know you shine down the lot of them.'

I laughed and waved him off. *Flattery.* Yes, flattery felt soothing to me having so recently suffered such a decimation of my pride, self-esteem, dignity...

'Still, too late for that now.'

I thought back to when I had had to make such a choice between him and Giles, after all the bad business. What a fool I had been to think I had made the better bargain. 'I am so much wiser these past months.'

He narrowed his eyes. They had a beautiful depth to them. 'Is it as bad as all that?'

'I have moved out of my husband's house, quite against his liking.'

'Yes, I did hear something like it.'

'Well, as a consequence, I have recently turned out to be the greatest source of gossip on-dit, scandalous child as I've become!'

'I'm sorry for you, Eleanor. I don't like to think you unhappy.'

'Don't be. I am happier now than I ever could be under his roof.'

He considered me a moment. 'And now I find you here, under mine?'

I coughed a little and was grateful for the pause it afforded me for I needed to collect my courage.

'Can I get you something to drink?' he said obligingly.

'No. Thank you. I did not come to sit, or to drink or prittle-prattle, but then I think you already know that, Mr Richards.' I watched his gaze grow still. 'I came here to make love to you,' I said so shockingly plain that we were both temporarily astonished by my speech. It did not linger; when I put down my reticule, stood up, unbuttoned my pelisse and pulled myself out of my dress, I noted the change in his demeanour, the vulnerability in his eyes. 'Will you make love to me, Mr Richards? God knows it's been an age since you did.'

I watched his expression darken and when I leant over to kiss him, *he* did not reject me.

'Oh Eleanor—' He pulled me into his lap and lifted my chemise over my head before burying his face at my décolleté. Small bumps rose up across my skin to meet his feather light kisses. Gentle. Breathy. Ticklish to begin with. Then I felt them at my breasts, the wetness of his tongue and it triggered deeper yearnings within me. A pulse contracting, coiling, demanding...

Oh, Annalise, how sweet your kisses would feel here. I pushed him back into the armchair and bought his hand between my thighs. The warmth of his palm against me made my legs fall instantly weak. Would he know how to handle me this way? Last time had been so rushed... Yes, he knew. I felt him stroke his hand against me, working all the tension *she* had conjured up in me. *I saw her then, a flash of her towel slipping in the water closet, the paleness of a breast reflected back in the mirror, a renegade lock of blonde hair obscuring one of her manilla brown eyes.* I pulled at his breeches and felt him ready for me. *Taut dewy skin stretched across a ladder of ribs, her waist tapered and slight. Below her navel...* I positioned myself and let him open me up as I sat back down upon him. *Slowly.* My body was still reluctant to give way, but it did not hurt like before and I was so ready from his handling, it had prepared me well for his entry. After a few cautious slides along the length of him, I found a rhythm and began to work it as he fed me feral groans and grunts into my ear. I held on to his shoulders. Kissed him harder on the mouth and ground myself against him until I could hardly catch my breath.

'Oh, Eleanor; god, you are a jewel.' I felt his hands stiffen around my hips to hold me firm as he bounced me up and down on his lap. He was deft in his handling of me and now I knew why. He was the secret plaything amongst the ton and so much used to the task. I might have felt offended by this knowing if my feelings were not so much elsewhere. *Oh Annalise.*

'Why do you stop?' I begged him as he slowed.

'I can't go on. Do not move, do not move a fraction,' he fret and so I obeyed him and relaxed upon his lap, stroked his face, tugged at his hair, kissing him slowly now, gently like I had kissed *her.* How much I wished I could kiss her now, touch her like he touched me, and reduce her to such helplessness. I imagined my delight to see the relief in her face. The shock in her eyes as she came undone. I imagined the scene: her pale breasts heaving with her laboured breaths, her hips rolling as I worked the spot, her eyes widened, her soft voice breaking into growls, begging me to release her from her torment as Mr Richards did now. I could not appease him any longer, I resumed the rhythm as vigorously as I could manage between his desperate imploring and attempts to slow me, and in moments, it was complete.

I collapsed against him and rested my head upon his shoulder as I recovered my breath. I heard the hammering of his heart as his chest heaved, my head rising with it. How could it be so easy to win him, any man, and with so much ease it was trifling, yet her: my beautiful Annalise did not want my kisses and there was nothing I could do to alter it.

I felt his hands stroke the lengths of my back and caress me, but it wasn't her touch and so much I needed it to be.

'Eleanor, are you crying?' he said, trying to pull me back to look at me. I did not want him to see my tears. I held fast and willed them to stop.

'Eleanor, what can I do?'

'Just hold me here and love me a while.'

In the morning, I awoke in his bed in a tangle of sheets and felt a deep and haunting sense of shame as I looked upon his sleeping face. I hadn't meant to spend the whole night. It was just as well there was no one to expect me home, I thought, as I unfurled his heavy arm from around my waist and stared into the ceiling. He was so handsome and so kind; he did not deserve such ill use as I had made of him. I felt ashamed as I remembered the brief interludes between our repeated love makings. It had proceeded through the night until I noticed the room come back into focus with the dawn of morning light filtering through the threadbare drapes. I had induced him to take me so many times, as if it would expel the heavy need within me to feel her touch. It had not. I realised soberingly now, that all it did was emphasise the void within me, not fill it.

But he had been tender in the pauses, cradled me gently as I wept upon his chest. Stroked my hair and paid me compliments I was not worthy of. It had felt nice then. But he was not her. And now, now I was saddled with the additional burden of my guilt to him. *This must not happen again.* He might be used to such encounters, but I was not used to feeling so much disgusted with myself. Besides, I had no wish to be an obstacle to him finding someone who could love him as he deserved. For whatever he said to dispel my suspicions, I felt certain that his affection for me could lead into a deeper state of dependency if I permitted it. I remembered his tender utterances in my ear. Now I understood so painfully the injury of unrequited affection, I would certainly not be the cause of his. So, I kissed him kindly, apologetically, as he slept and departed to Berkeley Square before he woke.

The Society.

October 1821. - Eleanor.

When I returned to Berkeley Square, the sun still breaking up the morning mist and half-light, Camille was asleep in my easy chair at my bedside. 'Camille,' I roused her gently, 'go to bed.'

'Madame!' she said, wiping sleep from her eyes. 'You are back. I was so worried. Where 'ave you been?'

'No need to worry. I—I visited a friend and we lost count of the hours. Go on up to bed now, get some proper sleep. I shall do the same,' I told her.

But I could not sleep. I tossed and turned and cried a little more in my attempts to persevere. But my mind was under invasion: images of her, images of him. It became clear to me as I went over things, circular, what a terrible mistake I had made going to him last night. It had been a comfort; a pleasurable distraction at the time. But now I felt hollow and more alone than ever.

By noon, I was perusing on Bond Street with Camille, looking mildly concerned at the number and variety of purchases I was making. 'It cheers me up to shop,' I told her when we returned to the carriage with bandboxes stacked in every space of the carriage about us. They were too valuable to risk outside of the carriage, so we sat with them rattling about at our feet and sliding from the seats beside us.

But I knew she was suspicious of me: how many people would buy six of the same gold pocket watches? The entirety of *Rundell & Bridges* stock of this particular kind. 'Gifts,' I had said in answer to her furrowed brow as she helped me unpack it all into a lockable trunk in my dressing room. 'It shall be Christmastide before we know it and I prefer to be timely.'

I would not take her with me again. I hardly had a reputation to protect nowadays so what should it matter if I was spotted shopping alone. This trip I may have managed to convince her of some mad-brained and somewhat over-indulgent gifting spree, but she would not accept my daily repeats of the same. Which is precisely how I spent each and every day now, becoming a favourite face to every merchant from end to end of the shopping district. My once empty trunk now stood half full of all manner of trinkets and my bills were already estimated somewhere in the region of eight hundred pounds. Which was still but a pittance of the dowry I knew my father had settled on me. I should have it all back, one way or the other, however long it took me to transfer it from his pocket to my own. And once I had, I could claim my ticket to freedom. Independence. Anonymity.

The trouble was, knowing how to go about selling it. I didn't know where to begin. Advertisements were one way, but they would take time and I would have to supply an address. There were no doubt shops and establishments that I could sell them to, but I did not think I would find such places in this district and would be vulnerable heading to other such districts where they might be found, alone. I should put my mind to all that after, and it was perhaps better I done so in some other place where I was less known. If Caitlyn accepted my request to go to Edinburgh, that should answer well enough, although I wondered how safe it would be to convey so many valuables on such a journey that would require so many stops and a higher probability of encountering highway men. Perhaps I would have to hire myself a brutish fellow with a talent for his pistols, like uncle's tiger, as an escort for the journey. But how I would go about finding such a fellow, and a trustworthy one at that? I had no clue.

But for now, I was to concentrate my efforts and subdue my melancholy thoughts, by procuring them, that was the most important part, the rest could be resolved in time, and it was upon passing that an idea struck me on how to minimise the volume, whilst increasing the spend. I thought back to Petworth and the rumours of how much the Earl had spent on his fine collection of art. I needed to procure those kinds of items. Wasting my time with trinkets would be nothing to the cost of a fine scene by Tinteretto, Turner or the like. So, when I was finished at the Western Exchange, I had the coach directed on to King Street to look at the catalogue at Christie's, remembering the address from sending off for their catalogue which was likely sitting on a stagecoach en-route to Cuddington by now.

There were all sorts of oddities listed; war medals and coins of old, rare manuscripts and antique books, but nothing of interest for my purposes. I wouldn't have the slightest notion of where to shift such items of acquired taste, well, not covertly anyway. So, I left upon the gentlemen clerk telling me to call back in a few days to view their new catalogues and receive an update on acquisitions, and so I made a mental note accordingly.

I received Lady W.'s card a week later and was pleased to accept her invitation to stay with her. Berkeley Square had been a painful dead bore in my melancholic mood and in a clash of considering the less of evils in remaining in London alone, I had packed for my return to Cuddington just an hour before her card came. *Sorry, Mama, I just cannot face returning yet.*

So, I left Camille at Berkeley Square to unpack them all again and headed over to Lady W.'s. I had no mind to take her to Grosvenor Square and risk her growing even more suspicious of my activities. I told her to take a week's leisure at my purse and to stay in Berkeley Square to send and receive my things as requested. Lady W. was not short of servants to prevail upon and with how cumbersome and protective Camille had become these past weeks, I preferred a stranger who would be too coy to level questions and impose unwanted comforts upon me.

Lady W. was in fine spirits and pleased to see me. I realised how much missed she had been as I settled back into comfort with her and we exchanged all our news since our last meeting. We filled our days with visits to the circulating library, more extravagant shopping trips on Bond Street and perusing the stalls of the Western Exchange. We took up tickets for the theatre and music halls, and even the odd exhibition as we stumbled across them. In the evening, Lady W. would host some small entertainment or other, from a salon to a card party, as usual composed of persons I had never before met, or had only the slightest of recollection.

On the surface, I begun to feel much like my old self and there was something comforting about the familiarity of it all. But deep down, in the rare but poignant moments that I was without distraction, I felt plainly how thinly it disguised the misery that lay dormant inside me. I knew if I let my guard down for the briefest moment, I would unravel from the tightly wound spiral I had twisted my emotions into, like a coiled spring.

It was on such a moment of contemplation Lady W. came to my chamber and bought a letter to me.

'Are you alright, Eleanor?'

I had slept ill and woken plagued by despair at how much my soul yearned to be close to Annalise that I had fought back so many tears for fear of never staunching them.

'Eleanor,' she said, sitting down at the window seat beside me. 'I am not in the habit of pressing a person when they have taken pains to conceal their troubles.' There was a seriousness in her expression she rarely gave away. 'But I must tell you, that whatever it is that has taken the bloom from that pretty face of yours, it cannot answer at keeping you so ill improved in so many days.'

'Oh Lady W., have I really made so poor a job of keeping my troubles out of the way?'

'My dear, I have seen you endure much that is unreasonable and yet I have never seen you so forlorn. I trust this is no regular spell of the blue devils? Pray, tell me that you are not in some desperate trouble?'

'No, no I am not in any trouble.'

'Then a matter of the heart I think.'

I cried then without meaning to let the tears come and she pressed a hand over mine. 'There, my dear.'

'Oh Lady W., I am sure I cannot bear it. I thought it must surely pass by now, but it does not abate, no matter how much I am determined that it must. No matter how many days go by, still I feel its violence as keenly as the day I awayed.'

'Is there no hope?'

'None. I wonder how I ever thought there could be; our circumstances so peculiar and yet I could not stop myself.'

'My dear, the heart does not speak the language of logic; it cares not for the arguments of reason or circumstance, it knows only how to feel.'

'I wish it would not feel so exceedingly.'

'Is it your husband that prevents it?'

'No, of all the obstacles between us, it is a matter of unrequited feeling that breaks the possibility.'

'Nay, I cannot believe it. Are you certain?'

'I own I believed my inclination returned, but I was so very much wrong I can barely believe I have been so foolish as to declare my own, and now, now I cannot see how I can ever go back.'

'Come, dear, it cannot be as bad as that. I assume then, we do not speak of Mr Richards?'

I flinched a little at the mention. 'No, not he.' I wished then, to tell her just how bad it was; to relieve myself of the whole. But no matter how accommodating Lady W. was in so many things, I could not expect her to sympathise with such a calamity as this. And even if she would, I could not bear the shame of confessing such a peculiar notion a second time around.

'You must go back eventually, when you feel restored to health enough and with good grace you will move on.'

'Will I? I am not sure I have the care to try.'

'Perhaps not just yet, but you will again. You are strong, Eleanor, but it is alright to forget the fact a while, as long as you don't forget it altogether. Until then, be patient with yourself.'

I tried to be patient as one day turned into the next and whilst I did not yet feel the restoration Lady W. spoke of, I at last mustered the courage to return my mother's letter and announce I would be home the following week in time to celebrate the news of Henry's impending heir. – The timing of which seemed rather expedient given the very recent wedding date.

But when it finally came upon me, it took less than three days of being back before it was all undone again and I insisted on my return to London. It had been too soon. Too difficult to fight the temptation to seek out Annalise and beg my forgiveness, beg her that we might at least go back to the friends we had become before I made such a mess of it all. I missed her so sorely I would have gladly taken her friendship back as some consolation, but even that possibility seemed altered beyond remedy now.

With the distance London put between us I could just about resist such urges, but without the leagues set physically between, I knew it was only a matter of time before I lost the fight against my will and risked breaking my promise and seeking her out. *That* could not happen. So, if all I could do to keep it was to stay abroad, then that I must.

I had expected another evening of Lady W.'s entertainments scraped from the thin society of London that were only just beginning to return with the late, but fast abating heat. But after dinner, she advised me that she was to be engaged in a committee meeting this night and I had leave to attend her should I fancy the diversion.

I had no notion of what the company would consist of when I was introduced to Lady W.'s guests, but any company seemed preferable to the solitude of my own.

It was a mixed party of ladies in attendance, mostly of the middling sort but some from higher and lower orders. None—I was pleased to note—I recognised.

They were a newly formed faction of the British Ladies Society for promoting the reformation of female prisoners. I was not ignorant of such causes and had some notion of Mrs Fry's much publicised work and vague memories of the astonishment that broke out upon her being heard by parliament a few years prior. For being the first woman to own such a triumph, she had a great deal of my admiration, although I could not greatly appreciate such interest in going on prison visits and trying to reform villainous types of persons. Her philanthropic involvement in

Newgate was well known, although I had very little interest in the news of it and understood the matter less still. But in spite of my bewilderment at Lady W.'s involvement in such a scheme, I listened on with interest at the exchange between the ladies as they gathered en masse in Lady W.'s large saloon.

A woman of middle age, in plain dress with her raven black hair tied back in a neat chignon, took the presiding role of the meeting.

'So, as you may know, our dear sister, Betsy, has had a much-strained year; the loss of her sister and now difficulties over her daughter's pending marriage. Still, she attends to many duties on behalf of the Society and as well as her own ministering at the Quaker Houses. But I think we must be mindful of her health and arrange to split our efforts between our new undertaking at Horsemonger Lane and continue to offer some assistance to Newgate at this time to ease her burden.'

This was met with agreement from the rest of the party and I wondered, as I looked about them, what had induced them to support such a cause. I was increasingly more philanthropically minded myself in the case of the poor and needy. My unpleasant awakenings of discovering Old Mill Street came to mind as I considered this. But to offer assistance to those sorts of persons seemed a natural duty, but to criminals? I could not be so much convinced. Betsy had told our set many a harrowing story from her father's duty as our local magistrate and none of them had yet induced me to feel anything beyond relief at their being apprehended and kept off the streets.

'Now, the magistrate of Horsemonger Lane, has already agreed to our admission and the gaoler, a Mr Honeyfield, expects us next week.'

I held in an involuntary laugh at the irony. It certainly did not fit with my expectation of a gaoler's persona.

'Miss Stanhope and I have been there this week to make preliminary inquiries and we have sixty-two females and twenty-eight children. We will need a substantial supply of sewing articles, linen, blankets and books for the school room to make a start. There are also a number of infants with barely a thread, so we shall need to procure clothing too before the colder season sets in. Is it possible we can manage this between us?'

'Yes,' said Lady W., 'I can see to sewing supplies, if you will furnish me with a list.'

'The ladies of my parish are already underway in the task of knitting and sewing children's things, but I shan't think it will be enough to cover half that number,' said a beetle-browed woman who appeared to be taking the minutes.

'I have also started taking in donations of clothes and blankets from the parishioners in Forest Hill. Perhaps Miss Ambrose, we can come together in this and see what remains to be done?'

Miss Ambrose smiled and nodded her agreement. She was a pretty, plain faced girl of similar years to my own I considered.

'Now, Mrs Carter, I understand you will organise the accounts.'

'Yes, my daughter will share the task with me.'

'Excellent. Now, our programme in Newgate works effectively, so I propose a similar format here, but our being already engaged in this work elsewhere will place limitations on our time. So, I ask you to extend our appeal to your benevolent friends and relatives, for we will be in need of all the assistance we can muster to bring this off. Whether it is the donations of things required or the donation of their time and activity, all will be gratefully received.'

I repressed another urge to laugh, although this was of a sardonic nature, as I imagined putting such a proposal to *my* friends and relatives. I'd as soon as speak in Swahili.

'Now since we have not procured any employment for these ladies and have no wish to diminish the work of the other successful prisons, we must, once again, seek to procure similar contracts as we have been fortunate in procuring at Newgate. If you have such connections that might come to mind to offer some undertakings in needlework or basket weaving or anything else industrious that might prove a suitable means for employment, please do petition them in this cause. You may direct them to the success of Newgate if they are sceptical. Mrs Carter holds the accounts and will be happy to meet requests for this information. You will see in front of you a piece of paper, please put on it what work you can undertake and what days you may commit to the task, so that we may draw up a rota and get things off the ground.'

A wave of silence prevailed whilst the women sat thoughtfully over their pieces of paper and scribbled them out. I looked blankly at mine, which must have been put there in error. I felt suddenly aware of my lack of participation and was relieved when Mrs Baxter collected them in and said we will take a break for tea whilst they reviewed them.

Lady W. rang the bell and an entourage of maids came rolling into the room with trolleys overloaded with teapots and crammed with trays of assorted pastries. The room began to break into bursts of chatter as the clang of teacups were arranged about the tables. I suddenly felt quite the outcast and was hoping for an opportunity to make my apologies to Lady W. and slip away, but she had busied herself in some discussion with Mrs Baxter as they thumbed through the submitted papers. I looked up as Hetty, the maidservant, offered me a teacup and selection from the trolley. Half-heartedly, I settled on a Redcurrant Puff with a strong brew of black tea. I could not just walk out and nor could I interrupt Lady W. at such a moment.

'Oh, aren't these delightful,' said a lady sat next to me, who I noticed on looking up, had made the same selection and had already enjoyed a bite of it.

'Yes, very good,' I replied, taking a nibble and reciprocated in some prittle-prattle to pass the time. 'So how did you come to know Lady W.?' I asked her when the introductions and pleasantries left a silence between us.

'Oh, I don't, well; I did not until today alas. But I have been with the Society for a few months and I believe Lady W., a recent patron of it, was good enough to host our meeting since the parish hall could no longer accommodate our growing number.'

'I see.'

'So, you are a new recruit yourself?'

'No. I am Lady W.'s guest; I have been staying with her.'

'Well then perhaps you might learn enough about us whilst you're here to consider so becoming?' she offered, finishing the remainder of her pastry as she awaited my reply.

'I shall not be in town for long.'

She dabbed some flaky crumbs from her chin. 'Shame. Where are you from?'

'Surrey.' I told her. 'Cuddington.'

'Oh, is it near Southwark?'

'No, near Epsom, like the salts.'

'Oh yes, I know,' she said satisfied. 'I don't know what gaols there are in that part of Surrey,' she said searchingly, and I could offer her no answer for I did not know myself. 'But there must be one in reach. Perhaps you might learn the ropes with us and start up your own committee when you return home, contact the gaoler there?'

I had no intention of contacting the gaoler of my local establishment or forming any such committee, but I smiled along with the suggestion. 'Mrs Neal, forgive me, for I have a great deal of sympathy with the needy, but I have to confess, I do not extend my pity to the fate of villainous sorts.'

She looked mildly astonished at this and then smiled kindly. 'Yes, I thought much the same myself. Indeed, I only came upon the Society by accident. I was helping at the shelter you see.'

I cast a blank expression for I was none the wiser by the reference.

'Mr Hicks warehouse in Cheapside? The winter shelter?'

I shook my head, sorry to disappoint the lady for I liked her natural warmth and charm, but these schemes were foreign to me and I could not please her. Then, gauging my ignorance, she went on to tell me the story of Mrs Fry, chancing upon a young boy dead in the snow in that harshest winter previous. A flash of regret surfaced in my mind, remembering little Lucy of Old Mill Street and I shook the image it evoked.

She went on to say that Mrs Fry had been so moved by this dreadful discovery that she held a meeting at the Quaker House to ask for assistance in running a shelter to offer warmth and meals for vagrants.

Now, this I could find great sympathy for, and my admiration for Mrs Fry grew a little deeper at this learning as it did for Mrs Neal as she explained that it had moved her equally and, being not far from Cheapside, had decided to join the cause.

'Mrs Neal, if there is to be another shelter this winter, I would very much like to help if I can. But pray tell me if you will, however did such a different matter cause you to extend your charity to criminals?'

'Oh yes,' she said as though remembering now, the point of her illustration. 'Well, of course, my time at the shelter had brought me many good connections to the Society: Ladies not just kind, but smart and skilled and organised in their endeavours. I learned a great deal about the work they had done at the prison and it had softened my scepticism just enough to agree, more out of curiosity, I own, to go and see for myself what they spoke of in such high esteem.'

'And you were similarly moved?'

'Yes. It was such a sorry sight, being taken down to the small school room, fashioned from one of the cells.'

'The children? Well, that is an unfortunate business that their mother's crimes might lead them to such an existence,' I said thoughtfully, seeing the injustice in this but thinking only harsher of these women who had permitted themselves to cause such a situation to bear so cruelly upon their offspring. 'If it is not ill enough to have a criminal parent, but to be made to suffer like one, it does not answer.'

'Mrs Craythorne, the "villains" you speak of, are often no more than a mother who felt driven to steal a trinket or pass a counterfeit note to feed her starving children. Of course, there are a great many others besides whose actions may be considered more reprehensible, but that is none of my concern. My duty is not to judge the actions of these females, for they have been so much judged and punished by others that they need no addition to that end. My endeavour is to find a means to serve them in their great suffering and hope they might learn to better their ways and their lives for having known a little kindness.'

I found such great sympathy and willingness to overlook their misdeeds both bizarre and compelling. Were women really imprisoned over such trifles? I could not quite believe it. And what of the others that had done much more vulgar things as to warrant such punishments? Could they be deserving of such help?

As Mrs Baxter called the meeting to reconvene bringing the chatter and clanging of teacups to an end, I searched the ladies of the room in quiet contemplation. Were they misguided philanthropists or the intelligent women of substance I had first considered them to be? Lady W., I could vouch for at least was no gull. She was an eccentric of sorts, yes; but of the best sort, I had long ago decided. A wise woman of such independence of mind, I could not see her involved in such a society on a whim. She was a well-reasoned creature in the least and yet she saw fit to bestow her charity upon more than the illiterate females I had seen in the library reading rooms, so there must be more to it than I could fathom in my ignorance.

So, when Mrs Baxter, upon reading out the submissions and declaring a short fall on Wednesdays and Fridays to meet the commitment, I surprised myself when I raised my hand and volunteered to the undertaking. Lady W., I noted from her quiet approving smile, was not surprised by my speech and I knew, that as mad brained as it had seemed to me to volunteer in something so foreign, I could rely on her guidance. So, as Mrs Baxter continued on her points, negotiating days and duties with the ladies, I paid more serious attention.

When the ladies departed Grosvenor Square much later than I had expected, and only Lady W. and I remained in the deserted saloon, she turned to me and said, 'Don't look so unnerved, my dear. You will be a great asset to the Society; I know it.'

'Is it that plain?'

'You look positively bewildered, my dear, but you will do well enough, be at ease.'

'I own I'm not sure what good my accomplishments will be in the teaching of such persons.'

'It is not your accomplishments that I refer to, but your kindness and good sense. And that head for determination will certainly serve you there.'

Kindness. I had not really considered myself kind. That was a virtue I had long beheld and admired in my beautiful, sweet Annalise, and sense had long abandoned me. But determined I could accept, however, I was in need of being certain of a cause before bestowing my will upon something with resolution and I could not yet feel convinced that this was a worthy one.

Horsemonger Lane.

October 1821. - Eleanor.

I had considered and reconsidered my decision at stepping foot into such a vulgar and notorious establishment several times before I finally trod the cobbled path through the prison gate. My blood was rushing beneath my skin. I felt the flush of heat in my cheeks, a film of sweat break out above my top lip. I dabbed it away with my gloved hand and sucked in a cooling gasp of air.

The journey here had been frightful enough, never knowing such a diminished district was in existence anywhere, less still just across the river. Air thick with fog from all the factories, its wooden hovels and roofless blackened timber buildings set out in irregular style amidst streets of chaos and traffic. I had never seen such poverty. It made Old Mill Street seem like Mayfair. I thought of Mother's horror at the prospect of knowing where I had come and was relieved she did not know.

I looked to Mrs Neal whose expression held no clue of apprehension and kept pace with her. But when I beheld the terrifying look of the gatehouse, scaffold perched upon its roof, I almost abandoned her in that instant. I had never been a willing spectator of such events, however popular they might be considered by some. I had, since childhood, held a great sense of foreboding at such scenes having once seen a riotous crowd bludgeon a man to death at the Pillory at Charring Cross, on passing in the carriage. I suffered nightmares for months and ever since, had a care to avoid any such events. A reassuring smile from her as the turnkey admitted us into the building encouraged me on. If a meek and genteel creature like her could walk in with so little concern, then I supposed I must be able to do as much.

So, I did not hold up my hand to shield my nose from the squalid stench of the place as it dawned on me, even though I felt instinctively to. Nor did I make any protest against the poor light as we became engulfed in the stifling darkness of the corridors, or as the breath seemed suddenly sucked from my lungs by the foul air as we came upon the musty ward. I followed her example precisely and walked on, outwardly unaffected, un-protesting at that which must be naturally felt by any person on entering such a place.

We arrived in a small dim courtyard with tall walls about the perimeter, housing cells within them, but they were not locked as I expected to find them. There were persons all about the place; talking, skulking, children hopping from flagstone to flagstone for their amusement. *Children.* I had not expected to see so many young ones in such a place. It disturbed me greatly.

'Thank you, Mr Bragg. We can take it from here,' Mrs Neal bid our escort and I felt a sudden resurgence of horror at being abandoned by him. However unsettling I found his demeanour, it seemed suddenly favourable to being left unprotected. 'It's quite alright, Mrs Craythorne. Remember, they are just people.'

I raised an incredulous eyebrow.

'Now, I will start on this cell, you take the one next to it and we will alternate. That way we will have it done in half the time and I'll only be next door to you. Alright?'

I nodded reluctantly, took my notebook and pencil from my reticule and with equal reluctance forced myself on through the doorway. I recited Mrs Neal's instructions: Take notes on the conditions, make enquiries on the capacity and the provisions.

As I stepped into its dimness, I could barely see the page to write upon, but was relieved to find it derelict. I began scribbling at my page; approximate dimensions, rudimentary items about the place: buckets, a few worn chairs, a makeshift kitchen area I supposed and a...a heaped figure upon the floor. I stood back in surprise and dropped my pencil on the filth ridden flags.

'Forgive me,' I said quickly, realising how close I had come to treading upon her as she stirred. 'Miss, miss? Are you awake?' I asked, and she lifted her head a fraction to see me.

''oo ar yer?' she said, blinking, taking me in.

I too saw her better now; she seemed not above sixteen years. She was lain upon a scant layer of straw upon the stone floor with no more than rags to clothe her half naked body. I was so astonished, I could hardly speak. 'I–I am from the Society.'

'Wot's that?' she said, sitting up to stare at me with widened eyes that seemed bright against the gloom.

'We are a charity. It is our duty to assess the standards here and try to improve them for you, just as we have done at Newgate,' I told her steadily.

''ave yer got anyfink ter eat?'

'No. I'm sorry, I do not. But once we have made our assessment, we will be able to help with that and more besides.'

She shrugged her disappointment.

'What is your name?'

'Tilly, miss.'

'I'm Eleanor,' I replied and instinctively, as she rose up fully from the ground, pulled my shawl from my shoulders and put it around hers. 'Here, take this.'

'Miss but this is yor own fine shorl?'

'It is of no consequence, your need I think is greater,' I told her and watched her cover her pale, bony body beneath it.

'Fank yer,' she said with some amazement in her eyes and I tried not to linger on the filthy look of her sooty smudged face and matted, once-blonde-hair, or the stink, as I took a seat on an upturned bucket and explained to her some of the improvements the Society had made to Newgate. She listened attentively but said very little and seemed to be as curious of me as I was of her.

She told me she had been gaoled awaiting trial on a charge of theft and that her case was to come to court this week.

'How long have you been in here?' I asked her.

''bout two monf now miss.'

I was astonished to think that if she might be declared innocent of the charges set against her, she would have already spent such a time in this dismal place.

'Did you steal, Tilly? You don't have to answer if you do not wish to.'

'I didn't, miss, I swear it. It wer that orful mister 'oo should be in the dock, not me. It wer a street urchin that nicked 'is wallet Miss. 'e said we were colluting—'

'Colluding? Working together?'

'Yes, miss. Said we were from some flash panney and operatin' out of it ter gull gentleman like 'im. But we weren't. I'd never seen the boy a day in me life, I swear it.'

'Flash Panney?'

'Um... an 'ouse of fieves.'

'And the man who accuses you?'

'A brute dressed in gentleman's clovin'! 'e were tryin' ter pick me up, miss. Wen I told 'im I were no street walker, 'e grabbed me by the arm and tried ter spirit me away. But I fought 'im hammer and tack, miss, and in the nickle of it all, that wee urchin of a foot pad came upon 'im and took 'is wallet and ran off frough the market.'

'Did they catch him?'

'No, miss. So 'e kept 'old of me whilst some bloke went for the peelers. 'e said I'd pay for this.'

'And you told the Justice this, when you were interviewed?'

'Yes, I did, but 'e didn't believe me cause that scoundrel paid men of straw ter speak against me, miss. Said they 'ad seen me and the urchin togeffer regular like.'

'Forgive me, Tilly, what do you mean men of straw?'

'Yer know, miss, the ones that 'angs about the gaol and court 'ouse wiv straw in their pocket or shoe. They speaks out in behalf of 'ooever pays them ter miss. But they believed 'im, 'is filffy lies.'

Were there really persons who would do such an abhorrent thing for money? A caustic retch of acid burned at my throat and I swallowed against it. 'Did you not have anyone to speak on your behalf, Tilly?'

'No. Well, at least I couldn't sink 'em into this business. I'll get out me spoons. Madam would ne'er 'ave me back if I did.'

'Madam? Tilly, I thought you said you were not a street walker?'

'I'm not, miss! Madam's 'ouse is a very fine place, not just any ole brutes! She gets us fine ones, 'oo like ter talk and dance and pay grand.'

'I see. And how did you come to be in Madam's care?'

'I 'ardly know miss, I bin 'er maid since I was six. Don't know much of 'ow I ended up there. But she told me once, I'd bin in the care of a baby farmer for a long while and that me ma 'ad perished before I were two years old.'

'So, you are a maidservant, Tilly?'

'Well, I was a tweeny before, but now I'm wiv the other girls, to learn their ways. But Madam is waitin' for a special fellow for me first, for she says I'm worff a very 'igh bargain and she'll not part wiv me until she finds such a gentleman worff 'is salt.'

I smiled along with her; though I felt a sting of tears glaze my eyes at her misplaced pride and was grateful for the poor lighting now. It seemed she was no better off at home than in this place. Could one person of so few years be of such repeated ill fortune? I looked out to the courtyard and wondered how many equally dire back stories might lay behind each one of these women.

'Wot yer lookin' at 'er ladyship? Wot yer bin up ter eh, ter end you up in 'ere wiv us?' said a woman who had met eyes with me across the cell room as she staggered in. Her sudden interruption surprised me and I gasped. Her speech was slurred and her body swaying, half supported by the wall.

'Don't worry about that ole fusty luggs, miss, she's always flord on the gin at this 'our.'

'No matter, Tilly,' I dismissed, turning back to her now.

I felt desperately afflicted when we left. The mood of the place was contagious and lingered on me even as I tried to shake it off with my footsteps. I half wished I could return to my prior ignorance and half wished I could do something more to be of aid. I had failed to be much use in my taking of the assessment for the Society, leaving Mrs Neal the lion's share of the work. I had intended to be more useful, but I had not expected to find myself so drawn into Tilly's story that when Mrs Neal gathered a crowd in the courtyard to make our purpose known, I had spent the entirety of the time with her. I assisted in taking notes as Mrs Neal questioned the women on their difficulties and needs which were as sorely neglected as one could imagine. But I could not remove my mind much from Tilly. So young. So simple. So vulnerable and alone. I even remembered to slip the turnkey some coins in exchange for his promise he would have some extra bread taken to the ward on our way out, remembering how hungry she complained of being.

I had seen much of what I had expected; bawdy and profligate persons with vulgar tongues and habits of vice, but I too had seen so much of injustice and cruelty in their treatment, it could not answer, even to the punishment of criminals.

'It is a just reaction, but do not despair: from every dark night the sun rises again, does it not? We must become the hope for these women, to help breathe some light back into the darkness of their days,' Mrs Neal said consolingly as we walked the journey back from Horsemonger Lane.

'Yes. You are right,' I agreed. And although I had been converted quite surprisingly to their cause after such a brief encounter, I was not certain that biblical readings and acquiring sewing works for them was the only way they could be helped. I had agreed to assist in both, but I was sure that sermons or needlepoint would not help turn Tilly from her fate, even if it did help them better pass their days there.

I pondered the entire journey back, what would become of her trial. Whether or not she was telling the truth. Whether or not it would matter a fig when she stood in the courthouse in front of a room full of men. They would unlikely trust the word of a coarse chit like her over that of a gentleman and his bought witnesses.

Mrs Neal had said, even though it was a capital offence, they would not necessarily hang her; it would likely be commuted to imprisonment or transportation. It all seemed so very severe, whether she was guilty of the accused act or nay. Having to sleep on that putrid stone floor in such a crush for two months was surely enough punishment to appease it in any case. Twenty to a cell the women had told us. Twenty!

When I returned to Grosvenor Square, I gave a full account to Lady W. 'How can I help her Lady W.? My brother is a man of law but he would not consent to helping such a person as she, even if I could beseech him in time for her trial.'

'I'm not sure what is to be done, my dear. Lawyers only usually work in the cause of the prosecution. Tilly must do her best to plead her case and hope the court is merciful. I daresay though, if she had someone to answer for her character, perhaps that would offer her a little merit?'

'But she cannot, she belongs to a bawdy house and fears the Madam will abandon her if she brings them into this.'

'I did not mean her...acquaintances.'

I frowned. 'Oh! You mean me? But I know not a thing about her, what could I possibly say to credit her after such a short acquaintance? I own I cannot be entirely sure of her innocence myself.'

'Did you not say that the accuser had paid witnesses to corroborate his story?'

'Yes. So, all I would be doing is redressing the balance. Thank you, Lady W., I will do it.'

'Mind, take care not to overdo it, it would be considered perjury to lie to the court. I think a simple and vague account of her credible character will answer well enough: a lady of your standing can afford to say few words and still yield a powerful influence.'

I was grateful for Lady W.'s counsel, for other ideas came to mind on my thinking over this one. If I could perhaps find this "man of straw" who testified against her, I could perhaps change his mind, or pay him a greater price than he was due, to withdraw his testimony. But how I would find such a man, I did not know.

I went back to gaol the next day alone, agreeing to take in a number of clothing donations that had started to come in from the Society. But I also bought with me a parcel of game pie and paper and pencil for my visit to Tilly, and took down detailed notes of her case. I tried to furnish myself with enough knowledge of her to lend support as a character witness, drawing heavily on the misfortunes I thought might best win some pity. I also took down a description of the strawman in question and asked her where I might find him. She did not know. If he was hanging about the court houses or gaols, it could be anyone's guess when or where.

So, on my journey back to Grosvenor Square, I made up my mind and had the coach stop on Albermarle Street and one of the grooms travel across to Brooks.

'You are to call upon my brother, Mr Edmund Ashlyn and give him our direction,' I told him and watched him cross the busied street and disappear towards St James'.

After what felt like a protracted wait, I leaned out of the coach window enough to see Edmund across the street, waiting for a passing coach to halt before he crossed it.

'Pray, what does my little sister want in this district?' he said with that father-like tone of authority I so much despised, as he climbed into the coach.

'Edmund, I came to call on you.' He looked as puzzled at this news as he ought since we had little time for each other beyond the obligatory family occasion for it. I had only seen him twice since my wedding breakfast, neither occasion proving congenial when I appealed for his help in the matter of gaining a divorce or separation from Giles, which was met with the expected outrage and distaste along with a lecture of the likely impossibility of obtaining such a thing, even if I was willing to drag my family's name through the mud in the trying.

I had considered whether the trying in this endeavour would prove worth the trouble too, but with no other person who could better furnish me with such information, I had considered the detour worth the attempt.

'Whyever would you call upon me here? Is anything the matter?' he said, settling on the seat opposite me.

'No, Edmund, all is as well as it can be.'

I watched the relief filter through his expression as if I had come to deliver him some tiding of ill family fortune or the like.

'Well, that's jolly good. But what do you mean by this?'

'I came for your counsel, brother, why else?'

'Oh, not this divorce malarkey again?' he said impatiently. 'You could have sent a courier.'

'No,' I corrected him swiftly. 'It is on behalf of another's situation I come. And I was passing in this direction so I thought it more expedient.' I didn't tell him that I doubted I would receive a response at all if left to a courier.

He checked his fob. 'Very well, I have half an hour at most,' he told me in a tone of mild irritation and tapped the coach roof and issued the driver an instruction to take a cant.

'So, are you going to enlighten me in this matter of such urgency you had to pull me from my club?'

'Yes. But I doubt you will favour my cause, although I do not ask you to take it upon yourself, just to furnish me with your counsel.'

'Very well,' he bemoaned and took the offered papers from me. I watched him scan the notes I had taken earlier at Horsemonger Lane. He had read no more than half when he looked up at me and frowned. 'What is this drivel?'

'It is not drivel, Edmund; it is a woman's life at stake.'

'You mean a pick pocketing harlot from what I can gather?'

'No, she is not. She is wrongly accused and this wretched accuser has paid a false witness to testify against her!'

'Eleanor, I don't know what maggot you have got into your head of late, but what has anything of this sort got to do with you?'

'She is the maidservant of a friend and wrongly accused,' I lied, for I could think of no other way he might accept my story and I was certainly not going to risk my mother finding out about my involvement in the Society.

'Then have her master deal with it, it is not your problem, and nor mine for that matter.'

'Please, Edmund, I do not ask you to approve, but I own, I will give my assistance with or without your help.' I waited for this statement to take the desired effect. Unlike our older brother, Henry, who could look to the future as the Ashlyn heir, Edmund had had to work harder for his lot and was no more a fan of scandals than my mama, since so much more of his standing in society depended on it.

'Very well, but I warn you, Eleanor; you will not sully your hands with such goings on if I agree to help you. You'll leave it to me. Damned shabby business for a lady to be tied up in! Now what is it you think I can do?'

'There are two things that I have in mind, but I am open to any other you might offer. The first, is I must find this strawman and have him repeal his statement made against her—'

'And how on earth do you propose we do that? There are dozens of strawmen about and I'm assuming you don't know who he is any more than I.'

'No, but I have a description, turn over the page. And I have no doubt that you could, through your connections, find out about such a person or case.'

'You are actually serious?'

'Perfectly. Now it's that, or I will not trouble you further and conduct the search myself.'

He shook his head despairingly. 'Do Mama and Papa know about your hare-brained involvement in such business?'

'Why should they? I am a married woman now.'

'I fear you are no better improved for it, Eleanor.'

'And nor would you be if you had an idea what my husband is. But let us not go over old ground. I'm sure you want to have this over with as eagerly as I so you can get back to your supper.'

'Fine. I will see what I can do.'

'Thank you, Edmund.'

'I make no promises, mind!'

'My thanks are for your trying. I am grateful for it. Now the next point is how might I best counsel her to plead her case?'

'Well, I can't imagine there is much to be said, except to stick to her original line, keep her speech polite and endearing if she might manage it, and to bring out any witnesses in her favour.'

'That is the best you can offer?' I could have managed as much myself without the Oxford degree.

'Well, what do you want me to suggest? A maidservant is hardly going to understand the workings of the law and manage to manipulate them to her effect in a ten-minute trial, is she?'

'But there must be something more she can do? Edmund, she might hang for it.'

'Must you always be so melodramatic? She won't hang; she'll probably be headed for the hulks at worst.'

'For something she is innocent of!'

He sighed. 'She must look for any inconsistencies in the prosecutor's or witnesses' testimonies; if there is something salient that might cast a question over their honesty, she might discredit him. But since I am not familiar with the particularities, I can hardly point out what they might be.'

I accepted this and bid Edmund a grateful farewell upon a promise that he would send word to me at Grosvenor Square with any progress on the strawman.

The next day, I headed to the Old Bailey and paid the admission fee to sit amongst the public gallery and see for myself what awaited Tilly. I took my seat on the wooden bench and sat patiently listening as defendant after defendant took the stand. First was a case of Mr Adams, accused of theft of monies from his master but was found by the jury to be innocent. This was proceeded by a young man and two young women jointly accused of coining offences, who were all found to be guilty and all sentenced to death. The next fellow was also accused of theft of a promissory note and found not to be guilty. The next woman, charged with assault, pleaded her belly and her death sentence was commuted, despite her guilty verdict. This was followed by a man sent to the gallows for buggery.

My head was in such a spin from the emotional tumult of the happy and despairing outcomes, the unbelievably short time in which such matters were argued and sentences passed. I did not know if my visit caused me greater hope or despair for Tilly. But I did know that I had a better understanding now of how these proceedings operated and when I returned to Grosvenor Square, I sat up late again in the library and made detailed notes of my observations whilst they remained fresh in my memory.

I was overtired and about to take to my bed when a courier came with a package for me. Inside it were copies of the court papers relating to Tilly's case. *Edmund! I will not forget this one kindness.* His note was brief, stating only that he had not managed to locate the strawman yet but would keep trying. I went back to my desk, my bed would wait.

'Now, Tilly, I am going to pretend I am the prosecutor and ask you to answer to the indictment. I want you to answer me as best as you can.'

'Alright, miss.'

We were sat in a disused anteroom which I had managed to procure on appeal to the turnkey to permit us some privacy for the price of a few shillings. I turned the chairs around to make a mock dock for Tilly to stand behind as I paced about in that intimidating method I had witnessed of some of the prosecutors at the Old Bailey. If I was going to have a hope of preparing her, I needed to be as authentic as I could manage.

'Miss Mullins, you say that you have never before seen the boy who stole Mr Dyke's wallet on the day in question?'

'No, miss—I mean, sir, I ain't never seen 'im a day in me life!'

'Then, I suppose you will also say that Mr Sheppit, who frequents Borough Market in his business of trade, is also a liar, when he claims to have seen you and the young boy frequently acquainted in the area.'

'That's a filffy lie and you know it! 'e's a strawman paid for by the mister!'

I held up my hand. 'Alright, let's do this again, Tilly. Now, this time, I will swap with you, and show you how I want you to make your answer.'

'Alright, miss,' she said obliging, and we took our new positions respectively.

'I can't remember 'xactly wot you said?'

'First you will ask me if I have ever seen the boy before,' I reminded her and let her ask me before rephrasing the answer she had given. 'No, sir, I had never seen the boy who stole Mr Dyke's wallet before that very moment.'

'Then you'll say that witness 'oo says he 'as seen you wiv 'im before, is a liar?'

'I say, sir, that the witness is mistaken, for I have never been in any acquaintance with the boy, either before or since, the theft, so it is quite impossible I could have been seen with him by any persons, for no such occasion ever occurred.'

'Wot shall I ask yer next, miss?'

'Let us pause a moment, do you see the difference in what was spoken?'

She looked at me a little bewildered. 'I fink so, miss; you said it a lot more fancy than I.'

'You are correct that what we said, amounted to the same account, but the manner in which it is said, makes it sound different. Makes it sound more even and credible, shows you are mild of temper and clear and confident of the facts.'

'Yes, I see it miss, but I'm not sure I can remember it all.'

'Have you ever been to the Theatre Tilly?'

'I did once, miss. One of Madam's gentleman took me and one of the other gurls.'

'Well then, you remember how well the actresses played their parts. How real it all seemed.'

'O yes, miss, it was such a splendid fing, i'd ne'er seen anyfing like it.'

'Well, let us imagine you are one of those actresses, Tilly; that you are cast in the play and these are your lines. It is your job to make the whole audience believe in the sincerity of your speech, your manner.'

Her eyes widened with delight.

'Do you think you can do that?'

'Oh yes, miss, I sha' try!'

'So let us practice it some more, until it becomes more natural to you.'

We practiced all day until the turnkey came to put our meeting to an end. Our progress was slow and arduous on both sides, but it was made, by degrees. How much easier it would have been if she could have read my notes and revised them. Of course, she could not. I did not know how much she would remember, so long it had taken to work through the likely scenarios I was not sure how much could be retained. But I felt some greater confidence that she had grasped the main points, learned to improve her speech, better contain her temper and maintain a more even and pleasant manner. This at least, I hoped would serve her well.

'This is for you,' I said to her before leaving her at her cell with the turnkey hovering at my side to hurry me.

'Wot is it, miss?' she asked, taking the offered package I had put together for her.

'There are clean clothes for tomorrow, soap, a hair wash and a comb. I want you to make an effort to look smart and well turned out alright?'

'Fank yer, miss! I will!'

I smiled and bid her goodbye, hoping and praying that our efforts may prove of worth tomorrow, but with a lurking feeling of doubt that if they did not, she might spend many months or years sleeping on this floor or crammed onto some prison ship. I shook the thought.

I was surprised when I took my familiar spot in the court gallery the next morning, at her transformation. She stood in a smart muslin gown I had picked from my own wardrobe, with freshly washed and neatly pinned hair and a brightness about her complexion I had not noticed beneath the grime. I fidgeted about to keep my view of her as a clerk walked about wafting nosegays of burning herbs. I had sat through four cases before hers was called and so I had had time to grow restless and doubtful between my moments of optimism. But as I saw the terror beyond her expression as she entered the dock, surveyed the room and was asked to confirm her name, I faltered a little and wondered if my coming had been too much of a torment after all.

The clerk read out the arraignment: 'Miss Mullins, stands accused, not having the fear of god before her eyes and being seduced and instigated by the devil, did on the third day of August eighteen-twenty-one, distract the attentions of one gentleman, Mr Dyke, in Borough Market, whilst a thief snatched away and set off with his wallet containing the sum of five pounds.'

I looked across to Lady W., who had come with me today, I think mostly to support me if all should go ill, but also with an interest in my cause and a consideration of what might be done for Tilly if things went well. She offered me a reassuring pat on the forearm as we watched on and Tilly made her plea.

'Not guilty, Sir.'

'Speak up, girl,' said the judge, a blubber cheeked man with sunken eyes and wiry brows that jutted out as he spoke.

Tilly repeated her plea with greater volume and it reverberated off the sounding board this time and carried into every corner of the room. A little chatter breaking out amongst the gallery to which I turned about and offered a look of disapproval in their direction.

'Very well. Mr Pembroke,' the presiding judge gestured to a hatchet-faced man I knew to be the prosecutor. He had been sat around the mahogany table rustling with his papers and now set them aside and stood up.

'Miss Mullins, do you accept you were in the vicinity of Borough Market at the hour of six pm on August third?' he asked her, approaching the dock to stare directly at her.

'Yes, Sir.'

I noticed how her voice cracked over the words. *You can do it, Tilly, keep your head.* I made some telepathic attempt to tell her.

'And what pray, were you doing there?'

'I 'ad been to Mrs Boskins' shop on Stoney Lane to collect a parcel of ribbons, Sir.'

'And yet you had no such parcel in your possession when the constable arrived at the scene?'

'No. I 'ad missed her by ten minutes. The shop were shut.'

'Unfortunate, indeed. Now, the gentleman to my right, Mr Dyke of Camberwell, proposes that he first noticed you talking to a boy outside the costermonger's stall. The same boy that some fifteen minutes later took off with his wallet, I might add.'

'No, Sir, that's impossible. I made no stops and spoke to no one until that man tugged at me arm.'

'I trust you know, Miss Mullins, what sort of trade is conducted along Maid Street?'

She did know. For this is the one part of her testimony we had rehearsed over and again as it was the only part that required some fabrication. For she did indeed stop in Maid Street, to converse with one of the girls who had been recently put out of Madam's establishment and had taken to working the Mint. But she would not testify to this effect, because she was adamant she would not speak of her Madam or their trade.

'Miss Mullins, Mr Dyke says you came upon him and offered him your "services" for which he flatly refused and attempted to set you on your way. But you refused to be put off and were intent on detaining him—'

'No, that's not 'ow it was. Mr Dyke came upon me, Sir. Not only me, as I passed him, he was beseeching another girl before me, but she would not entertain 'im. I made it clear to 'im when he offered me money for my "services" that he had made a mistake. I was not soliciting.'

'So, you deny that it was you that approached Mr Dyke and propositioned him?'

'I do. I told the gentlemen very clearly that I was not interested in 'is offer, but 'e would not hear it,' she explained and when she caught sight of me in the gallery, I smiled and nodded in her direction to let her know how well she was doing.

'A likely tale,' said Mr Pembroke with a smirk about his sallow mouth and the courthouse broke out in laughter. 'You grew up in the Mint, did you not, Miss Mullins?'

'Yes, Sir. I was orphaned young.'

'I put it to you, Miss Mullins, that you and the urchin, in joint endeavour, tried to gull Mr Dyke with this distraction to enable the theft from which you both intended to profit. A bulk and file, I believe it is colloquially termed.'

'Sir, I do not know the boy. I assure you. And certainly didn't try to profit from 'im.'

The conversation had read almost like a script from our rehearsals, with slight slip ups and variations on wording and order of questions with little of significance to alter from the facts. Then the prosecution, after puffing up Mr Dyke's character as a well-respected married gentleman in no need of such services as had been proposed by Tilly, he called to the stand a witness for his character: his wife. A woman of middling years, well dressed and meek who spoke on; exaggerating his many virtues as a husband and how outrageous such an idea that he would attempt to solicit a female's company, and how sorely injured were his whole family by such a wicked fabrication.

I wondered as her emotional plea filled the courtroom, if she was simply too ignorant to accept the actions of her husband, or if she purposely meant to cover up for him with her efforts. For now I knew him to be precisely the kind of scoundrel Tilly accused him of being. Where before I had only Tilly's word and my gut feeling to accept the truth of the story, now I had much more. For whilst I had been busying myself in preparing Tilly for the trial, Lady W., had, quite to my surprise, taken on her own inquiries with the details I had furnished her.

Through the Society, she had managed to learn of a former worker who had spent a spell in Newgate after falling in to trouble working from a similar establishment to Tilly's. She had agreed, upon recognising Mr Dyke's name, to testify as a witness to Tilly's cause. So whatever Mrs Dyke's beguiling speech had done in effect of the jurors, I did not feel overly concerned, knowing we had a better witness to dispute this fictitious character she was attempting to create.

It was the next witness, the strawman, whose impact I feared most as I heard him called to the courtroom. He was a professional at such guises and no doubt familiar with what must be said to good effect, even if they were lies.

'John Sheppit to the stand.' His name was called three times. A pause ensued, whilst the Beadle was sent for him but returned to the room alone.

'Mr Pembroke?' said the judge, clearing his throat. 'Your witness is not here.'

Edmund?

There were further whisperings between the prosecutor and the Beadle before he declared his witness absent.

'Your Honour, may I read out his statement given to the justice on the day of the event for the jury to understand in his absence?'

'You may,' the judge granted him.

I rolled my eyes.

'This is the statement taken by Jackson; steward of Geldings and Sir Reynolds, justice of the peace on August fourth of our present year. I read to you now his own declaration: "I, John Sheppit of Nelson Street, Bermondsey, did see the offence of Mr Dyke's wallet cruelly snatched from him whilst Ms Mullins distracted him in a seductive guise with a young foot pad I had often seen about the market..."'

The words made me mad as fire and I wanted so much to cry out, *liar, fraud,* as I listened. But once he had finished and Tilly was given leave to call her own witnesses, I felt hopeful once more.

'I call Miss Price, Your Honour.'

Mr Dyke shifted in his seat at the notice of her. *Yes, you recognise her now.*

'Please state your name to court,' the judge instructed her as Miss Price was led to the box. She was not at all what I had expected of such a person, demurely dressed and reasonably spoken.

'I am Miss Price of Nutkin's Corner, Bermondsey.'

'Please make your testimony, Miss Price,' instructed the judge. 'As quickly as you like before we adjourn for a break.'

This was met with laughter from the gallery and a look of relief from the barristers sat around the round table in the centre of the room. I hoped Edmund was not of this cut, for shame.

'I did not witness the events in question and I am not acquainted with the defendant. But I am well acquainted with the gentleman, Mr Dyke.'

'The gentleman to your right?' the judge pointed for clarification.

'Yes, Sir.'

'And how exactly are you acquainted with him?'

'I was one of the girls who waited on him at Madam Millard's bawdy house on Maid Street.'

I watched the surprise break out on expressions across the room and the scorn on Mrs Dyke's face answered my earlier question. It was a look of embarrassed shame not innocent surprise by such a revelation. *You vulgar breed of woman!*

'He was regular for a while, and procured many services, not only from me. But he fell out of favour with the Madam over an unsettled bill and she did not give him leave to return to us.'

'Miss Price, you are a self-confessed prostitute. You own you do not know Miss Mullins, yet you do not seem to mind coming in to court to make testimony on such an intimate matter, nor bring your lodging house into disrepute, is that correct?' said the prosecutor with so much innuendo in his tone, I wanted to cross examine him.

But the witness did not falter. She looked at him plainly and said, 'Sir, I have not been in that trade for the past three years, nor do I reside in Maid Street any longer. Those are the indiscretions of my past.'

A line of astonished faces perked up at this from the Judges Bench.

'And may I ask, if this is so, how you support your living now?'

I was hoping the judge would intervene and mark his comment irrelevant, but he seemed as eager to know the answer to this as the rest of the courthouse.

'I am a maid of all work, Sir. I tend my mistresses employ through the day and in the evening, I take in mending or weaving work as it's commissioned of me. Not that I see what it has to do with this matter, Sir.'

'Miss Price, let me take you back to your former career in that case. I presume such an employ involves a great deal of merriment, drinking, dancing and all sorts of goings on?'

'Yes, Sir, you describe it exceedingly well.'

Another peel of laughter erupted from the gallery at this and I felt a smile twitching at my mouth too this time. I watched the prosecutor colour a little at this implication before proceeding. She was no pushover. I did not know the full history of her engagements with the law, but I saw a steel beneath her calm composure that warned me she was well equipped to handle men like this with trifling ease and it reassured me greatly.

'So, it would be reasonable to suggest that you would have seen many men like my client, in such a house. In the midst of so much drinking and hubbub, I suspect it would perhaps be easy to mistake this gentleman from one of the many that frequent such a house?'

'Well, Sir, that's may be for some girls and even some gentleman, but one never forgets a fellow like Mr Dyke for he is known as a brutish warp. You don't forget a fellow like him, even after the bruises have faded.'

'A brutish warp?'

'Yes, Sir, a man of peculiar and rather violent tastes, if you please.'

'Miss Price, if Mr Dyke was attending the Maid Street establishment, or places of that kind, it is unlikely, don't you think, that he was also attempting to procure street walkers? I mean, it is a very different market, is it not?'

'Sometimes, but I saw him myself; tried to pick me up in Haymarket but I remembered him and stayed clear.'

'What were you doing in Haymarket?'

'Madam threw me out the house when I got with child and refused to let her medical man release me of the babe.'

A gasp of shock and disgust rose up at this.

'She washed her hands of me then and I had no choice but to take to the streets. The girls about the bridge know him well enough to avoid him, expect that's why he was sniffing about further afield where he weren't so well known. It's only the new ones that don't have the sense to avoid him. I reckon that's what happened to Miss Mullins over there. Was shocked by his rough handlings and tried to break away from him.'

'Miss Price,' the prosecutor cut in now with severity, 'your reckonings are not a subject of the court's interest—'

'I think,' cut in the judge, 'we have heard enough. Lest I remind you, Mr Pembroke, we do not have all day. Any further questions for the witness?'

'No, Your Honour,' he acquiesced and I could tell from his face that his confidence had faltered.

When Miss Price was dismissed from the stand, a furore of gossip broke out across the courtroom and the judge had to slam his gavel down several times and call it to order before he adjourned and rose, leaving Tilly and us no wiser on the outcome of her trial.

We had a torturous wait the remainder of the day to find out whether our attempts to assist Tilly had been enough to spare her. Lady W., decided we were to go for a walk around St. Paul's so she might regain the feeling in her limbs from sitting upon the hard benches, and when I raised concerns that we would be late and miss the verdict, she appraised me of the fact that there would be no rush. That the judge and his company would be dining in their comfortable parlours above the courthouse on fine food and drink whilst Tilly sat in a cell in the basement awaiting her fate.

I had never been more disgusted at persons of my own class than today and wanted so much to give them all a piece of my mind. I wondered what was going through Tilly's mind under such a strain. I thought of her being held in some colourless, bare cell upon the flagstones contemplating the hammer that was about to drop over her fate any moment.

The hours rolled on and by the time the jurors returned their verdicts to the court, I had quite forgotten who was who and wondered how on earth they had managed to process so many details and persons with adequate reflection in just a day. I had sat all day, just as the jurors had and struggled to distinguish the salient details of the earlier cases, since so many others had been tried. *Oh, Tilly, let us hope they remember yours!*

I sat stiffly upon the bench, Lady W.'s hand pressed lightly over mine as we listened to all the preliminaries. I jumped when I saw Tilly return to the dock looking anxious. I gave a sideways glance to Lady W., then took a deep steadying breath.

'Members of the jury, foreman rise. In the case of the defendant, Miss Mullins, have you made a decision?'

'Yes, Your Honour.'

'And how do you find her?'

'We find her not guilty, Your Honour.'

I leapt from my seat and almost let out a cheer. If it were not for Lady W. pulling me back down into my seat and containing me, I might have done it. 'She did it!' I whispered instead.

She smiled brightly at me, and once Tilly was released from the dock, we got up from our seats in the gallery and pushed our way through the crowds to meet her. I did not know if it was the lack of the strawman turning up, Miss Price's character assassination or a simple lack of clear evidence that gave Tilly back her freedom in that moment, after such a protracted and insufferable wait. All I knew was that I thanked the heavens that it had.

She flung her arms so hard around me when she caught sight of me through the crowded courthouse, I could not even congratulate her for several moments.

'Oh, miss, I can't believe it: it worked! All that time you spent on teaching me proper, it worked, miss. How can I ever fank yer?'

I pulled back to look at her and smiled. 'You did it, Tilly. You went in there and carried yourself just perfectly. You were remarkable,' I told her, wiping away streams of her tears and my own. I took her arm in mine and marched her out and over to the carriage with so much elation pulsing through me, I was certain I had not felt such genuine joy since prior to having parted with Annalise. More recently, there were times I thought I never might again.

Lady W. had her coachman convey us back to Grosvenor Square where she was to put the proposal to Tilly, after we had taken some refreshment and a little rest from the ordeal of the day.

'Tilly, you are a free woman once more,' Lady W. said to her across the small table we sat about in the breakfast room.

'Yes, ma'am and 'ow grateful I am to yer both, and that other gurl 'oo told them about that wretch.'

'We know you are, Tilly. But that is what I wanted to speak to you about,' said Lady W.

She listened on.

'What will you do with your freedom now you have won it back?'

'Well, I will go back to Madam o' course. Oh, you didnt fink I expected you to put me up 'ere for the night? No, I just wanted to fank yer, give miss back her fine clothes now I 'ave my own again, and then i'll be on me way.'

'You can keep those clothes, Tilly, something to remember me by,' I smiled.

'Oh, miss. I shall never forget yer a day o' me life, dress or no dress.'

I smiled and then said more seriously: 'Tilly, do you want to return to Madam, to your former life?'

'Yes miss, she'll be glad to 'ave me back at last.'

'And if that's truly what you wish, then you shall,' said Lady W. 'But before you do, I would like to offer you another possibility. I have a friend who is need of a chamber maid, Tilly. Mrs Craythorne tells me that you have experience of being a maid?'

'Well yes, miss. I was a tweeny before, for most me life. But you see, Madam says I am destined for better fings now I'm of age, she 'as great plans for me.'

'Tilly, you do realise what work will be required of you at Madam's...establishment, don't you?'

She looked a little bashful. 'Yeah o' course, miss. But it's not so bad. It's a respectable place, the girls get paid 'andsome and wear fine clothes, have fine things. And when they are not to work, they are at leisure, to do as they please, be waited on, even go to the theatre and on shopping trips. And it's a grand 'ouse miss, not as grand as this one to be sure, but it is very fine. I 'ave my own room with a good fire I can burn all day and night long if I wish it!'

'It does sound very fine, Tilly. I realise that, but it comes at a very heavy cost, do you see that?' I put in.

She shifted uncomfortably in her seat. 'Eliza told me it's not so bad. After the first few, yer get used to it and don't mind it so much anymore'.

I bit my lip. After my experience with Giles, I doubted that could be true. Having the accepted title of wife to gloss over lying beneath a man you did not wish to, drew little distinction between selling yourself as a prostitute and selling yourself into an unwanted marriage in my mind.

'And what if you were faced with waiting on a man like Mr Dyke? Do you think you could bear that?'

I saw the distaste cross her expression. 'We do what we 'ave ta to survive,' she said as if repeating words that had been given to her and were not her own. 'But I don't expect to 'ave dealings with 'is type. Madam has a fellow to take care of us if anyfing gets outta hand.'

'Well,' Lady W. cut in. 'It is your life and your choice, Tilly. But I want you to understand, you do have a choice. There are other ways open to you if you wish it. I can arrange a trial with my friend and you could see how it went, or of course you can return to Madam. But you have a way you can "survive" with or without Madam and her establishment.'

'Thank yer, miss. But I don't think I'm cut out for a maid's life. I've never liked it much in all me years. I doubt I'll start t' now.'

'Very well. I will have my coach convey you there after dinner if that is what you wish. But you can change your mind, be it sooner or later. Even after your return, if you find it is not what you hoped, you may call on me again and we can see what might be done. You can also call on Miss Price at Bermondsey who welcomes you to do so, should you wish it.'

'The lady who came to stand witness today,' I added in answer to her knitted brow.

'Oh. Well, fank yer. You 'ave all been so good to me, I can't believe me luck. I will see her. I want to fank her for what she did today.'

'Good. There is perhaps no one better placed to furnish you with an account of how she lives now, to how she did in her former career. Take a moment, will you child, to hear her story, won't you,' Lady W. said, nodding the footmen to begin serving.

'I will miss,' she said obligingly. But I knew it would not turn her head. She was resolute, drawn into the glamour of a life she had witnessed all the trinkets of and had yet to learn all of the labouring that accounted for them. I felt a deep pull in the pit of my belly. I felt it again when later we waived her off to Southwark, like a lamb to the slaughter, I thought.

I had been at odds with Lady W. on this matter. An uncomfortable circumstance, since we were never at odds in any matter of significance. I was minded we should be more persistent and persuasive in turning Tilly against the idea of returning to that house or that trade. But I realised now she was right after all. The way to give Tilly a sense of her own power and choice was not to take them away from her by imposing our wishes upon her, but to make her realise she had them, could make them and have her decisions respected, whatever they may be. What a gift it was to have such a learned friend of so much wisdom to guide me. I was certain if I had known her in my younger years, I may never have got myself into such pitiful scrapes as I now found myself living out the consequences of.

But as I sank against my pillow, I could not help but worry for Tilly, for what was yet to come. But I took a little comfort in remembering the cards Lady W. had given her with the direction of Miss Price and the charity houses of the Society. I also considered that if it had turned out differently, she could be spending the first night of a long sentence back on the floor I first found her on, or crammed onto a prison hulk, and remembered how grateful I was that she would sleep in the comfort of a bed on a full stomach this night and hopefully a great many more.

Homewood Bound.

October 1821. - Eleanor.

I had hardly thought much about Annalise, and had quite relinquished all thought of returning home. I realised now that in London I could be useful. That there was much work to be done. And that I could make a difference. Not in offering bible readings to prisoners or teaching them their letters, but in helping to instruct them on how to better defend themselves from being in there in the first place.

I would continue to assist the Society in practical matters such as assessments and donations, for there were some whose fate was already sealed and for those, anything that could make their lot more bearable seemed a worthy endeavour. But my primary concern now was to find the ones like Tilly, who still had a chance of a life beyond the prison gates and helping them find their way back to it.

I would need to get more familiar with the law and its nuances as well as spend a lot more time sitting upon the hard mahogany benches of the public gallery. But I was certain with a little time and application, I could gain a wealth of knowledge that could be put to good use, considering how much I had discovered in only a week.

So, I sent a note over to Berkeley Square to ask Camille to scan the library there for any books on matters of Law. It was possible there were some lurking there, just as I found some in the library back at Cuddington.

It was after two days of waiting without a return, that I grew concerned at having received no books or no answer. Lady W. and I were on our way back from an auction at Christie's where I had managed to procure myself some obscenely expensive art works to add to my collection of saleable things. I had the coach stop by the house and Lady W. waited outside with it whilst I went in to find out why I had received no reply and scan the library for them myself.

'Ah, Bentham,' I said upon him opening the door and admitting me into the house. 'Just a quick stop. Will you send for Miss Pascal for me?'

'Very good, ma'am. These came for you whilst you were away,' he said, reaching to the side table and offering me a salver full of letters. Why hadn't Camille bothered to send them on to me? I gathered them up, having no time to read them now with Lady W. waiting in the coach and headed straight for the library.

I discovered enough law books to collect a small pile for later perusal: The most part comprising of volumes of Commentaries on Law by a William Blackstone which seemed to deal extensively in the topic. When the door opened, I was struggling to manage them in one armful. 'Will you give me a hand with these, Camille?'

'Of course, ma'am, alas it is not Camille.'

I turned about to see it was Bentham at my side, arms outstretched to relieve me of the burden. 'Forgive me, Bentham, I thought you were Camille.'

'Ma'am, have you had any word from Miss Pascal?' he asked me, taking books from me and piling them up in his own arms.

'None, and I sent an express around just the other day asking her to send these over. I presume she is making the most of her leisure.'

'It seems, ma'am, that her bed has not been slept in and that no one has seen her about the place since yesterday morning at breakfast.'

'What?'

'Mrs Davy is gone to make a more thorough check on her room presently. Shall I tell her to find you here?'

'No. Show me the way to her room, if you will, Bentham. Put those down, they are too heavy to carry about. We shall collect them on our way back.'

It was immediately apparent she was gone. Her clothes missing from the drawers, her brushes and pomades from the dressing table. 'Did she not mention to anyone where she was going?' I asked Mrs Davy who seemed as nonplussed as I.

'No, milady. Not a word. But she didn't speak to any of us much.'

'I see. Well, I am in a rush, but you will send word over to Grosvenor Square if you discover anything at all?'

'I will, miss.'

'Thank you.'

It was later that afternoon when I was sat over the pile of letters that I received word from Berkeley Square. A note, addressed to me was found upon my dressing table by one of the housemaids. I knew immediately from the hand it was from Camille.

> *Dear Madame,*
>
> *Since you seem to have no need of me, I have taken the time to find myself a new position where I might be of some use.*
>
> *I hoped you might return so I could give you the news myself. However, you never come home anymore and I could not keep the registry waiting for my answer.*
>
> *So, this morning I am to travel over to Cheapside where my new mistress awaits me.*
>
> *I hope I can serve her well, where I was unable to do so for you.*
> *Camille.*

I felt a pang of regret in realising how redundant I had made her feel. And even though I had a scratching concern over how I was to travel now, I knew it for the best. For her and for me. For the truth was, I would always harbour some poorly concealed blame for Annalise discovering my feelings and she would always remain at arm's length, a proximity she was not satisfied with.

I hoped her new mistress was a better fit for her and only wished I had had a better understanding of her intentions so I might have kept a look out for a replacement in time to travel home. For the contents of my other letters had made it plain that I must do so now, even though I had no desire to.

Most of them had been from my mama, insisting on my overdue return, pressing me to accept an invitation to Beth's engagement soiree and finally threatening that my father would collect me himself on his way back from the House of Lords next week if I did not return by Thursday. But the one that sealed the decision had come from Giles; the usual style of demands and also asking after all my bills and threatening to write to all of these retailers with a notice not to extend any credit to me in the future if I was not beneath his roof as his wife. I realised I had been complacent in considering the time I could expect them to land upon his notice. When I had set upon my shopping sprees, I had been minded to return home before they would likely reach him. With the extension of my stay and my distraction with Horsemonger Lane, it had quite slipped my mind.

So having been discovered here and with my pressing work now done, I reluctantly headed back to Cuddington in the morning with only the briefest stay in mind.

I had much work to do in London in my newfound occupation that to return to the country felt so unhappily regressive as I beheld Cuddington's iron gates and all the memories of the business I had left behind me. I would stay no more than a week, just enough to throw Giles off the scent and to appease my mama. I had already made arrangements with Lady W. to return there with the maidservant she had loaned me to make the journey with and resume my society undertakings.

My parents were pleased to find me in improved spirits on my return even if they were less pleased at my plans to make a short stay of it. I told them that I had joined a society in London concerned with helping the needy with provisions, but left out the finer details they would protest against. I made clear too that the matter was both non-negotiable nor reliant upon my staying in Berkeley Square.

'I can't think why you must spend so much time in Grosvenor Square. With Betsy I might understand, but Lady de Whittaker-Hollingford? It is most unnatural; she is old enough to be my own mother. What must she want with the company of such youngsters?' Mama had said to this.

'She is a dear friend, Mama and I wish you would not speak so ill of her in my company. She has done more to help me than many friends I could name.'

'Help? Whatever can you need help with?'

'In fact, I need your help. I mean to employ a new maid as soon as possible now Camille is gone. I thought you could take the interviews with me,' I peeled off my gloves finger by finger as my trunks were offloaded by the footman. I took a fleeting glance at the one I knew to be Will and pushed ugly thoughts from my mind that arose at the sight of him.

'Very well. Mind, if you had took heed of my advice before, and realised that upsetting things with Miss Pascal and promoting a kitchen maid to such a position was a ludicrous notion, then you would not have to go to the trouble again. Now you have gone from two Abigail's to none! I have never known anyone get through maids so fast!'

'Yes, Mama, you were right.' I wish she would not bring Annalise up so soon. I had been making my best attempt at severing the association between her and Cuddington all the journey back. Being here at all was a test I was still not sure I would succeed in.

'Well, I suppose we could try the registry tomorrow, since you are in a rush.'

'Yes, we'll go tomorrow if you are free.'

'And talking of friends, have you had a care for your own since you've been away? The invitation I sent on for you? Did you R.S.V.P to Bethany?'

'Not yet,' I confessed. I still had not made up my mind on what to do over it. I had no argument with Beth, was happy she had landed her match at last and wished the best for her. But as for the rest of society, I had little desire or care to be amongst them. I had of late learnt the value of the company of genuine types of society, so far removed from that I had known, that the contrast was sobering.

'Not yet?' Mama frowned. 'The engagement party is on Friday. Oh, don't tell me you mean to decline it, Eleanor? You must see that Bethany is offering out an olive branch to you, a way back in.'

'I don't want a way back in, Mama. I am quite happy to be very much out of the way.'

'Nonsense, you are lonely and at a loss without your friends. We all see it. The decline in you. Now, why don't you think about what this could do for you? You know everyone is going. You can make amends.'

'I'll think about it. Now, if you will excuse me, I must change.'

It was being back in my chamber I blamed for the outburst of pent-up tears that befell me then. I could see her everywhere within it: in the chair opposite mine reading, at the washstand or in the reflection of the looking glass tending me, upon the right-hand side of the bed staring up into the canopy. Even the sight of my sewing box sent me into another inconsolable wave once I had recovered from the first.

I was not over it at all. It had been merely a pause and I wondered how I would get through the days stretched out before my departure. Perhaps I should go to Bethany's engagement party, for the distraction if nothing else.

I penned a quick reply before I changed my mind and before getting changed into my riding habit. It had seemed an age since I had rode out on Samson, and for whatever else that lent to misery here, the prospect of seeing him again, was a happy one. He might prove the only one truly pleased to see me too, I considered as I patted at his haunches and brushed out his mane whilst Thomas saddled him up.

I dreaded to think of all the people I would have to face out and do the pretty to at Beth's, having so long avoided such encounters and grown used to plainer behaviour in the company I now kept. I thought of Sheldon's family, Betsy and Anna, Mariella with a particular pang of disgust, as we pelted along familiar lanes and meadows, and my old life returned to my consciousness. It seemed severed in two of late, the demarcation of the pre and post wedded Eleanor, the out-of-love-in-love-unrequited-love Eleanor.

I had always counted on the season bringing great changes, but never could I have anticipated the nature or degree. My life had become unrecognisable in a matter of months. Little remained unaltered or untouched by it.

But for a brief moment, as I felt the wind rippling against my cheeks as Samson took full flight, I could almost convince myself that the last few months had been a fictitious imagining and all was as it ever had been. Certainly, on the surface, everything else seemed unchanged in Cuddington. Such was country life and it was both the thing I loved and loathed the most about it.

It wasn't until I felt the first spatters of rain drops against my cheeks that I realised just how far we had rode out. 'I think we must turn back, boy,' I said to Samson looking up at the curdling sky: swathing lines of drab purple and grey thickening menacingly over the trees. I slowed and pulled my seal skin raincoat from the saddle bag as we took cover beneath a bridge. *Thank you, Thomas.* He at least was prepared, even if I was not. I tied it beneath my chin and sprawled it out as far as it would reach in the hope of offering us both some protection as we set off for home. I didn't know precisely where we were, or how long we had been out. I could only hope we would be back before the violent looking clouds ahead erupted.

'Sir, forgive me for stalling you, but where is this place?' I said, slowing as I noticed a villager gathering up his lump wood in a barrow, ready to leave.

'We's in Headley Heath, milady.'

Headley? 'Thank you, sir.' My, I had not considered we had journeyed so far abroad. 'Well, boy, I hope you have it in you to make a dash for home after such a distance,' I said to Samson as we galloped off.

He did, and I was glad of it, for the clouds had erupted moments after with such violence I could barely see through the sheet of rain that streamed my face, swept against me by the wind. It was not cold yet, but I was not sure how long that could last.

When we finally kicked up the gravel along Cuddington's driveway, we were both exhausted. I dismounted Samson and handed Thomas the reins, discarding the sodden seal skin which had grown slimy with the rain beating.

It was pelting down so hard I ran into the stables to take cover in the hope it might break for long enough to make a dash back to the house. But it showed little sign of relent, and in the end, I took up Thomas' suggestion to send a stable boy to the kitchens to send for an umbrella. 'Make sure he is well rested, Thomas, and well fed, he has been put through his paces today,' I said as he led Samson off to his pen.

I sat alone on a barrel of hay in one of the empty pens, waiting. Thomas had disappeared with Samson and I tried, with little success, to wring the water from my heavy skirts that had soaked right through to my shift. When I looked up at the sound of a dash of waterlogged footsteps across the cobbles, I did not notice, until she came into full view, that it was Annalise below the hood of the umbrella. *Of all the servants he could have prevailed upon!* I sighed inwardly and composed myself. It had been an age since I had seen her; it seemed painful still, to dare to look.

'Forgive me, Tulley,' I said standing up; it seemed peculiar to address her so formally now. 'I did not ask for you to be sent here, I would have walked over myself if I had known you would be prevailed upon.'

'It's quite alright. I wanted to come.'

This astonished me so much I hid it poorly. 'Then I thank you,' I said, trying to compose myself, 'but you needn't have taken the trouble.'

'You are soaked through,' she said, feeling at my damp sleeves.

Please don't touch me. 'Yes, ill-timed of me,' I remarked, stepping back a little and brushing some more water from my face with the heels of my palms.

'Come, let me take you back to the house,' she held out her hand but I refused to take it.

It was a puzzle, this normality in her tone and manner. The last time I had seen her, she had wanted never to set eyes on me again. She had flinched at the slightest proximity to me. It had been the most injurious realisation, to be so much despised by her. To consider myself a source of vulgarity, when all I saw in her was beauty.

My absence had at least softened her anger with me, I supposed. But I was not sure I could bear this complication now. In some ways, it was better to be severed completely from her than trying for some uncomfortable imitation of normality. Like she was nothing to me. When she was everything.

'It is quite alright,' I said again. 'You go back and send another umbrella for me when you return. I'm not in a hurry.'

'I don't want to go back,' she said in a tone I couldn't quite make out the meaning of, until she found my hand at my side and took it into her own. 'And nor am I in a hurry.'

I pulled free of her instinctively. 'Annalise, I don't know what the meaning of this is, but I beg you go back now before things turn ill again.'

There was a note of a smile on her lips, she pulled my hand back into her grasp.

'Annalise, please.' I looked away. 'I have managed to keep to my promise, but you test me now.'

'You have,' she said sweeping a water weighed down curl from my face and stroking the residual wetness from my cheek. *Oh, to be touched by you again. How, how can such a simple gesture feel so soothing?*

'Sit back down,' she pointed to the hay bale I'd stood up from, and she pushed me gently back down on it and stepped up close between my knees. Either I had caught a chill and I was hallucinating, or returning home had proved too much and I was having some kind of deranged episode. *No.* I heard Thomas rustling about in the stable pen next door. *It was true.* I smelt flour and rosewater on her aprons as she gathered me in close, my head rested at her navel. I thought I might die. Even through all my astonishment and disbelief, my body responded to her and I wrapped my arms tight around her waist and buried my face against her.

'Forgive me, Eleanor. I have missed you so much,' she said and the earnest in her tone bought me quick to tears.

Was it true? 'I have missed you too,' I said through muffled mouthfuls of her apron as I inhaled her. I felt her stroke my wet hair and trace her fingers at the nape of my neck. *What did this intimacy mean? Was it one of friends or...*

'Come with me,' she said then and seized my hand, leading me out of the stables.

'The umbrella—' I reminded her but she did not pause, and led me off into the downpour at the pace of a run.

My mind raced but I did not speak a word as she pulled me on, not back to the house, but towards the woodland with the evening light near extinguished from the storm. An uncertain excitement rekindled in me: I was not sure what this meant or how it would turn out, but I wanted to find out.

When she slowed down and pulled me under the canopy of an overgrown Weeping Willow that's branches trailed the ground, I caught my breath. But what came next, I was not prepared for. She pushed me gently against its trunk and stepped in close to me. The branches swayed above us with the violence of the weather and twigs crunched beneath our feet. I could hear her heavy breaths but barely made out her face in the darkness and I could not read her expression for a clue. But I felt how close against my body she advanced, pressing me further into the trunk of the tree with another step. My stomach twisted with a knot of anticipation, though for what I was still uncertain.

'I'm so sorry,' she finally said, and interlocked her fingers with my own. 'I should have done this weeks ago,' she whispered, and I felt her gentle kiss upon my lips so suddenly, it took me a moment to understand it. *Can it be? My sweet girl, is it true?*

I reclined fully against the trunk, wondering if my legs would hold me up. *Could she mean it?* I wondered, almost frightened to let myself be drawn into such a trick. And then I felt her nervous tongue probe mine with a tenderness that bought me quickly to surrender. I moved my hands to her hips and pulled her in deeper to me until the warmth of our bodies penetrated through the wetness of our rain drenched skirts. *Oh Annalise, I think you have stitched me back together in one kiss.*

'You,' she said leaning back a fraction, 'must never set off and leave me like that again.'

'I won't,' I promised her, coaxing her back into another kiss that lingered even longer than the last. *I will never leave you.* I felt my skin tingle beneath her fingertips as she moved her hand from my cheek and traced her fingers down the side of my neck.

'I have wished for nothing else since you left,' she whispered, resting her head upon my shoulder and her breath against my neck brought me to shivers. 'It has been a painful realisation and I began to fear, too late.'

'Oh Annalise, what misery I have suffered without you,' I replied, grasping a handful of her hair and breathing in the scent of her.

'I think we have both suffered enough. Perhaps it is time for a turn.'

We held each other silently a while; it was an embrace that spoke so many undeclared words. It had been a long and uncertain wait for a moment like this, but now it was here, I didn't know how I had lasted so long without this intimacy.

I kissed her neck. 'What peace you have bought to my heart.'

'Oh, Eleanor. I have been such a fool and it has taken me far too long to realise it,' she said, brushing the tip of her nose across my collar bone. 'I did not know how to deal with the circumstance. I thought us both mistaken, and then when I realised not, I thought maybe it could be made to pass...but I see now—'

'Hush,' I told her gently. 'I would forgive you anything, you know that.' I leaned in to kiss her again but paused as the stillness was overrun with an ascending gallop of hooves. I pressed a fingertip against her open mouth and peeped through the swaying branches. The sound grew closer and a carriage flew past us at full pace. 'Who comes at this hour?' Mama had not advised me we were to expect company tonight. 'No.' I shook my head. 'No, it cannot be...'

'What?'

'That is my husband's coach!'

'It is?'

I nodded. 'I have nothing to say to that man, and I don't know what the devil he is about coming here like this.'

'Perhaps we should go in.'

'I'm not going back whilst he is there,' I said flatly.

Annalise turned to me. 'But won't they send someone to look for you?'

'Yes, they might, though I hope my father has the good sense to turn him out the instant he's announced, for he has no leave to call upon us.'

'Well, we can wait here then, no: if it won't take long?'

'Yes,' I said re-gathering her up in my arms and resting my head upon her shoulder to keep a view. It was impossible to see who disembarked from this aspect but I knew it was him. I could almost taste it in the air. He had come to bemoan the bills no doubt. Tell me to stop spending his blunt so readily even though I had not yet sunk even a quarter of my marriage portion. I felt even gladder for my spending now I had Annalise in my arms. Now there was a future worth investing in. That money was our ticket to freedom, to independence.

We waited patiently, beneath the windswept branches of the willow as they whipped around, scattering raindrops it had previously sheltered us from. The night now growing dense and black, and in what I estimated to be twenty minutes, still he had not left. I felt a little concern growing at the duration, and wondered what he had to say to them at such length, why they had not had him turned out instantly. The warmth of her embrace had kept me comforted throughout, but we were soaked through and she had begun to shiver.

'Let us make a dash back to the courtyard now. It's cold. You can slip back to the basement through that underpass and I will wait it out in the barn, no one will think to look for me there.'

'Let me go with you,' Annalise said, her fingers trembling in my hand.

I rubbed them between my palms. 'I would rather you wrapped up in the warm,' I answered and steadied a swaying branch to check if the coast was clear. 'Come,' I urged her. 'Let's make a try for it now.'

'Let me stay with you,' she said again between breaths as we slowed our steps to tread the cobbles as soundlessly as we could manage.

'No; it is too late and too wet. Go in, sit by the fire and get dry. Come to me later in my chamber.'

Reluctantly, she accepted this and I watched her disappear into the servants' entrance.

I trod delicately along the path taking pains not to disturb the ground beneath me. The stable keeper's cottage was aglow with soft light signalling the presence of activity beyond the windows and encouraging me to go cautiously if I wished to escape anyone's notice. Then a groom came out of the stables. I supposed he had been tending Giles' horses, so I ducked back behind a hay cart and waited out his passing. I was not minded to risk blowing my cover. Until that beast was gone from the house, I would not be bought to go into it, not for anything.

When I was sure the groom was gone, I went to step back out and jumped back again when I heard fresh steps along the path. But I realised as she grew closer, that it was Annalise.

'Over here,' I beckoned her, pulling her behind the hay cart with me and she gasped at the surprise.

'What are you doing? Did anyone see you come?'

'No, there is no one about. Shall we go, these will get soaked?'

I looked at the pile of neatly folded blankets held out in her arms, checked the pathway and stepped out carefully. But it seemed for all my pains at stepping around it, Annalise did not notice the rusty milk churn, knocking it crashing over against the wheel of the cart. I grabbed her arm and dragged her briskly towards the barn. 'Quick, go inside,' I directed her, holding back a nervous laugh and lifting the latch to release the creaky door. A curtain momentarily twitched from the cottage as I slammed the door back into place and burst into a nervous fit of giggles.

Annalise threw down a blanket on a thickly stacked expanse of hay, and looked across to me with a satisfied glance. 'Your bed, madam,' she jested, struggling to maintain a serious countenance. I think the nervous excitement had got the better of us both. I had forgotten what it was to feel such easiness.

'Why, and no finer bed have I encountered in these lands,' I replied, rushing over to her and throwing us down upon the haystack; we landed side by side and laughed a while staring up into the rafters, light pouring in through the roof panes.

'Oh, Annalise, you have made me feel light of heart for the first time in an age. How good it feels to be back in favour with you,' I said rolling over onto a perched elbow to look at her.

She turned to me and smiled. 'I have longed for you in ways I did not know possible, like a part of me was missing.'

I smiled into the darkness. 'I thought I had lost you.'

'No. I just lost myself for a while,' she sat up and reached for the remaining blanket that had been abandoned amongst the hay. 'Come,' she said, 'you must be cold. You are soaked through.'

I sat up and she wrapped the blanket around my shoulders and used a corner of it to dab the rainwater from my face. I lifted my arm and ushered her into the space, cloaking us both beneath it. We pulled it tight around us and shuffled in a fraction closer. 'You're beautiful,' I told her then and kissed her. 'You don't know how many times I have thought it and not been able to say the words.'

'Yes, I do, for I have considered you so many times I could not count them. I can hardly believe you must want me.'

'Silly. I would exchange the whole for you, you know.'

'But why? I don't understand it. You have admirers all about you, why me?'

I laughed a little at this irony. A hundred admirers or no, her admiration was all I needed for a lifetime. 'Annalise, don't you see? There's no one like you. Are you blushing?' I teased her, for the filtered moonlight cast us as shadows and did not permit my telling the fact, but knowing her character as I did, I could imagine the colour up in her finely set cheeks.

'You are to blame for it,' she said accusingly and I kissed her on the nose.

'Why didn't you tell me of your feelings?'

'I am, now... I was just a little slow in finding the courage to confess it, first to myself and then to you. I did try, but every time I went to speak, I faltered.'

'When?'

'The night before you awayed to London; when you pulled me up on the horse and subjected me to that fitful gallop home. I nearly came to you the next morning to plead with you not to go.'

'And there I was thinking you clung to me so tightly in fear of the animal,' I laughed.

'Well, I did to begin with. Only then it turned to something altogether different: The comfort of feeling you against me, as you are now. And I want to feel closer still,' she said with such conviction that I felt my breath catch.

I want you.

I found her lips and set upon them with more determination than before and in moments our gentle tender kisses made way for more fervent ones. *I need you.* I pushed her down onto the bed of hay, and lay beside her, glided my tongue down the length of her throat so feather light her skin prickled beneath it and a sigh escaped her lips. I took a tentative hand to roam her body through her clothes, pensively at first until I gauged her response and when I read the building passion in her sighs and breathy gasps, I found the hem of her skirts—still sodden from the rain—lifted them to her knees and climbed into the space between, sinking my weight against her. Her body stiffened at first and I almost relented thinking myself too fast. But when she began to kiss me harder on the mouth I ventured further, by degrees, until I found the nerve to place my kisses at her décolleté. To move against her as she curled her legs about me. To let my hand roam the shape of her waist and then her writhing hips. I wished so much to be up in my chamber with the warm fire roaring so I could strip us of our clothes, take her to my bed and feel her skin against my own. But for now, this was enough. More than I had ever thought possible. And every kiss, touch and movement of my body was imbued with a tenderness of such astonishing reverence. I wanted to undress her and I spent too long contemplating it for we were starkly interrupted by the sound of something outside by the time I had begun.

'What was that?' she fret, leaning up on her elbows. 'Could it be Mr Morris?'

I sat back upon my knees, listening hard and searching the darkness for a clue. I heard a rustling in the hay and before I could investigate it further, felt something wet and cold prod my ankle. I reached down to feel a bundle of fur beneath my palm. 'It's the puppies,' I told her with relief, holding up a golden bundle of fluff that sniffed the air, wagging its tail.

'Aww, how he has grown,' Annalise said when I passed him into her hands. She hugged him to her chest and laid back down.

'I wish you could keep him,' I said and snuggled up beside him.

'I wish I could keep you,' Annalise said, stroking my hair with her free hand.

We must have fallen into a doze after a time, me nuzzled in the space between her underarm and breast, the puppy curled upon her chest. I opened my eyes hearing shuffling about the stables and the coach driving around to collect Giles, I supposed. I wondered how long we had slept and how long overdue his departure was.

'Annalise,' I stirred her. 'He's gone.'

We went back to the house and parted ways. I was so dizzy with the beautiful disbelief of all that had passed between us this evening that I had barely remembered about Giles at all. I was handing over my riding crop and cap when Mama came storming into the hall with her hands about her hips.

'Where the devil have you been? Half the house has been looking for you.'

'I have been waiting for that vile man to be gone!' I told her flatly.

'Outside, in that downpour? Look at you, you are soaked through!'

'Mary, Mary,' she beckoned the maid who was just setting off to put my things away. 'Have the fire stoked in Eleanor's bathroom and the footmen draw a bath for her before she catches a chill. Whatever are you about staying out in the rain for such a time? Thomas said he stabled Samson but two hours ago!'

'I told you, I was avoiding him. What was he doing here?'

'He came to find you of course!'

'I gathered that, but why you admitted him, I cannot understand?'

'He said he was minded to bring a Crim Con suit against Mr Richards, so I had no choice but to hear what he had to say, giving off such threats.'

'Oh, what of it? He cannot prove anything—'

'Do you tell me that there is something to be proven? Is that the real reason you cannot keep away from the city?'

'No, don't be absurd. He is a friend. He helps me with my pianoforte sometimes. He is a music master after all.'

'Is that the way of things, or is there something more between you?'

'It's not important, Mama. I wish you would not ask me such questions.'

'So, he is right. I wish you had the sense to at least keep from prying eyes if you must persist in this way!'

'I have. I only saw him once and no one knows of it, for I shall speak no word of it and neither shall Richards, so he can go to the devil with his threats.'

'Well, that's pretty much what your father made of it and told him as much. But Eleanor, I wish you would take care!'

'So Father does not think he can bring about a case?'

'Well, he says he has little to make a worthy sounding try of it beyond conjecture, but Giles has a deep purse and your father is not a law man so I don't say he wouldn't make a try of it anyway. Perhaps we should write to Edmund? But in the meantime, I suggest you do not give him anymore cause to be irritated.'

'If he dares bring any such a case then I will turn it to my advantage and petition my divorce.'

'Eleanor!' she gasped and held a hand to her throat. 'You shocking girl!'

'Well, if he is going to make a public spectacle of our personal affairs then I may as well make the purpose suit my cause and not his!'

'Let us have a care that it does not come to all of that!'

I half wished that it would. 'I will take care, Mama. There is nothing between me and Mr Richards, so you may be at ease.'

This caused a change of expression. 'He says he means to journey to Ireland tomorrow and expects you to be at home by the time he returns. If you are not, he says he shall issue proceedings on his return. Hopefully, it will all blow over by then.'

I could only hope he would blow overboard on the sailing. 'Of course, it will, Mama. Be at ease,' I said, thinking of all the empty threats of the same he had made in his letters.

'Good. Now, go and see if that bath is drawn before you are in a high fever!'

'Yes,' I said obediently and made my way to my chamber.

Resignation.

October 1821. - Annalise.

Annalise did not make it as far as her room in time to change out of her wet things. She was apprehended by Cook outside the kitchen door before she got there.

'And where in the devil have you been?' she howled at her, the sound amplified by the reverberation of the basement walls.

'On an errand for Mrs Craythorne.'

She flung her teacloth over her shoulder and stuck her head out as she spoke. 'You are not in the employ of Mrs Craythorne now though, are you?'

'No, ma'am.'

'And what's more: you will not be in the employ of this household at all if you do not get yourself back in that kitchen this instant.'

'But, ma'am, I am soaked through. If you might permit me to change into something dry—I don't want to drip all over the food,' Annalise pleaded, knowing that where her own comfort would not succeed in such an argument, a risk to the dinner table would suffice.

Mrs Simpson looked her over thoughtfully. 'Fine. You shall have two minutes. And once dinner is served, you shall tend to the scullery on your own to make up what you've missed.'

'Thank you, ma'am,' Annalise said as Cook turned back into the kitchen.

It had become Cook's favourite method of humbling her; finding menial tasks beyond her duties to punish her with. She had aptly discovered the scullery was her least favourite of these punishments on account of the soreness of her hands after such a stint; angry cracks running through them and itchy rashes rising up over her knuckles. But to-day she couldn't have cared less whether she ordered her to milk the dairy cows herself and pluck a dozen game birds afterwards, she was so elated at Eleanor's return.

The truth was, it had been the only reason she had stayed on and accepted Mrs Simpson's unreasonable terms for her return to full time employ in the kitchen. To wait for her to come back.

The sale in Carshalton was expected to be finalised this week, the contracts being declared satisfactory by Mr Harrison's legal man and the banker's draft was at the ready. She had only until Friday to wait to sign the contracts and hand it over. An appointment was scheduled at ten-o-clock on Friday morning at Mr Morgan's offices at Mulgrave Road.

It had been all she could do to prevent herself telling Poppy the news that her pie shop was to be more than just an imagining, if she wished it. But she had held fast, just in case something had gone ill in the arrangements. It would be hard enough convincing Poppy she was not funning, even with the deeds in her hand, let alone without them. So, she kept her tongue and tried to hide from her all the letters that had been exchanged these past weeks in negotiating the matter.

She had been minded to toe the line with Cook until it was all settled even though so many times she had tested her to the point of almost quitting. She no longer needed the money and would soon have somewhere to live, but she had had no way back to Eleanor without her place here and now she had her back, she knew it had all been worth the bearing. With that in mind, she turned on her heel and headed back to the kitchen.

Mrs Simpson was flambéing a tray of roasted quails over the stove plates.

'Mrs Simpson,' Annalise called out from just inside the kitchen door.

She looked up and put down her flaming torch. 'What?'

'You can stick your scullery chores and your job. I have no desire to remain working under a tyrant,' Annalise called across the room as it fell deafly silent.

Cook coloured up speckled pink at the cheek and marched over to her.

Annalise stood firm.

'Who the heck do you think you are talking to?' she said through gritted teeth.

'A tyrant who has no idea how to treat her staff with fair regard. Hush, I am speaking,' she held up her hand at cooks attempt to cut in. 'You are a disgrace and it's high time my lady knew it, I think.'

She closed her open mouth at this but it was Poppy that cut in. 'Annalise,' she said sombrely.

'I'm sorry, Poppy, but we all know it is true and long overdue the saying. You should have her job once the Ashlyn's are done with her. We all loved working under you.'

'Annalise,' Poppy said more severely taking up her arm to lead her out of the room.

'Very well. I have said what I needed to,' Annalise relented and accepted her escort.

'What the hell are you doing?' Poppy said when they reached the corridor.

'It's alright, Poppy, everything is to be alright.'

'Are you in yer cups or somein? You 'ave no job.'

'I don't need one, Poppy, and neither do you. There is something I should have told you some time ago, but now is not the time for all the details. Just know I have money, lots of it and a job for us both if you wish it.'

Her face was a perfect puzzle. 'What?'

'Later, when you are off shift, I shall explain it all, I promise. But do not look concerned. It is happy news. Beyond what you might imagine. Now, go back before I land you in hot water. Tonight, we shall talk on it all.'

'But she'll 'ave you turned out before then after that display. Where will you go?'

'Nowhere, for now. I'm going to ask Eleanor for my job back and she shall have the say on whether I'm to stay or go.'

Poppy went back to the kitchen still looking unsettled by all this talk, and Annalise headed towards the stairs feeling lighter for having final-

ly had her say. She found upon them a group of housemaids arguing betwixt each other.

'No, you do it. I ain't never done a bath before and I don't even know
'er,' one of the young housemaids said.

'Mary asked you to do it, Mildred, and she won't be happy if you send
the littleun when you were given the order.'

'Well thanks a lot,' Mildred said, huffing her way past them and
meeting Annalise at the foot of the stairs.

'Mildred,' Annalise said in a sprightly tone.

'What?' she replied in irritated accents.

'Did I hear that you are to attend my lady in her bathroom?'

'Yeah, I'm going, aren't I?'

'No need. I shall go.'

'Will you?' she said, her features brightening and a kindness in her
tone now.

'Yes. Not for your sake though. You're all a bunch of prattling back
stabbers. But I should be neglecting my duty to permit such an incompe-
tent to go to her.' She turned about and headed back into the basement
along the hall where she found the door already ajar, Will and Jack heaving steaming kettles into the tub.

'Don't mind us,' Will said tartly, catching sight of her at the door.
This was how it was between them now, stiff and perfunctory. Ever since
the night he had dared to kiss her, she had kept her distance from him.
She felt a little sorry for him when he looked at her like that. She headed
to the towel store and begun loading the trolley just as Miss Pascal had
demonstrated to her before. Where was Miss Pascal anyway?

By the time she had selected the right jars and mixed the oils to go in
the bathwater, it was already full and Jack had disappeared.

'Anna,' Will said, hooking the last of the empty kettles back over the
fireplace. 'How long's it gonna be like this?'

'Will, please. I have no wish to be unkind to you but you must stop
pressing me.'

'I'm not pressing you. Not like that anyway. I just miss yer. I miss my
pal.'

'Truly?'

'Truly. I know when my feelings aren't returned and I've put the no-tion of all that out me 'ead. I just wanna be on terms with you again.'

Annalise smiled. 'Then we can be, friends.'

He smiled and his face seemed altogether transformed by it. 'I'll be as happy with that as I may. Ah come on,' he said playfully, 'no fella likes his pride injured.'

'I meant no injury Will. Look, you are the best kind of fellow. I too would like us to be on friendly terms again, if you can bear it.'

'Well, I can't bear this, so I'd say you 'ave a bargain,' he held out his hand to shake on it and she squeezed him into a hug and said: 'One day, Will, you shall make some fortunate lady very happy you know. That it is not me shall be but a trifle of a memory. But I hope that my friendship shall not be. I care dearly for you, in that way.'

He squeezed her back before releasing her and saying with the shine of tears in his eyes: 'Ah, you soppy thing. Well, then, I'm glad that's set-tled. I'd better get out the way with all this lady's business you're to deal in,' and he left the room.

Annalise sat upon the chaise and took a moment to process this. Wincing at the thought of him reduced to tears in her presence, smiling at the relief that they may return to kind regard for one another at least. It was better this way. He could stop wasting his efforts on her and move on and she could stop avoiding him. She stood then, took a breath, checked the temperature of the bath water, blew out a few of the candles to lower the lighting into a more somnolent glow and took the stairway up to Eleanor's jib door. She tapped at it and called through to her.

'But how?' Eleanor said opening the door up and frowning, 'I only just rang for you and here you are.'

'I was just getting things ready downstairs. I didn't hear it,' she said, noticing Eleanor was already down to her shift.

'Well, let us go then,' Eleanor said and once they had reached the bottom and she had taken care to lock both the doors behind them, she turned to Annalise and pulled her on towards the tub blindly as she kissed her on the journey.

It was precisely what Annalise had hoped for when she come, to be held again in her loving arms, so delicate and yet so strong that she felt strong when she was enveloped inside them. It was that she realised, which had given her the courage to stand her ground with Cook at last, knowing that so long as she had this to look to, she could handle anything else that reckoned with her peace.

She kept pace with her kisses and her steps until Eleanor was lent against the side of the tub, rosemary infused vapour rising from it beneath their noses as they continued in their embrace.

'I cannot believe you are still in these wet things,' Eleanor complained pulling back. My mama bemoans that I shall catch a chill and I find myself anxious that you shall.'

'I didn't get the chance.'

'Well, it's a good job you have me here to see to it,' she said and begun unbuttoning her dress.

Annalise felt uncommonly aware of herself as the weight of the damp fabric lifted from her. The slightest snag or brush of Eleanor's hands as she unclothed her made her tremble, the kiss she planted at her shoulder as she lifted her arms to remove her shift. A momentary doubt intervened as she felt conscious of her want to please her, conscious of standing there naked before her once her shift was thrown to the floor.

'You are so beautiful,' Eleanor said, pressing another kiss to her lips before she led her into the tub. The heat stinging at her ankles as she settled into the water. Eleanor stood before her, throwing her own shift to the ground before joining her. Her stomach spooled with expectation at the sight of her; steam rising in swirls and puffs about her thighs, Annalise waving it away from obscuring her view of her. She had seen her in this manner before, she reminded herself, but there was something new and changed about the experience now. She watched her sink back into the water, her breasts floating just above the water line. They were round and full and her skin had prickled to form small, neat bumps across its surface. She considered then what it would be like to touch them. She didn't know what to expect or what might be expected if she dared. Eleanor had been her first kiss and that had been a matter of guesswork. Yes, she recognised the stirring in her hips wanting something more. She recognised the oversensitivity of her body, the throbbing in delicate places, but how to answer to them was not so forthcoming. She waited for the water to settle around them before reaching across and taking up Eleanor's hand. They locked fingers instinctively. Then sat silently for a while taking in the strangeness of it all, contemplating the other's thoughts.

'You need not be shy of me, you know. I want you to look at me. I want to look at you,' Eleanor said eventually.

'I'm not shy. Well, perhaps a little,' Annalise confessed and Eleanor answered with a reassuring squeeze of her hand, then pulled it closer to examine.

'I'm sorry, they are rough and unkempt,' Annalise said withdrawing it.

'Don't be embarrassed, you need never be with me.'

'I can't help it. I am ashamed of the sight of them, all red and scratched to bits.'

Eleanor retrieved it from beneath the water and pressed a kiss to it. 'There is nothing about you I don't find charming, don't you see that?'

Annalise smiled and felt moved by this earnest gesture even if she couldn't quite understand her worthiness. To think it of Eleanor was easy, she was perfect; always neat and well-groomed and smelling of sweet floral waters. She, however, spent most her days covered in chicken feathers and fish guts and a good smattering of flour dust.

Eleanor reached round to the trolley, picked up a bottle and read the label with a squint. 'Now we shall both have to cast our minds back to Camille's teachings; which did she say was for dry skin?'

'The olive oil.'

'So, you were paying attention,' she grinned and found the right bottle, uncorked it, turned Annalise's palm face up and poured some into it.

'What happened to Miss Pascal? Did she go with you to London?'

'She did, but she did not come back with me,' she began massaging the oil into Annalise's hand between both of her own. 'She left me a note just yesterday saying she had found another place. It was entirely my fault, I left her sadly neglected.'

'She was a very good maid.'

'She was and I am a terrible mistress I know, but I mean to be a better one now, that is, if you will take your old job back?'

Annalise smiled at this. 'Well, it seems I am a terrible kitchen maid, or at least it shall be said so now, for I had the audacity to call Cook a tyrant and resign from my position before my coming here.'

'You did?' Eleanor asked with a note of surprise. 'Well, how did she take that?'

'She seemed rather stunned.'

Eleanor let out a laugh. 'Well, I own I understand it, you are such a mild creature. What power it wealds when you step into a high temper.'

'So, I was rather counting on you reinstating my position to tell the truth.'

'Well,' Eleanor said, switching hands and refilling her palm with oil, 'there is one condition.'

'Name it.'

'You are to accept the full wage that goes with it.'

'I don't care for the money, that's not why I want it. I want to be with you and I don't know any other way I can be.'

'My darling, you do not have to be my maid to find excuse to be with me. I will take care of you no matter what.'

'I want to take care of you. So, I shall take the position. For although Miss Pascal showed me well enough my shortcomings, I mean to care for you with everything I can.'

'Well, perhaps we can take care of each other then, for I am of precisely the same mind.'

And that is what they each demonstrated as they took turns in bathing each other, washing each other's hair and brushing it out by the fire as they sat wrapped in bath sheets.

When she returned to the servants' hall having dressed Eleanor for dinner, she expected to find her reception one of low whispers and pointing. But as she took her seat beside Poppy, she was met instead with the welcome of celebrity. Half the staff congratulating her on giving cook a well-deserved set down, the other half smiling and nodding their agreement.

Even those who had previously been staunchly camp Fanny, seemed impressed.

It was mildly disconcerting to have so much fuss made, but she was pleased it had not gone the other way as she'd expected, and she could be at ease as they sat over their supper.

When they had finished, Poppy returned promptly to her room with her, keen to hear her explanation for it all.

'She wants you gone by the morning,' Poppy said when she closed the bedroom door. 'Tell me you got your other place back at least.'

'I did,' Annalise said, sitting down upon the bed and gesturing Poppy to do the same.

'Oh, thank god for it,' Poppy said holding a hand to her chest, then recovering and breaking into a grin. 'That'll go down a treat when you 'ave to sup together in the fine parlour,' she laughed. 'She said she never wants to set eyes on you again so I should like to see how she manages sitting at the same table with you over breakfast.'

'I shan't dine with that snotty lot, Poppy. I shall dine here with you, like I always have. It will suit everyone better that way I think.'

'She'll make you give up your room though, you know, there's no getting 'round that.'

'Well, in the long run it wouldn't be fair to, but for now, Eleanor is to speak to Crawford about that. She is the housekeeper after all and her say will be final. Eleanor is proposing work to be done to the old nanny's room in the attic which hasn't been used for years. She shall insist that I shall stay here until it is complete and ready for me.'

Poppy smiled. 'Cor, Cook ain't gonna like that a bit. It'll get right under 'er skin knowing she can't do anyfing t'get at yer. She's come up trumps, your mistress, I'll give her that. Anyway, what's all this talk of money and jobs?'

'Well, you promise you won't be upset with me for not telling you sooner?'

'Oh gawd, Annalise, what 'ave you done. You ain't got yourself mixed up in some bad business 'ave yer?'

'Poppy, do you really think that's my line?'

'No,' she shook her head realising how daft it was to suggest it.

'Good. I can accept the rest of that lot thinking ill of me, but you know me better than anyone.'

'Well, I don't think any of 'em will dare after how you silenced Cook tonight. They'll be scared to cast you a wicked look, let alone say a nasty word. Anyway, what's all this about?'

'A few months ago, Poppy, I got a letter from Gint, asking me to go to him.'

Her face fell staid at this. 'What did he want?'

'Not what you suspect and something I am no less ashamed of telling you. I want you to understand, that is why I could not tell you before. I was in shock. I was ashamed.'

'What is it, luv?'

'He had something to tell me: he said he is my father.'

The astonishment in her face turned her into something of a carica-ture like she had seen in the papers in Rowlandson's prints. 'Do you be-lieve him?' she said eventually.

'Not at first. But you see, he said that he suspected he was dying and not long for the world—'

'Well, that'll save a lot a young girls their modesty. I know I shouldn't say it, for I am a Christian but, well, I'm not sorry to hear it.'

'I know. Anyway, he called me there to give me this parting news, but also to honour a promise he made to my mama, to settle upon me. And so, he gave me a draft for six hundred pounds.'

She almost fell sideways off the bed. 'Well, I'll be damned. That ole miser? You're serious, ain't yer?'

Annalise nodded.

'By gad, what will you do with all that? When you said a lot a money, I thought you meant you'd had a lucky spell, won a few shillings on that lottery you're fond of but—'

'Poppy, I have never played the lottery in my life,' Annalise laughed.

She frowned. 'You 'aven't?'

'No. Anyway, how do you like the sound of this: *Poppy's Pie and Pud-ding Shop?*'

She frowned again. 'You're still serious ain't yer?'

'Yes, and by Friday it shall be confirmed. I sign the papers for a sale of a dwelling house shop in Carshalton.'

Poppy smacked her across the knee then scooped her up and squeezed her.

'Ow, what was that for?'

'That was for keeping all them secrets from me,' she said. 'And this, is for being such a kind-hearted friend,' she added, squeezing her even tighter. 'What's that smell, you smell of something nice?'

Annalise laughed. I washed my hair.

'Ah, well I thought you seemed a little brighter.'

'Anyway, what do you say?'

'Is that really what you wanna do with all your money?'

'What, invest in my best friend, the best cook I know?'

She blushed and a tear rolled down her cheek a moment later.

'Oh, don't cry, Poppy, it is what I want: to invest it in you. In a proper future we can look to, free of tyrants.'

She wiped her tears from her cheeks on the back of her apron. 'You have that much faith in me?'

'Of course, I do, silly! Oh, don't start again or you shall have me joining you.'

She sniffed back her tears and smiled. 'Poppy's Pies and Puddings; it has a ring to it, don't it?'

'It does,' Annalise said smiling widely.

It had quick become something of a private joke between the two of them, a whisper in passing, behind a cupped hand at the table. "Poppy's Pie and Pudding Shop," they'd say and break into a laugh or smile.

Now Annalise was certain Poppy was keen on the idea and hadn't a care for leaving her position here to set out on this new venture, she grew increasingly anxious for Friday to arrive so they might both be put out of their misery and start on planning it all out.

As she journeyed to Mr Morgan's office by hack on Friday morning her stomach was all in knots and she needed the chamber pot every ten minutes, which was not ideal when in transit.

'Calm down girl,' Mr Harrison said to her before they went in, 'it's all agreed. Now you've nothing to do but sign the papers and hand over the draft.'

And he was right of course, and fifteen minutes after their entering, they walked back out with keys and deeds in hand.

'Oh Mr Harrison,' she declared throwing her arms about him as they waited for a hack for hire to collect them, 'thank you so much for everything you have done. It's all thanks to you.'

He patted her shoulder and smiled.

They took the hack straight down to Carshalton where he had arranged for the builder to meet them to discuss the works. It was not going to be cheap but she had enough to have the roof and beams attended, the shop floor rearranged and even for a small extension in the yard to be built to accommodate her sewing room. Today, he was to explain to her how it would all come about and how long it would take: A month for the refurbishments and another three besides for the extension in the yard. The white washing of all the walls and panelling would be included in the price.

She felt elated as they sat over another early meal at the Greyhound, discussing all the plans.

'I'll get this bill,' Mr Harrison said, when she got out her purse as they were leaving.

'No, it is the least I can do,' she protested.

'Ah uh, you need every penny you can to get this shop up and running. You still have furniture and stock to think of.'

'Yes, and I still have a little set aside for it. Plus, my wages have been doubled now I am trained.'

'Well, look at that. It seems your ma is sending down blessings from the heavens to rain upon you, lass.'

Annalise smiled and wondered if she might fit in a visit to the graveyard on her way home.

'Ah, Mr Harrison, Miss Tullier,' said the innkeeper as they approached him. 'I'll just get your bill,' he said shuffling through a pile of them. Today had been busier than the last time of their coming and they had been lucky to be squeezed into one of the parlours at all. 'Trust you've found everything to your liking?'

'Yes, thank you,' they choused.

'That'll be three shillings six pence if you please.'

Mr Harrison was the faster in putting his coin upon the salver and he pressed a hand over Annalise's, still fishing in her purse for the right change.

'Thank you very much, sir, hope to see you both again.'

'Ah, well, I think you might be seeing a lot more of us, or my niece anyway. You are now looking at the new owner of number sixteen,' he said with all the pride of a father.

'Well, my congratulations, miss. The next time you come in it shall be on the 'ouse since we're to be neighbours.'

'Oh, you are very kind, sir, I thank you. But there is no need for—'

'I insist. We's stick together 'round here as you'll come to learn.'

'Well, I thank you then, I shall look to it.'

'Any mind of what you'll do with the place?'

'Yes, it shall be a pie shop, a very good pie shop.'

'Ah, not too good I 'ope, don't wanna be at rivals with yer.'

Annalise stood stunned at this.

'He's funning with you, Annalise,' said Mr Harrison and they all shared a little laugh.

'Well, in that case, sir, you shall be the judge. I shall send one around to you once we are up and running.'

'Right you are, lass. I shall be expecting it,' he winked, then offered them a bow and they departed.

It was not until she was sat pulling weeds from about her mother's headstone that she felt the first shift in her merry spirits. She surely was raining blessings down upon her from every quarter and yet it seemed all the more painful knowing she could not be with her to enjoy it all. To have the easy retirement she was denied. She imagined her then, sat in the easy chair by the fire in the back parlour with her feet upon the stool. Finely dressed as she had always been in her younger days, giving her opinions on the pies as Poppy cooked them up.

'Oh, Mama, it feels wicked of me to find so much happiness without you,' she said and run her fingers across the copperplate letters of her mother's name which shone blinding bright in the sun.

By the time she was picking her way through the Cuddington trees, she had regained her buoyancy. The excitement at delivering Poppy the news hastened her steps, as well as the knowing she was already late returning to Eleanor as it was.

She knew she would not mind it. But also knew she had been in an anxious mood this morning at the dread of the party she was to attend this evening, and hated leaving her unattended in such a head.

'Poppy's Pies and Puddings is official,' she said to her when she had the hallboy go and fetch her for from the kitchen. Annalise and Cook had thus far managed to keep out of each other's way and she preferred it would stay that way.

'My love,' Poppy said, pressing a kiss to her cheek. 'What news! I can hardly believe I'm not dreaming.'

'Me either,' she said putting a key into Poppy's hand. 'But it is official and this key is your one.'

She turned it about in awe as though she had placed a handful of diamonds in it and not a rusty old key. 'You clever girl, you. I always knew something better was coming for you but never did I think I'd be joining you in it.'

'You are to be the main attraction, Poppy Gubbings. It is your pies that shall bring us repute, not mine. I can just about manage to stew an edible filling.'

'Oh, Annalise, thank you, luv.'

'Now, don't you start getting all teary on me again. You need to get back to the kitchen without blubbing over the master's courses,' she smiled. 'I just wanted to give you the news, so you can get to planning out your menus and we shall need to make up a list of all the things we shall need to buy later.'

'Eleanor, I'm so sorry I am late,' she said, finding her sat over her escritoire writing letters. She looked up and smiled but she could tell she was not in high spirits. She had wanted to find a way to share her own news with her, but thought it could keep for now, seeing how heavy things were weighing on her mind. A humble little pie shop was hardly the kind of news she could expect to lift her up. 'The time ran away with me this morning.'

'No matter. I'm glad you are back, though, I have missed you,' she said, putting down her quill and Annalise came up behind her and rested her head upon her shoulder.

'I've missed you too,' she said, planting a kiss upon her cheek to which Eleanor turned and placed one on her lips.

'You seem busy,' she said, standing up.

'No, not really, I was just trying to take my mind off this stupid party tonight. I really do think I should send a note of apology.'

'Is that what you were writing?'

'No. I was just writing out some advertisements. I have some things I mean to sell.'

'Oh. Well, can it wait?'

She nodded. 'It shall take me an age anyway. I shan't be finished to-day. Why, do you have something you want to do?'

'I thought a visit to the puppies might be good medicine for such a sullen face.'

'I'm sorry, Annalise. You are all the medicine I need. I shall snap out of this head now. Let us go and see how they do.'

By evening, Eleanor had changed her mind upon the hour. One minute she was going, the next she was to send a message with her apologies. A visit from her mother mid-toilette seemed to seal her attendance and she felt sorry to see the pressure put on her to go.

She had always thought Eleanor was lucky to be able to talk of her mama, to *have* her mama, but it was the first time she had ever wit-nessed them together and her impression of this encounter spoke a million words about their relationship. It had made her uncomfortable to witness it; the stiffness and formality between them, the perfunctory exchanges and her mother's hen pecking followed by Eleanor's eventual submission.

She folded her into the warmest hug when her mother left the room. Wanting to tell her she was sorry for what had happened. For how much tension was in the room, wanting somehow to shelter her from it. But Eleanor seemed to take it with such equanimity; it was that which really upset her. The normality of it all in her mind. Had she ever really known a mother's love? She wondered at it now. She knew that in these grand families they had nannies and other servants to see to the mundane tasks of parenting. But she had thought that must only lend to more time for the kinder things, not render the relationship devoid of anything she recognised of family love.

She had always known her relationship with her own mother to be special. They had only each other to rely on after all. But her heart swelled realising just how lucky she had been to have a mama that cared more for her happiness and wellbeing above all else and at any cost, she considered then, with a pang of regret.

But she shared none of these thoughts with Eleanor. It was not her place to bring her mind to such things when she was already troubled enough by this performance of graces she was to give tonight. So, she got her dressed prettily and sat upon the chaise with her, hugging and kissing her until she had to leave for the coach.

The cut direct.

October 1821. - Eleanor.

'Eleanor, you came,' Martha said, beaming up at me.

'Martha, how do you do?' I asked her, returning her smile. I had only been five minutes arrived and had expected to be standing alone a lot longer than this before someone had a kind word for me.

'Well, thank you. A little tired but I'm told that's to be expected,' she said holding the shape of her slightly protruding tummy in her hands.

'My goodness, congratulations, Martha. You are to be a mother. I had no idea.'

'Yes, it seems funny really.'

It did. I recalled it was not so long ago she struggled to manage her own affairs. I was happy for her though. To see her come along so far to a most unlikely outcome was heartening. 'Well, when shall we expect this little bundle to arrive into the world?'

'May, the very same as the name I have in mind if I should bear a girl. Bertram of course if it's a boy.'

'How lovely. How is Bertram? Merry at the news I expect?' I could see him romping around the lawns with it a few years along. He had the spirit of an overgrown child himself. I was certain he would make a very tender father.

'Very! I think he is more in a fidget for the arrival than even I. He'll be over in a moment, he's just speaking to his brother,' she pointed and I turned around to see the pair of them across the saloon.

'Are there any more of the family expected tonight?' I asked cautiously looking about.

'I don't think so, Mariella is already here. She is sat down on the sofa with Betsy and Anna. She says Giles is not come for he is away in Ireland,' she lowered her voice as if parting with some intelligence she was not meant to divulge to me.

'Yes, I heard the same.'

'You know Anna is married now, don't you? And Betsy engaged, waiting for the colonel to return in December.'

I wondered momentarily if that meant Sheldon too would return with him.

'They shall be having a Christmas wedding. A very grand one it seems, everyone's invited...' she said clumsily, realising that everyone would still not include me.

'Well,' I said quickly, pretending not to notice. 'How busy you have all been. I own I did hear of Anna's wedding and I knew the colonel had proposed but, well, it's all come about so quickly. No doubt you will not find yourself alone in your condition for long at this rate.'

'Yes, yes, I daresay you are right, although it doesn't look well for Clara. She has been trying since her wedding night and is sadly melancholy fearing she might be barren. She is to take the waters again next week to improve her chances. That's why I can't sit over there, the sight of me makes her burst into tears and I can't bear it.'

'How terrible. I daresay it is nothing and it will all come about soon enough. It has only been what? Three or four months?'

She nodded. 'I hope so.'

'Well, you have nothing to feel bad for, Martha. You have every right to be happy.'

'Yes, yes, I suppose you're right. Anyway, how do you do? I mean really, are you in better spirits?'

'I am in very good spirits, Martha. The best I have been in perhaps. I don't deny that having to come here tonight and face all the cuts hasn't taken the shine off my mood, but, well, I shall be happy when the night is over to say the least.'

'It must be very hard,' she said with a sympathetic look. 'But I am glad you are otherwise merry. No one thought you would come, but Bethany hoped you might. She wanted you to know that, well, not all of us are as unforgiving.'

'I know, and I am grateful to her for it, and that is why I have made the effort to come, in spite of everything else. But I haven't even had a chance to speak to her yet. She probably doesn't even know I'm here.'

'She is making the rounds I think, with Mr Dickenson.'

'Tell me, what is he like, her husband to be? Is he a good man?'

'He seems it and Bethany is thrilled with him. The others are not very impressed for he is a physician. But I can only think that quite a handy thing.'

I smiled at this. 'And I too. Of course, they would never think him up to scratch, but who cares what they think, so long as Beth is happy, that is what matters.'

'Very true.'

'Mrs Craythorne,' came a voice from behind and we both turned around accordingly, it was of course meant for Martha, for there were few who would seek me out as she did. I did not know the person who prevailed upon her but quickly found myself alone again, staring through the throng, considering if there was anyone beyond Delores and Miss Ponwiker I might prevail upon for a little company. It was then Beth caught sight of me and headed in my direction, what I assumed to be her husband-to-be walking close beside her, her arm looped into his.

'Beth, congratulations and to you too Mr Dickenson.'

'Thank you, Eleanor, and for coming,' Beth said as her husband bowed. 'Teddy, this is Mrs Craythorne.'

I dropped a curtsey. 'Well, when is the date set for?'

'Well, we did have in mind a Christmas wedding but since that put Betsy's nose so much out of joint, we decided to bring it forward to next month. Besides, we were pleased at not having to wait so long,' she said looking at her beloved with a twinkle in her eye that told me they were in love. It seemed being in love myself now, made the recognising of it in others easier. 'You will come, won't you?' she asked.

'I'd be honoured to, thank you,' I said, thinking that a wedding breakfast would be slightly easier to get through than tonight. *For one, you would have a permanent neighbour either side of you for the duration,* I considered as Mrs Jameson waved in Beth's direction, beckoning the couple over to receive more well wishes from someone she was talking to.

'Sorry, my mama is calling. I shall catch up with you later and have a proper chat then. Teddy, be a dear and introduce Mrs Craythorne to your sisters, will you, before you join me?' she turned and said to him and he said that it would be his pleasure and offered me his escort over to find them.

Before I knew it, the Dickenson sisters had not only adopted me for the evening, but they made it their mission to take me about the room introducing me to other friends and family that made up their portion of the guest list, and I wondered if Beth had put them up to it, fearing I would be alone all night otherwise. I was grateful for the pains taken, for it certainly felt easier to bear in company. And they were merry and spritely things, freshly out I suspected, recognising the over excitement and buoyancy of their enthusiasm. Particularly when the dancing started up.

Whilst I owed my first few sets to their meddling and persuasion, much to my surprise I had a number of other partners I hadn't expected, make invitations to me. Gentlemen of the ton, some of which I knew well enough to dance with, some I struggled to recall the introduction of prior. But it seemed they were much less inclined to hold me in disfavour than their female counterparts, who had mostly snubbed me with up-turned chins and pretences at not noticing me, the entirety of the night. This was Betsy and Anna's style as they caught sight of me upon the dance floor. *Yes, you didn't expect me to be dancing more than you tonight ladies, not now.*

A few of the old dames were little better, reluctant and barely motioned nods of recognition for my parent's sake I supposed. The Elmbridges were amongst them, the briefest involuntary acknowledgment followed by a swift turn in the other direction. I was certain they were pleased at the disaster my marriage had ended in. I could almost hear them saying: "Well, this would never have happened had she married Sheldon."

And it was probably true. But I was still grateful for how things had turned out, for I would likely have never known Annalise and found my true destiny, had it not turned out this way.

There were a rare few who ventured to bid me good evening at least, even if they took no pains to enter into pleasantries and a rare one now and then who bid me kinder smiles. But I was no doubt every part the pariah I had expected to be and if it were not for the Dickensons, I was sure I would have been deserted for the greater part of the evening.

I suspected them to be of the gentry and less familiar with my story as well as less haughty in nature. It was refreshing to have them about diluting the stiff and stagnant hauteur of the ton and bringing a little spirit into the saloon with their easy merriness.

Had it ended on this note, had I realised this would be the perfect time to leave, I might have come away concluding the night an unexpected success, and I would have felt my day of dread pointless and considered it all in all: a pleasant evening.

It was as I was chatting to the bridegroom's cousin—a Mrs Berry—at the buffet table, the clash came about. My former set were making their selections from the table when Clara and Mrs Berry reached for the same serving spoon at precisely the same moment.

'Sorry,' they both declared, Clara looking up and being confronted by the sight of me at last.

'Clara, good evening to you,' I said to her and only her, thinking she was not at all that bad and only towing the line for fear of the others' reactions.

She smiled back at me and said briefly, 'Good evening.'

'Clara,' Betsy was quick to intervene in a warning tone, it was one I knew so well the meaning of and I watched Clara shrink a fraction and turn back to the bowl that Mrs Berry was now finished serving her plate from.

'Clara, you can talk to anyone you want to. You don't need their permission. You are your own person,' I said to her, but angled my stare at Betsy.

'Oh, yes, like you do, anyone and everyone who's still willing to entertain you,' Betsy said with a menacing look about her expression and I wondered if she had been waiting all night for an opportunity to make some wicked comment to me.

'Well, I find most people are well mannered and interesting enough to bother with. Not everyone is so stiff-rumped they struggle to stand up from the sofa all evening,' I replied with my best smile.

'No, well some of us receive enough invitations that we must pace ourselves to get through them all,' she said, feigning smug indifference, but I could tell by the narrowing of her heavily soot coated eyes that she was in a fury.

The chatter in our vicinity had now sloped off and about half the room was covertly listening in on our conversation, which was not overly loud, but adequate for their hearing. 'I'm surprised you haven't tired of them altogether Lady Elizabeth since you've just run your third season.'

This was the tipping point for her. This time her voice was raised, although not in angry tones but an accent of mockery. 'Well, some of us are a little more circumspect and less hurried, not everyone wants to have one cried off engagement, one abandoned husband and at least one lover I could name, all in a six month.'

'Oh, do name him Lady Elizabeth, for he was the very same who rejected your wanton advances was it not? Yes, I do remember him mentioning how embarrassing it all was, having to throw you off him whilst your dear papa had him in his employ to teach you music. But we all know that was not at all the kind of lessons you meant to have from him, was it? Did you think even your father's coin would tempt him? He had not the least speck of interest in you, did he?'

Her façade came rapidly undone and I was surprised at it. The never before seen blush of her cheek, the look of surprise at what I had said; surprise at not knowing how to respond to it.

We had never crossed this threshold before. We had always been the quickest witted and most outspoken of our set, but whenever we had drawn close to a stand-off, we would only ever take it so far before relenting and preventing a real contest of our wits. Was she really so easily defeated? I saw the very same disappointment reflected in the eyes of Anna and Mariella who gave looks like they had been betrayed by her, by this pathetic show of stamina.

'Mrs Craythorne my dear,' said Mrs Berry, tugging lightly at my arm. 'Perhaps we should go.'

'I'm sorry. I daresay I have shocked you, and all you good folk. I apologise that I must, but those who know me, shall know this conversation has been a long time in the coming,' I said addressing the whole room now, crowded about with hands over their mouths, disgust in their expressions. 'You see, Lady Elizabeth and I were once friends.'

'What an oversight on my part,' she said to that.

'Is that what you shall tell the colonel, Bets—when he comes to hear of how you pawed over Mr Richards so wantonly whilst courting his affections? Will you call that an oversight too?'

Her colour returned so brightly now, for a moment it reminded me of Annalise's sunburned shade before it had settled.

'Enough!' Anna said bitingly. 'You've done enough damage.'

'Oh, Anna, I've only just got started. Congratulations on the wedding by the way. I know, my invitation must have got lost in the post. That was congratulations to you by the way, I offer commiserations to your husband.'

'Excuse me, ma'am,' said a fellow stepping forward that I assumed must be he.

'Ah, well of course. The question is can you excuse your wife of the lover she selected prior to your engagement?'

His face fell staid and Anna grabbed him by the arm, 'Come, do not listen to this,' she said, coaxing him away.

'No, I'll hear her since the rest of the room shall hear it,' he said. 'Who?'

'Mr Felix Craythorne. Not that I can confirm if things have fired off as well as Anna hoped them to. You shall have to ask her that. But what were your words back in spring? That was it, "Mr Craythorne would make a very poor choice for a husband, but an excellent choice for a lover."'

'Eleanor, we're leaving,' my mama came up beside me and tugged at me a lot less politely than Mrs Berry.

'Leave, Mama, if you prefer not to hear the truth. I daresay none of you like to hear the truth. You, Lady Elmbridge, how quickly you deserted our family when I cried off from your son's offer. You can go, ignore it, but everyone else shall have the hearing anyway. I understand that you were disappointed that the wedding you had in mind for him was not to be. I understand that you were hurt at seeing him sad. But did you ever wonder why I cried off? Did you ever consider how sad it made me to find him lying with Lady Caroline on the day I arrived to give him my answer? No. But still you cast your vote against my mama to cause her to lose her position at Almack's. You see, that's the problem with the ton, you all go about thinking you are so much better than one another when the truth is; most of you are up to no better, and often worse than the person you cut and sit over scandal broth counting their faults.'

'Eleanor,' this time it was Delores.

I pressed on. 'Yes, I did cry off from a very good match for a very good reason. And yes, my marriage worked out little better than that, for I had never expected that my husband would be bedding Mariella, something I was not willing to be a party to.'

This news was met with a wave of sighs and astonished glances and Mariella fled from the room. I realised then, they still thought them siblings, but did nothing to correct it. 'So, there it is: my side of the story. Now, I'm sure those of you who still have managed to keep your own little secrets close to your chest may now dish out the necessary punishment and ostracising that I have known in my troubled times, to these dear upstanding members who too have fallen from grace. I wonder how long it shall take for your own exposés?'

'I shall have to ask you to leave now,' said Mrs Jameson.

'I shall. I want only to say, Beth, Mr Dickenson and all the family, I am sorry for your having to witness this. You have all been very kind and I am grateful for it. I am sorry for any offense I may have caused you and I want you to know Mr Dickenson, your wife and yours too Bertram and Mr Radcliff, are the ones who may cast the first stone. For I know them to be good and decent women. Kind friends. I wish you all much happiness and hope you will forgive me for speaking that which no one else would. I bid you goodnight.'

'Mother, I shall hear nothing of it, not a word,' I said as we got into the carriage. 'If you want me to leave the house, then tell me and I shall, but I will not be lectured to like a child. Think what you may, but do not hit me over the head with it. You always told me when I was a child to tell the truth. I did nothing more tonight.'

Rum Business.

October 1821. - Eleanor.

I headed straight for my chamber when I arrived back home having exchanged not another word with my mother who was in a determined sulk and no doubt anxious for my father's coach to arrive from London so she could complain to him. I cared not. I felt a sense of peace with myself over what had passed. That I would have preferred the occasion not to have been Beth's party and in the company of the kindly family she was marrying into was too bad, but for everything else I felt not the slightest in error.

Annalise was waiting for me when I reached my chamber, and at the sight of her, I forgot everything else in an instant.

'How was it?' she said, looking concerned for my answer and as she undressed me for bed, I gave her an expedited outline of the evening, not wanting to linger on such matters when I had her to concentrate on. For she was all I had a care to fill my mind with. My eyes, my heart.

'Will you stay here with me tonight?' I asked her and she nodded, went over to the door and turned the key in it.

It was not the first time we had shared a bed together and yet it felt as novel as if it were. The nervous excitement was palpable. I felt it in the pit of my belly, heard it in the clumsiness of my speech and noticed it in the trembling of her hand when I reached out to grasp it.

Had those weeks of separation really jarred us out of comfort to this degree? Or was it because this time, when I was down to only my skin, I refused to step into the shimmy she had laid out for me. Or because when she reached for her own, I took up her hand and pulled her towards the bed. Even in the dimness of the fire's dying glow I could see the creeping hue of colour that rose up from her collarbone and flourished at her cheeks.

Tonight, it is not enough to delight in just the seeing of you. Tonight, I need to feel you.

She was so beautiful, but I did not know how to tell her. The observation formed easily in my mind but would not reach my lips. I think the thoughts somehow found their way to my eyes though, for I noticed how she studied my glances. If I could just speak the words, to reassure her...

I pulled back the coverlet and as we climbed into our usual spaces, I too found myself caught in a temporary paralysis. She was there. Inches from me. Her naked body beneath the brushed cotton sheets. Despite the trifling distance that set us apart, I did not know how to close the gap between us, even though every part of my being petitioned me to.

Don't lose your nerve now. I was not used to allowing my nerves to get the better of me; I was grateful how unfamiliar the feeling was, for it was shockingly powerful and disabling. I could barely imagine the conflict that a person naturally disposed to nervous episodes must endure on a regular basis, if this was its effect. I must overcome it, somehow. I must find a way to translate these rushing thoughts and feelings into actions. *But what actions precisely?*

I searched the dimness to make her out. She lay on her side facing me, her elbow tucked beneath her head, her chin nestled in the blankets. I wanted so much to release us both from this tormented, pregnant silence, and yet I hadn't a clue of how to approach her body, not in a tangible way. Yes, I knew what it was to feel Mariella's hands there—I shuddered and dismissed the memory quickly. I knew the effect of it, but not how to apply such workings. Besides, I did not only seek to pleasure her, I wanted something more than that: to merge with her somehow. To translate these deep yearnings into my tender handling of her, so she could feel upon her flesh, that which was aching in my heart to be spoken. I was not sure if such a thing was even possible, so insatiable and unquantifiable such depth of emotion felt. But after laying there a while in silence, unmoving, hearing our fractured breaths above the crackling of the fire, I managed to lift my hand from the quicksand of immobility, and find her forearm beneath the sheets. A gentle stroke along its length was all I could muster, a small gesture, but no less: a beginning.

I wondered what must come next and the fear of not knowing threatened to arrest my efforts once again, but then I felt her response; a timid twitching, her fingers entwining in my own. Relief washed over me; *She wants this too.* Was she waiting for me to take the lead, show her the way? How could I explain I did not know it either? Perhaps she thought, being a married woman, I would understand how to make love to another, yet I had never made love to anyone. In all those odd intimate encounters, feeling had not been a feature.

Nothing less than beautiful was worthy of passing between us, that much I knew; whatever other knowing I lacked. So, when I felt certain, from the gentle squeezing and flexing of her fingers, that she too wanted something more than we had managed to bring off, I dug a little deeper into that pit of quicksand and shuffled into those undisturbed inches of mattress, until it shifted with my weight and brought us both rolling into it. I felt the fullness of our breasts meet first, which shocked me. They were soft and weighty against my chest and in the instant of realising how close we had tumbled together, my breath caught and it took me a few moments to remember the other parts of my body. I adjusted my legs so our knees were not pressed uncomfortably together, sliding one of mine between hers and reaching around her waist a fraction to rest my arm in the recess. There was just enough light to make out her face, even though it was cast in shadow. Was it a smile I saw in her eyes? I did not pause for long, for fear of losing command of my actions again, so I seized the opportunity to draw her into a gentle kiss now we were close enough.

This we were comfortable with; tender sweet kisses—a savouring of each other's mouths. We had much practiced this art at almost any private opportunity we could claim. I felt her relax and as I breathed her in and tasted her, probed her with increasing longing, I found the courage to stroke the flank of her exposed waist; a smooth expanse of flesh and bone beneath my trembling palm. *Mon ciel étoilé.* My starry sky.

I reached further until my hand was at the small of her back and before I could talk myself out of the idea, scooped her in closer with the strength of one arm until I felt the full weight of her body pressed up against my own. Warm softness filled out the crevices and I felt her settle into the shape of me. *Jouissance.* Pleasure.

I heard her gasp; a gentle intake that momentarily sucked the breath from my own mouth.

'Are you alright?' I asked her; my voice sounded as though it had come from some other place, so long since I had dared to use it.

'Yes,' she nodded and kissed me back into silence and breathlessness. *Annalise, my sweet girl, have you any notion of what you are doing to me?* I felt as though she was near bringing me to the crest without any need for the manipulations that had previously induced me to such a state. Could that happen? Could someone stir your loins into such motion without even reaching for them? I certainly felt she might manage to. But I did not want this to end, not now, not ever. So, when the urgency of those longings kept surfacing, I fended them off. *Not now.*

This moment had a magic of its own, worthy of savouring for its own sake. So, I did not entertain its torment beyond the occasional pause to steady myself, remind myself that there would be time for *that* kind of magic too. But right now, it was enough to feel her against me, soft flesh and snug warmth.

The next night it was easier to reach out to each other's nakedness and find our warm embrace; limbs quickly tangled, folds of flesh shifting and merging as we gathered each other up. The instant I felt her, I remembered at once why the promise of bedtime had hung over me so impatiently all day. The hours stretched out until this moment had been difficult to bear in the ordinariness of the tasks and interactions that came before it; when all I longed for was this. This beautiful relief that filled me when our skin moulded and melded together so completely that it seemed interwoven: peeling slowly and reluctantly away when we shifted, before adhering itself back together in some altered shape.

Sometimes one of her breasts would sink into the gap between my own, at others I would feel them pressed against my chest and her ribs carving ripples in mine. Sometimes I could make no sense at all of how our flesh had settled; it was just all smooth warmth and weight pressed tight. But it did not matter. It mattered only that she was there. That I could feel the perfect curves of her. Stroke the lengths of her back and inhale the remnants of rosewater in her hair as I buried my face at her clavicle. This alone would have been enough to satiate the day's longings. If this was all there ever was to look to in a day, it was enough. More than I deserved perhaps.

But when she stirred me from our sleep-like trance, pulling her arm from around my shoulder and pushing me flat on my back before crawling on top of me and sinking me further into the feathered tufts of the mattress with her weight, I thought I must have been caught somewhere between a pre-sleep fantasy and an ensuing dream. But I was awake. She was really there: her face hovering above me in the shadows, lifted a fraction as she settled on her elbows, her breasts hanging from her chest, pooling in a heap upon mine. 'Is there no end to the delight of you?' I said, a whisper at her ear, her hair trailing my neck.

She made no answer, no vocal answer, but coaxed me into a kiss that felt somehow different from all that had passed before. *What was it?* I did not know, but I pulled her so greedily flat against me that the breath in my diaphragm was expelled as I found myself smothered in her flesh entirely. *Oh my.* The warmth. The pressure. The softness. It seemed almost too much to endure. Then as her tongue trailed my throat where my pulse violently throbbed, I recognised what was different; what had been unfathomable in her kiss. There was a promise in it, a purpose I could not distinguish in the movement or pressure of her mouth, but I could feel. By some inexplicable means, it spoke to me. I heard it, the message, conveyed in invisible tongues and it prompted me to dare.

I shuffled just a fraction to pull her thighs either side of mine until I was able to bring one knee up to nudge her further up my body, just enough to bring her breasts within my reach. When I unfurled my arms from around her back, she was forced to balance upon her elbows again and I took advantage of the gap and cupped them tentatively in my hands, their doughy weight falling between the gaps in my fingers as I grappled gently to stop them spilling from my grasp. I might have spent longer testing their weight, delighting in the sight of seeing them so closely, held in my own hands. But the heaviness of her sighs distracted my gaze and drew my eyes away. In hers, I saw the shock of the sensation as I drew circles with my thumbs.

'Are you comfortable with me touching you this way?' I asked her and she nodded. It was all the encouragement I needed. 'Sit up with me,' I said, pushing up from the bed and reshuffling us both, until I found her in my lap, her legs wrapped around me. I wished I could see her better, but was in part, glad that I could not. I feared it might be enough to unleash a wildness in my handling of her, when all I wanted was to show her such beautiful tenderness as befitted her.

My hands, in long smooth strokes, found their way around to her buttocks nestling in my crossed legs. I circled them a while before pulling her in closer to me until I felt a tickling fuzz of hair against my navel, then moist warmth, clammy against my skin. There was something reminiscent of a purr I noted in the rhythm of her breathing now, as I found the swell of her breasts once more, gentle strokes with occasional pressure as my fingers snagged against a nipple.

I could devour you entirely.

It seemed not to matter now, that I did not know precisely just how I would manage it. There was something building between us that reassured me, somehow, we would find just the right way if we continued listening in the darkness, to that subtle calling that had guided us this far. I trusted it. It seemed to have a wisdom all of its own. And whilst the nervous fluttering's at my core grew stronger, the questioning thoughts and paralysis began to dissipate with each new exploration of her, each blissful response I drew from her body as I traced my hands over almost every inch of it.

There were places I was still unsure about touching, not because I didn't yearn to, nor even because I was fearful of how—I just knew I would know when the time came. But each new level of exploration deserved to be cherished, each new advance felt like enough, for now. Besides, when I reflected on the previous night, replaying it over the day's banality so many times my mama would often chide me for having to repeat herself, I longed for the surprise of what would come next.

I enjoyed the sweet torture of walking innocently arm and arm with her about the park, knowing what it was to have our limbs tangled up beneath the sheets at night. Prattling on in the company of the Bartletts whilst admiring how beautiful she was as a smile beamed from her; her neat white teeth revealed for a moment. The seriousness that fell across her expression when she read what was really in my thoughts. *You. It is always you.*

Even when we were engaged in more serious endeavours such as the sewing work we were undertaking for the Society, or enduring one of the new curate's sermons at church, I could not be distracted from her for more than brief and punctuated spells. One moment I could be palms pressed, reciting prayers upon the pew and the next, transported to a memory of my mouth upon her doughy breasts as she sighed and panted beneath my tongue. Another, I might be concentrating hard on following her deft instruction on how to execute a hemstitch, as visions of awakening to her sleeping face—our feet still entwined—drew a reminiscent smile from me that was otherwise inexplicable.

'What are you smiling at?' she would sometimes ask me, her brows knitted as if she had missed some trick or detail.

'At how lucky I am to have you,' I would tell her and she would blush from collar to cheek before offering me a bashful smile. Not the ordinary kind she gave to others. This one had a slant to it that was reserved just for me, and I loved it even more for knowing it was mine. *She was mine.* The space beside me in the bed belonged to her, my kisses and my heart were fully and completely at her command. There was nothing I wouldn't do for her, nothing I could deny her, and even on the rare occasions when she scolded me a little for forgetting myself in public places or taking too much of a risk stealing kisses from her in the momentary gaps when a servant disappeared, I could not be cross with her for more than a few seconds.

Even her stubborn reluctance in learning to ride, which I would have grown quickly impatient with had it been anyone else, did not drive me to despairing of her. Because in whatever ways we might differ or disagree, I loved her so fondly it was unalterable by such follies or frustrations. So deeply run its roots, it could at worst sway my branches just a fraction, before I remembered just how deeply her roots had become entwined with my own. Just how much an extension of each other we had grown.

Not a day passed by without her beside me, nor a night without us beneath the same sheets. If nothing else ever altered in my life, I knew the remainder of it would be happy.

Even when the letters signalling Giles' return started up again: First apologetic, imploring, then increasingly demanding and threatening, I felt no fear. Only a deeper desire to sever ties with him and the shambles of a marriage contract I wished sorely never to have entered into. I could never be his wife now; even if I was foolish enough to accept his pledges of fresh starts abroad and promises of never giving me cause to be angered by him again. It mattered not. I was in love now. I knew what it was at last to feel so much absorbed in another being that it would be impossible to play at some loveless marital facade, even if I wanted to. Of course, I did not. After what he had subjected me to, I would as soon strike him down myself than have him aside me ever again. But it was for her I wished to safeguard my freedom now. It was for her I lived and breathed. Nothing else mattered and nothing else would be permitted to break apart what I had spent such a time longing for.

It was in this mind, despite all my doubts and reluctance, that when Edmund arrived home to break his journey on to Brighton, I seized the opportunity to try one more time to bring him around to helping me separate myself from Giles. This time, however, with Annalise in mind, I was willing to give the full account and make the most convincing try possible.

'Dash it, Ellie, not this again,' he sighed as I cornered him in the library. He shuffled about the papers he had been working on.

'Edmund,' I said, taking an uninvited seat and bracing myself to bring forth the subject. 'I know what your feelings are on the matter and I even find some sympathy with them. But if I told you what he did to me, you would perhaps find some greater sympathy with mine.'

'What could he possibly do to you that he has not earned the right to Ellie? You are his wife and you are playing absentee.'

I cleared my throat. 'He sodomised me Edmund,' I said as steadily as I could manage despite the shame that knotted inside me at confessing such a despicable thing to my own brother.

He put down his papers now and considered me.

'He had his cousin hold me down whilst he pinned me to the bed and fought his way to the task, to be precise.'

He seemed rendered speechless by this confession and I was glad at last to be taken seriously.

'What a beastly way to treat your wife,' he said eventually.

At last, you see.

'Eleanor, you do know what is meant by such a term?'

'Edmund, I might be young but I am no longer a child! And I confess I might not have understood it if it were not for the fact that when I was sat at the Old Bailey awaiting Tilly's trial, I saw a man sentenced to the rope for committing precisely the same act my husband did upon me.'

'You are quite certain then?'

'Certain? I could barely sit down! I assure you there is no mistaking—'

He held up his hand. 'Very well, I believe you.'

I resisted the sarcasm that lurked on the tip of my tongue. I needed his help and was sure it was worth biting in order to secure it. 'Can I prosecute him for doing such a thing?'

'Yes, husband or no, the law will look upon him no more favourably for such a crime.'

This was music to my ears. I had suspected as much, searched the books and newspapers relentlessly since that day in court, but could not find an example specific enough to be certain. It seemed always to pertain to men committing the act against other men. I had never considered that men might indulge their own sex, just as I did, less still be criminally tried for engaging in it. I would not ask Edmund if relations betwixt females were so treated. I had found nothing to confirm either way, despite my private attempts at trying to find out. 'Good. Is it enough to secure my divorce?'

'It most likely would be, if you were able to provide adequate testimony. But Ellie, you know, you have seen for yourself now, what that means.'

A fleeting memory of the full and chuckling gallery at the Old Bailey, briefly surfaced. 'What choice do I have?'

He sat thoughtfully a moment pressing his fingertips over the stubble of his chin before replying. 'A negotiation perhaps.'

'He does not seem to me like the kind of man who is used to negotiating unless it is on his own terms.'

'That's as may be. But I very much doubt he thinks you would have the pluck to share such details with your family, less still have them read out in an open court room. But if I approach him with the facts, call his bluff; I am sure he might have an altogether different mind to keep this matter quiet.'

'Do you really think so, Edmund? Do you think you could persuade him to agree?'

'Unlikely to trying for a divorce, he won't want the scandal either—unless, of course, he has hopes of remarrying, which would be by the by if this news broke out. But a separation of bed and board, agreed by both parties would perhaps manage this as quietly and as quickly as could be hoped.'

'Yes.' Expediency was needed. 'I don't care about the divorce; I have no desire to remarry. I only want to be free of him.'

'Well, that's may be, but don't forget, Ellie, you will not just be free of his person, you will be free of his purse and his lodgings for good, and with no option to marry your way out of such a circumstance, what will you do? I own the parents have some years left in them yet, but they won't be about forever to look after you. Then what? You won't have a feather to fly with. I can't see you hanging off of Henry's sleeves, even if he has forgiven you by then, and I can't see you managing as a Governess either.'

'I don't care,' I told him flatly. 'I would sooner live in poverty and have his claim to me relinquished.'

'I could just have a quiet word, warn him off such treatment?'

A sardonic laugh threatened to spill out but I quelled it. 'No, it will not do. I want a separation. I do not care for the consequences.'

'Very well; easier said than done, mind. Still, you will have to speak to Mama at least about this, better let her have it and soften the blow to Papa's learning it in the way you have given it up to me. I don't think he would ever be able to look at you again.'

I nodded. He could barely look at me now; I dreaded to think how it would be.

'Once he's taken it in and the negotiations are underway, he might be brought to drawing up a trust for you, if you can manage to keep on his better side from here on. Yes—I heard all about your stunt at the Jameson's. You've set the cat right among the pigeons there. It's not only your own marriage you've dashed apart now, is it?'

'What?'

'Lady Elizabeth, her wedding's been cancelled. Mr Barrington has moved back into his old London bachelor lodgings leaving Anna at Cavendish Square. Lady Caroline was said to be black and blue when she was last seen in town. Yes, you've set off a whole chain of events there.'

'No, Edmund, they did that themselves. I simply brought the truth to everyone's knowing, just as all my affairs have been so consumed.'

'Hmm. Bloody rum business, though. You'll get no blunt out of the old fellow if you carry on in that style.'

I couldn't care less whether he would settle some sum on me or nay, just so long as Giles was gone for good. With my Annalise beside me, there was nothing I could not face. No price I would not pay that would not be worth the sum total, so long as I could be with her entirely.

'I'll get on to it when I return from Brighton.'

'Thank you, Edmund. Truly.'

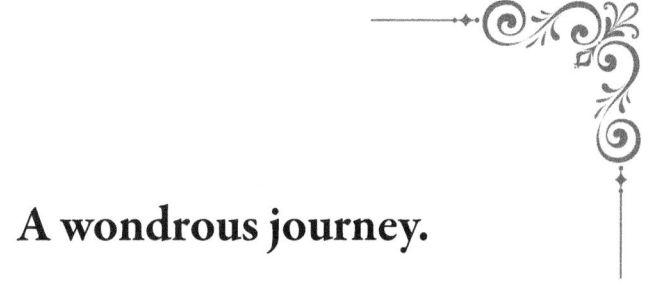

A wondrous journey.

October 1821. - Eleanor.

I was happy to depart the library knowing that however painfully, I had won Edmund's assistance. It was in his hands now and there was no one better to handle the negotiations than he, for whatever else, Giles knew him to be a man of the law with just the right connections to make this go very ill for him if he did not comply. As obstinate as he was, I did not think him foolish—not enough in any case—to risk his reputation more than he had to. Whatever he had of one had been sadly dashed in the gossip of him making a bed fellow of Mariella. Beth had told me people still believed her to be his sibling, even though Mariella had done her utmost to correct this deception of the Craythorne's own making. He had been cast in the light of Byron, with none of the status or poetic grace to soften this damnation, so he really could not afford to dice with it any further if he wanted to preserve what precious remained.

'What's got into you?' Annalise asked me as I sang my way through our three hours of sewing.

'You, of course, what else?' I answered. I could not tell her about my conversation with Edmund and the new hope it offered me. I did not know how to begin to broach the details of what exactly had passed in my short married life. I could have trusted her with the telling, if I could have bared to have her think of me so shamefully: so helpless and defiled as I had felt that night she met me on the basement stairs. I knew one day I must confess it all to her. I wanted no secrets between us. With her, I wanted only earnestness. But we still had so much more to discover and learn about each other that I did not want to taint this beautiful unravelling with the decrepit details of my former life, not yet. She was everything that was innocent, untainted loveliness, and to plague her with such details seemed abhorrent to me. She was happily set apart from what had passed and I would attempt to keep her so in what was still to play out in my separation. Once I had won it, I would tell her the whole. Once I could sweep it all away for good, as quickly as I set it before her, I would find a way to confess it all.

'Come,' I beckoned her, 'see what you think?' I held out my sewing for her to examine. We still had six more garments to piece together before we could package up the trunks of refashioned clothing we had painstakingly worked into mended, or entirely new garments to take to Horsemonger Lane. They had been donated to the cause from Miss Lockheart who had been collecting donations all year, only to find that this year, thanks to the money raised from the harvest raffle and all the generous sewing efforts of us and the other parishioners, they actually had surplus to requirements for a change. She had been minded to send them off to the Merton district, but was happy to donate it to our cause upon learning of it.

'You have been hard at work,' she said, holding out the infant sized dress that still had one sleeve to be sewn on to complete it. 'You have done a good job. See, I knew you were past needing my direction,' she said, handing it back to me.

'Well, I could hardly fail to improve with you as my teacher,' I told her, taking advantage of her proximity and stealing a kiss before turning back to my work with renewed focus. I was determined to work to completion this morning. We were due in London this afternoon for the Society's monthly meeting. Lady W. had written to remind me of the date, which was just as well, for my mind had been so much full of only Annalise, that I had quite forgotten the date, or my promise to return to London in time for it. I did at least have the sense to send her maidservant back last week. She had taken the coach with my father as he returned to Westminster.

It was our first proper journey out of Cuddington together, and Annalise's first trip to London since her childhood visit to the Tower menagerie. Her excitement was contagious as she spent most of the journey, faced pressed to the glass marvelling over some novel sight or the other. "Where are we now?" she would ask. "What's that building?" "Is it always this terrifically busy?" "Gosh, how many turnpikes there are."

To begin with, these places were of no significance and there was little commentary to offer her. But as we travelled through the Hamlet of Nine Elms and joined the Kingston Road, I was able to point out more and more places to delight her with: a quick stop for the horses at the Cumberland Tavern as we walked the gardens there, then through the turnpike onto Vauxhall Bridge, the boats passing up and down the Thames as we went over it, the hexagonal walls of the Millbank Penitentiary, The Queen's Gardens and Green Park, Piccadilly and Devonshire House.

I had never considered myself much of a tour guide, but for her, I would be anything at all that drew such wonder and amazement from her: Showering me with wide eyed smiles and childlike joy in her face. I had been back and forth on this route more times these past months than I could count. It had become such an irksome bore that I had not thought how even this could become such a happy adventure in her company. This confirmed to me, what I already felt; no matter what the circumstance, with her, it was always sunnier. And I knew that whatever consequences were to be borne in gaining this separation, it would be worth it.

By the time we pulled up at Grosvenor Square, I had formed a full itinerary of the places I would take her to during our stay, whilst simultaneously running a full and frenzied commentary of the inhabitants of the Grosvenor Estate as the coach took advantage of the quieter than usual roads and galloped along them, rattling us about in the back of it. I had earmarked Vauxhall Gardens on a fine day, the British Museum for a rainy one, and to see the pictures at the Royal Academy and the watercolours at Old Bond Street. To see the view of Westminster Abbey and the Palace from the bridge, then there was St. Paul's, and the Egyptian Hall to see The Great Belzoni's exhibition. Of an evening, I could take her to the theatre at Drury Lane or the new Haymarket and, I wondered if that opera staring Ms Vestries was still on at the Kings; I still remembered the hurrah over her performance in *Giovanni in London* last year. What a shame Mama would not permit me seeing it, it was too late now.

I had begun to wonder if our week's stay would be sufficient to cram it all in on top of the society work and visits I meant to undertake. Then it occurred to me on reflection of the busy streets at Piccadilly, how London might be the perfect place for us to settle to. On the one hand it was a place that posed the danger of bumping into every sort of acquaintance, especially during the season. But to its advantage, the busier it grew, the more invisible we would become, lost amongst the throng of it all. And I could not imagine London being such a place where it would be well noticed that two females were setting up house together, well, it perhaps might be in the Mayfair district, but all my collected trinkets were never likely to permit us anything in that locality. Perhaps we could go somewhere a little more out the way in our humbler search. I had always liked Tyburnia and the area about Mary Le Bone struck me as much like being in the country until you crossed south of New Street, if we were minded for something quieter. I would keep a keener eye out now. Of course, I could neither own or rent such a place, but in Annalise's name, there would be no trail or no husband to claim it from her.

When Lady W. met us in the hall, outstretched arms and happy greetings, I felt a pang of guilt having Annalise shown upstairs to unpack my things whilst Lady W. whisked me into her small sitting room for tea. We would have to play our parts again now and pretend not to be so much more to each other than our positions allowed.

'How well you look my dear! I am so happy to see the colour back in your cheeks,' she said to me when we were alone.

'I am so much better, I can hardly believe it myself,' I told her and explained it away detailing my conversation with Edmund and the new hope promised by his handling of the affair. It felt a terrible deception, not only for carrying off the joy duly owed to Annalise's restoration of my heart, but also in withholding such vital details from my dearest friend. I wanted to introduce Annalise to her as more than my maid, bring her into the room on my arm and declare the introduction as one between a dearest friend and the love of my life, but how could I? I could see it might, in time, become either plainer, or more possible to confide in someone like Lady W., but I was not ready yet, and I knew Annalise would not hear of it at all. She still suffered a great paranoia about our circumstance, that in private fell away more and more now, but in public remained a risk too great to be borne. I still had not managed to find anything that would suggest we would be treated criminally for such things, but I would never put her at risk, not for anything.

For me there was no real shame anymore, with her acceptance of us, my own shame had transformed into something more like muted pride. I wanted to tell the world she was mine, this beautiful girl who I felt so much undeserving of the happiness she had bestowed upon me. Of course, it could never be so. I knew it, yet I could not quell the instinct of wanting to share such a detail with my nearest friend. For Lady W., had become to me, in our short acquaintance, to be something between a favourite aunt and a best friend. If I was honest, I held her in more regard than many of my own relations, and all my other friends in sum. She had been there for me in my seclusion, never pressing or questioning me harshly, never judging me for my circumstances or decisions, just being a true friend, no matter what, no matter how I prevailed upon her. If there was one person I would wish to share my happy news with; if there was anyone I wanted Annalise to come to know: it was her.

Despite spending most of the afternoon absent from her, I knew Annalise would be welcomed to sit in on the Society meeting. Especially when I explained to Lady W. that it was under Annalise's direction and majority share in the efforts, that we were able to bring two trunks full of clothing donations with us.

'What a treasure she is,' Lady W. said of her. 'You have done well to find such a fine Abigail. She seems a very sweet natured girl and I can see she has a great regard for you.'

'I have indeed been most fortunate. I could not be without her. I own she has become as much a companion to me of late.'

'Well, I am happy to know you have someone at your side my dear. It puts my mind at ease knowing you have someone to confide in and to look after you, I must admit.'

That was as close as I was likely to come to a confession, I realised, glancing at Annalise with a similar sense of wonder to the one she had displayed through the carriage window on our journey. She was in conversation with Mrs Neal, and I was happy that amongst the Society, she could be at ease. No one cared whether you were in service, trade or landed; so long as you were in service to the cause, you were an equal here. When I showed Mrs Neal the products of our labour, she was quick to pass them about to the other ladies in admiration of Annalise's skilled workings. Tablecloths had been made into petticoats and shirts, curtains into infant sized quilted blankets and shawls, sheets that had been discarded by Mrs Crawford for carrying the slightest stain had been worked into skeleton suits and shifts, and yet the quality of the cut and the stitching would never have given away their original form, so clever she had worked them. There were some brand new things too, cut from the left-over fabric she'd procured for Old Mill Street: smarter coats, cloaks and jackets.

When the meeting was over and finally I had her to myself again, I was so overcome with love and pride for her, that I wasted no time in pulling her into my embrace and showing her.

'I think I should sleep on the day bed, what if someone comes in and finds us?' she protested as I lifted her chemise over her head and discarded it on the floor.

'No one will come in. Be at ease.'

'But what if the chambermaids come in to light the fire at some other hour here and we are found together in your bed?'

'Annalise, they light the fires here in the same pattern as we do at home. It is not a foreign land. I have been much a guest here and I'm quite familiar with the ways of the house. They will not come in before seven-o-clock, I assure you.'

'You are certain?'

I pulled her against me. 'What I am certain of, is that I have missed you so much today that now I am feeling very selfish of you and wanting to make up for all those hours I have been parted from or had to share you.'

She smiled a bashful, relenting smile and crawled into the bed beside me. I took a moment to reach for the drapes around the bed posts. I was not in the habit of drawing them, but I knew it would put her at greater ease to know we were shielded from view, should someone chance upon us, however unlikely I thought it.

As we settled into the bed, shrouded in pomona velvet with only a hint of still bright evening light seeping in through the seams, I gathered her up against me with an insatiable appetite for her. The initial rolling and fidgeting about to find a position that seemed to offer us the closest possible connection ensued; sheets twisted, blankets overthrown, trying to maintain our kisses and strokes as we tussled and tangled ourselves up. I felt her tender grappling at my shoulders as she kissed my neck, then long drawn-out strokes across my arms, my back, my buttocks. I writhed and rocked upon her gently, but was unprepared for what came next; she felt her way around to my breasts, sides first, until I lifted a little to make room for her hands. Then the magic, her fingers a gentle brush against my nipples; so light a touch, it was almost too painful to bear. A sigh escaped me. I looked down at her, her golden tresses a nest upon the pillow, her beautiful face concentrating on her task. These timid strokes made me shudder and flinch with exaggerated anticipation; she had never touched me here before.

I had made a habit of touching her like this since that first time in my chamber. I had not known if the delay on her part was due to her not wanting to touch me like this, or being too nervous to dare. I rejoiced at the confirmation of the latter. *Yes, she wants to discover me too.* I pulled up further still, holding my upper bodyweight above her, palms pressed into the mattress either side of her shoulders: an invitation.

With it, her timid strokes became more daring; gentle grappling and increasingly adventurous fingertips growing firmer, teasing, a deep longing contracting in my loins. I took pains to stifle the increasing volume escaping me. *Oh, Annalise, your effect on me is so disproportionate to the acts you commit. I am already close. I don't know if I can quell it this time.* A gentle kneading. *Try.* A twist. *Be steady.*

I climbed off of her and slipped beside her, realising how wildly I had been sliding myself along her body, pressing myself into her, faster, more purpose to my rhythm. I did not want to scare her off by pushing too far ahead before she was ready. I checked her expression for a sign and stroked her hair from her face to see it better. I could not read it: was it delighted surprise or shock upon it? There was no time to analyse, she was kissing me again. I tasted the promise in them once more. Was this her invitation? *Oh, to know your mind!*

Was she as desperate to be touched as I? I gathered my resolve and slid a palm across her navel and at the boundary I would usually divert it, went on, felt the tangle of hair beneath my fingertips until I felt her shudder, her fingers grip my shoulder, a deep sigh into my mouth. This I could interpret well enough. To induce such a feeling in her was almost enough for me to lose myself entirely. I refocused and drew another feather light stroke across the spot. A jolt this time. *Again.* A groan. *Slightly firmer.* A gasp so loud I looked about me a second. *Slightly faster.* Her breasts heaved with the arching of her back, pressing one of them to my cheek. I took my tongue to it, careful not to lose my rhythm in the distraction. An indistinguishable murmur of a word upon her lips. What was it? It was too quick. I looked up at her face, her eyes were closed, her face contorted in; pleasure, yes, I was sure that was the shape of it. *Slower.* One knee rising. My teeth grazing on the pinkness of a nipple. Her hand upon my arm now, forcing its direction.

Was I doing this right? What did she need? It was one thing to know the feeling applied and another to apply it. I worked on in a frenzy, combining all the things I had tried in sequence now, until the right purrs and movement of her body signposted the way. I side glanced my way down her body and watched her writhing beneath my hand. She was losing control now, her body making punctuated then erratic jerking motions, the rise and fall of her chest sharp and laboured, her face glowing, pink flourishes of heat at her cheeks, her features contracting and contorting. I had never seen her so wild and immersed. It seemed impossible she could become more beautiful, but this feral display somehow deepened the awe I felt looking upon her. *I love you. I don't know how to tell you, but I know it.*

I kissed her open mouth but she was too far lost to respond to it, or stay still enough to receive it. I felt her jaw jut against my teeth a fraction as she began groaning and then imploring. The words were mumbling and indecipherable but I could tell from the tone, the chaos and increasing volume of them, that she needed more from me. My arm ached with the strain, my fingers slipping clumsily from the moisture but I would find the resolve to appease her. I dug deeper, determination in my every movement, until suddenly, I felt her body lift an inch higher, a violent shudder and her thighs squeezing like a vice around my hand as a final unrestrained moan escaped her.

Then near silence filled the room and her body fell limp. *I did it. I managed to find my way.* I slipped my hand back to her navel and rested it there. I looked on in disbelief as I watched her swell with relief, listened to her recovering breaths, noted the clumsiness in which her limbs now rested in irregular positions, the bedding tousled and heaped beneath them. *My beautiful Tulley, you have tasted this pleasure at last, and I was the cause of it.* I was smiling into the Pomona green curtains, muted pride was the curve of it. I did not know whether to laugh or cry at my amazement. I rested my head against her shoulder and breathed with her. *I love you.*

Gaol fever.

October 1821. - Eleanor.

It was not the interruption of a chamber maid that woke us early in the morning but a dreadful nausea that roused me from a most blissful sleep with such violence I barely made it to the chamber pot in time to catch it in the bowl.

'Good grief, Eleanor, you are unwell!' Annalise shrieked, throwing aside the blankets and rushing to assist me. 'Here,' she said, pouring some water from the carafe and wetting a hand cloth to swab me with.

'Thank...you,' I said in a momentary pause before another dizzying wave possessed me and the retching caused my gullet to burn and scrape with the effort.

'I think I must go for help. Eleanor, you are seriously unwell.'

I shook my head. There was no need for such a fuss.

'But I think we must send for the doctor.'

'Nonsense,' I managed before my stomach growled again with an attack so prolonged, I could barely catch my breath for several moments until it abated. Her gentle strokes across my back helped me endure it with less complaint than it warranted.

'My love, I think it best.'

'It must have been the mutton,' I said finally, grateful to have recovered a little and wiping my mouth with the cloth she had been dabbing at my forehead. I stared into the spattered bowl and wondered how this had come about. I had not felt unwell last night. I had not taken any wine with dinner or eaten any of the crab, for that would have certainly accounted for such a reaction, so ill an effect if oft produced in me. But it was with precisely that in mind, I had passed on the course. My cheeks had stopped tingling and the excessive saliva that had built in them at last seemed dispelled. 'I am feeling much better,' I said now, releasing my grip upon the washstand and turning away to remove myself from the stench.

'You are?' she asked, mistrusting, shouldering me into my night robe and sending me over to the chair.

'I am, a great deal better, in fact,' I said as much to my own surprise for my relief was in the extreme so suddenly, like whatever needing purging from me had left.

She drew back the curtains and a beam of sunlight so bright flooded the room it blinded me a moment whilst my eyes adjusted.

'Some fresh air I think,' she said, lifting the sash window as high as its frame permitted and even though there was no breeze, a coolness filled the room, breaking up the stagnancy and stench. I rubbed my tummy in small circles and watched Annalise searching the floor for her shimmy and stretching into it, her arms reaching up into the sleeves, her breasts raised a fraction before they disappeared beneath the swathe of muslin as it settled about her.

'I shall get dressed and go downstairs to ask for the doctor to be sent,' she told me, lifting her long golden tresses from beneath the collar of her shift, dust motes illuminated by a sun beam dancing around her like confetti.

I wished she would not fuss so. 'Please, there really is no need. I feel quite myself again now.' It was true, I felt much improved save the soreness of my throat from all the retching. 'I think it must have been the mutton last night, or perhaps the crab was prepared with the salad and that proved enough provocation. I really do not have the constitution for shelled seafood, I always tolerate it poorly.'

'Your colour has picked up,' she said, studying me before pouring the remainder of water from the carafe and handing me a glass: 'Here, take a little.'

I complied, replacing the acidic tang of vomit with the slightly souring taste of water that had grown stale overnight. 'Thank you. Annalise, do not be concerned.' I reached for her hand as she pressed at my forehead to check my temperature. 'I do not feel feverish in the slight.'

'Well, perhaps bed rest will be enough, if there is no reoccurrence.'

'Bed rest? Thank you, no. Do you forget it is our names upon the rota for Horsemonger Lane today?'

'I do not forget. But I do not think you well enough to go.'

'Certainly, I am,' I insisted. 'Besides, we cannot let them down. You will see for yourself how much needed our attentions are. I shall not cry off and disappoint them.'

'Then let me go, whilst you rest. That will solve all matters.'

'Absolutely not. You have never been to the place before and it is not a place you should wish to visit alone on your first occasion.'

'I am perfectly capable—'

'I know you are, my sweet. I do. But I should not like to be parted from you another day.' It was true enough. I felt such anxiety at our separation, increasingly, the more I grew used to having her so selfishly at my side. But beyond that, despite thinking her even more adept than I in calamitous circumstances, I could not contemplate the risk of leaving her so vulnerable, should something turn ill.

'Mr Honeyfield, good morning,' I said as he admitted us into the gaol, the sunlight shut out with the closing of the iron door and only the gloom of the surrounding walls laying shadows upon the courtyard.

'Good morning, Miss Craythorne. Miss?'

'Tullier, sir; a new volunteer to the Society.'

'Miss Tullier,' he nodded and led us on, his chatelaine of iron keys clanging about his waist. 'I'm afraid the convict's wards are out of bounds today.'

'Out of bounds?' I said as we followed him on.

'There's been an outbreak; we've had to cordon off half the wards. Only the debtors and the ward for those awaiting trial can be accessed at present.'

'Whatever can you mean?'

'We've 'ad a woman and two babes taken down by a fever just this night, and two more showing worrying signs.'

'Taken down?'

He paused a moment. 'Dead as a doornail, miss. No choice but to keep them on lockdown 'til it passes.'

I was perfectly astonished, not least by his perfunctory manner. 'Passes? Mr Honeyfield, do you mean to tell me that these prisoners are unwell and have been shut up in their wards with no one to tend them?'

'Can't be 'elped, miss. Don't want the whole gaol going down with it.'

'Have they seen a doctor?'

'No need. No cure for this ill, miss. Seen it more times than I can count 'em.'

I slowed. 'Well, that may be Mr Honeyfield, but since you are not a physician, I think you shall call the prison surgeon at once, for you may be sorely mistaken and they may suffer where there is either a cure to be had, or some comfort at least in a little laudanum?'

'Too risky, ma'am. Spreads like wildfire, the least who are in contact the better.'

I stopped walking now and turned to him fully. 'Mr Honeyfield, if that is to be your logic then I must ask what you mean by keeping all the other prisoners locked down with them who are not *yet* ill? And with such poor light and air, I cannot help but feel you are inflicting the ill upon them, for how can they remove from it?'

'No need to take such a tone, miss. We're doing our best.'

Such a tone? Was he really taking offense at my speech having just relayed to me such information? 'With all due respect, sir, you tell me three have died in the night, that this malady "spreads like a wildfire" and it is not safe to send anyone into the place—yet you have locked up with the sick, what; a number in the region of eight and sixty on the convicts ward, and how many on the transportees?'

'Four and forty miss—'

'So, you are quite comfortable subjecting in excess of one hundred inmates to the very conditions that prevent you from allowing but one prison surgeon to be so exposed? One who might manage to bring some control of the epidemic—comfort at least—if not a cure to the sick? Damned shabby and wanting if you ask me sir, and it is Mrs, not miss!'

'Eleanor—' I felt a gentle tug upon my forearm and looked to see Annalise's gloved hand upon it, a graveness about her expression, and I knew she meant to warn me off such an outrage.

'A bit strong *Mrs* Craythorne,' Mr Honeyfield replied. 'No need for hysterics. I will call for the surgeon presently if it will...alleviate your concerns. For what good it will do, but it shall not be said I did not try.'

'Mr Honeyfield,' Annalise cut in now before I could form a reproach to his patronising acquiescence, 'may we perhaps make a few suggestions; to help you in this predicament? It is surely not an easy one with so many souls in your charge. I cannot quite imagine the burden.'

He nodded and I could tell in the relaxing of his expression that he was receptive of this kind of sympathetic sentiment: sympathy to *his* difficulties and yet none for those deserving of it.

She smiled and continued in those soothing accents that had a way of making any request or statement sound reasonable. 'Is there perhaps a place that could be made into a bay for the sick and only the sick? Removed from the rest of the ward? Where they might indeed be tended by the doctor and kept apart from the others?'

'We're full to the brim, ma'am, that's the rub.'

'The anteroom, sir, the one I have been previously permitted to hire on visits. Is that still vacant, as it was last?' I asked.

'Well yes, it is *Mrs* Craythorne, but it hasn't the facilities as a prison ward.'

'Perhaps not, but as a sick ward, with some basic furniture bought up to it, I think it will do well enough—no?'

'Think on it, Mr Honeyfield,' Annalise cut in again. 'I daresay it will make your load much the more bearable if it can be managed. I cannot suppose it is easy to contain so many under such circumstances.'

He looked mildly thoughtful. 'I will, Miss Tullier, you may count on it.'

'Thank you, sir. Perhaps we might get to the wards that are open before our morning is spent?' she said with that easy brightness in her face that came so naturally to her countenance.

'Thank you,' I said to Annalise when Mr Honeyfield deposited us at the upper debtors' wards. I had preferred we start our rounds here anyway before dissenting to the others, in part to break Annalise in more gently and in part to show her the contrast in comfort in which they were kept.

'What for?' she said, her brow furrowed as we walked the steps across the courtyard, this one receiving the benefit of sunlight and greater ventilation.

'For moderating me and handling Mr Honeyfield so well.'

'Well, I do know what a rage you can fly in to, and even though you were quite just in your reasoning, I thought better to stay on his right side if we want to assess the situation for ourselves.'

'Yes, quite right you are. I just cannot bear the hypocrisy. Three dead in a night and no more dust kicked up than if there were but three dead rats in the basement.'

'I know.'

'Still, I wish I had your disposition for managing it so well.' I had once had such abilities, but in opening my eyes to the truth, I had somehow cracked open so wide that such skill seemed now to evade me.

'Well, I think us better in tandem. I can play the soothing female to keep us on the inside and you can bring your clever mind and resolve to putting pressure on the magistrates on the outside. What a team we shall make,' she smiled and I permitted myself a gentle squeeze of her hand before we knocked at the first door.

'Good morning, we are from the Society and making calls today to see how you do here?' I said as brightly as I could muster to the well-turned-out gentleman who opened the door. His quarters, I noted as he invited us in, were very nicely kept. He welcomed us to take a seat on the slightly sagging sofa, which we did, whilst he sank into a well-worn armchair. The room was plain but comfortable, a window onto the courtyard letting in good light, a fire stacked but not burning on account of the clement weather I presumed. 'So, Mr Grenville,' I said, patting out my skirts, 'have you any concerns about the conditions here?'

'Conditions? No. The prices are a damned outrage though. Five shillings for a quart of ale. Daylight robbery I call it.'

I smiled. If he had any notion of what the other areas of the gaol were like, where there was no money to buy such comforts as a bed and a fire,

I was certain it might be otherwise. 'Have there been any restrictions of late, sir, on account of any sickness?'

'You mean other than my liberty? No. Not that I know of anyhow. I keep quietly enough to my papers for the most part.'

'Your papers?'

'I'm a pamphleteer, ma'am. You may be sure that if I had any complaints to make, I should certainly publish them for the world to know.'

'I see.'

'You may look them up if it suits your interests.' He crossed his legs and interlinked his hands upon his knee. 'You know I have long settled my debt that landed me here.'

I was puzzled by this. 'But why?'

'Why am I still here? Fifteen years on at that. Because these blaggards hold me to account for their extortionate fees for food and lodgings, taking my irons off, even turning keys. Although I don't go out much anymore.'

'They do?'

'Everything has a price here and they have a fairly captive market. It his hardly surprising that they make the prices up to suit them with no rivals to consider.'

'No, I suppose not.'

'And it's no use saying, as my aunt always did, that I must move into the plainer wards to stop the bills going up. I tried it you know. For all but three days. Not fit for habitation in the least.'

This much I could certainly vouch for and needed no persuasion that had I the option of dwelling here or in the alternative, which I would choose. I wanted to ask him how much his bill was with the Warden but I knew he was a man of sense and pride and had no wish to offend him. Instead, I asked, 'What sort of prices do they charge for such things here, sir?'

'Usually thrice their true value and less than half the quality or service, I always think.'

I took his answer as a wish not to converse on the details and so I pressed on. 'Well. Thank you for your time, sir. We will not keep you from your work.'

Our visits went on in much this fashion. There had been little above the ordinary to complain of in the high debtors' ward. As such, our rounds were swift, prevailing upon us to listen to a few further grumblings on the rising prices of Gin and Ale at the bar. Such were the luxuries of having means or wealthy patrons to keep your comfort. But when we descended upon the lower wards, that was when I knew the contrast would become easily apparent to Annalise.

It was at first the choking stench that took us by surprise, before the noise and chaos. Being only separated by a corridor from the ward for convicts, we could not fail to notice either as we journeyed. 'I know that smell,' Annalise said, covering her nose with the corner of her shawl and bidding me to do the same.

'Ghastly, isn't it? Even more than usual.'

'It is the smell of decay, decaying bodies, I fear.'

'You cannot mean it?' I said doubly horrified, pulling up the corner of my shawl a fraction higher.

We had not even the chance to go on towards any of the cells for as soon as we turned the corner, we were met by a wondering young lady, crying hysterically and turning in circles about the corridor.

'Are you alright?' Annalise asked her and I could see that she was rightly concerned.

'Will you let them out, miss? Will you? Have you come to free us?' she said, still pacing.

She was young, perhaps about nineteen. I could feel her distress so painfully it caught me quite off guard. 'Let who out?' I asked her gently.

'The dead ones miss. Can you smell them?'

I felt instantly nauseous. 'Are there any dead on this ward?'

'Not yet. Not yet is what they say but for how long is what I say.'

'Perhaps,' Annalise said, pressing a gentle hand at her elbow to try to calm her, 'you might show us the way back to your quarters and you can tell us more then.'

'I shall not.' She snatched her arm away and began pacing more furiously now. 'I shall not go until you unlock that door and let them out.'

'You mean the other prisoners, on that ward?' I pointed in its direction.

She nodded wide eyed and somehow begging with her gaze. 'Do you hear their cries, miss? All night they wail and scream and rattle the doors and bang their pots and nobody will let them out. They want to bury their dead. They cannot bear the smell and the flies any longer.'

I wanted to comfort her but was seized by a violence of retching and could do little more than remove a few paces and crouch at the wall in time for the waves of vomiting to engulf me. It was so violent, I could barely keep up with the raucous as the wondering prisoner renewed her wailing at the sight of me and Annalise was torn between calming us both and calling out for the warden.

By the time he was come back, I was recovering my breath and a spattering of vomit congealed upon the walls was pooling upon the flag-stones. Having given my apologies and furnished him with some coins to compensate the cleaning, we left under Annalise's insistence that it was not wise to continue on in my state of health. If I wasn't so fatigued by my spell and enraged by the prison conditions, I might have found amuse-ment in Mr Honeyfield's attempt at refusal of my coin, knowing how happy he was to extort from others who had less than I. But it was the least of my concerns.

I was still in such a fury when we returned to Grosvenor Square. La-dy W. was quite taken aback at my delivery of the news when I explained the whole. 'Forgive me,' I said more evenly now. 'I just cannot believe the apathy. Surely something can be done?' I sighed and I don't know if I had overworked my senses, for I suddenly felt quite dizzy.

'Miss?' Annalise said, taking me by the arm. 'Are you alright?'

I awoke on the chaise with Lady W. and Annalise sat upon chairs either side of me, wide eyed stares and anxious expressions.

'What is wrong?' I asked, lifting up and searching the room for a clue as to why I was here.

'You swooned my dear. Out for a good few minutes. You have given us quite a fright and poor Annalise here is convinced you have been struck down with the gaol fever.'

'Gaol fever?'

'Highly unlikely I think, since you were sick before you even set out. I wish you would have told me, Eleanor, I would have taken your place,' Lady W. said disapproving.

I darted a look across to Annalise but quickly lowered my gaze realising I could not blame her for apprising Lady W. of such details under the circumstances. 'Forgive me, I did not feel unwell at the time.'

'How are you feeling now?' Annalise cut in. I could see the distress in her eyes.

'Nothing out of the ordinary, a little fatigued perhaps.'

'Well, I think you have worked yourself up into such a temper you have quite exhausted yourself my dear,' Lady W. said, inching her chair a little closer and gesturing me to take up the cold cloth Annalise had just rung out.

'How silly of me,' I said apologetically and pressed it to my forehead. I had not meant to cause such trouble.

'Nonetheless, the doctor has been sent for and we shall have his verdict and set our minds at ease.'

'There really is no need,' I waved a hand in protest.

'Hush, we shall have our way and set our minds to rest if nothing else. Now, will I send for something to drink? You seem a little dry about the mouth.'

I accepted the offer and wondered why Lady W. did not ring the bell, but went out of the room. 'Oh, Annalise,' I turned to her now. 'Do not look so Friday-faced, my love. I do not have the gaol fever and I am certainly well. A little over excited and under hydrated perhaps, but nothing more. I should know it if I was ill,' I tried to reassure her.

'I do hope you are right,' she said, taking a pensive glance about the room and giving my hand a gentle squeeze on realising it was safe to do so.

'Of course, I am. Now, please, no more fuss. Let me see your smile again.'

When Lady W. returned, she sent Annalise on an errand of finding my bedclothes and robe and bringing me some more pillows before the doctor arrived.

'I'm sure I do not need to play the part of the invalid for the doctor's sake,' I protested.

'No, my dear, but he will want to examine you and it will be easier in your undress.'

'Very well,' I acquiesced and watched Annalise set about the task, shrinking inside at this formality that was brought to bear on us in company. I hated her being so referred to and treated as my servant, when alone we were partners in whatever duties may need tending, companions and friends through the most part, lovers by night. She was my equal and to see her so demeaned was painful to me.

When her footsteps had tapered off beyond our hearing, Lady W. leaned in and said to me with a graveness about her expression: 'Eleanor, will you have me stay with you when Dr Reeves is come?'

'Annalise can stay with me, she will not mind.'

'I do not think that a good idea my dear.'

'Whyever not?' I said incredulously, but before she could explain this peculiar notion, the doctor was announced and moments later Annalise returned with her arms piled neck high in clothes and pillows.

'Dr Reeves, perhaps you will take a cup with me whilst our patient is suitably attired?' I heard Lady W. say in the hallway.

'Can you sit up?' Annalise said, relieving herself of the pile.

'Yes, of course, I am perfectly able.' I swung my legs around.

'Slowly now,' she warned me. 'Let us not have a repeat.'

I obeyed and sat on the edge of the chaise as she instructed me, lifting clothes over my head and replacing them with night wear. 'Annalise, did Lady W. say anything to you when I was, out?'

'Only that she thought me quite mistaken and over-reacting to think you struck with the gaol fever, why?'

'No reason.'

'To own the truth, I think her a little concerned too, but perhaps too stiff faced to let on. Perhaps she didn't want to send us into a panic.'

It stood to reason, she was not the panicking type, but I had noted some serious concern in her too. Did she think I had the gaol fever? Should I be worried for my health? I was sure I had no need to be.

'Ah, are you ready my dear, for the doctor?' Lady W. came back into the room and Annalise fidgeted me about as she plumped pillows behind my back and pulled a sheet across my lap.

'Yes, I think so,' I told her, and in he came. Surprisingly, not an old puff guts of a fellow as our family doctor, but a young man, smart and serious looking, but with a kind smile and reassurance about his tone.

'Mrs Craythorne, I am Dr Reeves. I am told you have suffered an odd spell today?' he said, putting his bag upon the side table.

'Yes, doctor, although I do not think it a serious thing. I feel quite well recovered.'

'Well, that is a good sign,' he smiled, lifting the lid of his case and reaching for things I could not see inside it. 'So, is this the first time this has happened?'

I nodded.

'And you have been sick too, I'm told.'

'I must have eaten something bad,' I shrugged. 'I have a sensitivity to shelled fish.'

After a procession of irksome questions, he asked if he might examine me and as he began prodding about my neck and stretching my eyelids wide with his fingers and peering into them, Lady W. ushered Annalise out of the room and left us quite alone. *What was she about?*

'Eleanor, will you see me?' Came Lady W.'s voice as the door opened up a crack. I cleared my throat and wiped my cheeks with the sleeves of my night gown.

'Yes,' I answered her, my voice a mere whimper.

She came soundlessly into the room and sat beside me. 'It's not the worst thing, my dear.'

I frowned and lifted my head up better to see her face. 'You know?'

She nodded.

'So much for his confidence...'

'It was not the doctor, Eleanor. I suspected it from the moment your maid told me how violent sick you were this morning and how miraculously you recovered from it shortly after.'

'Forgive me,' I said more reasonably. 'I am quite out of my senses; I did not mean to speak—'

'No need for all of that, dear. Now, I take it this is the result of your dalliance with Mr Richards and not the issue of your husband?'

I nodded. It was a small mercy in the scheme of things, but one I was grateful for, for the idea of passing on Craythorne blood was abhorrent to me.

'Hmm, well, he shall not know any better unless you tell him, and I'm sure you are not so minded.'

'Lady W., he cannot find out at all. No one can know. It has been a hard-won battle to gain Edmund's allegiance in trying for a separation, and ahead, I still have the task of winning my parents. If they know of my situation, they will abandon the idea in an instant, and if Giles gets a sniff of it, well he shall know it isn't his and I do not think any amount of negotiation will contrive to bring him to a separation, and if they did...'

'You fear he would take the child from you?'

'Yes. I know it.'

'So, my dear, what will you do?'

'I hardly know, I am still taking it in; I can scarcely believe it to be true.'

'Well, perhaps you should sleep on it. It has been a long and vexing day for you, and you need your rest. Retire early, and in the morning, things may seem clearer.'

I nodded. 'How long do you think I have, before the condition will be noticed?'

'How far along did Dr Reeves think you?'

'A month or so he tells me, and my own counting back tells me about four weeks since...'

'Well, I am no expert my dear, as you know, but my guess would be some few months yet, perhaps longer still with that skilled seamstress of yours letting out your skirts.'

'She does not know, does she?'

'No. Why do you think I insisted upon leaving you alone for your examination?'

'Thank you, Lady W., you always think of everything.'

'Well, my dear, if that's what you think of my discernment, then you will take heed when I say that there is no possibility of you hiding it from her for very long.'

'You think her suspicious?'

'No. I think she is presently so relieved to know that her diagnosis of the gaol fever is without substance.'

I smiled a little at this.

'That much Dr Reeves did avail of, but the poor man hardly had a choice since she seized him in such a passion the moment he stepped out of the room.'

'What will I tell her?'

'Can you trust her?'

I nodded.

'Then you must tell her the truth, my dear, when you are ready. For you will need an ally, whatever else, and if you are certain of her, then there is no better person than your own Abigail to keep your secret and help you through it.'

I nodded again. I understood the sense in it. But how could I tell Annalise I was pregnant when I had only just won her back, when we were only just coming into each other's intimacy? This would surely change everything.

'If it is any consolation my dear, I think, from the little I have seen of her, that she holds your confidence in close regard and has an ardent concern for you.'

'She does,' I agreed and wished once more, to take the opportunity to confess all.

'Well hang on to her, won't you? Her care of you seems to have done you the world of good.'

'Yes. She has become something of a friend to me.' Something so sacred the thought of anything jeopardising it was inconceivable.

So, when she came into the room upon Lady W.'s departure from it, bursting in with anxious questions, I lost my nerve and waved them off.

'Likely the crab, the aversion of my constitution to the stuff. Apparently, the very exposure of it can be enough in some, to invoke such reactions.'

'Is he certain?'

'He is quite certain. I am perfectly well,' I said with my best effort, and I loathed the hearing of my own lies, the taste of them on my lips as I watched relief fall over her face.

The next morning, however, I woke in precisely the same manner, which did nothing to alleviate either of our anxieties. There was no crab to blame since I had taken only the thinnest of broth last eve, and I knew that my explanation that it was simply my body still trying to purge the contamination from me, would not last out beyond the day. I would have to find a way to break the news to her. Although it seemed the task grew increasingly monumental with each passing hour, each new lie I had to conjure in answer to the last. I should have just given her the truth at the time. Now it seemed impossible to broach it.

Since the doctor had forbade me return to the gaol in my condition with the threat of a fever about it, our plans for the rest of the week were now set asunder and I was resigned to putting to paper my complaints to the magistrate of the gaol and demands for sickly prisoners to be tended in the proper way. This, at least, we had from Lady W. who attended that afternoon to make her own enquiries with Mr Honeyfield, was confirmed. The gaol surgeon had been at last called and confirmed by way of rashes upon the skin, it was indeed the gaol fever afflicting these poor creatures. Some medicines had been instructed for them and upon applying enough pressure on the surgeon, Lady W. had managed to convince him to instruct Honeyfield to have the sickly prisoners moved to a makeshift ward with better ventilation and bid the Society volunteers cook up regular servings of broth and vegetables for them to strengthen their resilience.

This eased my mind a little, and once I had powdered and sealed the last of my letters—I had also undertaken the task of sending out an express to all the Society ladies in attendance of the gaol, to warn them of the recent epidemic, that they may take care with their own health—I got up and stretched. I considered we must not continue in such melancholy and idling and get out of the house. If Annalise could find a journey to Southwark entertaining, then I was certain she would delight in a visit to some of London's greater spectacles.

Confessions.

November 1821. - Eleanor.

We spent a happy morning walking down through St. James' park and over Westminster bridge to enjoy the viewing point from there to Westminster Hall, then back over to see the Abbey. Then I took her to Pall Mall to show her Carlton House, although we did not apply to go in. Then when it begun to rain as we left it, we headed for Old Bond Street to see the water colour exhibition and take shelter.

I had found myself unusually fatigued by this little exercise and was quite fit to go home and slump in a chair for the afternoon. To have the sick bowl to hand too seemed a welcome prospect, for though I had not vomited yet today, I had felt such dizzying nausea during most of our outing. I did my best to hide it from her, not least of all for not wanting to spoil her enjoyment. She was bursting with enthusiasm for everything we had done so far and everything we might yet do before the day was out.

It was this insatiable intrigue that induced me to agreeing to make a dash for the British Museum to catch the last entry. We hired a hack to take us there for I had not another ounce of energy in me and wondered still how I would manage all the stairs in the place. But I dug deep and triumphed over the first steps up to the vestibule. She was excited to see the Hans Sloane collections and I had a mind to see the manuscript gallery for I was sure they had a copy of the Magna Carta document there, and all the law books I had been reading from made ample reference to it.

I was just seeking the guidance from one of the curators on the direction of it when I heard my name.

'Mrs Craythorne, it is you.'

'Mr Richards,' I said, forcing a smile. The timing could not be more ill for such a reunion.

'How are you?' he said with a tenderness in his eyes I wished he would not give away so earnestly and in public.

'Well, sir, and yourself?' I said, perfunctory in my tone.

'Good, I am glad to hear it. It has been a while since I have seen you.'

'Yes, yes it has. I have of late returned to the country for the most part. I am arrived here but two days since.'

'I see. Are you in town for long on this visit?'

'A few more days, but dreadful crammed they are.'

Annalise shot me an incredulous look and I knew she had noted the exaggeration since our diary had now become in part annulled with the gaol outbreak. 'Miss Tullier, this is Mr Richards, a musician of great mastery.'

'Pleased to make your acquaintance, Miss Tullier.' He tapped his hat in her direction and she offered him a small curtsey.

'I own I am surprised to find you still in London, sir. I had thought you had a mind to remove a while.'

'It is true, I did. But—and I have you in part to thank for my recent good fortune—I have recently been contracted to give a concert at Buckingham House.'

Even I could not keep the joy from my eyes at this happy news. 'Mr Richards, this is quite excellent! I am so much pleased for you, for you certainly are worthy of such a place. How good to have your talents so justly recognised at last. But pray, tell me, why you credit me with such assistance?'

'Thank you, Mrs Craythorne. Your faith in me does me credit. It was through your efforts in introducing me to Lady D' Whittaker-Hollingford, that begun the connection.'

'Oh? How so?'

'She had made mention of me to one of her acquaintances who were in need of a last-minute musical soiree in which she offered the recommendation. Of course, I could not know that amongst the guests would be the Countess Greville, who also did me the kindness of inviting me to Spencer House where the King himself was guest of honour. I since seem to be wanted in more places than I could hope to undertake. So, I thank you.'

'You must not thank me for what you yourself have rightly earned, Mr Richards, but I am so much pleased for your turn of fortune.' I looked into those deep brown eyes of his, smiling at me as they did and for a moment, remembered: *I am to have your child. God knows I should be able to tell you, but it will do no good for anyone to know the fact.*

'I will also play at Lansdowne next week for Lord Petty, will you be there? I believe the Princess to be in attendance.'

Annalise's eyes brightened at the mention.

'I am sure I have had no invitation and I do not expect to receive one.'

'Well, if you would like it, I am certain I can procure your entry and yours too Miss Tullier should you fancy it.'

'Oh, Mr Richards, you know I do not expect such favours.'

'It would be nice to know you amongst the audience since it was made possible by you.'

I swallowed hard whilst I figured out how I might politely decline his offer. It was too much difficult to be in his company; knowing him the father of my child and Annalise not being wise to the true nature of our acquaintance. I glanced at her and saw how her expression seemed fit to erupt with the prospect of such an invitation. She had a misplaced regard for the royal family, thinking them quite the thing, when I knew they were little different from the rest of us but with more pomp and privilege than they deserved.

She was too polite and proper to interject, and yet her countenance told me how fervently she wished my answer be, yes. 'Thank you,' I said at last. 'Mr Richards, it would indeed be an honour to come, if of course it is no trouble for you to take pains over our admission.'

The pair of them were smiling widely at me. 'Excellent. I will send word to you at?'

'Grosvenor Square.'

Annalise, who I was grateful had her head in such a spin at the possibility of attending such a highbrow affair, had not much noticed how distracted I was for the remainder of the afternoon, and I was glad of it. For as we continued our tour of the museum, and stopped at Gunter's for ices on the way back, I could not put from my mind the growing reality of my calamity. It would have been enough to take in news of such gravity as becoming a mother so unexpectedly. But the complications of the pending separation I was determined to win, and the child being fathered by Richards and Annalise not knowing any of it: It begun to weigh ever heavier on my conscience and yet with it, the prospect of confessing it, became ever more implausible.

When Richards had bid us farewell, she had asked me how I knew him and remarked upon his fondness and generosity to me. It would have been a perfect opportunity to explain our past acquaintance and yet I brushed away her questions with such vagaries that even as I spoke them I regretted them.

I looked across to her; she was spooning the last of her ice, the sunlight setting her golden hair in a shimmer, her eyes seeming a shade lighter in its glare. *Tell her.* I dared myself. Just do it and it will be over with, I demanded. *No more deceit.* I had become such a skilled liar these past months that I wondered if I had acquired a talent and propensity for it. And yet at last I wished to be true and earnest with someone so completely, it seemed I did not know how. Or at least, that I was too much fearful of her being so disappointed in me if I confessed such misdemeanours, her feelings might be altogether altered. I could not bear to lose her, not again.

'Annalise...'

She turned to me and shaded her eyes with a hand cupped across her forehead. We were sat in the gardens of Berkeley Square. I had no wish to prevail upon the staff again after having so recently inconvenienced them with impromptu visits, nor did I want to risk running into my father, but I wanted to show her the family house whilst we were in its proximity.

'Yes?' she said.

'I...' I could not find the words. 'I want to tell you something, but I am afraid I don't quite know how,' I began.

Her expression changed and she put down her ice. 'Eleanor, whatever it is, just say it.'

I nodded but once again found the words evasive.

'Eleanor, you are frightening me, whatever is it that causes such a graveness to your expression?'

'I'm sorry, I—' this time it was not simply a lack of words that interrupted me, but a familiar stirring of nausea that flourished in my cheeks and sent me giddy. The flavour of the ice had seemed to suddenly turn sour on my tongue and it was all I could do to leap from the bench and rush to a bed of Dahlias to expel the contents of my stomach into it. I had been so desperate not to make a mess along the neat path I held my hand over my mouth until it came gushing through my fingers. Parmesan flavoured slush regurgitated.

'My god, Eleanor,' Annalise said, finding a handkerchief for me to wipe down with. 'You are sick. I mean, it is not just the crab, is it?' she said accusingly as I pulled my gloves from my hands and shook off the worst of the mess.

'I mean to explain it,' I said, looking about me, to see if there was anyone around to notice this grotesque display. Finding no one beyond a parked carriage on the street, partially concealed by the shrubbery, I let out a sigh of relief at that.

'It is the gaol fever, isn't it?'

'No. Listen, there is no need for hysteria. I closed my eyes a moment. 'Let us sit down again and I will tell you.'

She pulled me quickly on to the bench. 'Pray, I am so much concerned now, just tell me.'

'Then you must promise me something first.'

Annalise frowned. 'What?'

'Promise me, you will not despise me as I so despise myself. I couldn't bear it.'

'Eleanor, you are scaring me. Of course, I would never despise you. Now I beseech you, for heaven's sake, speak plainly.'

I reached for her hand before I continued, 'The doctor...he said that I am not at all unwell... He said that I am with child.'

'You are?' I saw her eyes glaze over with bewilderment.

'Yes, I am still adjusting to the news myself.'

'Well, I suppose it must be expected when you are recently married.'

I could see in her eyes, her turning over of the fact that I had been so intimate elsewhere and I hated the injury of it. The very thought of someone else laying their hands upon her beautiful body was enough to bring me to nausea once more. The memory of her kiss with Will, after all this time, still made me as mad as fire if I allowed myself to dwell upon it. And yet these things were nothing, nothing to account at all in comparison to what she must now be thinking. 'I disappoint you with this news. I am so much sorry.'

She squeezed my hand gently. 'Don't be sorry, Len. I am not disappointed. I am relieved to know you are not suffering some deadly malady.'

It warmed me when she called me that. I had noticed how she used this in our more intimate moments. She had taken it from my nephew's pronunciation of my name: "Lelanor". 'You are not upset with me then?'

'How can I be? You are a married woman and it is the most natural progression that you might bear a child. I own I had not thought of it since you have been so much apart from your husband, but...'

Here again came my opportunity to offer the rest of the story. 'I, I haven't been entirely honest with you, Annalise—about my husband.'

She wrinkled her brow.

'I am trying to seek a separation from him, negotiate an official agreement.'

'I see.'

'You know I do not love him and you know him responsible for my state that night. But you do not know that he has subjected me to some quite monstrous treatment, that I confess, I have not the stomach to recount the details of just now...'

'Oh, Eleanor,' she said, her eyes glazing over with tears, her hand holding firm in my own.

'I was too ashamed to tell you, forgive me.'

'My love, there is nothing to forgive and nothing for you to feel ashamed of. By god, I hope you succeed in this agreement, for I do not think I could bear to think of... My goodness, Eleanor; does he know of your condition?'

'No. And you see why he cannot.'

She nodded. 'He will demand you go back.'

'He will use the child to bind me to him and if I refuse to return, when the child is born, he will surely take it from me.'

'Oh, I wish you had not tried to bear this alone. It is too much horrid to conceive of.'

'So, you see, I must find a way to conceal this from everyone, although I shan't be able to manage it forever.'

'Hush, your mind runs away with you. Pray, for now, you can conceal the fact. I had not a clue and I have seen you unclothed. So, I think we have a little time to think on it.'

'We? Does that mean you won't abandon me?'

'How could you even think it possible? Len, I do not know what lies ahead and I cannot give you assurances that are not mine to give, but I tell you this in earnest; I shall never leave you, unless ever you should wish it, that is, and I hope such a day as that will never come.'

I gushed with tears of relief to hear these words. *Could I love you anymore?* I was close to forgetting us in public view, my heart swelling at her words as I took them in like salve, leaning into her, ready to scoop her up against me. I was only called to order by the notice of that nanny I had so often seen here, coming into the park with the toddlers running at her side. *Not here.* Richards would have to wait too. I was not about to spoil things now, feeling so much more at ease. 'I think we must go back,' I said, a gentle tug at her elbow as I looped my arm in hers.

'Yes, let us get you cleaned up and some ginger tea I think, will be just the thing.'

My confession eased things greatly in the coming days. Seized by so much sickness, it would have been quite impossible to keep it from her anyhow. Why I had ever thought I should seemed ridiculous to me now, and I wondered why I had been reluctant to take her into my confidence before. She knew more of my secrets than anyone, and yet there was still so many secrets I had yet to confess.

But I was not ready for those yet. They lurked in uncomfortable shadows that I feared would disturb our bliss. I had never known such happiness. It seemed impossible that I could love her anymore and yet our growing intimacy seemed to provoke another space inside me to open up and accommodate even deeper regard for her. Every time she bought me steaming cups of ginger tea that I complained at drinking for the pungent taste, every time she dabbed a handkerchief at the corner of my mouth as I finished retching, I saw it in her eyes, the earnest care, the love that had never been declared in words but spoken in these small acts and others that were not so small anymore.

Where I feared my condition, or at least the means by which it had come about, might make her flinch at such intimacy as we had of late been used to sharing, it had instead proved quite the contrary. The pace of such explorations had so much accelerated I was dizzy with anticipation every waking moment. We had become so fervent and impassioned in these moments, shedding the reluctance we had first been regulated by. Now I had shown her what delights her body was capable of producing, she took to the task of extricating such responses from my own. It was for the most part an easy undertaking, for I was so sensitive to her, that even tender caresses rendered me easily undone.

This night, I did not know how I might manage it, but I was determined to bring some new delight to her senses. I had spent the day considering how it might be done, what was still yet left to discover. So, when I glanced across to her, sat upon the dressing stool, untying the ribbons of her stockings, I put down my hairbrush and went over to her.

'Such impatience?' she said as I came behind her and began pressing kisses at her neck, my palms sliding beneath the neckline of her chemise.

'I have been patient all day,' I told her between kisses, seeing in the mirror her breasts exposed now, the ribbons slack and gaping at her décolleté. She had beautiful breasts, just the right measure full and pert and they seemed to fall at the most flattering angle when released from the support of her stays. Just the sight was enough to stir me to longing and despair. I watched her chest heave with the deepening of her breath as I run gentle palms over the expanse of them. Her head lolled back against me, her throat exposed, her face hidden in a mass of blonde tresses. I came around the stool to face her and knelt at her feet, kissed her on the mouth as I wrapped my arms around her to bring her closer to me, edging in between her thighs until I felt them pressed about my waist.

I cradled her in my arms as she leant back to steady herself on the corners of the stool, offering up her nipples to my ready mouth as her back arched. I meant to devour her tonight, not just in usual way, as I trailed my kisses from her breasts to her abdomen. I did not take my hand to her. Instead, I used them to push her thighs apart a fraction to allow my kisses from her knees to the crease of her inner thigh and it was then, when I felt the wet warmth of her brush against my cheek, the idea came to me. So natural a progression it seemed, where once the idea had filled me with anxiety, so depraved an act I had considered it before—the stuff of gentleman's books and fantasies—but tonight I was hungry to please her in all ways I had at my disposal. So, when she began panting and writhing at the proximity in which I edged towards the crevice of skin that demarcated the flesh of her thigh and the soft fuzz of hair at its border, I did not shy away from it. I willed myself on. Stretched out my tongue and took it to her deepest folds.

In barely a flick, she let out a gasp so loud and full of surprise. I went instantly back to taste again the salty sweet warmth of her. *Another gasp.* A wisp of hair tickling my nose as I sucked her into my mouth completely and teased the folds of her flesh until I found a rhythm that caused such jolts and shunting of her body against my face, I could barely breathe for its enthusiasm. *Oh, my darling, how good it is to know you so intimately, to know the very taste of you.*

I hooked my arms around her thighs to better control her thrusting. One moment teasing her with light strokes and flicks with the very tip of my tongue, the next drawing in every fold of her and suckling on it until she fought against me, fidgeting and lifting herself from the stool like a circus acrobat. *Groans, deep throated and promising imminent climax.*

Light strokes: tormented sighs and whimpers, her body relenting in its seizure momentarily. My face buried in increasing slickness, sucking her in: the seizure ensuing once more, the muscles of her thighs tense and heavy in my arms as I steadied her attempts to lift her bottom from the stool whilst maintaining my mouth so tight pressed against her as she fidgets and thrusts into the air.

'Oh Len...my god...how you torture me,' comes her breathy complaint as I slow.

I want to look up and see her face. I can picture it in my mind: flushed red and glowing, a strand of her golden hair caught upon the corner of her mouth, her eyes bleary slits rolling in and out of consciousness. But I dare not move. She is close now and whilst I want to toy with the final coaxing, I do not want to interrupt its beautiful flow. I can taste this flow upon my tongue. I am drinking her into me and this strange notion, of something of hers being inside of me, my body ingesting her essence, it delights me.

The limits of our sex have prevented me from thinking it possible to be inside of one another as I have so much longed, but now, a tiny fragment, a mere few drops of her is within me, somewhere, and I want more still: more of her inside of me, however we might manage it. Then as she pants more fervently and wriggles so forcefully, I must make a concerted effort to hold her still, I consider that I want also to be inside of her and release her left thigh, so I can find that tender place to slip my fingers in as I keep pace with her freer movement against my face.

'Oh...Oh... Len...do not deny me, hold fast..' she says as I am tempted to make another teasing decrescendo.

It is enough to prevent me. I can hear such desperation in her voice, breaking over the words she struggles to construct in her willowy breathless tones. It would be cruel to push her this far when I have never yet seen her so unbridled. Near violence in her movements as she gathers up a fistful of my hair and holds my face against her. I could suffocate with the obstinacy she grinds her hips against me and the firmness of her hand upon my skull, but I don't care. The only thing I can think of is how I have managed to reduce her to such depravity and desperation, and how intent I am to complete the task.

So, I work my aching arm with determined vigour, matching that which she impresses upon me in her erratic movements, and thrust my tongue along her folds with such repetition I must soon have a stiff and aching neck, strain the muscle of my tongue. But it is working in symphony: a lick inching her back, a thrust of my hand slamming her down upon it, and as I exhaust myself with this routine, my cheeks so wet they slide and slip and make my task more arduous than before, I feel the waves rippling through from her deepest core, a rumbling like distant thunder, inaudible and yet through some vibratory language I feel it coming.

Then in breaks of the slapping of her thigh flesh at my cheeks, I hear the primordial groaning ensue. I move with her lifting and jerking, steadfast in my task until I feel her pour into me, more fragments of herself, her movements relenting into steady gallops then jutting shunts, before falling away entirely.

Her legs limp now upon the stool, her pale flesh spread flat, her elbows bowing with the effort to hold herself up on it.

I smile at her now, sitting back upon my heels. She's a wild and beautiful mess and it thrills me to watch her recovering from what I have laboured to bring about.

She catches my eye and smiles back, 'I love you, Len,' she tells me then. I think tears might come forth as I take in her words. I had felt the words, but had not yet heard them, and it paralysed me a moment, before I returned them to her, bought her down to the floor with me in a tumble of kisses, undressing us both fully in the pauses. Wrapping up our limbs in each other's and rolling upon the rug. Flesh sliding and slipping as I glide my body up and down the length of hers, until it all becomes too much, and I slide a leg out at an angle, half hovering in the air, that allows me to press my delicate parts against hers, until the warmth and wetness of this union shocks us both and we share a glance; surprise and then delight at this new discovery.

I hold onto her calf and begin to build a rhythm, kissing the pale flesh of her ankle until I find it; it is tricky at first, to manoeuvre in such a way, reshuffling and twisting our bodies until they yield; it takes our joint collaboration to bring it about. But after a few fails and blunders, we work it out, find the motion that brings relief, and I am bouncing now, upon her and against her, in much the way Richards had bounced me upon his own lap. I look down at her as I move back and forth, up and down. Beauty, such beauty it was almost too much to behold.

Upon her elbows she holds her body, a twist at the waist to entwine with mine, her breasts lolling with the motion we are building, her hair trailing and heaping upon the pile of the rug, her eyes fixed upon mine, delight dancing in them. She is watching me, taking in the sight with concentration, making a study of the way I rock and writhe upon her, letting out involuntary sighs here and there, but refusing to draw her eyes away from me.

She conveys such longing and passion through them that I can hardly believe it is meant for me, so engrossed she seems, to behold me. I recognise it, for it is the way I feel, making such a study of her. Taken. In entirety. Possessed by her. Unable to look away even though my consciousness is slipping from my grasp, taking me into raptures and universes beyond this one.

I forget myself. I forget the house I am in and the people within it. I am moaning with such volume she has to press a finger to her lips to remind me of the fact. But it is too late. I am trembling now, my body jerking and shuddering in a rhythm I have no command over. It is the wisdom of my body itself that holds the reins and directs such erratic and determined motion. It knows how it must best satiate its longings and brings it about in any which way it must find.

And the sighs and near screams at the peak of it that escape me, are not mine to command either now—they too have been taken over. The sounds are distant, as if I'm under water; I can hear them, but from some other place. Then I hear her voice, the reckless ramblings I can't make out as I ride the last waves of my own eruption. Slowing. Rocking gently now as I watch her final collapse upon the Persian wool, no longer on her elbows, her face the centrepiece of a corn-coloured nest of hair, chin turned up to me, mouth open, clutching for breath.

I kiss the flesh of her calf before climbing off of her, my hips aching now, my legs reluctant to refashion themselves as though moulded and set into this new shape and they tremble as I force them to alter, crawling upon my hands and knees to lay down next to her. I hear my heart pound against the floorboards as I sink upon the rug and wiggle myself into the crook of her elbow.

'Eleanor!' she cries and I start from the alteration of her tone, the urgency in it.

'What?' I say, lifting up my head, but she is already scrambling up from the floor.

'Someone is coming, don't you hear?' she says, gathering up clothes from about her, panic set across her flushed face.

'No,' I tell her, but following suit, picking up discarded stockings and ribbons and searching about me for my Pegnoir.

'I hear footsteps,' she whispers, and I hear them too at last.

'Mrs Craythorne?' The door begins to rattle in its frame as it is pounded with an urgency that confirms my fears: *We have been heard.*

'Yes?' I say as nonchalantly as I can contrive to. 'Go into the dressing room,' I mouth to Annalise and tie my belt about my waist, opening the door just a crack.

'Is everything alright, ma'am?' Bradshaw says to me, her brows knitted, her glance lingering over my shoulder to see better into the room.

'Yes. Quite well thank you, Bradshaw.'

'You are certain? We did hear a terrible raucous. I was sure I heard screaming. Lady W. thought someone was being murdered up here!'

I feigned a laugh, convincing enough I thought it. 'Oh that,' I said, hearing the latch of the dressing room door close softly behind me and opening up the door wide to let her in to the room. 'Would you believe, there is a monstrous big spider that I am certain means to taunt me. I was just finishing up my toilette and my maidservant screams, noticing it rush out from beneath the washstand. I too scream in response and see it dash across the rug with such haste it was all I could do to hop onto the stool until it was out of sight!'

'Oh,' she said, hand pressed to her chest, relief washing over her, a smile turning up the corners of her mouth. 'Thank goodness. I was scared what I might discover with you being so recent unwell.'

'Forgive me for distressing you, I should have had a care but I—well, you know how a fit of panic can seize you when you are not expecting it. Silly really, it is only a spider after all, but I cannot persuade myself to bear them well.'

'No, indeed, ma'am. I own, the spiders do not much provoke me, but if I see a rat, well...'

'Heaven forbid.'

'Would you like me to look for it?' she offered, searching the room with a narrow gaze and I was pleased to see that everything appeared to be in good order. The bed still made up and the uncleared clutter about the washstand corroborating my story.

'You are very kind, Bradshaw, not to mention brave, but I think it has long since scarpered to some crevice along the skirting.' I pointed.

'Very well, miss.'

'Thank you, Bradshaw. You will give Lady W. my apologies for the disturbance. I should hate to interrupt her further at such an hour.'

'I will, miss. She is herself to bed, so I shall pass it on.'

'Goodnight, Bradshaw,' I said, closing the door behind her and resting my forehead against it a second as I at last let out a sigh. *That was close: too close!*

Discretion.

November 1821. - Eleanor.

When I rose the next morning, I found Lady W. hosting a society meeting in her breakfast room. It consisted of only half a dozen of the society ladies, the majority of them senior ones from what I could tell catching sight of Mrs Baxter at her side. 'Come in, dear, join us. We have only just started out,' Lady W. beckoned me, breaking her address to the group at my lurking in the doorway.

I found an empty chair and settled to it. It seemed this was something of an emergency meeting called in the wake of the gaol fever outbreak and I realised then why I had not known about it before.

There was talk of the death toll now being at eleven, most of them infants and the hospital ward now at capacity and having no other notion of what might be done to prevent the wards being locked down again. There was a great deal of talk about petitioning members of parliament and ministers about the situation and a general consensus it would likely take too long to go about it that way and half the prisoners would be likely already sick—or worse, dead—by such a time.

'Perhaps then, we might make appeal to the chief justice to have all prisoners who are awaiting trial or transportation to be released, an amnesty of sorts, so the sick can be well cared for and the others spared from falling so,' suggested Mrs Carter.

Lady W. nodded, 'Yes, that might be worth the trying for, although I think a transfer might be more realistic. I propose we try for release and prepare to be negotiated down to transfers, but yes, that route might certainly prove quicker.'

'Do we know the number, Miss Carter; of those categories of prisoner, so we might understand the impact on the overcrowding?'

'Let me check my notes, Mrs Baxter,' she said, reaching down to her leather satchel slumped beside her on the floor and fiddling through her papers. 'W'argh,' she screamed suddenly and jumped out of her chair so fitfully I thought something terrible had happened. I caught her chair as it fell back since I was sat beside her and watched her dancing about in fantastic style.

'Spider!' she said. 'In my satchel.'

My sigh of relief was shared by the rest of the table and I said: 'Shall I find it for you, Miss Carter?'

'Oh, yes please. I had a frightful notion it had crawled up my sleeve but thankfully I think it's still in there.'

'Alright,' I said picking up her satchel and moving it away from the table entirely to prevent another spectacle if it should run out in her direction. I tipped it onto the carpet and papers scattered all about it. But after waiting for some horrific tarantula sized beast to rush out at me, nothing came. So, I looked back into it and found an average looking house spider clinging to a corner of the lining. 'Will someone get the window for me?' I asked and when Lady W. stood and opened one behind her, I scooped it up in cupped hands and dropped it onto the window ledge and closed it.

'Oh, thank you, Mrs Craythorne,' said Miss Carter, recovering her papers from the floor and looking more collected now. 'You are ever so brave.'

'Indeed,' Lady W. said with a gleam in her eye. 'How swiftly you have mastered your phobia. You must tell me your secret some time: I am ghastly afraid of wasps.'

I chuckled at this but only to hide the horror that would have otherwise been apparent. 'To be sure,' I said lightly. But it had took less than half a second's breath for me to understand my faux pas. The excuse I had given Bradshaw of a spider causing the raucous from my room. *Damn it!* What a fool I had been to try to gull Lady W. of all people. Of course, I had only done so in a moment of panic, but what else was I to say? *Sorry, Bradshaw, was our love making too loud? Please give your mistress my apologies, we'll have a care to be quieter next time.*

Oh, I hated to keep such a secret from her. I had took her entirely into my confidence in every other matter, however intimate, however shameful, she had the measure, except in this one. This I felt cornered by, unwilling to disclose the details and yet struggling to keep them from her notice, loathing myself for the deceit. It was painful withholding and yet the prospect of confession seemed impossible. What could I expect her to say upon such an admission? Oh, that explains your recent change of spirits? Congratulations? I pressed my palms against my face and sighed. *I'm sorry, Lady W. Truly. If there was anyone I would dare to confide in, it would be you.*

But I could not have my dearest friend in disgust over what must surely be seen as an unnatural attachment. And how could I convince her that it was not? That if she understood just how perfectly we went along, how easily we supported each other, comforted each other, how deep our regard; she would too understand it a most natural thing after all.

Once the coaches had been called and the teacups cleared and it was just me and her left sat about the table, a silence falling upon it now, where only moments ago it was alive with the hum and clatter, I instantly felt uncomfortable.

She was at liberty, if she so wished, to demand a private explanation of the spider excuse; and I too was afforded the opportunity to volunteer such an explanation whether she sought it or not. I fiddled with a straying thread at the corner of the tablecloth and stared into the pattern of it. It reminded me of a habit of Lizzy, our childhood pet dog, who would often hide her face beneath a table or sofa when she had been up to some mischief, as if her being unable to see us was akin to us being unable to see her there, despite her large shaggy body stretched out upon the floor in plain sight. This logic seemed momentarily to have rubbed off on me, absurd as it was. 'Lady W.,' I said eventually when the silence grew too loud and prickly for me to continue feigning a daydream.

She was sat peering up at the mantle and slid her gaze towards me. 'Yes, my dear?'

I was relieved to find her smiling, that comforting easy smile I was familiar with. 'I feel that I owe you an apol—'

'My Alfred,' she interjected, glancing back up to the mantle and only now I realised the focus of her stare: A portrait hanging above it of a young and handsome looking gentleman. I did not ever think to ask who was in the portrait since houses such as these were full of exhibitions of such ancestral ghosts. It was one of the few things I disliked about Cuddington: the vastness of the place afforded so much more wall space for the hanging of such portraits.

Art in the form of landscapes or scenes, I had a great fondness for, but portraits of ancestors long since departed I had never grown comfortable with, despite a lifetime of their oil painted eyes following me up staircases and through corridors as I passed them and staring at me as I supped across the dining room table. As a child I would often run past a few I found particularly curious or disturbing. "There is nothing to be frightened of, it is but your great, great, great uncle Frederick," Mama or Delores might say as if this unknown and long since buried relative being bought into context might dispel the shivers that crept over me upon the sight of it.

'It is the anniversary of his death today,' she said then and drew me back into the present.

'Oh, Lady W. I am sorry, I did not know.'

'How could you? I am not sad, only grateful.'

'For the time you had together?'

'Yes, and for knowing such a man.'

I smiled with her. 'It sounds like you were very fortunate in your husband. You must have been very happy.'

'I was fortunate. Of course, at the time I did not really understand just how fortunate I was and we had only a couple of years together and they were not particularly happy ones, although there were happy moments.'

'That seems so terribly short. For a happy marriage I mean. Unjust that such a match should be cut short.'

'You mean when bad ones seem often to have such longevity?'

I nodded. 'Was you in love with Alfred before you wed, or did it come later?'

'Alfred and I were never in love. But we had a gentle regard and a great deal of fondness betwixt us.'

I was stunned to hear this. It seemed absurd she would ponder on his memory with such reminiscence and after so many decades of his absence, if they were not even in love.

'I shock you, I think.'

'I confess I had assumed yours to be a love match, given your choice to remain unmarried all these years.'

'Yes, many think as much—the long-suffering loyal widow—and I am happy to let them think what they choose. I was indeed a young widow and I have certainly been made enough offers since that I might have taken at least a dozen husbands over the years if I had wished it. Not that I flatter myself that my fortune wasn't to blame for at least half of the applicants.'

'Then what prevented your accepting them, if not for your husband's regard?'

'Independence, my dear. Something so sorely lacking amongst our sex it seemed a stupid thing to consider giving up, since fate had dealt me it at such a youthful age, however unfortunate it was in coming about.'

'Yes. I see the sense in that.' Indeed, I would have guarded mine more carefully if I knew what I know now. 'But, if you were of such an inclination, then I hope you will not mind me asking: whatever induced you to marry in the first place if you were in favour of your independence and not in love?'

'I was young, I did as bid. Alfred seemed a good choice—admittedly, our marriage was such a short one, we had hardly begun to know each other well, so who's to say how it might have gone. By the time of our first anniversary, we had not long come past the awkwardness of sharing a bed together and being at ease in each other's company. You know how it is to begin with. And remember, in the days of my youth, there was none of this protest on romantic grounds; we were betrothed with little care for argument and we had sat around a dinner table and danced a set perhaps only thrice before taking our vows. We were as good as strangers on our wedding day and these things take time to overcome.'

'Yes,' I nodded my agreement, remembering the horror of my own wedding night with a wince.

'But I was certain enough that Alfred was the type of man I could one day come to love, in earnest. Not because any particular romance had blossomed, even by then. The sad amount of miscarriages I had within weeks of finding out the news had not left much room in my mind for romantic thoughts...although it did encourage a tenderness of understanding between us, I think.'

'I'm sorry, I did not know.'

'It was not meant to be and I have long since made my peace with the fact. Anyway, Alfred was a good man, a rare type amongst our set and I know I can say that to you without being misunderstood.'

I nodded. 'What was he like?'

A mist of reminiscence hung over her a moment before she smiled and turned back to me. 'Honest and good. That is my most pertinent memory of him. Of course, five and forty years is a long time for such things to fade about the edges. He was not extraordinary in looks, as you see,' she pointed at the portrait.

'I see a kindness in his features, a brightness in his smile.'

'Yes, and I thought well enough of him, for it was his character that shone through. Not that everyone could see the gift in it: he was a sad disappointment to his father as he had paved the way for him to make a career in politics. But he never could have been a success. His heart was far too big, his sense of decency and justice far too entrenched to be suited to such tasks, although he did make a try, for his family's sake but... Well, if he had not, he might still be here today—'

'What do you mean?'

'Come, Eleanor, you are not green. You come from an ambitious line yourself. Your father in the Lords, your mama presiding over Almack's applications.'

'Corruption?'

'Indeed. But Alfred wasn't corruptible you see, and there is no place for such virtues in *that* world. In fact, I believe it a prerequisite that you must be quite without virtue altogether to be involved in such a charade as a government at all, don't you agree?'

I did agree. I had never understood why such a thing was so called. I had studied my Latin with enough diligence to make the connection, although I suspected my understanding to be much more ignorant of the scale of it than her own. 'So did Alfred step down from these engagements?'

'He tried, love him. But his family were determined to keep their influence and his father was growing too old and too marred by gout to hold his seat any longer. So, he went along with it a while to appease him. But he was not like his family, not a bit. In fact, he was so singularly irregular I am not sure how he was bred from such a family at all. I have never met anyone like him since.'

I smiled at this, because now the image of his character was becoming clearer in my mind. I realised just how similar her description of Alfred was to how I might describe her if I was asked to, and it seemed suddenly so sad to me that they were parted so early, for even though they were not in love, they surely would have blossomed so very naturally into each other's hearts, being so much of the same mind. 'He sounds very special to me, if you will not mind me saying so.'

She nodded. 'He was; at least, that's always how I saw him. Sadly, he did not place votes in the House of Lords the way he was told he must and he upset a lot of people, the wrong sort of people, and he was always a black sheep amongst his family and amongst the ton after that. They seemed to consider the very things I thought marked him out as special as the very things that bought them shame and disappointment. His father was always telling him he was "too soft", and yet he was quite the opposite in my mind, for it takes a great deal more strength and courage to stand up to and apart from the status quo, don't you think?'

'Yes, it is a lonely path I think, that only the strongest may tread.'

'Well, that's what he did—much good that it did him—and whatever they did to try to cover it up, I know it was that which got him killed, for I shall never believe in the accounts they gave to me of him having that accident; he was too good a rider.'

I saw a glistening of tears at her eyes and felt suddenly deeply bereft for her. 'You think he was murdered?'

She nodded and dabbed a corner of her handkerchief to her eye.

'Good grief. It is too dreadful to take in.'

'I did try to push for greater investigations at the time, but I was young then and much more easily frightened into acquiescence than I have ever been since. So, I did not pursue it nearly as fervently as I wished I had, even though I had an idea of who was to blame, but no proper evidence of it.'

I did not wish to press her although I felt the questions burning on my lips.

'Anyway, it was all a very long time ago now and we have digressed.'

'Yes. And yet I fear that some things, such things as these have not much changed amongst our class.'

'Well, my dear, you and I come from a, shall we say, a class of persons who are not much minded for changing their ways, even when they are in dire need of reforming them.'

I nodded, understanding her better than I wished. For however much I had been made to feel so much ashamed and irregular these past months, the truth and the irony was, that I was so much ashamed of them. Their selfish, shallow, self-indulgent ways that they were blind to. The wilful ignorance. The lack of empathy.

'So, you see, I never had a mind to re-marry, for I knew there would never be another like Alfred. Men like that are near to non-existent in our circles and my family would never have permitted me marry outside of such circles.'

'Was there ever anyone you wished to marry but did not?'

'No, and I am glad of the fact for I know few women that have been as fortunate and satisfied with their lot as I have. Of course, there were times I felt loneliness and envy—in my younger days moreso. But I did not go without...companionship.'

'You did not?' I was quite astonished to hear such a confession.

'Why my dear, of course not. I daresay it is hard for you to take me seriously in my dotage but, well, let us just say that I have known a few Mr Richards of my own over the years.'

We both broke into a bubble of laughter which was welcome, dispersing the sobriety of such a subject like an emerging breeze through a stuffy room.

'The difference my dear is that you have a lot to learn in the mastery of discretion if you are to successfully get away with it—and you still have a living husband in your shadow, so you really must learn to have a care.'

'I know. I have been so foolish.'

'It's a rite of passage to be so at your age. Just, have a care to get better in your management of them.'

'Yes. I realise it now, not to mention regret a great deal of it.'

'Ah, now that is indeed true folly.'

'What is?'

'Regret. Of course, we must take the lessons of our misgivings forward, but there is little sense in my mind, on brooding over that which cannot be altered.'

'I suppose that makes sense, but I fear easier said than done.'

'Well, practice makes perfect, I should know.'

'I cannot imagine you having many regrets, Lady W. I have to say it seems I have accrued more in the past months than most manage across the span of a lifetime.'

'Only because I chose to give them up. Don't be fooled into thinking the version of me you know is the same one through the years. We grow and shed so many versions of ourselves throughout our lives that you will soon begin to lose count of them, as I did long ago.'

If that was true—and I had fair cause to consider it could be given how unrecognisable my former self of only six months prior seemed to me now—then I wondered, how long this version would be around for.

'So, my dear, if you are minded to take advice from a wise old owl, I have to tell you for fear that nobody else will and you will waste precious time indulging regret or in making confessions that nobody has the right to exact from you.'

And there it was. How had I forgotten so quickly the subject we had originally digressed from, the very one I had painstakingly decided to broach. Could she really be referring to what I thought she was? Or perhaps it was a reference to Richards? I studied her for a clue. 'What if you feel it your duty to confess?'

'Your only duty my dear, is to yourself and your own conscience, do not be gulled into thinking otherwise. Discretion is not only a skill that will serve you well once you have mastered it, but a right you have to exercise over your own private affairs. The world and our society particularly, is a dangerous place to speak *too* freely. But if you get the chance to be happy—take it. If you get the chance to find someone of virtues that align with your own, don't dismiss that, whatever other differences there might be and especially not for the sake of societal or even familial disapproval. But do my dear, take care with keeping your cards close to your chest in matters of high stakes.'

I felt the burn of tears in my own eyes at this speech. 'Thank you,' I said, my heart aflood with gratitude for such words, such wisdom, such...acceptance.

Revelations.

November 1821. - Eleanor.

It turned out that Richards' intervention in procuring us invitations for Lansdowne had not been necessary, even though they were promptly sent. Lady W. had proposed our going upon her own invitation to this affair the very same evening. She had a mind to scratch at a few of the ministers who she knew to be present, with her society concerns. 'Much better,' she told me with a wink in her eye, 'to catch them in a comfortable setting and at ease than trying to get through the official channels.'

She thought it a little bit queer that I should want to bring my Abigail with me, but accepted the notion, providing we introduced her simply as my friend come to visit from the country. It was of course as I had planned to anyway and it felt a little easier to be in Lady W.'s presence as we sat in the grand ball room of Lansdowne to listen to Mr Richards' concert.

I had still not fathomed who of the ton outside of our parish might have heard about my outburst at the Jameson's. Thankfully, furtive glances along the rows of chairs about us confirmed there was no one from Cuddington here at all.

It put me greatly at ease and when the concert broke for the interval and the room dispersed into the adjacent one for refreshments and dancing, I felt a little less conscious for knowing I need not fear bumping into anyone who had been present. As a few late arrivals begun to join the throng, I kept an ear out for the calling of the announcements as best I could amongst all the chatter.

Richards had played wonderfully and by the look of his continuous accosting since standing up from the pianoforte, had been duly received as deserved. I was grateful he was obstructed from coming over to us because I had meant to slip away soon enough, now Annalise was appeased of her wish to see the Princess who had claimed a superior aspect at the front row with her entourage.

I was only waiting for Lady W. to break her conversations with some acquaintances who had spotted her on our way over to the buffet table.

Annalise and I continued on to it and began to fill our plates. I filled mine more to be perceived as too busy to be interrupted by conversations or dance invitations, for I could hardly stomach more than the occasional mouthful. I was increasingly finding my taste so much altered by this nausea that things I had once enjoyed fondly now caused me to retch at the smell or sight.

I nibbled on a plain cracker, for after the parmesan ice cream, I could not consider the cheeses a sensible choice. I found a corner for Annalise and I to hide away in as we ate and I marvelled at the look of her, so astonished and intrigued by the company and the grand house. She fit in so well amongst us in her beautiful pink and apple green gown that she had altered and re-trimmed from one of my season gowns. I was certain no one would suspect her in the least as being anything other than good ton, her manners and grace so mild she cast my own into shade.

I was certain she was soon to be flooded with petitions to her dance card, which was the only clue that might give her away. I had tried at showing her some of the steps in the run up, but it was difficult to show her and play the music on my own, and Lady W. had been rarely about in the daytime since she was busy now in helping to set up winter shelters for one of her other societies.

So, Annalise was insistent that she would not dance tonight for she had not practised enough, and even that which she had mastered would likely slip from her memory under such anxiety. It was a shame. I had hoped to see her dance and make merry tonight for at least the first set, although having caught Richards' enthusiastic smile for me as I took my seat for the concert, I hoped instead we might slip away once we had finished our plates and the dancing really fired off. For now, most were content in chatter and refreshment, but I knew after the second half of the concert, Richards would be at greater liberty to join us and I could not let that happen.

'What are these?' Annalise said to me holding up a small pastry.

I took it from her and nibbled a mouthful and handed it back. 'I do believe it is a lemon mince pie.

'Oh,' she said taking a tentative bite from it and considering the flavour. 'It is quite pleasant,' she said after her mouthful, but the only thing I hankered to taste this evening was her. She looked so striking with the glow of adventure and excitement in her face. Her hair curled in glossy ringlets piled upon her head, her complexion enhanced by a subtle dash of rouge to her cheek bones and lips and her blonde eyelashes sooted black. As she brushed a fallen crumb from her décolleté, she drew my eyes in with it. I thought how much I looked to returning home with her tonight.

'What?' she said looking up at me and frowning.

'You—I do not think you conceive of what a high fidget I am in trying to compose myself around you tonight.

She broke into an understanding smile revealing her neat white teeth and I returned it with a sultry one.

It was in this distraction that I had allowed my guard to slip and found Richards heading purposely in our direction. I looked about me wondering where we may flee to before he reached us, but I had ushered us into a corner and the only way to escape it was in his direction.

'Mrs Craythorne, Miss Tullier,' he said, dashing a bright smile between us and then fixing his eyes on mine, 'I am so pleased you made it.'

'As are we, sir, you played so very finely. I'm sure everyone has told you so.'

Annalise nodded her agreement. 'You have a very rare talent, sir. It was a delight to hear you play.'

'You are very kind, I thank you.'

'Anyway, I'm sure you must have the entire room in want of offering you congratulations, do not let us detain you from it,' I said.

'Yes, well, I would rather be with you,' he said pointedly and I looked instantly to Annalise to see if she had detected his meaning. I saw the slightest furrow of her brow.

'Ah, well they would all think us very ill-mannered to be so greedy of the star guest tonight, though you do us honour. We must go and find Lady W. anyway now.'

'Very well, Mrs Craythorne, so long as I may go away having claimed your first set tonight?'

'Oh, I do not mean to dance at all tonight, Mr Richards. I own I am so very tired. Miss Tullier here has kept me quite busy walking all about the city taking tours that it is a wonder I am still standing.'

'Please, Eleanor, one set is all I ask. You must know I have my heart set upon it.'

'Mr Richards, please,' I said lowering my voice, 'I cannot dance with you tonight and I wish you would not press me so.'

'Are you worried about what everyone else will say? The rumours are long dead and there is nothing better to counter them than an innocent dance.'

I knew now that Annalise had understood so much more than I had wished her to. If his ardent looks in my direction hadn't given it away, his speech now surely had.

'Alright,' he held his hands up in surrender having read my expression, 'it is very un-gentlemanly of me to press you so. It's only because you are dear to me, but I see you are minded not to. I shall come and find you later and see if you will at least take a turn with me?'

'Very well,' I said as he bid us both a bow and I placed a hand to my cheek.

'Eleanor what on earth was that about?' she said the instant he was gone.

'I am too tired to dance but I couldn't tell him why, could I?'

'Not that, I am perfectly capable of reading between the lines, but that was no ordinary regard he spoke to you in. What is all this about rumours? Is there something between you?'

I put down my plate and sighed into my palms. I knew I had yet to make this confession but I had felt it would be better to manage it after this engagement. 'It is a long story—'

'Then you may start on telling it instantly.'

'Annalise, this is not the time or place for such a conversation.'

'Eleanor, I want to know it, so if you can't tell me here, then take me somewhere else.'

I could tell from her expression she was not trifling and so I led her back over to the empty concert chairs in the next room. 'Annalise, I should have told you as much before. My...acquaintance to Mr Richards, is not, well it was the case before, but of course is not now, because I did not understand the way things stood between us, I mean how they would come to, in the end—'

'Eleanor, you are making no sense.'

'Forgive me,' I said, swallowing against the constriction of my own throat. 'Annalise, Giles did not father my child.'

She tilted her head to the side and knitted her brow as if I was speaking in a foreign tongue she could not quite comprehend. 'What? I don't—' she said in bewildered tones and I felt a queasy stirring within me that could not be blamed on my condition.

I swallowed hard and cleared my throat. 'Richards is the father of my child, although he does not know it.'

She said nothing but glared at me in some paralysed fashion that seemed as if she was altogether somewhere else.

'Annalise?'

She came back into focus.

'Forgive me; I am trying to understand how this is possible? You tell me you are expected to be around five weeks into your confinement and yet—'

'It happened when I left Cuddington, after I thought you lost to me.'

I saw her recounting the occasion. 'I see. So, whilst I was in anxious turmoil over what had passed between us, you took your solace in Mr Richards' bed. Is that about the shape of it?'

'Annalise,' I reached for her hand to comfort her, for I feared such a sad decline in her mood it frightened me. 'It was a foolish thing to do, I know it. But I thought you lost to me, entirely, and I could not bear it.'

'So it is my doing?' She pulled her hand from my grasp and when I stepped forward to reclaim it, she edged back.

'No! How could it be? Annalise, I was foolish and not in my right mind. I was heartbroken to think how sincerely you wished to away from me. So much you were ready to abandon everything and leave your place at Cuddington. I own I had never known such rejection and I dealt badly in it. Very badly.'

'I was in shock, Eleanor. Trying to understand what was between us. I had no notion then that I was in love with you or even what it was to be in love. Less still amongst my own sex.'

'And if I had the slightest hint of that being the case, I should never have ventured to commit such a stupid act. I swear it. But I thought you despised me.'

'Stupid? You are having his child, it is hardly a trifle.' Tears shined in her eyes and I felt instantly the prickle of them in my own.

'I know. I can scarce believe it myself. But you must see it alters nothing. There is nothing between us and he will not find it out.'

'Perhaps in your mind, but I see now, how his kindly glances are meant for you. I feel sick to my stomach to think he shares in the intimate knowledge of you, I thought belonged to me.' A tear rolled down her cheek and I caught it on the satin tip of my gloved thumb.

'Do not cry. It does belong to you, Annalise. Because what we have shared is beyond any feeling or deed—'

'And why should he not know he is to father a child? What a cruel trick it is to keep him from the knowing.'

'Because there is nothing to be done for his knowing but the cruelty of him learning another man has ownership of his issue and that I do not return his inclination. Tell me it is not a crueller thing to break his ignorance with such calamities which lie beyond his power to resolve and yet would vex him sorely.'

'If you truly do not return his affection, how, how could you do it, Eleanor? How could you lie with him so freely? I own I cannot make sense of it, for I cannot even bring myself to imagine letting anyone else touch me the way I permit you. Yes, I am not green enough to think a married woman would not know her way around the bedroom, but in that you had little choice. But this...'

I did not know how to answer this. 'I am ashamed of what I did, Annalise, and I wish I could convince you to understand that the meaningless of that night and the intimacy we enjoy are so wholly set apart. Annalise, I love you, in every way it is possible to love another.'

'I thought you did, but I cannot imagine that having such conviction in your heart for me would permit your doing such a thing with him, whether you thought my cause lost or otherwise. God, Eleanor, the very idea is too much—'

'My love, I am so much sorry—'

'Ah, there you are,' I turned to find Lady W. slip into my peripheral vision. 'Whatever is the matter?' she said, a quiz about her expression as she took in ours.

'Nothing,' I said quickly, making a conscious effort to recompose myself.

'I have called for the carriage. I don't wish to alarm you my dear, but I have just been detained by that antiquated fogie Dowager Birdwhistle, and well, I shan't need to explain to you how she does love to gossip. Anyway, she had a particular interest in knowing what you were doing here and having seen you in Mr Richards company—'

'Oh no,' I sighed into my gloved hand. 'This is very bad.'

'What is?' Annalise said, the glow of anger in her cheeks beginning to wane like dying coals.

If I could be grateful for nothing else about this disastrous turn of events, then I must at least be grateful for its timely diversion. 'Annalise, she is Cuddington's biggest prattlebox and scandal mongerer. You may trust she knows all about my marital circumstances and the old rumours about me and Richards.' This, I realised as I said it and from her strobing glance, would cause us to resume our prior conversation at a more private opportunity. I had not considered how I might break to her that it had not been an isolated occasion. Her reaction to the notion of the one occasion had been so unprecedented, I could not bring myself to go into that now. And certainly not here.

'So, I think better to away before Richards breaks free of his obligations and starts dangling after you in the company, or she will have too much fuel to add to that fire,' added Lady W.

'Yes, to be sure. Thank you, you are always so quick minded. But you need not break your engagement here, not on my account.'

'I think I must my dear, it would look awful queer you scurrying off without me as if you have something to hide. I already told the old battleaxe I was feeling quite fagged and gave her some hint that my arthritis was playing up and I must be forced to beg you see me home.'

'Then we must get you home in that case, I shouldn't have encouraged your coming if I had understood you to be ailing.'

'Ailing? My dear you cannot believe for a minute I was in earnest!' she exclaimed in horrified accents. 'I own I might be considered passed my prime, but I'll have you know that I'm in fine fettle and could outlast most of my generation.'

I took up her arm and laughed. 'I do not doubt it in the least Lady W. You are quite the most formidable lady I know.'

When we returned to the house, there was little left to chuckle at. Annalise, for all my attempts at reassurance and apology, remained disconcertingly remote, and Lady W. was persuaded that given my condition, and being in little doubt that Dowager Birdwhistle would return to Surrey with a ready—and likely over embellished—account of seeing me with Richards, I should look to departing both London and my hometown before any on-dit could really fire off that might substantiate it.

'Surely that will only lend suspicion to my disappearance?'

'Perhaps it might be taken that way,' she said considering the likelihood. 'But here is how I see it: The fact of the matter is, if you are, as you are minded I think, to attempt to keep this news away from your husband's learning, then you shall have to away at some point before there is a clue to your condition.'

This much was true, although I had been too distracted to fathom out the finer details of exactly where I was to go and when I must make such a journey. Until tonight, it had seemed I had time enough to consider these things.

'And think my dear, if you should stick around a few months more, you will have given ample opportunity for such rumours to take root, and then vanish away to make some impromptu holiday when everyone else has already drawn their own conclusions. Now, I think that might prove the more suspicious, than you going away now ahead of them.'

I considered these possibilities. It was indeed the case that if I was to depart now, nothing out of the ordinary would be thought of the circumstance, since we were soon approaching the Christmastide season and many would take trips elsewhere in time for it. Well, perhaps not quite so lengthy as mine would necessitate, but what's to say I would not extend such a trip to say, Edinburgh to stay with my sister's family? That was my original plan after all, before all of this came about. But now I saw that that would not answer. Wherever I was to go, I must be unknown, anonymous and unsuspected to be there. I had no clue where that might be...but my departure at this season would be a timely one. 'Perhaps I should go now,' I said in answer to her waiting expression.

'I think it wise, on balance of the likelihood. That is not to say some would not take the line that you suppose. But I imagine that old harridan to be in town for the rest of the week, and if you were to go now and beat her to Cuddington, making some small appearances in the public way to explain your taking a holiday and having only delayed it for your want of keeping to your invitations, well, who could fail to understand your reasoning? And I'd venture to say, that you shall beat her to the telling of your being there and can give your version ahead of hers. I mean, what a dead bore she will find it to persist in such spreading of scandals when it's already been had from the horse's mouth directly. You might blame me for the invitation to Lansdowne and keeping Richards altogether out of the way of things.'

'Yes. Yes, I see it the preferable alternative to having such ideas as the Dowager would like to set in their minds then disappearing for no apparent logic other than to escape their slights and lend substance to them. Not to mention the dust Giles will kick up at the learning once she has had her say. Any hopes of Edmund's negotiation will be quite futile if he has a suspicion that things between Richards and I are not at last extinguished.' He might well disapprove of Giles' treatment of me, now he understood it plainly, but if he thought me likely to throw myself upon Richards, I was certain he would disapprove enough to reconsider helping me altogether. I had seen for myself how my earnest reassurance that I was not minded for remarriage comforted and no doubt influenced his decision to assist. It could not be for nothing I had finally bought him around.

And so, the decision to go was settled. I would depart for home at first light tomorrow and spend a brief spell in Cuddington, apprising my parents of my intention to make a holiday and letting about the news to a few of the scandal broth sippers about the place who could still be relied upon to tolerate me in their parlours and Lady W. would put the same line about in London. I would take care not to extend my stay beyond a few days, since from my recollection, Giles was to be in Dublin until then, and I could not risk the news of my departure reaching him ahead of my executing it. The problem, the only problem I could not find a happy solution to, was where on earth I was to go.

'You might take my house in Bath my dear?' Lady W. had offered to this dilemma. 'Or there is a dower house at a pretty country seat in York you may remove to? A bit out of the way though and a dreadful long journey, so I never go there. But it might be just the thing?'

'Thank you, you are very generous to me and I should think it just the thing to answer, but I fear Lady W. that the first place Giles will look to once he realises I am gone, is to anywhere he may connect with you.'

'Hmm, well that takes Bath out of the running, for there is no secret in that now, but I'm sure he will not so easily make the connection to York. I mean, it is no particular secret since it was my late Alfred's country seat, but I have not removed there for so many decades I can scarcely imagine anyone would be of a mind to think of it. The family don't make much use of the estate either since the heir is still at Cambridge. So, you shall be quite left alone and no one about to ask questions.'

'Anyone excepting Giles perhaps, and that irksome valet of his who has a penchant for sneaking about and sniffing out such details.'

'Ah yes, I had quite forgotten that dreadful slyboots. Well, if time would favour us, I might manage to apply to a trusted acquaintance to put you in the way of some vacant seat or letting that may not be so readily equated, but I shan't be able to account for the place or the keeping of your secrets, and it shall take a great deal longer than a few days to make such enquiries if I am to keep them in the private way.'

'Lady W., please do not concern yourself. You have done quite enough; more than I deserve. I shall bring no more of these calamities to bear on you. It is my quandary to solve and so I shall. Be at ease.'

'My dear, I do hate to see you in a scrape, although I own, you do seem to rather make a habit of getting into them.'

We both laughed at this understatement and when the ripples waned, I said to her in earnest: 'I truly am grateful for all you have done for me. I should have lost faith entirely with my peers had it not been for you.'

'Stuff and nonsense. I have done only my duty as a fond friend and as for the rest of those stuffy philistines to which we may be classed amongst their set, well, I never considered myself one of their number in any case and I scarce think you may be counted amongst them either.'

Another peel of laughter escaped me. 'No, that is very true.' I cupped an affectionate hand over hers. 'Oh, Lady W., what shall I do without you for such an age? I shall miss you so very sorely and then there is the Society work I was keen to set about on.'

She returned my kindness with a gentle pat. 'You will do just dandy my dear. For unlike most of these chits our sort insists on bringing out in the world with little idea on how to manage its calamities, you, are one of substance. And when you are not losing your senses and getting into these impassioned scrapes, you have a wise head on you, if you would only learn to keep it.'

I smiled at this gentle chide for I knew it to be meant both in earnest and in jest.

'It will be a difficult time for you my dear, whatever you decide to do and I am certain that whatever that proves to be, will be for the best. But, you have that clever maid to take away with you and I do not doubt she will be your greatest ally, and I am always here, if I am needed. Who knows, I may even make a journey to see you before the term is out, providing you are not beyond a day's travel and I am confident of hiding the scent from your husband.'

'I would like that a great deal. And I shall write to you, even if it must be in some other hand and under a pseudonym.'

'Well, my dear, I think you must set about your arrangements for to-morrow and get an early night. You have a taxing few days ahead of you to bear yet.'

'Yes,' I said, getting up off the sofa and when she rose with me, I flung my arms around her.

When I returned to my chamber, I found Annalise fast asleep on the day bed and understood this slight to be a sign that her fury with me had not yet expired. I sat down gently beside her as she slept and stroked her cheek. 'I'm sorry, my love. So sorry,' I whispered and placed a kiss up-on her cheek before snuffing out her candle and taking my own into the dressing room to begin on packing up our portmanteaus.

Morning came in a blink, so late the task of packing had kept me. Despite the nights brief reprieve, which I prayed would prove enough to soften Annalise's pain and disappointment. I was still so fagged I struggled to get up. And once I did, I noted little improvement from her punctuat-ed answers and evasive demeanour to suggest the twilight hours had had any mollifying effect on Annalise at all.

She sat across from me at the small table, chewing silently on a break-fast of tea and plum cakes, staring blankly out towards the window as I studied her over my steaming cup, an oversized knuckle of ginger root bobbing against my mouth as I sipped tentatively at it.

'Annalise,' I said gently, clicking my cup back into its saucer and try-ing to catch her gaze which she was determined to avert, 'I am truly sorry for all of this.'

'Please, do not...' she said, her words and her brief and fleeting glance capped with icy exactitude.

'I don't mean to anger you, Annalise. But surely, we cannot go on in this fashion,' I said reasonably, I thought, considering I felt like either scolding her in return or bursting into a fit of tears. I was not certain which would prevail if I permitted myself.

'Eleanor, I shall travel back to Cuddington with you and see you safe-ly off to wherever it is you mean to go. But I shall not travel with you. I intend to move on within the week. I have somewhere in mind to go but it likely shan't be possible without a little notice and so, if you will do me the favour of permitting me to stay at Cuddington until you go, I would be most grateful.'

I seemed suddenly to have turned to lead. 'You cannot mean it?'

'I wish it were so,' she said with a hint of regret in her face, but no sign of relinquishing her position. 'I only tell you so you might account for getting someone else to go in my place. I realise this whole arrangement is rushed and I hate to think of you in a fix under the circumstances, but I am persuaded I am to stay behind.'

'But why?'

'In truth, I cannot bear to look at you.'

I had underestimated her disgust at me. I could do so no longer now I had seen it upon her face.

'I am sorry for it,' she added. 'I cannot feel right in saying such things to you when you have so much else to think of. But I cannot lie to you, Eleanor. I fear, if I was to go with you abroad, far from being there to help and comfort you, I may prove only to distress you further in such a head and that things may turn even more sour betwixt us.'

I bit down upon my trembling lip. 'I know you are mad as fire with me, and why shouldn't you be? You are every bit correct; I should not have kept such secrets from you, kept anything from you. It was fear, not malice that permitted me to do so. But in time, we might get over this and I shall never keep a thing from your knowing ever again.'

'How long was your affair with Richards? How many times did you lie with him?'

I took a sip from my cup to collect myself. *No more lies, not this time.* 'Well, do you truly wish to know the details?'

'I do. I need to know the truth.'

I nodded. 'Very well,' I said, replacing my cup after another steadying sip. 'It was never really an affair per se—more like fragmented occasions.'

'Well, how many of these such occasions?'

'Only two of that particular nature.'

'So, you lie with him not once, but twice?'

I regretted what I must say next but knew that I had to. 'Once on the first occasion, which was before I ever knew you. I did it to get back at my husband I suppose. He was sleeping with someone else—someone I had thought a friend who deceived me very cruelly.'

'And the second was to get back at me?'

'No. Not that. I was lonely. I was lost. I felt like nothing. Empty. A sad failure. So, I went to see him. I shan't pretend that it was for any other purpose for I knew. I knew what led me there: the desire to feel *something* when all I felt was numb.' I wiped tears from my cheeks. 'I spent the night in his lodgings. We were intimate throughout it and so the number is not only two. Although I cannot recollect precisely, but perhaps double that.'

'How could you be so loose?' she said through gritted teeth as she tried to hide the welling tears in her own eyes. 'If you were in love with me, how could you give yourself to him?'

'I don't know. I disgust myself. I wish I could explain it. But it meant nothing.'

Silence ensued.

'In the morning, I left before he had risen and I had not seen him until that unfortunate meeting at the museum. I wanted to refuse his invitation to Lansdowne—honest. But I saw how keen you were to go, to catch a glimpse of the Princess and I did not think it could do any harm to stay for just a little while so you could.'

'Ah, how thoughtful of you,' she spat in acerbic accents and I began to howl with sobs at this acidity in her speech. The venom in her contorted features as she looked at me so wickedly.

'Forgive me, Eleanor, truly,' she said in a gentler tone. 'I do not wish to cause you any distress under such circumstances and I mean you no injury, for I understand how it bruises. But trust is a fragile thing and you have broken it.'

'Very well,' I said, staunching the flow of hot stinging tears that promised to re-erupt if I dared stay in the room a moment longer. 'I understand,' I told her and fled from it as quickly as I could before a bout of customary morning sickness, erupted from me.

When she followed me into the dressing room to offer me her assistance, I sent her away with a wave, even though it took me twice as long to set myself to rights without her help and caused us a delay in leaving.

I was coming down the stairs at last, having called myself to order and Annalise and Lady W. were waiting for me in the hall where the footmen relayed our luggage to the carriage, when at the very moment Mr Richards came into view in the open doorway.

'Good morning,' he said, lifting his hat three times to account for all of us, and looking a little surprised. First at finding the door wide open, and second at noticing our imminent departure. A serious look overcame him at this notice and I read the unspoken questions on his face.

'It is alright, I have a moment to spare,' I said as Lady W. contrived excuses to send him away.

I took him into the small parlour and closed the door.

'Well, I had come to find out why you made such an early departure last eve and now I find you making yet again another,' he said to me and I could not mistake the disappointment in his expression.

'I am sorry to have rushed away like that. Lady W. was not feeling well and I wanted to see her home safely.'

'Shame. I had hoped to spend a moment in your company, find out how you do? So little I see of you of late. I see that will not be possible now.'

'Mr Richards, I am very sorry to disappoint you and wanted to tell you the truth last night. But it was not the occasion and with how much I enjoyed your playing and how much it pleased me to see you so well situated. It becomes you.'

'Thank you, Eleanor. Hearing so from you is a compliment I hold dear indeed. But I must press you now, and come directly to the point, for I know I interrupt your departure. Eleanor, I cannot help but ask it, have I done something to offend you?'

'No,' I said alarmed at this. 'No, you have done nothing of the sort. Look, I cannot give the whole right now, but I have gotten myself into

quite the scrape and matters concerning my marriage are greatly compli-
cated for me at present.'

'So that is why you have been determined to keep away.'

I was not sure if it was relief I read in his face at this evaluation. 'Mr
Richards, I fear I have done you a great disservice in tangling you up in
my affairs. I feel very ashamed of doing so for you are such a good fellow
and I am such a calamity, and of late such a quiz.'

'A quiz I will allow,' he said, smirking. 'Eleanor, I don't know what
trouble you are in and I wish it were otherwise, but you must know, that
to me, well, I'm fond enough of you just as you are.'

Oh no, not this and not now. 'Mr Richards, you are, as ever, all flattery.
But—'

His kiss was so forthcoming he must have leapt at me in one swoop
to deliver it without my prior notice. I pulled back instantly. 'Mr
Richards, please...'

'Eleanor,' he said, permitting my release from his kiss but not from his
embrace. 'Forget your husband, abandon your troubles and come away
with me.'

I felt for his hands about my back and gently peeled them away. 'I
cannot, sir. You flatter me sincerely, but I simply cannot.'

'Of course, you can. I know you haven't a care for your husband and I
understand your reservations, indeed it was the very reason that prevented my asking you before. What had I to offer in support of such an irregular elopement? But my circumstances are much changed now; I have
means and engagements to last out beyond the year and into the next.
Come with me, Eleanor. I can take care of you now and you must know
how much I have longed to.'

I was so dizzy it took me a moment to construct a reply. 'Oh, Mr
Richards, I am so much sorry you waste your goodness on me. I cannot
accept your offer.'

'Whyever not? I know how unhappy you have been dealt in your
marriage bargain. You cannot pretend you wish to stay true to it and, I
fear I am in love with you, Eleanor. You must know I will do everything
I can to give you the happiness he deprives you of.'

My heart could not bear another word of this and yet to break him so cruelly with unrequited sentiments was agonising. Instead, I said, deciding upon it at the last. 'I cannot go with you Sir, you do not understand, I am to bear my husband a child.'

He looked so much stunned at this he was struck a moment speechless.

'I am sorry I did not tell you so before. It was wrong of me to come to you in such knowledge of my condition and spend the night with you as I did.'

'You mean you already knew it then?' he said astonished.

I nodded. 'You see, Mr Richards, what a wretch you place your kindly words and affection on. I am not worthy of either and I told you so before, but I think only now you see it.'

'Does your husband know?'

I shook my head. 'No. Barely a soul knows it and I trust you will keep my secret. I was hoping to win a separation from him, and of course this news will surely put paid to such an attempt.'

'But still, you mean to try?'

'I do not know what to do, Mr Richards. If I persist in that direction and win my freedom, he still has the rights to my child and I must stay with him anyway, and of course if I do not, the result is I shall never see it.'

'Then dash it. Come away with me before he learns of the circumstance. I will stand by you and your child.'

His words scratched like razor blades against my eardrums and I struggled to take a steadying breath. *You would stand by me. One day I shall tell our child about you, about its father.* A tear rolled down my cheek and I wiped it promptly away. 'Mr Richards, the last time I heard from my husband, he made a threat to bring about a Crim Con suit against you, but he had little hard evidence to pursue it beyond trifling on-dit. If I were to run off with you, well, it would be all he would need to take you down and lose everything you have worked so hard to only recently gain.'

This at last had the effect upon him I had been anticipating, and even though the relief of getting my point to him without an outright cruel rejection was at last arrived, the grave disappointment in his face now sent me to shivers.

'I don't care about all that, only how could I look after you if—'

'If you had neither means or reputation to rely on. Indeed. For he would take it all from you without a care.'

'You poor creature,' he said to me eventually, the feeling reflected in his eyes and in his tone, shifting now, from one of bereft disappointment to a pitying sobriety.

'I made my bed and now I must work out how to lie upon it, for it was my doing and mine alone. You, however, have a future bright and beckoning you to move into its adventure. I bid you follow such a course and find a good wife to share in it with you. For you deserve it and it will make me so much happy to hear of it one day, when all these troubles are long behind me,' I said, embracing him gently now. 'Thank you, Richards, you have been of so much comfort and a true friend to me. I shall not forget it.' I kissed him on the cheek and went out of the room and directly to the carriage.

'I am sorry Annalise, to have had to entertain Mr Richards, but you were right: I owed him some explanation,' I said as soon as the carriage pulled away.

She looked up at me and I noticed the redness around her eyes. 'You told him?'

'No. I spared him that ordeal. He thinks I bear my husband's child, but, well, I have set things straight between us, in so far as I can, and I shall not see him again.'

'Why did he come?'

'To see why I disappeared so abruptly last night...' I considered then the potential of creating yet another secret if I did not give her the whole. 'And he wanted me to go away with him, suggested an elopement.'

Her eyes flashed at this and I wondered if I was mistaken to tell her. 'You should consider his proposal, Eleanor. It would perhaps answer to your predicament.'

I was astonished. I shook my head in stunned disbelief before I could recover my ability to speak. 'How can you say it?'

'So it is I who is the unfeeling one now?'

'No, Annalise, and I understand your anger, your disappointment, even your disgust at me. All of it I must own to be in line with how I would feel in such a situation. But, I do not believe, that even feelings of such gravity are enough to break what is between us. You cannot just *decide* upon not loving someone when your heart has already attached itself to their affections. You cannot just *decide* to abandon those feelings.'

'No,' she said steely toned and looked away and out of the window, 'I suppose that is why it is so excruciating. Because you know my heart, Eleanor, you know that I could not have allowed what has passed between us unless I was in complete understanding of my regard for you.'

'I do. And I am so much sorry I cannot say it any more than I have.'

She turned back to me. 'I don't want you to say it. It alters nothing.'

'Perhaps. But in time, if we wait for the dust to settle; you know Richards is gone...'

'But is he gone, Eleanor? I know you remain firm in your argument that you hold no feeling towards him, but I cannot believe it. You have been four times intimate with him, voluntarily. Either you would have me think you very indifferent in matters of sharing your bed or, and more to the likelihood I think, you do care for Richards and it is that which led you to such a course.'

I felt entirely cornered by this ultimatum. It was of course a trap wherein either answer would incriminate me and justify her scorn. 'Fine. I did feel some kindness towards Richards, once.'

She rolled her eyes. 'Well, he is a handsome looking kind of rake.'

'But it was only the kindness of a friend at a time I felt friendless. Indeed, I shall always think well of him, for he has only ever shown me such regard. But as for his handsomeness, or any other more serious attachment you may be imagining, I can tell you in earnest, there is none.'

She searched me with an inquisitive gaze, as though testing the truth of my declaration by some invisible instrument. 'So, you do not think him handsome?'

I sighed out my frustration. Little did she know that I would not suffer any such trifling and circular examination from any, but her. 'Of course, I see as anyone can that he is a perfectly handsome man, Annalise. I am neither blind nor trying to gull you. What I mean is, that though I see it, I do not feel drawn to it, enchanted by it as others do.'

'So why did you do it then?'

'You really want the truth of it, Annalise? You really want to know the workings of my mind to that degree? Fine. You will not like it a bit.' I took a steadying breath and looked her over. 'Because I knew I could. It was to console me. I felt torn to shreds at your rejection, not because I expected you to reciprocate on my terms, but because I knew I had felt the warmth in your regard for me, growing as mine did. I saw the ways your eyes lit up at finding mine upon you. How, you too, inched a fraction nearer to me when we lay upon the grass reading. How you started placing goodnight kisses at my cheek. How we had both grown impatient with the absences between us, and I knew it, I felt it to be sure in my heart that I was not imagining it, but seeing in you, what was bubbling inside of me.'

She snivelled and I noticed a tear escape and roll down her patchy cheek.

I wanted to reach across to her but I daren't. 'I would never have had the courage to approach you with my affections if I had not been utterly convinced of yours. So, when you rejected me and would not see me, talk to me, look at me; it was the most violent pain I had ever known, for it took so much to dare. I would have tried to bear it out one way or the other, although I had no notion how it might be managed. But then you left and the horror of it was unlike anything I'd ever felt. It was the first time it had occurred to me with any true conviction, that you truly did not reciprocate. That I had perhaps got it all so terribly wrong. That even my presence under a roof so large as Cuddington was too much for you to bear. It was in that mind, Annalise, one of despair and such low feeling that I went to Richards, not from any notion of revenge or earnest affection towards him. I never expected to have to explain myself to you, for I thought I might never again set eyes upon you beyond a passing in a corridor in some distant time. So no, I was not thinking of vengeance, nor of the consequences. I was not thinking of Richards and that I may come to bear him a child. I was thinking how much I wished him you. How much I wished his handsome face might cure me of my want of you. Of course, it answered to neither...'

She closed her eyes against this hearing and a frozen silence ensued until I grew uncomfortable with it. I waited for a less rickety spell along the road and dared to lean forward and reach for her hand. 'Annalise, all I want in the world is you. The rest can go to the devil.'

Inertia.

November 1821. - Eleanor.

The journey back from London was the polar reverse of the one setting out just a week ago when we were both so effervescent with wonder and anticipation. The remainder of it was endured in painful silence, noisy with thoughts. I felt mentally drained by the time we arrived and wanted nothing more than a day of sleep to take refuge from it, but Mama had other ideas and kept me to talking in her sitting room for far longer than I could cope with.

When I settled early to my own bed at last, too fatigued to even bring to my mama the topic of setting out on a 'holiday' and having been too distracted with Annalise to think on where this holiday might be, I felt everything had caught up with me and I was sinking beneath its weight.

I had meant to be thinking ahead of my calamities, acting with a swift and practical mind to construct a fitting plan. The bones of it had already been plotted by Lady W. and myself. Yet it seemed suddenly as though I was to be taken under in a wave of immobility. Ill-timed inertia.

I was tired: tired of running from Giles, tired of deceiving others, tired of trying to convince Annalise that my affections were engaged only in her direction. *Why must everything be such a battleground.*

My body seemed caught in a chronic bout of lethargy and wished only for the relief of sleep. But the early evening light had kept me tossing and turning and permitting unwanted time for protracted replays of the day's events. When I had allowed them free reign to torment me into fitful sobs, I finally persuaded myself to find the energy to pull the curtains about my bed and shut out the little slants of light that crept from about the edges of the window drapes. Of course, I could have rung the bell, but since I was now—once again—without a lady's maid, I thought against drawing attention to the fact by summoning someone else.

I had still not wholly given up on Annalise going with me, despite her words. Not because I meant to press and cajole her into going. I knew better than to think that conducive to winning her around. But because I had learned something from the last time we were at odds; that neglectful absence had a power that dogged persistence did not. And so, I meant to let her have her way. Let her indulge in her solitude as I did mine. I had made no protest to her request to take leave to sort out her affairs, made no demands that she attend me in my toilette despite her offering to continue to fulfil these obligations until my departure. Nor had I uttered another attempt at persuasion since the carriage journey. I had stated my case as openly and as honestly as I had ever been bought to doing and I was of a mind that if she did care for me as she had declared both in word and in body, then I was certain she could not let me go off alone for several months without her.

With this silent challenge, I knew I carried the risk of discovering not only if she did truly care, but also if she did not. The latter gripped me in a knot of crippling fear that I refused to let prevail. It seemed something I could not permit such reign, seeming so impossible to believe having spent the last weeks in such blissful intimacy together.

But this modicum of doubt grew harder to repress and proved haunting to me at times as the days went on. Often, they would begin with a strength of conviction that she must be missing me as painfully as I her. That she was surely changing her mind at every moment and when not in the contemplation of that, in recollection of our newly made memories and bonds.

It had certainly been the pattern of my private thoughts, whether I had been busy paying calls to lace the scandal brewers with my version of attending the London soiree ahead of the Dowager, or news of my anticipated 'holiday' to Edinburgh to spend Christmastide with my sister's family. This, I had decided on as not the actual plan, but a perfect decoy to leave in my wake to throw Giles entirely off of my trail, should he think to have his slyboots valet pursue my direction.

I was half in hope that he would be kept away from the idea, just by the notion of stepping up uninvited to a man of Lord Docherty's standing. My sister's husband was a man of such great consequence, being the Marquis of Walden, that I hoped even Giles might be tentative about bringing such tantrums and protests to the door of his household. I could not be certain of it, but knowing, as he would in due course when Edmund got to his negotiations, that I had confided such intimate details to my brother, he must be left to assume that I had done as much to my sister's family. In suspecting this, he must also be brought to assume I would be under the protection of my sister and the Marquis and any attempt to accost me there would be met with the height of incivility.

So, with this cover story adequately set about the parish, I had now to contend with the greatest of my obstacles yet: Bringing my mother into my confidence and contriving to arrange the actual plan of my departure.

I found her busied in the library, sat behind her writing desk in deep concentration. I was reluctant to disturb her, but had no time to delay; if I did not approach her now, she would likely hear the gossip of my awaying from someone else. 'Mama,' I stepped into the room and took an uninvited seat opposite her. 'I am sorry to disturb you, but there is something I must ask that cannot wait.'

She put her quill back in its pot and pushed her papers aside.

I peered down at them. She was going over the kitchen orders and making entries into account ledgers. 'I have come to ask you to give me leave to go to Stapleford Hall.'

She frowned and tilted her ear as if mishearing me. 'Stapleford? Whyever would you wish it? You have never cared for the place.'

I pulled my chair up a fraction closer to the desk and leaned forward in order to lower my voice. 'I need somewhere out of the way to go, somewhere quiet and inconspicuous.'

She took her spectacles from her nose and placed them on the table. 'Why?'

'I am with child.'

Her face lit up.

'And I do not want my husband to know,' I pressed on before she could burst into congratulation.

'But, Eleanor, this is happy news. Perhaps this will be just the thing to set things right between you and bring an end to all this enmity.'

'I don't want to set things "right", Mama. I cannot bear the sight of him.'

'But, Eleanor, you are to be a mother, you must try to overcome this; you are going to be a family now.'

'No. I shall not tell him. In fact, Edmund is to take an interview with him presently and try to negotiate for a separation of bed and board.'

'What madness is this? Edmund would not dare to contrive to do such a thing without our knowing!'

'No. In ordinary circumstances, he maintains he would not, but in the light of recent understanding, he has undertaken to for my sake.'

'For your sake? And what about the child's sake, Eleanor? You cannot mean to abandon your child to Giles' care?'

'I don't mean to. He does not know of it and I have no intention of telling him. He cannot seek what he does not know to exist.'

'Come, Eleanor, he will find out eventually. You cannot hide his own child from him and you cannot deny the child his rightful claim to his position, inheritance, father. Even if he is not the best of husbands to you, it does not prevent him from being a good father to your child. It may improve him in fact, as often these things do once a wife has done her duty.'

'It is not *his* child, Mama.' This produced the necessary shock that I was relying upon to obtain her agreement.

'Good god, Eleanor, you cannot mean it!'

'Well, since I have been away from him for months now, Mama, how could you suppose it would be so. Besides, I have never had *ordinary relations* with my husband, so I can assure you, it is the truth and what's more, he will know he cannot be the father.'

She scrunched up her nose. 'Ordinary relations?'

'Mama, I will be as plain in the matter as I can for clarity's sake, but I warn you; you will not be well disposed to hear what I am about to tell you. Nothing I could ever contrive could be so wholly unbelievable, and yet it is so.'

She leant forward in her chair and I could see the shock and anxiety settling into her features at the anticipation of what was to come.

'Giles, when he attacked me that night I came home, did not assault me in the common manner. It was in a way I now understand to be of a criminal nature.'

'No!' She held her hand to her throat and I was glad she was sitting for I thought she might otherwise fall down so much colour had drained from her cheeks leaving her complexion suddenly sallow.

'I own, I did not know then that it was a criminal act, and by no means did I consent to it. But on learning this since, I have thought of setting criminal charges for Sodomy against him, but Edmund tells me that nothing will be kept private in such proceedings, so in pursuing such a course, I will injure us all in making the details plain. So, it is his suggestion that instead he calls Giles' bluff with a threat to issue proceedings and attempt to win his agreement for a separation in exchange for keeping this business out of open court.'

'Oh my, tell me it is not true, surely he cannot be such a menace?'

'I wish I could. Anyway, he is due back from Dublin any moment and soon to be accosted by Edmund, so I've no doubt *that* will send him looking for me. With your protection, we might again fend off his attempts to bring me home to him. But if he knows I am with child, Mama, he will in spite go after the child, and no doubt he will go after Richards as he threatened to before, except this time, he will have the proof he has been waiting for. If it comes to such a circumstance, I will have no choice but to bring the criminal charges against him to prevent this. You must understand, if I am left with no better choice, I will do what I must.'

She nodded slowly taking it all in. 'Mr Richards, so *he* is the child's father?'

'Yes, he is.'

'Oh, Eleanor.'

This was hardly the time for class snobbery. It was not Mr Richards that had violated me, but Giles, after all. 'He cannot know either, for there is nothing he can do about it as far as the law is concerned, so I see no sense in tormenting Mr Richards with such news. It is best no one knows.' I could see we were in agreement on that at least. 'Stapleford Hall is far enough away to conceal it, and besides, Giles has no knowledge of it being owned by Papa as it is un-entailed. I have put about the notion that I am to away to Edinburgh to see Caitlin over Christmastide, so he will likely send his spies and poison pen letters to Scotland, which of course will prove fruitless.'

'But Eleanor, even if we were to go through with such a scheme, and manage to conceal it, whatever will we do when the child is born? Will you give it up?'

'I fear I must, for how else can this be mended?'

'Perhaps Mr Richards' family could take the child? A clandestine arrangement of course—'

'He has no family, Mama, don't you remember? He came from one of those foundling hospitals.'

She looked as though she was searching her memory for a clue. She seemed so pale and withdrawn. 'Eleanor, it cannot answer to abandon it, whatever were you thinking to get yourself into such a scrape as this?'

'I was not thinking, Mama, and nor would you be right thinking if you had endured all I have these past months. Besides, Mr Richards is a very good sort of man, a much better one than my husband, but is of no position to support a child.'

'We could pay for the child's upkeep, I'm sure...'

'No, my father cannot know about Richards. He can barely look me in the eye as it is. You must promise to keep that part of the story between us, Mama. There is no need for my father to know precisely why I have gone, only that it is to escape Giles, whilst Edmund deals in this negotiation.'

'I see that for now, but what about the many months you must be gone thereafter? We must think of something else.'

'Yes, but whilst we are thinking, you must help me get out of the way, or it will be too late to do anything at all.'

She nodded. 'I will send a courier to Stapleford presently and have the house opened up. I will go with you and your father will think it nothing to answer since I have been meaning to go. Of course, we will have to tell him, eventually. Perhaps I can write to him as if we have only just discovered the news. Then of course we must come up with a plan for when the child is born.'

'Mama, you must not come. Just think what a rattle there will be about the town once the villagers learn that Lady Helena as you were once styled, is in residence after so many years of the family's absence. It will cause such a raucous, Giles will have little trouble getting wind of it and discovering me there. It must be a most clandestine occupation, with no one beyond my maid in attendance. No alterations to the staff that are resident and they must be sworn into absolute discretion. I think it is only then, we may be at ease.'

And so, everything was arranged as quickly and as quietly as could be managed. After some protest on the matter of me venturing to see if Delores might go along, to which I reminded her as I often must, she was now a married woman, it was agreed that she would let me go with my Abigail. She had also suggested that we might bring my sister into my confidence with a view to placing the child with her family at such a time as necessary.

I slept easier for having Mama onboard. She had turned out more reliable than I had expected, even though I could see the pain behind her pragmatic planning. I had always been the difficult child. But I'm sure none of us could have anticipated the magnitude of ways in which I had come to shame and fail my family. For the most part, I no longer cared much for their complaints, since they had cared little for mine, but in this, looking at the heaviness that hung like a shadow over my mama, I felt quite desperately sorry for bringing this to bear upon her.

My father, I still had little to do with since our last run in, but my mama, for all her failings, I could not help feel was in some genuine despair and not only for the scandal for a change, but actually, for once perhaps: for me.

I was glad that when Edmund's coach rattled up the driveway at a quarter past eleven that night, I was the only one still up to receive him. I wanted the opportunity to speak alone with him and to warn him that Mother was now aware and ready to bring my father into some of the knowing. I got up from my escritoire where I had been writing my diary and grabbed my shawl and pounded down the stairs and out onto the vestibule to meet him.

'Edmund! Do you bring news?' I said as soon as he climbed the steps.

'I do, but let us go inside. I need a drink and a warm fire after that brutish journey.'

I walked anxiously beside him as we went into the house and he handed Grantley his coat and hat, issued orders to have some Brandy sent to the small parlour and for his portmanteau's to be offloaded.

'Eleanor, sit down,' he said gravely when we arrived at the parlour and I instantly felt concerned.

'You have been to him?'

'I have,' he gestured again to the chair as he held his palms out to the fire's warmth and rubbed the heat into them. But I wasn't inclined to sit. I felt the anxiety pulsing through me, a flush creep over my skin.

'Well?' I said to his silence.

'It did not go as well as I hoped.'

I sighed into my palms. Some part of me suspected he would be an obstinate fool and force my hand. 'What happened?'

'He denied it. Played the perfect part of ignorance. Apparently, you are delusional and in want of a spell at the Bedlam, which he hinted was within his power to affect as we know.'

'Well, you hardly expected a confession, Edmund. But how did he take your proposal?'

'With equal indifference. He won't give you a separation, Ellie. He is adamant.'

I felt my lip begin to quiver. 'Bastard.'

'No need for that kind of talk.'

I ignored this. 'Well, then, I have no choice but to report him to the magistrate and see him swing for it. I had tried to be reasonable but he has left me no choice.'

'Ellie—'

'No, Edmund! I don't want to hear another word of your protests against this course.' I leant palms pressed upon the table. 'He brutalised me, he tries to threaten and trick me into going back, he sends his valet to spy on me. Where do you think it will end if I do not make it end?'

He sank into a chair now and poured himself a cup. 'He won't swing for it, Ellie.'

'What do you mean? You said it yourself; the court would look no better on it for him being my husband.'

'And it's true enough. The difficulty is—I've had my solicitor looking into it and it seems that any hope of such evidence has long since expired.'

'What do you mean?'

'Please, Ellie, sit down, won't you.'

This time, I did. Not because of his insistence but I had started to feel unstable. Like some wave of insatiable anger was rushing to every extremity with such a violence that the effort of containing it would either strike something down or strike me down in the effort to restrain it.

'The threshold of proof is very high for such a charge.'

'I will give them the testimony. I will even submit to an examination of a physician if I must—whatever it takes to go forward, Edmund, I do not care.'

'There is no defence to such an act, it is indisputable. The problem is one of threshold. It requires the, well there is no other way to put it than bluntly: "the emission of seed" as evidence. That is the only proof that will suffice for the courts.'

'You cannot be serious!'

He nodded. 'Ellie, I have no wish to gull you. This is the way of it, 'pon my honour. Without such evidence, there can be no conviction.'

'I see. That is how justice is served in our lands, is it. Unless I am to present myself in such a state of disarray at the very moment, then it did not happen.'

'I do not say it is just, Ellie. I say simply that it is the Law.'

'Then the Law is sadly lacking, Edmund. It is a disgrace. A nonsensical disgrace!'

'That's may be, but it is the way of it and there is nothing to be done.'

'So, what will happen if I make complaint to the magistrate, he will simply not hear it?'

'He will no doubt hear it from a lady of your standing. But without the evidence required, he is unlikely to be able to proceed beyond taking interviews—'

'Unlikely?'

'Well, it is not in my power to determine how the magistrate sees fit to deal in it, Ellie, but the result will be the same either way. Whether he concludes it upon the interviews or attempts to put it forward to the court, at some point, it will fail before a court trial. The only difference I see is that one way will make it possible for the details to leak into the public ear and one will not. Either way, you won't see him swing.'

'Fine,' I said getting up from the chair.

'Ellie?'

'If I won't see him swing then I have no other recourse than to publicly disgrace him.'

'Have you gone queer in the attic? You will publicly disgrace yourself! All of us with it. Damn it, Ellie, haven't you done enough damage already?'

'Oh no, Edmund. I have only just begun!' I snarled.

'Where are you going?' he stood up.

'To the Magistrate!'

'Have a care, Ellie, it's nearly midnight. Will you think about what you are doing?'

'Oh, I have thought long and hard. I thought you were going to help me!' I burst into sobs.

'It is out of my hands, but I own that if I knew that it was going to result in you flying into such rage and behaving so nonsensically, then I would not have made the attempt.'

'Well, you are relieved of your duty, Edmund. I shall deal with this my own way now.'

I marched out of the room with him keeping pace, nipping and pecking at me with a torrent of pleas. 'Grantley,' I said once I reached the hall where he was still supervising the luggage. 'My bonnet and my spencer please.'

'Yes, ma'am,' he said puzzled but obliging.

'Ellie, just calm down and give me a chance to think about other options.'

'Other options?' I shrugged into my spencer sleeves and turned around to face him squarely. 'Only a moment ago you told me you regretted ever helping me and now you offer other options? Forget it.'

He reached and held my arm. 'Please. Give me a little time to think and if I do not come back to you with something before I go, then you still have the option to go to the magistrate.'

I considered him a moment; there seemed to be an unusual sincerity in his eyes. 'You have till morning,' I said and I handed my bonnet back to Grantley.,

Poppy's Pies and Puddings Shop.

November 1821. Annalise.

Annalise crept into bed unseen by anyone other than the footman who passed her on her way in as they headed out to unload the coach. Will had tried to catch her eye but she kept her gaze to the floor and walked quickly. She knew her face would give away all the heartache she was trying so hard to contain and couldn't bear questions or congeniality now.

Poppy was still at work in the kitchen when she slipped into their room and slipped as quickly into bed without undressing. She spent the first few hours between exhausting sobs and fitful dozing. Then when the evening fell and the room grew dark, she got up for the chamber pot, undressed properly and sunk into sleep right through to the morning.

She felt slightly calmer by the time it came about, but a check in the looking glass as she washed her face, gave away the violent pink swell of her eyes. She looked over to Poppy who was still fast asleep and picked about the room quietly in the half-light so as not to wake her. When Poppy woke to find her already risen and set off, she would think nothing of it; only that she was tending her mistress as was usual for the hour.

Where she headed to though, was not Eleanor's chamber but to Watts' room, which she had discovered was just along the attic corridor from the one being prepared for herself. *What a waste of effort,* she thought as she passed it now, the door ajar, dust sheets laid out upon the floors and furniture and the walls primed for painting. What a waste it had all been; her trust, her sacrifice, her love. She had been a fool to think it could have turned out differently.

She took a breath and composed herself before tapping lightly at the door and waiting for the sound of shuffling about the room before a bleary-eyed Watts opened the door a crack and looked her over in a puzzle. 'Yes?' she said tartly.

'Good morning, Alice, sorry to disturb you, may I come in a moment?'

'What for?'

'I have a proposal for you.'

She looked Annalise over with a sense of curiosity then stood back to allow her room to come in. 'Well?' she said, pulling her shawl about her shoulders and sinking into a chair without offering Annalise one.

'You know I am Mrs Craythorne's Abigail now?' she begun, still standing.

'Yes, and what of it?' she said impatiently.

'Well, the thing is, I cannot tend to her today, or for the next couple of days for I am called on urgent personal business—'

'Forget it.' She lifted a hand in the air. 'I know what you're gonna say and the answer is no. I have enough on my plate seeing to my own mistress. Do you think someone of my years has it in me to keep up with a young madam like yours now? Well, I tried it and it was impossible, so no. I have my back to think of, which proves enough of a gripe in managing with her ladyship. So, no favours.'

'I understand, although I did not expect you to take it on as favour. I had meant to pay you for your trouble, but it is no matter, I shall ask one of the housemaids—'

'How much?'

'I'm sorry?'

'How much you paying?'

'Well, whatever you think suitable compensation for your trouble I suppose, but if you are not up to it—'

'Three days you say?'

Annalise nodded.

'Five bob and I'll do it.'

Annalise reached for her purse inside her pocket and nodded. 'There's half a sovereign, for your trouble and my gratitude,' Annalise said passing the coin to her.

She turned it over in her palm with a look of surprise at this unanticipated generosity. 'Thank you,' she said in a tone more gentle than any she had used on her insofar.

'Thank you. I bid you good morning.'

'Ah, Miss Tullier,' said Mr Benson stepping down from his ladder in the newly adapted shop floor.

'Mr Benson, my goodness you have been busy,' Annalise said looking about the place with a genuine smile upon her face, the first she had bestowed on anyone in what felt like an age.

'Aye, well, hope to be finished by the time the week's out. In 'ere I mean. We'll get started on the yard work and extension then o' course, but, well, least you can move in and get going whilst we're seeing to that.'

'Thank you, sir. It is just as I had hoped and why I came. I thought I'd better take some measurements for furniture so we can get prepared to move in. By the end of the week you say? We might move in then?'

'Aye, should be finished in here. We've done all the plastering and woodwork now, just the painting to see to down 'ere—all the upstairs has been finished and this shouldn't take long once me nipper gets down to join me. He's just at the builder's merchants.'

'That's wonderful news. And what a wonderful job you have done,' she said, considering how improved the space was. It was as though he had taken the back wall and counter and seamlessly pushed them back a few yards without a clue to it having ever been any other way arranged—excepting the fact they only ran half the width of the room now; the other half reaching to the rear of the house on the right hand side to accommodate some tables and chairs for eating at.

The generous size of the space it had given way to surprised her in its new L-shape formation. She suspected they might fit three of four round tables into the new space, or one exceedingly long one like the kitchen table they worked at, at Cuddington. She pondered what would be the better choice and then she had an anxious thought for the diminishment of the back parlour that had been sacrificed for it. 'Do you mind if I go and take a look about?'

'Course not, ma'am, it's your 'ouse,' he smiled and the sound of it brought it home to her. Yes, it was her house. All of this now belonged to her and it seemed too preposterous to believe, even though she had signed the documents herself.

She headed through the concealed panelled door and stepped inside the parlour room. It was indeed greatly diminished, but it seemed to no dire impediment. The fireplace and mantle remained just as it was with its fireside chair and foot stool draped in a dust sheet. She lifted it and scraped the pair of them along the floor to the opposite side of the fire to check there still remained ample room for another: one for her and one for Poppy. Yes, it lended to a nice cosy spot with just enough room to navigate around them.

This is where the pair of them would relax after a day of work, a cup in hand and the crackle of the warm fire in the background of their chatter, she considered a moment, taking a seat. Then she walked over to the opposite wall—the new mock wall that had made way for the new L-shape in the shop front. The panelling having been skilfully recreated to match the original style, but standing out bright against the rest of the room in its freshly planed raw colour. *The colour of sand or straw,* she thought. It would soon be all washed white and bright and she was certain that would lend to opening the space up a fraction too.

She followed the wall towards the rear boundary wall where she found a new door etched into it. She opened it up to find a tiny walled box of a room she first considered must be a store cupboard of sorts, but then remembered what Mr Benson had explained to her and Mr Harrison on the day they had commissioned him for the work. This was to become the door to the new extension, to her dress making parlour. She was to have a new front door on the extension, opening out to the yard space, where her customers could enter it along the yet-to-be-laid yard path, so she might keep the two different trades quite separate. And she imagined then a vision of her first customer ambling up a path of newly laid stone lined with shrubs and beds of colourful flowers, welcomed by their fragrance and pleasant sight before tugging at the bell.

There, they would enter her small but purpose-built parlour equipped with a long worktable for laying out patterns and cutting reams of fabric to the rear, and two fine plush sofas for them to sit upon to the front by the small wood burning stove that would heat the room and where she could offer them warm drinks without the need to disturb the pie kitchen.

The walls facing the garden would be studded with large windows and smaller ones would be inlaid into the roof to make for as much good sewing light as possible.

She would have a small bureau to keep all her order notes and paperwork organised in and she could pull the lid down to sit at it and answer letters or update ledgers when she needed to. There would of course be hanging rails fitted across the length of the back wall, some to display fabrics and some to hang new commissions ready for their final fittings.

It all seemed so exciting in her mind, even if a little harder to imagine in the barren patch of unkempt yard space that the only window in the room looked out onto. More still since it had been turned into something of a builder's yard with piles of sand and sawdust and wagons of tools strewn about it.

She closed the cupboard door, which in fact was to become the door through to her sewing parlour once the new room had been built, allowing her a private entrance through the back of it.

She stared out of the window a moment trying to picture the new view, then turned around and considered whether a dining table for her and Poppy could still be accommodated beneath the window as was first planned. She was certain it could be if they kept to a table no larger than for four—or perhaps one of those extending types that could pull out to accommodate extra settings when needed. For it was not only she and Poppy to think of. There would be staff, perhaps not above a couple, but no less, they would need somewhere to sit for their rest breaks and take their meals and it would not be professional to have them out front with the customers. And she meant to invite Mr Harrison over for supper once a week if he could make it and was certain Poppy would have folk she might like to invite from time to time, since she still had many living relatives about the county.

She popped back to the shop floor now.

'Well, what do you say?' asked Mr Benson, turning about at the creak of the opening door.

'It is a marvel, sir. I cannot believe how well it all looks even without the finishing touches.'

'I'm glad you're pleased, ma'am.'

'Mr Benson, I don't suppose you happen to have a measuring tool I might borrow, to work out the furniture dimensions? I seem to have forgotten my tape measure.' She hadn't forgotten it, she had tried to get it out of her sewing box without waking Poppy but it was too noisy and she abandoned it.

'Certainly, I do. Let me just finish this panel so it doesn't start up all tacky and I'll fetch it from my wagon and bring it through to you,' he said.

'That's very kind, thank you.'

She disappeared to the upstairs rooms now and it was here she begun to really see how transformed the rest would soon look. The stairs freshly sanded and varnished, letting off a deep shine as she trod them, the walls and timbers dazzling white and the stifling gloom of the mahogany quite forgotten—the ceiling seeming higher, the walls a breadth wider. Then as this style continued into the upstairs landing and in each of the three rooms it opened on to, she continued to gasp in astonishment and delight at the sight of each new room. The old tatty furniture and junk having been cleared so you could see the shiny floorboards stretch from wall to wall now, the mouldy and part-rotted window frames replaced with fresh beads of wood and painted crisp white like the panelled walls, the glass polished clear so the light streamed in un-obscured.

It was like they had been built anew and she hardly recognised them as the rooms she had last viewed.

Yes of course the new addition of furniture would show up their true size which was modest in the smallest of the three but generous enough in the other two, certainly three times the size of the room she and Poppy shared now.

Poppy would have the first pick of them she decided, since she would have the benefit of her sewing room to work or write in. She would take the next and the smallest would be reserved for one boarding staff member. She hoped it would be Maggie, but knew the decision would be Poppy's, as would all of them relating to the pie making side of things. She had no mind to meddle in the matters where Poppy was expert, no more than she expected Poppy would meddle in her sewing room once it was underway.

She looked forward to helping though, in whatever ways she might to get things fired off: Peeling, chopping and washing pots and pans, wiping down the tables and sweeping the floors until they could afford to hire someone else to pitch in on it and certainly by the time her sewing parlour was complete and ready to set to work in.

Things would be a little tighter now she was not to have her service wages to look to. She had accounted for having them to top up the deficit the renovations had cost and to go towards procuring the furniture, linens and ingredient stock they would need to open up. If she was careful, it might all be managed and if she focussed on the bare minimum to start with: the beds and the shop front furniture, she could add to the rest later once they had started seeing the coin flow back to them.

When Mr Benson came up and handed her a folding tin ruler, and a larger fruitwood one, she got to work on the smallest room first. This was the room that seemed almost not worth the retaining in its former state, but now she was glad that it had been. She had taken some measurements from the furniture in her room at Cuddington with her sewing tape measure, just before setting off to London with Eleanor. It afforded her a rough idea of the dimensions she must accommodate, in the minimum. She took out the crumpled piece of paper she had noted it on and began drawing lines of chalk upon the floor according to them, another item Mr Benson had been good enough to borrow her and to explain how best to approach the task.

It seemed there was only one way a bed could be made to fit and that was to the left-hand side of the room which was undisturbed by the door opening on the right. It would at least accommodate one a little wider than her own, if not an inch longer. And there was a built-in closet sat high over the rise of the stairs which had been boxed in to look like it was part of it. Its door swung open wide now as did the window, she supposed to clear the paint fumes which still hung pungent in the air, even if dry to the touch.

She worked out in the end that beyond the bed, the most that could be made to fit in it would be a comfy chair in the corner closest to the window and a small washstand and hide-away stool. There would be little room left beyond a strip in the middle that permitted you to get to everything, but it would be pleasant, she was sure, with some pretty paper added to the walls when she had the money for that addition, a few watercolours and a looking glass hung upon them. Pretty heavy drapes at the window frame since this was the only bedroom without its own fireplace—something Mr Benson assured her would not be an issue given its position over the kitchen and the rising heat from it as well its small size which would contain it well if the door was kept shut on wintery days. She would have a nice soft rug placed from wall to wall and make up some thick quilted coverlets for the bed, just to be sure it was as snug and comfortable as it might be.

And she tried to remind herself that the choice of staff was to be Poppy's, but she could not help imagining Maggie in it, being delighted to have a room of her very own, and such a pretty, cosy one as she meant to make it.

She carried on in this style for another five hours, taking down notes and sketches, chalking the floors, then washing them down with soapy water afterwards. At least the floors downstairs had not yet been swept from all the sanding, still having a layer of thick dust upon them, so she was able to leave them as they were and get over to the Greyhound before she suspected an afternoon rush of supper diners. She wanted to catch the innkeeper when he was not too busy, although she found that he was and she was made to wait a quarter of an hour in a little parlour until he came to her.

'Ah, Miss Tullier, what can I do for you?' he said, looking over her dust and chalk covered plain gown, rightly assuming she was not here to take up his offer of that dinner on the house.

'Sir, forgive me, I know you are busy and I know I am in quite a shabbier state than you are used to finding me,' she said quickly. 'I have been inspecting the works in the shop and it is thick with work dust at the moment.'

'Aye, I can imagine. How's it all coming about?'

'Very well. I thank you for your recommendation of Mr Benson, he has done a wonderful job. Only, well, I have a little dilemma I was hoping you might help me with?'

'Oh?'

'Well, Mr Benson says the work shall not be finished until the end of the week and I need to move in by Wednesday. You see, I must be about to arrange the furniture and unpacking before it can be moved into and yet it shall not be habitable by then with all the wet paint and varnishing fumes.'

'No indeed,' he said reasonably.

'I wondered, sir, if it would be possible I might hire one of your rooms here to lodge in for a few days until it was ready for moving in to?'

He let out a sigh that sounded more like a hum and looked thoughtfully before saying, 'You mean on your own, miss?'

She nodded. 'I know it is not your policy to let out rooms to lone females, but you see, I am in a bit of a fix and so I thought I must ask.'

'I'm sorry, miss, for I really would like to help you out. But I have my reputation to think of, and yours. I mean, I know you are a fitting guest, but my other guests shan't know it and will wonder why an unmarried female is about the place without the protection of some honourable fellow like your uncle. Unless, of course, he could take up a room, then it would be nothing to answer.'

'Oh no, sir, I'm afraid he is too busy with his own bookshop to be called away at such length. But I do understand, and I thank you for considering—'

'I'll tell you what I can do, though,' he interjected. 'There's an old widow down by the pond at Wandle Cottage that lets out lodging rooms to tourists. She's a highly respectable lady, if a bit of a stickler, and has some pretty tight house rules but, the rooms are nearly half the price of mine and twice the size. Here's what I shall do if you would wish it; I shall make her a recommendation of you and see if she has anything to answer to the purpose, how about that?'

'Oh, would you, sir? That is very kind.'

'No trouble at all. Mind, it'll 'ave to wait till morning now, we're up to our ears here with a hunting party. But if you leave me your direction, I'll send you word, either way.'

This she could not do or he would get the notion she was either far haughtier than she had led him to believe or she would be discovered to me no more than the Ashlyn's servant. She scribbled down Mr Harrison's direction instead and handed it to him; 'I am staying at my uncles presently. I thank you.'

'Not a problem dear. I do hope she has vacancies: much more fitting place for a lady like you too, miss, than a place crammed with young sporting gentleman.'

The reply was quick to come the very next afternoon and she was grateful it came bearing good news, for it had now been confirmed that Eleanor would indeed be departing on Wednesday and setting out on a journey. She was surprised she hadn't called on her to give her the news herself. She had had it from Will who had overheard Mrs Crawford appraising Grantley of it and asking him to give directions for the footman to deal in the luggage and the grooms to ready the coach when the time came.

It stung to hear it in this second-hand fashion. It stung that she had not rang for her even once in the two days they had been back. But it was for the best; that much she knew. For even though she had kept her days chock full of chores to divert her mind from the matter, she spent the night-time crying into her pillow to the point of exhaustion. If it were not for her freedom to be in bed earlier than Poppy now, she was certain she would have questioned her about the state of her puffy face. But she had either been asleep or feigned sleep at the time Poppy had retired to the room.

Ordinarily she would be sorry to be so evasive with Poppy, especially after having been away, but she was heartened by the fact that in a matter of days they would be moving out of Cuddington and have all the time in the world for catching up. Besides, she hoped by then the worst of her melancholy would have shifted—enough at least, to keep it private and undetectable. It would be easier once they had their own rooms too.

Today she was on a mission to make sure they were furnished so they weren't sleeping on the floor at this rate. Mr Harrison had given her the direction of a house sale he had heard about when she stopped by on her way back from Carshalton yesterday. The sale itself was not until Saturday, but he had taken the liberty of enquiring as to whether the gentleman would have any objections to a private pre-sale ahead of it, to which he had agreed in exchange for the favour of Mr Harrison agreeing to put up his posters in the shop window advertising it. So, Annalise was to have first pickings and since Mr Harrison was expecting a delivery of books this morning and could not accompany her, she had prevailed upon Miss Lockhart instead, on his insistence that she must not go to a gentleman's house alone—an unfamiliar one at that.

Although he sounded respectable enough and it was on this basis she hadn't minded. He had been a local doctor in training and now his mentorship was complete he was travelling to the continent to set up a new life and his own practice there. It all sounded very exciting Annalise thought, but incredibly brave to desert your homeland like that. She had always thought the same of her mama, but the choice had never been her own and she was young enough at twelve, when they left France, to adapt to it better.

She met Miss Lockheart at the Rectory gate at ten as he directed her and found her full of congratulations for the news. 'Well, Annalise, I think it marvellous what you are doing,' she said, 'setting up an independence for yourself like this. How lucky you are. You shall never have to marry now, unless of course you wish to.'

Annalise shook her head as if she had suggested something unappetising. She knew now that she never wanted to marry. The only love she had known had broken her heart into so many shards, she meant never to love romantically again. Her life was to be filled with the love of good friends here on and nothing more. If she did ever succeed in nursing herself back to a state of equanimity, she would certainly not risk it being so cruelly dashed again.

'I don't blame you. Why hand over everything you would have worked for to some fellow who might cheat you out of the lot and dictate your life to you when you are capable of getting along perfectly as you are?' she said this with a bitter resentful edge to her tone and Annalise began to wonder if she too had had her heart broken before. She did not ask. If anyone asked her such a question, she was sure she would never wish to talk about all the pain, all the disappointment and worthlessness. No. It was to be a closed subject and one she intended to take to her grave.

'Unless of course you want children that is, and then, well I suppose you must hope for a decent man for many reasons.'

No, even children would not induce her, she thought half-heartedly, but was too resolute to start up a debate in her head just now on such a topic.

'Anyway, I hope you don't mind, but I kept these by for you.' She handed her a basket full of linens. 'They were surplus donations I haven't found homes for yet and even though I know you far from a charity case—tradeswomen that you are now—I thought they might come in useful as you are just starting out and they seem to be in very good order. There are a few tablecloths and sheets and a number of balls of knitting yarn I thought you might be able to make use of?'

'Thank you, Miss Lockheart, that was very thoughtful of you.'

'Not at all. If you don't want any of it, then you can donate it all back to me, I suppose,' she said with the hint of a laugh about her tone and Annalise was surprised at it, for although she was always very amiable and kind, she was also very serious and of quite formidable presence. She was sure she had never seen her laugh before in all the years she had been acquainted with her mama.

'Well, shall we go around to the stable and fetch the wagon then?'

'The wagon?' Annalise said frowning.

'Yes, of course, what else will we carry all your furniture back on? I own I am all for a challenge but if you think I mean to lug things between here and Epsom on foot, my dear, that is a little past the mark for me.'

Annalise laughed at this. 'Of course not. I meant to hire a hack if there was anything there I wanted and I don't yet know if there is, so I shouldn't like you to go to so much trouble when I might not come out with much at all.'

'Nonsense. It is no trouble. You are amongst friends and very well regarded for your kindness—yes, do not think I do not hear your name often from the generosity you bestow on folk—so for a change, you shall have a little in your own direction. I have spoken to the folk at Old Mill Street and you have a dozen strong fellows ready to help with any heavy lifting should you need it.'

'Oh miss,' she was too fragile for such emotional talk today.

'Let's see how we get on, shall we? We'll only call on them if they're needed. We can stop on our way back through to collect them. I'm sure we can fit at least a couple on the trap with us if in need be.'

It turned out it was just as well Miss Lockheart had the foresight to bring the wagon, Annalise having found a number of pieces of excellent quality furniture at very fair prices. The doctor needed a quick sale so he could get on his way and asked only a reasonable price for things so they could contribute to the replacements he must seek out when he arrived in Switzerland, where he meant to set up home. For most of the visit as Annalise went about the rooms inspecting things; lifting up ornamental items and opening out draws, Miss Lockheart stood in engrossed conversation with the doctor over his setting off to such a place.

Had he been there before and if so, how many times? Yes, he had been thrice, first upon his tour where he fell in love with the irregular landscape and stunning views. Was the air as fresh and clear as it was so rumoured Miss Lockheart wanted to know. Indeed, it was the finest air to be had as far as his knowing went and the climate very congenial for an Englishman compared to many of the places he had travelled to where the heat grew unbearable at the spring and summer seasons. In Switzerland, it was but a few degrees above what he was used to in a good English summer season at most and there was the advantage too that even that could be retreated from by going up higher into the mountainous regions. Yes, he spoke both French and German so he should do well enough for business there and yes, he had an acquaintance out there who was to help him settle into the place...

By the time they had completed the sale, she felt she knew as much as there was to know of Doctor Shaw's life, despite having only the briefest exchanges with him herself. She came away happy for the visit though, for she had got herself a fine pair of wardrobes and a matching bureau of drawers in glossy cherry wood, a heavy oak table, oval in shape with an extendable leg that lifted out and supported an extra leaf if it was needed with a pair of matching carver chairs. Of course, she would have to add to that number but two would do for now for her and Poppy to dine at it. Sadly, the writing bureau she had hoped to buy was not for sale on account of it being a particular gift and rarity of craftsmanship, and the only thing he had been willing to pay the carriage to take with him to Switzerland.

Her disappointment was soon forgotten when she caught sight of a handsome easy chair she knew would be perfect to match the one around the fireplace. Not in fabric, but in style, with fine Queen Anne feet and a winged back. Yes, they would seem a mismatch for the time being, but eventually she would reupholster them both to match and give them a little extra padding where they sagged a fraction in the centre to bring them about as new.

She reserved the only bed frame in the house but not the mattress. That much she meant to have new and was willing to go to the expense to know that when she sunk into it, it had never before been slept upon and she needn't be in fear of bed bugs or fleas. Not that she thought it likely in the least Dr Shaw's mattress would be so infested for everything was in very good order indeed, but she had already settled on that promise to herself and allocated a budget for three new mattresses. Which now she would have to alter to one single sized and two doubles, rather than the three singles she had planned to commission. But she couldn't be sure she would find another bedstead for sale in time and so to have a double to start, since there was only one for sale, would at least permit them both to bed down in the meantime. And if she was to have a double, so was

Poppy. There was no hope of such an upgrade in the third room and so that at least would run to budget.

Her final substantial purchase was an unexpected one and somewhat of an indulgence and fancy if she allowed herself to admit the fact. It was an extravagant looking sofa upholstered in Chinese style fabric which was bright and exotic looking in both vibrant colour and unusual design. She had no need for sofas yet with not even the foundations dug out for the sewing parlour, but stretched to the expense of it thinking she would likely never find such a handsome piece again, nor at what she was certain must be a very reasonable price for a sofa as fine as this. For now, it could go handsomely along the refashioned wall beside the new door. *It will just about fit,* she considered, and if it did not, it would have to go upstairs in the largest bedroom, for the time being.

This and the bed, she arranged to pick up on Saturday—the day of the official house sale—for the cart would not take everything and he needed something to sleep on until then. It was just as well too for when the four of them—Dr Shaw's valet joining in the effort—began to load the wagon, it soon became clear that it would not take so many heavy things in one trip and one of the pair of wardrobes would also need to remain behind if it was not to prove too heavy for the horses to pull.

It was decided that Dr Shaw would reserve the bed, the wardrobe and the sofa and she could pay him for those upon collecting them Saturday morning. The rest she paid for there and then in coin, for which a heavy purse thick with sovereigns actually proved worth the carrying of on this occasion.

She hired a hack to convey her on to Carshalton to lessen the burden on the Lockhearts' horses and to pile up with all the smaller items she had found: a fine pair of silver candlesticks, a brass lantern clock for the fire mantle in the back parlour, a handsome gilt framed looking glass that could hang above it, a tapestry firescreen so faded the image could no longer be made out, and a handful of things for the kitchen: a decorated porcelain meat platter, a set of wine glasses, an assortment of cutlery and crockery that seemed finer in both quality and condition than the ones she had found in the dresser at Carshalton. Although, on the whole, the kitchen had been the best stocked place in the house with very little requiring any urgent refurbishment or replacement.

Most of the smaller things fitted snugly into a purchase she had debated long and hard over: a copper bathing tub, that only just about fit inside the hack, providing she lifted her legs to rest inside it too. It reminded her painfully of Eleanor and the night they had been caught in the rain and sat in the steamy filled tub together. She cast the image of her out of her mind and stared out of the back window to check that Miss Lockheart was keeping pace with the wagon.

It had not seemed worth the trouble of stopping in Old Mill Street for help given that the heaviest of items were to be collected on Saturday, with the exception of the wardrobe which she was sure Mr Benson and his son would help them with. The table and chairs and the bureau of drawers they could easily manage together and the tub full of small items they could manage single handed. But on Saturday, she would take up the offer for it would be much trickier to get such large things up the narrow staircase, she realised as she watched Mr Benson and his son manoeuvre the first of the wardrobes up them.

Everything had had to go upstairs for now, except the smaller items and the copper tub that fitted in the kitchen, which was the only room that was not having any work done on it. A good scrub down from floor to ceiling was all that room required and a polishing up of the wooden dressers and copper pans hanging from the racks where they had grown dusty and dull.

The shop floor was now complete but they couldn't go in there on account of the drying floor varnish that had only just been painted on this morning, so Annalise walked Miss Lockheart around to the front of the building so they could look in through the windows.

'Wonderful!' Miss Lockheart declared, cupped hands pressed against the glass and her face pushed against them. 'It shall make a very charming pie parlour indeed!'

'Well, Miss Lockheart, you shall be amongst our friends invited to come and try it on our opening day for a complimentary feast of our offerings.'

'Well then, I thank you. I shall look to it indeed. Although, I must confess, I am not overly partial to a pie—'

'These are not ordinary pies, Miss Lockheart, but very fine ones. But Poppy has decided there are to be soups and stews and even a few pastries to be enjoyed upon the menu too, so I am sure we might find something to your liking.'

'Well certainly,' she said, stepping away from the glass and peering up at the bare metal hanging rail where a sign was to be placed. 'All that is missing now is the sign above the door,' she said.

'It is being crafted as we speak, although it may not be ready for a couple of weeks yet. But I think we shall need at least that time to get everything furnished and spick and span anyway.'

'Indeed, what a busy time it shall be, but very worthwhile, I'm sure. I confess I am quite envious of you and Poppy. I shall likely wither away under my father's roof for the rest of my years.'

'I do not think you withering away at all Miss Lockheart—you are the lifeblood of the community and the importance of your work must not be understated.'

She smiled. 'You are kind, Annalise. I do try and I suppose there is truth in what you speak. Only, well, don't you ever just wish you might do something wholly radical and selfish once in a while?'

'Yes, yes I do. I suppose we might call it balance?'

She laughed merrily her agreement at this. 'Indeed.'

'On that subject, Miss Lockheart, do you think, I mean, I know you are very busy and I would be very happy to pay you for your time and trouble of course. But when things are up and running here—do you think you would be interested in visiting us once or twice a week to teach Poppy and our other staff their letters and numbers?'

'Why of course, I should be happy to.'

'That would be wonderful, for I think it would be useful for everyone to be able to know at least the basics if we are dealing in orders and bills. And I had a thought that Poppy might one day like to make a receipt book to record her dishes and make the training up of new staff even simpler.'

'Why, certainly it will. How many do you expect?'

'Not very many to begin with, Poppy of course, a young boarding maid and another living out, but I too mean to take an apprentice further down the line—I was thinking of the Bartletts' eldest, Jane, if she should fancy it.'

'A wonderful idea and very generous of you. Do let me know when you are ready to commence. I'm sure you shall have many things to think of presently, but once you are settled, we may find a suitable time for lessons.'

She was kind enough to convey Annalise back to Cuddington on her journey back to Ewell. She would spend only another two nights beneath this roof, Annalise considered as they approached the gates and Miss Lockheart set her down just outside them.

It was a sobering decrescendo to her very productive and otherwise exciting day when she caught sight of Eleanor's windows as she cleared the woodland. She looked quickly away in case she might be sitting at one of them. How was it possible to hold such contradictory feelings simultaneously? She at once wanted to rush on up there and throw her arms about her whilst as earnestly wishing to berate her for the heartache that she had caused. She both wanted to see her this very instant and never see her again. It was all such a head scramble and she wondered how she would have gotten through from one day to the next if were not for having so much to do.

She kept to the task when she was back in her room, both for the sake of time ticking on and the sake of her own sanity. This time she spent circling advertisements for house auctions and private sales. She found an oak table and a number of chairs that were of particular interest for the shop floor as well as a few auctions she meant to go to next week.

Then when she had written out a batch of enquiry notes to the sellers, she set upon packing up some of her things to take to Carshalton with her tomorrow. Mainly her mama's things. There would be too much to take and not enough time to take it all if she did not begin on it soon. She had accumulated an impossible stash of boxes and bags beneath her bed, growing thick with dust and dead spiders where it was impossible to sweep beneath them now.

She went carefully through them all and reorganised them as best she could. She would need to ask one of the farm hands or hallboys to fetch her a barrow to wheel them out to the gate for when the hack came to collect her in the morning. Most mornings she had walked the journey over to Carshalton. It was time consuming but the exercise seemed to help un-clutter her thoughts, and even though the weather had long since turned chilly, it was still fine enough walking weather in the peak of the day if the sun was up bright, even if a little crisp. But she had taken the trouble to book the hack for nine-o-clock tomorrow since it was Poppy's morning off and would be her very first visit to her new home. It seemed sensible to make the most of the expense and convey the lion share of their things along with them.

Tears was Poppy's overwhelming response as she took her about the nearly finished house. Intermittent with bursts of gratitude manifesting in impromptu hugs, ear to ear smiles and inevitably, another wave of sobs. 'I just can't believe it, Annalise, it is all so...perfect,' she said as they stood in the yard, Annalise explaining to her how the extension would look once completed.

'It shall be. I think we will be very happy here once we are all settled in. But we will have our work cut out getting to that phase,' she added, leading them back into the kitchen where they pulled out two of the rickety stools from beneath the table and sat around it. Annalise was keen to stay as much out of Mr Benson's way as possible since he was running ahead of schedule, the parlour ceilings and walls already having had the first coat of paint. She knew there was still the floor to do and so she wasn't expecting to move in far enough ahead to prevent her prevailing on the widow at Wandle Cottage, but she was hopeful her stay there might be shorter than planned. After her extravagances at Dr Shaw's the other day, she was growing ever more mindful of her withering bank balance and every penny saved would help go towards something else they needed, and there was still so much they needed.

'We'll manage well enough, luv,' Poppy had said to this. 'The steward shall 'ave to settle my wages before I go and you will still have yours for the moment, so I'm sure we'll get along alright. Rome wasn't built in a day—isn't that what they say?'

'Yes, it is,' Annalise smiled but felt unable to deliver her the news that they would not have any wages of hers to rely on. There would be too many questions and she had no wish to burst their merry bubble. 'Well, how about we start by taking an inventory of what we have here in the kitchen already and what we need to get in?'

'Well, we shall certainly need to get to business, but we shall 'ave to 'ave a brew to keep us going, and a bit of grub. Why don't you let me pop down the road and see what I can find? There seems to be plenty o' choice along 'ere so I'm sure I'll find us something.'

Whilst Poppy was gone, Annalise found her way to the water well which was at least conveniently located toward the back of the shop dwellings, just past the yards. She rinsed out two buckets there and filled them up. They were heavy and the winding made her arms ache. She had been spoilt with the hand pump and taps at Cuddington and was a little out of practice now in lugging buckets of water about. Still, it was but a stone's throw in distance at least, and for that she was grateful, for they would certainly need a good supply with a kitchen to run. She put two of the four kettles on to boil using the first rounds to wash out a few mugs, plates and some of the cutlery in nothing but warm water since she had nothing else to do them with—not even salt or a teacloth to dry them, so she set them beside the sink to drain and shook her hands in the air until the worst of them were dry. She started her list with: soft soap, soda, scourers and rags and knew this was going to end in a very long list and winced at the prospect of the bill that would accompany it.

Poppy came back shortly after with a small jar of tea leaves, a quart of creamy milk, half a pound of butter, a good slab of cheddar and a fresh loaf—still warm—filling the air with its malty scent.

'Goodness, Poppy, tea? What extravagance,' Annalise said, holding up the jar as Poppy finished unloading the basket onto the table.

'Well, I thought it'd make a nice change from the thrice brewed leaves that come down from the upper parlour, and anyway, we're celebrating, aren't we?'

Annalise smiled, 'Yes we are. I'll see if there is a teapot about and put another kettle to boil.'

Aye love, you got some warm water for me to wash me 'ands in?'

'Yes, but we haven't a drop of soft soap—or a cloth to hand.'

'Never mind, we'll manage for now and I'll pick some up from the grocers before we leave. He's given us an account with him you know and so did the baker. Didn't have to pay for a penny of all this yet. Told 'em we were their new neighbours and that was that, they wouldn't take my coin and got their books out.'

Annalise had a mind to settle with them promptly, the last thing she wanted was to start out running up debts.

'Good folk round 'ere and it looks like we got everything to hand: the grocers well stocked and there's a butchers I didn't stop at, just poked me 'ead around the door to say good morning, but it was all nice and neat in there from the glimpse I caught. Then there was the costermongers and an apothecary and all sorts of other fancy places I didn't get a chance to nose at. A bit pricier than we're used to but looks like its all good stuff—nice and fresh—and I daresay we can strike some better bargains with them when we'll be buying so much to keep the kitchen going.'

'Yes, I shall leave the negotiations to you,' Annalise said, thinking her the better person for the task. Poppy had a knack for making a friend out of anyone when she'd a fancy to and she was certain to come away with a far greater bargain than Annalise. Annalise had no stomach for bartering. Indeed, she had paid Dr Shaw on the nose for everything she wanted without even trying to knock him down a penny. Perhaps, she wondered then if she should have sent Poppy to manage that too.

She rinsed a tired looking teapot with a crack running down its spout with a little warm water to freshen it up and also to check the crack was not leaking before she risked spooning the precious leaves into it. It was fine and she soon set a brewing pot on a griddle rack on the table with a jug of the creamy fresh milk and the best of the mugs aside it.

Poppy too got busy, slicing bread and cheese and warming a plate for the butter by the fire. They were soon sat about with Mr Benson and his son, enjoying a hearty break with strong fine tea to sip on.

'This is very good of you ladies, we were just coming towards a rest break too,' said Mr Benson who was still washing clinging strings of congealed paint off his hands in the bowl of warm water Poppy had set out for them.

'Well, yous been working 'ard and you need to keep your strength up,' Poppy said pouring tea into all their mugs. 'Go on then little un, 'elp yourself and get stuck in,' she said to his son, who introduced himself as Tom. He seemed a pleasant mannered boy with sandy hair and a freckly nose, not above fifteen Annalise supposed, but hardly a little 'un as Poppy had referred to him.

They came away from Carshalton with a whopping big list of essentials just as Annalise had expected. But once she had the hack drop Poppy back to Cuddington in time to report to cook, she took it all the way on to the market near Old Mill Street where she knew she could get at least half of the items on it for far better prices than she could from the High Street vendors in Carshalton. She returned back with so much stuff she had to have the hack drive her right up to the basement door for there was no hope of carrying it all.

'What's all this for?' Cook came out with hands on hips as Will helped her offload it all.

'Things my mistress asked me to get for her journey,' she said flatly and marched straight passed her with two heavy baskets on her arms whilst Will filled up a barrow.

'What does your mistress want with a broom?' she said unconvinced.

'I don't know Mrs Simpson, it is not my place to question her, but I shall call her down if you so wish to ask her?'

She stomped back into the kitchen with an inaudible mumble upon her lips and Annalise exhaled, thankful her bluff would not be called. The last thing she needed was to have Eleanor prevailed upon to save her skin. If it came to it, she thought she might rather head off a day early to Wandle Cottage, considering the less of the two evils. For this was to be her last night here and it felt so very strange considering the fact as she sat upon her bed ticking things off her list and circling those most urgent she must pick up tomorrow. Then she started sorting her clothes from the hanging rack, separating those she was to take with her from the heavy work gowns Mrs Crawford had issued her from the fine dress-es Eleanor had commissioned for her. It made her melancholy to look at them, thinking of all the fine places in London she had worn them, how happy they had both been then, before it was all cast in shadow. It would not be right to keep them now and so she made a separate pile to set in a box that she would leave marked for Eleanor's attention. She kept only the beautiful Pelisse she had given her as a birthday gift after some pri-vate debate. She would not be received into Wandle Cottage if the wid-ow really was such a stickler as the innkeeper hinted, dressed in her own shabby, dated clothes. The fine Pelisse would hide them from her view and hopefully overcome the issue, especially if she took the trouble to do her hair up fancy as she had grown used to doing in London. If she was too busy looking at her pretty pelisse and hair dress, she would likely not notice her worn boots and tatty skirt hems.

She sunk into bed once this was done, feeling dragged under by a fresh wave of melancholy as the reality dawned close. This was the last night she would ever be so close to her again. For they were both to be gone in the morning, neither of them knowing the others direction here-after since she had no clue where Eleanor was headed and had never told her about Carshalton. The link was to be severed here and whilst she knew it for the best, she could not help feeling the full force of this im-pending separation as she wept into her pillow.

Stapleford Hall.

November 1821. - Eleanor.

When my final morning at Cuddington dawned—a bird upon the window ledge awakening me to its chirping song—I felt a sinking feeling at the realisation that I remained unforgiven. In the days of her absence, I had told myself she would eventually come about. That there was no need to make last minute arrangements for a new maid. That she would not last out the day, and then the next. *But she had.* I had now run out of days. I had almost run out of opportunities to hope. It seemed I would leave today...alone.

I sat up in bed and searched the room for any sign of her having been up; an indigo hue of still breaking morning light veiled the room. The washstand lay empty as did the breakfast table. It was too early yet for even servants to be about the business of filling hot water jugs and teapots. Not that she had performed this service since our return, even though she had offered to carry out such rudimentary duties until I was gone. I had forbade it altogether in the hope that complete separation would speed up her wish to reconcile. Again, it seemed I had been mistaken and I felt instantly full of regret that those possible last moments together, however perfunctory, may have been wasted. The opportunity to change her mind...gone.

I sunk back onto the pillow and exhaled a deep throated sigh. What was I to do? The prospect of leaving her behind was too terrible to accept and yet I was powerless to effect it. I knew deep down that I must not try to sway her with desperate pleas and petitions, however much I felt tempted to. I must instead turn my attentions to accepting the fact that I must leave her behind and face this alone. I squeezed my eyes shut against the tears that tried to bleed their way through my clenched eyelashes. *Oh, Annalise, are the measure of our feelings not enough to help us come through this?* Could the pain of our separation really be the lesser pain to bear than that of forgiveness?

I must have fallen into a doze once I had lost the battle against my tears and given into them to the point of exhaustion. When I opened my eyes now, blinking against a shaft of brilliant sunlight, stretching into a yawn and rolling on to my side, I saw that the washstand was freshly stocked and noticed steam rising from the cup upon the small table. I pulled myself up and went over to it, wiping a crust of congealed tear debris that was stubbornly attempting to glue the corners of my eye together. *I know that smell.*

I sat down and peered into the cup to see a nobbly stem of ginger bobbing about in the water, its tangy aroma pungent beneath my nostrils. *Annalise?* There was no one else who would bring it to me and I had taken a care not to request it out of fear of raising any suspicions amongst the staff. Much to my own peril, as however much I disliked the taste of it, the sickness had exacerbated without its regular dosage. I took a tentative sip on it. *Annalise, what does this mean?* I dared not excite myself with fantasy notions and yet I could not help but read into it as a sign. My stomach churned with excitement anyway, as I poured the hot tangy liquid into it, realising I must hurry if I was to be ready on time for an early start. The sun had only just fully risen and it was the perfect opportunity to set out; ahead of busy roads, and prying eyes. I rung the bell.

When the call was finally answered and I heard footsteps coming up the hall, I pinched my cheeks and flattened my hair with my palms. I considered what must be the best expression in which to greet her; the gleeful smile I felt already building in my cheeks as the footsteps grew nearer. Perhaps something more solemn to reflect how sorely missed she had been. I had not finished considering the competing emotions and expressions of them when the door swung open and into the room came a servant I did not recognise at all. *You are not my Annalise.*

I realised from the perplexed expression upon her face as she closed the door behind her and bobbed a curtsy, that my own had been one of utter disappointment. There was a time I had been so well trained in keeping my feelings from manifesting upon my face that I remained always perfectly unreadable. Lately, I seemed made of glass; and whilst I was grateful to align my inner and outer worlds in greater harmony, I too hoped to maintain enough balance betwixt the two.

'I'm sorry, ma'am, I was told to come to help you dress?'

'You was?' I said, finding my voice at last.

'Yes, if you please, ma'am, you did ring, did you not?'

I smiled. 'I did.' I said turning from her now to hide the quiver of my bottom lip. *Oh Annalise, I thought...* 'Thank you for coming.'

She bobbed a curtsey and went over to the washstand.

I wanted to ask on whose orders she had come, but I could not. She already seemed quite unsettled by what was no doubt, a very unwelcoming reception. I knew it was not personal; but she did not. By the time she had poured the water and set out my clothes, I had, by some means unknown to me, managed to regain my composure before presenting myself for my toilette.

'You must forgive me, I do not know your name. I think you must be new here?'

'Yes, ma'am, I am. Everyone calls me Spinks.'

'Spinks. Well, thank you for coming. I am not sure why Watts did not answer, but thank you for stepping in. I am to leave early to journey to Edinburgh today, so I have little time to spare.'

'Much obliged, ma'am,' she said, pouring water from the jug and adding rosewater to it. 'Watts is not well so she couldn't come—put out her back she has, and that other maid said I was to fill in for her.'

'Mrs Crawford?'

'No, miss.' She paused and turned her head at an angle thoughtfully before adding the face cloths to the bowl. 'Tulley, I think she's called.'

My heart sank. She was so much bent on avoiding me she could not even bring herself to cover her own duties on my last day! She despised me *that* much that she would not even take the trouble to say goodbye, wish me well on my way? I could not bear to take it in. *Do not take it in. You cannot fall apart now. Change the subject.* 'Oh dear. I do hope Watts is soon recovered,' I said, and I meant it, for despite my having little patience for her, I had come to learn that a servant's life was not an easy lot and I had perhaps not always been as kind to her as I might have.

Servants that were swayed by bribes had always been easy to disregard as lacking in loyalty and virtue, and yet I had come to realise that they were no more guilty than I had been in commissioning them. Besides, if I was to exist upon their incomes, I should likely not pass up the opportunity to earn extra coins either. I would send some of my firm, feather tufted cushions up for Watts in the hope of her being made to feel more comfortable, and some of that soothing herbal salve that always put me to rights after a little massaging of it. These were the thoughts I kept resolutely to as I lifted my arms in the air, spun around to be laced, and balanced on one leg as my stockings were rolled over the heel of my foot. For if I dared, for even the briefest moment, to allow myself to think more of *her*, to accept in all its full horror that she was not coming to me after all, I should definitely fall apart on the spot and find myself quickly incapacitated.

So, I stuck carefully to this compression of my thoughts as I tied my bonnet beneath my chin, kissed my mama upon her cheek as she stood in her dressing robe on the landing, and when I stepped out onto the vestibule as the coach was loaded up, sagging with the weight of hefty trunks—I was not travelling lightly this time—I tried to focus. I would be gone the better part of a year. I would not see this view again in such an age and I could not afford the risk of sending back for things.

I would not see her face again for so long, I ached at even the anticipation of such a prospect. I should go and seek out at least a final farewell, I considered as the last few trunks were lifted. The prospect of not even having a parting glance of her to hold on to was unthinkable and yet so was the likelihood that if I dared, even with the utmost of good intentions to seek her out, I would not be able to leave at all. And I must, leave.

It was this that propelled me on towards the coach when a footman swung open the carriage door and awaited me. I took a reluctant step towards him, slow, stalling, looking about me, behind me, for any sign that she might yet come running up the driveway to say farewell. But there was no one else, only a glimpse I caught of my mama waving to me from the parlour window, a look of uncertainty upon her expression. I waved back and marched on. I could not have her realise I was setting out alone and complicate things further. Giles was back in town now and no doubt this would be one of his first stops. *I have to go now.* I lifted a foot. I will write to her when I get there. Perhaps she might still be persuaded to join me later on, once she realises, as she had before when I had gone to London, just how torturous such a separation would prove.

I stepped onto the footplate, taking one last, desperately hopeful glance behind me before turning back with the heaviest of hearts. An ache building in the back of my throat, constricting it as I ducked my head to get into the carriage. Then I almost fell back out of it in shock; the footman holding fast and supporting me to prevent it. *Was it true?* I steadied my footing, thanked the footman and burst into a fit tears as he slammed the door shut and I moved towards the seat.

'No, sit with me,' Annalise said, shuffling up to make more room for me beside her.

I could barely speak, it was all I could do to steady my breath, as I settled next to her, a tentative distance left between us. That beautiful scent of rosewater in her hair catching in the morning breeze that came rushing through the window. Just to see her again was like sunshine breaking through heavy clouds. 'You came?' I said.

She nodded.

Her expression was a solemn one and I wasn't sure what to make of it. 'Are you here to see me off or—' *Dare I ask it, dare I presume?* However much I wanted to, it occurred to me that she might mean to simply offer a farewell or see me off safely for the first leg. I was to take the family carriage only as far as Islington before switching to the post, in the hope of such a conveyance attracting no particular interest in my arrival in Cambridgeshire.

'I am coming with you, silly.'

I exhaled my relief into my gloved palm which I had, in astonishment, held cupped across my mouth without realising it until now. 'Oh, Annalise, thank god...'

'Come now. No tears. Your mama is watching. Wave her off so I may hold you at last.'

I leaned out of the coach window and smiled up at my mama, waving as the gravel shifted beneath us and the horses took off. *Goodbye, Mama, we may not have rubbed along perfectly, but I shall always be grateful for this.* And when first she, and then Cuddington faded into the distance, I turned back to Annalise and found myself quickly enveloped in her waiting embrace.

'I've missed you, Len,' she said and I smiled into the expanse of her shoulder. To be close to her again, to smell her and feel her gentle kisses upon my salty cheeks was beyond my capacity to contain myself. 'I'm sorry,' she said.

'I'm sorry too.' I squeezed her a fraction tighter before drawing back to see her face. 'I thought you would not come. Why didn't you tell me you had a change of heart?'

'I didn't know. I only decided upon it this morning. When I brought up your tea, I was minded only to bid you farewell and see you had your ginger before such a long journey. By the time I returned to the basement, holding the sleeping image of you in my mind and realising I was not to see such a sight again for months, well, let us just say I have never packed up and said my goodbyes so quickly.'

So, you did bring me the tea and you did mean to say goodbye. I smiled, there was gratitude in its curve. 'I had thought you lost to me.'

'It was like you said, Len, when you are in love, you cannot just *decide.*'

She was in love with me. For wasn't that what love was: to accept not only the perfections but imperfections of that one? I gushed with more tears now; happy tears. I had fallen in love with her so deeply, I realised now, how superficial every other feeling or fancy had been that had passed before. It seemed ridiculous to me that I could have ever fancied myself marrying Sheldon, or considered there was something of romance in my encounters with Mariella, or any true solace in my interactions with Richards. It had all been great folly of one kind or another, now that I knew what it was to love. Now I could see how these past fancies paled into insignificance in the midst of true feeling and attachment. It was an energy so vibrant it coloured every aspect of life, invigorated every breath, soothed any ill prospect and filled with purpose even the feeblest of tasks. If I could have married her, I would have gone through any court and house to petition my divorce—to the devil with the complication and scandal, so certain I was that I could make a lifelong attachment without ever wanting to be free of the connection. She was worth any price. Perfect to me in every way.

Every day I found something new to admire in her, something more to love her for, and just when I thought it impossible I could feel anything more profound, she would win another inch of my heart that I did not know was vacant.

I looked at her now, sat meekly in her pale grey travelling coat and bonnet, the motes of dust dancing around her pretty face as the sunlight streamed in through the carriage window. I found her hand on the seat and stroked it lightly and received her neat smile; luminosity dancing in her eyes. No matter what was wrong in my world, everything seemed right whilst she was part of it.

Stapleford Hall was a pretty little place, set in ancient parkland, with the River Cam coursing through it and old-fashioned formal gardens which were well kept and alive with their autumnal bloom of colour. It was, by comparison to our other homes, a small place of no great consequence, with its five-window-wide façade set in twenty acres, which included an impressive walled garden and small farmyard. It had been the Dower house Mama had spent the second part of her childhood growing up in, after her father's untimely death which caused them to leave Wimpole Hall and all its pomp and grandeur.

I at last understood its charm now, as the groom drove us up to the house in the cart. Rattling along the winding driveway, parting through a copse of trees as it came fully into view. Weather beaten brickwork cutting angles against the softer shapes of a colourful cottage garden flounced about its perimeter. I saw instantly, the promise if it's cosy and more private refuge. Mama's sentimentality became clear to me now; I could see why she had preferred it over the mansion she was born to. It was small, but perfectly formed, nestled away like a consecrated secret.

Despite its humble size, when we were shown to our rooms by the housekeeper, with only us to occupy it, it seemed so vast in its emptiness. The household staff who had been on board wages for many years, comprised of a butler, housekeeper who also served as head cook, one footman, three maids of all work, plus a groom that lived in the stable cottage and a farmer who occupied the farmhouse with his family, tending to the land and gardens. It seemed so very quiet above stairs, so private. How freely we could exist in such a place.

If we lived quietly here, it was unlikely a soul would suspect the place occupied at all. No calls to receive or make. No standing upon ceremony for one occasion or another. Mama had already written to inform the staff that they were to keep my residency concealed as best they could, and with only a handful of staff remaining in the whole establishment, it should certainly help to keep matters quieter since there were less persons to point the finger at if something got out. If my presence was innocently noticed by the locals, it was to be told that the house had been let to a widow of no consequence. All I could do now was hope that all these precautions proved enough.

The vacant circumstance of the house had also made it easy for me to explain to Mrs Wright the housekeeper, that I should like my maid to take up the rooms directly next to my own so she was close at hand should I require her, and me, not left up here so much alone in the night. Of course, I knew I had no intention of having her more than a hairs breadth away from me, but this explanation satisfied Mrs Wright and we unpacked into the adjoining rooms without suspicion or audience. Of course, in a house like Cuddington, or even Stapleford if it was at capacity, such an arrangement would seem ludicrous. Servants were not offered rooms fit for their masters, but with so many to spare it could not be considered such a transgression or oddity.

We decided on a leisurely afternoon after such a tiresome day of travel and feeling so shook up in the carriages. So, before dinner we took an exploratory stroll about the grounds for as long as the waning evening light permitted us, and en route picked an impromptu basket of Hawthorn berries that had ripened in the woodland.

'They are surprisingly sweet,' I said to Annalise, sampling one from our small bounty. 'You must try,' I said and passed a plump berry from my lips to hers. We were sat atop a wall that provided a balustrade for the patio whilst forming one of the elevations in the walled garden below us. The sun's warmth was still upon our cheeks as a pinkish halo began to form around it in preparation for it setting. I had not felt so much contentment in all my life. No Giles to keep eyes on me, no one nagging at me, no disapproving glances from Father, no societal niceties to stand attention to. Just us, here, together, free.

To be continued...

Afterword

Thank you for reading Appetence! I hope you have enjoyed reading it. I would be very grateful if you could help spread the word and leave me a review.

The next instalment is in the works and anticipated for release in Winter 2022 and will be available for pre–order, shortly.

To keep up with the latest news on new releases, you can find information on my website: ccburns.co.uk or follow my Facebook Page: @bluestockingbard

Thank you,

Claire.

Coming Next...

Diary of an obstinate, headstrong female: Volume 3: Cicisbeo.

A cosy country Christmastide.
An ill-timed quest to expose injustice.
A determined pursuit that sets everything asunder.

When Eleanor and Annalise arrive at Stapleford Hall and begin to acclimatise to the slow rhythms of a secluded country life, they expect the remaining months of Eleanor's confinement to continue as uneventfully as they began. But then a Christmas outing sets them on an unexpected mission to seek justice for the women of Cambridgeshire who are subject to the tyranny of the University Proctors and the questionable practice of confining them to The Spinning House without reasonable cause or a fair trial.

Their quest to expose this unlawful custom leads them on a path of spontaneous adventure, new acquaintances, and a chance to test their thespian skills and new disguises.

It would be risky business in any event, but with Eleanor lying low and Giles expanding his countrywide search for her, the timing might have been better.

As the Midwinter winds set over the frost-bitten Fens, unforeseen danger begins to crystallise in the powdery snow trails of their perilous footprints.

Out Now!

Also by C. C. Burns

Diary of an obstinate, headstrong female.
Appetence
Midwinter.

Watch for more at www.ccburns.co.uk.